LAUREL

HORN OF AFRICA

"One hell of a fine book. . . . A masterly success on multiple levels. . . . A fascinating tapestry of a remote region of the earth and the people who live there. . . . A rousing and completely successful adventure story. . . . An illuminating exploration of the nature of violence and the darker corners of the human soul. . . . The test of time may even accord it a ranking near that of *Moby-Dick* as a landmark of American literature."

—*The Houston Post*

"Told with immense narrative drive. . . . Caputo's descriptive power is such that you will feel your lips crack and your skin crawl with fear."

—*The Detroit News*

"An extraordinary, passionate novel. . . . A devastating book reminiscent in its passionate style and moral intensity of the best of Joseph Conrad."

—*Newsday*

"Breathtaking . . . a compelling story . . . a brutally vibrant, arresting achievement."

—*Publishers Weekly*

"Caputo brings to *Horn of Africa* the uncompromising honesty that distinguished *A Rumor of War,* as well as an intuitive grasp of human motivation, a flair for the theatrical, and descriptive acuity. This novel prods us into a startling reevaluation of man stripped of personal illusions and denied civilization's ethical restraints."
—*Saturday Review*

"A hard, cruel, cynical novel—and a good one."
—*The Washington Post Book World*

"Adds an unexpected moral depth to the tale of mercenary adventure that is in itself as eventful and authentic as, say, something by Frederick Forsyth. . . . The strata of behavior Philip Caputo is mining belongs not to adventure writing, finally, but to people like Conrad, Melville, and Dostoevski."
—*The Denver Post*

"A powerful, shattering novel that challenges our neat systems of rationality; it reveals the savage lurking just beneath our thin veneer of civilization."
—*Nashville Banner*

"Remarkable . . . a splendid book combining taut narrative with remarkable characterization. . . . A vehicle for plumbing the depths of evil in man's soul."
—*St. Louis Post-Dispatch*

"Like Conrad, it is brooding, adventurous, alive with exploits that trace the inner torments of the human soul. . . . Like Hemingway, it is spare, briny, punching deep inside the fragile ferocity of machismo. . . . Like Crane, it is vivid, ironic, sensitive to the instabilities of human beings under stress. . . . The result is remarkable, a potent, impressionistic fusion of physical derring-do and psychological tension. *Horn of Africa* studies evil's hypnotic power."
—*The Charlotte Observer* (N.C.)

"A blockbuster . . . this is the stuff of which the best adventure yarns are spun, and there will undoubtedly be comparisons with early Hemingway, Kipling, and Conrad. . . . I doubt that women readers will fail to be as spellbound as men."
—*Chicago*

"Caputo has created fascinating psychological portraits of . . . three men and enriched them with a hard-edged plot of intrigue, duplicity, betrayal, and death. He has created a work that transcends categorization, a work of brilliance."
—*The Hartford Courant*

HORN
OF
AFRICA

HORN
OF
AFRICA

PHILIP CAPUTO

A LAUREL BOOK
Published by
Dell Publishing Co., Inc.
1 Dag Hammarskjold Plaza
New York, New York 10017

This book is dedicated to the memory of

STANLEY A. CLAYES

A decent, civilized man whose very existence
was a reproach to the violence and absurdity
of this age.

AUTHOR'S NOTE

The incidents and characters in this novel are fictional. There is no province in Ethiopia called Bejaya, no tribe known as the Beni-Hamid, and no town in the Sudan named Nassala. These are inventions, purely the products of the author's imagination. To avoid confusing the reader, I had considered creating an entire country in which to set this story, but decided that that would be carrying literary imperialism too far. No doubt there are people who will feel I've gone too far as it is: what arrogance to place a nonexistent province on the map of one of Africa's oldest nations, and then populate it with an imaginary black-Arab tribe. To them I offer my apologies and this explanation: my inventions were designed to create an effect and to further the main purposes of this narrative, which are to present my personal vision of the nature of violence and to show what happens when a certain kind of man is free to exceed the bounds of acceptable human conduct.

I have also played fast and loose with American geography and history. Anyone who searches a map of Minnesota for Jeremy Nordstrand's birthplace, the town of Walton, will not find it. I built the town out of thin air. The expedition led by Nordstrand's great-great-grandfather, though loosely based on an actual event, the 1862 Sioux uprising in Minnesota, never took place. Likewise, though Operation Atropos had its genesis in a real incident, which was related to me when I was covering the rebellion in

Eritrea for the *Chicago Tribune,* its details are solely my creation. A novelist who attempts to fashion literature out of contemporary events runs the risk of having his work read for its supposed informational value. Anyone even vaguely familiar with the current situation in the region from which the title of this novel is borrowed will see that the rebellion in the fictional province of Bejaya bears certain resemblances to the one in the actual province of Eritrea. They are, however, superficial resemblances; the incidents described in this novel are in no way intended to be facts thinly disguised as fiction. In so stating, I also hope to avoid criticisms from various experts for factual or chronological inaccuracies contained in *Horn of Africa*: these inaccuracies are deliberate, and again, designed to achieve an effect.

PJC

April 1977–March 1980

ONE

KHAMSIN

He was thick-chested and light-haired, with sloping shoulders joined so smoothly to his neck he seemed not to have any neck at all, and a head whose size made his shoulders look narrower than they were, a wide round head which he cocked slightly forward when he walked, swinging his arms as if he meant to smash through whatever stood in his way. Just over six feet tall, he reminded you of a bear, and I do not mean some tame and shambling circus bear. The impression was heightened by his eyes, close-set in that washtub head of his, glowing an animal green and vaguely slanted by the high cheekbones he had inherited from his Scandinavian ancestors. They seldom looked to the sides, those eyes. They were almost always fixed straight ahead, and their cold green fire, like the roll of his shoulders and the swing of his tensed arms, suggested an inner turbulence straining for an outlet. His voice was level, as level as the northern prairies that had helped to form him. But it was not a dull voice. It was interesting by virtue of its unnatural calm, beneath which you caught an undertone of menace, a warning that the calm could easily burst into a rage. It aroused the expectancy, mixed with dread, of a still August day in his part of the country, when you hear in the lulled air the far-off rumble of one of those summer storms that sometimes savage the plains.

Jeremy Nordstrand was now and then mistaken for a primitive: the ex-football player, ex-infantry officer who

was all claws and teeth, good only for bashing skulls or
leading suicidal charges. He was much more than that, or
much less: his style of barbarism made a true primitive's
unconscious savagery seem refreshing by comparison. He
was, though, a remarkable man. I will give him that much;
he was remarkable. His claws and teeth were guided by
a high, if warped, intelligence; his capacity for cunning
and deception would have made him stand out in the courts
of Medicean Florence; above all, he had an implacable will
and a gift for making others bend to it. He bent me to it,
and Moody, who at least resisted for a time, and Kasu
Murrah, who righted himself near the end, when it was too
late, and Osman, the old fighter who died for him. Even
Muhammad Jima, a willful man himself, gave in and violated one of his people's most sacred codes. "I see things
through," Nordstrand once told me, "right through to the
end." I will give him that, too. He saw things through. And
I am sure his determination, combined with his talent for
making others do what he wanted, would have ensured
him a brilliant military or political career if the fabric of
his mind had not been woven on a faulty loom. I am not
trying to place all the blame on him. This story may be an
exorcism of sorts; but it is not an apology for the things
we did and the things we allowed him to do out there. In
the end, it was by choice that we bowed to Nordstrand's
will, each for his own reason. Murrah because he had lost
his particular faith, a loss that left him without any principles on which to make a stand; Moody because he did not
know how to deal with a man like Nordstrand; Osman—a
product of the past—because he had an outmoded belief
in white men and a need to associate himself with their
supposed powers; Jima because of ambition—he had flattered himself into thinking of Nordstrand as his own personal instrument, the device that would transform his fantasy kingdom into reality and raise him to its throne. As
for myself, my reasons were no better than theirs, perhaps
worse. So Nordstrand did not overthrow the inner gover-
nor—call it conscience, call it will, call it a standard of
behavior—that had once ruled us. We permitted it to
abdicate; we surrendered to him, and made ourselves his
accomplices.

Certainly we would have been indicted if everything had happened in a place where lawyers and judges stage the little dumb-shows we call justice; but it all took place in the empty desert in the midst of a revolution, neither of which allowed the slow workings of the law. Each eventually dispensed its own form of justice, crude and unfair, but forms of justice nonetheless. The last few days on the desert were the worst, racking us with agonies more exquisite than could be inflicted by the worst prison in the world. The wilderness, however, was not entirely merciless; it allowed me to escape, to bear witness, and to experience a kind of expiation. The professional moralists, from their pulpits, from their editorial offices, from their speaker's dais littered with half-eaten dinners, might say it was not a genuine expiation and call for investigating commissions, inquiries, punishments. Let them chatter. We paid whatever debt we owed. Nordstrand and Moody paid all a man can pay, Nordstrand with interest because his liability was the greatest. I took his last installment and closed his account.

Colfax was the exception. His penalty was very light: exile to an obscure province in the bureaucratic empire. He is there today, reading boring journals out of which he produces boring reports for his division chief. He will rise no further in the hierarchy. He will inhabit his stuffy little cubicle until he is pensioned off. He will never be anything more than a glorified clerk, and his name, if it is spoken at all, will be spoken only in whispers accompanied by shakes of the head and comments that he ruined his career by "overreaching." That was the word our resident in Khartoum used after I made it back to the Sudanese border.

Colfax, amid the wreckage of his career, probably regards his as the worst punishment. His career was the only important thing in his life. He belonged to "The Craft," as he liked to call his business, and the men of The Craft, as anxious to conceal their mistakes as they are their secrets, could not have afforded to have him publicly whipped. Nor could they have fired him, for he might then have felt released from his oath of silence. They had no choice but to bring him in and banish him to a dead-end job where he could be kept quiet and on a short leash. But

if I had had anything to say about it, I would have made
Colfax pay a great deal more. I would have made him pay
and pay and pay. My revenge would have required certain
scientific equipment which, I believe, has been developed
by the patriotic scientists who work in the experimental
laboratories in the building where Colfax now writes his
pointless reports. If I could get my hands on it, I would
wire it to our heads, flip the switch, and transfer to Colfax's brain some of the images engraved on mine. Then he
would spend his nights with the lights on, yearning for
sleep and dreading it at the same time. Then, once sleep
came, he would see in troubled dreams all those butchered
bodies, those smiling dead whose taut-drawn grins would
not fade when he woke up in a trembling sweat.

They appear to me three or four times a week, their
faces as clear and real as the pictures on my wall. There are
the faces of the villagers who died in the bombing, the face
of the man I killed in what is usually called the heat of
battle, and the faces of the men Nordstrand killed in another kind of heat. The last trouble me most of all. Their
ghosts haunt my dreams because they know I should have
seen Nordstrand for what he was much sooner than I did,
and done something to prevent their slaughter. Nordstrand
executed them. He executed and beheaded them because he
had thrown himself into the abyss, the moral abyss where
a man becomes capable of anything. And I had done nothing to curb him from satisfying his violent lusts until it
was too late. My own ethical antennae were blunted,
blunted even before we went out there, blunted further by
the months we spent living among primitive men on the
African desert, eating their vile-tasting mush, drinking from
wells half-dried by drought the putrid water that never
slaked our thirst, while the sun clubbed us daily and the
winds slapped our faces raw. Moody had taken such great
care to bring enough medicines to protect us from malaria,
dysentery, and hepatitis, but nothing to inoculate ourselves
against the diseases of the spirit men are prey to in such
places.

The frightening thing is, I know how close I came to
becoming like Nordstrand. Given a few more weeks of
heat, isolation, and stinking water, a few more weeks of

feeling myself surrounded by a world barbarous and alien, I would have followed him in his fall; it is an awful knowledge to live with, more awful than the knowledge of death, the knowledge that you could be capable of the worst under the right circumstances. Perhaps that is another reason why Nordstrand's victims haunt me: to remind me of my capacity for evil. Whenever I see their hideously grinning mouths and blind staring eyes, I also see, in a kind of waking nightmare, the earth opening into a chasm as black as the desert when there is no moon and the dust clouds raised by the wind have extinguished the stars. I am standing at its lip, simultaneously horrified and fascinated as I watch Nordstrand plunge down, his arms outstretched, not in a plea for help, but in invitation. A terrifying dizziness comes over me.

And I would have Colfax tormented by such visions, not because that would change anything, but because it would balance the scales. Gogol once said, "I call the devil, devil, and do not dress him in a splendid costume à la Byron, and I know he wears a frock coat." Thomas Colfax wore pinstripe suits, a costume which lent authenticity to his playact role as the Cairo manager of a company called Inter-Arab Development Ltd.; but he was as much a devil as Gogol's frock-coated gentleman, so I think his life should be a living hell rather than the purgatory it is now. After all, the project—being fond of classical allusions, Colfax had code-named it Operation Atropos—was his idea. It was the child of his brain, born deformed and nurtured by that other demon, Nordstrand, into a monster that maimed or destroyed everyone it touched except its parent.

———

I have begun to ramble again. I may even be raving, with my talk of nightmares and ghosts. The doctor would probably blame it on my drinking. A man in my nervous condition, he says, should avoid the world's oldest and most reliable anesthetic. Perhaps he is right, but whiskey works a wonderful magic on me. It puts me to sleep by blurring the images of the dead whose joker grins keep me awake. In any case, the confusion in my mind is not important;

the history of Operation Atropos is. And chronologically, Atropos began with the phone call from David Harris.

That was nearly two years ago, and will sérve as a traditional beginning. For it was through Harris that I met Colfax, and through Colfax, the remarkable Nordstrand. It was also through Colfax that I helped to ruin Harris, who was among the operation's first casualties.

Harris and I first met in Beirut in the days before that outburst of mass homicidal mania known as the Lebanese Civil War. Ours was one of those expatriate friendships, which do not arise out of a commonality of needs and interests but out of shared circumstances. In our case, we were Americans who had been thrown together in a strange part of the world. Harris was then Middle East representative for the Endicott Bank, which was seeking its share of the billions generated by Arabian oil; I was a correspondent for the *Los Angeles Post*, which was seeking its share of the Middle East's other natural resources: the headlines generated by endless wars, terrorism, and human suffering.

During that time in Beirut, before the war, before the phone call, we met fairly often. Harris was entertaining company, although he tended to be too confessional after a couple of drinks. He was a short, slight man with dreams of riches as big as he was small and a pretense of taking nothing seriously, including his dreams. One afternoon on the veranda of the St. George Hotel, he told me he regarded life as a circus and most men as mere performers who spent their lives jumping through hoops. This came in a tone of genial cynicism, as if he were some jaded old Levantine trader who had seen so much folly and greed that the human condition amused rather than saddened him. I said I found his views neither original nor interesting. Ignoring me, he went on, describing about how he had jumped through "the Jewish liberal hoop" in his early twenties, marching with blacks in Mississippi and working with the AID program in Laos. Both experiences had disillusioned him and led him into a brief flirtation with the New Left—"the Jewish radical hoop." Finally, nearing the watershed of thirty, he had responded to an opposing call in what he termed his Semitic genes, joined Endicott, and began to jump through "the Jewish banker hoop."

It was one of the few times I had heard him emphasize his ancestry, about which he was confused and self-conscious. His father, the descendant of a Russian Jew, had changed the family's original name after he'd become a successful executive. He had married an English Catholic while serving in London during the Second World War. The couple, unable to decide in which religion to raise their son, made a shaky compromise: Harris attended Hebrew school as a boy, then went on to Georgetown for a healthy dose of Jesuit Catholicism. Unsure of which God to worship, Harris had decided to worship none at all. He maintained his atheism until joining Endicott, a citadel of WASPism that caused him to undergo a Pauline conversion. He told the personnel director he was a Protestant, a fiction to which his sandy hair, blue eyes, and aquiline features gave a convincing, if false, testimony.

We were drinking gin and tonics that afternoon in Beirut. Holding his glass in one hand, Harris swept the other across the serene bay as if he owned all the ships anchored in it, and described his vision of the future. It was a rather vague vision, which made it all the more captivating.

He was making plans to jump through yet another hoop: that of the independent entrepreneur. His job with the bank, he said, was temporary, a prelude to the day when he would strike out on his own. He gave himself another five years to acquire the capital and contacts; then he would become what he called an "overseas consultant," a middleman between Middle Eastern oil kings and Western businessmen, fixing international deals, winging between capitals in a Lear jet. He boasted of the contacts he had already made with shipping magnates, gold smugglers in Dubai, ministers in various governments, and Saudi Arabian princes who entertained him lavishly. He saw himself as a financial adventurer, a modern-day Marco Polo searching for his personal silk route. Finishing his drink, Harris swirled the slice of lime around in the melted ice and grinned impishly as if to say, "Don't take what I've just said too seriously. I don't." I knew this flippancy was a pose adopted to protect himself against any possible failure. He took his job with the bank more seriously than he

would ever let on. It was the only thing he had done well
in his life; at thirty-one, he was the youngest overseas
branch manager in Endicott's history.

"Well, what do you think, Charlie?" Harris asked,
sucking on the gin-soaked lime.

"About what?"

"My plans."

In so many words, I told him to forget them. Brokering
deals in the Middle East were a tricky business requiring
a ruthless singlemindedness. Whether a pose or not, his
flippancy was a drawback. I recognized several of the
names he had mentioned in his list of contacts; they were
typical of the characters then hustling in Beirut, tough-
minded men who did not see life as a circus or themselves
as performers jumping through hoops.

"What're you driving at, Charlie?"

"That you're out of your league. Stay away from those
characters. They've graduated *summa cum laude* from old
double-cross U. Get mixed up with them and you'll get
yourself jammed up. Stick with the bank. Play tennis in
your spare time. They've got some great clay courts over
at the Renaissance Club."

I did not expect him to listen to me—the atmosphere of
greed in Beirut was as thick as the fumes pouring from the
thousands of clapped-out Mercedes taxis that choked its
streets—and, in fact, Harris was in trouble when he phoned
me a long time after that conversation. That was not why
he called. He didn't know about the fix he was in; nor did
I, although we both found out soon enough.

I was living in Cairo by then, having been blown out of
Beirut after the civil war started. I had also left the *Post*,
not entirely by choice, for the uncertain future and low
pay of a free-lancer. The bank had meanwhile transferred
Harris to London because the fighting had made the
orderly pursuit of profit impossible in Lebanon. I'd already
had one letter from him telling me of his involvement in
"maritime financing," the granting of loans to ship buyers.
He relished his new job. It gave him the chance to match
wits with all sorts of seagoing hucksters out to cheat the
bank, thereby fulfilling his need to think of himself as a

clever operator, which he was not. He was intelligent but not clever.

Now, on the phone, he said he had just come up to Cairo after a hard week of wit-matching with a Greek in Alexandria.

"The guy's what Onassis would've been if Onassis had been a small-time crook."

"Congratulations," I said, hoping to be spared the details.

"Didn't catch that, big guy."

"I said, 'Con-grat-u-la-tions,'" I shouted. Next to the pyramids, the Cairo telephone system is one of Egypt's greatest wonders. Harris was staying at the Meridien Hotel, only a few hundred yards across the river from my apartment, but sounded as if he were calling from New Guinea.

"Yeah, he was diverting charter-hire." There was a pause as he waited for me to ask what "diverting charter-hire" meant. When I did not, Harris said, "Listen, Charlie, that isn't why I called."

"What?"

"This connection is awful. Look, hang up and I'll call you right back."

"You might not even get through next time. I can hear you if you shout."

"I don't think I should shout."

"What's the matter?"

"Nothing. Somebody told me the Gyppos bug all these hotel rooms."

"I doubt it. But if they do, you can figure the bugs work like the phones. What's with the intrigue? You got another big deal in the works?"

"Uh-uh. I was saying I didn't call to tell you about Alexandria."

"Well, I hope the hell you're not going to offer your condolences."

"About your job you mean."

"Right."

"No, I wasn't going to offer you any condolences. You were kind of mysterious in your last letter. I got the impression you had to quit."

"Yes."

"I thought you were one of their heroes after what happened in Beirut."

"You used the right tense."

"What?"

"Never mind."

"Listen, big guy, it's your business. But since you brought it up, maybe you could explain it to me."

"You know what happened in Beirut?"

"Sure. A shell or something . . ."

"An RPG. Rocked-propelled grenade."

"Okay. You're still a stickler for accuracy. An RPG. An RPG hit your office and killed your secretary. The story I heard, you were in another room and weren't even scratched."

I did not say anything at first. As if they were an incantation, Harris's words resurrected the image from the mental crypt where I had buried it. I saw my office on Hamra Street, the glass blown out of the windows, the walls pitted from shrapnel, smoke everywhere, and through the smoke, Leila's typewriter crushed as if by some giant's hands, her desk tipped over, she lying beneath it, one leg protruding with a new Charles Jourdan boot still on it, the boot intact, as if to demonstrate the superior survivability of French leather over human flesh. I saw myself in the Telex room, whose thick walls had shielded me from the explosion. The Telex was tap-tapping away, the copy paper filling up with the lines of the story I was filing to Los Angeles. I was sitting on the floor, stunned, half-deafened, and wondering how the machine could go on like that, tap-tap-tapping away, wondering against all reason why it did not stop in acknowledgment of the horror in the next room.

I had seen worse things, in terms of numbers of dead. A gallery of grotesques hung in my mind. It was my very own private, portable collection of the disasters of war, begun when I was a paratrooper in Vietnam and added to each year as a correspondent in other wars in other places. But the picture of Leila was the worst, the Mona Lisa of my collection. The horror of her death did not lie in the fact that she had been dismembered, for I had seen plenty of that as well, but in its utter randomness. She had come to work that day because a cease-fire had been declared. The city had been quiet all morning. Then someone, probably some teenage moron who had grown bored, fired the RPG from the Moslem quarter above Hamra Street. He could not have been aiming at anything; he fired blind. The rocket arced over the roofs and, guided by pure chance, smashed through the window of the *Post*'s office while Leila was typing up my expense account.

"Big guy, did you hear me?" Harris shouted.

"I heard you."

"That's the way it happened, isn't it?"

"That's the way it happened."

"So you were a hero. I saw some of the *Post*'s stories reprinted in the *Herald Tribune*. 'Our man narrowly escapes death' and all that. Why'd you have to quit?"

"Situational reaction."

"What? Jesus, it sounds like there's a wind blowing through this phone."

"I said, 'situational reaction.' It used to be called shell shock. A nervous breakdown. After what happened, they had to send me to an American army hospital in Germany. All the shrinks up there specialize in people who crack up in wars. I was there for a month."

There was a long pause, then: "Christ, Charlie. I didn't know that. I can't even believe it. Old hard-ass Charlie Gage having a nervous breakdown, spending a month with the wig-pickers. I don't suppose Allison shoving off on you helped either."

"That didn't make any difference. That's why she asked for the divorce in the first place. She felt she never made any difference. I guess she didn't."

"Well, that was nice of her, taking off on you like that. And that was nice of the *Post*, to squeeze you out just because you cracked up."

"That isn't exactly the way it was."

The way it was. After the doctors released me from the hospital, the paper gave me a month's leave and then transferred me to Cairo. The editors considered the assignment a reward, their idea of Cairo being the Cairo of travel brochures, a sensuous, graceful Paris-on-the-Nile, and not the Cairo of reality, a fly-plagued, decaying mess, Calcutta-on-the-Nile. Still, it was better than Beirut, where those who survived each week's fighting stuffed sprigs of mint in their nostrils to block the stench of those who had not. The trouble was, I had lost the ability to function. The doctors had certified me to be of sound mind, but I had begun to suffer from another kind of malady, one I could not name. Its principal symptom was a profound indifference, a monastic sense of detachment from the world that was relieved only by fits of anxiety whenever the memory of the explosion and Leila's fractioned body rose up out of the nightmare depths of my mind. Then, to calm down, I would take a couple of pills the doctors had given me. Their effect was to leave me so dazed it required an effort to do the simplest things. As for the more complicated things, I did not do them at all. I failed to keep appointments, missed interviews, forgot to attend press conferences. I filed only two pieces during my first few months, but felt none of the guilt I was supposed to feel; the stories the editors regarded as so critical seemed totally unimportant to me.

The home office indulged me for a while, ascribing my silence to the usual problems of adjusting to a new post. Then messages began to come in, expressing the foreign desk's impatience with my performance, or lack of it. There were only one or two a week at first, couched in polite language. I picked them up at Reuter's dingy office on Shiriff Street, where I rented desk space and a mailbox. Later, the messages—they are called "rockets" in trade jargon, a term I found disturbing—took on an increasingly threatening tone, rather like those computerized warnings credit-card companies send to customers who have not paid their bills.

GAGE: FILE SOONEST YOUR VERSION NYT STORY ON POSSIBLE DISPATCH ARAB-LEAGUE PEACE-KEEPING TROOPS TO LEBANON. CHEERS, HANSON.

GAGE: AGENCIES DAYLEADING SITUATIONERS EGYPTIAN-SYRIAN MINI-SUMMIT UPCOMING NEXT WEEK. WHERE YOURS? REGARDS, HANSON.

GAGE: COMPETITION FRONTING ALEXANDRIA RIOTS
SAYING BIGGEST TEST YET FOR SADAT REGIME. WHY
YOU UNFILING AND UNRESPONDING OUR QUERIES?
HANSON.

I found it impossible to explain to Hanson, the foreign
editor, why I was "unfiling and unresponding." I could not
explain it to myself. My only defense would have been to
say I had snapped under the strain; but I was too proud
of my reputation. Sending no reply to the last message,
I awaited the final rocket. It burst two days later:

GAGE: YOUR RESPONSE OUR LAST QUERY UNRECEIVED.
LETTER FROM MACMORRIS FOLLOWS. HANSON.

MacMorris was the managing editor. His letter reached
me after a three-week voyage through the Egyptian mails.
It opened with a couple of paragraphs praising my past
achievements, my "track record," as MacMorris called it
with the athleticism American executives are so fond of.
This was followed by expressions of sympathy for what I
had been through in Beirut, which were prologue to a
recitation of the facts of life: he had a newspaper to put
out, he needed copy from me, I was being paid to supply
him with it, I had not done so in weeks; therefore, effective
the first of the following month, I was to be replaced and
transferred to the copy desk in the home office.
I recognized this for what it was: a gentle suggestion
that I quit to spare them, and myself as well, the pain of
a sacking. I had known several older correspondents, men
who had lost the wind and the legs to stay with the pack,
who had received similar letters. All of them accepted the
demotions to desk work and all of them were out on the
street within a year. Deciding there was no point in pro-
longing the inevitable, I submitted my resignation. It was
accepted, with regrets of course, and an offer to pay my
fare back to the States. I declined. I had been abroad too
long to go home, I dreaded the thought of facing old col-
leagues and all their petty gossip, I was in no condition to
go through the ordeal of writing résumés and fielding silly
questions from personnel directors. So I stayed on in Cairo,

free-lancing now and then to pay the rent, but mostly living off my savings.

Several weeks passed before the reaction set in. I was thirty-five years old, in the dead-center of my life, and I began to suffer all the self-doubts that come from being unemployed at that unsettling age. Perhaps it was my blue-collar background, but I believed a man was what he did. I was doing nothing; therefore I was nothing. For a while I sought refuge in self-dramatization, playing the part of the dissolute white man living in exotic exile. I drank heavily, gambled recklessly in the hotel casinos, and paid frequent visits to a hash den in a quarter called Bulaq, the rotten heart of rotting Cairo. But the attractiveness of that way of life diminished with each withdrawal from my bank account. My old feelings of indifference started to give way to desperation, desperation for a job, any job. It was not only the need for money, but for some activity that would give at least the appearance of a purpose to my existence.

On the other end of the line, Harris, barely audible through the static, said, "Charlie, Charlie, Charlie. Your life has been a series of disasters lately."

"Yeah."

"Listen, I know a guy who wants to talk to you. I think there might be something in it for you."

"What, for example?"

"Money, for example."

"How much?"

"I don't know. Does it make a difference?"

"No. Just curious."

"The guy's got a lot of contacts. He might help get you a job somewhere."

"What kind of job?"

"Don't know that either."

"Then why in hell does he want to talk to me?"

"Look, Baby Dave is just passing on a message and trying to help out his old buddy at the same time. Okay?"

"Okay."

"This guy, Jack Gardner, I met him a long time ago, when I was working with AID. Didn't see him for close to ten years, then I bumped into him in Beirut, just before I got sent to London. Turns out he's managing a company called Inter-Arab Development. You've probably heard of them."

"Sorry. Can't say I have."

"You can't what?"

"I've never heard of them."

"Jesus, I hate all this shouting. You sure there's no bugs in these rooms?"

"No, I'm just sure they don't work."

"Uh-huh. Well, anyway, a couple of weeks ago Gardner phoned me in London. Said he heard I was going to Alex— don't ask me how he found that out—and that he wanted to talk to me if I got up to Cairo. So I saw him this morning and he said he wanted to talk to you. This outfit he manages, they do development projects. You know, building factories and irrigation systems. The A-rabs put up the bread and Inter-Arab gives them the equipment and technicians to teach them how to use it. You know, technical expertise. Give the wogs a shovel and then show 'em how to dig a ditch."

"Dave, I'm pretty much a wog myself when it comes to building factories. Don't know a thing about it. So what does this Gardner want to talk to me about?"

"Let me give you a little advice, Charlie. Gardner's a cockroach."

"That's a terrific recommendation."

"What I mean is, he doesn't like bright lights. There's only one difference between him and a real cockroach. Shine a light on him and he won't slip into a crack in the wall; he'll tear your head off. Follow?"

I said I followed, and felt a buzz of fear and excitement.

"Here's what he said. He said: 'You know that Charles Gage fellow'—there's another mystery, big guy. How'd he know we're friends?—'You know that Charles Gage fellow, and I'd appreciate it if you told him I'd like to talk to him if he feels it wouldn't compromise his journalistic integrity."

Saying nothing, I looked out the window, down to where the trees on the riverbank shaded a moored riverboat, then on across the liver-brown Nile. The Meridien rose at the tip of Roda Island near the opposite bank, all glass, stone, and steel glinting in the hard sunlight.

"Charlie, are you listening to me?"

"Your friend Gardner isn't a cockroach. He's a comic. My journalistic integrity! If he knows so much, he ought to know I'm not exactly long on journalistic integrity these days."

"That's what he said. And that he wants to pick your brain about that place in Africa you wrote about a while back."

"What place?"

"I'm not supposed to mention it on the phone. But since you don't think these bugs work, I'll tell you: Bay-Bay something."

"Bejaya."

"Right. Bejaya. That's it. He wants to talk to you about Bejaya. His outfit's got some development project planned there."

"A *project*. Dave, the place is the end of the world. Nothing but sand and mountains and hardly a road in it. And they've got a war on there, a rebellion. Been going on for five years. What's your man going to do? Build a dam in the desert and then pay the rebels not to blow it up?"

"Charlie," Harris said in an exasperated tone, "you're no sweet young thing anymore. You've been around the block a few times, so I can only assume you're being deliberately difficult. What do I have to do, write it out for you on the blackboard? *Officially*, it's a development project. All he wants to do is talk to you. Maybe he can help you get a job. Anyway, you're in no position, after what you've told me, to ask a lot of nit-picking questions."

"Just trying to preserve my journalistic integrity. I really like that. It's a great line."

"Look, Tom's a strange guy."

"Tom?"

"Give me a break, Charlie. I meant Jack. His name's Jack."

"Right, and he's a strange guy."

"Kind of formal sometimes and, well, you know, he's got to be careful about dealing with newsmen these days, even ex-newsmen. Listen, I've got an appointment and I'm running late. If you're going to talk to him, he wants you

to be in front of the Hilton at two. Two sharp. I told him
I'd let him know how you feel about it."

"Tell Tom I don't feel my journalistic integrity will be
compromised."

Harris paused, then answered in a somewhat nervous
voice. "I said his name's Jack Gardner."

"Dave, when did you start getting mixed up with
spooks?"

"*Charlie, goddamnit.* I'm sticking my neck out, talking
to you on the phone like this. We're supposed to be friends,
so stop playing games with me. Yes or no?"

"Yes, I'll see him in front of the Hilton at two."

"Okay, great. That was really like pulling teeth. Hey,
let's get together before I leave. I'm flying out Wednesday,
so let's make it for Tuesday night at the Cinq à Sept Club.
Say nine. Okay?"

I said that would be fine and hung up without asking
for a description of Mr. Gardner; because he appeared to
be in the business of knowing things, I assumed he was
familiar with my face and would recognize me. Also
assuming he wanted accurate information, I refreshed my
memory by rereading the stories I had written about Bejaya
two years before, then looked for the notebooks I had kept
while there.

All of my old notebooks, several dozen of them, were
stored in the bottom drawer of the mahogany campaign
desk Allison and I had bought in London when the *Post*
first sent us abroad. The shopkeeper, to justify its battered
condition and extravagant price, claimed it had belonged
to a brigadier fighting Afghans on the old Northwest Frontier. Looking at it, heavy and solid, with brass handles and
brass-tipped corners, I remembered how we had worked
to refinish it and how we had been then. Remembering,
I felt an aching; the ache of loss, of the always mysterious
loss of love.

Well, in our case it might not have been so mysterious.
I was always too long away from home, in places where
I saw things I could not express to her—or to anyone, for
that matter. There had been the time I jetted back to our
Chelsea town house after weeks on the Golan Heights,

where the stench of the Syrian dead leaked like a gas through the rocks covering their shallow graves. I had been up on the Golan one afternoon and in London the next. With no time to decompress, I suffered a bad case of the emotional bends. A record was playing on the stereo, logs crackling in the fireplace to cut the house's chill, my books neatly stacked on the shelves flanking the fireplace; and Allison, sitting on the couch with her legs tucked under her, was chatting about the lecture on Hardy she had heard at the American Women's Club. That smell was in my nostrils. It seemed to be on my hands and in my clothes, and I wondered that Allison had not noticed it or if she was just too polite to mention it. She went on and on about some professor's brilliant analysis of Hardy's use of color in *The Return of the Native*. I wanted to scream, "How can you talk about Victorian novels while they're lying out there, thousands of them, and their stink is all over me?" But I just sat, smiling stupidly and saying, "Uh-huh, yes, I see," the way you do when listening to someone speaking in a foreign language you pretend to understand.

We were transferred from London to the Rome bureau, and from there to Beirut. Whatever city I called home, I was always leaving it for the dark and violent regions of the earth: Ethiopia, Rhodesia, Cambodia for two weeks before the Khmer Rouge took over, Cyprus to record the Turks and Greeks renewing their ancient blood-feud. Allison meanwhile lived in the capsule of the American wife abroad. Live-in maids. Clubs. Cultural study groups. Occasional forays in tour buses to look at the natives or the ruins of dead civilizations. In time, it became impossible for me to speak to her, to listen to her. She was a few years younger than I, not long out of the tidy Catholic women's college where she had been taught that the world was basically a reasonable place, man the paragon of animals, and all his problems solvable. Everything I had seen had taught me the opposite. There were moments when I felt malicious impulses to show her the pictorial evidence— the photographs I had taken for the *Post,* the ones the editors had refused to print as unsuitable for a family newspaper—of the brutal and bloody age we lived in. But I did not want to be the one to shock or persuade her out

of her traditional humanism, to inflict my bitterness on her.
(And I was bitter because I had left Vietnam convinced I
had lost all my illusions and plumbed the depths of human
darkness, only to learn that that was just another illusion;
there were always greater depths, there was always something more to lose.) I began to behave strangely whenever
I was at home, falling into long, gloomy sulks and snapping
at Allison if she tried to cheer me up with some enthusiastic
description of her latest trip to the (museum) (gallery)
(palace) (cathedral) (mosque). Finally, and naturally,
she found it unbearable to live with a man who was gone
half the time and who returned full of a secretive silence,
as if he had done something shameful. I think she may have
suspected me of infidelity and was bothered by it despite
her assertions that she didn't care what I did when I was
away as long as I came back to her. Whatever, our marriage
became the major casualty of my peculiar life.

Sitting at the desk, I saw her on the day, months before
Leila's death, that she left Beirut for the States. She was in
line at the airport, a tall woman as slim and graceful as a
cypress when she stood, but still girlishly awkward when
she walked. Her shoulder-length chestnut hair was pulled
back because of the heat, and, with an elegant movement
of her arm, she handed her passport to the green-uniformed
guard at the gate. He glanced at it, waved her through, and
she walked toward the plane without looking back. The
recollection flooded me with all the emptiness and desolation I had felt then. *Charlie, Charlie, Charlie. Your life
has been a series of disasters.* I supposed Harris was right.
The divorce had been one of the disasters, like the shrapnel
that had shredded my legs in Vietnam, like losing my job,
like the rocket that had killed Leila and driven me into a
psychiatric ward. It was a dismal record, and as I sat there,
absently rummaging through the drawer, a voice in the
back of my mind whispered that these events had not been
the acts of a malicious Providence; I had secretly wanted
them to happen, the voice said, somehow willed them to
happen. Disaster was drama and I had the journalist's penchant for drama, a coin whose opposite side was a fear of
normality. Perhaps I had subconsciously done everything
possible to sabotage my marriage because I knew it would

inevitably lead to children, a mortgage, everyday responsibilities. Oh, the hell with that, I thought. The hell with self-analysis. Maybe the unexamined life is not worth living, but there are some of us whose lives would be intolerable if subject to too close a scrutiny. So the hell with thinking, find those notebooks, and keep your appointment with Jack Gardner, whose real first name is Tom.

Bound in green vinyl, the Bejaya notebooks lay at the bottom of the pile. There were two, filled with what scraps I'd been able to pick up in the week I had spent interviewing Bejayan rebels and refugees near the province's border with Sudan. I slipped them into my pocket and started down the stairs. Having been tutored by MacMorris to believe in what he called the "adversary relationship" between the government and the press, I felt uneasy, as though I were about to do something forbidden. It was MacMorris's policy to fire any correspondent caught moonlighting as an agent and to refuse to rehire any staffer who had quit to work as, say, a press aide for a political candidate. I had severed all ties with the paper, but the years of regarding Them as a kind of enemy could not be wiped away in a few months. On the other hand, it would be a lie to pretend I was not flattered by their interest in me, flattered, curious, and excited—excited enough to go bounding down the stairs two at a time, nearly tripping because the steps were slippery from the sand that had insinuated itself through the cracks in the windows. I had been a soldier for three years, a correspondent for nearly a decade, and those occupations had provided an adrenal stimulation that had become an addiction. I did not have the temperament for a sedentary existence; it made me morbid. I had a need to act, and in Mr. Gardner I sensed the promise of its fulfillment.

With plenty of time and little money, I walked to the Hilton. Zamalik, the neighborhood where I lived, was on Gezira Island, a green, quiet refuge separated by the river from the slums of Bulaq, in whose dust-strangled streets Cairo's millions patiently endured their misery.

It was spring and the *Khamsin*, the hot wind that comes out of the desert, had just begun to blow. *Khamsin* means "fifty" in Arabic and the wind blows for that many days.

Crossing the Nile over the Twenty-sixth of July Bridge, I could see a faint brownish-gold mist hovering over the river and the city—sand, tons of it, blasted in from the wasteland they call the Great Sand Sea. Each grain glittered in the light like a tiny shard of broken glass. There would soon be more of it in the air, so much more that what was now a mist would become a dense pall, darkening the sun at noon to a dusky orange and at dusk to a deep, unnatural red, the color it will have in the distant age when it begins to burn out and die.

Traffic choked the bridge. Fumes rose from thousands of rusted-out exhaust pipes to mingle with the sand, a smothering mixture that made me wheeze like an asthmatic. The buses, the red and white buses the government had bought new from Spain two years before but which already appeared ready for the scrap heap, were so crowded you wondered how the passengers avoided suffocation before reaching their stops. Taxi drivers leaned on their horns futilely, cursing as only Arabs can. The devout had their radios tuned to the station that played the daily prayers, so amidst the honking and cursing there was the high, strange cry of the *muezzin*.

Once over the bridge, I headed along the Corniche, the wide boulevard that parallels the river. Black and white taxis were hurtling down the street, rattling like tin cans filled with pebbles when they went over the potholes. It was a long walk beneath an oppressive sun. The puny trees, dust-paled and spaced wide apart, offered little shade. The sidewalk, full of holes and cracks, had buckled in places. Every day, there seemed to be more holes and cracks, more buckles, more chips in the curbstones; and the buildings on the opposite side of the Corniche, begrimed to an almost uniform grey-brown, looked a little more run-down. Cairo was a city whose disintegration appeared to be progressing at a geometric rate. Walking, I wondered when it would reach the point of collapse, when the decay would reach critical mass, creating a scene out of a Hollywood disaster movie. I could see it happening one day—the hotels and casinos, the mosques and museums, the villas of Zamalik along with the shacks of Bulaq, all quitting the struggle to stay upright and crashing down into heaps of

stone and brick, the rubble sliding into the river to create
a huge dam against which the Nile would back up, drown-
ing the fertile valleys along its banks, then cutting itself a
new channel through which it would go on flowing, as it
was flowing now. It was filled with the silt of centuries,
with the dissolved mud of all the towns swept away by its
perennial floods, with the feces and garbage of all the
masses who had lived up and down its great length; but
it was still flowing, the way it always had and always
would.

Halfway to the Hilton, I suddenly felt tired and stopped
to lean against the embankment wall. The water below was
flat and brown, dark brown now that the sandy mist had
dimmed the brightness of the sky. The Information Ministry building stood behind me, its tall TV transmission
tower a symbol of an illusory progress, its entranceway
guarded by a worthless parapet of rotting sandbags, against
which a squad of militiamen lolled indifferently. Gezira
lay almost directly across the river, with the Cairo Tower
rising above it and the flamboyants blossoming red, like
fresh bullet wounds puncturing the body of the green trees
lining the island's streets. Looking at the Nile, so wide
there, its current so slow and majestic you could not see it
moving except where it pushed against the pilings of the
bridges, I thought of how long it was, and how long it had
been there, and how many civilizations it had seen rise and
fall, and I felt almost overcome by a sense of the futility
of all human effort. Nothing we did, individually or col-
lectively, seemed to matter compared to the great river
that was like a god in its eternity, in its power to give life
and take it away. Less than half an hour before, I had left
my flat hoping for a chance to act; now all action seemed
without purpose. The quick change in mood was not unusual. Ever since Leila's death, my emotions tended to have
as many ups and downs as a sine wave moving across an
oscillograph.

I might have brooded there until well past two had it not
been for the street-hawkers and beggars. The Corniche
was one of their favorite beats. They preferred stationary
targets and started to swarm around me within minutes

after I had stopped walking. Boys and old men dressed in filthy *gelibiyas*, they offered to sell me trinkets, or to shine my shoes, even though I was wearing buff desert boots, or simply held out their hands with the look I had seen in the eyes of beggars in other eastern cities: the wide, haunted stare of a hopeless poverty seeking a useless charity. I began walking again, keeping them off with waves of my arms and shakes of my head. They all quit except one persistent old man whose right eye had been turned into a gray smear from trachoma. He was pushing a cart with a few bruised oranges in it, and shuffled beside me, asking if I would buy one. No, I would not. Would I then give him a few piasters *bakshish*. No, he had performed no service, so why should I *bakshish* him? He fixed me with his good eye and gave me a yellow-toothed grin. "Because *bakshish* is a custom here." Knowing he would never believe that I, an American, was nearly broke, I said, "*Allah yatik*—God give you something," and he backed away, mostly out of surprise at hearing the phrase from a westerner.

The Hilton was now just across the way, sleek and modern and oozing meretricious glamor. I crossed the Corniche at a run and then went up the hotel's curved driveway. Covered by a marquee, it was full of the usual tour buses and limousines, the latter for privileged tourists who were treated deferentially by a doorman dressed to look like a retainer in some nineteenth-century pasha's court. It felt good to be out of the kindless North African sun. My feet were hot from the walk, my eyes raw from the windblown sand. Seeing me waiting, the costumed doorman asked if I wanted a taxi. I shook my head. What I wanted he could not give: a drink to cool my parched throat. Maybe Mr. Gardner would be good for a few gin and tonics, in exchange for an education about Bejaya. I hoped for more, but a few gins would do as starters. Waiting, I looked at every male western face that passed by and watched for a glance of recognition. None came. Maybe he did not know what I looked like after all. It was already a quarter past two. I took a few steps toward the doorman, thinking to ask him if he knew Gardner, then rejected the idea out of an instinct that Mr. Gardner was not the sort of man who would want his name, if that was his name, dropped indiscreetly.

After another fifteen minutes, I returned to the scorched street and started pacing back and forth in front of the hotel. Sweat was breaking through my khaki jacket and I was considering calling it quits when the Arab appeared alongside me.

"Good afternoon, my friend," he said in English. I went on walking back and forth, like a sentry. He kept pace with me and repeated, "Good afternoon, my friend. You're new to Cairo. I can see that. My name is Ali Mahmoud. As we say, *Ahlan wasahlan, mit ahlan wasahlan.* That means—"

" 'A thousand welcomes,' Egyptian dialect. Syrian dialect, it's *Ahlan wasahlan, alf ahlan wasahlan.*"

"Ya-ah! You speak Arabic. And very well."

"Right. And I'm not new to Cairo. So shove off, as we say. That means 'shove off.' "

The hotel grounds were off limits to the hustlers who worked the street, so I turned to go back up the Hilton's driveway. But the man who called himself Ali Mahmoud hopped nimbly around me to block my path.

"I know that phrase. It's American. You are an American. I *am* right about that?"

"Right."

"Ye-es. 'Shove off.' That's American. An Englishman would say, 'Bugger off.' Bugger off," he said, imitating a British accent and smiling at his mimicry.

He was tall, almost as tall as I, and dressed in tight trousers and a clinging cotton shirt opened to reveal a jungle of black chest-hair. Except for his height, he reminded me of one of those dark characters who lurk around the piazzas in Rome, trying to look like every middle-aged divorcée's fantasy of the Mediterranean male. For a Cairo peddler, he appeared remarkably healthy; trachoma had not clouded his eyes, his olive skin was not pitted, and he had a set of white, perfectly aligned teeth. He flashed them, saying, "So, you see I also know languages. A knowledge of languages is useful in my craft."

"Look, Ali Mahmoud, I'd appreciate it if you got out of my way," I said evenly. "I've got to meet someone here."

"Well, perhaps I could help. I know most of the foreigners who come here. Who are you to meet?"

"No, you can't help me, and it's none of your goddamned business who I'm going to meet."

He leered like a pimp, and I fought the urge to smash those pretty teeth of his. "Ye-es. I understand. A woman. Perhaps you would like to buy one of these for her."

He patted the brown paper-wrapped package he was holding under one arm. It was an exceptionally muscular arm. If I did take a swing at him, or tried to shove him out of the way, he would probably fight back, creating a scene. Not wanting a scene, I started walking toward the corner, where the Arab League building stood.

"This would be just the thing for a woman," Ali said, striding beside me.

"It's not a woman. Look, friend, I don't want whatever you've got there. And I don't want to see the belly dancers or the pyramids. And I don't want a girl or a fresh young boy or whatever else you're peddling. All right? Go find another customer."

He affected an expression of insulted pride. At the same time, I saw something else in his mud-black eyes: an appraising look.

"My friend, I don't deal in belly dancers, or in girls, or in boys. Boys! By God, that's abominable. I only wish to show you these. You only have to look. It's only my hope that you will look and then come to buy at my shop."

"My ass your shop. Your shop's right there under your arm. What've you got? Stolen watches?"

"I told you, Ali Mahmoud doesn't deal in things like that. It's jewelry. Berber jewelry from Algeria. Here."

He handed me a business card, printed in Arabic on one side and in English on the other. It declared him to be a dealer in metal crafts and "Oriental curiosities," the proprietor of a shop called the Valley of the Kings in the Khan al-Khalili bazaar.

"So you see I'm quite legitimate," Ali said, slipping around the corner and furtively opening the package as if it really did contain hot watches. But it was Berber jewelry after all, or at least a fair imitation of it. "Please, my friend, have a look."

"If it'll get you off my back. But I'm broke. No money."

Handing me a bracelet of hammered silver, he said, "You are most welcome."

I looked at it because I was curious, not about the bracelet but about him. Ali Mahmoud appeared a little too vigorous, a little too smooth and articulate to be a mere bazaar-hawker. And I did not like that concentrated, appraising look in his eyes. Pretending to an interest in the bracelet, I saw, out of the corner of my eye, Ali glancing over his shoulder at a new Fiat that had just pulled into a no-parking zone near the entrance gate of the Arab League building. When the policeman guarding the entrance walked over to tell him to move, the driver said something. Nodding, the policeman returned to his sentry booth. Farther on down the Corniche stood the old Shepheard's Hotel. It had been wrecked in the food riots, one of those rare instances when the famed Egyptian patience, strained by resentments too long repressed and sufferings too long endured, burst into a collective dementia of looting and arson. The ruins reminded me of Holt, the *Daily Telegraph* correspondent who had been killed during the disturbances. The government blamed it on the rioters, but no one believed that. His body had been found in a car in Old Cairo, his hands tied and a single bullet hole in the back of his head; an execution, not a random murder.

"What do you think of the bracelet?" Ali asked.

I handed it to him, but he kept his arms at his sides.

"What will you offer for it?"

"Nothing."

"Then this perhaps." He pulled out a heavy elaborate necklace that made a jangling sound when he held it up. "Also Berber. 'Barbarian,' as they call it in Algeria."

"No, not that either."

"But mister, I've worked all day without selling a thing. All-l da-ay and nothi-ing."

"*Essabr' muftâh elfa'rah.*"

He grinned his white grin. "Ye-es. 'Patience is the key to gladness.' You know the proverb. There's truth in it, but I've been patient all day and no gladness has come to me."

" 'God is generous. May he open the gates of sustenance unto you.' That's another one I know."

"Incorrect if said to someone like me. That's something you say to beggars."

"Look, patience is something I'm running out of. You said I didn't have to buy. Well, I'm not buying. Now take this thing and get out of here."

He snatched the bracelet with a grimace of feigned anger, feigned because I saw no anger in his eyes, only that cool, studious stare. Looking at him and at the dark green Fiat parked half a block away, I again thought of Holt. It was difficult to see how Ali could force me into the car in broad daylight, with thousands of people on the street. Still, I felt nervous, exposed, vulnerable.

"I regret you didn't like these," Ali said, squatting to rewrap the jewelry. "God willing, another time."

"God willing. Tell me something, dealer in Oriental curiosities."

"If I can."

"You're something of an Oriental curiosity yourself, aren't you?"

He stood. "Hey?"

"It's curious the way you keep looking at me. And your interest in that car, that's pretty damn curious, too."

Ali smiled again, a true Cairo hustler's smile if I'd ever seen one, bright and profane, suggestive and false. "What car?"

"The one behind you."

He glanced at the Fiat, then turned his eyes back to me. "How observant you are. Let me make another guess about you. You are a journalist."

"Was. Why are you so interested in the car?"

"It's possible the man in it is my associate."

"I'd say it's certain."

"As you wish. So let us say the man in the car is my associate and that, together, we deal in some other thing than Oriental curiosities. An Oriental commodity. You are, perhaps, interested in this commodity?"

"I'm interested in getting back to the hotel."

"To await your friend."

"To await my friend."

"But this commodity in which you may be interested. *I* know where it can be bought. It can be bought in Bulaq, in the coffee shop of Ismail Hijazi, where no one goes for coffee but only for this commodity."

Surprised, I said nothing. I saw in my mind the narrow, nameless street where there was no light except from the kerosene lamps burning in the one-room hovels and from the fluorescents in the coffee shop, their bluish glow dulled by the dead flies plastered to the glass tubing. Men sat or squatted along both sides of the street, staring glassily into the semidarkness. Boys in cotton pajamas were coming out of the shop with the long, curved pipes made of brass and wood, then lighting them and fanning the embers as we drew on the stems and sparks flew with a crackling from the bowls. Hijazi sold only the best stuff and, the penalties for drug-trafficking being rather severe in Egypt, the location of his place was a closely guarded secret. You needed a map to find it through the rat's maze of alleyways and dead-end streets. So who could have seen me and how did this trinket-peddler Ali know I had gone there?

"Not interested," I said with a composure I did not feel. "I'm going back to the hotel now. You bother me any more and I'll break your jaw."

I went around the corner and headed back toward the Hilton. Despite the warning, Ali followed, then, lithe as a ballet dancer, got ahead of me.

"My friend, I know you're interested in this commodity," he said, walking backward. "You use it. Oh, ye-es. I smoke it too, you see, and recognize the look. It's in my eyes"— he fanned his fingers in front of his eyes—"and in yours." His fingers moved toward my face, fluttering like brown tentacles. I had had enough. Slapping his hand away with my left, I swung for his jaw with my right and stopped cold when he dropped the package and deflected the punch with the neatest, fastest block I had ever seen. Or felt. My arm was numb from the wrist to the elbow.

At that moment, a platoon of sunburned German tourists marched past, clutching glossy guidebooks from the Egyptian Museum. It had happened too quickly for any of

them to notice, although two men slowed down to gaze at
Ali and me facing each other like boxers.

"It's okay," I said to the Germans. "Go on ahead."

"English?" one of the men asked.

"No, American. Everything's okay. Go ahead."

He looked at us, his wide brow knitted quizzically. I
smiled at him, rubbing the welt on my forearm at the same
time. "No trouble. *Verstest?* Alles ist okay."

This bit of fractured German seemed to satisfy him and
his friend; they fell back in with the others. When they
were well away, I said to Ali:

"Well, you bastard, where'd you learn that?"

"I told you a small lie, Mr. Gage. A half-truth. I've another craft besides the selling of metal crafts. A craft that
requires some knowledge of self-defense. And self-control.
You noticed I didn't retaliate. Ye-es, if patience is the key
to gladness in life, self-control is the key to success in The
Craft. Self-control. You must learn it. You have a bad
temper, Mr. Gage."

We were standing below the Hilton's pool and tennis
courts, which had been built on a low, artificial rise and
concealed from the street by a wall and thick shrubbery. I
could hear the splash of swimmers diving into the water,
music playing in the poolside bar, and the rhythmic
thwack-thwack of a tennis volley. I recall these irrelevant
details because they are associated in my mind with Ali's
words: "Self-control. You must learn it." And I remember
his words because self-control was the one quality Jeremy
Nordstrand did not have. Whenever I look back on the
chain of events that led me to become involved in the
operation, I see at one end an Egyptian lecturing me on
self-control and at the other an American who lacked that
attribute, lacked it utterly.

"You saw how your behavior attracted attention," Ali
was saying. "That's a good lesson. From now on you'll have
to learn to control yourself. That would include avoiding
places like Hijazi's. As you must know, Mr. Gage, hashish
is an excitant."

He picked up the package, but he was no longer the
slick, leering, obsequious street-hustler. He stood confidently before me, hands resting on his lean hips.

"Does Gardner make a habit of theatrics like this?" I was trying to sound cool, wise, and knowing, though my heart was beating fast, bubbles of anxiety rising in my throat. It had to be Gardner. How else could Ali have learned my name? Unless I'd been wrong about the taps and someone had picked up the phone conversation between Harris and me.

"Not theatrics at all," he said. "*Not at all.* You see, none of us had seen you before. . . ."

"Then how the hell did you know I'd been to Hijazi's?"

"Let us say someone saw you there. But that was at night. Besides that, we had only a photograph, a copy of your photograph from your newspaper. It wasn't very good, so I had to make sure it was you."

"Well, I think you prolonged things a bit, Ali."

"Perhaps." He nudged me and we started back toward the corner. "But I was sent here to do more than rendezvous with you. You're an unknown, you see. We had to test you. Mr. Gardner is an unorthodox man and he has unorthodox methods of testing his recruits."

"Recruits?"

Ignoring the question, he said, "I was your examiner, so to speak."

"I still think it was theatrical. And unnecessary."

"As you wish. I *was* enjoying the game. Ye-es, I do enjoy practicing the art of distimulation."

"Dissimulation."

"Ya-ah! Ye-es. Dissimulation."

"Well, examiner, did I pass?"

Ali reached into his snug, sweat-spotted shirt for a cigarette. "Smoke? They're American."

"I don't smoke."

"Yes, you passed, though you could have done better." He puffed thoughtfully; apparently, he took his role quite seriously.

"You failed when you lost your temper, which showed poor judgment. And lack of self-control. On the Corniche! By God, if you're going to bash someone, Mr. Gage, you bash him from behind on a back street, preferably at night. Not on the Corniche in daylight. Mr. Gardner told me

you had a reputation as a hothead. It caused you some un-
pleasantness in Beirut some time ago. Correct?"

"Your Mr. Gardner seems to have been interested in me
for a long time."

"He's a man with many interests."

"I'm sure."

"But, correct, you struck a Lebanese customs official
some time ago, and you were sent to jail?"

"Only overnight, till the right people were paid off."

Ali shook his head. "That won't do any longer. Self-
control, Mr. Gage. A foreigner who practices The Craft
in this part of the world must keep his head or risk losing
it, so to speak. Please."

The Fiat had pulled around the corner, out of sight of
the policeman guarding the League building. "Please," Ali
repeated, opening the door and sweeping his arm like an
aide ushering a minister into a limousine. The driver was
a paunchy, unshaven man in a threadbare suit. He looked
harmless, but I hesitated nonetheless.

"Please. Fear nothing."

"This is exactly how Holt bought it. The last time anyone saw him, he was getting into a car with an Arab."

"Bought what?"

"That's a colloquialism, knower of languages. It means
'got killed.' 'Lost his head,' so to speak. Part of it anyway."

"Ya-ah! The English journalist who was killed. Well, I
can promise you that you're safe. I do represent Mr. Gardner and we're going to meet Mr. Gardner." Ali gave me a
reassuring pat on the shoulder, which I found patronizing
and offensive.

"I'll sit in the back, alone."

"As you wish."

I climbed in. The Fiat was very hot inside and filled with
that leathery, new-car smell. Ali Mahmoud slammed the
door and, sliding into the front seat, told the driver, *"Yalla!*
—Let's go."

We pulled slowly away from the curb, went around the
hotel, Ali checking the rearview mirror now and then,
drove through El Tahrir Square, with its chaotic traffic and

tramcars so crowded and rickety they went down the tracks
leaning like sailboats heeling in a high wind, then crossed
the Qasr al-Nil Bridge over the everlasting river and
headed toward Giza.

I sat sweating in the broiling back seat, my clothes stuck
to the upholstery. Ali was combing his curly black hair in
the mirror.

"Would I fail one of your examinations if I asked where
the hell we're going?"

" 'Patience is the key to gladness,' " Ali answered, and I
could see his lustrous smile in the mirror.

The driver bullied his way through the berserk streets,
beseeching his God to condemn to eternal torments the
children of all motorists who blocked his path. He heaped
even more elaborate curses on the peddlers whose horse-
drawn wagons slowed traffic to a near-standstill. When we
were at last free of the city, he gunned the Fiat down the
Upper Egypt Road, toward the village of Badrshein. An
endless, dusty procession of men, vehicles, and animals
plodded along the blacktop. Weaving around creaking
carts and through herds of goats, we passed things that
looked like walking brush piles—donkeys loaded with
heaps of twigs and straw that covered every part of them
but their hooves. A string of four camels crossing the road
held us up for a few minutes. The driver gave them a
couple of blasts of the horn, and the caravaneer, yelling
hut! hut! hut!, whacked the lead animal's haunches with his
crop to hurry the string across. The camels picked up their
pace, the bundles of alfalfa on their backs bouncing in
rhythm to their swaying, rocking gait. We passed them,
got stuck behind a stopping-starting-stopping bus full of
women wrapped in funereal black, went around that and
another train of straw-laden donkeys, and slid back into
the right lane, just missing a truckload of *fellahin* trundling
down the left. It was moving all along the road, from one
village to the next, the slow and ceaseless traffic of the Nile
Valley.

Off to the left, the river glinted dully in the hazy sunlight. Bean, cotton, and barley fields, watered by the Nile,
stretched away from each bank for a short distance before

ending in the desert, where the river surrendered its power to nourish and renew the earth and all was given over to the killing sun. In places, the straw roofs and mud-brick walls of a *fellah*'s house showed through the date palm and feathery tamarisk trees that shaded the fields. An old man was squatting not far off the road, cranking the handle on an Archimedes' screw to raise water from a canal to irrigate his bean field. The beans lay in rows separated by water-filled ditches shining silver in the sun, like strips of polished metal. An ox, yoked to a wooden well-wheel and blindfolded with what looked like a dirty bed-sheet, was clomping in monotonous circles, around and around, turning the wheel. Behind the ox and the man working the screw, the *gelibiyas* of the peasants in the distant fields were varicolored specks against the gold squares of barley and patches of green cotton.

"Isn't it wonderful?" Ali asked rhetorically. "My wonderful, backward country. It looked just like this in the time of the pharaohs. Wouldn't you say so, Mr. Gage?"

"How would I know?"

"On the walls of the tombs there are painted scenes just like this. Nothing's changed. Nothing since the pharaohs' times."

"Well, your friend Gardner does development projects. Maybe he ought to start right here."

"His work is in political development."

"Political development. That's what you call it?"

"Yes."

"I wonder what a political development project looks like."

"I think you may see one. I think that's what Mr. Gardner wants to discuss with you."

"I don't suppose you have any details."

"No. I know only what I need to know. 'Need to know.' It's one of Mr. Gardner's favorite phrases."

"I need to know where we're going. That's what I need to know."

"Are you afraid?"

"Curious."

"No, not curious. You journalists like to think of your-

selves as curious, but what you call curiosity is really an
inability to withstand the unknown or uncertainties. Oh, I
know. I was once a journalist."

"Before you became a dealer in Oriental curiosities?"

"Yes." He turned around, resting his round chin on his
arm. Sweat had beaded beneath the line of his knotty
hair, and the dust blowing through the window had mixed
with the sweat to form a paste on his forehead. "I worked
for *Al-Ahram*, translating English articles into Arabic.
They got rid of me for making indiscreet remarks about
the Russians. That was what? Oh, a number of years ago,
when it was fashionable to say we loved the Russians even
though we hated them. I didn't know the art of dis—
dissimulation. It is 'dissimulation,' Mr. Gage?"

"It is."

"I don't know why I have such trouble with that word.
Dis-*sim*-ulation. So, I was young then and not so good a
dissimulator. I hated the Russians and said so and my
editor got rid of me. That gives us something in common."

"Can't say I hate the Russians."

Ali gave me one of his gorgeous grins. "Now you are
the dissimulator, Mr. Gage. You know my meaning. We
both worked for newspapers and we've both been got rid
of."

"Did Gardner tell you that?"

"Oh, ye-es."

"Where're we going?"

We had by that time traveled some ten or twelve miles
out of Cairo and were moving slowly through a village.
Above its huts of sunbaked brick, kindling piled on their
roofs, round dovecotes rose like castle turrets. The villagers
did not keep doves in them, but fertilizer, whose acrid smell
soured the good odors of woodsmoke, brewing coffee, and
baking bread issuing from the huts. "We're going there,"
Ali said, pointing beyond the village to where the limestone
plateau called Abusir rose above a broad stretch of palm,
the forest of Badrshein. The line between it and the desert
plateau, between green and beige, between fertility and
desolation, was as sharp as the line dividing land and
sea. Abusir, in fact, looked like a huge wave poised to en-
gulf the forest, and the fine sand which the *Khamsin* was

scouring from its surface resembled a spray. Through it, I saw the high step-pyramid, the tomb of King Zoser Neterkhet.

"That's Saqqara," I said.

"Yes, Saqqara. That's where we're going. Your next question, O journalist, would be: 'And why are we going to Saqqara?' My answer: 'Because Mr. Gardner is there.' Your next question: 'And what is Mr. Gardner doing in Saqqara?' My answer, a question: 'Do you know what Saqqara means?' "

"Soqarit was the ancient Egyptian god of the dead."

"And Saqqara means 'the domain of Soqarit.' "

"The domain of the god of the dead. I don't find that very reassuring."

"Don't worry. You aren't going to join them. Mr. Gardner wants to speak with you there because he has a passion for secrecy. I would call it an obsession. A useful obsession when dealing with us Arabs. We talk too much, we are too much in love with our language. With us, a thing spoken is a thing done. Further, that which has not been spoken or written first cannot be done. Now, at this time of day and with the wind blowing, there should be few people there. Perhaps no one. No one but the dead, who cannot betray a secret. Could you think of a better place to ensure privacy?"

I shook my head, not in answer to Ali's question, but out of disbelief.

"I think Mr. Gardner is a little whacko."

"*Shu?* What?"

"I think he's mad."

"I wouldn't say Mr. Gardner's mad. Oh, no. As I told you before, he is unorthodox."

———

The unorthodox Mr. Gardner was wearing an orthodox perma-press suit with grey and white stripes, a pale blue shirt and blue tie. Under the circumstances, the conventionality of his dress did reveal a certain unconventionality in his character. What kind of man, I wondered, would wear a suit and tie in that weather, out on a desert?

He was sitting on a pile of ancient rubble, outside the crenellated wall that enclosed the step-pyramid. King Zoser's tomb had been built in tiers, the widest at the bottom, and resembled a series of stairs leading to nowhere. Beneath it, Gardner looked as small as a doll. He gazed at the structure, then scribbled something in a notebook. I guessed he was posing as a student of pharaonic burial practices. Not that a pose was necessary; as Ali had figured, no one was there, no one except three ragged Arabs. One of them ran up as we left the car and offered to guide us through the tombs for five pounds Egyptian. Ali told him to move along; then, in a more deferential tone, told me to wait while he talked to Gardner. I watched him walk, hunched against the wind, his feet sinking in the limestone marl, to where Gardner sat serenely in his suit. They spoke for several minutes, the Egyptian gesturing, the American sitting on a stone slab with his legs crossed. I could not hear them for the hissing wind but assumed Ali was reporting on the results of my examination. Huge and mysterious, pyramids rose all around the vast plateau. Beyond, the wastes of the Western Desert stretched away beneath a pall of blowing sand.

It was more than unreal, crazier than insane. And when Ali returned and said, "Mr. Gardner will see you now," as if he were a receptionist in an executive's suite, I broke out laughing.

"You find this amusing, Mr. Gage?"

"Oh, no. I'm quite accustomed to meeting people in graveyards. That's what this is, isn't it? The world's biggest cemetery."

"Don't laugh in front of Mr. Gardner. He's a serious man."

Ali walked back to the car and drove off, leaving me feeling stranded.

Trying hard to accept the improbability of the situation, I introduced myself to Gardner. He stood, shook my hand, then sat down again in the same pose as before: right leg crossed elegantly over the left, clasped hands resting on one knee. He perched amidst the ruins, an unlikely figure all got up like a man about to address a sales meeting.

"Aren't you uncomfortable?" I asked just to say something.

"I believe in maintaining standards, Gage."

"Well, the days of the raj are over, you know. The natives don't care how you look."

"I believe in maintaining standards because these parts of the world tempt a man to dress sloppily. If he dresses sloppily, he begins to think sloppily. If he thinks sloppily, he gets careless. Carelessness is not forgiven in my craft, Gage."

Having explained the metaphysics of his dress code, the man called Mr. Gardner asked, no, ordered, me to sit down. I did, on one of the limestone slabs next to his.

"Mind if I smoke?" I asked, smiling.

"No, I don't mind. But from what I've learned about you, you don't smoke."

"I don't. It was just a joke." I gestured at the landscape. " 'Mind if I smoke' is something you'd say to a man in his office. Get it?"

Gardner, with his hands still folded over his knee, looked down at his dangling right foot, which he was twirling in slow circles. He wore desert boots like mine, his only concession to the environment. The wall stood behind us, gold-white in the sun, worn smooth by fifty centuries of weather. Rising high above the wall, the ledges of the pyramid were covered with sand, which was continually swept off by the *Khamsin,* then replaced with new sand whipped in from the desert by the same wind. There was a steady, dry hissing in the air, as if an invisible giant were exhaling with its tongue clamped between its teeth. Studying his foot as he might a strange object, Gardner sat without saying anything. I began to squirm, made uneasy by his silence and by the impression he gave of being a man under an unnatural self-control; his every word and gesture, however slight, seemed rehearsed.

In appearance, he was the most ordinary-looking man I had ever seen, as commonplace as his suit. A verbal portrait of him would read like a description out of a passport; color hair: light brown (cut short and flecked with fortyish grey); color eyes: blue; height: five-feet-ten; weight: 160

pounds; build: medium; distinguishing marks and scars: none. He looked like anyone, which is just another way of saying he looked like no one; it was as if nature had designed him for a life of anonymity. Even his voice was neutral, a television reporter's voice. The only thing unusual about his features were his lips. They were very thin and turned down at the corners, giving his face the bleak, nasty expression you see on the faces of plains farmers or southern mountaineers in those old daguerreotypes of the American frontier.

"A joke," the man called Gardner said finally. A faint smile broke on his tight little mouth. It was as empty of mirth as his voice was of expression. "Yes, a joke. May I suggest that you're not in a position to make jokes? And I have a very good reason for bringing you out here."

"Ali told me you have a passion for secrecy."

"My passion is for security."

"Security, then."

"I'm considering you for a project of mine. A very special project. I didn't want the slightest chance of the wrong people seeing us together."

"Dave Harris told me your company builds dams and things like that. I don't suppose this project has anything to do with dams."

"That's correct. It's more in the nature of . . ."

"Political development?"

"Well, yes. That's perceptive of you, Gage, Yes, you could call it a political development project."

"Do I get to hear the details?"

"You will in time."

"I will in time," I said, suddenly angry. "All right, fine. Now I want to know why I've been dragged out here. And I'm not making any jokes because all this cloak-and-dagger doesn't seem very funny. It just pisses me off. In the first place, Dave Harris phones me this morning and tells me you'll meet me at the Hilton at two. Fine. I'm there. You're not. Instead, there's this loony Egyptian making like he's a street-hawker—"

"Correction."

"Listen, I don't like people making an ass out of me."

"I said, 'Correction.' "

"Correction what?"

"Harris told you to *be* at the Hilton at two. Think about it. He didn't say a thing about my meeting you there. You were simply told to be there."

"What's the difference? So let's say he said that. So what? It wasn't unreasonable to assume—"

"Yes, it is. It's unreasonable to make assumptions in this business. Assume nothing. As for being made an ass of, you did that to yourself, from what Ali told me. What's wrong, Gage? Does it embarrass you to know other people know you're taking hash? Does it make you nervous? Afraid of the police?"

"Let's get back to the point."

"Which was?"

"Which was that Dave led me to believe I might be interviewed for a job. Which meant I expected a quiet talk over a few drinks. Instead, I'm dragged out into the middle of nowhere by an Egyptian who likes playing games."

"You mean you're bothered merely because you find the circumstances unusual?"

"Yeah, unusual. And undignified, Tom."

His only reaction was to give up the contemplation of his foot and look at me with raised eyebrows.

"So just for the record, who the hell are you? I think, after all this, you owe me your name."

"Well, it looks as if you pried something out of Ali. I'll have to have a talk with him."

"You couldn't pry anything out of him with truth serum. It was Harris, and I didn't pry it out of him. He made a slip."

He was smiling again, his thin lips stretched across his face like two strands of flesh-colored wire.

"I guess that's what I get for dealing with amateurs."

"I guess so. That's your problem. I want to know who you are."

"Not what I am? Or have you already assumed what I am?"

"I have."

"My name's Thomas Colfax. Now you know. And now that you know, let me caution you about something. That secret is very important to me. Important, Gage. You know, there's a kind of virus going around, confessionalism. Everybody is confessing their sins. That includes people in my craft. They've discovered that money can be made by making a confession and selling it for twelve-ninety-five a copy in hardcover editions. Let's say I recruit you for my project, and let's say when it's done you feel the urge to confess and reveal who I am. Something will happen to you. Do I make my point?"

"Yes."

"I'm not sure I have."

"You have. Let's get on with it."

"I'm not really sure I've made my point, Gage, and I want to be sure. So I'm going to underline what I've just said."

An emotion had upset the neutrality in Colfax's voice; it was anger, subtle and rigorously controlled, but the sudden change in pitch was as startling as a loud noise in a previously quiet room.

"You know what I do, but I want to impress on you right now, from the start, that I don't pander to this . . . this . . . ah . . . what? This sickening moralism we've got today. This sham decency. I am not going to allow anyone to compromise me or my plans. I'll stop at nothing to prevent that."

His voice slipped back into neutral, then again assumed that tone of tautly reigned anger.

"I'm in a serious business and I take things seriously. Seriously enough that if you mention my name or anything we discuss to the wrong people, I'll hurt you, son. I'll hurt you." He pointed his finger at me like a scolding schoolteacher and his voice became very tight and low, as if his jaws had been wired half-shut.

" 'Son'? Look, nobody ten years older than me calls me 'son.' "

"I might be only ten years older, but I'm fifty years smarter. Do you understand that? And do you understand that if you ever cross me, the best thing, the very best thing, that could happen to you would be to die quickly. Now then, I think I've made my point. Have I, Gage?"

In any other period of my life I would not have tolerated

a threat like that. I would not have tolerated that patronizing tone. But Colfax had caught me at a time when the
mainspring of my nerves had worn out, leaving me with a
lack of confidence and that sense of inner fragility survivors
of heart attacks must feel. I said and did nothing, startled
not only by the threat but also by the contrast between
it and Colfax's innocuous appearance, between the pater-
nalism in "son" and the menace in "I'll hurt you." It made
the situation seem even stranger, heightening the dis-
orientation I had been feeling ever since meeting Ali.
"The best thing that could happen to you would be to die
quickly" might have sounded natural coming from a gang-
land boss, not from a man who looked like he belonged in
a Dubuque insurance office, sitting at a desk with a citation
from the Jaycees on the wall. The restrained anger in his
voice had been just as unsettling, for it had given his words
a frightening sincerity; there wasn't the least doubt he
would carry out his threat, or try to.

"For a change, you seem at a loss for words," Colfax
said. He had resumed his normal, sterile tone. It fascinated
me how his feelings were expressed with his voice alone,
and how he could seemingly modulate it at will. "I asked
you a question."

"The answer's yes. You made your point, Tom."

"I'm pleased to hear that. By the way, address me as
Gardner. I even want you to think of me as Gardner. Not
as Tom, not as Jack, not as Colfax, not as Mr. Colfax,
but as Gardner. Understood?"

"Gardner it is."

He stood and brushed off his suit. "As David told you,
I'm interested in hearing about Bejaya. You spent some
time there a while back and I'd like to hear about that."

"I was there a week, and only got a couple of miles over
the border. And that was two years ago. The situation's
changed some since then."

"I read the papers, Gage. I'm interested in hearing
everything about your adventure in the bush regardless of
how things have changed. Everything you can remember."

"What's your interest worth?"

"A flat fee of two hundred fifty dollars, considerably

more than I pay my local informants. After you've satisfied
my interest, we can discuss something more permanent
and a regular salary. Is two-fifty equitable?"

"A pretty word, equitable. Yes, it's equitable."

"Good. Now let's get out of this wind and chat inside."

"Inside?"

"In there." He pointed to the entrance that led through
the wall into the courtyard where the pyramid stood.

"You want to talk in there?"

"You waste a great deal of time with your questions.
You're not a journalist anymore, so stop behaving like
one. Yes, I want to talk in there."

"All right—Gardner."

"That's better, Gage. That's much better."

We went through the passage, narrow, musty and dim,
and spent the next hour walking in and out of the shade
of colonnaded galleries, up and down ruined staircases,
with the terraced pyramid always above us. Sand billowed
over the worn bastions of the enclosure wall and our feet
made a crunching sound against the limestone. The sun
was intense, despite the crystalline brownness that splintered and refracted its light. I was soon sweating heavily,
but Colfax's face remained dry.

He jotted in his notebook as I tried to answer his questions about the rebellion in Bejaya, a land of dry plains
and grey mountains bounded by the scorching brilliance
of the Red Sea and separated from Sudan by a border
that was only a line on a map.

No detail was too small for him. He wanted to know
everything about the climate, the terrain, the availability
of water, the conditions of the roads, what few roads
there were, the rebels' morale, the kind of weapons they
carried. He even showed an interest in a few tidbits I had
picked up about the customs of the nomadic tribes who
roam those deserts in a ceaseless quest for graze for their
herds. He asked how I had withstood the rigors of the
brief time I spent on the border. Could westerners, if they
were in condition, endure, say, several months on that
desert? Probably, I said, but it would be a trial. The guerrillas were used to marching thirty miles a day in crushing
heat on no more than a cupful of water. They lived on a

diet of dried dates and a kind of mush called *durra* and
regarded a few slabs of stringy goat or gazelle meat as a
luxury.

"But they could do it, if they were determined enough?"

Yes, I answered, they could. The rebels had once kidnapped two American technicians from Albara—the big
communications base the U.S. maintained in Bejaya—and
held them for six months. Both men survived the ordeal
well enough.

"Kidnapped."

"I've got the details somewhere in here," I said, taking
out my notebook.

"I'll take that."

"If you'll hold on a minute, I'll find the notes I made
on the kidnapping."

"I said I'll take that, Gage."

I handed the notebook to him. He put it in his pocket,
then looked off into space and said, "Of course, kidnapped.
It's so obvious. Why hadn't I thought of that?"

"What the hell are you talking about?"

Colfax gripped my upper arm, squeezing it with more
strength than I would have imagined in such an average-
sized man.

"Just thinking out loud. You don't realize it, but you've
already made a contribution to my project."

"Glad to be of service."

Colfax let go of my arm and paused to make some more
notes. I resisted the temptation to look over his shoulder
to see what he was writing.

"Now then, tell me what you know about the factions,"
he said when he had finished.

You could say of the Bejayan rebels what Orwell had
said of the Spanish anarchists: they suffered from a
plethora of initials. The largest and best equipped faction
was the FLN, the Front for National Liberation. Their
politics were a stew of nationalism and Marxism. Most of
their officers had graduated from revolutionary finishing
schools in Libya, Iraq, and Russia, where they had learned
the leftist catechism with all its fatuous slogans, and had
their heads filled with notions of turning their desolate
homeland into a socialist state. And their ideological edu-

cation had hardened their hearts, so they could, when the
time came, commit without qualms of conscience those
acts of cruelty required for establishing the New Order.
First, they would win independence from Ethiopia, then
revolutionize Bejayan society, such as it was. Purges, reeducation camps for the politically ignorant, a few exemplary executions to motivate slow learners. . . .

"I feel the same about those people as you do," Colfax
interjected, "but I'd appreciate it if you left out the
editorializing. Go on."

I went on. After the FLN came the PLF, for People's
Liberation Front, a faction whose genesis lay in a tangle
of tribal antagonisms and rivalries among the guerrilla
leaders. The PLF, dominated by Bejayan Christians, also
called itself Marxist, but it tended away from the FLN's
orthodoxy and more toward New Left lunacy. The FLN
and PLF were theoretically united under the RCC, the
Revolutionary Command Council; in fact, the splinter
groups were often at each other's throats when they were
not fighting the Ethiopian army.

"It's kind of ridiculous when you think about it," I said.
"All those initials. Alphabet soup. You wonder how they
can take themselves seriously."

"Do you, Gage? I don't wonder. I know why they take
themselves seriously. Because they don't have a sense of
irony. That's their great strength. They're not self-conscious, the way we are. They come from primitive societies
and don't have a mob of intellectual darlings eating at their
spirit with mincing ironies—" He stopped himself abruptly,
then asked, "Have you heard of the NIIF?"

I said nothing. The question came just as I was shifting
mental gears to follow his argument about the virtues of
lacking a sense of irony.

"Gage, the NIIF. Did you ever hear of them?"

"No. What is it? Another faction?"

Yes, he said, it was, a new one spawned by the recent
change in Russian policy, a change that had been cynical
even by the Kremlin's standards, but in keeping with the
history of Bejaya, a history of betrayals and geographical
grand larceny.

More than a thousand years ago, the Arabs stole Bejaya

from the aboriginal inhabitants, then the Turks took it from the Arabs, the Italians from the Turks, the British from the Italians. After World War Two, the English handed it over to Haile Selassie, who annexed it to his Ethiopian empire. The Bejayans later rebelled against His Imperial Majesty, and had been fighting ever since to make the province an independent state. The Soviets had supported the rebels, mainly because the Americans supported the Emperor, whose oppressive rule was mitigated by its inefficiency. Then a band of leftist officers calling themselves the Dergue, which means the "committee," deposed the Emperor, proclaimed his threadbare empire a people's republic, branded the rebels as reactionary bandits, and appealed to the Russians for aid. Moscow responded generously: it abandoned the Bejayan guerrillas. Soviet tanks, guns, and planes poured into the old imperial capital, along with Russian advisers and Cuban pilots. The latter were soon bombing rebel supply lines from Sudan. The Russians meanwhile taught the Dergue the art of efficient repression and helped the Ethiopian army organize a ruthless counteroffensive that, in six months, had pushed the guerrillas back into the deserts and mountains where the rebellion had begun.

"You can guess how that confused our Bejayan friends," Colfax said. "One day the Russians are their patrons, the next day they've got Soviet MIG's strafing them. It's turned their whole world upside down. They'd been hating us for so long, when we were behind the emperor. Now they've got to learn to hate the Russians. No understanding of the way big-power politics work. At any rate, some of the rebels got fed up enough to make another break with the Command Council. They'd been wanting to all along. They're led by one of their sheikhs, a fiftyish character named Muhammad Jima.

"They're devout Moslems over there, you know. Devout. And all that Marxism of the FLN and the other lot was sticking in their throats. Until then, Jima had been fighting for the FLN. Even that faction was too left for his taste, but at least they were Moslem, unlike the PLF. Well, the Russians gave him the chance he'd been looking for. Jima told both factions, 'You've gone along with the Russians and now they've betrayed us. What else can you expect from Communists?' So he broke off and formed his own group, the National Islamic Independence Front. Clever name, because 'independence' and 'Islam' are words that mean something to those tribesmen. They've been free-roving nomads for centuries.

"The core of the NIIF is the Beni-Hamid. Jima is a Beni-Hamid. You must have heard of the Beni-Hamid when you were there?"

I had, but knew little about them.

Sounding professorial, Colfax explained that the Beni-Hamid were a highland tribe whose men never went any-where without guns in their hands and knives in their belts. Partly descended from Yemenite Arabs who had migrated to the African Horn in the Queen of Sheba's time, the Beni-Hamid had more Semitic blood in them than the darker-skinned tribes, whom they despised. In the past, they formed a warrior caste that had raided over vast stretches of Ethiopia and the Sudan, and were known to this day for their Moslem fanaticism and ferocity in battle. "They can really hate," Colfax said admiringly. "I'd say they hate the FLN and the PLF almost as much as they hate the Ethiopians. Jima himself is quite a fellow, looks his part, a real desert falcon. I've met him. I'm telling you that in confidence, Gage. I met him in Khartoum just after he made his split, a few months ago."

"Since you know so much about the way things are over there, why're you paying me two-fifty to tell you what you already know?"

"Would you prefer I not pay you the two-fifty?"

"No."

"I didn't think so. Input, Gage. I require input from a variety of sources, even if it's something I already know. I'll tell you something else I already know. I already know there'll be a civil war among the factions once the Bejayans have won independence. My man Jima knows that too, and he wants it all."

I said nothing, wondering at Colfax's use of the pos-sessive pronoun.

"He hasn't had much education beyond reading the Koran, but he understands what's going to happen, and he wants it all. He doesn't want some muddled-up compromise, because he understands you can't compromise with those people. He means to win it all."

"What's he going to do with it once he's won? It's a lump of sand."

"This is serious, Gage. Jima means to turn Bejaya into an independent Moslem state. You see, the FLN and PLF leaders treated him rather badly. They kept him at the bottom of the Command Council, called him a reactionary and all that other nonsense. He didn't like being bossed around and insulted by all those young ideologues. He's a proud old bird, and he didn't like that at all. That was another reason he broke off and formed the NIIF. The council's a bit worried about him. He's only got about six hundred men, but he's gaining followers. The council wants a reconciliation, kiss and make up. He'll probably go for it as a tactic, but after they've whipped the government, he's going to try and grab it all."

We were walking down a flight of chipped, crumbled stairs, stairs so old they had been ancient ruins when Herodotus first came to Egypt. Colfax stopped and sat down. He looked at the ocher-colored wall above us, the wall topped by a limestone slab on which a frieze of carved cobras flared their hoods in menace.

"There's one other thing, and I'm telling you this in the strictest confidence," Colfax said conspiratorially. "Albara."

I was growing as weary of his cryptic talk about strange tribes, an unknown desert chief, and revolutionary politics as I was of the sun and beating wind.

"Albara?"

"When I met him in Khartoum, Jima assured me we'd be allowed to maintain our base at Albara if he wins. When he wins. Despite their current chumminess with Moscow, the Ethiopians haven't ordered us out. Not yet anyway. They're keeping their options open. But if either the FLN or the PLF comes out on top, we'd be out of there in a week regardless of what the Russians do. The FLN and those others might not like the Russkies anymore, but that doesn't mean they'll start loving us. The point they're at now, they hate all foreigners. And the main objective of

my project is to make sure we keep that base after the
guerrillas win. Don't get the idea Jima's a fan of the west.
He's a Moslem fanatic, but of the lot, he's the best chance
we've got to hold on to the base. You realize how vital
that base is to us?"

"I thought it was just a communications station."

"It's more than that. Take it from me. It's vital to us.
Vital. I think it's clear that Jima is presenting us with an
opportunity and we have to seize it now."

"Sure. Clear."

"Clear to me and clear to you," Colfax said, missing the
sarcasm in my voice. "But it's not clear to Washington.
I know that. I know it's going to be hard, selling them on
the project, because they're scared bureaucrats. Scared of
any daring or innovative idea because of what you newsmen have done with all your petty investigations. All this
publicity. God, it disgusts me. But I'll sell the project. I'll
show them what can be done. I'll convince them yet."

"Them?"

"It will be a model," Colfax went on, without answering the question. "A model operation. In the future they'll
study it as an example of what can be done."

I guessed he was thinking out loud. Certainly he was
talking to himself rather than to me. His voice had again
lost its blandness and taken on that sound of a strong inner
rage held in check by a powerful self-discipline. And then
I noticed a change in his eyes that matched the change in
his voice. An intense light appeared in them, making them
seem strange and not strange at the same time, like a familiar object viewed from an unfamiliar angle. I had seen
that light before, but, unable to recall in whose eyes I had
seen it, wondered if I was just imagining things.

"The point is, I know it can be done. I have to convince
them it can be done in the right way with the right people.
Resolute people. That's the key to everything, Gage. Resolution." He clenched his fist resolutely and the light in his
eyes burned still brighter. "Before anything else, you have
to understand the importance of resolve today. The age of
compromise has been dead for decades. We live in an age
of totalism, and only the most resolute will prevail."

"Look, most of this doesn't make any sense to me. I'd

appreciate it if you gave me the two-fifty now, and maybe we could talk about a job tomorrow."

He unclenched his fist and held up his palm like a teacher signaling a pupil to be patient. "Don't be so anxious, Gage. I want you to hear my ideas." He grinned his tight little grin, a grin which seemed to want to be a sneer or a snarl but which Colfax somehow forced to become a smile. "In any case, you're a captive audience, unless you want to walk back to Cairo. Now, where was I?"

"On the age of totalism and the death of compromise."

"Yes, totalism. Maybe I should have said we live in an age of extremism. Our enemies are extremists. We saw that in Vietnam. You were there. So was I, and for a lot longer than you. You saw what we did to the Viet Cong and you saw how they withstood it and endured it and went on to win. What explains that but extremism? An inhuman self-discipline and dedication, asceticism pushed to its logical extreme, and the resolve to do anything, suffer anything to win. It's the zealotry of the modern revolutionary, Gage. That's what I meant about their not having a sense of irony. A sense of irony implies a sense of proportion, but they don't have that. They don't have any notions of limits except the limit of necessity—they'll do whatever's necessary to win. That's what our civilization is up against, and it's going to take some extremism on our part to keep them from coming over the walls."

Colfax went on in that vein for the next quarter of an hour, never pausing, the light in his eyes never dimming. I sat, mesmerized by his voice, teased by the familiarity of that ocular brilliance, trying to recall where I had seen it before, and thinking, Jesus, I was right, he *is* nuts. He seemed to be delivering a speech to an invisible audience. He never looked at me, but into the distance, as if an attentive crowd were sitting out in the desert, listening to his every word. Surrounded by the rubble of one dead civilization, he delivered a monologue riddled with Spenglerian visions of the impending doom of our own. His disjointed ideas leapt from ancient to modern times and back again, from Periclean Greece to Mandarin China to contemporary America. He covered whole centuries, spanned continents, crossed oceans of space and time; and slowly, his apparently unconnected brushstrokes came together to form a disastrous and lurid portrait of black, brown, and yellow revolutionaries playing Visigoth to our Rome. They would soon be coming over the wall, hordes of them, armed with their Kalashnikov rifles and their lack of irony, if the West did not stiffen its rotten backbone. Vietnam was only the beginning, a telltale flapping its warning in the winds of history. *They* had the will, we did not. To defeat *them* we would have to become like them, extremists ourselves, minds cleaned of all notions of moderation and compromise.

Colfax's lofty, if confusing, ideas about revolution and the fate of western civilization seemed in some unfathomable way connected in his mind with an obscure rebellion in a desolate corner of Africa and an even more obscure tribal sheikh named Muhammad Jima. By the time he finished his soliloquy, I felt wrung out and slightly afraid of him. For while he was speaking I had realized he was not at all mad, a realization that had come with the sudden recollection of where I had seen the odd light in his eyes. It had been in the eyes of some radical Palestinian guerrillas I had once interviewed in Lebanon. I had not immediately recognized it in Colfax's eyes because they were blue and that light was associated in my mind with the Arabs' dark brown. The difference in color had confused me. But the light was the same, and it was not the luster of insanity. It was the gleam of something darker than madness—belief, an absolute belief in the rightness of one's religion or political dogma or personal destiny, the faith that creates saints and demons alike, that inspires both the martyr and the murdering bigot, that gives a man the power to destroy others because he is willing to risk his own destruction in its name. Thomas Colfax had already undergone the transformation he recommended for us all; he had become like the people he called "our enemies." I knew it by his shining eyes: he was a fanatic.

Gazing at the frieze of cobras, Colfax asked, "Does what I'm saying confuse you, Gage?"

"Let's say I can't see what it's got to do with me."

"It has everything to do with you."

"That clears up things nicely."

"I'll make things a little clearer." He reached into his pocket, took out a comb, and drew it carefully through his hair, then picked the grains of sand from the comb before putting it back in his pocket, an act of fastidiousness that amazed me. "I don't want narrow-minded people working for me. I can always recruit those, men who are good at what they do but without an idea in their thick skulls. Mercenaries, in other words. I want people who understand the nature of the struggle. That's why I've gone into all this. So you understand that my project has a guiding philosophy behind it. It's going to be part of something much larger, the struggle that's going on all over the world today. And you'll be part of it if you sign on with me. You won't be observing events, Gage. You'll be part of them, you'll be helping to shape them."

"That's quite a pep talk. You mean in my own little way I'll be helping to save western civilization?"

"Yes, you could put it that way," he said, dead serious. And I knew then you could not accuse him of having a sense of irony, or of proportion.

"All right, let's put it that way, Mr. Gardner. What does a savior get paid these days?"

"I'll ignore the sarcasm, Gage." He paused for effect. "I wanted to get to the money part later, but since you've asked, the salary will be twenty-five hundred a month plus expenses."

My throat swelled a little. "Twenty-five hundred American?"

"Of course American. Two thousand five hundred in cash, tax-free, on a one-year contract. I know that's a little shy of what you were making with your precious *Post,* but I think it'll see you through."

"I think so too." Oh, did I think so. Twenty-five hundred plus expenses for a year. Tax-free. Thirty thousand dollars. No fortune, but it seemed like one then. And under the intoxicating influence of the time-tested vice of greed, I began to feel a little better about the zealot in the striped perma-press suit.

"Okay. We've got that settled. Now maybe you could tell me, nice and clear, what I'll be doing for twenty-five a month."

"Act, Gage."

"What?"

"I'm going to pay you two and a half thousand a month to act, and I don't mean playact, although you might have to do a bit of that from time to time. No, I mean you will *act*, and if I know your type, you need and want that more than you want or need the money."

He smiled in a superior way. His perception was so accurate that I wondered if he had installed a wiretap in my brain.

"Isn't that right?" he inquired. "What you need to do is, well, to *do*. I know your type. You feel useless. But it's more than just that. You think a lot about death, don't you, Gage?"

"I've seen quite a lot of it."

"And you think about what you've seen when you're not doing something. You think about all the death you've seen and it depresses you, doesn't it?"

"It'd depress anybody."

"You've seen a lot of death and you think about it for the simple reason you have the time to. You have nothing to do except, maybe, knock out some free-lance piece of trash now and then. You're not chasing all over the world anymore, at the center of events, meeting deadlines, covering wars, and you miss that. You miss that action because action stops you from thinking. Acting for you is a kind of drug. You need it, Gage, that release, that freedom from thought—"

"Okay, stop it."

"You need it."

"I said to stop it."

"You need to act. Action is your narcotic, and I, in a manner of speaking, am offering to be your supplier."

"I think that's enough."

"I'm offering to be your supplier and all you'll owe me is loyalty. Simple loyalty, Gage, and I'll give you the opiate you need."

I wanted to hit him, to break that spare little man like a dry stick; but his air of superiority and his seemingly mystic ability to read my mind gave him power. He had begun to exercise over me the iron control he exercised over himself.

"What am I going to be doing for twenty-five hundred a month, specifically?" I asked in an attempt to get him off psychoanalysis.

"Specifically, I'm not at liberty to tell you yet. All I can tell you is that you'll be acting. That should satisfy you for the moment, that you'll have a chance to act."

"Will it compromise my journalistic integrity?" I was trying to gain some advantage over him. "I wouldn't want to act if it'd compromise my journalistic integrity."

"Are you worried about that?"

"Only joking."

"I asked you not to make jokes."

"Sorry about that."

"And I'm sorry I even had to use that phrase. Journalistic integrity. It shows you how much things have changed. Twenty years ago—no, ten years ago, even ten years ago I wouldn't have had any worries about recruiting a newsman. Now I have to make sure they don't feel their integrity will be compromised." He pointed at the frieze. "Do you know what those represent?"

"Cobras," I said. "Snakes."

"You're a master of the obvious. Of course they're snakes. But do you know what they symbolize? They symbolize the Goddess of Buto, protectress of the Northern Kingdom in ancient Egypt."

"I'll say this for you. You're versatile. Two minutes ago you were psychoanalyzing me. Now you're on archaeology."

"No. I'm going to make an analogy. An analogy."

I resigned myself to listening to another Colfax monologue.

Phrase by phrase, it came from between his compressed lips, in a voice as dry and dead as the wind. He compared himself and the others in his craft to the cobras on the frieze. They were protectors of the kingdom. A cobra, he said, is a repulsive creature, but the ancient Egyptians had not seen any contradiction in using it to symbolize the defender of their state. They could have chosen a more noble beast, a lion or an eagle, say, but they recognized that the fearsome power of their guardian goddess was best evoked in the form of a poisonous snake. In that sense, the cobra was a thing of beauty to them, and, to his way of thinking, proved the Egyptians of that age were pragmatists. We had once been pragmatists, had known the defense of our civilization required men expert in the serpentine ways of The Craft. Occasionally, it was necessary to depose a prime minister inimical to our interests, or to "terminate" some revolutionary who might cause us problems, or to elevate a foreign political leader friendly to us. It was never pleasant work, but the purpose, the overriding moral purpose of protecting the Republic justified whatever had to be done. In the good old days, when we were pragmatists, no one had thought it unethical to recruit journalists. How he missed those days. He longed for the clarity of that era when we had certain villains to fight and there was no doubt as to where a man's first loyalty lay: it lay in his duty to his country.

"But now, now men like you, Gage, you newsmen, feel your loyalty belongs to your newspapers, or magazines, or networks. To the so-called ethics of your profession. What hypocrisy! An ethical journalist is a contradiction in terms, and yet men like me are being portrayed in the press as repulsive, like the cobras on the frieze. And no one any longer sees the beauty behind the repulsiveness. . . .

"I'm using 'you' in the editorial sense. I'm a good judge of men and I think you're a fine American."

"Thanks."

"You served your country in wartime. You haven't misplaced loyalties. I think you're an honorable man."

I nodded, benumbed by the heat and his droning voice, confused by his analogy, which I found a tortured one. He and his fellow craftsmen were cobras, spitting their deadly poisons in the name of preserving our purple mountain majesties and amber fields of grain. I did not particularly agree with his view of himself and his business, but I thought it had been offered with sincerity. That proved one of two things: either I was a worse judge of men than I thought or he was a master of what Ali Mahmoud had called the art of dissimulation.

In retrospect, I can admire the fitness of his choice of our first meeting, the tomb of King Zoser in the domain of the god of the dead. It had struck me then as a strange spot for a meeting, and Colfax looked ridiculously out of place in his suit and tie. In light of what I learned at the end of Operation Atropos, I can see he was not out of place at all. There was a symmetry between the setting and his character, for the great enclosure wall surrounding the tomb is known to Egyptologists for its facsimiles. The stone blocks forming the roofs of the galleries have been carved to resemble the trunks of palm trees. The wall has fourteen double doors, none of them real. They are all imitations carved in the limestone, complete with fake hinges and handles. Even the entrance itself is a mere passageway, with the leaves of a mock open door chiseled on each side. The temples and altars inside are likewise artificial: although they look like the real thing, only their exteriors have been fashioned, their interiors being lumps of ordinary masonry. And those architectural deceptions formed the perfect backdrop for Thomas Colfax to present himself as a patriot and zealous guardian of western civilization, to expound his abstract, high-flown ideas about loyalty, and to explain the guiding philosophy behind his project. All of that was a sham, every word of it as counterfeit as those phony doors and false temples. His reason for bringing me out there was another lie, or a half-truth at best. He had given me the idea he wanted to keep our meeting secret from the KGB, or the Egyptian Mukhabarat, "the wrong people." He never gave the slightest hint that the wrong people included his own boss, the Chief of Station in Cairo.

In moments when I am inclined to give him some benefit of the doubt, I like to think he believed in his grand ideas. I like to think that he had lived so long in a twilit world of ruses and aliases and double crosses and all the other hocus-pocus of his craft that he had lost the ability to distinguish truth from falsehood, even when it came out of his own thin-lipped mouth. That is what I like to think. In fact, he was conscious of his lies. I am not implying that my first impression of him as a fanatic was mistaken. My only mistake was to think him fanatical about his politics;

in fact, his zeal was directed at no cause other than self-advancement. Although he sought to project an image of moderation in his dress and manner, he was a very immoderate man when it came to promoting his career. If greed was the principal vice of the last century, the lust for power is the principal vice of this one; and Thomas Colfax was possessed by a need for power, a possession so strong it had consumed his morality, his compassion, and his sense of personal responsibility. His ideas, his talk of loyalty and honor and all that, were just so much plating to conceal the base metal of his ambition. The only time he spoke the truth that afternoon was when he said, "I'll show them what can be done. It will be a model. They'll study it as an example of what can be done." For showing them what he could do was the real guiding philosophy behind his project.

"So, I'd like to hear your thoughts," Colfax was saying. "I'm considering you for the project. I'd like to know if you're going to sign on."

"You know, when I joined the army, even the recruiters told me more than you're telling me."

"We've been through this, through it. I'm not at liberty to give you any details yet."

"I can't seem to get a straight answer out of you. *I want to know what I'll be doing.*"

"Whatever I tell you to do. That's what you'll be doing. Is that straight enough for you?"

"Back to the army, huh? Doing what I'm told."

"Back to the army. You want to act, but you're not in . . . oh, shall we say, the correct psychological condition for acting on your own, are you?" He was smiling in his knowing way again.

"No, I suppose not."

"Then you've decided? You'll sign on?"

"I've decided, yes. Okay. Yeah."

But it was not a real decision, the lack of one rather. It was not an act so much as it was the absence of an act. I had agreed without conviction, without thinking why. I had drifted into it simply because the alternative seemed worse. What did I, an unemployed gypsy journalist, have to go back to?

"That's good, very good," Thomas Colfax said. He squeezed my upper arm again, about as friendly a gesture as he was capable of making. "You're going to be useful, Gage. Useful. I'll have the contract ready for you tomorrow."

"All right. Now maybe you could give me a few details. A hint would do."

"I managed to get hold of copies of your military records. They interested me. They're one of the reasons I decided to consider you for the project. After you were wounded in Vietnam, you were transferred to a headquarters unit, weren't you?"

"They put me on limited duty because of my leg. 'In the rear with the gear where there is no fear.' "

"Specifically, they assigned you to a section in intelligence, G-2. More specifically, you were part of a team that inspected and identified captured enemy weapons. Russian-made weapons mostly. Correct?"

"You saw the records."

"What I'm driving at is this: if I were to give you a Russian training manual—translated, of course—and a few of these weapons, let's say a Sagger antitank missile or an AK-47, do you think you'd still be able to field-strip them and train someone else how to use them?"

"Run that one by me again."

"I said, if I gave you a Russian training manual, let's say a manual on the Sagger, do you think you'd be able to disassemble and assemble it and teach someone else how to use it?"

"Wait a minute. You're going to give me a Sagger *missile*?"

"They're not very large. As I recall, a single infantryman can carry one. They come in a case no bigger than an ordinary suitcase."

"I'm not talking about their size. I mean, where in the hell are you going to come up with a Russian antitank missile?"

"That's no concern of yours. Just answer my question."

"With the manuals, sure. I used to be pretty good at it. Sure, I suppose I could do it."

Colfax stood, dusted off his suit, and again combed his

hair, which the wind immediately ruffled. We walked in silence for a while, passing the entrance to a mortuary temple from whose dim recesses came a smell that combined the odors of a cellar and a crypt. The stale stink of death and petrification.

"You can do it," Colfax said. "Good. It's what I hoped to hear. Well now, we've had a long talk. A long and satisfactory talk. Time we headed back."

"Hold on a second, Colfax—"

"Gardner. I insist on that."

"Okay, Gardner. With the hint you've given me, I think we ought to have another talk about money. I'm afraid I'll have to ask you for more."

Colfax's laugh was all ice. "You've got more nerve than I've been giving you credit for. I've just hired you and you're already asking for a raise."

"I'm going to be running guns, right? To this Jima character in Bejaya."

"Running guns. How romantic."

"That's a dicey business and I think it's worth more than twenty-five hundred a month."

"Who said anything about running guns?"

"You did. Just now."

"I didn't say anything about gun-running."

"For Christ's sake. You must take me for an idiot. After what you just told me, it's a natural assumption that you're talking about running guns."

"I thought I told you not to make assumptions."

———

Ali Mahmoud had left with the Fiat, so we drove back to Cairo in Colfax's air-conditioned Mercedes. The car, which must have pulled up while we were talking, was one of the perquisites he enjoyed as a fictitious executive with Inter-Arab Development. I did not bother to ask why, after he'd gone to such lengths to make sure we were not seen together, he now felt safe riding in the same automobile with me. When he had said, "I thought I told you not to make assumptions," there was something in his voice that told me to avoid asking any more questions. I was already

acquiring Ali's ability to suppress natural curiosity. Need
to know. I would know only what I needed to know,
which need would be determined by Thomas Colfax.

The guardian of western civilization sat with his legs
crossed, gazing at the landscape that flashed past the windows like footage from a travelogue with the sound turned
off. Hermetically sealed in the Mercedes, we could not
hear the wind blowing through the trees. The trees swayed
and shuddered silently, reminding me of weeds in an
ocean current. We could not hear the wind, or feel the heat,
or smell the thick, warm smell of the Nile Valley farms, or
the odor of the flat bread baking for the evening meal.
We saw the smoke from the clay ovens where the plump
wives of the *fellahin* baked the *aish baladi*, but we could
not smell it on the wind. Inside the car, there was only the
hum of the engine and the cold odorless blasts of the air
conditioner.

We were riding back by a different route, following the
Pyramids Road along the sharp frontier between the desert
and the sown land. It was nearly dusk. A few farmers were
still at work, winnowing grain. They went at it with wood-
en pitchforks, bowing and lifting rhythmically in yellow
clouds of flying chaff that blew away in the wind. A gently
winding line of trees in the distance marked the course of
the Nile. I could not see the great river, but knew it was
there by the line of trees and could sense its enduring
presence. Later, we passed by a village. It was the time for
the prayer before sunset, the *salât il'asr'*, and on the village's only street, its dun-colored dust printed over by
sandaled feet, by donkeys' hooves and camel tracks, a
dozen *fellahin* kneeled on bits of old cloth that served as
prayer rugs. We could barely hear the *muezzin* through
the closed windows. With their imam in front of them, the
men bowed again, up and down, submitting themselves to
the will of the implacable God whose name the *muezzin*
repeated again and again in a prolonged, hypnotic chant.

Colfax looked at them silently, his hands folded primly
on the knee of his crossed leg. Then he leaned forward to
glance in the rearview mirror, took out his comb, and once
more tidied his plain brown hair. His lips were drawn
into threads by a smile, the smile of a man thoroughly

satisfied with himself. Turning to me with that smug expression, he asked if I had any financial obligations to Allison. I said I did not. She had not asked for alimony. How about emotional attachments? No, I lied, I felt nothing for her.

"Does she still feel anything for you?"

"I doubt it."

"So, chances are she wouldn't make any great fuss in case something happened to you?"

The phrase, delivered in his neutral TV reporter's voice, sent a jolt of fear through me. At the same time, I was disgusted with myself for feeling fear, and hated him for his ability to make me feel it. The emotions got mixed up together and, through some chemistry, produced an instant of rage. I came very close to wrapping my hands around his priggish little neck. Then I thought of the thirty thousand dollars I had coming if I played his game, a thought that calmed me, for money can tranquilize as well as incite passion.

"What's going to happen to me?" I said. "Or is that Classified, Top Secret, Eyes Only, Burn before Reading?"

"I trust nothing will happen to you. But you'll be taking some risks for me. In case something does happen, I don't want some hysterical woman asking a lot of questions. I don't want to have to deal with that."

"Yeah, that would be a bother."

He reached into the inside pocket of his jacket. After his last remarks and all the peculiar happenings of that day, I half expected him to pull out a pistol. Instead he handed me a plain sealed envelope, through which I could see a welcome and familiar green rectangle.

"Your first paycheck. There's five hundred inside in fifties. Two-fifty for the information you gave, and a two-fifty advance on your first month's salary."

"*Allah karim,*" I said, giving him a mock bow. "God is generous. Why the advance? I haven't signed the contract yet."

"I'm not Allah and I'm not generous. The advance is to induce you to avoid having second thoughts about signing. Anyway, I trust you, as I hope you trust me."

I did not say anything and slipped the envelope in my pocket.

In Arabic, Colfax told the driver to turn on the radio.

He did, filling the car with the moaning, dissonant chords of some Arab love lament.

"Now, then, you'll find your first couple of months with me an easy adjustment," Colfax said without raising his voice above the radio. "You'll be working as a journalist again, or pretending to. You know the *Arab Digest*, don't you?"

I said that I did.

"Yes, of course. You fellows quote from it whenever you can't get a story on your own. 'The authoritative monthly *Arab Digest* said today blah blah blah.' I think that's the stock phrase. Officially, you're going to be working for them. Your contract will be with them. They'll pay you, give you a press card, an I.D., all the usual camouflage. But your assignments will come from me. You might say I'll be your editor. You won't get anything from me directly, but through a fellow named Iskander—"

"A buffer. Giving orders through a buffer. Like the Mafia."

"I can't say I care for that analogy, Gage. But yes, Iskander is a buffer. Iskander Ahmed Iskander. Grand name. He publishes the *Digest*. I think you'll like him. He understands things and doesn't ask a lot of questions. He'll pass my assignments on to you. The only one you'll get directly from me is the one I've got for you tonight."

"*Tonight?*"

"What's wrong with tonight?"

"Nothing's wrong with tonight except that I'm drained after today."

"That's nothing a hot shower won't cure."

"The hot water's been off in my building for three days."

"A cold shower then. Nothing a cold shower won't cure. I want you to have a talk with someone who's just come up from Alex. Greek fellow named George Boxavenides. Consider him an interview. He has a story to tell. He's also got a request to make. You can consider carrying out his request your assignment. Your first one for me.

You can consider it an order from me. The army must have taught you about orders."

"They did that all right. You said this Greek's from Alexandria. Does this have anything to do with Harris?"

"It has something to do with my project. George will explain a few things to you. Not everything. Just a few things. Don't press him. Don't take your make-believe role too seriously. He's waiting to hear from me. We weren't sure if you'd sign on, you know."

"I haven't signed anything yet."

Colfax laughed his polar laugh. "You might not feel you've learned very much, Gage, but you've learned enough to make signing that contract a necessity. You don't and you *will* be in trouble."

"What's all this got to do with Harris?"

He ignored the question. "When we get back, I'll phone George and tell him to meet you for dinner at the Hilton at nine. He'll pick up the tab."

"Look, Harris told me he'd been dealing with some Greek down in Alex. Is he mixed up in all this?"

"Nine sharp. The main dining room of the Hilton. Just ask the maître d' for his table. Boxá-va-needeez."

We were riding past the Giza pyramids, Cheops, Chephren, and Mycerinus, three huge triangles against the brownish-blue sky. For all their massiveness, they did not look quite real to me. I had seen them on so many postcards, on the covers of so many guidebooks, on the glossy pages of so many travel magazines that they seemed mere stage props, as if they had been constructed for the sole purpose of being photographed. The petty, multicolored figures beneath them were tourists, taking last-minute pictures of each other astride mangy camels before the buses took them back to the city. There were not many tourists because of the late hour and the stiffening *Khamsin*. The lower quarter of the sky was brown as teak, and the dying sun swollen and dark.

"Let me get something straight," I said to Colfax. "I'm supposed to interview this Boxavenides and then . . . what? Write a piece about him for the *Digest*?"

"Gage, if things work out, you aren't going to write a word about that man for anyone."

The older women, adhering to tradition, discreetly veiled their faces with their shawls when I walked by. All of them, young as well as old, were wearing the black *tarha* on their heads. It made them look like mourners as they stood in a long line behind the well, holding earthen jugs or rusty cans in hands so work-cracked and dirt-crusted you could not see much difference between the hands of a girl of twenty-five and those of a crone of seventy. One by one the women stepped up to the well—a faucet attached to a pipe in the ground—drew their water, then walked off balancing the jugs and cans atop their heads.

A few boys were playing soccer up the street. Barefoot, they kicked the ball indifferently, sometimes slipping on patches of dung that had been flattened and mashed into the ground by the traders' carts. They played with none of the shouting you usually hear from boys at a game, and their children's faces were old with the defeated expression worn by the women at the well, by the men idling in the coffee shops, by all the people in Bulaq. I imagined infants there were born with it, as if, from the moment they first breathed the air of that slum, they knew they had no hope of ever breathing any other.

I walked on down the street, dim in the shadows of the buildings that sagged at odd angles and seemed to be propping each other up. There were one-story shacks and taller houses with latticework windows and intricately carved porches from Ottoman times, the wood dry-rotted and the porches dangerous-looking. The soccer ball rolled tiredly to a stop in front of me. I kicked it back. The boys briefly stared at me with a dumb, animal gaze in their black eyes, then resumed their joyless game. Overhead, in the narrow space between the buildings, the early evening sky was the color of sulfur; and in the yellow dusk the homeless were lighting cooking fires beside the tents and scrapwood shanties they had built smack up against the houses in which the more fortunate lived ten to a room.

Turning a corner, I headed through a market, passing a very old woman who sat on the ground as one dead or paralyzed. She did not try to brush away the flies clinging to her face. The stalls were closed now, the market empty except for a single cart drawn by a donkey and driven by a slump-shouldered *fellah* who now and then flicked the animal's neck with a stick. The wind was blowing at full force, sand falling on the city like a dry mist. It had grown much hotter in the two days since I had met Colfax, a smothering, choking heat that made me feel claustrophobic. The air was dense with the stink peculiar to Bulaq, an odor composed of the smells of urine and excrement, of the orange rinds and vegetable scraps rotting in the gutters of the market, and of the stagnant pools where the women had emptied the day's dirty water.

I walked slowly, waiting for dark. I kept one hand in the pocket where I had put the letter I'd typed earlier in the day. I must have looked like a man carrying a concealed weapon. In a sense I was, the letter being the figurative knife I was to stick in David Harris's back.

After another fifteen or twenty minutes of threading my way through the slum's labyrinth, I rounded another corner and saw the shaft of blue fluorescent light falling across the otherwise blackened street. The smell reached me on the hot breeze gusting fitfully between the rows of houses, the smell whose thick sweetness blotted out that other stench of misery. The smokers were sitting or squatting against a wall, in the darkness at the edge of the pool of light. Sometimes a pipe flared redly, illuminating the face of a man sunk in a welcome oblivion, of another man sucking hard on a stem in a desperate attempt to reach oblivion. Hijazi's boys, flitting in and out of the coffee house, waited on those wretches as if they were princes. They tamped the hash into the bowls, lighted the pipes, brought fresh ones. Hijazi himself stood in the entrance, pocketing the pound-notes the boys handed him and looking at his customers benevolently. He wore a skullcap on the back of his shaved head.

A look of surprise passed briefly over his plump, round face when he saw me. Then his oval eyes widened like a child's and he smiled.

"Mr. Charlie! *Marhaba!*"

"*Marhaba*, Ismail."

"*Ahlen,* Mr. Charlie. *Ahlen ah-ahleeennn,*" he said embracing me and, standing on tiptoe, kissing me on both cheeks. He smelled of garlic and old sweat. "Welcome. Welcome."

"God give you a happy evening," I said, thinking he seemed a little too glad to see me.

"All my evenings are happy, but you have made this the happiest by your presence. Welcome, welcome. And how is your health, Mr. Charlie? I haven't seen you for so long, I thought something had happened to you."

"Something did happen, but I'm quite well, praise be to God. And yours?"

He touched his hand to his forehead. "Praise be to God. Oh, Mr. Charlie, I have had a great longing for you."

He was laying on the Arabic poetry with a trowel. I had come to him for his hashish—that is, for the courage to do what I had to do that night—but his unusually effusive manner told me he knew something that might answer the questions I had been asking myself since meeting Colfax. Ali had said, "Let us say someone saw you there." Who else could it have been but Hijazi? He knew something, all right, and I decided on the spur of the moment to stay straight until I learned what it was.

"You, Ismail Hijazi, have been longing for my money."

"Your skill in Arabic has improved."

"I beg God's pardon. I am so full of faults, you have no reason to praise me."

"Well said, Mr. Charlie. But it's true I have had a great longing for your money because you are an American, and an American is his money, his money him. I have, therefore, in my longing for money, had a longing for you."

"And that's cleverly said. What happened to me was the lack of money. I was out of work."

"And this misfortune is at an end?"

"Praise be to God."

"Praise be to God. But it is difficult to believe there is in all the world an American who lacks money. This scum you see here"—he gestured at the smokers—"have no work and little money. Nevertheless, they come to Hijazi with what money they have. Oh, Mr. Charlie, I was made desolate by your long absence."

Bullshit, I thought.

"As my misfortune is at an end, so is your desolation."

"Praise be to God. Please, sit down. Sit down and smoke a little."

Turning to one of the boys, he dropped the obsequious tone and snapped. "You! Bring two chairs and hurry." The boy scurried into the shop and brought two rickety wooden chairs from one of the tables. We sat down, Hijazi with his back half-turned to me so he could keep an eye on his customers.

"I've had good luck," he said. "Just yesterday I received a small shipment of the very best. Of a quality beyond describing. There is only a little, and I'm reserving it for my most favored customers. This refuse here are smoking what I have from the Bekaa and Morocco, which is good, but this that I received just yesterday is from Afghanistan. Well dried. The purest leaves of the purest Indian hemp. You will do me an honor to smoke a little, Mr. Charlie. It is without equal."

"I will, but first I'd like some information. Truthful information."

"Truthful information. Ah, the truth is as rare and valuable as the hashish from Afghanistan."

"You will be rewarded."

"Please. Ask."

"We will speak in English now."

"As you wish."

"Do you know a man named Ali Mahmoud?"

Spreading his hands and tilting back his head, Hijazi tsk-ed. "Mr. Charlie, I know ten times a hundred Ali Mahmouds. You should ask if I know Ali Muhammad, for of Ali Muhammads I know ten times a thousand."

"This Ali Mahmoud is a tall man, like me, and strongly built and not dressed in rags like these here, but like a European. I think he's been here. More than once."

"No such man has ever been here," he answered too quickly.

"The truth is as rare and valuable as the hashish from Afghanistan."

"I'm not lying."

"How valuable is the truth?"

"That depends on the truth."

"Ten dollars American."

"*Ya Allah!* That's a cheap truth and not worth the telling."

"Fifteen then. You could double it on the black market."

"Please, sit down awhile and smoke a little and forget your truth." He had taken his worry beads from his pocket and was fingering them in a fleshy hand, like a pudgy monk saying a rosary.

"Twenty dollars."

"Thirty. It is a thirty-dollar truth."

"Twenty-five for the truth and one pipe of the Afghanistan hashish."

"Twenty-five for the truth."

"I'm too tired tonight for this bazaar-bargaining."

"Then why bargain? If you don't wish to bargain, don't come to the *souk*."

I folded two tens and a five and pressed them into the hand that held the clacking beads.

Pocketing the bills, Hijazi said, "There was a man like that here several times. First he came to smoke alone and only a little. He watched. He was a watchful man. That was about three months ago. Then he came again with a dark man and they smoked a little and talked a lot in a strange language. I don't know your Ali Mahmoud, Mr. Charlie, but this man looked as you've described him. I remember him because he came with the dark man and then, another time, with the dark man and an American, and another time again with the American and a man who I think was a European."

"An American?"

"Yes. The only American who has ever come here besides yourself."

"What did he look like?"

"Like an American. That's all I remember. He looked like an American."

"Nothing else?"

"The American was always combing his hair. I remember only that about him. I can't remember his face. It was just an American face. But he was very worried about his hair."

"And?"

"And they had a strange conversation, the American, the dark man, and the man you call Ali Mahmoud. He paid me some money to ensure no one else came into the shop. A very good price, too. In dollars. Only the boys could come into the shop, and me, of course. But we were to stay away from their table. So they talked. Ali Mahmoud talked to the dark man in a strange language, then to the American in English."

"And they said what?"

"I didn't understand the strange language."

I figured he was angling for more, so I slipped him another five, making it a thirty-dollar truth. "But you understood the English."

"The English was as strange as the strange language, Mr. Charlie. I heard Ali Mahmoud speak to the dark man in the strange language, then say to the American, 'The prophet needs twenty lengths of pipe.' And the American wrote this down in a notebook. Then again Ali Mahmoud spoke to the dark man and said to the American, 'The prophet also asks for five hundred water pumps.' I remember that clearly. I overheard them and I remember that, because I thought, What manner of prophet is this who asks for lengths of pipe and water pumps? That's all I heard. A prophet needed twenty pipes and five hundred water pumps. It cannot mean anything. It's nonsense."

"It is not nonsense if the pipes are not pipes, the pumps not pumps, nor the prophet a prophet."

Hijazi shook his head and jiggled the orange beads. "All very strange."

"Now, tell me about the European."

"That is another truth, Mr. Charlie."

"No more money, Ismail. I'll smoke two pipes and pay you for that, but no more bargaining for the truth."

"Very well. This truth cannot mean anything at all. It means even less than the last truth. The European was here with the American and your Ali Mahmoud only . . . oh, I think two weeks ago. Perhaps less than that. . . . Mr. Charlie, you must tell no one about what I'm saying to you this night. I could get in trouble. . . ."

"No more. You've been paid. The European."

"A man with black hair," Hijazi said tiredly. "Again, I was paid to keep everyone out and to keep away from their table. Again there was talk of the prophet and pipes and water pumps. All in English. But in quiet voices, so I heard almost nothing and what I heard was more nonsense. I know English well, Mr. Charlie. I had to in the old days when I worked in Port Said. French, too. We had to. English and French in the old days in Port Said. . . ."

"What'd they say, Ismail?"

"As I told you, I heard almost nothing. The only time I heard anything was when the European and the American got into a small argument and made loud voices. And when the European said 'two and a half million dollars.' Of course, when I, Ismail Hijazi, hear such a sum mentioned, I pay attention. . . . Mr. Charlie, I have had second thoughts. There must be a greater payment, even if you smoke the two pipes. We have gone beyond the realm of the thirty-dollar truth."

I haggled with him, but, my curiosity whetted, ended up paying him ten more.

"So," Hijazi said, "the European said this: 'She's insured for two and a half million dollars. I can arrange everything. Ten percent will go to you.' Then the American said, 'All right, you know I've had to something to pay for the pipes and pumps. I can something the books for a few months, but the company is something every year and I'll have to put the money back."

"What are all the somethings?"

"English phrases I did not understand and cannot remember. Truly cannot remember. No amount of money could make me remember because I cannot remember."

"All right. What about the argument?"

"It was not a bad argument. They just made their voices louder. The American said something . . . oh, I think, 'Nothing should happen to the crew.' The European laughed in a cruel way, which made the American angry. The European said, 'They're all Pakis—' What is a Paki, Mr. Charlie?"

"Pakistani. Men from Pakistan."

"Ah yes. Pakistan. So he said, 'They're all Pakis and no one will miss them.' Then the American makes his voice

loud and he said . . . well, now what did he say? Something
something, then 'go down with her' then the word *investigation*. Yes, there's a word I know. Investigation. Then another word. Pub, pub something. Oh, my English is not
so good. I cannot remember."

"Publicity?"

"Yes! Publicity. He said 'too much publicity.' What is
that?"

"Never mind. What else?"

"*Ya Allah!* All this remembering foreign words tires
me."

"I've paid you forty dollars not to get tired. What else?"

"Oh, after that the European said, 'Don't worry, it's
arranged.' Then more talk I could not hear. Then the
American said something that made the European stop
laughing and smiling. I remember that about him. All the
time, even when they argued, he laughed and smiled. A
jolly man. But then the American said, again in a loud
voice, so loud that Ali Mahmoud had to caution him to be
silent, he said in this loud voice, 'You are a something
bastard, George, and you might be tempted something
something your part of the bargain.' The European, this
George, was still smiling and said, 'Yes, I might be
tempted.' Then the American. 'Don't give in to it, George.
Because if I don't get that money, you won't be missed
either.' That's when the European, this George, stopped
smiling." Hijazi sighed and slumped into the chair, expanding his already rotund belly. "*Khalas*, Mr. Charlie.
Khalas, khalas. Finished. Never have I had to do so much
remembering. Come now and buy one pipe of the Afghanistan hashish."

"You haven't told me everything."

"Oh, yes. Everything."

"Ismail, I find something strange in what you've just
told me. How did the American and European know about
this place? I can guess. Ali Mahmoud brought them here.
And Ali Mahmoud knew about this place because he's been
here before. So you know him. You know him so well
that you told him I come here."

"Oh, Mr. Charlie, I hope I haven't done you a disservice. Yes, I know Ali Mahmoud. He used to come here."

"What did you tell him?"

"It was an accident. After the time he first came here with the American, I only mentioned to him I had seen but one other American here. Ali acted very disturbed. What American? he asked. What was his name? I told him your name. Then he told me I was to never say what I have just said to you and I was to telephone him if I saw you here. It was strange, but he behaved as though he knew you. He seemed to know your name."

"And you called him?"

"Yes, the last time I saw you here. What? Two months ago. I saw you and told him you were here. You see, Mr. Charlie, I thought Ali had gone to work for the Mukhabarat. So I did as he asked."

"For a good price, I'm sure."

"You are not in trouble, Mr. Charlie? I haven't done you a disservice? I'm so worried now I've done you a disservice."

In a voice I hoped was sufficiently low and menacing, I said in Arabic, "You owe me a debt."

"I have done you a disservice. And you. You, one of my most favored customers."

"You owe me a debt for informing on me to strangers."

"But I thought he was from the Mukhabarat. My business, Mr. Charlie. I must cooperate to stay in business."

The round fingers fluttered frantically over the beads.

"Your business," I hissed. "*Quss ummak.* Your mother's vulva."

"Please, Mr. Charlie, there's no need for insults."

"You owe me a debt."

"If I have done you a disservice, I'm sorry."

"Sorrow is not rare in Bulaq."

"How can I repay this debt?"

"With something rare."

Hijazi puffed his cheeks and expelled a long breath. "How much?"

"Two pipes."

Without hesitating, he called to one of the boys: "You, Mazzan! Come here and hurry!"

The boy ran up, a scrawny kid of twelve or so in a dingy *gelibiya*.

"Bring this gentleman a pipe of my best, that which is in the green package in the back, and accept no money from him. When he asks for a second, bring it to him and again accept no money. Go on now."

Nodding, the boy turned to go into the shop.

"But if he asks for a third, make sure he pays," Hijazi said.

———

I did not ask for a third. I even declined the second. The hash was as pure and potent as Hijazi had advertised, and I knew one pipe would give me the edge I needed to do what I had to that night. A shower of sparks burst with a popping sound from the bowl of another smoker's pipe. My senses heightened, the crackling sounded as loud as rifle shots and startled my heart into a frenzied beating. I whirled around in my chair and made a start toward the man, whose face looked diabolical in the flare of the pipe he was inhaling with long greedy drags. There was prickling behind my eyes, a painful burning sensation, as if coals had been set alight inside my head. My fists were clenched, and I wanted to beat the man's face into jelly. It was strong stuff all right. Very strong. I had to talk myself down. Wait. Wait. This part won't last long. This is just the first stage and it'll pass.

Waiting, I leaned back in the chair, my head resting against the warm hardness of a mud-brick wall. Gradually, the good feeling came over me: I could no longer feel the wall against my head. There was a numbness in my face and the sensation, thrilling and frightening at the same time, that the back of my skull had been separated from the front and was floating in midair. I wanted to giggle, picturing the bland Thomas Colfax plotting and conspiring in this same hash den. I could almost hear him, speaking in that nondescript voice of his, then the voice taking on its note of constrained fury as he said, "Don't give in to it, George. Because if I don't get that money, you won't be missed either." I could hear him making the threat in the same tone he used to threaten me—"the best thing, the very best thing, that could happen to you would be to die quickly." It was odd; I could remember his voice, but not his face. When I tried to picture his face, all I saw was a featureless outline topped with short brown hair. The American was always combing his hair. The image made me want to giggle again. Combing his hair in Hijazi's fly-spattered drug palace. The ordinary Mr. Colfax among the hash-eaters. Well, he practiced his craft to the hilt; you could say that for him. Clandestine rendezvous in a hashish den with a dark-skinned man—apparently a Bejayan contact man in Cairo—and with the Greek gun-runner, George Boxavenides. Code words. The prophet (which must have been Muhammad Jima's cryptonym) needs twenty lengths of pipe and five hundred water pumps. Code words, cryptonyms, and secret meetings; he was doing it all by the numbers, by the book. And yet, something seemed wrong, dreadfully wrong.

It was safe to assume, Colfax's admonition notwithstanding, that he had been put in charge of a project to arm Jima's faction. But why, with all the logistical support that could be his for the asking, was he relying on a fly-by-night smuggler like Boxavenides? For some reason, he needed Boxavenides, and Boxavenides needed to reclaim his freighter, and reclaiming the freighter required ruining Harris. That was my assignment. Why was it necessary? Thinking of myself, I wondered why he had recruited me, a rank amateur, in the first place. If the project was so special, why hadn't he gone to the professionals who were trained for—what? Back to my original question. What was I going to be doing?

Sitting there, dreamy-dazed, I felt like a patient trying to solve one of those puzzles psychologists give to determine intelligence. Riddled with riddles. The pieces seemed on the verge of juggling themselves into place. It might have been an illusion induced by the drug, but everything seemed so close to making itself clear. The answers were on the edge of my conscious mind, just beyond its grasp, teasing it. In retrospect, I sometimes think I ought to have been able to figure things out. If the hash had not been so strong, I might have been able to think with a clearer head; I might have picked up on the clues Colfax had, unwittingly I am sure, supplied on the day I met him. It had been his use

of pronouns. "My project." "When you sign on with me."
"All you'll owe me is loyalty." *I, me, my, mine.* Never
once an "our" or a "we." Yes, if I had combined that with
the facts Hijazi had given me and the little I had learned
in my phony interview with Boxavenides, I might have been
able to figure out what Colfax was up to. I might have
made the one assumption he most definitely would not
have wanted me to make.

After I had waved the boy away, Hijazi asked, "Why
aren't you going to smoke the second?"

"I don't need to."

"And what of my debt? You said two pipes."

"Yes, I did. Two pipes. That's what I said. Two pipes
in repayment." I could hear my own voice. It sounded
familiar and yet peculiar, the way I did when I heard it
played back on a tape recorder.

"The debt is repaid then?"

"No, you still owe me the second installment."

"I don't like being indebted."

I rose from the chair. The movement seemed to take a
very long time, and when I stood I could barely feel the
ground beneath me. It was as if I were levitating, a sensation that gave me an exaggerated awareness of my height.
Hijazi, paunchy and short, looked small as a gnome to me,
a grotesque little figure toward whom I could feel nothing
but contempt.

"Maybe you should learn to keep your mouth shut."

"But Mr. Charlie, I thought he was from the Mukhabarat."

"He could have been from the Red Cross for all you
cared. He gave you some money to inform on me. That's
all you cared about."

"Believe me, I thought he was from the Mukhabarat."

"Believe me, he's not."

"Mr. Charlie, I think you are in a hurry. I think it's
time for you to leave."

"Yes, I think it is."

"God willing, I shall see you back in good health."

In the suffused light of the fluorescents, Hijazi's puffy
face had a pale, greenish cast and reminded me of a
swollen melon. I repressed an impulse to slap it.

"Ismail, if you tell Ali about tonight, you won't be in good health when I come back."

"Mr. Charlie, I'm not stupid. I know this Ali and the American and the dark man, they are all making a conspiracy. I'm an Arab and I know about conspiracies."

"I'm not talking about them. I'm talking about me. *I'll* see that you lose your health. Do you understand? I'm offering you a better price to keep quiet than Ali can offer you to talk. Your continued good health."

"I think I understand."

"Your continued good health. That's my offer. I'm offering you your health for your silence."

The hash was working, almost too well. I felt an exciting release from all inhibitions.

"I understand. It isn't necessary to make threats."

I bowed low, touching the tips of my fingers to my forehead. "You understand. In the name of Allah, the all-merciful, the all-compassionate."

"Nor to make blasphemies."

"Peace be upon you."

"And upon you, peace."

"Somehow I doubt it," I said, switching back to English. "*Ma'assalame*, Ismail."

"*Ma'assalame*, Mr. Charlie."

I walked unsteadily out of the circle of light and into the darkness. No stars were visible overhead, only a curtain of sand through which the shine of the waxing moon barely penetrated. Walking into the seemingly endless blackness of the street, I was aware of being surrounded by people, millions of them, millions of people I could not see. They huddled in their wretched houses, which showed as almost shapeless forms, ranked thick as the trees in a jungle, festooned with laundry hanging from poles stuck out the windows. From inside came the murmur of voices, incomprehensible mutterings, the squalling of infants, yaps of dogs and chuckling of chickens, bangs, rattles and scrapes. Sometimes, through a half-open door or the chinks of a broken shutter, I could see a kerosene lamp glowing and someone's shadow, huge and misshapen, cast on a wall. My heart was beating unnaturally fast from a senseless fear and anger, which were both intensified by the dark and all those invisible people, all that life, hidden, unknown, and menacing. Every sound, every vague movement I caught out of the corners of my eyes, startled and infuriated me at the same time. I wanted to lash out at something, but did not know at what. The hash had aroused the violent, irrational side of my personality, the part of me where blind hatreds and primal terrors sleep, usually to be awakened only in nightmares. And all the while, the other part of my mind, the part that had remained lucid, kept repeating, Stay calm, it's only another stage, it'll pass like the others. And I heard Ali saying, "As you must know, Mr. Gage, hashish is an excitant." Yes, I knew it. It mimicked a condition I had experienced a few times in the war, in those moments under fire when my emotions became so extreme they created their polar opposites. Panic grew so high it gave birth to the resolution required to control it, resolve grew so intense as to become indistinguishable from desperation until, finally, these conflicting emotions neutralized each other and I felt nothing at all.

Nothing is what I wanted to feel. That had been my original purpose in going to Hijazi's. It is possible I could have achieved a similar numbness with whiskey. I am, however, a traditionalist, and traditionally, in the Middle East, hashish is the intoxicant one takes before committing an assassination. The one I was to commit did not involve any physical violence. It was to be more in the nature of a character assassination, which is violence of another kind. It was violence nonetheless, demanding a degree of callousness. Because the victim happened to be a friend, it demanded more callousness than I had in me. So I had taken the narcotic that deadens, better than any other I know of, the nerve ends of conscience.

The agitation passed as I emerged from Bulaq's tyranny and, dry-mouthed, dry-eyed, anesthetized, headed down Ramses Street behind the Egyptian Museum. I was clutching the letter again. Boxavenides had asked me to write it two nights before. That had been the request I was to consider an order from Colfax. I thought of Boxavenides when I saw the side of the Hilton facing Tahrir Square, the rows of light and dark windows making the hotel look like an enormous chessboard standing on edge. I wondered

which were the windows of his suite. I knew they faced the
square because he had complained about not getting his
usual room on the Nile side. He had been slightly molli-
fied by the complimentary bottle of champagne the man-
agement had placed on the dresser, along with a note informing maids, room-service boys, and visitors that Mr. G.
Boxavenides was a VIP. Looking at the embossed note
and the bottle, sweating in its bucket, he'd said: "You
know, Mr. Gage, my mother wanted me to be a priest. She
was a very devout woman and she wanted me to be a priest
so I would do good in this world. I'm no priest as you
know, but I have done well, ha ha ha."

Despite his sense of humor, Boxavenides was a charming
man. At least he seemed so in contrast to the image I had
had of him before our meeting. I had expected either a
swarthy buccaneer or an aging Levantine Greek, some
ponderous crook wearing a cheap shirt with the stench of
corruption oozing from every thread. Instead, he turned
out to be a lively man in his late thirties or early forties,
trim and tanned from almost daily tennis games, with a
relaxed manner that put you automatically at ease and a
face handsome in a slick, dark way that reminded me of a
1950s nightclub singer, the kind who crooned commercial
ballads in Miami Beach hotels and who were always
thought to have vague connections with gangsters. I could
understand how someone like Harris, the eternally innocent—or, more accurately, stupid—American, could be
taken in by him. Also, his shirt was not cheap, and rather
than the stink that is as unique to his kind of hustler as a
certain foul, oily stench is to a barracuda, I caught the scent
of an expensive cologne. It concealed the odor of his corruption as the reality of his business was concealed by its
legitimate-sounding name, the Arab–East Africa Trading
Company Ltd., AEA Trading for short. He said it dealt
in "reexported products," meaning smuggling. When I
asked what sort of products, he replied, "Oh, a great di-
versity, but we specialize in those that fire seven hundred
and twenty rounds per minute, ha ha ha."

We had gone to his suite after dinner to discuss his request. Ignoring the champagne, Boxavenides ordered up a
bottle of aniselike *arak*. Maybe he thought the powerful

brandy would make me more receptive to his request. For a while, he talked about Lebanon; he wanted to know if I thought the Syrians could keep what passed for peace there. I said I wasn't sure. Boxavenides nodded. "Yes, yes, no one is sure. But for all practical purposes, I think that war is over." There was a note of disappointment in his voice. "That was quite a market. I've never seen such a market, Mr. Gage. The Christians were paying anywhere from five to eight hundred dollars for an M-16. If it had a sniper-scope, a thousand dollars. Imagine. For one M-16! A thousand dollars! We didn't do quite as well with the Palestinians and the Moslems. They had the Libyans, the Russians, the Iraqis, oh, everyone behind them. But we did well enough, considering the competition."

"An RPG hit my office when I was over there. Blew my secretary to pieces. She was only twenty-six."

"Oh. I am sorry to hear that, Mr. Gage. Maniacs, all of them. Christians, Moslems, all maniacs. Only twenty-six, you said. Really, I am sorry. A bad war."

He sounded sincere. I believe he was sincere. I believe he was, like a technician in a napalm factory, incapable of making a connection between his reexported products and what they produced.

When Boxavenides had finished discussing the commercial advantages of slaughter, he turned to the problem of his ship, a freighter called the *Galaxy Challenger*. The Endicott bank, from which he had secured the loan to buy the vessel, had confiscated it after he defaulted on his payments, then instituted a suit against him and put the ship on the market. Boxavenides responded with a counter-suit, thereby in effect blocking any sale until the litigation was resolved. The bank was now stuck with a useless ship that was costing them thousands of dollars a day.

The story of how matters had arrived at this point was a long and complicated one, full of financial technicalities I only half understood. I was not surprised to learn that David Harris was one of the story's central characters. Knowing Harris, it also did not surprise me to hear he had finally got himself into the kind of trouble against which I had warned him that afternoon on the veranda of the St. George Hotel.

It was not, as white-collar crimes go, a felony, but it was serious enough to cause him and the bank considerable trouble if it became public. Some time ago, he had falsified a report on AEA's financial condition, thereby enabling Boxavenides to obtain the seven-figure loan. That is, Harris had defrauded his own bank. In exchange, the Greek had persuaded one of his contacts to finance a fleet of small tankers through Endicott. Harris was delighted with bringing in the business, which helped his career considerably. Since then, there had occurred not only what Boxavenides termed a "misunderstanding" over the loan scheduling, but Endicott had discovered the freighter was being used to smuggle guns to A rican rebels. But, Boxavenides said, "It's none of their goddamned business what I ship.

"And all this is really unnecessary," Boxavenides said. "It'll be years before those lawsuits are resolved. This whole matter can be settled out of court—and they know I can't pay off the loan without the ship anyhow. So here's what I want. I want them to reschedule the loan and give me back that damn freighter.

"I've explained all this to them several times but those tightasses in New York and London won't listen to me. They're going to need a little extra motivation. Maybe they're solvent enough to absorb the losses of holding on to my ship. But there's one thing they can't afford to lose and that's their reputation.

"That," Boxavenides went on, "is where Harris comes in."

Over Harris's name, I was to write a letter of resignation to the bank, explaining his culpability in the affair and instructing them to drop the suit and to return possession of the ship to Boxavenides. If they did not comply, the full story would appear as part of an *Arab Digest* article on Middle East bribery scandals, which would cause the bank to suffer more than just embarrassing publicity.

Boxavenides said: "Mr. Gardner told me you'd be agreeable. So I can be assured you'll write the letter."

"Why do *I* have to do it?"

"Because you know him. Mr. Gardner told me that. You have his confidence. He'd be more likely to listen to you than me. And, of course, Mr. Gardner can't do it. He can't have his name and the name of his—what?—his organization associated with this. You're the logical choice. Do you see?"

"I see all right, but what makes you think Harris will sign it?"

"Harris will sign because he'll be named in the article and that would ruin him completely."

"Yeah, and you'll be named too."

"Mr. Gage, you're not stupid. You know that *any* kind of publicity will do a man like me good. When are you going to see David next?"

"Tuesday night at the Cinq à Sept Club."

"Tuesday night. So that gives you two days to write the letter. It also gives you two days to think about things. Thinking is unhealthy. I know you're under orders, but I also know you and David are friends. Your friendship might cause you to consider not finishing the job. So, so"— Boxavenides held his glass up to the light and looked through the clear liquor like a scientist studying a solution in a test tube—"so I think you should be impressed with how badly Mr. Gardner and I want that lawsuit dropped. Mr. Gardner and I, we also want the ship back. You should know that and you should know this—you won't be doing your friend a favor if you don't finish this job. I know what David is, and if that letter isn't signed by Tuesday night, I'll see to it some other people know our friend has been masquerading."

"As what?"

"I'll see to it they know he's a *yehud*, Mr. Gage. A dirty little Jew who's been flying about the Middle East pretending he's something else, and seeing oh so many important Arabs. I think that would look very suspicious to some people, don't you?"

"He's only half Jewish."

"Oh, come, come. The people I'm talking about don't trouble themselves about technicalities."

"Look, you start suggesting he's an Israeli agent, you could get him arrested."

"Yes, arrested if the hints are given to people in a legitimate government. If you're talking about people in some other organization, then something worse might happen to

him. These other organizations, I'm well connected to
them. They're among my markets, Mr. Gage."

"Strictly business, is that it?"

"Strictly business. I would say to them, 'My friends, I
appreciate your business, so I'll tell you something. There
is this American banker, David Harris, who travels all
over the Middle East. He sees this man in Jeddah and
this man in Beirut and this man in Cairo. And this David
Harris, my friends, is a *yehud,* a Jew boy. He doesn't look
like one, but he is, and on all his visa applications he says
his religion is Christian.' Do you see, Mr. Gage? I wouldn't
need to tell them any fables, just the truth, and let things
take their natural course. They'd think he's a spy for the
Israelis and deal with him accordingly. They might kidnap
him, shoot him, mail him an explosive letter."

"I can't believe that freighter of yours is so damned important you'd get Dave killed over it."

"When you've finished the letter perhaps you'd like to
get in some tennis. I'm very fond of tennis, play it nearly
every day. It reduces tensions. Keeps this flat." He patted
his stomach. "I think a few sets would do you good. The
physical activity would stop you from thinking."

"I don't play tennis."

"Too bad. But you do drink. I can see that. A little
more?" He held up the bottle of *arak,* white and clear.
I nodded.

"Well, perhaps this will stop you from thinking," Boxavenides said, refilling my glass.

"So it's that important?"

"Stop interviewing me, Mr. Gage."

———————

I did not begin to think about it, really think about it,
until the next day, after I signed the contracts.

The *Digest*'s offices were in the same building as Reuters,
one of two slate-colored buildings facing each other across
a small courtyard. Their shadows made the courtyard dim
on the brightest days, and on that afternoon, with the sun
half-eclipsed by sand, it looked especially dismal. An array
of signs hung outside the doorway, one declaring the *Arab*

Digest to be on the fourth floor. Another hung near it. I must have seen it every time I had been in the building, and I wondered why bells of recognition had not rung in my head the night before in Boxavenides's suite. The sign read, in English and Arabic:

6TH FLOOR. AEA TRADING LTD.
ALEXANDRIA—CAIRO—DUBAI—PORT SUDAN.

Isn't this getting incestuous, I thought, walking into the lobby, where most of the lights were burned out. The antiquated elevator refused to respond to my repeated buzzings, so I took the stairs. There were no lights at all in the stairwell. Groping my way up in the darkness, I had an uneasy feeling, mingled with giddiness, that reminded of the way I had felt in the amusement-park haunted houses of my boyhood. But underneath those emotions was the depression, the sense of death and decay that building always aroused in me. The giddiness had become unpleasant by the time I reached the fourth-floor landing, my breathing labored, and though I tried to lay it off on poor conditioning, I knew another of those periodic attacks was coming. Pressing the doorbell to the *Digest*'s offices, I nodded to the old woman washing the stairs. She did not return the gesture. Back bent, wearing a black shawl over her head, and stirring the water in her bucket with a mop, she looked like a witch. The woman swabbed each step carefully, her efforts useless. The grime was so embedded no amount of scrubbing could ever get it out. All she accomplished was to turn the dirt into mud, a rivulet of which flowed down the steps, like a black river descending a terraced waterfall, to pool in the cracks of the landing below.

The *Digest*'s offices were likewise somber and shabby. The windows faced the courtyard. Some were still covered with blue blackout paint from the last Middle East war, not because anyone expected another war soon, but because no one had yet mustered the energy to scrape it off. The dust that smoked the panes of the other windows obscured what little light came from the courtyard. The room itself was reminiscent of a newsroom of fifty years

ago: rows of battered wooden desks, vacuum tubes for
sending copy from one desk to another, writers hunched
over antique typewriters, a layer of acrid-smelling cigarette
smoke hovering below the ceiling lights, and three old
wire-service machines clacking out tales of conferences,
border conflicts, floods, fires, plane crashes, speeches,
clackety-clackety-clackety. Hearing that sound, I felt the
attack coming on stronger, my heart beginning to race, my
nerves drawing taut, bracing themselves for the roar and
shock of a bursting rocket. I knew no such thing would
happen, told myself the reaction had been caused by an
association of sounds: there was no danger. But my nerves
did not respond to these instructions from my mind. They
seemed to possess a life of their own, over which my will
and reason exercised only a tenuous control.

Feigning calmness, I walked up to Iskander's secretary,
a plump and sullen girl immersed in an old copy of *Paris
Match*. She showed me into his barren office. I was relieved
when she closed the door behind her, muting the insistent
clatter of the Telexes.

Iskander Ahmed Iskander, he of the grand name, was a
short man with curly white hair, a white mustache yellowed by the pipe he smoked constantly, and blue eyes
that betrayed some European blood in his ancestry. There
were the usual greetings, all in compliance with the Arab
obsession with formalities. In compliance with the Arab
obsession with hospitality, he had his secretary bring in
two cups of Turkish coffee *masbut*—that is, half-sweetened
—then glasses of tea. Iskander said he had been expecting
me, he was pleased to have me on the staff, I would be an
asset to the English-language edition. I answered that I
was happy to be back in journalism and hoped to do my
best for him. We kept up this polite charade for fifteen
minutes or so, pretending to an ignorance of the real reason for my being there and concealing our uneasiness
with a lot of small talk. Was the tea all right? Yes, it was.
Would I care for more? No, thank you. Would I like a
cigarette? No, I didn't smoke. Ah, that was very good. He
had quit cigarettes two years ago, but, as I could see, he
had been unable to give up his pipe. Did its smell bother
me? No, it smelled rather good in fact. Yes, it was fine

tobacco, a custom blend made by a London tobacconist
and shipped to him at some expense, one of the few
luxuries he permitted himself.

When we had run out of banalities, he handed me the
contract, which I signed, feeling a bit the way I had when
I'd signed my enlistment papers. Committed. An irrevocable choice made. Iskander said, "We won't let it out
what you're earning. Thank God it doesn't come out of
our pockets. But if the staff knew your salary's three times
mine, I'd have a revolution on my hands." That said, he
gave me a packet containing my camouflage: a card identifying me as a staff member of the *Arab Digest* and the
black press-pass, like a pocket-sized address book, issued
by the Ministry of Information. The pass had already been
stamped and had my photograph in it. I asked where he
had found the picture. He answered that the ministry still
had several extra prints on file; he had gone there personally to get the pass for me. I thanked him. "Don't
mention it," he said with a casual wave of his pipe.
"Finally there is this." Iskander walked over to the safe,
opened it, and gave me an envelope containing $2,250.
"The rest of your first month's salary in advance. Mr.
Gardner wanted you to have it. I can't tell you how relieved I am to have that off my hands." Pocketing the
money, I felt the bonds of commitment tighten. Iskander,
anxious to get rid of me, then walked me out of his office
and through the newsroom to the front door. We shook
hands, and in a stage whisper just loud enough for a few
nearby reporters to hear, Iskander said, "I look forward
to seeing your first story, Mr. Gage." But when I stepped
through the doorway into the twilit hall, his voice dropped.

"You should write something for us now and then,"
he said, smiling in a way at once rueful and resigned. The
banging of the cleaning woman's bucket came from the
shadows below. The still, stale air smelled like the crypts
at Saqqara. "I hope you appreciate my position. It's too
long a story to tell how I got into it, but I hope you appreciate my position."

I nodded.

"Just a small article now and then, to avoid people here

asking questions. To keep up appearances. Can you promise that, Mr. Gage? A small article every now and then?"

Promising him I would, I said good-bye and headed down the stairs.

The woman was working on the flight just below. Hunched over, she mopped the steps with a slow, even rhythm, the mop handle moving with the regularity of a metronome. I stopped for a moment, waiting for her to stand aside. She looked up. I could hardly see her face. It was just a dark oval shrouded by the darker folds of her shawl. Her eyelids sagged at the corners, so that her eyes, set in the scarcely visible face, looked like two white triangles suspended in a void. Flapping her hand in a beckoning motion, the creature spoke. "Descend, descend." She dragged the bucket out of the way. "Mind," she said hoarsely, "it's wet. Take care you don't fall." That was when the attack struck. The sight of the woman and the sound of her voice caused a wave of irrational panic to rush hotly from my feet, through my legs, and into my face. My head started swimming. The stairwell looked like a mine shaft, on whose edge I stood precariously balanced. For a few crazy moments, the woman seemed inexpressibly evil. I thought she wanted me to fall, to tumble into the shaft. Terrified of her, I grasped the railing; the feel of its cold, solid metal restored some of my grip on reality. It's just another one of those attacks, I told myself. The doctors said you'd get them from time to time. Just another dizzy spell. It'll go away. The hag flapped her hand again—you could not call that spastic gesture a wave—and repeated, "Descend, descend." Her croaking voice was more insistent. "I've my work to finish. Come down now." Holding the railing tightly, I raced past her and took the remaining stairs two at a time until I reached the safety of the lobby floor. Outside, an image of the old woman remained on the retina of my inner eye. I saw her for what she was, a harmless old lady. I had been terrified of a harmless old lady for no reason at all, and the fact that I had felt terror when there was no reason frightened me all the more, and my knees were water as I walked through the heat and dust of the street.

I spent most of the next day in my flat, staring at my typewriter, wondering how to compose the letter and what to say to Harris when I gave it to him. My first assignment. The only thing good about it was that it prevented me from indulging in any romantic fictions about my new career.

It would destroy his illusions, those captivating visions of a rich and glamorous future. It is true I never thought much of them; they struck me as being as unrealistic as the glossy portraits of the good life presented in the slick men's magazines he liked to read. Harris was too guileless to be truly venal. He was, rather, romantically fascinated by money and the illusory independence he imagined it would bring him. But my opinion of his vague and frivolous dreams did not matter. They were important to him. They gave his life a dimension it would have otherwise lacked; they give it a purpose, or the appearance of a purpose, which amounted to the same thing. To destroy them would be to destroy the purpose; and there was the chance he would be unable to replace his old illusions with new ones and do something self-destructive.

Perhaps I was being melodramatic. Harris was a naturally exuberant and resilient man. He did not seem the suicidal type. But if he did something desperate, I could not escape responsibility. Yet neither could I escape responsibility for whatever happened if Boxavenides carried out his threat.

I put a sheet of onionskin in the typewriter and began the letter. My motives were a mystery to me then, though I have since been able to sort them out.

It wasn't the money, and it wasn't because I thought I was saving him from Boxavenides's thugs. I had chosen to play my part in the wrecking of David Harris because I lacked the will to oppose Colfax. It was the same lack out of which I later capitulated to Nordstrand, an affliction that reflected a loss of control over my life. Somewhere amid the wreckage of all my losses of the past decade, I had lost the last remnants of my belief in the idea that

some order governed the world. The explosion that had
shredded Leila, I knew, had shredded that belief as well.
She had been blown to tatters for no reason that I could
see, and being the product of a faithless age, I was incapable of relegating her annihilation to the will of a just
but inscrutable God. It had become to me an example of
the terrible chaos that seems to lie at the heart of life; and
its emotional aftereffects had, finally, caused my perceptions to become so disordered that I had seen a threat in
a frail old woman. A man who cannot be certain of something so basic as his physical senses cannot hope to be
certain of himself. Lacking certitude, I could not exercise
the will to direct my life and, subconsciously, I sought to
submit myself to someone who would stop the spinning
of my psychological compass and fix it on some azimuth.
That was the ultimate reason why I had enlisted with
Thomas Colfax. Unable to assert my own will, I had made
myself the instrument of his. I was not the operator, but
the tool; not the criminal, but the accomplice.

And resigning myself to that part, I finished the letter.

When it was done, I addressed the envelope and folded
the four single-spaced pages into it without sealing it. Then
I sat staring out the window. My apartment building had
gone up the year before Nasser's death. It was one of the
tallest in Cairo and commanded a view of the entire city,
its only virtue. It had been slapped together hurriedly and
with only a little more care than a child would exercise in
building a sand castle. The *Khamsin*, now blowing so hard
it raised white caps on the river, moaned constantly through
the ill-fitting window frames. The late-afternoon sun slanted
through the sand-fouled air, the sand fracturing the light
into a million pieces, the light reddening the sand so that
each grain resembled a droplet of blood. They fell into
the great, rust-colored artery of the Nile, upon which a
barge and two feluccas were heading upriver. The barge
cleared the Twenty-sixth of July Bridge, between whose
black girders traffic moved incessantly. Each felucca had
earthen jugs pyramided on its decks, and the pyramids,
white against the brown decks, seemed dangerously near
toppling as the boats rocked in the barge's wake. Then,
their yellowed sails bellied in the wind, they went under

the bridge and past the quays by the old Port of Bulaq. The slum stretched away from the riverbank, into a thick haze through which the laundry hanging from the windows and balconies looked like flags of surrender.

The letter written, I was left with what Colfax might have called a procedural problem but which I chose to call an emotional one: how to confront Harris with it, how to summon the resolve to complete the act. Various approaches occurred to me; none seemed satisfactory. Taking the letter out of the envelope, I read it over, as if it might contain a solution. "In view of my implication in the matter explained above, my only course is to submit my resignation. . . . I cannot see how I could justify appearing as a witness when the suit comes up for trial . . . urge you to give serious consideration to Mr. Boxavenides's request to settle out of court . . . full account may appear in the press here . . . pursuing the present course, in my opinion, would risk a scandal that would be more harmful to the bank's interest than any losses it might incur by ceasing all legal actions against Mr. Boxavenides. . . . Very Truly Yours, David R. Harris."

The crisp phrases sounded as if they had been written by someone else, a commerce-school student practicing business English. I felt my nerve slipping and a simultaneous and contradictory determination to get the job done. Turning the problem over in my mind, thinking, thinking too much, I gazed out the window once more, toward Bulaq. A quarter of a mile away and eight stories below, the slum's rooftops made a dark mosaic of greys, browns, and dull yellows that appeared to be pegged to the earth by the spikes of the minarets. Thinking. Thinking, It amounts to a kind of character assassination. "*Assassination: Assassin* 16th cent. Arab. *hashshāshīn* (pl. of *hashshāsh*, one addicted to hashish). 1) One of a secret order of Muslims that at the time of the Crusades terrorized Christians by secret murder committed under the influence of hashish. . . . *Assassinate*. 2) To injure or destroy unexpectedly or treacherously." Leaf of the Indian hemp, the marvelous leaf that overcomes reluctance, frees the brain from the oppression of thought, and lifts the burden of conscience. Oh, yes, the leaf of the hemp plant;

if thought paled the native hue of resolution, a few tokes
of hash would restore its complexion. It had provided me
with temporary solutions to other problems; it would
provide the solution to this one. Slipping on my khaki
jacket, once part of my foreign correspondent's getup, I
put the letter in one of the big side pockets and left for
Hijazi's.

———

An Egyptian friend who had been one of my regular informed sources when I worked for the *Post* once told me,
"There are only two cities in the world where a man can
lead a civilized life—Paris and Cairo." My friend was
partly misinformed in this case. Parisians, even the poorest
of them, lead princely lives compared to most Cairenes.
Eight million people squeezed into a city built for one-
fourth that many, they exist in quarters like Bulaq, subsist
on black-bean paste, and are plagued with bilharzia, an
intestinal disease that leaves them semisomnambulant and
makes them die young. They stand in long lines for such
staples as sugar and salt, chronic shortages of which prevent them from devoting themselves to any pursuit more
civilized then surviving from day to day. Those like my
friend, who have never suffered from shortages of anything, who have people to stand in line for them, and who
comprise about one percent of the city's population, live
very well indeed.

The Cinq à Sept Club was one of the places where they
gathered to celebrate their good fortune and to be civilized
together. It was discreetly hidden on a narrow side street
off Qasr al-Nil, with stained-glass in its one window so no
one could peek inside and a heavy wooden door guarded
by a big ugly character whose main function was to keep
his own kind out. Like its *haute bourgeoisie* patrons, the
club suffered from a cultural identity crisis. It had been
a British watering hole in the colonial days, and its leather
chairs, brass ashtrays, and wainscoted walls, decorated with
fox-hunting scenes, made it resemble a Mayfair men's club.
It was named for the time of day when Parisian men visit
their mistresses. The bar served Scotch, German wines,

Russian vodka, and, when it was available, American bourbon. Keeping pace with modern trends, the half-Turkish, half-Egyptian owner had declared Tuesday and Wednesday to be "disco nights." Music was provided by a third-rate Italian band that had memorized the lyrics to American songs. Oriental entertainment was reserved for the weekends, when the customers could watch the fleshy writhings of a Greek belly-dancer about whom the only thing Arab was her stage name, Aisha. The club was Harris's favorite night spot in Cairo. He liked its wood and leather and what he called its "cosmopolitan ambience"; it made the perfect setting for him to indulge himself in fantasies of wealth and international wheeling-dealing.

I had some trouble convincing the sentry to let me in. He kept saying "no tie" in English, shaking his head and pointing at my neck as if he meant to drive his thick finger through my windpipe. I showed him my press pass and said the words that could get you shot, kidnapped, or arrested in some parts of the Middle East, but which had more pleasant effects in Cairo, where Americans were loved for their money: "*Sahafi Amerikai.* American journalist."

The doorman scowled at the pass, checked the photograph against my face, then grudgingly pressed a buzzer. The door was opened by a chubby man in a shiny black suit. He also made a fuss about allowing me in until I told him I had an appointment with Mr. David Harris.

"Oh, yes," he said, "Mister Har-ees. Yes, *tfaddal, tfaddal.* Please, please. This way. But you will please wear a tie next time?"

I nodded. He led me through the crowd which, because it was "disco night," was mostly young. There were twenty-ish actors who all seemed to be trying to look like the youthful Omar Sharif; girls with eyes that provoked and repelled at the same time, that expressed both desire and the repression of desire, a natural lust at war with a determination to preserve virginity; young men who referred to themselves as intelligentsia, meaning they had university degrees, no jobs, but enough family money to lead civilized lives. A few older people—chaperons, for Egypt is a Moslem country and guards its unmarried daughters vigilantly—were sitting at the tables. The men looked like

high-level bureaucrats, sleek and complacent. Their wives
were bovine, heavy-haunched women over whose gross
bosoms jewelry glittered and clattered.

The long walk had straightened me out a little, but the
hash was still working; it had altered my depth perception,
so that, afraid of stumbling, I moved through the press
with the exaggerated caution of a drunk trying to prove
he's sober. Even inside, I could feel the heat of the *Khamsin* against which a small vintage air conditioner hummed
ineffectually. Through the smells of perfumes and colognes
came the musky odor of stale sweat: a reminder that these
people, for all their conceits, were made of the same common, corruptible clay as the wretches I had just left in
Bulaq. It made me want to smash the pretentious furniture,
rip the incongruous fox-hunting scenes from the wall, and
drag everyone through the slum whose dust continued to
cling to my shoes.

The chubby man pointed to Harris, then left. Small,
dressed according to his idea of how an international banker should look—that is, in a suit conservative enough to
project an image of solidity, but with just enough flair to
show he had a bit of the gambler in him—he was sitting
in one of the leather-covered booths against the back
wall. As always, his dark hair was trimmed short and
carefully parted. Just above his well-barbered head hung
a print titled *The Find,* and next to that another called
The Pursuit. As I moved toward Harris, I noticed a third
scene, *The Death,* depicting a fox about to be executed
by the pack. It struck me as appropriate, but the sight of
Harris did not evoke any of the pity I had felt earlier.
There was only the anger that made me want to tear the
place apart and contempt for him, the sort of contempt
you feel toward an adolescent who refuses to see things
as they are, ignores all adult advice, and suffers the consequences.

This is how I expected it would go: Harris, unsuspect-
ing, would smile, shake hands, and ask how things had
gone with Colfax. I would say I was working for him.
Then we would order drinks, over which Harris would
deliver a pornographic narrative about some new girl
friend in London. I would interrupt him, take out the let-

ter, and tell him to read and sign it. He would be stunned at first. When the initial shock wore off, he would try to squirm out of his predicament. Relentlessly, coldly, I would cut off all avenues of escape, pointing out with cruel clarity his lack of an alternative. At last, beaten, he would sign and everything would be over.

Reality did not live up to my expectation. It never does. Harris did not smile when I slid into the booth across from him. He did not extend his hand, but kept it wrapped around his glass. He had been nursing his drink: I could tell by the way the melted ice had bleached the Scotch almost to the color of gin. Holding the glass in his small hand, he glared in a way that told me immediately he knew what was coming. He looked at me for a long minute without saying anything. His eyes, cold and accusatory on the surface, bore an expression of pain underneath, the pain of betrayal. My anger, my contempt, and with them my resolve, started to peel away.

"Well, I guess someone told you," I said nervously, unable to bear the strained silence any longer. "Who was it? Gardner or Boxavenides?"

Harris made a show of looking at his watch. "You're late, Charlie. Half an hour late. What was the trouble? Working up the balls to come here?"

"I got tied up."

"You mean doped up. I know your vices, Charlie, and I'd say you've been doping it up again. All right, fine. Some guys get theirs from booze, you get yours from drugs. Fine."

"Since when did you get interested in drug enforcement?"

"Your eyes look like Little Orphan Annie's, Charlie."

"Okay, I blew a little hash. So what? Look, none of this was my idea."

"Tell me something, Charlie my boy. Did you get yourself doped up before you went off on those hot-shit war-correspondent assignments? Is that how you got the balls to do it?"

The aggressive manner was not at all in character, and it threw me off-balance as much as his apparent knowledge of why I was there.

"C'mon, big guy. Tell me. Did you smoke dope before you went out to play war correspondent? Or maybe you got yourself doped up and hallucinated all that crap about ducking bullets in Lower Boongiebungieland. Maybe you made it all up. Winged it. Maybe that's why you had to quit. You couldn't make things up anymore."

"If you're trying to get me to take a swing at you, you're doing a good job of it."

"If you're trying to scare me with that, you're doing a lousy job."

"Somebody told you. Gardner probably. What'd Gardner tell you?"

"Colfax. His name is Tom Colfax. I mean Thomas Colfax. He doesn't like 'Tom.' Virginia aristocracy."

"He doesn't like being called Colfax, either. The great spook wants to be called Gardner."

"His name's Colfax."

"I know his name's Colfax."

"So, we'll call him Colfax. His name's Colfax, that's what we'll call him. We'll keep everything out in front. You won't be able to stab me in the back, Charlie. 'Charlie my boy, oh Charlie my boy, you thrill me, you chill me with moments of joy.' Uh-uh, Charlie my boy, you'll have to stick it in my chest."

"What'd he tell you? If he told you everything, then we can just get all this over with."

"What did he tell me? He told me real good news as far as you're concerned."

"I got the job. I'm working for him if that's what you mean."

Harris smiled sardonically. "Don't glamorize yourself and don't bullshit me. You're back in the hack racket."

"What the hell are you talking about?"

"You're working for the *Arab Digest*. That's one of the things Colfax told me. He helped get you a job with the *Digest,* but don't try and tell me you're working for him."

"For Christ's sake, that's only a cover."

I realized how silly and melodramatic the phrase sounded even as I said it.

"You've really doped yourself up. You're having delusions. 'That's only a cover.' Blow my cover, Maxie, and

you're a dead man. Do you think just because you gave
Colfax a little info about Bay . . ."

"Bejaya."

"Bejaya. Do you think just because you gave him a
little info about Bejaya you're some kind of spook?
Where's your leather coat, Charlie? Your Walther automatic?"

I remained silent, afraid of saying something sillier.

"Okay, you wanted to know what Colfax told me. Here
it is. You gave him some information about that place.
He's got a contact on the *Digest,* and repays you by getting you on the staff. The *Digest* has been picking up on
those stories back in the States, about how all of us
Yankee businessmen over here are bribing every Arab in
every ministry from the janitor on up. They'd already decided to do their own bit of scandalmongering. You come
along and they assign you to do it, I guess because you're
an American. Now comes the first twist. They've been
talking to greasy George Boxavenides, who's told them
some juicy tales. They send you over to finish up interviewing him and he tells you the same tales. About me
and what happened between me and him. So I'm going to
be mentioned in the article. Maybe. It might be only a
couple, three paragraphs, but it'll be enough to get me fired
if it ever gets to the bank, which it will. I guess if I wasn't
the target, I'd find it all pretty damn ironic. I helped you
get back on your feet and what's the first thing you do?
Knock me off mine."

"Wait a minute."

"I knew you were hard up. I didn't think you were this
desperate. Anyway, the hell with it and the hell with you.
I misjudged Colfax. I called him a cockroach, didn't I?
Well, he's not. You are. You're the cockroach, Charlie
my boy."

"Dave, hold on a second. He's giving it to you all wrong.
I don't know why, but it's all wrong."

"I'm not done yet. Here comes the second twist, the
one that really gets to me. Greasy George and you and
whoever you're working for at the *Digest* cook up a little
deal. You're going to do me a favor. My name and the
bank's name stay out of the article if I tell the bank what

happened, resign, and convince them to drop the suit so greasy George can get his ship back. I guess he's paying you a little something for that and that's what I meant about your being so desperate. At least Colfax had the decency to warn me. Let's play Let's Pretend, okay? Let's pretend you are working for Colfax. What difference does that make? At least he had the decency to warn me so this thing wouldn't hit me out of nowhere. That's the least, you know, the rock-bottom minimum I would've expected from you, a guy I've known for—what is it now? Four years. To warn me. Instead, I have to hear it from Colfax."

"Jesus. When did he tell you all this?"

"An hour ago. He called me at the hotel. Said he'd just found out what you were up to. I didn't believe him at first. Couldn't believe it, but he convinced me. Apologized, too. Said he was sorry he'd got you the job. Wouldn't have done it if he'd had any idea about what you were going to do."

"Jesus."

"Do you want a drink? Maybe the hash isn't enough for you. Maybe you need a drink, too."

"I don't need a drink."

"Are you afraid it'll react with the dope, make you incoherent, foul up your brain cells?"

"Colfax is giving it to you all wrong. He's lying. I can't figure out why you believe that lying S.O.B."

"Well, I need a drink."

"You've got half of that one left."

Harris emptied his glass. A light drinker, even the watered Scotch hit him hard.

"There. Now it's gone and I need a drink. I'm going to the bar to get a drink. That'll give you time to work out an alibi, in case you haven't worked out one already. I mean some other story than this crap about doing it for Colfax."

"Alibi for what?"

"Why you're doing this. I mean, greasy George gets his ship back out of the deal, you're going to get whatever he's paying you to blackmail me, and what do I get? I get my name out of the article. Zero, in other words. Zip. Nothing. That's what I get. Now I'm going to get a drink so you have a little time to dream up some reason why you're screwing up my life, you bastard."

"Go on, get your drink."

"Are you sure you don't want one? I'd like to buy a drink for the old buddy who's going to screw up my life."

"Get me a plain tonic water and lime."

Harris slid out of the booth and, with the aggressive swagger small men often adopt in crowds, walked toward the bar. I sat, trying to think of why Colfax had concocted that story. The man had more unexpected twists in him than a mountain road. Maybe this was another of his un-orthodox tests, maybe an attempt to disassociate himself from the scheme to get the suit dropped. Maybe this, that, or a dozen things. I didn't know. Angered by his duplicity, I considered calling him for an explanation; then I re-membered that his home telephone number was another thing I did not know.

Harris returned and put a tonic down in front of me. A slice of old lime the color of algae floated among the ice cubes.

"Your drink, sahib," he said, crinkling up his face. "It is a playzure to serve the sahib in this oh so very Breeteesh-looking club. Oh my, yes. Such a great play-zure to serve the sahib who screws his friends."

I took a long swallow, but the tonic only made my mouth feel drier.

"So, would the sahib now be pleased to tell me his alibi? I am so very anxious to hear it."

"If you don't think all this is Colfax's idea, maybe you ought to know that Inter-Arab's got a charter with Box-avenides."

"I know about the charter and that Colfax-sahib has a connection with Mr. Boxavenides. That is how he discov-ered what you are up to. It is Colfax-sahib's business to make discoveries. But perhaps you should know that Inter-Arab is a legitimate company. Oh my, yes. It is true it serves as a front for Colfax-sahib, sahib, but it also does legitimate business, if for no other reason than to main-tain appearances. Hence, its charter with Mr. Boxavenides. But oh, sahib, I simply cannot believe it has such an interest in the vessel that it is going to these lengths."

"Do you know what they're shipping?"

"Irrigation equipment. To make the deserts bloom, sahib."

"Knock off that Hindustani crap."

" 'Knock off.' That is an Americanism, I believe, and I am unfamiliar with its meaning."

"Do you know what Inter-Arab's going to ship in Boxavenides's rust-bucket?"

"And how do you know, sahib, that Mr Boxavenides's vessel is, as you put it, a rust-bucket?"

"He didn't seem like the type who runs Cunard Lines."

"You are so very right. My goodness, the Greek sahib's vessel is in the most deplorable condition. Oh yes, most deplorable."

"He's shipping guns. Colfax isn't sending irrigation equipment so the bedouin can grow string beans in the sand dunes. He's got some kind of deal with one of the rebel factions in Bejaya. He's going to run guns to them. Boxavenides is his supplier and shipper. That's why he wants the freighter out of wherever your bank has it locked up."

"Monrovia."

"That's why he wants it out of Monrovia and afloat as much as Boxavenides does. Part of this project of his. He's behind this."

"Now don't tell me Colfax told you he's running guns," Harris said, finally dropping the Hindu mimicry. "He's not the kind of guy who goes around saying things like that."

"No, he didn't tell me. It's my guess. An educated guess. A damned good guess."

"It's a damned bad one. You're really reaching, Charlie. That outfit of his—not Inter-Arab, the other outfit—they own *airlines* for Christ's sake. They own Air America. They own shipping companies. They've got more weapons stacked up in arsenals than most armies've got. That's been in the papers. So let's say Colfax is planning to ship arms to these fuzzy-wuzzies in Africa. With all that behind him, airlines and ships and arsenals, why should he have to hire some half-assed operator like Boxavenides? It doesn't add up."

"No, it doesn't. But that's what he's done."

"Why do you keep trying to pin this on Colfax, Charlie my boy? You think I'm a little naïve, don't you?"

"I never said that."

"But you think so, don't you?"

"All right. Sure. A little."

"Well, I'm not that naïve. I know that you don't get hired right off the street by people like Colfax. He isn't running a day-labor agency. You've got to go through background checks. You need clearances, you get sent back to the States for training. You're trying to tell me Colfax just hired you off the street? That doesn't add up, either."

"Okay, what about this?" I reached into my pocket and slid the press pass across the table. "And this." I flipped my I.D. at him. He looked at them. "What about those, Dave? If I'm not working for Colfax, how do you suppose I got those so quickly? They were ready for me when I went to the *Digest* yesterday. It'd been planned all along."

He tossed the documents back at me. "Do you know how I analyze all this? I'll tell you how I analyze all this. His Greasiness is paying you a nice chunk of bread to blackmail me. You feel guilty about it, so you go and get your head screwed up with some hash and dream up this story that you're really a spook for Colfax. You figure that that'll make it legitimate. 'Sorry old boy about shoving this knife into you, but it's all in the name of Her Majesty's Secret Service.' You're going to screw up my life, you don't have to lie to me on top of it."

"I'm not lying to you. I'm working for Colfax. He works for the government, so that means I'm working for the government. And yeah, I guess that does make it more legitimate."

"You've been overseas too long. You're out of touch. Nobody thinks spooking for any government is legitimate anymore."

Harris was rolling his glass in his boy's-sized hands. Noticing they had got wet from the condensation, he dried them on a cocktail napkin, which he then wadded into a soggy ball.

"Even if it were legit, it doesn't help to tell me that. All I know is that a guy I've known for years is going to screw up my life." Then he started singing quietly to himself, "Charlie my boy, oh Charlie my boy," wadding the napkin into a smaller and smaller ball.

I wanted to give him some explanation, but could think of nothing. I stared at the sconce on the wall next to the fox-hunting scene above Harris's head. The light seemed to be expanding and contracting, swelling into a ball of diffuse white, then compressing itself into a brilliant pinpoint that made my eyes ache. So I did not see the wadded napkin fly over the table in a low, fast trajectory. I only felt it strike my forehead, where it stuck for a few seconds before falling off like a leech touched by a lighted match. Water, smelling faintly of Scotch, beaded above my brows, then dripped into my eyes, further blurring my uncertain vision. It was not, however, so uncertain that I could not see Harry's malicious grin. "You thrill me, you chill me," he sang quietly. "You thrill me, you chill me with moments of joy. Oh, Charlie my boy."

"I hope that got something out of your system," I said.

"It did. A little. It felt good."

Drying my forehead with a handkerchief, I looked around to see if we had drawn any attention. We had not. The couple closest to us, a young man with a glossy city-Arab's face and a girl whose body, though voluptuous now, carried omens of the starchy corpulence into which it would expand in a few years, stood babbling about her family's last trip to Geneva.

"It felt good?" I said. "Well, good. I'm glad it did. It's going to make this easier." I took the letter from my pocket and handed it to him. "Here, read this and sign it. It's your letter of resignation."

"My letter of resignation? I didn't write—"

"I know. You didn't write a letter of resignation. I did. I wrote it."

"*You* wrote my letter of resignation?"

"What did I just get through saying? Sure, I wrote it. I wrote it this afternoon. It was my first assignment."

"I can't believe this, Charlie. I really can't believe you'd go this far. You mean I don't get the chance to write my own letter? I don't even get that?"

"No."

"No. Just like that? No."

"That's right."

"I really can't believe this."

"You'd better start. Read it and sign it, and don't think about not signing it. You don't sign it, you'll lose a lot more than your job."

"Like what?"

"Boxavenides said he'd spread the word about your ancestry. He said he'd let a few people know you're a dirty little Jew. His phrase, not mine. The implication being, Dave, you're over here spooking for the Israelis."

"That's not going to scare me into it, Charlie. You think I'm a little naïve, huh? I'm not that naïve. I know things aren't black and white over here. Do you suppose my contacts don't know I'm part Jewish? Sure they know. Even my Saudi contacts know, and the Saudis don't even let Jews into their country. But I get in. It's business, Charlie."

"He's not going to your contacts, but to his. He's going to pass the word to his terrorist pals, the ones he peddles guns to. Tell me things aren't black and white with them."

"So he sells guns to them. He hasn't got so much influence with them that they'd knock somebody off for him. Anyway, I only spend a few weeks out of the year in the Mideast. I spend most of my time in London now. I've got family there, from my mother's side. They couldn't get me there."

"Okay, you spend most of your time in London. You and your mother's family. Here's how they'll get to you: One day you'll be sitting in your office, all safe and cozy in London. Your secretary will bring in your personal mail. You'll open it. One of the letters you open will go bang and blow your hands off and mess up your face and rip your guts open."

Harris attempted, without success, to avoid showing any emotion.

"Is that greasy George's plan?"

"He suggested it."

"At the rate you're going, maybe you'll be the one to send it. Why not? For a few lousy bucks you write out my letter of resignation, you screw up my life. So maybe for a few lousy bucks more you'd mail me a letter bomb."

"Don't *you* give *me* shit about doing things for a few lousy bucks. Boxavenides clued me in on the little game you played with him."

"Is that in here?"

"Yes, all of it."

"Son of a bitch."

"Read it. It's in there. All of it."

"Son of a bitch, Charlie."

"Read it and sign it. As a friend, I'm telling you it's in your best interests to sign it."

"Our friendship's over, Charlie. That's why I threw that thing in your face. Your rotten face. Just in case you hadn't figured it out. I threw it in your face to let you know our friendship's over. I'm just sorry I didn't know you'd written the letter because then I would've tossed the whole drink at you. I don't mean just the Scotch. I mean the glass and all. Right into your rotten face."

"Okay, we're not friends. As your enemy, then, I'm telling you to sign this goddamned letter."

"I'll look at it, then we'll see."

With a flourish that made the sleeves of his suitcoat rise up on his arms, Harris unfolded the letter and began reading, his face pinched into the critical, concentrated expression it must have worn whenever he went over a balance sheet.

"This isn't a letter of resignation," he said when he was finished. "It's a confession."

"That's the way they want it. They want the bank to know all the gory details."

"You've left out a few details. You know that?"

"What details?"

"For one, Boxavenides lied to me. Did you know that?"

"No," I said, amazed at the outrage in Harris's voice, at his invincible innocence. Boxavenides lied to him. What had he expected?

"I didn't think you knew that. He lied to me all right. He said he wouldn't have any problems meeting the payments. He didn't at first, but the bank didn't see a dime from him after that. We gave him a grace period, sent him all kinds of letters, warnings, you name it. He still didn't come up with a cent. So the bank finally had to issue papers ordering the ship impressed. It's kind of like fore-closing on a mortgage except that a house stays in one place. Greasy George just kept the *Challenger* on the move. She was a phantom ship, a regular *Flying Dutchman*. She never put into port. She'd anchor outside some harbor, where we couldn't get at her, and smaller boats would off-load her. Boxavenides kept that dodge up for damn near a year. He didn't maintain that freighter, though. Her steering mechanisms broke down off Liberia a few months ago. She had to be towed into Monrovia. Lucky for us, we had a man there. He heard about it and got to everyone before Boxavenides could pay them off, and we impressed the ship. Then we went to court and slapped His Greasi-ness with a suit for back payments."

"What the hell does all this have to do with anything?"

"He *lied* to me, Charlie. He lied about the papers, he lied about the payments."

"What're you talking about? What papers?"

"He had a five-year charter with some Belgian outfit to ship machine parts to the Mideast and Africa. The charter was collateral for the loan. It looked like a damned good one. Profitable, I mean. There wasn't any question in my mind about his ability to pay off the loan. I figured he was as good a risk as any, so I made those changes in the report. Then he brought me that tanker deal, and I said, 'Okay, George, I did you one and you did me one. We're even.' And he said, 'Of course, David, we're even.' He lied about that."

"And that surprises you?"

"You think I'm being naïve again, don't you? Well, I'm not. I knew he wasn't completely on the straight, but I didn't think he'd lie to me like that."

"I guess he feels you double-crossed him."

"Double-crossed him? The bank was suing him. The bank confiscated the ship, not me. We were even. You've got to understand that. We were even."

"No, I don't. I don't have to understand that. Here's what I understand—you went ahead and did what I told you not to do a long time ago. Got yourself mixed up with a real beauty. A regular kinky bastard and now you're going to have to pay the bill."

"Hey, Charlie my boy. Cliché me no clichés. 'Pay the bill.' 'I don't want to be the one to say I told you so.' What else? I suppose, 'This hurts me as much as it does you.'"

"I don't like doing it."

"Don't make me sick."

"Here's something else I understand—you're a fool, Dave. An ass. You've always been an ass."

"How's that again?"

"An ass."

"In hashish veritas. It's all coming out now. Now I'm getting the truth out of you."

"Are you?"

"You thing I'm a fool because I didn't listen to your peasant wisdom, you, the old Michigan country boy. Now you're punishing me. You're secretly enjoying this. That's your cheap dirty peasant's secret. Right? Level with me."

"Sure." I took the letter and put it back in my pocket. "I'll level with you. I'm taking this without your signature and shoving off. I'll give you three pieces of advice, the benefit of my peasant wisdom. Number one, I'd avoid making any more trips to this part of the world. George's friends'll have an easy time nailing you here. Number two, hire a suicidal secretary to open your mail for you. Number three, the next issue of the *Digest* comes out in ten days. The story'll be in there. All right, you can believe what you want about Colfax, but the old cockroach gave it to you straight about one thing. Your story won't rate more than a couple, three, maybe four paragraphs in the article, but there's enough meat in it to interest AP and UPI, especially if it's a slow news day. So here's my third piece of advice—don't spend the money to buy the papers because I can write their leads for you. I'll write it for you right now: 'An executive for one of America's largest banks falsified an official report to help obtain a substantial shipping loan for an alleged smuggler believed to be a major arms supplier for guerrilla and terrorist groups in the Middle East and Africa, according to the *Arab Digest*. Want to hear the second paragraph?"

Harris said nothing.

"Here's the second paragraph: 'In a major article on Middle East bribery scandals, the authoritative monthly said that David R. Harris, formerly the Beirut branch manager for New York's prestigious Endicott Bank, falsified the report so George Boxavenides, identified by the *Digest* as an illicit-arms trafficker, could purchase a freighter recently discovered to have been carrying weapons hijacked from a Belgian armory by an unknown terrorist group.' Like to hear the third paragraph?"

Again, Harris said nothing.

"Dave, the third paragraph. Want to hear it?"

"No."

"Okay. You can figure the bank wouldn't want to hear it, either. Any of it."

"Blackmail. A guy I've known for four years is blackmailing me."

"He's also saving you a lot of grief. If Boxavenides meant what he said about his terrorist pals, the same guy is saving you from getting your ass blown off."

"Nice rationalization. You're cutting my throat to save my neck. Why are you doing this to me, Charlie?"

"It wouldn't make any sense to you. Look, it's best if you just sign."

"I really don't see why I have to resign. I mean—"

"Dave, c'mon. You can't tell them all this and not resign. Look, you're being given an out. You resign and you won't have being fired on your record. The bank's name stays out of the press. They drop the suits and reschedule the loan. George drops his countersuit—"

"But we were even. He said so himself. We were even."

His voice trailed off, losing its angry edge. The resistance in him crumbled all at once, and he seemed to shrink down into the booth, growing smaller before my eyes, as if he were reverting physically to the child in himself, the child who believed it was possible to be even with men like George Boxavenides.

There was the sound of heavy objects being moved. The Italian band, dressed in clinging black trousers and lurid shirts, were setting up their speakers and amplifiers. Their hair, shoulder-length and the color of their trousers, gave them a barbaric look. Huns with electric guitars.

"Dave, you might as well sign this now."

"I guess you're never really even with anything."

"I guess not. Have you got a pen?"

He gestured at the stage. "You ever heard them?"

"Once."

"They're lousy."

"Have you got a pen?"

"I don't know why the guy who owns this place started this disco-night bullshit. This used to be a quiet place to have a drink."

"I haven't got a pen. Journalists never carry pens."

"Who said you're a journalist?"

"I can borrow a pen from one of the waiters."

"Don't exert yourself. Give me the letter." I handed it to him. Without saying anything more, Harris pulled an expensive Schaefer from his inside pocket. He always carried a fountain pen, said they had more class than ballpoints. After he had signed, I replaced the letter in the envelope that bore the address: "Mr. Allen H. Greenway, Manager, International Operations," et cetera, et cetera.

"Boxavenides wants you to stick around until he's heard the bank's decision. Colfax, too."

Harris, his hands quivering, brought the glass up to his lips, then put it down without taking a drink.

"Colfax, too. You keep trying to blame the poor old cockroach. Look, what more do you want? You've finished me and now I'm supposed to stick around here until he's heard."

"Dave, don't say that. About being finished. You're only thirty-four."

"Thirty-five going on thirty-six. It's going to be fun, being thirty-five and with this on my record and looking for a job. Okay, I'm thirty-five. I'm thirty-five and finished."

"You'll come out of this all right." I said it with little conviction, knowing that, in his case, his relative youth was only a marginal asset.

"You're crazy and he's crazy if you think I'm going to stay here. It'll take weeks for that letter to get to London."

We were momentarily deafened by a long, dissonant chord that ended in the shrill whine of an amplifier with feedback problems. One of the guitarists was bending down, adjusting dials with one hand and tuning his instrument

with the other. Already couples were crowding at the
perimeter of the dance floor, waiting to do their self-
conscious, clumsy imitations of the dances they had seen
on their European vacations.

"I'm not supposed to mail it. I'm to give it to Boxavenides tomorrow. An educated guess, Dave: he'll give it to
Colfax, who'll have some messenger boy pigeon it to
London. It'll be on Greenway's desk by Thursday morning."

"I've got a flight out tomorrow and I intend to be on it."

"Another educated guess. They'll find something wrong
with your visa and you won't get past passport control."

"There's nothing wrong with my visa."

"Jesus, you're hopeless. I know there's nothing wrong
with your visa. They'll find something wrong with it because Colfax will have paid them to. But maybe you ought
to try it and see for yourself. Maybe that'll prove to you
Colfax has a hand in this. It's for sure Boxavenides
couldn't arrange something like that on his own."

"I don't understand it. Not any of it."

"They want to keep you under wraps, I guess. Keep
you under wraps until the suit's been dropped."

"Suppose the bank doesn't? Suppose they don't give in
to this kind of strong arm? Do you have any guesses on
that, Charlie? You're so full of guesses tonight, what's
your guess on that?"

"Odds are they'll give in to it. They don't want that kind
of publicity over one lousy freighter. Ten to one they'll
play along."

"I asked what your guess is if they don't."

"I don't have any."

"You don't have any. That's fine. Charlie, I wish you'd
get the hell out of here now. I wish you'd get out of my
sight."

"All right. I'm just advising you not to try flying out
tomorrow. You'll only make things harder on yourself."

"More of your advice. I'll Telex London tomorrow, tell
them I have to stay another week or so. How's that?"

"That's fine."

"You know, I was just thinking, some guys in my fix
would kill themselves. Now, suppose you're right about

Colfax being behind all this and that it's all got something to do with some secret project of his. If I went and did a half gainer off the Meridien, that would cause quite a stir, wouldn't it? Lots of publicity. Blow everything, maybe. I was just thinking I ought to leave a note and do that just to fuck up whatever's going on."

"Listen, I don't want you even joking about it."

"What's wrong, Charlie my boy? Conscience needling you?"

"Don't even joke about it."

"Don't worry. I'm a dirty little Jew, remember? A Yid. A professional survivor. It's in my genes. Professional survivors don't kill themselves."

"Look, Dave—"

"Charlie, you don't exist anymore as far as I'm concerned. I asked you to get out of my sight. So do it."

"Listen, there's something."

"I'm going to take a swing at you. Make a scene. Make a mess. I know you're big enough to wipe the walls with me, but I'm going to take a swing at you if you don't please please get out of my sight."

I stood to leave. Harris seemed very small and vulnerable, and, remorse suddenly flooding me, a cold tightness gripped my chest. It was as if every branch in my lungs had been filled with ice water. The band was still tuning up. Disparate chords and notes occasionally joined to form a few bars of a recognizable melody, then broke off into cadenzas of senseless noise punctuated by the rasps of the snare drum. Profiled to me, Harris sat watching the red-shirted Italians as if I had already left, as if I did not exist. Looking at him, broken, and knowing my betrayal of our friendship had helped to break him, I felt cut off from everyone and everything familiar to me, lost, isolated, and as alone as I had ever felt. Then I turned and walked outside, where the street lights shone pale amber through the translucent sand.

TWO

THE DAUGHTER
OF THE NIGHT

Squatting on his heels, Patrick Moody rummaged through the equipment he had laid neatly on the warped wooden floor of the hotel room while Nordstrand looked at him from behind with raging eyes.

Moody, a fussy, obsessive man, had emptied the rucksacks we had spent half the afternoon packing; he wanted to be sure we had not overlooked anything before we left for Nassala, the border town that served as a sanctuary for the Bejayan rebels. With all the care of a good soldier preparing for a barracks inspection, Moody arranged the contents in three orderly rows: the big nylon rucksacks strapped to their aluminum frames, the lightweight sleeping bags tightly rolled, emergency rations, lensatic compasses, maps in canvas cases, survival kits and first-aid kits, extra sets of clothing and boots, water bags, and wide-brimmed hats to shield us from the sun. The only item left unopened was a small canvas bag of Nordstrand's. It had a lock attached to its zipper and appeared, from the bulges in it, to contain some paperback books.

To all the gear we had brought from Cairo, Moody had added a duffel bag filled with canned goods, toilet paper, and enough medical supplies to equip a medium-sized clinic. He had scoured every bazaar and pharmacy in Khartoum for them. Tins of Vietnamese pineapples, Georgia peaches, Polish hams, Spanish beans, and British corned beef were stuffed in with vials of tetracycline, enterovia-

form, halizone, iodine, and penicillin. The bag was propped
in a corner, beside a worm-eaten armoire faded to the
color of driftwood. A porter had lugged it in the day before, its weight bending him over so that he looked like
a crippled peddler as he hobbled across the room. When
we saw what was inside, Nordstrand reminded Moody of
Colfax's instructions to travel light. Atropos was to be a
paramilitary operation, not a Sierra Club camping trip.
Cheerfully Moody replied that, having been born in the
Sudan and having served as an adviser in Oman, he knew
a bit more about desert hardships than Colfax. We would
need the tinned food to keep up our strength and the medicines to ward off the assaults of African bacteria. As for
the toilet paper, well, we didn't have to go *completely*
native, did we? A soldier's first duty was to make himself
as comfortable as possible.

"General, you aren't going to last," Nordstrand said,
finishing the sentence with a burst of mocking laughter.

The remark was the beginning of Moody's torment. He
was a lean man of average height, with a fine nose, an
elegant English jaw, and a mouth whose firmness was betrayed by his watery grey eyes, which sometimes wore a
look of doubt and gave him the air of a schoolboy not
quite sure of his answers. This undergraduate appearance
was heightened by flawless skin that took ten years from
his age—thirty-three. His manner of speech was occasionally indirect and equivocal; he had a laugh that sounded
more like a cough and a habit of slurring his words to the
point of incomprehensibility.

Nordstrand despised him.

He had despised the Englishman ever since the briefing
in Colfax's office in Cairo, despised him in the unreasonable, instinctive way one kind of nature despises its antithesis. In the three weeks since, he had made some effort
to control his feelings; but Nordstrand was a man unaccustomed to self-restraint, a man who shared with many of
his generation the notion that self-restraint was unnatural
and unhealthy, a man with little resistance to the urgings of
his personal demons. The struggle to repress his rancor
only increased it; and the confinement of the small, shabby
room we shared, the tensions that always precede the doing

of something dangerous, the sheer strangeness of Khartoum, an overgrown African village whose dark alien faces made us painfully aware of our whiteness, aggravated it still more. Now, on our last day in Khartoum, it was beginning to come out, not explosively but more like a jet of gas released under extremely high pressure.

Nordstrand was lying on one of the beds, an old sagging bed that sagged further under his weight, his huge figure striped by the sunlight falling through the louvers of the shuttered windows. He lay looking at Moody's back. Having noticed during his inspection that we were short of halizone tablets, Moody had asked him to buy an extra supply. It was that simple request which ignited hatred and contempt in Nordstrand's green eyes.

"They've a lot of chemists here," the Englishman was saying. "Saw them when I passed by the *souk* this morning. Must be one on every corner. You'd better get moving now, Nordstrand. The afternoon snooze is over and the shops'll be reopening."

Moody kept brushing his sandy hair out of his eyes as he spoke, a tic I found a little irritating myself. Nordstrand said:

"What d'you mean a chemist?"

"Pharmacist. I suppose I must get used to these American phrases since I'll be working with Americans. 'Pharmacist' rather than 'chemist.' Must learn to pronounce 'schedule' *sked-jewel* instead of *shed-yule*."

"Right, Moody. You do that."

"Well, then. Get along to a pharmacist and pick up some halizone. A dozen more packets should do it."

"It bothers me when somebody doesn't look at me when they're talking to me."

Moody stood and turned around, squinting slightly in a bar of bright sunshine.

"This suit you?"

"Sure, General."

"I'd prefer you drop that 'general' business. Afraid Colfax put me in charge of this show. I know you don't like that, but that's the way things are. Do yourself and us a favor by making the best of it."

"Speaking of generals, do you suppose when Gordon

came here to fight the Mahdi he made sure he had enough halizone tablets with him?"

"Don't believe they had invented halizone back then, but I should think they took precautions. Boiled their water most likely."

"Do you think if they had invented halizone Gordon would've been worried over whether he had enough?"

There was an unpleasant note in the question, and Moody, looking at the American's bulk stretched across the bed, laughed nervously.

"What sort of question is that?"

"The answer to that question would demonstrate the way national traits can change in a relatively short time. Gordon came here in 'eighty-four, less than a hundred years ago."

"Afraid I don't see what that's to do with us."

"Feature this. General Gordon is packing up to come to Khartoum to fight the mad Mahdi and his ten thousand screaming niggers. He looks at his gear and says, 'Oh, dear, can't leave yet. Don't have enough halizone and I hear the water's bad. I say, Leftenant Hargreaves, do run off to the chemist and see if he has some.' Feature that, Moody."

"Feature?"

"Picture. Picture that."

Nordstrand propped himself up on his elbows, and even that slight movement gave you a sense of the enormous leverage in his body.

"Very well, I've pictured it. Afraid that still leaves us short of halizone. We'll be four to six months in the bush. Schistosomiasis, you know. It's passed on by the snails in the rivers and the wells."

"Feature Gordon worried about the water like some tourist from Dipshit, Iowa, going to Mexico for the first time. 'Must have our halizone, Hargreaves. Can't fight the mad Mahdi and his ten thousand screaming niggers if we have the runs.'"

"Nordstrand, your penchant for calling these people niggers isn't going to help us much. And it's not the simple trots I'm worried about. It's dysentery and schistosomiasis."

"Schis-*to*-so-*mi*-a-sis. Now feature that. Gordon worrying about what these scummy little snails might do to his guts before he comes to fight the mad Mahdi and his ten thousand screaming *nee-groes*."

"Let's get the stuff," I said. "We'll probably need it. Moody's right."

"Did you hear me say he's wrong?"

"Then what're you doing, giving this speech about Gordon?"

"I just told the General a minute ago. An example of rapid change in national traits. Generational degeneration, Charlie. Gordon was an Englishman."

"Awfully clever of you, Nordstrand."

"He was an Englishman and you, Moody, hold a British passport."

"Brilliant. You're quite brilliant for an ape. Gordon was English and I'm English."

"Didn't say you were English. I said you hold a British passport. There's a difference. The pure and the dross."

"This conversation is ridiculous. What's got into you, Nordstrand?"

"You hold a British passport. You're a tame one, Moody."

Moody's face colored and his voice rose, crackling.

"Get the hell on your feet and pick up the halizone."

Nordstrand clasped his hands behind his head and, tilting his chin at an insolent angle, smiled strangely by drawing his upper lip to bare the top row of his teeth and curling the lower over the bottom. His irises, hard, brilliant, and darkly green, shone like two chunks of polished malachite.

"You just can't see the difference, can you, Moody?"

"We're wasting time," Moody said.

"Guess I'll have to give it to you straight."

"The only thing you have to do is pick up some halizone."

"Gordon was an Englishman while you, General Dross, are a welfare-state limey."

Moody did not say anything. He stood, silent and transfixed, his jaw tight and trembling from humiliation, or fear, or anger, or all three. Nordstrand had delivered the insult with the venom of an unregenerate bigot saying "nigger" or an anti-Semite spitting out the word *kike*, but I don't think it was the insult itself that had stung the Englishman. It was the malice in Nordstrand's eyes, alight with a cruelty made all the more malign by its apparent lack of motive and suggesting depths of hatred which the words alone had not expressed. They were merely code words for something he found inexpressibly disgusting. Moody tried to meet the American's glance, but failed. He looked at me, his own uncertain eyes asking a question I could not answer.

"What d'you say to that, General?"

"Afraid it doesn't deserve a reply."

"You seem to be afraid an awful lot, Moody."

"That so?"

"You're afraid of me, for example."

"Oh, paralyzed with terror," Moody quipped. But the intended irony did not quite come off. His voice lacked conviction, and another peal of scornful laughter burst from Nordstrand's throat.

"There is one thing I am afraid of. I'm afraid we're off to a rather bad start. It bothers you that I'm running this show, doesn't it? I've sensed it these past ten days. I've been expecting you to say something—"

"That isn't it."

"I think it is. And you don't like it that I've asked you to pick up some halizone. Feel as if I'm making an errand boy out of you? I'm beginning to think that's all you're mentally capable of, running errands."

Without saying anything, Nordstrand rose and walked toward Moody, his shoulders rolling, his chin tucked in, his eyes riveted on some imaginary point in front of him, his head swaying from side to side. The effect was that of a charging grizzly, but his movements had none of the clumsiness associated with that animal. The smaller man stood his ground, but betrayed himself by flinching when Nordstrand raised an arm and wrapped it around his shoulders. The gesture could not have been more condescending or better calculated to trivialize Moody.

"You know, I've been unfair," Nordstrand said, grinning again. "I didn't realize you've got such a conventional mind."

Moody wrenched himself free of the disdainful embrace.

"I've made you feel like an errand boy. I've deflated your overblown opinion of yourself."

"I don't feel like an errand boy. You're giving yourself too much credit thinking you could make me feel like an errand boy."

"Then what is it? You'd best give me a reason. We're going to be out there for months, so if we have any differences, let's get them settled now."

"There's nothing to settle."

"Jolly good. That ends it. Now go pick up the halizone and be careful not to scrape your knuckles on the ground."

Nordstrand shook his great blond head.

"Moody, you're missing the point. We've got our differences, but we can't settle them. They're unsettleable. You and me, General, are positive and negative, black and white, oil and water, the cathode and the anode."

"Rubbish."

"Think about it. Get that conventional little mind of yours to think about it. The cath-*ode* and the an-*ode*."

Moody started laughing, a tinny, slightly manic laugh.

"My God, you're trying to provoke me. It's as simple as that. You're nothing but a schoolyard bully, Nordstrand, and you're trying to provoke me with your cheap adolescent insults. You want an excuse to bash me."

In his prairie-level voice, Nordstrand said: "I'm never going to lay a hand on you unless I absolutely have to."

"You want me to make you have to. You want to provoke me into starting a punch-up. Go back to the schoolyard with that."

"No. All I want to do is explain what it is about you that offends me."

"I've heard enough, and I'm not interested in why I offend you. You offend me. You've offended me enough that I'm thinking of cabling Colfax to have you taken off this mission."

"Wouldn't waste my time, General. Colfax isn't going to take me off."

"If I do cable him, you'll be on your way back to Cairo tomorrow."

"Why do you think Colfax picked me? Because he knows I'm the only one who'll do what we have to do to bring this thing off. I get things done. I see them through, Moody, right through to the end."

"I'm not bad at seeing things through myself. You don't want to be reasonable, fine. You're out of this show as of now."

Distracted, Moody made a start toward the telephone; then, realizing he could not send the cable over the phone, turned and left the room, slamming the peeling age-rotted door so hard I was surprised when it didn't crack in two.

"Feature that," Nordstrand said, shrugging and smiling. "Thought the English were supposed to be so cool." Walking over to the nightstand, he picked up his wallet and put it in his pocket. "Let's go."

"Where?"

"To pick up the halizone, of course. Let's go."

It was neither invitation nor request. It was a command, and there was in its peremptory tone an implicit assumption of obedience that rankled me. And yet, responding like a soldier to an order, I got up and followed him out the door. Nordstrand was not a man to argue with, even in small things.

I think my compliant attitude also arose out of admiration for him, admiration I had felt from the moment I first saw him, standing in the entrance to Colfax's flat after Colfax had answered his insistent ring, standing with no more than a couple of inches between each shoulder and the molding of the door. Always so in command of himself and others, Colfax suffered a rare attack of uncertainty in Nordstrand's presence. He hesitated briefly, unsure of what to do; then, closing the door, he extended one arm to make introductions. Ignoring the gesture, Nordstrand greeted him with a nod contemptuous in its brevity and lunged through the foyer toward Moody and me. We were sitting at the far end of the long living room, in a pair of wicker chairs, which, along with the rattan footstools, the ceramic elephant table, the dragon-shaped ashtrays, and the Montagnard crossbow mounted on the wall beside a painting of a Balinese orgy, were among the plunder Colfax had shipped out of Saigon just before the city fell. Still stand-

ing near the door with his arm out, the guardian of western
civilization looked like a butler offering to take a guest's
coat. He did not appear to know what to make of Nordstrand's rudeness. I enjoyed seeing Colfax with some of
that annoying self-assurance knocked out of him and felt
like congratulating the blond giant who had demeaned
him and who was charging across the room in a straight
line, without seeming to care what lay in front of him. He
was obviously a man who took life head-on, confident he
was big enough and strong enough to survive any collisions.

He was walking like that as we went down the hotel's
long dim corridor, passing room doors with only the outlines of their old numbers still showing. A clump of
bleached-looking Europeans were handing their passports
to the desk clerk in the lobby. Outside, an ancient peddler
sat beneath the arcade that ran along the front of the
hotel. He squatted beside what looked like an armory for
a Bronze Age army—crudely forged daggers, animal-hide
shields, spears, and long swords in scabbards of dried,
cracked leather—and turned his old eyes on everyone who
came out of the currency exchange at the far end of the
arcade.

The heat struck us as soon as we were outside. Heading across the unshaded terrace, its tables packed with
sweating Sudanese guzzling iced bottles of Jemel beer,
Nordstrand and I made for the refuge of the tree-shaded
street fringing the Blue Nile. The air was more oppressive
than anything I had felt in Cairo, even at the height of the
Khamsin; though Khartoum was surrounded by desert, the
breezes from the river carried a hint of dampness, of the
equitorial lands to the south, of jungle and swamp, savan-
nah and swale.

There were no taxis, so we headed for the *souk* on foot.
My shirt was stuck to my skin by the time we passed the
People's Palace, guarded by soldiers in heavy, hot-looking
blue uniforms. Its white walls were beautiful against the
clear sky. A few old Krupp cannon rested in the embras-
ures of a wall near the river's edge. The guns pointed
across the Nile to where North Khartoum rose above the
trees bordering the far bank.

Nordstrand stopped suddenly.

"That's where Gordon died," he said, pointing at the palace. Then, apparently on impulse, he climbed a short flight of steps to an esplanade fronting the palace lawn. Walking up to the wall and leaning with both hands on the breechblock of one of the guns, he gazed over the water.

" 'The man of England circled by the sands.' "

"Gordon's epitaph," I said.

"Gordon died here. On the spot where I'm standing." His mood and voice had changed abruptly. He sounded reverential. "I can feel him here. I've read everything written about that man, and it's like I know him."

I started to laugh, then saw he was utterly serious.

"The fort's near Omdurman," I said. "This was probably one of the Mahdi's positions. Those guns are Krupps. I read somewhere that the Mahdi had used Krupps when he put Gordon under siege."

"This was Gordon's position. He died here." Nordstrand's tone told you he would brook no argument. And as it did not seem a point worth arguing, I said:

"All right. He died here. So what?"

"Gordon stood right here. You ever had that feeling? Being in touch with someone you never knew, someone who died before you were born?"

This was a new side to him: Nordstrand the mystic.

"No," I said, noticing that one of the guardsmen was watching us suspiciously. I have always been plagued by a fear of uniformed authority. "Let's shove off, Nordstrand. I don't think we're supposed to be here."

"But we're here."

"I don't like the way that guard's got his eye on us."

"What's he going to do, arrest us for trespassing?"

"We're supposed to keep a low profile, remember? Avoid attracting attention."

"Gordon was a great man."

"Jesus."

"Think about it. He came down here when there was nothing and he conquered this place."

"I think the books credit Kitchener with conquering the Sudan."

"Think about what it was like, coming down here in those days. Disease and savages. Completely cut off from the outside world and then going on to conquer it all. Then holding out at this fort for a year against the Mahdi. No help from anyone. No radio, no telephone, no helicopters to come in and fly you out. Nothing. And no hope of that relief column reaching him on time. But he held out. Gordon saw the thing through, right through to the end until they broke through and finished him."

"They also finished everyone else in the fort. If you've read everything about Gordon, you've read the new histories about the siege. There's evidence Gordon had orders to evacuate. He wasn't that cut off. He got orders to pull out but he ignored them and got a lot of people killed for nothing. Your hero was a megalomaniac as far as I'm concerned."

It was as if I had insulted Nordstrand personally. He turned to face me, a huge hand gripping the breech of the gun tightly, that furious glare igniting his eyes again.

"That's why he was a great man, Charlie Gage. Because he ignored the orders to pull out. I know why he decided to make his stand here. Because he was the pure metal. Because he wanted to prove he could do it, orders or no orders. Because those tame house-cats who issued the orders were dross." Nordstrand was almost shouting, the words cracking rapidly and a little manically. "Any mediocrity would have obeyed them, evacuated this place, run out. Any mediocrity can get people killed for a reason. Any piece of dross can do that, but Gordon was the pure stuff. He didn't just risk his own neck, but everyone else's too. He proved he wasn't ordinary because he proved the ordinary rules didn't apply to him. He had a natural right to do what he did. He didn't need a reason."

The booming voice carried a little way over the endless Nile, and then was lost on the wind. In the middle of the river, its waters brown as fried butter, a palm log drifted on the steady, sluggish current, twirled slowly in a strong eddy, then continued on downstream.

"What're you getting so excited about?" I asked. "Gordon's been dead for a century. What was he, an ancestor of yours?"

"A spiritual ancestor."

"I see."

"That's how I know why he disobeyed his orders."

"Tell me if I've got it right: he disobeyed them because they didn't apply to him. He was what you call 'the pure stuff'; therefore he could do what he damn well pleased."

"Only men made out of the pure metal are capable of acting without motive. The motiveless act is the most beautiful of all acts, as the motiveless killing is the greatest of all murders."

"You don't really believe that."

"Not a question of belief. It's self-evident."

"You sound as if you've been reading Nietzsche."

"Read every word he's written."

"So Gordon was a superman."

"He wouldn't have accomplished anything if he hadn't been. And don't give me any of that conventional humanitarian bullshit about how he got people killed for nothing. He gave them a great gift, the gift of heroic death. Suppose he had evacuated and those people survived? What would have happened to them? They would have gone on living, a few more years, a few more decades, what's the difference? They would have gone back to their insignificant little lives, got old and senile, lost control of their bowels, and died in bed with shit in their drawers. Gordon saved them from that. By allowing them to be destroyed in battle, he elevated them to his level."

"I'm sure they appreciated what he did for them."

"Listen, Charlie Gage, listen. The trouble with the dross in the world isn't that they follow the rules. They have no choice but to follow the rules, because that's the nature of things. The pure are also bound by the nature of things *not* to follow the rules. If everyone understood this, there would be no conflict. Conflict arises when the dross attempt to impose their petty standards on the pure. It's the difference between what Nietzsche called 'the morality of masters' and 'the morality of slaves.'"

I listened to this with a mixture of fascination and bewilderment. On one level, it was the worst sort of muddled, fascistic nonsense, but on another, it had a certain logic and an appealing simplicity.

"Is that what that business with Moody was all about?"

"Do you remember what Colfax said about Jima's people at the briefing?"

"They're a tough bunch."

"I remember it verbatim. I wrote it down and memorized it. 'The Beni-Hamid are to this day a tribe of warrior nomads with a heroic view of life. A boy is not regarded as a man until he has killed at least one man in personal combat. The weak, the ineffective, are sometimes tolerated, but are always treated with contempt. In the Beni-Hamid's world, might *is* right, and they honor only those who are powerful and successful.' Those are the kind of people we'll be living with for the next six months. Not just living with, but training and leading. Now, what do you suppose their reaction is going to be when Moody shows up with his grab bag of goodies, with his portable grocery store and his pills and his air mattress and his toilet paper? Toilet paper, for Christ's sake. They'll see him for what he is—a weak sister. And if they think for one minute that he really is in charge of the operation, they won't respect us any more than they'll respect him, and this whole mission is going to fail."

"I didn't ask for a speech on native folkways. I asked what that business in the room was all about. Look, all he did was ask you to pick up some halizone. You attack him, insult him, and then end up doing what he asked in the first place."

"The two are not connected, Charlie Gage. We're leaving for Nassala tomorrow. I felt it was time to begin reminding General Dross of his place in the scheme of things."

"That was only part of it."

"Right. And you know the other part."

"No. I don't."

"You're playing games with me."

"No. No games."

He threw back his wide head, cocking his chin at the same arrogant angle I had seen in the room.

"Yes, games. You know the other part. Right, Charlie Gage?"

His cocky assurance that I knew "the other part" irritated me. Fresh beads of sweat erupted on my forehead and, streaming down my face, burned my eyes. Blinking, I looked out at the Nile. The log had floated out of sight, and the slow-flowing river was flat, empty, and serene.

"He gets on your nerves, too, doesn't he?" Nordstrand went on, pursuing his point. "That accent of his, the way he mumbles sometimes, like he's got a mouthful of marbles, and always brushing his hair out of his eyes, and his grab bag of goodies and pills. A weak sister. Hell, I'll bet he'll want to stop for high tea when we're out in the bush."

"I suppose I've got my share of irritating habits."

"That's very liberal of you, Charlie. Your liberality is to be commended. *Co*-mmended. Point is, you fought in Vietnam, you know what it takes to bring off an operation like this, and you know Moody hasn't got it. You know it and I know it. We have a few things in common, more than you think. Right, Charlie?"

"Go to hell."

He laughed loudly and his laughter exhausted the tolerance of the palace guardsman who had been eying us. Gorgeous in a Gilbert-and-Sullivan uniform as blue-black as his skin, he marched up to the balustrade at the edge of the lawn and with brusque waves of a white-gloved hand signaled us to leave.

"I think we're being kicked out," I said. "Unless you'd like to stay to prove we don't have to play by the rules."

"I don't fight meager battles."

We headed for the *souk*, walking through the old colonial quarter with its wide avenues and shade trees, its old walled villas, its traffic circles ringed with drab office buildings—monuments to the modernity that was supposed to have come with independence. Nordstrand went down the street with his military stride: back braced, arms swinging, heels digging rhythmically into the pavement as if he were keeping step with a drum beating inside his head. We soon crossed an invisible frontier into a part of the city where the streets were all beige dust, and the houses hardly more than huts made of sun-hardened mud. Mud walls enclosed their disorderly gardens, and the gates to the walls were painted blue as a protection against the evil eye.

"They still believe in that in this neck of the desert," I said, thinking aloud.

"Believe in what?"

"The evil eye. They paint the gates blue because that color is supposed to ward off the evil eye."

"Who gives a sweet damn what these ragheads believe?"

"They believe the evil eye is caused by envy."

"You playing games again?"

"No games."

"You implying I'm jealous of Moody?"

"Colfax did put him in charge."

"Listen up. You heard Colfax at the briefing. It wasn't his idea to make Moody the boss. My guess is some worm in Washington wanted that little limey in charge. Not that that makes any goddamned difference. Natural selection. Nature'll select who's going to run things once we're in the bush."

"But you're going to help nature along, aren't you?"

"You're a smart man, Charlie Gage."

"You're going to try and break him."

I am not sure how I arrived at that conclusion. Certainly it was not the end product of a logical process; an insight, rather, vouchsafed by some malignant element within me that understood Nordstrand instinctively. We did have a few things in common, more than I had thought, more than I wanted.

"I'm not going to try," he said. "I will."

"What the hell for?"

"A number of reasons. One of them is freedom."

"Freedom?"

"Freedom of action."

"To do what?"

Nordstrand stopped walking. He put his hands on my shoulders, gripping them just tightly enough to make them hurt, just lightly enough to let me know he had plenty of strength in reserve. It was odd how, standing face to face with him, sensing the power in his hands, my three-inch advantage in height seemed to shrink to nothing.

"Between you and me, understood?"

I said nothing.

"Gage?"

"All right, all right," I said, feeling conspiratorial. "Our secret. What the hell are you talking about?"

"I'm talking about the freedom to discover myself, to explore my limits, to be myself completely without any interference. That's the chance I'm going to have in Bejaya because it's an empty place, one of the very last empty places left. There is nothing there, no one to stand in my way except Moody. Moody will try, either by saying something or doing something, or both, and he'll try because that's in the nature of things, just as it's in the nature of things for me to get him out of the way."

"Wait a goddamned minute—"

"Be easy, Charlie Gage. Easy, easy. I'm not going to get rid of him. Moody has his uses. He speaks that tribal dialect of theirs, what do you call it?"

"To-Bedawyi."

"To-Bedawyi. *To-Be*dawyi. He speaks the local lingo, which'll make him useful. All I'm going to do is make sure he understands his place in the scheme of things, stays there, and stays out of my way. Do you see, Charlie?"

"No, and I'm not sure I want to."

"Listen. The ultimate power is to be yourself so totally that other people don't even exist for you. I keep thinking of how Gordon must have felt when he ignored his orders to evacuate, knowing he was condemning himself and everyone else to death. He did it on his own authority, without a thought about public opinion, or the history books, or duty, or obligations, or those little vermin in London who'd ordered him to run out. He must have felt totally self-fulfilled and self-possessed at that moment. He must have felt like a god."

Nordstrand paused, shaking me by the shoulders to stress his point. A wind that did not relieve the heat hissed past us, raising a dust devil that danced a whirling jig down the middle of the street before it spun into a wall and disintegrated.

"He was able to experience that feeling," Nordstrand continued, his voice again solemn and reverential, "because he was free. And he was free because he was cut off, as isolated as a man on an island. Listen, the beautiful thing about war is that it strips a man of his pretenses. He discovers just what he's capable of, and some men discover they're capable of anything if they're given the chance. Once a man learns that, none of the rules mean a thing to him, and he can never be the same again. He has got to act on his discovery. If he knows he can do anything, then he is bound to do it, if he's made of the pure stuff. He cannot go back. He's bound to see the thing through to the end. I learned that about myself in Vietnam. Jesus. The things you could learn about yourself over there. You must have. Things you never imagined."

"Some of them were things I wished I never learned."

"Don't give me that liberal garbage, Charlie. I'm grateful for what I learned. The only thing I regret about that war was that I never got the chance to act on what I'd learned because it had to be the most oversupervised war in history. Rules-and-regs men all over the goddamned place. Always some inferior looking over your shoulder to make sure you didn't do anything that would upset some scumsucking senator's breakfast. That's not going to happen where we're going. It'll be war in an empty place. It's the chance I've been waiting for for years, and Bejaya's the place I've been looking for, and I'd be a goddamned fool to let some inferior like Moody interfere. Now do you see, Charlie. *Do-you-see?*"

All I saw clearly were his face and his disproportionately large head, with its thick hair wind-whipped into a wild tangle of gold and brown. Beyond that, there was only the glimpse he had just given me of what went on inside that oversized skull of his. It was a fuzzy glimpse, but revealed enough about his thinking to make me uneasy. His ideas were not unfamiliar to me. I had encountered them before, in books written by harmless men of thought, in undergraduate debates carried on within the safe confines of college campuses, in places where there were checks and balances. The uneasiness came because I had never met a man who believed in them so ardently, who would have the opportunity to translate them into action, and who was obviously determined to do so.

I wanted to tear Nordstrand's hands away, but a kind of paralysis had come over me. A force stronger than his

grip locked me to him. My mind, recognizing the danger
in his ideas, was repelled by them; but my heart was captivated by the conviction with which he had expressed them.
There had never been a hint of doubt in his voice, not the
slightest suggestion that his beliefs were open to question,
or were anything but perfectly clear, logical, and right.
Sometimes I see Nordstrand as the ultimate egotist, an
exponent of old-fashioned, red-white-and-blue rugged
American individualism pushed to its logical extreme. He
obviously included himself among those elect who were
made of pure metal; therefore Moody, who was not, had
no importance beyond his usefulness to Jeremy Nordstrand. And the war in Bejaya had no significance beyond
its providing the conditions for him to discover himself
and explore his limits, whatever that meant. The tenets of
his personal creed—he believed in them absolutely. Believing in nothing, not even in myself, I envied the strength
of his faith, an envy that existed simultaneously with a disgust for the faith itself. I was drawn to him and away from
him at the same time, held motionless between poles of
attraction and repulsion.

I remained in that emotional magnetic field for less than
half a minute, though it seemed much longer. Then I
grasped Nordstrand's wrists—if you could call them wrists:
his forearms extended in a straight line from his elbows
to the heels of his hands—and pulled myself free. He
grinned to let me know he could have hung on to me as
long as he wished.

"You see, all right," he said.

"And I can't say I like the picture," I answered, wondering what concrete form his abstract ideas would take, how
he would conduct the exploration of his limits. (I wonder
if even he knew that that would be an expedition into a
boundless inner space, for he had no limits.)

"No one asked you to like it," Nordstrand said as we
began walking again toward the *souk*. "Just accept it."

We could hear the noisy crowds in the marketplace before we saw them, and mingled with the noise, the notes
of a mysterious chant being sung to drums and flutes and
screeching bedouin fiddles. We turned a corner and were
in the market. It was the most African part of the city,

thronged with people from a dozen different tribes: Beja, Dinka, and Nubian; white-robed Baggara horsemen and fine-boned Ethiopians; Hadenowa with bushel-basket heads of hair leading bellowing, farting camels; Moslem women in dark veils, and pagan women unveiled and wearing flowing *taubs* of turquoise and yellow. There were no trees to break the racking sun. The sky had the remorseless clarity of truth. Dust raised by the ceaselessly moving swarms hung overhead, too thick to be blown away by the wind. It seared our throats, and breathing it made my chest ache. Smells, of sweat and hides, of spices and decaying vegetables shrouded by humming flies, of the burlap sacks stacked high beside the stalls and shops, and the musk of dried urine rising from the walls against which men and animals had pissed, assaulted our nostrils, blending into one indefinable odor, as the clamor of voices bargaining in a dozen different tongues beneath the stalls' tattered awnings merged into a din unrecognizable as human speech. A carnivallike spirit pervaded the air, charging it with that special excitement, that sense of freedom from the familiar and predictable which strange places still evoked in me.

It aroused in Nordstrand a mood of belligerent exuberance. "I love this," he said, plunging into the crush of humanity. He swaggered his way through, shoving people aside with rolls of his muscle-bunched shoulders, his combat boots making corrugated tracks over the imprints of the barefoot crowds.

———

We found Moody in the bar when we got back to the hotel. He stood drinking a beer beneath the ratty skins and moth-eaten heads of trophies shot by white hunters long dead themselves. Looking at Nordstrand, he said quietly, "One for you," and handed him a Telex.

"Told you," Nordstrand replied after reading the message. He stuffed a halizone packet in Moody's shirt pocket. "And there's one for you, General. Now you don't have to worry about those scummy little snails."

"You'll note that he asks us to reconcile our differences.

Which means you ought to stop behaving like some school-yard thug."

"You can't reconcile the irreconcilable, but why don't you try by buying me a beer?"

"Bugger off, Nordstrand."

I picked up the cable from the bar. Except for the *noms de guerre* Colfax had given Moody and Nordstrand, it had been sent in the clear to Inter-Arab's Khartoum office:

TO: A. J. ANSON
FROM: J. GARDNER INTARCAI
IN RESPONSE TO YOUR MESSAGE OF THIS AFTERNOON, FREDRICKS IS TO REMAIN ON THE TEAM. I REGARD HIM AS VITAL TO THE PROJECT. YOUR DIFFERENCES APPEAR TO BE A PERSONALITY CONFLICT WHICH YOU SHOULD MAKE EVERY EFFORT TO RECONCILE. REMIND YOU TO CONFIRM YOUR ARRIVAL NASSALA TOMORROW AND TO WAIT THERE FOR MY MESSAGE ON ETA IRRIGATION EQUIPMENT. REGARDS AND GOOD LUCK. J.G. ENDS.

A personality conflict. I supposed you could call it that; and yet the phrase seemed too commonplace for the opposing chemistries in whose clash I now sensed a potential for disaster.

———

I slept badly that night. The room was stifling. I could hear the taunting sough of the Nile breeze blowing through the trees; not a breath of it came through the window. Though they had been laundered that morning, the bedsheets felt gritty; the grime and odors of all the people who'd slept on them over the years clung to them like a bad memory. Once, I was awakened out of a restless doze by a rustling crackling sound in the bathroom. I got up, switched on the bathroom light, and saw a file of roaches marching from the drain in the shower-stall to feed on some scraps in the wastebasket, which was lined with wrapping paper. The noise was made by the insects' legs, scratching on the paper as they tried to climb out. Startled by the light, the roaches still on the floor skittered in retreat back toward the drain, antennae waving, bodies reddish black, hard and shining, as if they had been freshly varnished. I got one of my boots, and using it as a club, bludgeoned most of them to death. Then I dumped their crushed corpses, together with the live ones still in the basket, into the toilet and flushed it. A quick body-count revealed they had suffered fifty percent casualties. The rest had been routed. Total victory.

Turning the light off, I went back to the room and lay with my head propped against the tarnished metal bedstead. The sound of the battle had not awakened Moody or Nordstrand. Even in sleep the bad chemistry between them seemed to be at work. It had assumed a life of its own, becoming a fourth presence in the room, a presence that would not let me rest. My vision had not yet readjusted to the dark, and looking toward the high ceiling, I could see only a blackness which seemed infinite. With nothing to arrest or distract my eyes, an image of Nordstrand rose unsummoned from my mind to hover between me and the invisible ceiling. I saw him stomping through the marketplace with his conqueror's stride; I saw his eyes green as weathered copper, and heard again his extraordinary speech, the confession of his faith, and the vow, "I'm not going to try. I will."

I'm not going to try. I will. The words cracked inside my head as they had cracked from his mouth: with the malevolent sincerity of bullets from a rifle. As my night vision returned, the details of the room slowly reappeared: the paddle fan overhead, so choked with greasy dust it could barely turn, the remade packs leaning against the armoire, Moody's bulging duffel bag beside them, Moody himself, in sleep even more boyish and vulnerable looking. It occurred to me that I ought to warn him of the American's intentions. *I'm not going to try. I will.* By making that admission to me, Nordstrand had in effect handed me a contract for a secret covenant. A failure to warn the Englishman would amount to my signature; I would be playing the accomplice again, and every moment of silence would be an act of conspiracy. Then, as always, I began to have doubts and second thoughts, and the whole matter started to seem silly. What was I to say to Moody? It was all too vague and abstract. If the big man had said something like, "First chance I get, I'm going to put a bullet in that limey's back," I would have had something sensible and concrete to warn Moody about. On the other hand, you did not have to kill a man to destroy him; you could smash his spirit. On the other hand. But. Perhaps. I was a master of ifs and buts and perhapses and on the other hands; and with those qualifying words swirling in my brain, I did nothing.

Agitated, I reached over to the nightstand, took one of Moody's cigarettes, and lit it. It was my first cigarette in three years; the first few drags nearly gagged me and made my head reel. I drew the smoke deep into my lungs nonetheless, hoping it would eventually settle my nerves or make me so sick I could think of nothing else. But I thought anyway. The cigarette's glow revealed the upturned corners of Colfax's message, which Moody had left on the nightstand, and the memory of its sterile wording reminded me of Colfax's toneless voice in Cairo three weeks before.

Inter-Arab's offices were in a stucco building with curving balconies not far from the Ab-Din Palace. It was after working hours when we went in. The outer office was empty, its desks covered with blueprints for factories, dams, and half a dozen other futile schemes of progress. Inside the *sanctum sanctorum,* a small meeting room concealed behind Colfax's private office, all the props had been put in place. Papers marked "Top Secret" had been stacked on the Formica-topped conference table; a slide projector had been set up to show us photographs of the people we would be dealing with; a large relief map of Bejaya Province hung on the wall behind Colfax's chair at the head of the table, where he sat with an open attaché case in front of him. It was all there, everything designed to create a simulacrum of a genuine briefing. Colfax even had a rubber-tipped pointer, perhaps another souvenir from Vietnam. I have to credit his thoroughness, his eye for detail, and his energy.

The toneless voice began instructing us about "Operation Atropos." (Atropos. Oh, what a lovely name, Thomas Colfax. Atropos, last of the three fates who control the destinies of men, the daughter of the night who severs the thread of life.) As its creator, Colfax had been named case officer. The three of us had been classified as "contract PMs," or paramilitary operatives, or "free-lance soldiers of fortune if you gentlemen prefer the more romantic term." Without pausing and in the same monotone, Colfax then revealed the mission: we were to infiltrate into Bejaya over the Sudanese border, make contact with Muhammad Jima, then arm, train, and organize his faction with the object of making it a "viable force" in the secessionist movement. Armed with the most modern weapons, in some instances weapons the two larger factions had been unable to obtain, the NIIF would have the strength to score victories, which would make it a factor the FLN and PLF could no longer ignore. With a credible army supporting him, Jima would be able to secure a seat on the Command Council's ruling Directorate. He would no longer be an outlaw, but in a position to influence the movement's policies and, if he played his hand right, to win the interfactional conflict that would certainly break out once the Bejayans won their independence. Click. Click. Click. Everything fell into place. It sounded less like a briefing and more like the synopsis of a movie script, with each scene leading inexorably to the happy and foreordained conclusion.

"In simple terms," Colfax continued, "you three are going to take a mob of savages who are a couple of decades out of the Bronze Age and turn them into a modern army."

This was followed by a repetition of what he had told me on the day I'd met him at Saqqara. Maintaining the base at Albara vital to U.S. interests. Timing could not be better. Rebel casualties in recent Cuban-Russian-sponsored counteroffensive heavy. Defeat had diminished the guerrillas' appeal to the populace. Rumors circulating that elements in PLF and FLN had made secret overtures to Ethiopians through Cubans. Want to strike deal, bargain for Bejayan status as autonomous province. Though probably unfounded, rumors had created atmosphere of mistrust among secessionists. Fearing sellout, some guerrillas had already begun switching allegiance to Jima's NIIF. By moving now, we exploit the discontent and enhance NIIF's stature. . . .

At that point, Moody, bent over his notepad, shook his head and muttered:

"Still at the same old stand. Quite amazing."

"*What* is quite amazing?" Colfax asked, bristling at the interruption.

"I was merely reflecting on how the more things change, the more they stay the same."

"That isn't very clear."

"Here it is, the last quarter of the twentieth century, and we're still selling at the same old stand. It's as if nothing's changed in Africa, only the peddlers and the products. Now instead of us, the British, I mean, and the French and the Portuguese, it's the Americans and the Russians with their Cuban gurkhas. But it's the same old stand, isn't it? White men peddling weapons—missiles now instead of mausers—to black tribes, which are now called 'factions' and have initials instead of names. Peddling guns and taking advantage of their tribal feuds for our own ends. It's really quite amazing."

"Would you like to back out of the project?" Colfax asked in a way that implied backing out would not only be an act of cowardice, but tantamount to treason as well.

"Look, Colfax—"

"No, *you* look. You're talking nonsense, and I'll be damned if I'll let any of my people even *think* such nonsense. Especially not you—you're in charge of this mission in the field. Though God knows if I'd had my way, you wouldn't be."

"Just what the hell is that supposed to mean?"

Colfax leaned toward Moody, and for an instant, I thought he was going to hit him. Then the moment passed. Drawing back, Colfax snapped out, "Never mind. Let's go on. Here are the nuts and bolts."

Nordstrand and Moody, under the cryptonyms of James Fredricks and Allen Anson ("forged passports and other documents supporting fictitious identities will be handed out at the end of the briefing") to fly to Khartoum posing as hydrologists contracted by Inter-Arab to drill for artesian wells near the Sudanese-Bejayan border. Establish

credentials as such in Khartoum before flying on to Nassala. While in Khartoum, arrange for clandestine contact
with one Hassan, a member of the Bejayan underground
in the city and an NIIF sympathizer. "Hassan will give you
a letter of introduction to your contact in Nassala, a man
named Kasu Murrah. This is Hassan." The lights dimmed
and the slide projector, whirring, flashed on the wall beside
the map a photograph of a very dark, middle-aged Bejayan
whose pained expression made him look as if he were suffering from a perpetual migraine. "And this is Murrah."
Whir. Click. A photo of a short young man with nasty
black eyes and a buck-toothed grin. "Murrah is Jima's
political officer. Right now he's staying in a refugee camp
outside Nassala. Keep your eyes on him. He recently de-
fected from the FLN. Loyalty's uncertain. He may be an
FLN agent sent to keep tabs on the NIIF. All right. Now
for Gage. Already has journalistic cover, so no cryptonym
is needed." Gage to accompany Nordstrand and Moody
under the guise of an *Arab Digest* correspondent assigned
to report on their expedition as part of a general article
on Sudan's agricultural potential. (Colfax had gone so far
as to give it a title: "Sudan—Future Breadbasket of the
Middle East?")

The weapons were already in shipment from Dubai to
Port Sudan in crates marked as irrigation equipment. An
Inter-Arab cargo plane would fly them on to Nassala, where
they would be off-loaded onto trucks to be used in our
phony search for nonexistent artesian wells.

"Method of infiltration will be a kidnapping. The story
will be that you three were captured by NIIF guerrillas
when your convoy accidentally strayed over the border."
(I felt startled for a moment, then a warm glow of professional satisfaction. A kidnapping. My contribution.) "For
that reason, you'll be unarmed while you're in Sudan. Once
over the border, Murrah will help you make contact with
a guerrilla patrol that will escort you to Jima's base, some
two hundred miles away. You are to guard your identity
as captives throughout the operation, avoiding compromise by confining yourselves to Jima's camp as much as
possible and avoiding direct participation in military actions. This for two reasons, gentlemen: one, it would harm

the NIIF's image if it became known that you were acting
as its advisers; you would be seen as white mercenaries,
who don't have much cachet in Africa these days; two, it
is absolutely essential to avoid even the suspicion of American intervention in the rebellion. That's why only three
of you are being sent in instead of the usual army we use
in operations like this. And that's why the weapons are of
Soviet or East European manufacture, thanks to the re-
sourcefulness of our arms supplier." Colfax gave me a
conspiratorial grin with his thread-thin lips, and, remembering what he had done to Boxavenides in Dubai the
week before, I felt sick.

Colfax continued for another hour, standing with his
hands braced on the table while we sat and scribbled like
students at a lecture. Communications: twice-weekly situation reports via a burst transceiver that would be delivered
to us in Khartoum. The radio, which operated like a
battery-powered Telex, was set for high-speed transmissions, so no one could get a fix on it. Its signal would
bounce off a satellite and be transmitted to a Telex Colfax
would have installed in his private office. Code: a simple
book code would be used. Book codes are all but impene-
trable without the cipher key. Hugo's *Les Miserables*. He
crisply laid a copy of the novel in front of each of us, with
the key enclosed. Moody, who had served part of his British army tour as a signals officer, would be in charge of
the radio.

Colfax then turned to the map, tracing our infiltration
route in red grease pencil from a rebel camp near the
Sudanese frontier to the Malaka Highlands and Jima's
base at Bab el Howa, a remote tableland at the edge of a
vast dry salt lake called the Malaka Depression.

Finally, the conclusion, in which Colfax came close, as
close as he ever came, to admitting the real reason why
he had breathed life into this bastard child of his brain.

"I came to the Middle East determined to achieve something and this project is it, gentlemen," he said. "And I'm
determined to see it turn out successfully. Atropos is as
important to me personally as it is to Washington. It will
be a model of efficiency and cost-effectiveness. I—*we* are
going to show how much can be done by only three men.

You'll be building an army out of a mob of backward tribesmen, and that army, if events turn out as I predict, that army is going to be the nucleus of an entire nation. I expect only one thing from you: results. You'll be taking risks. A lot of things could go wrong. I expect you not to allow setbacks to deter you. Accomplishing this mission won't be easy. It'll require a bit of rough stuff now and then. I am, however, giving you the discretion to act as you see fit and I promise any actions you take will have my support. In a phrase, I don't give a damn how you do this job so long as you get it done."

The last words elicited a faint chilly smile from Nordstrand. He turned with an inquisitive glance to Colfax, who responded with a barely perceptible nod and then tapped the table lightly with the pointer three times. *Tap, tap, tap.* I can still see those two at that moment, making their vague gestures, their silent signals of a mutual understanding. I see them, not as two individuals, but as two aspects of the same entity, as the mind and the will, the will with its questioning look asking if those last words had granted it license, and the mind with its slight nod and the taps of the pointer replying *yes, yes, yes.*

———

Lying on the sweat-dampened sheets, I had begun to drift down to within seconds of sleep when I saw once more the smile Colfax had given me at the briefing, and was jerked awake to an image of the quay at Dubai.

I saw myself walking on the quay beside the Creek, an inlet that doubled as a sewer for the city and as a harbor for a fleet of Arab dhows. It flowed in sluggishly from the Persian Gulf, its waters darkened by the silt of the coastal salt marshes whose odor mingled with the sewage to produce a stench strong enough at floodtide to make your eyes tear. Bright new buildings rose on both sides of the brown Creek—banks, offices, hotels. "We now have twenty-one banks, Mr. Gage, *twenty-one*, and fifteen of them are international," the press minister had told me that afternoon. To cover the actual purpose of my trip to the emirate, I had presented myself to him as a reporter doing a piece on Dubai's future as a financial center. "We will not be a center, but *the* financial capital of the Middle East," the minister predicted. Walking to keep my appointment with Colfax, I considered the minister's prophecy and wondered if the Creek's stench ever penetrated the shining buildings that attested to his optimism, and if it did, if the men haggling over contracts inside paused to reflect upon how well the stinking residue of their business lunches blended in the dark waters with the smell of the marshes' primordial silt. Remember, man, thou art feces and unto feces thou shalt return. I could hear Allison, with her propriety and belief in man's destiny, criticizing that scatalogical thought as vulgar and pessimistic, "typical of your newsman's cynicism and misanthropy." Ah, but Allison dear, when one's nostrils are filled with the foulness of mud and shit, one's thoughts naturally turn to mud and shit. Mine also turned to hell, the weather being hellish. The Tropic of Cancer slashed through Dubai, it was the height of the Gulf summer, and my clothes stuck to the adhesive of dusty sweat clinging to my skin. I watched with gratitude the sun dropping toward a minaret on the far side of the harbor and went on down the long quay, past a coastal freighter with rusty water streaming from its bilges.

The dhows were moored farther down, three-deep in places, their crowded masts resembling a forest of stripped trees against the reddening sky. They were not the most beautiful ships in the world: with their sharply pointed bows and high, square sterns, they looked like a cross between a Spanish galleon and a Chinese junk; but the planks of their curving hulls had been hand-hewn and hand-fitted, and they had the grace, the quality of being alive, which only sailing vessels possess. They seemed to belong not in that hot, rank harbor, but out at sea. They looked like trapped things, bound by heavy hawsers to the prison of the dock; and I fancied I heard in the creak of the lines the sound of the dhows straining to break free. Sailors swarmed over their decks, piratical-looking characters in turbans and dirty robes beneath whose folds you occasionally caught the dull glint of a *khanjar*'s ornamented hilt. Here one caulked a loose plank, there another carved with an adze a new helm for his ship, and there three others, chattering in Persian, repaired a broken spar. Cargo bulked in pallets all along the quay, making it an obstacle course. Ragged stevedores unloaded still more cargo from trucks spewing blue fumes and swung them with groaning winches into the holds of the ships. The voices of deckhands and dockhands made a constant hum, punctuated by the rapid invective of immaculate merchants arguing with captains. I spotted the corner of a poorly camouflaged ingot showing from beneath a load of dried fish. That's what most of the noise and activity quayside was about: gold. Dubai had a field of offshore oil, but it was a flourishing illicit trade in the traditional symbol of wealth that had erected the gleaming buildings and put Rolls-Royces on the emirate's streets.

I found Colfax near the end of the quay. He was wearing his suit, but the 110-degree heat had convinced him to take off his tie. Standing with one foot on a dock cleat, he leaned over to talk to a boatman in an ancient launch with a new Yamaha outboard.

"You understand? You'll be here at midnight," Colfax said in almost flawless Arabic. "If I'm not here, you will wait."

"Inshallah—If God wills," the boatman answered.

"No. There will be none of this 'if God wills.' You will be here at midnight and you'll wait."

"Aiwa!"

The boatman, standing in the bow, shoved off, then scampered to the stern and took hold of the outboard's tiller. The launch backed off, swung away, and headed over the harbor, its wake churning the brown water into a bilious green. Turning to me, Colfax said:

"Gage. You're on time. Let's go."

We started walking. I had not seen him since my recruitment months before and that was all he had to say in the way of a greeting.

"Go where?"

"Dinner, of course. You're hungry, aren't you?"

"Was," I said, crinkling my nose and pointing my thumb at the Creek.

"Yes. Smelly, isn't it? Just as well if you eat lightly. Might be a bit of rough stuff later on."

I knew better than to ask what he meant by "a bit of rough stuff." Evidently it was to be very rough stuff: I caught a reflexive movement of his hand toward his right side, and saw he had not worn a suit jacket solely out of an adherence to his rigid dress code. My gut tightened, a not unwelcome sensation. The previous months had been extraordinarily dull. All I had done was play courier, Thomas Colfax's messenger boy. I would go to the *Digest* offices, pick up a letter I was not allowed to read, fly off to someplace like Nicosia or Damascus, and deliver it to someone whose identity I was not allowed to know. In between my rounds as a postman, I wrote boring articles for the *Digest* to keep up appearances. So I wanted something to happen that night in Dubai, some violent action, and the setting sun struck my sight as a new wound, lanced by the minaret and bleeding its red into the cirrus clouds streaked low on the horizon.

We ate in an imitation English restaurant full of men with blanched faces jabbering about construction projects and drilling rights. The place was air-conditioned to a fault; the sudden change from intense heat to cold hit me like a malaria attack. We sat at a large table facing the entrance with three Lebanese whom Colfax introduced only as "gentlemen from Beirut." One held an attaché case with a combination lock on his lap. All three were wearing suit jackets for the same reason Colfax wore his. None looked like a gentleman. They spoke among themselves in French the whole time.

While they talked, Colfax, in an unusual, nostalgic mood, reminisced about his early career—a year training anti-Castro guerrillas in Guatemala followed by two years with Montagnard tribesmen in the wild hills near the Laotian border. Over our London grilles, he described the day the Montagnards initiated him into their tribe. He recalled the gongs ringing in the village, the sun slanting through the jungle canopy, the throb of buffalo-hide drums, and the village chief, clad in scarlet, anointing his head with rice wine and the blood of a freshly slaughtered chicken. Those were, he said, the best years of his life. Things had been so simple and clear then, and Indochina seemed to hold so much promise, so many chances for a man to achieve something extraordinary. His voice trailed off, and he stared silently into space, his blue eyes fastened on something only they could see.

I sat without talking, trying to picture the guardian of western civilization with chicken blood streaming down his forehead.

"I'd like to go back someday," he said in a distant voice. "I'd like to walk down those trails again—we used to see the pug marks of tigers on them. And I'd like to hear the way the jungle wakes up. You could almost set your watch by the noise, monkeys and birds screeching, thousands of them, all at once."

"This sentimentality doesn't sound like you."

"Do you think of me as an insensitive man?"

"No, but that doesn't mean I think you're sensitive, either. The adjectives don't apply to you, any more than they'd apply to a machine."

"I see. A machine." He snapped out of his far-off mood. "Perhaps I am, although I like to think of myself as an artist. I feel the same satisfaction when a project turns out the way I've planned it as a composer does when a musical score turns out the way he's planned. And I feel the same frustration when things don't turn out right. I am seldom frustrated, Gage."

Colfax signaled the waiter for the check; then we left with the three gentlemen from Beirut. After the air conditioning, the heat and stench outside were overwhelming. Kerosene lamps glowed orange in the deckhouses of the dhows, their light reflected in the harbor, which was as smooth and black as a pool of tar. We walked down the street opposite the quay, one of the men about five paces in front, the second an equal distance behind, and the third, carrying the attaché case, beside us. Point man, rear guard, flank security. All three were big men, with an air of lethal competence and the relaxed but watchful manner of professional bodyguards.

"You expecting an ambush?" I asked, hearing the tautness in my voice.

"I'm expecting a double cross which might involve an ambush."

"Let's drop the mystery. Who's going to double-cross us?"

"Boxavenides."

"Who tipped you off?"

"My quick wit, aided by some documentary evidence I managed to get hold of."

"Your quick wit?"

"A felicity of perception arising from a thorough knowledge of a man's character that gives one the ability to predict what actions that man is likely to take in a given set of circumstances. Applied to the case at hand, our Mr. Boxavenides is greedy, shortsighted, and an amateur when he works outside his limits. He doesn't realize he's an amateur, which leads him to presume an amateurishness in others and to believe he can outsmart them. Unfortunately for him, he's had limited experience in dealing with real professionals."

"Such as you."

"The difference between him and me is the difference between a competent novice at chess and a grand master. Where George can see only one or two moves ahead, I can see five or six, sometimes the entire game right up to check and mate."

"You think a lot of yourself, don't you."

"I told you, I like to think of myself as an artist. All artists have big egos."

Passing through a brightly lighted *souk*, where the pungency of spices and mustard seed diluted the stink of the harbor, I saw a potential assassin in every shopkeeper squatting beside his scale, and even in a bedouin girl whose black eyes glared at us through the masklike veil worn by the women of the emirates. The market led into a narrow dirt street, which we followed to a quadrangular building with high, whitewashed walls. It was an old caravanserai that had been converted, according to the sign above the gateway, into warehouse number two of AEA Trading Ltd. In the courtyard where camels once knelt by the hundreds, several big trucks were parked beside the fountainlike trough where the camels used to water. The drivers and loading crews lounged about, listening to a mournful Arab song on a transistor radio. One of the gentlemen from Beirut took a look at the half-visible figures and at the two-story, arcaded walls surrounding the courtyard and pronounced it *"Mauvais pas."*

"Non, non," Colfax assured him. *"Il est sans danger ici."*

"Regardez! Mauvais pas."

"Du calme. Je connais ses petits manies."

The Lebanese shrugged as if to say, "All right, if you say so, but I think you're wrong," and went in with the other two, the three of them walking as though through a minefield. They never took their eyes off the men crowded around the trucks. With its high walls, the courtyard reminded me of an abandoned cloister. It would have been a spooky place even without Colfax's warnings about double crosses and ambushes. A light burned in the window of a ground-floor storeroom.

"You said you know his little ways. How do you know he isn't going to pull it off here?" I asked in a whisper. "It's the perfect place for it."

"Boxavenides is not the type to foul his own nest."

Colfax knocked at the door of the lighted room. Boxavenides let us in. A surprised expression came over his face when he saw the three Lebanese, but he caught himself and flashed one of his charming smiles, greeting Colfax and me with his usual false and unctuous friendliness. Dressed in two-tone shoes, lime-green trousers, and a tennis shirt set off by the gold medallion hanging from his neck, he did not look ready to spring an ambush, but as if he had just stepped off a cruise ship. Shaking my hand, he apologized for not having thanked me; he hadn't had the time. I did not say anything. Boxavenides asked if David had taken it all right; David was a nice fellow, he bore no personal animosity toward him. I told him that David was taking it just wonderfully. The last I had heard of him had been in a letter from a mutual acquaintance: Harris was back in New York, was looking unsuccessfully for another job, drinking heavily, and popping antidepressants like gumballs.

"I see," Boxavenides said. "Well, it's not the end of the world. David's young. He'll get over it eventually."

Then, turning in Colfax's direction, he remarked:

"I knew Gage was coming, but I didn't expect you to bring an army with you, Tom."

"I know you didn't, George."

"Who are these people?"

"These gentlemen are from Beirut. They're going to help Gage inspect the consignment. Make sure I'm getting my money's worth."

"Very well, then. Shall we go?"

"Here."

"I thought we'd agreed to do the inspection aboard ship. You said you personally wanted to see the consignment loaded on the ship."

"I do and I will, but we'll have a look at it first."

"I hadn't expected this."

"I know."

"Tom, I've got the crews of three dhows waiting—"

"Where is it, George?"

Boxavenides cocked his head in the direction of a door that led into another storeroom. We went in. It was a large, musty-smelling room with exposed wiring banded to its stone walls. At one end, a hundred-odd wooden crates of various lengths were stacked beneath tarpaulins. Immediately, the three Lebanese pulled off the tarps and began to break open the crates with crowbars and hammers. There was the smell of Cosmoline and of the linseed oil that had been rubbed into the stocks of the AK-47s.

"You told me some months ago you could remember how to field-strip these weapons. Let's see if you can. Field-strip one of these rifles and you tell me if it'll function."

He handed me a Soviet manual, with English translations pasted into the chapter on assembly and disassembly.

I removed an AK, wiped off the Cosmoline, and laid the rifle on a tarp. Its polished fore and butt stocks gleamed richly in the light.

Boxavenides complained that it would take the rest of the night and all the next day to inspect every weapon. He expressed anxiety about getting the arms loaded aboard the dhows, which were to carry them to the *Galaxy Challenger*, lying-to offshore. The weapons had to be loaded before daybreak, when the freighter was scheduled to take on her legitimate cargo.

"We're just going to take random samples," Colfax said soothingly. "A sort of spot check. We'll be done in an hour or so."

"Tom, all this, and those three men. I don't understand it. I thought we trusted each other."

"In the sense that trust is an assured reliance on someone's behavior, I trust you."

It took me only a few minutes to break the weapon down into its basic components. I liked the way they felt in my hands, the smooth shining wood, the solid, well-machined metal parts of the barrel housing and receiver groups.

"All right," I said. "Field-stripped."

"Now detail-strip it."

"I'm not sure I can."

"You might have to once you're out there."

"Out where?"

"You'll find out when I brief you in a week or so. Detail-strip it, Gage. Just follow the book."

I got down to work. It was difficult. My hands were slick from the Cosmoline. Okay, we have the operating rod, recoil spring, and gas piston. Barrel-housing group first. Ease the spring. Remove the piston and operating rod. Next, the trigger housing. Here's the selector switch for firing full automatic. Selector switch connected to the hammer spring, hammer spring to the full automatic sear, the hammer to the trigger. *Oh them parts, them rifle parts,* I sang to myself. *Now hear the word of the Lord,* and you better believe you'll hear the word of the Lord when all those connected parts work together and there's a round in the chamber and twenty-nine more in the magazine. What a piece of work is the modern automatic rifle, how simple in design, how destructive in action, in the movement of its parts how efficient, the paragon of the industrial age! All you had to do was flip the selector switch to automatic and pull the trigger. The weapon would fire as long as you kept the trigger depressed, fire so rapidly that you could empty a thirty-round magazine in under five seconds; and just one of those pieces of lead, traveling with tremendous velocity, could end forever all the countless mental, emotional, and physical operations of the paragon of animals. What a triumph of engineering! Dr. Kalashnikov with his AK-47 and Dr. Colt with his M-16 had achieved what designers in other fields still sought: the perfect synthesis of form and function. They had built a machine without an excess part or a single frill, a machine total in its specialization. The automatic rifle could not, like a war club, be used to hammer a nail or, like a knife, to open a can, or, like a bayonet, to drive a screw, or do anything other than what it had been made to do; and it looked like what it did.

As I fumbled to disassemble one of these marvels, one of the Lebanese quickly and expertly took apart an RPG-7, another marvel. One man could carry it, but it could cripple a tank. Or disintegrate a secretary, I thought, looking at the slim, tubular launcher. The shell exploded again in the ear of my memory, and with my memory's eye, I saw myself down on the floor of the Telex room, my nostrils filled with the stench of high explosive and burned flesh.

Remembering, my hands shook as I made a stab at reassembling without consulting the manual.

"Memory a little foggy, Gage?"

"I wish it was."

Keeping my mind focused on each small mechanical task, pushing away the image of the mangled Leila, I managed to put the AK together. I felt pleasure as my old skills came back to me. When I was finished, I cocked the bolt and dry-fired.

"Not a screw missing," I said. "It'll fire."

The Lebanese gave a similar prognosis for the RPG. We went at it for another two hours. The three gentlemen from Beirut gave me quick refresher courses on the RPD machine gun, the big 12.7-millimeter DSHK, the Sagger, with its metal case that converts into a small launch platform, the shoulder-fired SAM-7 anti-aircraft missile, or Strella as it was code-named. I found it all incredible. There was enough there to fully equip a Soviet regiment.

"You're impressed, Mr. Gage?" Boxavenides asked.

"It looks like you raided a Russian armory."

He gave a self-satisfied laugh.

"I have my sources. I have my sources."

The inspection finished, we returned to the small room Boxavenides used as an office. He sat at his desk, crossed his legs, and dusted off his two-tones.

"So, Tom, now that you're satisfied that you're getting what you're paying for, it's time for me to get what's due to me."

"You certainly will, George."

"A quarter of a million."

"Don't forget that it's a loan. I wouldn't forget our arrangement if I were you. Your payment was getting your ship back."

"Of course, of course. But I need the money now to pay my sources. You do have it?"

At a gesture of one of Colfax's elegant surgeon's hands, the Lebanese spun the combination lock on the attaché case, laid it on the desk, and opened it. And only the most devout member of the Order of Saint Francis could have looked at all those five-hundred-dollar bills without feeling his throat tighten.

"There are five hundred of them in there, George. Would you like to count them now or wait till we're aboard?"

"We should have the consignment loaded before daybreak and it's getting late. No, I'll wait, Tom." He stood to leave. "You see, I trust you."

A little minuet took place then. The three Lebanese formed a perimeter around Boxavenides's desk; Colfax walked to within an arm's length of him and laid a hand on his shoulder. One of the gentlemen picked up the case.

"Please, sit down, George. I'd like to read you something before we go."

Colfax's eyes gave off a glow like that of the decomposing wood I had seen in the Vietnamese jungles, a blue phosphorescence, a light without warmth. Boxavenides opened his mouth to say something, but one look at those cold eyes made him think better of it. He sat down.

"This'll only take a few moments," Colfax said, pulling a sheet of paper out of his inside pocket. The Greek shifted in his seat when he saw the checkered grip of the 9-millimeter automatic holstered on Colfax's belt.

Unfolding the paper, which was filled with typewritten Arabic, Colfax read:

" 'The Falcons of the Palestinian revolution claim responsibility for the liquidation of the American spies Thomas Colfax and Charles Gage. This action was carried out on August sixteenth on the instruction of our high command, resolutely fulfilling its mission to strike at U.S. targets throughout the Middle East. The spies Colfax and Gage were executed by our freedom fighters in Dubai, where they were conspiring with the reactionary elements in the United Arab Emirates to deny the Palestinians' demands for national rights. . . .' It goes on in that vein. Shall I continue, George?"

Boxavenides shook his head. He showed no signs of nervousness, and Colfax told him he was carrying it off very well so far.

"Carrying what off, Tom? That has nothing—"

"What do you think of this document, besides its having nothing to do with you?"

"Think of it?"

"Yes. What do you think of it?"

"Well, evidently—what I mean is that there's—it appears some Palestinian group is—"

"Forget it. I'll tell you what I think of it." Colfax's voice lost its balance, rose to its pitch of restrained rage. "I think it's interesting. For one thing, today is the sixteenth. For another thing, there is no such group as the Falcons of the Palestinian revolution. That's very interesting. I think the Falcons of the Palestinian revolution, like this communiqué, are inventions. And I think you're the inventor. You were smart enough to figure my assassination would cause certain people in the States to try to find out who killed me and why. You were also smart enough to figure the trail would lead to you. So you dreamed up this red herring to throw them off. Smart, George, but not smart enough. Not by half."

Colfax said something in French. The Lebanese holding the case began to swing it by its handle. Boxavenides, no longer carrying it off so well, fidgeted with his medallion.

"Tom, that's completely fantastic. You can't possibly believe I—"

The sentence ended abruptly in a cough and a sound like air hissing from a bicycle tire as the Lebanese swung a corner of the case square into Boxavenides's solar plexus. He went bug-eyed and, half-paralyzed by the blow, slumped in the swivel chair. One of the other gentlemen pulled him upright and held him by the shoulders.

"What infuriates me about this isn't the fact that you tried double-crossing me," Colfax said in a tremolo of anger. "Double crosses are an occupational hazard. It's your clumsiness, your stupid assumption that I'd be foolish enough to come flying out here with a quarter of a million dollars without taking precautions. Do you take me for an amateur? Do you think I do what I do as a hobby? Do you see me as some kind of dilettante? I'm a professional. I've been one for nearly twenty years. I've outsmarted and outthought people who make you look like a cretin. Do I make my point?"

Boxavenides gasped out a yes just before the Lebanese again knocked the wind out of him with another measured swing of the case. He sank halfway to the floor.

Colfax and the three gentlemen from Beirut then danced another minuet. It was more intricately choreographed than the first, and faster in tempo. It happened so fast that I have never been able to recall how they did it. Colfax ended up in the swivel chair, Boxavenides on his hands and knees on the floor, his lime-green trousers and underwear pulled down to his ankles. Two of the gentlemen, one with a hand clasped over Boxavenides's mouth, held him in that position while the third, after bolting both doors, knelt behind him and pointed a small-caliber pistol at his trim, athletic bottom, a white circle between his tanned waist and legs.

The guardian of western civilization, calm restored, began the interrogation in his most passionless voice:

"Due to your limited ability to articulate, you'll answer my questions by nodding or shaking your head. Understood, George?"

Boxavenides nodded.

"I have several hypotheses. You were going to use at least three men, armed with handguns with silencers. The most convenient place of execution would be the dhow after it was out of the harbor. *Pop, pop,* and Charles and I were to be dumped overboard. Our bodies would be carried into the Creek on the incoming tide. They would be found floating there, so it would look as if we had been killed ashore and then shoved off a dock. Then the communiqué would be issued to the press. Correct, George?"

Boxavenides, neither nodding nor shaking his head, made a groaning noise through the Lebanese's hand. The gentleman kneeling behind him then did what I had been afraid he was going to do with the pistol. Boxavenides jerked as if he had just received a high-voltage shock and let out a stifled cry. Feeling a dry heave coming on, I turned and faced the wall.

"It hurts now and I want you to think of how much more it will hurt if I tell him to pull the trigger," Colfax said from behind me. "It's only a low-velocity twenty-two, you know. The bullet will travel up into your guts and tear them up a bit, but you won't die quickly. You'll die slowly of internal hemorrhaging. The pain will be extraordinary. Now answer my question."

Boxavenides must have twisted his head free. I heard him say in a rapid, wheezing whisper, "Won't pull trigger . . . need me." This was followed by an awful, gagging noise. I suppose the man with the pistol had twisted the barrel a bit. I don't know. I was looking at the white stone wall and wanting to cry out, "Stop it!" But every time I was on the verge of it, an invisible noose tightened and choked me off, as in those strangling nightmares when you want to scream but the scream dies in your throat.

"Listen carefully," said the voice of the guardian of western civilization. "Even before I got hold of this communiqué, I figured you were going to try to pull something off. So I took appropriate measures. Redundancies. Backup systems so to speak. Every arrangement I counted on you making, I made on my own. I've hired a launch, so Gage and I don't have to ride in one of the dhows. My three friends will make that trip. For another example, I've arranged to have our financial agreement covered in case you have to be killed. There isn't time to go into details now. I just want you to realize I don't need you. You're a convenience, George, not a necessity. Now, then, if you don't answer this time, I'm going to tell him to pull the trigger. Was it to be three men with silencers in the dhows?"

Boxavenides must have nodded because Colfax said:

"Good, George. Now, are there more than three?"

A pause.

"Less than three?"

A pause.

"Two?"

A pause.

"I see. Two was all you could get. All right, I was close. Next question: those two are either on the dhow or among the truck crews outside. Answer with a nod or by shaking your head. Are they aboard the dhow?"

A pause.

"Outside?"

Another pause.

"What was the game plan? Were they going to get aboard the dhow when we weren't looking? Masquerade as part of the crew?"

Another pause.

"Okay. I'm going to let you talk now. You'll answer my questions quietly. What are their names?"

A convulsive sob was all that came from Boxavenides's throat.

"George. Their names."

"Musa and Ibrahim," he whispered.

"Here's what I want you to do. You'll go to the door and tell your Musa and Ibrahim to come in. You'll speak in a normal tone of voice. You'll leave the door open. You'll return to this desk, unless you want to get hit. All right now, stand up, pull your trousers up, compose yourself, and call them when I tell you to. I trust you've gained some wisdom and won't try anything stupid."

I heard Boxavenides get up from the floor. He was still crying.

"Compose yourself, George. You only have to maintain your composure for a few minutes and then you can have yourself a good cry."

After another pause, Colfax asked me what I was doing.

"Looking at the wall."

"I can see that. You'll have to learn to be a little less squeamish, Gage. Turn around."

I turned around. Boxavenides was buckling his belt, and I could not recall ever having seen a more tormented-looking man, a man more humiliated, more defeated. The Lebanese, wiping off the muzzle of his pistol, made a disgusting joke in French. He holstered the revolver. Colfax handed him his own pistol, its barrel elongated by a silencer, then deployed his troops: one of the gentlemen crouched in a corner beside a filing cabinet; another genuflected in a corner opposite, while the third sat on the edge of the desk and faced the doorway to the courtyard, crossing his arms to conceal the automatic beneath his jacket. Triangulation.

"Since you're so squeamish about this," Colfax said, "stay out of the way."

I squatted in an empty corner while Colfax got behind the door. Boxavenides called to the two men in a cracking voice. There was no response from the courtyard.

"Call them again, and a little more firmness in the voice, George."

"Musa! Ibrahim!"

"That's much better," Colfax said softly.

"Na'am?" a voice called from outside.

"Come in here. I need to talk to you."

"Coming."

Boxavenides quickly walked to the desk and sat down.

"Very good, George."

The two men walked in warily. Colfax flung the door shut and threw himself down and there was a series of noises that sounded like someone uncorking wine bottles.

I stood when it was over. Musa and Ibrahim lay a few feet from me. They looked quite young, in their mid-twenties at most; and to make sure they had absolutely no chance of ever suffering the indignities of old age, one of the Lebanese put a finishing round into each of their heads. Colfax instructed him to stuff their *keffiyehs* in the crack of the door to prevent the blood from flowing outside and drawing the attention of the men in the courtyard.

"Were these two chummy with anyone outside, or were they imports?" Colfax asked when this was done.

"Imports. Lebanese Moslems." Boxavenides's voice came in rapid gasps.

"That should please my Lebanese friends. They're Christians. Have you got a couple of empty crates, George?"

Nodding, Boxavenides gestured vaguely at the door to the storeroom.

"I'm curious. Did you have a buyer for the weapons?"

Boxavenides did not say anything.

"George?"

"Rhodesian guerrillas. I was going to sell them in Mozambique."

"I see." Combing his hair, Colfax glanced at the bodies. They looked like dummies from a wax museum.

"Those nine-millimeters are very effective, but they do make a mess. Some of that might leak through the crates. We'll have to cut up the tarps and wrap them in that. You don't mind if we cut up your tarps, do you, George?"

———

Riding in the launch across the black mouth of the Creek into the blacker reaches of the gulf, where the running lights of distant tankers appeared to be floating in mid-air, I heard two faint splashes as the bodies were dumped from the dhow directly astern of us. Then there were only the sounds of the Yamaha outboard and the launch's bow-wash hissing. I was sitting in the thwart. Colfax, bracing himself with one hand on the gunnel, stood scanning the waters for the freighter.

"We should be coming up on her soon," he said. "Boxavenides said she'd be blacked out about three miles off-shore. Do you see her, Gage?"

In the moonless night, the gulf was one with the sky. We seemed to be plunging into a void in which nothing was visible except the lights of the far-off tankers.

"No."

"You sound sullen."

"I'm tired."

"Are you troubled by what happened tonight?" He sat down.

"I said I'm tired."

"Past your usual bedtime?"

"Shove it."

"Your nerves are probably strained, so I'll overlook that last remark. Just think about this: those two splashes you heard a moment ago could have been you and me. Had it not been for my percipience, you and I would now be serving as snacks for various forms of marine life. In a phrase, I saved our necks."

He bumped against me when the launch began to pitch and roll in invisible swells. The movement and the engine's fumes made me a little queasy.

"That could be her wake. Do you see anything now?"

"No."

"I hope that cretin doesn't have her out in the tanker lanes."

Thick with the vapors of the salt marshes and the fetid Creek, an inshore breeze blew over us. The boatman, staring into the horizonless night, asked where the ship was. His launch had not been built for the open sea. Colfax assured him we would see the freighter soon.

"*Inshallah,*" the boatman said.

"God wills it. Stop worrying."

"That business with Boxavenides, it bothers me."

"Why this tender conscience?"

"Even a son of a bitch like him didn't deserve that."

"Would you have preferred due process, Gage? A grand jury? A counsel for the defense? Cross-examination of witnesses?"

"Forget it."

"The Craft is governed by one immutable law: that which is effective is good, that which is ineffective is bad. That method is very effective."

"If I were Boxavenides, I'd spend the rest of my life finding a method to nail your ass to a wall."

"No, you wouldn't. You see, once you've done that to a man, you have humiliated him totally. He is yours forever because you've stolen every last shred of his self-respect, and he'll hang on to you like a slave hoping that someday, somehow, you'll give him back what you've taken."

"Got it all figured out, don't you?"

"Yes."

We heard a dull, muffled thudding at an indeterminate distance ahead. A fine cloud of soot started falling on us.

"That's her. She's clearing her stacks. Do you see anything now?"

Except for the lights of the tankers crawling across the horizon, I could not see anything ahead; but from behind, in the darkness beyond the unearthly whiteness of the launch's wake, a spotlight flashed four times from the lead dhow. Three answering winks came from in front of us and slightly off to the left. There were three more flashes from the dhow, the spotlight's beams revealing the vessel's dipping bow. It and the others were sixty-footers, but the heavy cargo made them ride dangerously low in the water. Two flashes from the freighter, one from the dhow, one more from the freighter, the water greenish brown in the flickering light.

"Confirming signal," Colfax said, standing. "And there she is."

The *Galaxy Challenger*'s silhouette rose hugely out of the sea two or three hundred yards away. Her thudding engines fell silent, and the silence was filled by the screeching and banging of an anchor chain.

"Very good. Right on the money. George does all right when he stays within his limits. That was Boxavenides signaling from the dhow, Gage. Hardly the act of a man thinking about nailing my ass to a wall, is it? Yours forever."

"That is the ship?" the boatman asked.

Colfax replied that it was.

"Ilhamduilla—Praise be to God."

The *Galaxy Challenger* now loomed almost straight above us. Fast lines, with which the dhows would be held alongside, hung from the freighter's iron rails like vines. Attached to powerful cables, rope slings dropped down from creaking deck winches. A derrick swung out, dangling a cargo net between us and the sky, so that the stars themselves appeared ensnared.

Moving forward in a crouch, the boatman lashed the launch to the accommodation ladder which had been lowered for us.

"You know," I said, "there was a time when I would've just shoved you overboard."

"But that time is gone. I want your commitment, and I feel confident that I'll get what I want."

"Don't feel so goddamned confident," I said, climbing out onto the ladder platform.

Colfax, with one foot on the bow and the other in mid-air, lost his balance when the launch rolled unexpectedly. Instinctively, he reached out a hand. Just as instinctively, I took hold of it and pulled him aboard.

"What was that you just said, Gage?"

———

The cigarette went down more easily, and I was beginning to rediscover the psychological benefits of nicotine. An image of the dhows, heading into the lightening east after they had off-loaded, the crews paid for their services with ingots the *Challenger* had brought in from Europe, slowly dissolved in the smoke I blew toward the ceiling. I remembered how fine and free they had looked, running with their lateen sails raised, and how badly I had wanted to go with them. They would pass through the Strait of Hormuz into the Arabian Sea, then catch the summer monsoons for the coast of India. Bound for India in an Arab dhow with a cargo of smuggled gold: a pure, straightforward adventure. No double crosses, betrayals, or ambiguities. And if the adventure involved violence, it would not be sadistic, but quick, man-to-man; the knife swiftly shoved in the belly.

Hopeless romanticism.

Quitting the struggle to sleep, I walked to the window and looked out at the forks of the Nile. Moonlight plated the river. Its far bank formed an intensely black line shaped like an inverted V where it divided into the White and Blue Niles; the White flowing up from as far as Uganda, the Blue winding across the Sudan into the old, old mountains of Ethiopia. "The river of destiny," the Egyptians called it. Destiny: the invincible necessity no man can escape.

And it's necessary for me to go through this, I thought, looking at the silvered river.

I was sick of the demoralized state I had been in since Beirut. Each man owns to a paramount dread: some fear poverty, some failure, some illness, some the loss of love, or of fame, or of youth. The list is endless, but how lucky are those who can name their dread; for in naming it they objectify it, and are therefore better able to fight it. Mine was a dread without object or sense, a free-floating horror of something I could not name. It varied in intensity from day to day, but it was always there, the lurking fear that had made me panic at the sight of a harmless old woman and tremble at everyday noises. If allowed to go un-checked, I thought, it would eventually unman me entirely and I would end up cringing at everything in existence. It was important to prevent that from happening. It was im-portant to be unafraid again. Goddamnit, I had been a paratrooper and war correspondent. I had been decorated. I had been wounded, on a day when there had been so many wounded the doctors ran out of morphine when they got to me and had to take the shrapnel out in the good old-fashioned way, without benefit of any anesthetic except a local, with a few shots of whiskey and three medics holding me down: and I had not cried out. I wanted to be that way again. I wanted to be the man I had been.

Still gazing at the river, its dark edges gilded by the lights of Omdurman and North Khartoum, I dreamed there would come a distinct instant when fear and weakness would pass from me like a fever. My mind began to work with the clarity which sometimes graces us in the wakeful dark, and I came to a recognition. Nordstrand had per-sonal reasons for going into Bejaya; so did I. I saw there a chance, a hope for a homeopathic cure. One war had sud-denly infected me with baseless terror; therefore another war would just as suddenly rid me of it. *Similia similibus curantur.* I had a presentiment that if I went on, on into Bejaya, I would find in its deserts and primeval mountains the formless beast that haunted my days and troubled my nights. I would name my dread, face it, fight it, subdue it, and win a personal victory.

It would require, however, a collective victory. The mission had to be successful. I could not afford to take

part in any more failures. We would have to carry off the
mission. But how difficult that would be. When I considered
it with a cool head, it struck me as bordering on madness
and made me wonder why the presumably sensible men
in Washington had approved it in the first place. Three
men in a wilderness, cut off from the outside world, were
expected to teach tribesmen accustomed to the sword and
spear how to use rocket launchers and anti-aircraft missiles.
Three men in a wilderness, with little chance of survival if
events turned against them. It would be a leap into the
dark.

"And he's the only one who can see us through." The
words burst in my mind with the brilliance of a revelation.
Turning from the window, I looked at Nordstrand. In the
shadows, his body appeared all of a piece; it was a form
not entirely human, as if it had been hacked out of a block
by a sculptor who had begun to fashion the figure of a
man and then gave up when he was halfway through. It
was a body that looked invulnerable and indestructible
and, even at rest, it seemed to emit waves of a furious
energy. Whatever kind of man Nordstrand was, he possessed an elemental drive, that ancient human drive for
completion. If anybody could see us through, he could.
Certainly I couldn't, not on my own depleted resources.
Nor could Moody.

Moody had had some experience leading Arab troops
when he served as an adviser in Oman. But I thought the
Englishman was too—what? Too reasonable even to be
on a mission like ours, let alone to lead it. I had seen
enough of war to know it devoured the man of reason.
Brute force won in the end; then the men of reason could
argue fine points about right and wrong.

Oh, the lucidity that compensated for my insomnia, the
light in the darkness that revealed the lie behind the second
thoughts I had had earlier. They had been nothing but
rationalizations. I had not warned Moody simply because,
subconsciously, I had not wanted to. I had more riding on
this roll of the dice than I had realized, too much to risk
it with him in charge. I needed a personal victory and was
pinning my hopes for it on Nordstrand. He wanted to run
Atropos. Fine. He would get no opposition from me.

Flipping the cigarette out the window, I watched it ꞏ
like a signal flare into the shrubbery below. Then I fe.
back on the bed, feeling the liberation that comes when
you have unearthed truth about yourself. It might not be
a pretty truth, an admirable gem, but it is a truth nonetheless and therefore more valuable than the lovely glass lies
we like to tell ourselves. And so, witnessed by no one but
myself, I signed the secret covenant with Jeremy Nordstrand. He was right about Moody. An old and exhausted
civilization had refined out of him the natural ferocity
without which no man can take on a wilderness. He was
just too reasonable to see us through. It was as simple as
that; and looking at him pitilessly, I knew I had no intention of ever saying a word to warn him or of doing a
thing to help him.

———

"Lay-ee-deez and gentlemen, this is your one and only
captain speaking," Raymont said, affecting a silk-scarf-
flying-in-the-wind, hotshot, bush pilot's voice. "Please fas-
ten your seat belts and pucker your bung holes. We are
about to land at Nassala International Airport. For your
information, the weather in Nassala is so hot you could
cook waffles on the sidewalks if the place had sidewalks.
You are now approximately one thousand air miles from
Cairo, two hundred from Khartoum, and twenty from
enchanting Ethiopia, where you'll meet people who like
to eat people. In short, welcome to the ragged edge."

"Well, I guess that's home to us ragged-edgers," Moody
remarked to me.

Raymont brought the twin Otter down as if he meant
to strafe the airfield instead of land on it. My ears popped
and my stomach tried to squeeze through my throat. Below, the shadow of our wings moved across a patch of low
square buildings and the black line of the Khartoum-
Nassala road. All was hemmed by a hopeless desert that
went on forever. The only natural landmarks were a few
enormous rocks in the distance. They stood high as small
mountains and were sheer as cliffs, grey oblong things
which rose out of the desert for no apparent geological

reason and which looked like the pillars of some gigantic, ruined temple.

The plane touched down on the runway—nothing more than a strip of sand flattened by rollers—and taxied to a stop. Earphones hanging from his neck, Raymont came aft and asked if we needed help with our gear.

Moody, holding his pack in one hand and shouldering the duffel bag with the other, pointed to the radio. It was concealed in a drab metal box that resembled a large suitcase.

"You could give us a hand with that."

"We don't need any help," Nordstrand cut in, taking hold of the carrying handle and lifting the case so easily you would have thought it was empty.

"Okay," Raymont said. "Look, gents, all I do is fly charters for Inter-Arab. I don't know a damn thing about irrigating deserts. But let me tell you something before you shove off—God didn't forsake this place, he never even considered it. There ain't no artesian wells inside of a thousand miles. You might as well go look for the Wizard of fucking Oz."

"Thanks for the advice, but we've got preliminary evidence of underground water sources near the Wadi Takazi," Nordstrand said in an authoritative voice.

"The Takazi would put you near the border. I'd watch my young ass out that way. Got beaucoup bang-bang going on in Bejaya, and the border isn't marked."

We climbed down the steps into a sunlight that pierced our eyes like a needle. Raymont stood in the hatch, smoothing his thick drooping mustache.

"We'll be careful," Moody called up to him. "We've got six months. Plenty of time to get the lay of the land."

"*Six months.* Shee-hit, if you're going to be out here that long you'd best watch out for something else, gents." Raymont tapped his temple with a forefinger. "Watch out for what happens up here. Six months is plenty of time for that, too."

With that warning, he closed the hatch. I saw him profiled in the cockpit window as the beige and white plane rolled down the runway.

In the terminal, an adobe-walled building resembling a

stagecoach station on the Arizona frontier, we were met by a stocky Sudanese who overplayed his part in the game. Glancing furtively over his shoulder with nervous, flicking eyes, he asked for the letter.

Moody handed over the letter of introduction Hassan had given him in Khartoum.

The Sudanese read it, holding it close to his chest, like a poker player with a pat hand. Every now and then, he looked suspiciously at the ticket agent who sat behind the counter yawning and swatting flies.

Returning the letter, the Sudanese said quietly in English: "This is in order. My name is Suleiman."

Moody extended his hand. "I'm Moody and these—"

"*Shhhhh!* Please, don't speak your names here. This must all be on the hoosh-hoosh."

"The what?"

"Hoosh-hoosh. Your boss said it must be on the hoosh-hoosh."

"Suleiman, I'm afraid you've been spending too much time at the cinema."

"*Yalla imshi*—Let's go quickly," Suleiman said urgently.

We followed him outside to a dirt parking lot where a couple of taxis waited for the once-weekly commercial flight from Khartoum to land. Moody hobbled along with the duffel bag slung over his shoulder, the bottom of the bag bumping against the ground.

Suleiman opened the tailgate of a much abused pickup truck.

"Please, quickly."

He kept casting his jittery eyes toward a border guard standing nearby at a relaxed parade rest. The policeman was watching us from beneath his broad-brimmed hat. Three white men made a conspicuous sight out there, and Suleiman's shifty manner convinced him we were worth closer examination. As we loaded our gear into the back of the pickup, he came marching across the lot with that mixture of suspicion and cockiness found in policemen everywhere.

"Congratulations, Suleiman," Moody said. "Your James Bond theatrics are now going to cause us some problems."

"Relax, General."

"I'm not in the mood for any of that, Nordstrand."

The border guard exchanged a few words with Suleiman in the rapid, almost incomprehensible Arabic spoken in the Sudan. Dissatisfied with whatever explanation Suleiman had given him, he turned to us.

"Passports."

We handed him our passports. He read every line on our visas, which took a good ten minutes. Returning them, he spoke again to Suleiman.

"Now what the devil does he want?"

"I told him you are here for the water work. He wants to see the papers from the ministry permitting you to do the water work in this area."

Moody gave these to the guard, who studied them with his brows knit in a way that made me question the level of his literacy.

There were only two names on the documents, he said when he was done, Mr. Anson and Mr. Fredricks. Who was I?

I was a *sahafi Amerikai.*

"Papers."

I presented my press credentials. He looked at my photograph, then at me, then again at my photo. I figured that the life of a border policeman in a town like Nassala wasn't very interesting and that he intended to stretch the process out as long as posssible. We were making his day. After handing the pass back to me, he demanded to know what was in the metal box.

"Bloody hell, we can't let him see that."

"Relax, Moody."

The guard pointed at the box with the countenance of a man accustomed to obedience.

Moody told him the box contained delicate equipment used in irrigation work. It would be of no interest to him. The policeman repeated his order.

"Damn it, this is a fine start. Things are breaking down already."

"The only thing breaking down is you."

"Listen, Nordstrand. . . ."

Again, the border guard gestured toward the box. For emphasis, he stagily unsnapped the flap of his holster.

"Well, I guess there's nothing for it except do what he says. We'll just have to convince him the radio isn't a radio."

"Don't touch it, Moody. It's time I taught this Nilotic tar baby his place."

Nordstrand handled it neatly. Drawing himself to his full height, expanding his wrestler's chest, he belabored the policeman with that demeaning invective for which Arabic seems to have been invented; but he was careful to hurl only those insults that would intimidate the guard without pushing him to the point where he would feel compelled to defend his *muruwwa,* the manly honor that is sacred to an Arab.

We were engaged in important work on behalf of the Sudanese government, Nordstrand told him. This work would bring progress to the country. We had to get on with it, and who in the name of God did he think he was to stand in the way of progress? As for the box, we would be pleased to open it, but only in front of the policeman's commanding officer. He, the border guard, might be fit to examine passports, but he was obviously too ignorant to know anything about the complicated equipment in the box. He might, in his ignorance, damage it. However, we intended to comply with the law. If the law required opening the box, we would open it, but only in front of an intelligent man such as his commanding officer. In fact, we demanded to see his commanding officer. We wished to inform his commanding officer that we had been hindered in our work for the government by a miserable policeman who lacked the honor to extend the hospitality due to guests of the Republic of the Sudan.

Somewhat stunned by the tirade, the policeman replied that his commanding officer was at station headquarters in town.

Then, Nordstrand retorted, we demanded to be escorted to headquarters.

The guard answered that he could not give us escort because his duty required him to remain at his post.

"Then we suggest you do your duty and leave us alone."

Attempting to preserve at least the appearance of dignity and authority, the policeman braced himself and said we did not have to open the box. Instead, he wished to see what was inside our packs.

"Clothes," Nordstrand snapped. "Shirts. Shoes. Trousers."

"Open it."

"Certainly."

Nordstrand took his pack, unzipped the compartments, and threw it at the policeman's feet. The latter bent down decorously to rummage through the contents.

"There, you see now, O policeman, shirts. Shoes. Trousers. Please look at them. Look at them as might an old woman shopping in the marketplace."

The last remark struck the border guard like a backhanded slap, but he restrained himself.

"And is this also shirts and shoes?" he asked, holding up Nordstrand's canvas bag. "Like an old woman, I'm curious, my friend. What's in here?"

For an instant, Nordstrand's synthetic anger became real.

"Books," he said.

"What kind of books that you have to put a lock on them?"

"I'll open the lock so you can see for yourself—if you can read."

Sensing that he had regained enough lost ground, the border guard did not make an issue of it. He merely smiled, dropped the bag atop the pack, and with a curt wave commanded us to *"ruh, ruh—go, go."* Then he turned on his heels and marched off, a very smart figure in his khaki shorts, creased shirt, and rakish hat.

"Well done!" Suleiman exclaimed when the guard was out of earshot. "You showed him."

He offered his hand in congratulations. Nordstrand took it, then wrenched the stocky man's arm into a hammerlock, shoved him to the opposite side of the truck, out of the policeman's view, and slammed him against the cab.

"And I'll show you, you yellow son of a bitch. Your behavior almost gave it away for us. Who the hell are you?"

"Suleiman. I am Suleiman," he said, thoroughly terrorized.

"And what are you?"

"Like you, I am free-lance man."

"And just where do you intend to take us, free-lance man?"

"To the Bejayan refugee camp. East of town. You're to meet your contact there."

Nordstrand, holding him in the hammerlock, grabbed a handful of his knotty hair and banged his head against the window.

"And who's our contact?"

"Murrah. Kasu Murrah."

"Then you take us to Mr. Murrah, free-lance man, and behave normally. If you do anything to attract the attention of any more policemen, I'll break your goddamned neck."

A dazed and trembling Suleiman nodded. Opening the door, Nordstrand shoved him behind the wheel.

Moody and I loaded our gear and climbed onto the bed of the truck.

"Carried things to a bit of an extreme, didn't you?" Moody said as Nordstrand came around. Without picking up his pack, he leapt in beside the Englishman.

"That's only natural. I'm a bit of an extremist."

"I'd suggest you avoid any more displays like that last one. And you ran it very close with that policeman. Too close."

"Are you speaking in your capacity as field agent in charge?"

"That's beside the point. The point is, you can't go pushing these people around."

"But you can. You *can*. I just did. I just taught you a lesson you welfare-staters have forgotten. How to handle the wogs. You've forgotten how to use that white skin of yours, Moody. You've been conned by all this United Nations bullshit about human dignity. If you take that for what it's worth, which is nothing, you'll find that this white skin of yours can still put the fear of the Lord into these tar babies."

"You know, Nordstrand, your ideas are so revolting they're fascinating. Where did you pick them up? From those books of yours?"

"From observing the way things are."

"It's remarkable. The other day you climbed all over me for bringing extra rations and medicines, and now I discover you've brought your own portable library."

"I wouldn't go crossing any lines, General."

"Planning to catch up on your summer reading, Jeremy?"

His face framed by the rear window of the cab, Suleiman was looking at us in bewilderment.

"I think our driver's getting anxious," I said. "Let's get moving."

"Sure, Charlie Gage. Just as soon as Moody picks up my gear."

"Excuse me?"

"You're excused."

"You just said that we'll go as soon as *I* pick up *your* gear."

"That's right."

"I'm afraid that is out of the question."

"You afraid again, Moody?"

"Know something, Nordstrand? You could have had a fine career as a circus strongman."

"When are you going to pick up my gear?"

"Pick up your own gear. I'm the one giving the orders and that's an order."

"Go ahead and give them. What'll you do if no one obeys them?"

"I'm going to order Suleiman to get a move on. How's that? You can come back for your gear, though I think it'll all end up in the market."

"Don't talk about it. Do it. Order him. Then I'll order him to stop. Who do you think he'll listen to?"

"Listen, you told me you don't fight meager battles," I said. "Is this your idea of a major one?"

"Stay out of this, Charlie Gage. Any contest between me and the General is major."

"I'll pick up the gear."

"You'll do no such thing, Charlie."

"Listen to him, Charlie. He said he's giving the orders. Obey the General's orders, Private Gage."

"Look, be serious will you?"

Nordstrand gazed at me and I saw that he *was* being

serious, deadly serious. He viewed the childish argument as a crucial contest of wills and meant to see it decided if it took all day, all night, all week.

Meaning to end it, I climbed down, picked up the pack, and threw it into the truck.

"Look at that, Moody. Even Charlie isn't obeying your orders. You've got a mutiny on your hands."

"It's settled as far as I'm concerned." The Englishman tapped on the cab window and told Suleiman to get moving.

The truck lurched forward. Without warning, Nordstrand bellowed "Mutiny!" and drove his fist into the cab with such force that he put a sizable dent in the metal. The Sudanese slammed on the brakes, tossing us against each other, and Nordstrand, hollering that he abhorred mutiny, lifted the pack with one hand and flung it back into the dust.

"You bloody insane bastard."

"I served in the United States Special Forces, renowned for its discipline. I believe in Special Forces discipline. I hate mutiny, so I've returned matters to the state they were in before Private Gage's flagrant disobedience of orders. *Flay*-grant. Pick up my gear, Moody."

Nordstrand's mouth stretched into a grin as white and cheerful as bone.

The Englishman did not move, except to turn his head to glance at the dent. I supposed he was thinking about what a blow like that would do to his jaw.

"And what will you do if I don't? Give me a bashing? Very well, give me one, because I'm not going to play batman for you. Before you start swinging, you think about our policeman friend over there. If you cause a row, he'll be back here straightaway."

"You're too limey to be true. The bobby on the corner."

"Yes, the bobby on the corner. Go ahead, Nordstrand. Bash me. Then all three of us will be hauled down to the station. There'll be questions and that will be the end of the mission. All of it over absolutely nothing."

"That cop makes you feel pretty safe, doesn't he?"

"I don't need policemen to feel safe."

"But it's nice to have him around, isn't it? You know, you strike me as the kind of weak sister who doesn't know what it's like to be in a fight that doesn't stop. If you ever got into what you limeys call a 'punch-up,' you could always count on somebody to stop it. Like that cop. You know if I start to work on you he'll be over here with his gun and his uniform, isn't that right?"

Moody did not say anything. I looked out over the lot, which was just an extension of the patch of desert between the airfield and the town. There was the dusty lot, the taxis with their drivers dozing behind the wheels, the border guard in his cocked hat, the square houses of Nassala, the wind sock at the airfield straightening then drooping in the spasmodic breezes, the sun whose light seemed strong enough to sear your retinas, and all around the pointillist glittering of a reddish-brown desolation. The ragged edge.

"Well, Moody?"

"You said it before. Don't talk about it. Do it."

"But you know that I'm not crazy enough to do something that'd bring officer tar baby running back here. Isn't that right?"

"No, I don't know. You're rather like a six-year-old in your impulses."

Nordstrand continued to grin his skull-like grin, but the malice had faded from his eyes. Through the window, I again saw Suleiman's sweating face, looking at us as if he was convinced we were all mad.

"You should thank your policeman, Moody," the big man said. Then, in what was not a series of movements, but one fluid graceful motion, he leaped to the ground, landed on the balls of his feet, heaved the pack into the truck with one arm and with the other flipped himself over the side panel like a man hurtling a fence. Sitting on the wheel well, he let out a laugh.

"One for you, Moody. One for you. *Ya Suleiman!*"

"*Aiwa!*"

"Let's go."

"Praise be to God," the driver answered, and Nordstrand laughed again.

Suleiman took the truck across the lot and onto the Khartoum road, tires making a sucking sound on the viscous asphalt. Shimmering in the mirage, the straight road

looked like a black canal leading through the town to end
abruptly in the dry emptiness beyond. The grey, pillar-
shaped rocks rose in the far distance, breaking the otherwise perfect joint between desert and sky.

"You must be feeling pretty good, General. You won
one."

Bowing his head and cupping a match between his
hands, Moody lit a cigarette.

"How does it feel to have won one?"

"I don't feel as if I've won anything, Nordstrand. The
whole thing was incredibly stupid. Look, the arms are
supposed to arrive tomorrow afternoon, and we are scheduled to cross the border that night—"

"*Sked-jeweled*, Moody, not *shed-yuled*. Pronounce it the
American way."

"Shove it along, Nordstrand."

Moody ran a hand through his tousled hair and gazed
blankly at the mud façades of the squat shops lining the
main street. From the shade of the buildings' sagging
porches, from beneath faded signs in Arabic, dark and
enigmatic faces stared at us. A black-cloaked woman
squatted in a market behind rows of round, clay jugs that
resembled huge petrified eggs.

"Ah, General. You won one thanks to your policeman."

Moody shook his head as if indulging Nordstrand.

Standing, the American looked over the roof of the cab
to where the desert stretched endlessly eastward.

"And that way lies the border. We're *sked-jeweled* to
cross tomorrow night. Bejaya. The back of the beyond.
Think about it, Moody. Think about where we'll be by
tomorrow night."

"I know where we'll be."

"Moody."

"You'd do us all a favor by shutting up for just ten
seconds."

"Mooodeee."

"Bloody insane bastard."

Sitting again on the wheel well, Nordstrand glanced at
Moody with an expression that was almost coquettish.

"Think about it, Moody. There won't be any policemen
where we're going."

The closer we came to the refugee camp, the closer I felt
to the edge of things, to the point where the strands tether-
ing us to civilization would stretch, fray, and cease to hold.
From a distance, the camp appeared to be part of the
desert. Its low huts, made of sand bricks hardened in the
kiln of unremitting sunlight, were reddish brown; the walls
of the courtyards enclosing the huts were the same color,
as were the treeless streets, and the only relieving shade
was the blue of the courtyard gates.

The place looked deserted in the midday heat. Everyone
had fled the sun to huddle behind the courtyard walls,
which divided the settlement into a maze of private com-
pounds and protected the people from the sight of a surrounding desert whose arid emptiness inspired a disconsol-
ate feeling of one's own insignificance. Behind the walls, a
man could tend his garden, eat his meals, scold his wife,
play master to his children, and preserve the illusion that
he mattered.

The only men we saw were two nomads mounted on
light-limbed riding camels and leading a string of heavier-
built baggage camels. They were a wild-looking pair,
stringy-muscled warriors with hair like black brush piles.
Wide leather belts pinched their waists, and they wore
smudged white robes sashlike over their lank shoulders
and chests. One had a two-handed sword sheathed across
his back, the other carried an old Lee-Enfield. Each sat
with an easy grace on his twin-horned wooden saddle, one
leg curled over the front horn, one hand resting on the
knee while the free hand held a riding crop of braided
leather. Their bearing made them look as haughty as their
mounts. Bodies moving in rhythm to the camels' slow,
swaying gait, they rode down the street gazing disdainfully
at the huts that housed displaced villagers and farmers.
The wandering children of the desert, men who could
look the emptiness full in the face unafraid.

Suleiman stuck his head out the window and gave them
the traditional greeting:

"*As-salaam aleikum*—Peace be unto you."

The formula required them to reply, "And unto you peace," but the rider closest to us responded only with a stony stare, the studied indifference in his black eyes expressing contempt for this fat driver of trucks who had just spoken to him.

"Not very friendly," I said, leaning toward the window.

"No," replied Suleiman. He pointed at the baggage camels. "Smugglers. And probably *shifta*—bandits—too. Bad fellows."

Nordstrand, his belligerence instantly changing to fascination, stood to get a better look at them through the dust raised by the truck. He pronounced them "magnificent."

"They're Hadendowa," Moody explained. "The fuzzy-wuzzies Kipling wrote the poem about. Nasty lot. It's a toss-up who's nastier—them or Jima's Beni-Hamid."

"They're the most magnificent men I've ever seen."

"Before you go making noble savages of them you ought to know they suffer from endemic tuberculosis, smallpox, trachoma, and liver diseases."

"I'd figure you to say something like that." Nordstrand did not take his eyes from the retreating figures. "Guess you'd like to make welfare-staters out of them. Enroll them in the National Health Service and let them live happily ever after, healthy and tame as house cats."

"Oh, for God's sake. Very well, then. They're magnificent, TB, trachoma, and all."

We stopped in front of a compound at the far end of the settlement, where the huts seemed to huddle against the threatening vastness beyond. Even as we unloaded our gear, Nordstrand's eyes remained fixed on the Hadendowa, now shrunken figures hardly visible in the dust.

Suleiman knocked at a metal gate upon whose blue leaves barbaric symbols were painted in blood red. I couldn't tell what they were—charms, talismans, or mere decorations; but they appeared to be out of another time, like cave paintings, and their mystery heightened the feeling of being on the threshold of a world full of incomprehensibilities.

Suleiman had become nervous again. The camp was full of partisans from the other factions, he said; it would jeopardize the plan if any of them saw us entering the house, which he grandly described as the headquarters of the NIIF underground in Sudan. He told us to enter quickly, quickly, as the gate was opened by an old man in a snowy *taub*.

The old man, who was holding a crude hoe, had a dreamy smile on his face.

"Buongiorno," he said. *"Benvenuto. Benvenuto a la casa mia."*

I told him we spoke Arabic. No need for that, he replied, he understood Italian perfectly.

I looked around. The compound was fairly large, with a garden, a well, an outhouse, and an L-shaped building that had small shuttered windows cut into its adobe walls and a straw-roofed veranda supported by palm-log poles. It was still except for the murmuring of pigeons and the sound of the wind.

"La casa mia," he said proudly. *"Là, giardino mio. Anche, ho un pòzzo con l'acqua pura. Pura, signóre. Pura cóme l'acqua al' montange. Una casa, un giardino, e un pòzzo con l'acqua pura. Tutti. Io chiamo Abdul."*

"Charlie, what the devil's he saying?"

"He says that this is his house, that he has everything, a house, a well with pure water, and a garden, and that his name's Abdul."

"Why is he speaking Italian? That is Italian, isn't it?"

I said it was, and conjectured that Abdul, who appeared old enough to have been an adult in the days when Bejaya was a colony in Italian East Africa, had probably grown senile and thought all white men spoke Italian.

He opened a door in the short leg of the L, and we entered a room that looked dark as a cell after the bright sunlight. It was furnished with four straw beds, a table with a kerosene lamp on it, and a wicker chair.

"Piace?" the old man asked, sounding like a hotel-keeper. *"Bène?"* He opened the shutters, and in a shaft of dusty light, the pink of a scar showed on his lower leg, just beneath the hem of his robe.

"What's he saying now?"

"He wants to know if we like the room."

"No. I should like one with an ocean view."

"He was just being polite."

"In that case," Moody said. dropping his duffel bag on the floor and his pack on a bed, "inform our host that it's not Claridge's but it'll do for one night."

"Sì. Piacciamo. Tutti bène."

Abdul gave me his benign, vacant smile and asked if we were hungry. Yes, we were. He read off the day's menu— eggs, olives, bread, and vegetables from his garden—and said he would begin cooking immediately.

"Dóve Signór Murrah?" I asked.

"Chi?"

"Kasu Murrah. Vogliamo parlare con Signór Kasu Murrah. Lui qui?"

No, Abdul replied, Kasu Murrah was not there. He knew no Kasu Murrah. This was his house, not the house of any Kasu Murrah. Now, if we would excuse him, he would go to the oven to cook. Abdul shuffled out the door, picked up his hoe, and resumed tending his garden.

"Suleiman," I said angrily. "What the hell is going on here? That old man says he never heard of Murrah."

Suleiman held up his hands in a placating gesture and assured me Kasu Murrah would arrive at any moment. Abdul, he explained, was a refugee from a highland village that had been bombed by the Ethiopians five years ago. After the air raid, government troops moved in and herded everyone who had survived the bombs into the ruins of the local mosque. The soldiers then poured machine-gun fire into the crowd. More than fifty people, including Abdul's wife, his children, and their children, were massacred. He had been the only survivor and, though wounded in the leg, trekked across the desert to this refugee camp. It was only through the will of God that the old man survived the journey and did not lose his leg.

"But, as you can see, the experience took his mind away. He forgets everything. He probably doesn't know who you are, even though we explained to him just yesterday that three foreigners would be coming here. He's probably forgotten that. He was hospitable to you because he is a Moslem, and he could forget that at any time. Beyond that, all he remembers is his name and how to speak in Italian."

"That's why we've been fighting those bastards for

seventeen years, and why we'll fight them for another seventeen, and seventeen more after that."

The high-pitched voice came from a short, wiry young man who had appeared in the doorway in true guerrilla fashion, suddenly and without a sound, as if he'd sprung from the earth. He had a small head, a black, curly beard, and buck teeth that gave him a perpetual humorless smile.

"Ah, I told you he would be here at any moment. Gentlemen, Kasu Murrah." Suleiman sounded as if he were introducing a celebrity. He handed the letter to the small man, who put it into his pocket without looking at it. "So, Kasu is here. I'll leave you now. I'll see you tomorrow night."

Exeunt Suleiman. Enter Murrah, who, following through on his dramatic appearance, hooked his thumbs into his web pistol belt and swaggered into the room like a sergeant into a recruit barracks. Everything about him, his walk, his ready voice, his mean little eyes, made him instantly offensive.

"A village bombed. Fifty-four people massacred in a mosque. Yes, very nice, the Ethiopians. And three years ago, to prove they don't discriminate against Moslems, they murdered one hundred and twelve of our Christians in a church." He paused for effect. His jet-black eyes flicked about, then rested on Moody.

"You are one of the two Americans?"

"No, English. They're the Americans."

Murrah focused on Nordstrand and me.

"A village bombed," he squealed. "Fifty-four people massacred in a mosque. One hundred and twelve machine-gunned in a church. The planes were American. The bombs were American. The machine guns were American. The bullets also American. All made in the USA."

I had the impression he had rehearsed this abrupt, accusatory speech well ahead of time. Whether he had or not, it took us by surprise, a sort of verbal ambush.

"Yes, yes, made in the USA," he repeated.

"So is that," Nordstrand said.

"What?"

"That pistol belt you're wearing. It's U.S. Army issue."

"Yes, also made in the USA. I took it from the body of a dead Ethiopian."

"Look Mr. Murrah, aren't you being a bit sudden?" Moody asked.

"What?"

"Sudden. Abrupt. Blunt. Too quick to the point, whatever your point is with all this."

"I don't understand you."

"You might try being a bit more diplomatic."

"Was it diplomatic when the Ethiopians bombed that old man's village?"

"The Ethiopians bombed it. We didn't."

"You work for the government that made the bombs."

"Maybe you ought to walk out and start over again."

"Ah! Yes, now I understand you. You expected me to greet you with the Moslem hospitalities. 'Peace be upon you.' 'And unto you peace.' 'May Allah prolong your life.' 'And may he prolong yours.' 'How is your health?' 'I am well, praise be to Allah.' With the Moslems, it takes half an hour to say hello because they are always praising Allah. I haven't time for that, Mr. . . ."

"Moody. Patrick Moody."

"I haven't time for that, Mr. Patrick. I'm a commando, a revolutionary. If you want the hospitalities and the praises of Allah, you will hear all you want from Muhammad Jima. Muhammad Jima believes in all the old ways. But I haven't the time for them. I'm a revolutionary—"

"You've already told us that. Jolly good for you."

Temporarily talked out, Murrah paced around the room with jerky, self-conscious movements. Then, in a less hostile tone, he said:

"Gentlemen, I have nothing against you. Only against your government."

"Damned good of you. I'd like to remind you that that government is now assisting you. That's the reason we're here."

"I'm against your being here. I wish to make my position clear from the start. Your presence here is Jima's idea. I argued against it. The movement doesn't need mercenaries."

"We are not mercenaries."

"What are you, then?"

"Advisers."

"It's the same thing. I wish to make my position clear."

"Fine. It's clear."

Murrah whipped the letter out of his pocket.

"So, you are Mr. Patrick?"

"Yes."

"Who is Mr. Charlie?"

"What the hell is this, roll call?"

"You are Mr. Charlie?"

"Yes."

"And you are Mr. Jer . . . Jer-ah-mee?"

"Jeremy. Short for Jeremiah."

"Isn't Jeremiah a prophet in your Bible?"

"The Old Testament. A Jewish prophet."

"Don't say that in front of Jima. He hates the Jews. He thinks the Zionists are trying to destroy Islam."

"I'm not Jewish."

"That's good."

"But I was made in the USA."

"Yes, yes." Murrah laughed a screechy, grating laugh. "You and Mr. Charlie. Both made in the USA."

Then, with a quick, windup-toy motion, he pulled the wicker chair to the table, sat down, and read the letter as if it were a piece of incriminating evidence.

"Mr. Patrick, Mr. Charlie, and Mr. Jeremy," he mumbled reaching into the pocket of his khaki shirt for a cigarette. His dislike of things made in the USA did not extend to tobacco: he was smoking Salems. Turning suddenly in the chair, he announced that he was Kasu Murrah, political officer of the National Islamic Independence Front.

"Of course," Moody said.

"Didn't you just hear Suleiman introduce you?"

"Yes, yes. But I wished to introduce myself. It's done. The hospitalities are done. Now, business. The weapons will come tomorrow?"

"Yes."

"This is the plan. We have hired six trucks which will

take them from the airfield to the border. We have very little motor transport, so the weapons must be loaded on a caravan at the border. We will go across the border with Suleiman. At the correct place, we will make the rendezvous with the caravan. We will leave his truck. Suleiman will drive it back to here and tell the police that our fighters captured you, but let him go. That is the plan. As I've told you, I'm against it, but I am a revolutionary, under discipline, and will see that it is carried out."

"Jesus," Moody said, rolling his eyes toward the ceiling.

"Also, you will remain in this compound until tomorrow night. You must not be seen in the camp. Perhaps it will accustom you to being prisoners. Are you hungry?"

I told him Abdul had promised to cook lunch.

"Did he? If you look outside, you will see Abdul cultivating his garden. He doesn't remember anything. He is full of forgetfulness. I think that's fortunate for him."

"I suppose so."

"The American machine guns that massacred his family massacred his memory."

"Mr. Murrah, I don't believe the nationality of the machine guns is relevant."

"What?"

"What about lunch?" I asked.

"I'll see that you're brought something to eat."

He left, cranking off like a little mechanical man, and began talking to Abdul.

"How extraordinary," Moody remarked, looking at the bright rectangle of the doorway. "One gets the impression he hasn't much use for the home of the brave and the land of the free."

"I can't say I'm crazy about him."

"Really an extraordinary performance. If he keeps that up for the next six months, he's going to be a problem."

Nordstrand lay down on one of the beds, propping his head against his pack.

"He won't."

"Won't what?"

"Won't be a problem."

"You sound awfully confident. Jeremiah the prophet."

"Underneath all that 'I am a revolutionary' Marxist bull, he's just another tar baby who doesn't know his place in the scheme of things."

"I suppose you intend to fill that gap in his education."

"We'll see."

"I'd like to see you stop behaving like a six-year-old."

Moody then opened the radio case, plugged in the battery pack, and powered up the transceiver. "Think it's time to let Cobra know we've arrived safe and sound." Cobra was Colfax's radio code-name.

Moody consulted the cipher key for the page number of *Les Miserables* containing the code for that day, encoded the message, and sent it through. There was a ten-minute pause, followed by a rapid clacking as Colfax's response came in from a thousand miles and a world away. It seemed incredible to me, incredible and comforting to know we were not totally isolated. Outside, the pigeons chuckled.

"Shit!" Moody said when he had finished decoding. "Shit and double shit."

"Troubles, General?"

"Charlie, look at this. We've already got a balls-up."

He shoved the message at me. It read:

> Proatropos one Excobra: Freighter had developed engine problems which will delay consignment's arrival Nassala. Remain your present location. Come up tomorrow at 1000 Zulu time for further word from me.

Rising, Nordstrand took a look at it, shrugged, and said he was going to the well for a drink. While Moody and I talked over the problems the delay might cause, Abdul suddenly flew into the room brandishing his hoe in a fury. Who were we? he demanded in a demented voice. What were we doing in his house? Who was the man stealing water from his well? Before we could recover from our surprise and answer him, he flew out, his white robe swirling behind him. Now in Italian, now in Arabic, he began shrieking that strangers had entered his house, a stranger was stealing water from his well. A rifle, O brothers. Give

me a rifle to kill the strangers who have invaded my house
and defiled my well. We heard Murrah tell him to quiet
down. Abdul shrieked again. Strangers in his house. A
stranger at his well. A rifle, O brothers. Murrah, apparently forgetting his pity for the old man driven mad by machine guns made in the USA, squealed, "Be still, you useless old idiot!" This was followed by several sharp slaps
made by a stick or riding crop vigorously applied to human flesh. Half an hour later, Abdul returned with a tray
full of food in his hands, the dazed smile on his lips, and
a welt rising redly on the smoke-colored skin of one arm.

"My guests," he said, speaking in Arabic this time. "Do
me the honor of eating in my house."

We thanked him. He went out, limping slightly on his
injured leg.

"This is all turning out quite marvelously," Moody
said. "Wouldn't you say, Charlie? Oh, yes, quite marvelously."

———————

As instructed, we came up on the radio at the appointed
time on the following day. The guardian of western civilization had no new information for us and told us to
come up at the same time two days hence, again to await
further word. Altogether, we spent four days and three
nights confined in that scorching compound, attended by
the amnesiac Abdul, whose erratic behavior made us feel
as if we were locked up in an asylum. Murrah's moods
also changed abruptly. He seemed to harbor two distinct
personalities: Murrah the curt, slogan-spouting revolutionary, and Murrah the man, full of uncertainties. We had
already seen the first Murrah. We met the second during
the following days, when, for motives that were never
clear, he lowered his defenses and became quite intimate.
On the last day, he reverted to his former hostility.

On that first afternoon, the news of the shipment's delay caused the bud of revolutionary paranoia in his mind
to bloom forth dark petals of suspicion and imagined conspiracies. There was no shipment, he claimed. This matter
of a delay was a plot. What sort of plot? He didn't know,

but it was obviously a plot. We were probably spies sent to Bejaya under the pretext of aiding the revolt, our actual mission being to sabotage it. He had found us out. Why didn't we confess now, while we had a chance to go back where we had come from? He would gladly let us go. The movement did not need mercenaries. It did not need the weapons, for that matter. In the people's struggle, it was not the quality of arms that counted, but the quality of the men.

His rantings might have been less offensive if his voice had not been so shrill; it often struck a register that drew your nerves to the breaking point. His appearance did not help him either. The handsomeness of his fine-boned, Hamitic features was ruined by the protruding teeth, which made him look distinctly like a rat.

Moody, the man of reason, argued with him for a solid hour, gradually calming him. The Englishman then took him outside for a long, private chat. I was grateful. It was very hot, the room stifling, and I felt sure another minute of listening to Murrah's squealing about plots and betrayals would have made me murderous.

I don't know what the two men said to each other. Somehow, Moody managed to break down the Bejayan's antagonism. Murrah was a different man the next day. The animosity, if not the shrill tone, had gone out of his voice. He apologized for having made rash accusations. Mr. Patrick had assured him we were not engaged in any conspiracy. But if Moody's assurances had made him less nasty, they did not make him less talkative. Murrah loved to talk, and for the next two nights he conducted a kind of political seminar combined with a partial account of his career as an African revolutionary. Politics, politics, politics—he spoke about nothing else. His political beliefs, his political doubts, his political hopes. He was easily the most politicized man I had ever met, the flesh-and-blood manifestation of the ascetic, humorless radical Colfax both feared and grudgingly admired.

All of Murrah's youthful passions seemed to be channeled into the attainment of an ideological saintliness. Like a medieval monk seeking an impossible cleanliness of soul, he sought a purity of political motive. He wanted to purge not only himself but all of his people, of greed, self-interest, and personal ambition. He decried the provincialism that sullied the ideological chasteness of the movement, the narrow-mindedness of some of its leaders, the petty factionalism, the tribalism that turned many of them into nothing more than local warlords.

"All they ever talk about is independence from the government. Independence is fine, but it's only the first step. They can't see that." Murrah, who was sitting on the floor, pounded his tiny fist against the hard-packed earth. "They think we're fighting this bloody revolution just to change the color of a flag."

This statement led him into a description of the future he envisioned, the new society that would be built beneath the differently colored flag. It was the standard Third World vision of instant progress, of deserts blooming and water running in riverbeds now dry and new apartment blocks rising where brushwood huts now stood. The centuries-thick crust of backwardness would be broken, the layered dust of ages would be swept out by the New Order. Murrah went on in that vein for hours, speaking, not in sentences, but in a series of Marxist clichés. Resolution of societal contradictions. The nationalist struggle precedes the socialist struggle. Strike alliances with bourgeois elements to form a united front.

He had learned this stilted vocabulary in the Soviet Union, where he had also acquired his vision of Bejaya's future. Ten years ago, when he was seventeen, the Socialist Motherland had plucked him out of Africa and pressed him to her bosom. This embrace had been arranged by a friendly Russian cultural affairs officer in Albara, the provincial capital, where Murrah had been raised in a Coptic Christian orphanage. His father, a Beni-Hamid warrior, had been killed in the first year of Bejayan resistance against the emperor. His mother died of tuberculosis less than a year later; drought and famine claimed the rest of his immediate family. A UN Relief team rescued him and placed him in the orphanage when he was thirteen.

When he reached high school age, the directors, having tried without success to teach him Christianity, decided it was time for him to learn a useful trade. They put him to

work in the institution's printshop, where type was set for
the newspaper published by the American soldiers at the
nearby base. At first, Murrah's job was that of a copyboy.
He would take a bus to the base, pick up the typewritten
stories, and run them back to the shop. Later, he learned
to set hot metal and to operate the press. In time, he became a competent linotype operator; however, he was always the one who had to pick up the raw copy. It was a
long, tiring trip on the crowded bus, and he began to find
the job demeaning as he grew older, nearer the age when
a Beni-Hamid boy would be initiated into manhood. Instead of learning a warrior's skills, he learned to set type,
to read and speak English, and to endure the patronizing
kindnesses of the soldiers in the newspaper office. He also
learned that he harbored an instinctive dislike of Americans. Traveling to the base, he would see Bejayans, wasted
by malnutrition or debilitated from bilharzia, lying still as
corpses in Albara's streets. He would see them in the baking sun of the dry season and in the brief downpours of the
monsoon; and no matter how many times he made the
trip, he would never fail to be stunned by the comparative
comfort in which the American soldiers lived. Though
spartan by most standards, the base looked obscenely
luxurious to one who had lived either in a goatskin tent or
in a rundown orphanage. But it was the soldiers' drunken
behavior that offended him most, for he had been born to
a faith that taught modesty and abstention. The Americans
revolted him when, on their weekend passes, they raced
their cars out of the main gate to whore and drink in town.
The sight of them, swaggering down the streets as if they
owned the city, their faces flushed, their white hands ca-
ressing the black flesh of Bejayan whores, filled him with
a helpless fury. He felt like killing them, cutting them to
pieces with the great sword his father had carried. The old
Italian colonials who still lived in Albara did not behave
that way, which led Murrah to conclude that Americans
were a brutal and disgusting race apart.

One day in his sixteenth year, riding through a slum
quarter on his way back to the printshop, he spotted a
crowd being harangued by a speaker. He got off his bus

and joined in, mostly out of curiosity. He had never seen a
demonstration before. Curiosity quickly turned to anger
when he learned why the protest had been called: four
drunken soldiers had run their car onto a sidewalk, killing
a Bejayan. The police arrested them, but turned them over
to the U.S. military authorities on the condition that they
pay reparations to the dead man's family. This they did—
five hundred Ethiopian dollars, the equivalent of about
one hundred American. Was this all a Bejayan's life was
worth? the speaker shouted from the roof of a truck. What
kind of government was it that let foreign murderers go
free? The Americans must be tried and punished. Who did
they think they were to kill a man and then pay for his
life with their money? Albara belonged to the people, not
to the *ferengei*—the foreigners. The rhetoric was as a wind
to the smoldering rage in Kasu Murrah; the word *ferengei*
stirred his natural xenophobia; the indignant cries of the
small crowd sent a surge of energy through him, and transformed him from an onlooker into a participant. He began
to shout and shake his fist along with the others. Then,
suddenly, he felt compelled to say something, to release
through words his pent-up fury. Without another thought,
he shouldered his way through the press of agitated people,
mounted the truck, and grabbed the speaker's bullhorn. It
was a bold act for a sixteen-year-old boy, but the blood of
a warrior race was in his veins. Carried away by his own
audacity, he told the demonstrators who he was, and that
the orphanage where he lived had forced him to work for
these Americans and their newspaper. The speaker tried
to wrest the bullhorn from him, but several people yelled,
"No, no. Let's hear this boy." Murrah went on, describing
the luxury the Americans enjoyed while Bejayans starved,
and how they had turned Bejayan women into prostitutes,
and how they had killed a man and thought they could
get away with it because they were rich. He would work for
these disgusting people no longer! With the born orator's
gift for the dramatic gesture, Murrah then flung the thick
packet of copy he was carrying against a building wall.
Announcements of promotions and transfers, stories about
dances to be held at the enlisted men's club, and accounts

of charity drives sponsored by officers' wives went fluttering over a mass of upraised fists and faces contorted
by the special fury of an incited mob.

"They should go, all of them!" he shouted. "They are an
arrogant and shameless people. I have learned from these
Americans that they have a place called the Far West
where there are cattle herdsmen who behave recklessly and
without shame. I say this: if these Americans wish to behave like their cattle herdsmen, let them go to their Far
West and leave Bejaya. Americans, out of our land!"

Because it got a response from the crowd, Murrah
shouted the last phrase again. It was the simple cry of a
simple boy, but he had uttered it with all sincerity, and the
passion in his voice was transmitted to the demonstrators,
stirring their rage. They began to repeat the phrase, the
repetitions exciting their rage further, the excitement making them yell the words louder, until they reached that unstable point where a protest threatens to turn into a riot.
This was the last thing the organizers wanted—it would
bring the imperial police down on them—and it required
all their persuasive powers to stop the people from going
on a window-smashing, auto-burning rampage.

Murrah, climbing down from his rostrum, marveled at
himself. He, a boy, the orphaned child of desert nomads,
had sent a crowd into a frenzy. An entire crowd had been
incited by his voice. He wanted to repeat that heady experience, to feel again the connecting current of anger between him and them, to see them moved by his voice to
the point of violent action. It was a turning point in his
life. He had discovered within himself the thrilling power
of the born demagogue, the power to sway masses merely
by saying the right words.

The police arrived shortly after Murrah's speech, but
the demonstration was breaking up by that time. He
escaped arrest, which could have ended his career just as it
was beginning. But if he did not draw the attention of the
authorities, he did attract the eyes of the protest organizers, a cell of urban guerrillas who were always on the
lookout for promising recruits. They got in touch with
Murrah and, after assuring themselves he was not an
agent provocateur, inducted him.

It was the beginning of Kasu Murrah's education as a revolutionary. The cell members put him through ideological grammar school. He learned, for example, that his hatred of Americans was a politically correct emotion. His reasons for hating them, on the other hand, were incorrect. It wasn't their white skin or their whoring with black women that made them despicable; it was the fact that they represented the forces of imperialism. Therefore, Murrah's hatred should be based not on race but on class; it was the natural antagonism of the oppressed for the oppressor.

After a couple of months indoctrinating him, the cadre introduced him to the Russian cultural affairs officer, who in fact worked for an organization that had nothing to do with sponsoring folk festivals and readings by visiting poets.

They met in the shabby building where the cell meetings were held, alone except for a cadre member who acted as an interpreter. The Russian said he had heard impressive things about Murrah. He had courage, oratorical gifts, great promise, and he was so young! What were his plans for the future? Murrah, awed by these compliments from a representative of the distant and mighty Soviet Union, answered that he intended to leave the orphanage, which was run by unbelievers, return to his tribe and his faith, and fight the Ethiopians as his father had done. Yes, of course, the Russian said. Quite understandable. That would be the patriotic thing to do, and politically correct as well. But did Murrah realize there were nonviolent means with which to fight the government and the Americans who supported it? No, he did not. There were, replied the Russian. He understood that Murrah used to work for the Americans at their base and had quit in protest. Quite understandable. Politically correct, et cetera. However, it could be of benefit to the Bejayan cause and, the man of culture stressed, to the freedom-loving nations that supported the cause, if Murrah returned to his old job and, for example, supplied the Russian with whatever bits of information he picked up on the base. Information was a weapon, often a more powerful weapon than any rifle or machine gun.

Through his oratorical gifts, the boy managed to persuade the orphanage director to return him to the print-shop. His suggestion that he was beginning to believe the gospels had more merit than the Koran might have helped sway the director, a Coptic priest who held Islam on the same level as the devil.

Murrah followed his old routine for the next year. There was only one change: every Sunday, when he and other "converted" Moslem boys were given a free day as a reward for attending mass, he met with the man of culture. Their usual meeting place was a park in what was still called the European quarter. Murrah filled his ears with tidbits of gossip, none of which had any intelligence value. Murrah did not know it at the time, but the Russian had never expected him to deliver significant information. He was testing the boy. At the end of the year, satisfied with Murrah's performance, he handed the youth an application for admission as a foreign student to Moscow's Friendship University. It left Murrah almost speechless. *A university. In Moscow.* Was this true? he asked the cadre member present at the time. Of course it was true. It was done all the time. He, the cadre member, had himself gone to school in the Soviet Union; that was where he had learned to speak Russian. But there would be problems, Murrah pointed out. He did not have a passport; the government would never grant a Bejayan permission to study in Moscow; he could not get out of the country let alone to some place as far as Russia. The man of culture soothed him: obtaining a passport for him would pose no problem, and there were ways of getting him out of the country. Murrah filled out the form.

Two months later, with a cardboard valise and a passport containing a Soviet visa, Murrah began his pilgrimage to the Vatican of revolutions. On foot, muleback, and camelback, he traveled over desert and mountain to Sudan. From one village and oasis to the next, the rebel underground passed him along like a precious package until he reached Nassala. They put him on a bus for Khartoum, which then struck him as the grandest city on earth, and then onto a plane for Cairo and a connecting flight to Moscow. The son of nomads was too bewildered and exhausted to be either frightened or excited by the novelty of flying.

He spent four years at Friendship University, studying political theory. His instructors were skilled in the art of conversion, and their daily sermons on the Marxist-Leninist gospels worked on his unsophisticated mind, succeeding where the Christian orphanage had failed. They wooed him away from the holy Koran and made him embrace a new faith that promised heaven on earth for all mankind. Like most converts, Murrah's zeal exceeded that of one born into the faith. Impressed by his enthusiasm for the doctrine, his professors tended to overlook his poor performance in other subjects. Thanks to their indulgence, he passed his courses, which made his stay fairly pleasant. But the Moscow winters were long and harsh to a young man who had lived all his life near the equator, and Moscow was a vast, intimidating city, the Muscovites were a rather chilly people who evidenced no love for his dark skin. After a while, the interminable lectures began to bore stiff a young man ardent for violent action. He was buoyed through it by his classmates—Asians, South Americans, and Africans like himself. He met Bolivians who spoke of jungle skirmishes and Che Guevara, Vietnamese who described heroic battles against the Americans, Arabs who told lurid tales of smuggling bombs across the Israel border. As the product of a tribal society, Murrah understood blood ties; but in Moscow, he experienced comradeship for the first time, a sense of kinship based not on blood but on common ideas, experiences, and aspirations. His classmates seemed to think as he thought and to feel as he felt. He saw them as he saw himself: as fighters in a worldwide struggle to rearrange the world. That view gave him a sense of importance and self-respect he had never known before. Anger still burned in the youth, but it was no longer impotent.

After graduating, he and a group of carefully selected students from other Moslem countries were taken on an extended—and rigorously supervised—tour of Soviet Central Asia. It was the sort of propaganda show at which the Soviets excel. The students saw the legendary cities of Bukhara and Samarkand. They were shown the miraculous transformations the Great October Revolution had wrought among the once-backward Uzbeks and Tadzhiks. Hydro-electric dams. Irrigation systems. Collective farms. Cities that had been squalid collections of mud hovels less than fifty years ago. The stone-walled palace of the emir of Bukhara, who had oppressed the masses in the midnight be-fore the revolution's Bright New Dawn. Murrah was shown sights, bombarded with statistics, and fed a mish-mash of truths, half-truths, and outright lies that had de-ceived minds far more educated and skeptical than his. His mind was dazzled, and he was filled with a glorious new hope. If so much progress could be achieved in such a backward region in less than half a century, then surely the same could be done in his country. Bejaya could be wrenched from the Middle Ages into the twentieth cen-tury in a little more than a generation. He had seen ir-refutable proof in the form of soaring cities, roads, dams, and modern farms. It could be done. Those four words inspired him as no others ever had. *It could be done.*

When the tour ended, those of Murrah's group who had not displayed sufficient enthusiasm, or who had asked too many embarrassing questions, were flown back to Moscow, given their degrees, and sent home. The others, Murrah among them, were packed off to a special training camp in the remote Kara Kum desert of Turkmenistan. There the sons of other deserts learned the practical meth-ods by which they could hasten the Bright New Dawn in their countries. It was a kind of postgraduate course in applied political science: how to fire the Kalashnikov rifle, how to interrogate prisoners, how to indoctrinate recruits, plant plastic explosives, garrote a sentry with piano wire.

The course lasted three months. After his matriculation, Murrah, now a trained young man of twenty-one, was al-lowed to return to his homeland. He was infiltrated back into Bejaya, where he joined the PLF. The ultra-radicalism of the predominantly Christian faction had more appeal to him than the FLN's mixture of nationalism, Islam, and Marxism. He was filled with a vision of creating a new society of progress, equality, and justice, a vision so over-powering he was ready to commit any injustice in its name.

As a Moscow-trained man, he was considered too valuable to fight on the front, a decision that happily coincided with Murrah's new view of himself. His lust for action had cooled as he had grown older. It was not that he was afraid; he thought of himself, rather, as a man of vision, and men of vision were more important to the movement than men of action. The PLF assigned him to headquarters as deputy political officer. His job was to indoctrinate recruits—"raising their political consciousness," he called it. He was also made a member of the faction's internal security committee, which acted as an ideological watchdog and as an organ for investigating cases of suspected treason. Murrah thus became both political preacher and secret policeman. His talent for speechmaking and his love of seeing others respond to his voice had not diminished. He exhorted and harangued the recruits with such fervor that most of them could not wait to become martyrs for the cause. (Murrah referred to all the rebel dead as martyrs, to distinguish an exalted sacrifice from the routine deaths suffered by the paid soldiers of the Ethiopian army.)

"I made them willing to die," he told us. "What a powerful weapon that is, the man who is willing to die."

But if the men were willing to die, they were not willing to see their families suffer. In the manner of a detective reminiscing about his first big case, Murrah recalled a matter that had come before the internal security committee a few months after he joined.

It involved a Christian guerrilla named Michail. The Ethiopians had enlisted him as a double agent by threatening to massacre his family if he did not cooperate. The PLF suspected as much, and Murrah, assigned to investigate the matter, eventually got a confession out of the man and brought him before a drumhead revolutionary tribunal.

"Some of them wanted to be lenient," Murrah said, not looking at us, but at the yellow disk the kerosene lamp cast on the sloping ceiling. "They argued that this traitor had had very little choice. I argued very strongly that he be put to death. If Michail was not executed, the Ethiopians would have a powerful new weapon to sabotage our movement: they could blackmail every fighter by threatening his family. It would have been politically incorrect to be lenient. Every fighter would have to know he would die if he betrayed the movement. It wasn't enough for them to be willing to sacrifice themselves. They had to be ready to sacrifice others, their parents, their wives, even their children."

"So you made an example of this poor devil," Moody said.

"Yes. I persuaded the committee to execute him. It was done in front of a group of new recruits, to teach them a lesson. I remember Michail crying to the head of the firing squad, crying about his family. How would his family survive without him? He was told not to worry about them. They did not belong to him any longer. They belonged to the revolution. The revolution would take care of his family. Then he was shot."

"And did the revolution take care of his family?"

"Of course."

"That was awfully sporting of the revolution."

"We're not barbarians."

"Never suggested you were. You were just doing what was necessary for the revolution. Can't make an omelet without breaking a few eggs and all that."

"What?"

"Nothing. Just an expression. I'm curious, though. The committee had a point. That poor devil didn't have much choice. Doesn't it ever bother you, executing him?"

"It didn't then."

"And now?"

"I don't know, Mr. Patrick. Really, I don't know."

The answer surprised me. Having listened to him spouting doctrinaire slogans for two nights, I expected him to reply with a flat, ruthless no.

Murrah looked haggard in the lantern light, and I wondered what had moved him to confess so much of his personal life to strangers, as I wondered why he was now fighting for an Islamic fanatic like Jima. Colfax had warned he might be a spy for the FLN; but if he were an agent, he would have made a greater effort to conceal his dislike of the old sheikh.

The answers came as Murrah talked on and on well past

midnight. It became clear he was no spy, but rather a man of confused loyalties. Cracks had formed in the edifice of his adopted faith, fissures of doubts opened by the realities of African politics, which stubbornly refused to fit in with the abstract concepts he had learned in Russia. I had the impression he'd decided to talk to us precisely because we were strangers: we were safe; he could air his doubts without fear they would be reported back to some committee or other. In effect, we were convenient sounding boards as he reflected on his past in an attempt to figure out what had gone wrong, what had prevented him, and the movement, from attaining the ideological grace for which he yearned.

The first major shock came a couple of years after his return from the Soviet Union. To Murrah's profound dismay, the creed of revolution was not strong enough to prevent the followers of Jesus and those of Muhammad from cutting each other's throats: an internecine war broke out between the PLF and FLN. After something like three thousand guerrillas had been killed or wounded on both sides, the strife was settled by a "democratic dialogue" at which ethnic and religious "contradictions" were resolved and a "united front" formed among all "elements genuinely seeking liberation," et cetera, et cetera. Despite all these sanguine phrases, Moslems were thereafter regarded with suspicion in the PLF, were moved out of high posts and replaced with Christians. Murrah lost his job as deputy political officer. He was banished from the center of power to become an itinerant evangelist of the revolutionary gospels: the faction's executive committee sent him far into the bush with the mission of "raising the political consciousness" and "eradicating the negative traditions" of the desert nomads.

Having lived four years in the capital and four more in the Soviet Union, he had all but forgotten what life was like among the wandering tribes. Naïvely, he began to indoctrinate them with the same language he had used with the PLF recruits, most of whom had been educated boys from the cities and towns. The children of the desert listened to his sermons with utter incomprehension. They would have found it easier to understand Chinese than Murrah's talk of masses, proletariats, and the class struggle. That failing, he tried to appeal to their patriotism: the rebellion was being fought to make Bejaya a free and independent nation. Again he failed, for the nomads had no concept of nationhood. He then appealed to their tribal loyalties, but their tribal loyalties were about as permanent as the goatskin tents they pitched and pulled up according to the season. Alliances made in the summer were broken in the winter. At last, quite against both his will and his principles, he exhorted them with the one idea that stirred their indolent souls: the Ethiopians were infidels, and it was the tribesmen's obligation to fight them, even to die fighting them; for it was written that he who dies for the faith shall have eternal life in a garden where rivers flow.

The phrase drew a favorable response, so Murrah repeated it over and over in every nomad encampment he visited. And something peculiar began to happen to him. He began to believe it, or to half believe it himself. He had set out to convert the tribes politically; he had begun to reconvert himself religiously. The age-old phrase from the holy Koran echoed out of his early childhood, when he had heard it uttered by warriors around the fires in the high mountain camps of the Beni-Hamid. His father had said it when he left the family to fight with nothing but his sword and an antique Italian carbine. "He who dies for the faith shall have eternal life in a garden where rivers flow." The ancient and beautiful words, striking an atavistic chord within him, warred with all the catchphrases and slogans drummed into his head in Moscow; and he wasn't sure any longer which had the greater power to move his spirit. The words from the Koran aroused in him politically incorrect emotions; he had a need to confess these feelings to his old comrades in the cadre, in deep need of the self-criticism sessions that, in their youthful enthusiasm, they used to hold to keep their thoughts on the right track. But he was alone except for the small security patrol and the medic who accompanied him. He was alone on the desert; and at their night camps in desolate wadis, Murrah, for the first time in his life, began to undergo the painful, confusing process of thinking for himself. Thinking, he tried to figure out how a man who had come to show others the path to paradise on earth was now showing them the way to the paradise of the God whose existence he denied.

He was also unsuccessful in eradicating the tribesmen's "negative traditions." Preferring the familiar charms of witch doctors to the strangeness of a hypodermic, women in some settlements ran away shrieking when the medic tried to inoculate them or their children. Patiently, Murrah explained that herbal brews could not prevent smallpox or cure typhoid. The women did not appear convinced. Murrah counted it a great victory when a girl who had cut her foot allowed the medic to inoculate her against blood poisoning. That was one of his few triumphs.

As he struggled to overcome deeply rooted practices that were followed simply because they had always been followed, Murrah began to wrestle with a growing despair in himself. What could be done with people who preferred the superstitions of witch doctors over the efficiency of medical science? His visions of creating cities, highways, and collectives began to seem as illusory as the mirages he saw each day. And in the winds which blew over the vast sere plains he thought he heard a mocking voice whispering, "No hope, no hope." He also missed his old life at headquarters. He missed lecturing the young recruits, the intelligent boys whose minds were not sunk in the invincible ignorance of these tribesmen. It pained him to recall the committee meetings and planning sessions, the exhilaration of being at the nexus of power. He felt like an exile.

Finally, the medic reported to the PLF's executive committee that Murrah was preaching Islam, not Marxism, to the tribes. Rather than face the sort of tribunal that had convicted the traitor Michail, Murrah deserted and joined the FLN. With the bitterness of the factional civil war still fresh, they gave him a chilly reception. What, they asked, had a Moslem been doing with that lot? Had he pulled the trigger of a rifle that had killed one of their fighters? Murrah assured them he had taken no active part in the war, had, in fact, been among those who tried to stop it. His arguments eventually won the FLN's trust. Accepted into their ranks, he was again assigned as a political officer, this time at a rebel training camp near the Sudanese border. Again realities frustrated him. Tribal strife constantly threatened to unstitch the fabric of the FLN's unity. Handendowa and Beni-Amer looked at each other through a prism of centuries-old rivalry. Both sneered at the few Christians in the FLN, who insisted on proclaiming their religion by tatooing crucifixes on their foreheads. And the mountain-dwelling Beni-Hamid, full of the clannishness found in highland peoples, regarded everyone with suspicion and contempt. Murrah delivered his usual sermons on the evils of division and the necessity for unity. They had some effect, but it was superficial. Around the campfires at night, he would hear the guerrillas talking of scores to be settled when the war was over, making vows to avenge insults and to kill their rivals.

Then an event occurred that shook the temple of Murrah's belief so violently it was a wonder it did not collapse entirely. One afternoon, four government planes strafed the camp, strafed it with such efficiency that none of the rebels believed Ethiopian pilots were in the cockpits. As the camp's anti-aircraft guns hammered at the swooping planes, Murrah glanced up from his foxhole for an instant. Expecting to see the familiar, dartlike silhouette of an American F-5, he thought the blasts of the planes' rockets and cannon had driven him into hallucinations. The planes were MIGs. For weeks, there had been rumors that the Russians had switched allegiance and were supplying the government with tanks, aircraft, and Cuban advisers. Now the rumors had been confirmed in the most emphatic manner possible. *MIGs*. Planes from the nation which had embraced him as a comrade and sent him to a university, which had supplied the insurgents with the very machine guns whose rapid rattle now filled his ears, Russian planes were strafing their camp. One was hit by anti-aircraft fire. The pilot ejected before it crashed, but he was too low for his chute to brake his fall. After the raid, the rebels found his broken body. He was no African, but a white man with olive skin and dark hair. Though he carried no identification, his features identified his nationality. The fact stunned Murrah and the others. Russian planes flown by Cuban pilots had bombed them, killing or wounding two dozen of their comrades.

Murrah found it incomprehensible. He spent the next several days trying to make sense of it both to himself and to the recruits for whose political education he was responsible. He could not dredge up an explanation from his confused mind. The world he had so carefully arranged into immutable concepts had suddenly and inexplicably rearranged itself into something wholly different and alien. He felt as a devout priest might upon discovering that God was Satan and Satan God. Just as he had been taught to speak in slogans, he had learned to think only in terms of rigid ideological axioms; no matter how hard he tried, he could not stretch them to accommodate this absurd and incredible event. They had been bombed by Russian planes flown by Cuban pilots. And no stage-frightened actor could have known the awful muteness of Kasu Murrah on the day he stood before an audience of fresh recruits, opened his mouth to deliver the lecture he had delivered dozens of times before, and found that he had nothing to say.

He suffered more serious consequences. The squadrons of Russian MIGs and T-54 tanks had brought disaster to the insurgency, wiping out in a matter of months gains the guerrillas had taken years to win. Now, with Russia as much a villain as the United States, the FLN's leaders began to take another look at its young political officer's Moscow education. His years with the rival faction had made him an object of suspicion from the beginning. These misgivings on the part of the leadership grew more intense after the government's counteroffensive.

Murrah found himself the subject of an uncomfortable scrutiny by the FLN's internal security committee, and the object of a number of contradictory accusations and denunciations. He had been trained in Russia; therefore he was pro-Russian; therefore he had played a part in the rebel defeat. The committee had also checked into his background, discovering he had worked at the U.S. base in Albara. So he was probably pro-American as well. Murrah protested, how could he be both pro-Russian and pro-American? That was a contradiction. No, it wasn't, replied a committee member. It was well known the two great powers often worked together, dividing up the world between them. Murrah then heard the committee tell him he was suspected of a new political crime: acting as an agent of superpower hegemony. There was also the matter of his tribal origins. The catastrophe of the counteroffensive had contributed to Muhammad Jima's decision to form his own faction. Jima's split had further weakened the movement, at a time when it needed unity above all else. Jima was sheikh of the Beni-Hamid; Murrah was a Beni-Hamid; therefore, he had in some way played a part in fomenting the schism. Again Murrah protested the contradiction, pointing out that Jima had broken off to protest the insurgency's dependence on the cynical Russians. How could they accuse him of being an agent of the Soviets on the one hand and of Jima on the other? The committee answered with a collective smile. Yes, it was a contradiction, but it was obvious that Murrah was a contradictory, inconstant fellow. A Moslem raised by Christians, a man who changed factional allegiances as if he were changing a pair of sandals.

Murrah knew what they were up to: they were on a witch-hunt for traitors to explain to the rank and file why they had been so unprepared for the counteroffensive. And they were determined to find traitors on the flimsiest evidence. Sensing the case being built against him, Murrah had his most incorrect thought. He considered the ultimate denial of the optimism demanded by the creed. He thought of killing himself.

"I had served the movement for eleven years," he told us. In the lamplight, his eyes were shining. "Yes, ever since the day of the demonstration, I had served the movement and it had come to nothing. The best years of my life wasted." His voice hit a piercing note that was not shrill; poignant rather. "Eleven years wasted."

But there was an out, a last chance to redeem those years, to win back the sense of purpose he had lost, and, on a more practical level, to escape the possibility of a firing squad. He packed his meager kit one night, slipped past the sentries, and started across the wide indifferent desert. He was headed for the barren mountains where he had once heard warriors speak of a garden where rivers flowed. He had nowhere else to go.

When he arrived after ten days of traveling, he did not

receive a prodigal son's welcome. The Beni-Hamid and the NIIF were even more suspicious of his loyalties than the FLN. Desperate, Murrah demanded an audience with Jima. He pled his case and explained his circumstances, but his persuasive powers did not work on the sheikh. Then, in total opposition to his principles, the younger man appealed to Jima's sense of *'asabiyah,* an almost untranslatable Arabic term meaning blood ties, family tradition, clan solidarity, and tribal loyalty all rolled into one. In so many words, it meant Jima had to accept him back into the fold because he was a Beni-Hamid, the son of a warrior who had died fighting the unbelievers. The argument swayed the old man, and Murrah was enlisted to fight under a new set of initials.

He had to pay a price, however. Propagandizing being his principle skill, Murrah was once more made a political officer: but Jima would not permit him to teach the creed of which he had once been a devoted apostle. Instead, he was to advocate the sheikh's personal philosophy, Islamic socialism. It was a mixture of fundamentalist Moslem doctrine and the primitive communism found in most tribal societies, with the emphasis on the former. Jima, Murrah said to us, fancied he had been elected by God to lead Bejaya into an era of independence and religious purity.

Later, Murrah learned from a member of the old man's inner circle that Jima had been moved to split with the other factions for reasons more earthly than a summons from Allah. His true motives lay, first, in a personal feud he had with the leader of the FLN and the chairman of the Revolutionary Command Council, a man named Omer Hassab. Hassab had kept Jima at the bottom of the council hierarchy simply because his clan had been an enemy of Jima's for so long that no one could any longer recall why. The two men were just enemies, their hatred of each other regarded as part of the natural order of things. Secondly, and more galling to Jima, he had suffered an insult at the hands of one Adam Bairu, a Christian and the chief of the military arm of the PLF. It had happened after a battle nearly two years before. The PLF forces under Bairu overran an Ethiopian outpost that an FLN battalion, led by Jima, had besieged for weeks but had

failed to attack because the position was ringed by mine-
fields. Bairu's guerrillas infiltrated through Jima's lines at
night, found a path through the mines, and in a surprise
attack, took the outpost without suffering more than a
dozen casualties. The next morning, the FLN battalion
started down from their positions in the surrounding hills
to claim their share of the victory and suddenly found
themselves under fire from the other faction. An hour-long
skirmish followed, a miniature civil war within a civil war.
A truce was finally arranged, the shooting blamed on a few
hotheads overwrought by battle; but when Jima went to
congratulate Bairu, the Christian humiliated him. After
making a few blunt comments about FLN fighting qualities
—you Moslems had the Ethiopians bottled up for weeks,
we Christians took the place in an hour—he refused to
shake Jima's hand and questioned the legitimacy of the
sheikh's ancestry. It was one thing to be insulted, but quite
another to be insulted by a *kafir*—an unbeliever. Furious,
Jima raised his rifle, but his men restrained him. This was
not the time, these were not the circumstances for taking
revenge, they told him. But there would be a time, Jima
said. In the Beni-Hamid's traditional manner of swearing
an oath, he grasped his rifle barrel in both hands. There
would be a time, the right circumstances would come along,
and he would take full advantage of them. He vowed it.

It was nothing but a vendetta, Murrah thought when he
heard this story. It was the same tired, timeworn, idiotic
business of blood ties and blood feuds, insults and injured
pride. The movement had been split because of a feudal
sheikh's pride and archaic code of honor. The NIIF had
been formed merely as an instrument of the old man's
revenge. Murrah was sick of it. He wanted no part of it,
though he knew he had no choice but to be a part of
it. The NIIF was his last chance. He made some attempts
at reconciling his feelings with his circumstances, settling
finally on an expedient hypocrisy. He continued to cling
to his own vision of Bejaya's future, the future of enlightenment and progress; more accurately, he clung to the hope
that his vision would one day be restored to its former
clarity. In the meantime, he played the sycophant to Jima
and preached the old man's philosophy, which was so shot

through with religiosity that Murrah often wondered if he was a political officer or a theologian. But he could do little else. There was nothing for it but to play along and attempt to moderate the sheikh's religious fanaticism. Jima was about fifty-five, an advanced age in the desert, and he had no sons. Murrah would wait.

The Bejayan suddenly fell silent, either because he was exhausted or because he was afraid to go further.

"Wait for what?" After hours of hearing Murrah's voice piping like a calliope, I found Moody's soft tone sounding faint as a whisper. Nordstrand, as he had throughout Murrah's monologues, remained in an attentive silence. Sitting on the edge of the bed, he had weighed every word, studied them, like a general listening to an intelligence report.

"Wait for developments," Murrah said.

"Wait for the old boy to die?"

"It's two o'clock." Murrah squinted at his watch in the dim light. "I've been talking all night. And all last night, too."

Breaking his silence, Nordstrand said:

"Moody asked you a question. He asked if you're waiting for the old man to die."

Murrah stood slowly and stretched the dark stems of his arms.

"Jima will live forever."

"The implication was that you're going to wait for Jima to die, or for something to happen to him and then you take over the NIIF."

"Nordstrand, try being diplomatic once in a while."

Nordstrand gestured to Moody to keep quiet.

"Let's hear it, Kasu."

"I have no ambitions for myself. I only want to see the movement united again."

"All right. You've said that for the record. Now let's hear the rest of it."

"The rest of it? I've talked enough. I don't know why, but I've talked and talked. There's nothing more to tell."

"I think there is."

"You're not here to interrogate me, Mr. Jeremy."

"It would be pretty convenient for you, wouldn't it? The weapons come in, we train your men how to use them, and you've got a ready-made army. Then we leave and you arrange a little misfortune for the old man."

"Nordstrand, I think you've gone far enough."

"You started it off, Moody. Let's say I'm curious. Kasu's given his autobiography, so I think it's time he told us about his future plans, his ambitions."

"I told you, I have none."

"A real idealist, are you? You're a good talker, but you make a lousy liar."

Murrah looked at him silently. His face, which had showed a range of emotions while he was speaking, now showed none at all. With its small size, its taut brown skin yellowed by the lantern light, its pink gums and buck teeth bared in a mirthless grin, its eyes staring rigidly, it resembled the face of a shrunken head. And like a shrunken head, it kept its secrets. Saying only, "Good night, gentlemen," Murrah turned and walked out.

———

"Splendid," Moody said. "A splendid performance. You sounded like a barrister on cross-examination." He tossed his sleeping bag onto the straw bed. "Really a splendid performance."

"Just following through on your question."

"You followed through all right. The trouble is, you don't know when to stop. Accusing him of wanting to assassinate the old man. God."

"Your conventional brain is working conventionally again."

"My conventional brain tells me we'll have to be working with that man for six months. A few days ago, he was as hostile as I've ever seen anybody. I won his trust. Why do you suppose he told us all that about himself? And why do you suppose I listened to all that ideological claptrap without arguing with him? To prove he could trust us. It would be helpful to have him on our side."

"Your getting warm, Moody. Turn that around and you've got it."

"Then you come along with that tactless accusation

and now we're probably back to square one with him. Do you have any other masterstrokes planned?"

"You're not listening. Listen. It would be helpful to him to have us on his side."

"You're speaking in riddles."

"Get that conventional brain of yours to think. That calculating little bastard didn't give us his life story because he trusts us. Think about it. Made himself out to be a pretty sympathetic character, didn't he? Kasu Murrah, the frustrated altruist. He was even ready to shed a few tears over his wasted life. Very tender. And he made Jima out to be the big bad feudal warlord. Listen, conversion's been his stock-in-trade, and that, Moody, was what he was trying to do—convert us to seeing things his way."

"To what end?"

"In case his chance to get rid of the old man comes up before we leave. He figures if he's won us over, we'll turn the other way when he makes his move. He's waiting all right, but he's not waiting for Jima to die of hardening of the arteries. And I'll tell you why. First, Albara. My guess is that Murrah opposes the deal Jima made with Colfax. He figures that if Jima's out of the way, the deal will be null and void. Second, personal safety. Or maybe you could call it job security."

"What the devil are you talking about?"

"First he joins the PLF, then he has to desert them and join the FLN. They don't care much for him, and he goes over the hill again and joins the NIIF. From what he said, they aren't too high on him either. But if he has to leave them, he'll have nowhere to go. He's run out of factions. He'll be an unemployed revolutionary with no openings anywhere. The best way for him to keep himself in business is to be the boss. With Jima out of the way, he has a shot at that. You heard him. The old man has no sons. Once he's gone, the top spot will be up for grabs."

"Nordstrand, your thinking has become feverish. A man merely tells us a few things about himself and you've got him plotting a coup."

"The superior man always puts himself in the mind of his enemy. Take it from me, that little bastard is our enemy. Albara is what this mission is all about, but if Murrah ever ends up in the driver's seat, we'll be out of that base the next day."

"What absolute rot."

"General, it bothers me to see you always living up to my worst expectations of you."

"Then I shall continue to do so. It comforts me to know that something bothers you."

Nordstrand laughed superciliously.

"And what about you, Charlie Gage?"

"I'm tired."

"What do you think of our ugly little friend?"

"I think Murrah was trying to sort things out, to get the train back on the track. Maybe his candor came from whatever it is that makes us reticent with those closest to us but frank as hell with perfect strangers."

"You believe that?"

I unrolled my sleeping bag and lay down.

"I'm not sure what to believe."

"Know something, Charlie Gage? The trouble with you is that you're never sure about anything."

With that fillip, he walked out, his huge shadow, distorted by the flickering light, moving along the wall.

Nordstrand had taken advantage of the delay to accustom himself to the rigors of the desert. He had slept outside every night without his sleeping bag, unmindful of the scorpions. He simply lay down in the sand beside Abdul's garden and slept with the soundness of a man who is always sure of everything.

Saying it was late, Moody rolled onto his side. Within a few minutes, his back was moving with the measured breaths of deep sleep.

I lay looking at the insects flitting around the lantern. whose light magnified their shadows. The days of confinement had begun to work on me. I sensed a growing tautness in my nerves, and knowing those outsized shadows would arouse terror if I looked at them long enough, I rose and blew out the light. Lying down again, I stared for a while at the arched blackness of the ceiling. The night was silent with the utter silence of the desert. Then I fell asleep.

It was still dark when I woke up one or two hours later in a panic. There was a rapid fluttering in my chest, a tingling in my arms and legs, and my mouth tasted of brass. I had had a nightmare, but could not recall a single detail of it. All that remained was the horror it had aroused. A powerful urge to get up and do something, anything to shake off that inner trembling, was countered by a feeling that something awful would happen to me if I moved an inch. Outwardly paralyzed, inwardly agitated, I struggled to raise the nightmare up from my subconscious. A few fragments floated to the surface. I saw Murrah's face, then Nordstrand's. I saw a blindfolded man kneeling, a rifle pointed at the back of his head. Michail? The dream had had something to do with him, but my mind refused to yield any more. It held the rest of the dream secret, and the dread it had awakened flooded me like a psychic poison. I knew then that the nightmare, whatever it was, had only been a trigger for an assault of the nameless, formless terror. While I wrestled with it, I heard something or someone enter the room. Padding almost soundlessly across the floor, a dark shape darker than the blackened room was moving from the doorway toward the table. In a near-delusional state, I thought for an instant that my bête noire had at last materialized. At last I was going to see the thing that made me quake like a frightened child, see it, face it, and fight it. My muscles tensed, ready to spring and wrestle with the phantom; fear became mingled with the lunatic giddiness I used to feel before a fire fight. There was a hissing, the smell of sulfur, a sudden, blinding brightness. Both terror and elation drained from me when, in the match light, I saw that it was Nordstrand.

Rational again, I watched him, wondering what he was up to poking around in the predawn darkness. He lit the lantern with the match and walked quietly to where our packs were propped against a wall. His tall shadow was bent at the middle by the joint between the wall and the ceiling. Anyone who saw it from the doorway would have been unable to tell if it was the outline of a man, a bear, or some huge, slouching creature between beast and man. Squatting, he opened the zipper to a compartment in his

pack. With the sensory acuity that always accompanied
my attacks of bad nerves, I heard a click as he unfastened
the lock to his canvas bag. He took from it a book about
the size of a pocket dictionary, then stood, and swinging
the lamp in an arc, checked to see if Moody and I were
still asleep. I pretended to be, cautiously opening my eyes
only when I heard him move the chair to the table. He
was sitting at a slight angle to me, writing. After several
minutes, he paused, chewing on the end of the ballpoint
like a student stumped at an examination, then began
writing again, rapidly and with intense concentration.
Moody, stirring in his sleep, interrupted him once or twice;
he glanced nervously at the Englishman, obviously afraid
of being caught at whatever he was doing. What an odd
sight he made. The pen looked ridiculously small in his
hand, his broad back dwarfed the chair so that it looked
as if it had come from a doll's house. He stayed at it for
half an hour or so, then returned the notebook to his
pack. Closing the zipper slowly and quietly, he extinguished
the light and left.

I lay still for a while. I had not heard the click of the
lock. Moved by an invincible curiosity, I crept over to my
pack, got my penlight, opened the compartment to his
pack, and removed the canvas bag. The hasp to the lock
was open: it was difficult to imagine a man as thorough
as Nordstrand overlooking something like that. Feeling like
a burglar, I took out the notebook. His name and the
words "Vol. Eight" had been printed on the buckram
cover. About half its small, ruled pages were filled with a
cramped backhand, and each entry had been dated. The
last was headed "Sept. 21st"—today's date. The rest was
an all but incomprehensible scrawl, a jumble of scribbled
sentence fragments in which I recognized the words "Murrah," "no word yet on shipment," "only a few miles from
where I want to be, on the threshold." The last phrase was
repeated at the end of the passage, printed in capital letters and underlined. "ON THE THRESHOLD." The
preceding entry, dated two days earlier, contained some
musings on Nietzsche that related to his, Nordstrand's,
attitude toward Moody. Some strange idea that they were
by nature antagonistic; therefore, he need make no effort

to get along with the Englishman. Moody represented the Apollonian forces of restraint, harmony, and moderation while he embodied the Dionysian power of the irrational.

Afraid of being caught prying and unable to make much sense out of Nordstrand's scratchings, I put the note-book back. As I fumbled in the bag, I felt another note-book at the bottom, then another, and another. There were eight altogether, all of a set, bound in the same buckram, marked with his name and volume number, and written in the same tight backhand. Paging through them quickly, I noted the dates. There were often gaps of several months between entries, some of which contained the names of the places where they had been made—Cairo, Beirut, Tel Aviv, Saigon. It amazed me to see that the first had been written thirteen years ago in a place called Walton, Minne-sota, presumably Nordstrand's hometown. It began with the phrase, "Have begun this diary because have read I.B.'s and I know now what I must do." This was followed by more illegible scrawl.

A diary. It seemed as incomprehensible as the writing itself. Nordstrand, the wisecracking bully, was the last man I would have expected to maintain a record of his life. It wasn't consonant with his character; it required an introspectiveness I would have thought beyond him. That he had kept one for so long and had brought it all with him, a record going back to when he was seventeen, heightened my surprise. It suggested a perverse fidelity, a warped sense of continuity. The only connection I could make between my own boyhood and the man I had be-come was purely biological; two different personalities united only by a tenancy in the same body. One had moved out when its lease expired and the other moved in. And when I considered all the adolescent memorabilia I had thrown out or had left buried in a trunk in my fam-ily's house—the fragmentary diaries I had kept, love let-ters and poems to girl friends, report cards and letter sweaters—I could not understand why a man of thirty would carry with him an account of what he had done, thought, and experienced as a boy of seventeen. Sentimen-tality? I doubted it. There was not a single cartilage of sentimentality in that mass of hardened tissue. No, it was something else. Nordstrand must have perceived some connection between what he was then, was now, and would become. An idea, an ambition, a desire, something that, like his handwriting, would not change. I was sure of it. A unifying thread bound the first cryptic line—"Have begun this diary because have read I.B.'s and I know now what I must do"—to the last, equally cryptic, "on the threshold."

The urge to read every line and discover the connecting thread was almost irrepressible. The lack of time and the fear of being discovered were all that inhibited me. I did not in the least feel that reading his diary constituted an invasion of privacy. For the few phrases I had been able to make out had found an echo within me, had awakened a sense of a peculiar kinship. It haunted me to read the name of that Minnesota town in the first entry. Like me, Nordstrand came from the upper Middle West, that gloomy land of flat plains and flat pine forests encompassing small farms. Even more haunting was the last phrase of the last entry. It was as though I had written it, for I too saw myself on a threshold, about to embark on a mission of self-rescue. The purpose of Nordstrand's personal mission was different—he was seeking what he called the freedom to be himself—but the emotion implicit in those words was familiar to me: the anticipation of an experience that would profoundly alter the course of one's life.

I browsed through the diaries, picking out a sentence here, a word or two there, until a faint light pressed through the window and the *muezzin* began trilling the call to the prayer before sunrise. Muttering to himself, Abdul stirred in the next room and went outside. Looking through the glassless window, I saw him kneeling in the dust and facing the grey shimmering above the compound's eastern wall. As he bowed low, forehead touching the earth, his *taub* rode up, revealing the full length of the pink, jagged scar on his leg. His prayers done, he put on his sandals and shuffled to the outdoor clay oven. In a few minutes, the smell of baking bread was on the cool, otherwise odorless, air.

Moody lay snoring. His face was placid in sleep, with a suggestion of a benign melancholy in its expression. It

was a romantic, doomed-youth face reminiscent of those
elegiac photographs taken of RAF pilots before they were
shot down in the Battle of Britain. You could picture him
gallantly flying off in his Spitfire to a blazing self-sacrifice,
but he seemed completely unsuited for this clandestine
work. For a moment, I wondered what had driven him
to it, though that wonder was overcome by a greater
curiosity about Nordstrand. I wanted to go on reading,
but heard the author of the diaries huffing and grunting
outside. Responding to his need for physical activity as
automatically as Abdul responded to the call of the
muezzin, Nordstrand did calisthenics every morning. He
started them the moment he woke up. He never lolled
through a drowsy interlude between sleep and full consciousness, but opened his eyes and instantly began pumping out push-ups, sit-ups, and deep knee bends. Even
with him awake, I felt a strong aversion to replacing the
diaries. I was sure I would never get another chance to
read them. Nordstrand was unlikely to commit the same
oversight twice—if his leaving the lock open had been an
oversight. The thought had occurred to me that he had
known I was awake and had deliberately not closed the
lock because there was something in those books he wanted
me to see.

Reluctantly, I put them back, got my shaving tackle,
and went to the well. Smiling in his feeble way, Abdul
said, *"Buongiorno."* He was heaping round, wafer-thin
loaves on a platter while tea brewed on the fire. I lowered
the goatskin bucket into the well, filled it with the warm,
iron-colored water, and began to shave in the polished
tinplate I used for a mirror.

"This water is bad," the old man said. again in Italian.
"Don't drink it."

"You told me it was pure, like the water in the mountains."

"I could not have said that. This is the water of the
flatlands, and the water of the flatlands is never good.
Only the water of the mountains is good. It makes a man
strong. This weakens him. It's woman's water."

"I see."

"My village was in the mountains."

"I know."

"The Ethiopians destroyed it."

"Yes, I know."

"Everyone thinks I don't remember how the soldiers destroyed it, but I remember, as I remember how the water was there."

"I understand."

He piled some eggs and a bowl of *homus* onto a platter with the bread and tea. Starting toward the house, he said over his shoulder: "Don't drink that water. It will make a woman of you."

"I won't drink it."

Looking at the lame figure clad in white, I tried to imagine what it had been like that day in the mosque. Machine-gunning defenseless civilians in a mosque, a typical episode of the epoch. Our own dear murderous twentieth century.

Nordstrand had meanwhile begun the karate katas that he had restored to his exercise routine after our arrival in the compound—there had not been enough room to do them in the hotel in Khartoum. He performed ritualized workouts twice a day with total concentration and self-containment, with devotion, I would say. He was stripped to the waist; sweat varnished his skin, and I could see the mark left on his upper arm by a shrapnel wound he had suffered in Vietnam, a long, dark, crooked line which from a distance looked like the tattoo of a serpent. He made an impressive sight, leaping, lunging, and twirling, throwing frontkicks and spinning backkicks, thrusts, jabs, and blocks; a fluid, graceful, lethal ballet. The martial art Nordstrand practiced was called Hwrang-Do. It was, he'd told me a few days earlier, the art of the "total" warrior. Its ultimate objective (Nordstrand enjoyed using words like *total* and *ultimate*) was the attainment of a spiritual state called *ki*, in which a man could accomplish remarkable feats of strength and have the power to control other men's minds. I had thought that so much mystical nonsense, but now, watching him, I was inclined to believe there might be something to it. I am not saying my mind had fallen under his control, but an unmistakable aura

surrounded him as his arms snapped mock blows, any one
of which could have shattered a man's skull, and his legs
lashed out in kicks reaching higher than his head. It was
an aura of dominion. The singleness of purpose in the
movements was matched by the unequivocal expression
in his eyes. He looked as though he were actually fighting
someone, not sparring with thin air, and the eyes told the
imaginary opponent, "I mean to kill you," and there was
a kind of splendor in that extraordinary union of brute
force, grace, and will.

Moody and I had breakfast on the thatch-roofed porch,
serenaded by cooing pigeons whose droppings splashed
uncomfortably near our plates. Digging into his duffel
bag, the Englishman added a tin of corned-beef hash to
the bread and eggs. He urged me to eat some as well. It
would help maintain my protein level. Lack of protein
was the cause of the tuberculosis that ravaged the nomads.
This bit of dietary advice and the somewhat prissy way
he ate got on my nerves for some reason. Maybe it was
the heat, the uncertain waiting, and the vicious flies, which,
half-starved on the pristine desert, swooped at our food
with ravenous whines. Nordstrand joined us after his
workout. Though he was as lathered as an overworked
horse, he permitted himself only one cup of tea and half
a cup of water. Like his sleeping on the bare ground, this
abstemiousness was part of his effort to discipline himself
for the ordeal ahead. Sitting on the bench, he looked at
Moody's tin in the morally superior way of a fasting
ascetic looking at the scraps left by a glutton. I waited for
him to make some sarcastic comment, but the violent
exercise appeared to have quieted his belligerence. He rose,
went into the room, and came out with a paperback copy
of *Beyond Good and Evil*. Nordstrand meditated over the
book for an hour or two each day, with the same self-
contained air as when he practiced the deadly choreog-
raphy of Hwrang-Do. He allowed nothing to disturb him.
If you spoke to him, he pretended not to hear.

Leaving him to his studies of the high priest of heroes,
Moody and I, like prisoners in a yard, paced around the
compound and waited for the day's word from Colfax.

Abdul hoed his garden. The sun mounted, each degree of its ascent accompanied by what felt like a ten-degree leap in temperature.

Murrah appeared, his mood again antagonistic. Moody, trying to soothe him, apologized for Nordstrand's remarks —a little too profusely, I thought. He had something of the modern European's oversensitivity to Africans and Asians, a heightened tenderness that was a reaction to the cruelties Europe had inflicted in the past, and in its own way just as dehumanizing. His act of contrition had no effect on Murrah. The latter maintained an attitude of studied indifference. I tend to think he enjoyed hearing a white man singing a litany of regrets, and hoped his demeanor would elicit more of that unfamiliar but pleasant music.

He expressed less contrived emotions after Colfax's message came through. It said repairs on the freighter would delay the shipment at least two more weeks, and instructed us to cross the border that night, move on to Jima's camp, explain the situation to him, and wait for word as to when and where the arms would be delivered.

"What the hell kind of marching orders are those?" Moody asked rhetorically. "We can't go trooping up there empty-handed."

He sent a reply to that effect. The Cobra answered:

Proceed as instructed. Have faith. Send no further transmissions until this time tomorrow.

Moody shredded the message.

" 'Have faith.' Not much cause for faith so far. You'd think the USA could find itself a seaworthy ship." He folded the antenna, unplugged the power pack, snapped the case shut, and half carried, half dragged the transceiver across the floor, setting it beside his lumpy duffel bag. " 'Have faith.' He's sitting in bloody Cairo, we've got to muck it across a desert and somehow explain to the old man of the mountain that all he's getting for the time being is our three warm bodies, and Colfax tells us to have faith. What an ass."

Murrah, who had no faith whatsoever, had meanwhile

fallen into another fit of paranoia. Having been schooled in a doctrine which taught that nothing occurred but by man's design, he could not accept the pure happenstance of a ship's engines breaking down. Once more, he began to rave about plots. He raved about what he would do with the trucks he'd hired. Moody begged him to be reasonable, and asked him to get hold of Suleiman and tell him to pick us up for the drive to the border. There was nothing else for it. Murrah refused. He would not allow us to set one foot in Bejaya until the arms arrived.

"Keep your head about this, Kasu. We've got our orders. We must cross tonight, so get hold of Suleiman and tell him to be here as soon as it's dark."

"No. *You* call your boss on that wonderful radio of yours and tell him you are not being permitted to cross until the arms are here."

"He's instructed me to maintain radio silence until tomorrow."

"Then wait until tomorrow."

"Look, I should think Jima's the one who has the say about the conditions under which we'll be permitted to cross."

"You don't understand. Jima has already had his say. From the beginning, he thought something like this might happen."

"I guess we don't understand."

"Jima is a strange man. A suspicious man. I think he's not well in the head."

"And what has his mental condition to do with all this?"

Murrah, moderating his strident tone, then unveiled his surprise.

"Jima was always a little suspicious about your boss. He thinks there is a chance your boss is working with the Zionists. He issued orders to the rendezvous party who are to meet you at the border that if you come without the weapons promised, you are also to be considered Zionist spies and made hostages."

"You can't be serious."

"I am. So is Jima. You will be made hostages. The ransom will be the weapons promised. So if you cross tonight, you will not have to play at being prisoners, gentlemen."

"I can't believe that. It's absolutely irrational. Zionist spies, for God's sake."

"Jima believes he is a target of the Zionists."

"I can't accept this. This is completely—"

"Then don't accept it, Mr. Patrick. Cross the border tonight. Then you will have to accept it. I think it will be better for you if you stay here."

"And just why are you doing us the favor?"

"Because I don't think we'll ever get the weapons if you're held hostage. And we need the weapons."

"Oh? I thought only the quality of the men counted."

"That is just a saying."

"Kasu, it simply isn't feasible for us to stay cooped in here for another two weeks."

"Are the accommodations unsuitable, Mr. Patrick? You would prefer something more comfortable?"

Nordstrand intervened then. He shouldered Moody aside and cracked Murrah across the face with the back of his hand, knocking the small man against the wall. Murrah slid to the floor, blood trickling from his nostrils, over his upper lip, and down the row of his protruding, tobacco-yellowed teeth.

"Nordstrand! For God's sake!"

He turned on Moody savagely. "You say one word about how to treat this little bastard and I'll break your fucking neck, weak sister."

Then to Murrah: "Now, what's this about not letting us cross?"

The Bejayan looked up, and the way he grimaced when the blood dripped onto his tongue told me its salty taste was new to him. He had probably never been hit before. He certainly had never been hit like that.

"*Get up,*" Nordstrand said, implying another, harder slap if he wasn't obeyed.

Murrah stood unsteadily. No anger, no hurt, no fear showed in his eyes, only a stunned look rather like that of a man who has run into a lamppost. He wiped his nose with his fingers.

"Are you ready to listen to us now?"

"What is it?" The Bejayan held his hand to his nose and tilted his head backward.

"Are you ready to listen?"

Suddenly Murrah started gagging. Moody said he would not be a party to this "revolting exhibition" and stalked out.

"Kasu," Nordstrand said with a mocking kindliness, "by holding your head back, you're forcing the blood to run into your throat. Bring your head forward a little, let the blood flow out of your nose. It'll clot in no time at all. Did you understand that?"

Nodding, Murrah leaned his head forward, pink and scarlet leaking between his fingers.

"One more time. Are you ready to listen to us?"

Murrah nodded again.

"That's better. We want you to contact Suleiman and tell him to be here at nightfall, ready to take us across. That's all we want you to do. You can do that, can't you?"

"Yes."

The initial shock had worn off. Murrah was looking at the American with a sullen submission, with a mixture of obedience and defiance that disquieted. It promised he would not forget this humiliation. Nordstrand sensed it too.

"Listen, Murrah. After we're across, you might feel more confident with all your friends around. You might encourage them to go ahead with this cockeyed plan to hold us hostage. You just might do that, so let me ask you a question. Did that hurt?"

Murrah said nothing.

"Did that hurt, Mr. Kasu?"

"Of course it did."

"Then think about this. We have a blow in the martial arts which is delivered with the heel of the hand against the bridge of the opponent's nose. Like this."

The fingers of his right hand bent like talons, his arm shot forward. With perfect control, he stopped the blow a fraction of an inch short of the Bejayan's face. Nordstrand smiled when Murrah jerked his head back.

"No need to be scared. I was just demonstrating. If I wasn't demonstrating, I would have driven your nose through the base of your skull and into your brain, like a nail. Instant cerebral hemorrhage. You would have been dead before you hit the floor."

His green eyes flicking coyly, Nordstrand handed Murrah a handkerchief. The Bejayan pressed it to his nose and, sounding like a man with a cold, said:

"And what will you do tonight? The men in the rendezvous party, they're all armed."

"You said it. It's not the quality of the weapon, it's the quality of the man."

Murrah held out the blood-soaked handkerchief. It was the blood of a warrior tribe that had never been subjugated, and he looked at Nordstrand levelly.

"This is yours, Mr. Jeremy."

"Keep it."

"I don't need it."

He let it slip to the floor, then walked out, leaving a faint trail of red on the dirt floor.

Moody reentered the room a few minutes later. Without speaking, but radiating disgust over what had happened, he began to roll up his sleeping bag.

"Well, General, now I suppose you're going to give me a lecture on how to treat the wogs."

"You seem to have a psychological need for confrontation."

"I get it. No lecture. Analysis instead. Proceed, Herr Doctor."

"No lecture. No analysis. Just a bit of advice. If this Zionist spy madness turns out to be true and we have any problems, I will handle them. Do you understand? I will handle them. We won't be dealing with any educated Murrahs, but some very tough, very unsophisticated tribesmen. You start trying to bash in noses, and you'll get us all shot."

"I got the job done."

"That's indisputable."

"I get things done."

"Just what was all that? The first lesson in the reeducation of Kasu Murrah?"

"If he's a receptive student, the first and the last."

"I saw him when he left. He didn't appear all that receptive. I've the feeling he isn't quite the pushover you think he is."

"I relish challenges. Resistance tones the muscles."

"I couldn't help overhearing you. That business about killing a man by hammering his nose into his brain. I believe you're capable of something like that."

"I'm happy to hear that, Moody. Belief is one of the noblest of human emotions."

"And because I believe it, I'm going to hold you in check, even if I have to do it at the point of a gun. You're not in the schoolyard anymore."

"And you don't have a gun."

———

In the darkness before moonrise, the face of the desert was a cadaverous grey pocked by the black clumps of thorn bushes and acacia thickets. The truck's headlights gave to the trees and brush bunched by the roadside an unnatural color that made them look like plastic vegetation; and that artificial appearance reinforced the impression, given by the barren reaches of sandy gravel separating the islands of sparse greenery, that nature never wanted anything to grow in that dead land. Occasionally, reflecting the headlights, the minerals embedded in the rocks strewn across the road shone with an adamantine glitter. Suleiman, with Murrah in the cab beside him and the three of us riding in the back, drove slowly, keeping the headlights on the road. It was not a true road, but a camel track, a narrow, shallow depression worn into the desert by the passage of caravans, and Suleiman followed it with the caution of a ship's pilot navigating a tight, dangerous channel. There were no reference points out there; if he deviated even a short distance from the trail, he would lose it and have little chance of finding it again. Other tracks, dozens of them, crisscrossed the desert, and we could not tell one from the other. They wound in every direction, meandering into oblivion. The sole landmarks were the pilaster-shaped buttes in the distance, and even those made unreliable guideposts at night. We could mark their position only by the absence of the stars whose light they effaced;

and if we looked at them long enough, the dark blots they made against the sky would shimmy and waver until we weren't sure if we were looking at solid objects or at some kind of enormous night mirage. A jackal cried dismally.

As we jounced across the flat and featureless desert, I felt as I had the first time in Bejaya: like a castaway aboard a rocking boat upon an arid sea.

Seeking a fixed beacon to guide on, I gazed up to look for the Southern Cross among stars so numerous they spread as a white dust across the sky. I found the constellation, and the sight of it comforted me. It was familiar. I had lived under it most of my adult life—in Indochina and in parts of the Middle East and North Africa. I had seen thousands die, cities fall, and governments collapse beneath it, but the constellation always appeared at its appointed place in the heavens, its cold white crucifix offering no consolation save the proof that all of man's wars, his great conquests and tragic defeats, had not the slightest effect on the order of the universe.

These cosmological reflections were interrupted when the truck hit a rock and gave us a particularly hard jolt.

"Rotten ride," said Moody, looking at the rooster-tails of dust whirling behind. "Feels like it's going to knock the teeth out of my head."

"It will seem cushy enough when we start humping it on foot, maybe as real hostages."

"I suppose, Gage. Yes, I suppose it'll seem cushy then."

Moody fingered the amulet Abdul had placed around his neck before we left; he had presented it to the Englishman, murmuring the Arabic farewell, *Allah yisal'limak*— God save you. It was a cylindrical leather bag, attached to a leather thong and filled with what looked like either crushed stone or fragments of bone.

"Odd, his giving me this," Moody said. "It's supposed to protect one against the devil. They still believe in that in these parts, spirit-possession I mean. The Moslems wear charms to ward off Christian spirits, the Christians to ward off Moslem spirits, Moslems and Christians both to protect them from pagan spirits. And since the whole lot believe in one sort of demon or other, they've all got charms against the devil."

"We haven't been in the bush half an hour and Moody's already going over the edge."

"I forgot, Nordstrand. You're a fan of Nietzsche, the man who wrote God's obituary. God is dead and all that. And I suppose if God's dead, so is the devil."

"Half an hour in the bush and you've got religion."

"Awfully odd, Abdul's giving me this."

"What's so odd about it?"

"I meant it was odd what he said after he gave it to me and Murrah laid into him. You didn't pick up on it because they were speaking in dialect. Murrah screeched at the old man, told him he was weak-minded, a fool, and that there weren't any devils. Abdul put his hand against his chest and said, 'There are. In here.' Odd, that."

"Why's that so odd? What's with all these oddities, Moody?"

"I thought it a lucid comment for a madman, for one thing. The devil's in a man's heart. For another, it seemed to me Murrah protested a bit much. As if he believes in devils, or half believes in them, but is afraid to admit it."

"He probably does. You can take the boy out of the bush, but you can't take the bush out of the boy."

"Put with your usual crudity, Nordstrand."

They stopped speaking, and the silence of the desert closed in around us again, the awful, absolute silence that was interrupted only by the jackals' cries. There is no more dismaying sound on earth, or off it for that matter, than the howl of those wild, carrion-eating dogs.

We went on down the sinuous track, bouncing over gullies, skirting ravines, plowing across wadis where the sand lay as thick and fine as beach sand. At an undefined distance ahead, desert and sky were bonded by a band whose blackness, as total as the blackness of outer space, inclined you to believe the earth was flat after all and to feel you were approaching its edge. Once in a while, we passed the fires of nomads encamped a short distance off the trail, large fires that kept hyenas from attacking the hobbled camels and which revealed the outlines of goatskin tents and the figures of the tribesmen, lounging against their saddles. The children of the desert—men who did not fight it or seek to conquer it, but who had made their terms and lived in harmony with it. They built no cities, no highways or railroads; they did not plow fields, or erect monuments to their dead. They buried their dead as prescribed by the Koran: in unmarked graves. One generation after another was born, spent its years wandering in search of water and grass, then died, leaving no sign or record of its time on earth except caravan trails and the ashes of campfires which the winds soon scattered.

The truck banged and jounced over the emptiness for perhaps another hour. We drew closer to the giant rocks, then passed them and went rolling over a plain that resembled the bottom of a vast gravel pit. A jaundiced moon rose, gradually whitening as it climbed. We could see the tops of the acacia by its light, perfectly flat, as if they had been meticulously pruned.

The trail passed between two large boulders. A short distance farther on, a barricade of palm logs and brush lay across our path. Suleiman slammed on the brakes, throwing us forward, and two men popped up from behind the obstacle, stepped out of the headlights' glare, and stood pointing their Enfields at the truck. One said something in dialect; Suleiman switched off the lights. Murrah climbed out of the cab. He called to the two men who, now only half-visible forms, approached cautiously, their carbines leveled. Then, identifying him, they lowered their weapons and embraced him.

The greetings over, Murrah ordered Suleiman to flash the lights twice. This Suleiman did. Another pair of lights winked in the darkness a few hundred yards ahead. An engine sputtered to life and a large truck rattled toward us. It was a captured Ethiopian army truck. A half-dozen guerillas were sitting in the back.

Murrah came round to the rear of our pickup and opened the tailgate.

"Please come down, gentlemen."

"Can I assume we are finally in Bejaya?" Moody asked

"You have been for the past half an hour."

We climbed down and unloaded our gear. My breath

caught in my throat and I flinched when one of the rebels, from behind the barricade, fired a couple of rounds into the windshield. He laughed derisively. The other guerrilla smacked Suleiman on the side of the face with the flat of his rifle butt, Suleiman staggering sideways, his knees buckling.

"Ai! Ai!" he cried, cradling his jaw in both hands. "Ai! Kasu, this is too much authenticity. He's broken my head."

Laughing—the first time I had seen him laugh—Murrah clapped a hand on the driver's shoulder.

"Ya Suleiman! You've been ambushed. Three men have been captured. You can't return to Nassala looking as if you've been to a party."

"Altogether too authentic," Suleiman repeated. "He's broken my head."

"Your head was broken from birth," said the man who had struck him, a thickset man with a broad face.

"You play your part too well, you, whoever you are."

"Osman ibn Rahmān."

"Ibn Rahmān? 'The son of the merciful'? How were you ever given such a name?"

"Why, because my father was Rahmān. Why else would I be called the son of Rahmān if Rahmān were not my father?"

"Your father was a goat. Your mother laid with a he-goat and you were the issue. You are Osman the goat's son."

"Any more of that, and I'll give you another, more authentic than the first."

"Ya Osman, you son of a goat," shouted one of the rebels in the truck. "Give it to him anyway."

The others exploded with laughter, the kind that comes from men who seldom find anything to laugh about, with an edge of cruelty in it, the laughter of war.

Convinced of the authenticity of Osman's threat, Suleiman made no more insults. Cupping a hand over his jaw, he extended the other and shook hands with each of us, saying, *"Allah yisal'limak."* I thought it a decent gesture, and feeling a bit sorry for him, apologized for the trouble we had put him through.

"It's nothing," he replied in English. "I'm a free-lance

man, like you, and this is part of the game. Again, *Allah yisal'limak.*"

"*Allah yihfazak,*" I said. "God keep you."

He climbed into the cab and drove off. The pickup's taillights soon shrunk to a pair of red pinpoints, then vanished altogether. The sound of the engine diminished until all we heard was the wind, rasping like a prolonged death rattle through the dry branches of the acacia.

At the end of our training in the paratroops, we were taken up for the first of the five jumps we had to complete to earn our wings. Each soldier leapt with the conviction he would be a different, better, man once his boots touched the earth again. He would be a man who had triumphed over his fears, and the prize of that conquest would be a greater sense of self-esteem and self-possession. When I heard Suleiman's parting words and watched him drive off, I felt a measure of the emotions I had felt before making that baptismal lunge into space: a sense of irrevocability mingled with hope. Now, the only way to go back was to go forward. I saw the ordeal ahead as a test, like the jumps we had to make.

The ordeal began immediately. The guerrillas' mood turned ugly when they learned about the arms shipment. An argument broke out between them and Murrah, the former talking all at once in the fluty voices of men raised in the highlands, the latter's voice rising to a shriek as he tried to make himself heard above their clamor. They argued for a quarter of an hour. Because they were speaking in dialect, neither Nordstrand nor I understood a word.

"All right, Moody. Colfax hired you on because you understand that gibberish," Nordstrand said. "It's time to earn your pay. What're they saying?"

"It's not gibberish. It's a Beja language called To-Bedawyi. And Colfax didn't hire me on just because I understand it."

"What're they saying, Moody?"

"In sum, Murrah wasn't bluffing about Jima's orders. It seems the stocky fellow, the one called Osman, intends to hold us for ransom, the ransom being the weapons. Murrah's told him that if he does that, the Americans will react by not sending any arms. This Osman chap said he realized that, but he has his orders and orders are orders. His mates in the truck agree with him."

"What about Murrah?"

"Told you. He's pleading our case. It appears he's convinced Osman to talk the problem over with us. I suppose it gratifies you that Murrah's taken our side."

"General, you're gratified only when a hope is fulfilled. I never hoped that little bastard would learn his lesson. I knew he would."

"I wouldn't go into a victory dance, Nordstrand. The only reason he's backing us is because he thinks that's the best way to get the guns. And I still don't think he's a pushover."

"Like I said, I relish challenges."

"And here comes one."

Murrah and Osman, his thick chest stuck out aggressively, walked up to us. Osman was well into middle age, the grey in his knotty hair thick enough to see even in the dark. Fine, deep lines crosshatched his face, and he had an air of authority combined with a certain tiredness. He reminded me of a veteran top sergeant who could still exercise command but who had lost his zest for it and was thinking of retirement and a pension. But there was no retirement or pension in his army and no discharge in his war. He looked us over for a moment or two, then tested our handshakes to see whose was the strongest.

"You must be the head," he said to Nordstrand in a British-accented English and with a faint note of deference in his voice.

"No, he is," Murrah corrected, pointing at Moody. "Mr. Patrick."

Osman looked puzzled for a moment, then: "You will please come with me, Mr. Patrick."

"Tell him we all settle this together, Moody."

"Sorry, Nordstrand. This matter requires a bit of tact, not threats about smashing noses."

"You will come with me, please. You two sit down and stay here."

Osman, leading Moody to the truck, snapped an order to his men, who piled off and surrounded Nordstrand and me. All wore motley uniforms, carried rifles from a number of different countries, and had broad-bladed knives in hide scabbards hanging from their cartridge belts. Four V-shaped scars, like sergeant's stripes, were branded on their faces—the Beni-Hamid's tribal markings. The scars, the rebels' ragged dress, and the long knives gave them a savage appearance I would have found colorful if, say, I had been a photographer for *National Geographic*. We sat on our packs beneath their watchful eyes. None looked much older than nineteen or twenty, and I was uncomfortably conscious of a youthful restlessness in them, an eagerness for violence. One, in a playful mood, squatted and tapped me on the shoulder with a long, heavy herdsman's stick he was carrying.

In Arabic, he said that he found us rather useless: we were gunrunners without guns.

I stayed quiet, looking at the truck beside which Murrah, Osman, and Moody sat palavering. The wind rasped ceaselessly through the trees, carrying the notes of a jackal yipping far off.

"You, did you hear me?" the guerrilla asked. "No weapons. Why are there no weapons?"

"That's being discussed with that man over there. Osman."

"Where did you learn to speak Arabic so well?"

"At mission school," I said in English.

"Eh?"

"In school."

He tapped me on the shoulder again, a little harder than the first time. A smile of incipient madness cracked across his face.

"Are you Zionist spies?"

"Don't be silly."

"Jima says we Moslems have two enemies, the Communists and the Zionists." The rebel soldier duck-walked closer to me, resting the stick on my shoulder and rubbing it against my neck. "Jima says the Israelis help to train the Ethiopians. Did you know that?"

"Not any more, not since the Russians moved in."

"No! The Israelis are still there. And also the Russians. They're working together. Jima says this proves the Communists and the Jews are making the conspiracy against the Moslems in Bejaya."

"Do you believe everything Jima tells you?"

"Jima is a great man. Before we left our base, he told us that the three *ferengei* are not Communists because they are Americans, but they could be Zionists because it is well known the Americans support the Zionists. If the three *ferengei* come without the weapons promised to us, it will be a sign they are Zionist spies."

I looked away from his crazy grinning face and up at the frozen moon and the Southern Cross.

"I myself doubted this until just a short time ago. Then I saw you behave nervously when the rifle was fired. 'If this man is our friend, why does he jump at the sound of a gun?' I thought to myself. 'And why is he afraid?' Again, I answered myself, 'Because maybe he is a spy.' When Kasu told us you did not have the weapons, I was sure of it. I thought to myself, 'It is as Jima says. The three *ferengei* are Zionist spies.' "

"It must have been difficult for you, all that thinking."

"Put your hands behind your head."

"No."

He struck my shoulder a third time, hard enough to make it hurt.

"Behind your heads. Both of you."

Nordstrand said: "If you hit him with that stick once more, I'll make you eat it."

The guerrilla paused to absorb this seemingly empty threat.

"Ya! What's this? Brothers, did you hear? We are six men armed and the large one says he will make me eat this stick."

"We heard," answered one of his comrades. "Perhaps he should to make you still. You talk too much, Yassin."

"Large one, do you think I talk too much?"

"My name isn't 'large one.' "

"And how are you called?"

"Jeremy."

"Jer-ah-mee. I asked you, Mr. Jer-ah-mee, do you think I talk too much?"

"I haven't heard women who talk more."

"You listen to me. I, Zein Yassin, have killed four men, and you say I'm a woman and you'll make me eat this stick?"

"You'll be shitting wood for the next week, Zein Yassin."

The others laughed at this, which moved the young man called Yassin to find some way to save face. He pointed the cudgel at Nordstrand, who grabbed it by the end, effortlessly tore it from the guerrilla's hands, and tossed it a good ten yards with not much more than a flick of his wrist.

"Your supper, Zein Yassin."

Yassin just squatted there, temporarily immobilized by the astonishing ease with which he had been disarmed. To my everlasting relief, Murrah, Osman, and Moody, their negotiations ended, came up to us at that moment. Like a boy caught stealing from the cookie jar, Yassin stood quickly and assumed an innocent air.

"Afraid I've bad news," the Englishman said redundantly: his tone, his rheumy eyes, and his nervous hands, fluttering through his hair, told us he'd gotten nowhere.

"Let's hear it," I said.

"In so many words, we're under arrest. We're to be taken to Jima's base tied up and blindfolded, I'm afraid. This chap Osman is going to send a message stating their demands to their man in Karters and he'll pass it along somehow to Colfax. When the shipment gets to them, we can consider ourselves free men. I tried to persuade him that this is all nonsense. Odd thing is, he agrees with me, but he's the head of the old man's bodyguard. Chief of staff, so to speak, and his orders were to regard us as spies if we showed up empty-handed. A fine balls-up. I guess Jima isn't quite as chummy with the Cobra as we thought."

"Your tact has worked wonders, General."

"My tact, Nordstrand, probably saved us from getting shot. This mob was prepared to do away with us if we acted up."

"No, they weren't."

"Think what you like. It's settled. They're camped just

over there, in the wadi. They've got a supply caravan going up with some ammo they've smuggled in from the
Sudan. We'll be going with it, tonight. Afraid the truck
stays here. One of the few they've got and they need it for
bringing in whatever they get from the Sudan. Which
means we'll be mucking it on camelback."

"Tied up and blindfolded," I said. "Two hundred miles
on camelback tied up and blindfolded."

"Be a rough go, but we can look at it this way—it'll
lend a bit of authenticity to our cover."

"Right," I remarked. "Suleiman can tell you about that.
This mob is big in the authenticity department."

"Khalas, khalas," Murrah interjected. "There's been
enough talk. None of this would have happened if you
listened to me and remained in Nassala. If the weapons
arrive, everything will be all right."

"And just the opposite if they don't."

"That's correct, Mr. Charlie."

"Hands behind your backs," Osman ordered, but there
was a lack of firmness in his reedy mountaineer's voice, a
strangely apologetic tone. Nordstrand, whose antennae
were tuned to pick up signals of weakness, perceived this
irresolution and slowly, pointedly, crossed his hands in
front of him.

"You. I said *behind.* Behind your back."

One of the guerrillas was already cinching my wrists,
tight enough to numb my arms. Beside me, also being tied,
Moody whispered:

"Nordstrand, do what he says. We're not in the schoolyard and these aren't schoolboys."

Nordstrand did not move.

"Ya! You! What's wrong? Don't you understand Arabic?"

"I understand."

"Then put your hands behind your back!"

Nordstrand remained still, hands folded over his groin,
pale hair paler in the moonlight.

"Yassin, Hamad. Put this one's hands behind his back
and tie him up."

"I'll kill the first man who touches me."

The sheer audacity of this statement, its insane sincerity, made Yassin and the other man pause. Yassin, perhaps, was thinking about the ridiculous ease with which the big man had wrenched the stick from his hands. Perhaps he had seen Nordstrand slowly and subtly shift his weight to his left leg and bring his hands to his sides, tucking the thumbs into his palms, bending the fingers at the second joint so that they resembled thick claws. Another change had accompanied the change in physical position: Nordstrand's emotional atoms had undergone some sort of rearrangement and were nearing critical mass. He radiated an inner fire that could be felt but not seen, like the heat from an active volcano just before it erupts.

"You can't behave this way!" Osman exclaimed. "I'll shoot you if I have to."

"No, you won't. Because if anything happens to me or these other men, you'll never get your weapons and you know that."

Osman gestured with his Enfield, and Yassin, standing behind and slightly to the side of Nordstrand, raised his rifle to club the American in the head. But the movement was tentative and halfhearted. Catching it out of the corner of his eye, Nordstrand whirled, letting out a scream. What happened next was as swift as the explosion of a shell and almost as destructive. It was too dark and Nordstrand moved too fast for me to see anything but his legs, feet, and fists smashing with lovely coordination and economy of motion into groins and faces. Yassin, the guerrilla named Hamad, and a third man went down, seemingly all at once. The American grabbed one of their rifles, leaped back, and, crouching, pointed it at the three guerrillas who were still standing. In an ecstatic rage, he bellowed at the top of his lungs:

"The only reason I didn't kill was because he didn't touch me, but *I'll kill all of you if you don't drop those weapons.*"

Like soldiers hit by a surprise attack, the three were utterly bewildered. Everything had happened with such speed that none had had time to unsling a rifle. One made the mistake of trying. Nordstrand lunged and caught him in the jaw with a horizontal buttstroke. The guerrilla's head snapped back, like a dummy's pulled by a string, and he collapsed facedown into the sand. I thought his neck had been broken.

"Drop them, I said, or I'll kill all of you."

The two remaining men were convinced. Their weapons clattered to the earth. Osman could have easily shot Nordstrand at that moment. I was so sure he would that I threw myself down to get out of the line of fire. Lying in the dust with my hands bound behind me, hearing one of the injured men gagging as if he were being strangled, I waited for the crack of Osman's Enfield. It never came. For some reason, he lacked the nerve to pull the trigger.

"Yours, too," Nordstrand said, turning to him. "Put it down."

The older man hesitated.

"Put it down."

Murrah then did something unexpected and puzzling. He took Nordstrand's side.

"Do as he says," he told Osman.

"I can't. Jima's orders were—"

"Jima isn't here. This man is. Do as he says. He's beaten you."

Osman dropped the rifle. Nordstrand ordered the others to move away from their weapons. I heard the scuffle of their sandals against the earth, moans and gasps from the injured men.

"Good! Good, Osman! All of you, good!" Nordstrand hollered suddenly. "This is the second time I've had to use violence today. Why don't people believe what I say? Why, why?" Rolling onto my side, I saw he had turned his face toward the sky. He was howling at the heavens, howling on the empty desert like some crazed prophet. *"Why, why?"* he repeated, dropping again into a crouch and holding the Enfield in the position for assault fire, with the butt jammed in his armpit. "Why do I have to demonstrate?" He lunged at the Bejayans and laughed a lunatic's laugh as two of them recoiled. Yassin, kneeling, began vomiting. "Look! Look what you made me do to this poor boy." The rifle in one hand, he took Yassin by the hair with the other and yanked his head up. A bilious liquid dribbled from the youth's mouth. "Look at him. It's disgusting." He released Yassin and dropped back into his

crouch, grinning, and he seemed so far gone I was sure
he was going to start shooting. But the fit was all theater.
Walking over to me, he grasped the ropes around my
wrists, pulled me to my feet, and winked. Winked and
whispered:

"*L'audace*, Charlie Gage. *Toujours l'audace.* These wogs
believe madmen have special powers."

Yassin retched again, and Osman, his voice more uncertain than ever, asked Nordstrand what he wanted.

"To talk," Nordstrand answered quietly, the swift change
from crazed rage to calm as unsettling as the sudden onset
of rage had been. The rapid shift in mood gave him the
special authority of unpredictability.

"Talk about what?"

"About this business of holding us hostage."

"That's already been talked about."

"The circumstances have changed." Turning, he waved
the rifle at the guerrillas. "All of you, move over there
and sit next to Osman. Go on, *move, move.* I hope you
believe I'll kill the first man who doesn't." The men helped
the casualties to their feet, moved off, and sat down. Nordstrand untied Moody and me, then handed us each a rifle.

"This, my dear General, is what's called negotiating
from a position of strength."

Moody, cradling the rifle in the crook of his elbows,
rubbed his wrists.

"You belong in an asylum, Nordstrand."

"You just watch what this crazy is going to do for you,
Mr. Reasonable." Facing Osman he asked if the older
man was ready to talk.

"You can't do this," Osman protested in the face of
the irrefutable evidence of his senses. He had remained
standing to preserve at least a vestige of dignity. "This
isn't done. Our camp is in the wadi over there, not five
hundred meters away. A number of our men are there.
. . ."

"And what will you do? Call for reinforcements? Five
hundred meters is a long way, and you know I'll shoot
anyone who makes a sound. You do know that, don't you,
Osman ibn Rahmān?"

Osman, folding his thick arms over his chest, did not answer.

"Do I have to make another demonstration?"

"No."

"Then you believe me?"

"Yes."

"So we can talk about this problem?"

"Yes. Yes. Talk. Go ahead. Talk."

Talk he did, eloquently and almost without pause for nearly an hour. He spoke in Arabic, a language that lends itself to eloquence as much as to invective, and his speech was as audacious as his actions had been. He seemed to know instinctively the right things to say, the right emotional buttons to push. He seemed to read their hearts, as if he were one of them.

"Are you fighters," he asked rhetorically, "or mere terrorists who commit kidnappings? Are you warriors and men of honor who extend hospitality to foreign guests, or bandits? We are more than guests. We have been sent, by the will of God, yes, by His will, to fight alongside you. Is this, then, the way to treat brothers-in-arms, to make prisoners of them? It violates all the laws of hospitality. It is an offense against God, who will exact a retribution for it."

The Bejayans' initial reaction was hostile. It was obvious from their stares, stony and vigilant at the same time, that they were waiting for the American to lower his guard and give them a chance to redeem their disgrace. Nordstrand, however, did not relax his guard. He kept the rifle pointed at them, and his eyes never left them, and gradually, the invocations of Allah's name, the appeals to their manly honor and to the nomads' belief in the sacredness of hospitality began to touch them. I don't doubt the change in them was partly caused by the sheer fascination of hearing a foreigner speaking their language so fluently. There was also the language itself, their magnificent Arabic with its hypnotic rhythms. And there was their worship of the heroic and their inbred gravitation toward the strong man. In the end, though, there is no rational explanation for the transformation Nordstrand wrought in them. He simply had a gift. It was the gift of the charlatan, of the cult leader, of the confidence artist, of the magnetic politician. You can call it charisma, or presence, or mystique, or anything you like. By whatever name, it was a personal magic, vouchsafed by his size, his willingness to use his strength, his air of certitude, and above all by his unstable, unpredictable violence. In its way, that violence was as unnerving as madness and as arresting as great beauty, and it was the source of his talent for bending the minds and will of others.

He talked on and on, the rebels' hostility evaporating in the heat of his presence. He knew they were acting on Jima's orders, as he knew Jima was a great man. But even great men made errors in judgment. The arrival of the weapons had been delayed through no fault of our own. As in all things, it had been God's will. *Allhau akhbar*, he said—God is great. The sacred phrase rolled off his tongue as piously as it would off the tongue of a *mullah*. God is great. He had sent us to aid in the fight against the Ethiopians, even though we were not of the faith. Had they never heard of the great English soldier Lawrence? Lawrence had also been an unbeliever, but God had sent him to lead the Arabs in their battle against the Turks. As this Lawrence had been sent, so had he, declared Nordstrand, switching to the singular. He, Mr. Jeremy, had been sent to lead them in their fight against the Ethiopians, and he, Mr. Jeremy, personally guaranteed the weapons would arrive; he, Mr. Jeremy, would stake his life on it; yes, they could shoot him, stab him, hang him if the arms did not arrive, the arms in whose use and maintenance he, Mr. Jeremy, would teach them, God willed it. On and on, constantly appealing to their simple faith, manipulating it, calling on their deity until he began to sound like a messianic preacher and his audience to look like a spellbound congregation. In the end, his sorcery worked; he transmuted their enmity into its opposite. (I except Murrah. Throughout Nordstrand's monologue, he had stood off to one side, coolly detached from the others; it was as though he saw Nordstrand's presence as a physical entity, like a magnetic field one could not step into without being trapped by its force.)

Nordstrand stopped finally, probably out of sheer exhaustion; he had been speaking in a difficult foreign language for close to an hour, an effort that taxed even his energies. Sensing he had a captivated audience, he finished his oration with one of those histrionic gestures so beloved by the men of the desert: he threw the rifle down and declared in a booming voice: "I do not need it any longer. I believe myself to be a guest in the company of honorable men, and no guest need fear for his safety or liberty when among honorable men. All I need is your word. You can consider us prisoners if you wish, but there's no need to tie us. Where could we run to in this desert? I want only your word that we will be allowed to make the journey as free men."

The guerrillas, puzzled and charmed at the same time, gazed at him silently.

"Osman, do I have a word?"

"Ya, Mr. Jer-ah-mee, it isn't a matter for my word. I was ordered by Jima—"

"I think you should do as Mr. Jeremy asks," Murrah interrupted. "Give him your word."

"Eh? Kasu?"

"What he says makes sense. They can't run away. Do as he asks."

"And what of the ransom demand?"

"Don't send it. If we start making demands, we might not receive a single cartridge."

"But Jima—"

"Jima, Jima, Jima. Mr. Jeremy has said it. Even men like Jima make mistakes."

"Who will explain this to Jima?"

"I will."

"And you'll also take the responsibility?"

I very nearly laughed. Osman, who, with his weathered face, makeshift uniform, and crisscrossed leather bandoliers, looked every inch the veteran guerrilla, was passing the buck like some nervous bureaucrat.

"Yes, I'll take the responsibility," Murrah answered.

Osman paused, rubbing his forehead in the manner of a man wrestling with a grave decision. To him it was. His tired, wind-cracked face reflected the war within him, between his fear of Jima and his awe of the improbable Mr. Jeremy. In the end, he decided in favor of the more proximate danger.

"Very well," he said. "I can't allow them to carry weapons. I'll leave it to Jima to decide on that. But they won't be tied. On that they have my word."

I wanted to applaud. I wanted to cheer. I wanted to shout, "Bravo!" I wanted to hug Nordstrand the way you do a running back who has made the winning touchdown. There aren't a handful of men in the world who could have carried off that remarkable performance. I envied his gift and felt my judgment of him vindicated. He would see us through. Carlyle said it long ago: follow the man who can do something. Nordstrand could, and I was ready to follow him anywhere.

He took his moral victory with grace. Looking as smilingly confident as a politician among his constituency, he shook hands with Osman, then with the four men who had been the victims of his violence. He then picked up his pack and the sixty-pound transceiver. The now-chastened Yassin offered to help him. Nordstrand handed him his pack. Yassin, the self-styled bad actor who claimed to have killed four men, slung it over his shoulder and followed the American like a porter.

Murrah watched them. In the darkness, it was difficult to tell if his teeth were bared by their malformation or in a smile of secret satisfaction.

THREE

DRY SEASON

The Wadi's edge teemed with thirsting trees sinking their broad roots to suck what little moisture was held in the earth beneath the dry riverbed. The thick-clustering trees eclipsed the moon. Led by Osman, we stumbled through them as through an unlighted tunnel. A low campfire gleamed nearby. A gust of wind stoked its embers, and the flare gave a mahogany cast to the faces of the rebel soldiers who squatted beside it, sipping tea. I caught the glimmer of other fires, the outlines of bell-shaped shelters camouflaging foxholes, the silhouettes of two guerrillas sitting behind a machine gun. The fecal odor common to all military camps thickened the air. Osman brought us to a palm-frond hut beside the wadi. Moon-bleached, the fine sand in the riverbed looked white as salt.

"You will wait here," Osman said. Apparently to prove he was an honorable man who extended hospitality to guests, he asked if we wanted tea. Moody said we did.

"Yassin. Jib chay."

Yassin scurried off toward one of the campfires.

"So, now I have to explain to the head of the caravan that we won't need all his camels. No weapons, no camels. He brought more than a hundred."

"And I suppose that'll cause more problems," Moody said.

"Problems? Oh no. He won't care as long as he's paid."

Osman trudged out into the riverbed. A short way upstream, or, to be precise, a short way in the direction from which water flowed when it rained—roughly once every three years—a herd of camels knelt, bawling, braying, farting, and making a hollow gurgling noise that sounded like bad plumbing. Parties of guerrillas moved among the forest of oblong heads and curving necks, lashing ammunition crates, goatskin water bags, flour sacks, and other supplies to the animals' backs, the hobbled camels sometimes turning their heads to bite at the men in indignant protest, the men whacking the camels' snouts with herding sticks. The caravaneers, tribesmen who were not part of the rebel army but who provided it with a transport service, sauntered about with an air of proud detachment. They were even more wild looking than the two we had seen in the Sudan, men refined by the desert to an economical leanness, with long hair hanging in thin braids past their shoulders and broadswords slung across their backs. One of these atavisms stood a few yards from us, resting one leg by bracing his foot against the inner thigh of his opposite leg and supporting himself with his spear, driven point-first into the sand. He held a stick in one hand, and, in silhouette, the stick and the spear shaft appeared to grow out of his bony frame. We sat outside the hut, the night earth cool beneath us. I felt the tensions of the past day draining from me and a desire for sleep that was partly overcome by a sense of expectancy roused by the sight of the camels and the lanky caravaneers. On the threshold.

Yassin returned carrying a kettle of tea and a pot of awful-looking, awful-smelling mush. I asked what it was. He said something that sounded like "gargosh" or "gargoosh." It was stale bread, good old-fashioned hardtack, softened in boiling water and seasoned with soggy peppers. Its taste was as unpleasant as its appearance. Moody took a bite, swallowed hard, and pulled a can of pork and beans out of his duffel bag.

"Think I'll stick to this until it's absolutely necessary to eat that."

Nordstrand dipped his fingers into the gruel, wolfed it down, and wiped his mouth with his sleeve in what struck me as a deliberate effort to be as disgusting as possible.

"You aren't going to last," he laughed, shoveling in another mouthful. "What're you going to do if you lose your portable supermarket? Starve?"

"Are you going native already? Is that why you're eating like that?"

"You just aren't going to make it, General. You and your tact."

"I suppose you expect me to give you a cheer for your methods."

"I don't expect anything from you."

Yassin, made docile by Nordstrand's methods, squatted beside us and listened to the exchange without comprehension. Pouring tea into our canteen cups, he said:

"I knew you weren't spies."

"That isn't what you said before."

"Oh, I knew. I was just going along with the orders, Mr. Charlie. We were all angry because you didn't have the weapons. But it is as Mr. Jeremy says, God's will. We are all instruments of God's will."

"Did you hear him? 'It is as Mr. Jeremy says.' "

"I heard. Wouldn't go playing white god quite yet if I were you."

We relaxed for a while, not talking, drinking the tepid tea greedily. Osman came up with a few tribesmen whom he ordered to load our equipment. Moody cautioned them to be careful with the transceiver, and gave explicit instructions as to how they should pack his duffel bag, taking care to secure it in such a way that it would not chafe against the camel's flanks and be torn open. Nodding, the men trundled off with the bulky gear.

A few minutes later, Osman said with great ceremony:

"Gentlemen, prepare yourselves. We're moving."

The laden camels woofed and snorted as the drivers untied their hobbles. The animals heaved themselves to their feet with a powerful, rocking motion, rising first on their forelegs, then the hind. Standing, they had a look of arrogant stupidity, like aristocrats who are the products of too much inbreeding. Leading them by rope halters, the drivers cut them from the rest of the herd, still kneeling,

then cinched the halter of each animal to the harness of
the other, stringing them together nose to tail in a long
line. A squad of guerrillas, rifle slings jiggling, jogged to
the front of the caravan and stood in file behind two Beni-
Hamid guides. Another squad formed the rear guard. Seeing all was ready, Osman called, *"Yallah! Yallah!"* The
guides started off, walking with the easy, loose-limbed
gait of the desert nomad, their spears held horizontally
across their backs. The column followed. The men remaining behind murmured farewells to those departing. The
caravaneers, with clicks of their tongues and swats of their
herding staffs, urged the camels forward. Joining Osman
and Murrah, the three of us marched at the flank. It was
tough going in the wadi's deep soft sand, but the caravan
soon turned, pushed its way through the smudge of trees
on the far bank, climbed a gentle slope, and headed out
across the pavement-like surface of the desert. It went on
without end, gravel and sun-hardened sand, thornbush and
stunted trees, endlessly on beneath a sky dusty with more
stars than most city men see in a lifetime, endless, empty,
and utterly still save for the wind and the occasional,
drawn-out cry of a jackal. The beige camels looked white
in the moonlight, as white as the robes of the caravaneers,
trodding effortlessly alongside. Ahead was the dark mass
of the point squad, slung rifles bobbing in rhythm with
their step, and beyond them, the guides loping along with
their hands hanging over the ends of the spears braced
across their shoulders. The wind blew as steadily as a wind
at sea, and in it the dry branches of the acacia sounded
like rats' claws scratching. The camels snorted once in a
while, or made that hollow belly-rumble; their hooves
crunched in the gravel, their swaying loads creaked. The
sandals of the guerrillas and caravaneers, cut from old
automobile tires, scuffed softly against the rocks. We were
not following any trail that I could see, just plunging into
a void, featureless except for the thorn-bristling branches
of the trees, grey and crooked in the moonlight, shudder-
ing in the wind. Then, as if to defy that intimidating vastness, the drivers took up a lilting caravan song. And how
brave and beautiful their voices sounded, chanting against
the dark emptiness, flinging a song of man into the teeth

of the hissing wind to counterpoint the jackals chorusing over heaps of scavenged bones.

Nordstrand marched as if he were leading a victory parade. His linebacker's legs took long strides, his arms swung vigorously, and beneath his wide-brimmed hat his face was flushed with exuberance.

"By God, I love this. I love it, Charlie Gage." He held his arms out wide, as if he meant to envelop the desolation in a possessive embrace. "This is where I've always wanted to be. This is the place I've been looking for. I can feel it."

He lunged ahead toward the point.

"Ya! Yassin!" he called. "It's me, Mr. Jeremy."

"Ya! Mr. Jer-ah-mee."

Supercharged with a kinetic energy, Nordstrand pirouetted, executed a few frontkicks, and pummeled the air with a flurry of punches.

"O Mr. Jer-ah-mee, you must teach me to fight like that." He flung an arm around the youth. "I already gave you your first lesson." And he laughed loudly.

Moody and I walked at a slower pace, falling behind Osman and Murrah. We had been on the move less than half an hour, and I was already beginning to feel how badly out of condition I had become in Cairo. Despite the cool night air, sweat broke out on my face. My legs were tired, my throat dry. I wanted a drink and a few hours sleep. Moody was in even worse shape, breathing as if he'd run the past couple of miles.

The camels rocked along beneath their creaking baggage. Ungainly in repose, the animals were oddly graceful in motion. Moody stumbled on a rock and cursed. Recovering his balance, he remarked that "our Mr. Jeremy" was in high spirits. I muttered in agreement.

"I hate to admit this, but it was quite remarkable, the way he convinced them. Did you know I used some of the same arguments and didn't get anywhere?"

"I knew you didn't get anywhere."

It was difficult not to feel a measure of contempt for him and his ineffectiveness, that ugly, instinctive contempt we feel toward anyone who has failed.

"I suppose our Mr. Jeremy understands them on an instinctive level. It really was remarkable, what he did, but

I meant what I said. I think the man belongs in an asylum, not out here."

"But he's here."

"Yes. Which means we'll have to find some way to curb him from his tendency to excess."

"What did he do that was so excessive?"

"Compared himself to T. E. Lawrence, for one thing. Said he was sent by God to lead this lot against the Ethiopians, for another. That's egotism gone amuck, Charlie. It also contradicts Colfax's explicit instructions. We're supposed to train these people, not lead them."

Gesturing at the desert, I said: "Right now Colfax seems irrelevant."

"Maybe he is. The mission isn't. One is given a mission to perform, one performs it. We've got to have some standard to go by in a place like this, and the mission is it. I have the impression Nordstrand's got an expanded notion of what the mission is and I think he fancies himself taking over."

"From you."

"That and more. I don't think that business of comparing himself to Lawrence was a rhetorical flourish. I think he was dead serious about it. I think he fancies himself playing Lawrence to Jima—you know, a sort of adviser and chief of staff. Rather think he could pull it off, too. The man has some kind of . . . of . . . oh, I don't know what to call it."

"Gift?"

"That's as good a word as any. Yes, a gift. It's like a talent for painting or whatever. Inexplicable. Knew a chap like that when I was in Oman. British mercenary. Commanded one of the Sultan's battalions during the rebellion there. Ruthless bastard. Had the morals of an East End skull-basher, but those Arabs loved him. He had the gift. Should think Lawrence did as well. And Gordon when he was in China. . . ."

"Gordon's one of Nordstrand's heroes, you know."

"I guessed as much. Gordon was another egomaniac with that odd gift of just dropping in on some foreign country and somehow winning the confidence of soldiers from another race and religion and culture. I rather think that's what Mr. Jeremy has in mind."

I rather think. I should think. Really. Quite. Fancies. Chap.

The hard walking had made me short-tempered. I did not feel like talking, and Moody's British English scratched my nerves.

"What do you think, Charlie?"

"I don't know."

Moody removed his hat, wiped the sweatband with his finger, combed his hair with his hand, and jammed the hat back on. He took the talisman from beneath his shirt and glanced at it briefly.

"What do you make of Murrah taking Nordstrand's side all of a sudden?"

"Don't know what to make of it."

"Awfully puzzling, that."

Aw-flay.

"What's so puzzling about it? You said it yourself. Murrah wants the guns. He knew they'd never get them if they went through with that screwball plan to hold us. So he backed Nordstrand up."

"Yes, yes. That was part of it. But there was something more to it. I had the impression that Murrah was encouraging our big friend to play Nordstrand of Arabia. Not in character."

"Maybe Murrah was thinking about that bloody nose Nordstrand gave him."

"Maybe, but I doubt it. I rather think Murrah is not the sort to be intimidated by a smack in the nose. Wouldn't you say, Charlie?"

"Just don't know."

"Oh balls, Charlie. Bloody balls. Is that all you can say? 'Just don't know.' Can't you just once give a categorical yes or no?"

Bawls. Blud-day bawls.

"No. That categorical enough for you?"

"That isn't the sort of categorical I had in mind, actually."

Ek-shulay.

We tramped all that night, laid up in an overgrown wadi
at dawn, rested there for the day, though the heat made
sleep impossible, struck camp at dusk, and trudged on for
a second night, and a third, and a fourth. The homicidal
sun and the manmade murder of the Ethiopian air force
made marching at night a necessity. Led by the two stringy-
muscled guides, who could have hiked across the Sahara
on a cupful of water a day, we walked until I felt half-mad
from walking. Because of the darkness and because the
baggage camels were sluggish, sometimes balky animals,
we counted ourselves lucky to cover more than twenty
miles in a march. The slow pace nipped at everyone's
temper. "I hate escorting these supply caravans," Osman
grumbled one night. "On a mission once we made forty
kilometers, attacked a police barracks, killed every bastard
in it, and marched back again—in one night and half a
day. But with these damned camels, it's slowly, slowly,
slowly, always slowly. Damn them." And to vent his
frustrations, he smacked the haunches of the lead animal
with his rifle butt, shouting, "Hey-ya! *Imshi! Imshi!* You
galled bitch!" The whack spurred her into trotting a few
yards; then she fell back into her plodding gait.

The landscape was as monotonous as despair. It was no
picturesque desert full of scenic fantasies, but infinite
reaches of thornbush savanna, sand, and rock; rock that
had been pulverized into sand by eons of wind, sand hardened by eons of sun back into rock; a bare land that had
never known, and never would know, the ancient rhythms
of the fertile regions, the hope of seedtime, the fulfillment
of harvest. Night made it worse: we could not see the shifts
in color of the desert floor, and everything looked as
achromatic as the surface of the moon. By the fourth
night, my desires had reduced themselves to the basics. I
wanted a drink of the pure mountain water crazy Abdul
had talked about and a few hours' solid sleep. The guerrillas had begun to mumble something about the gardens
of the Balaka—the oasis on the Wadi Balaka near Adi
Abbas, the district capital of western Bejaya. The gardens

were not far, the rebels said. And in the gardens there were an artesian well, groves of date palm, banana plantations, fields of corn, of peppers, of tomatoes. I did not believe it. It sounded like a tribal legend to me, a mythological paradise. I could not imagine anything flourishing in that blasted desolation except thornbush and gnarled acacia. An artesian well. I pictured a pool of clear, crackling cold water. No, it couldn't be. Ever since arriving in Nassala, we had been drinking the putrid stuff from desert wells, which were holes dug in the wadis. Dug deep, too, because drought had diminished the level of ground water. Thirty, thirty-five, forty feet or more the holes went down, as black as the night and looking as if they plunged straight to the core of the earth. A goatskin bucket would be lowered down with a rope, then hauled up distended by a goo as brown as strong tea, and damn near as hot, gritty with sand and stinking so much of sulfur you thought it had come from the rivers of hell. A palmful was all each of us got. The water stank, but it was life itself to the nomads whose tents always clustered near the wells. The headmen shared the water with us only because we had them outgunned, though they pretended their generosity arose from loyalty to the *jebha,* as the insurgents were called in dialect. A palmful of water, and then it was "*Yalla, yalla,*" and the caravan started off for the next well, which might be twenty-five miles off. Ah, but in the gardens, Mr. Charlie, in the gardens of Balaka the artesian water flowed constantly from a pipe. *Aiwa!* From a pipe. And a man could drink all he wanted because the gardens were once plantations owned by Italians who had left because of the fighting, and now everything in the plantations had been taken in the name of the revolution and was for everyone. Pure water. Bananas. Dates. Tomatoes. I added bananas, dates, and tomatoes to my fantasy of pristine water. For our diet was no less dreary than the landscape: always the same stale bread, or a porridge called *bosh-bosh,* which had an orange-ish color and the consistency of overcooked oatmeal. Moody threw it up one night. The camel drivers had followed his packing instructions so thoroughly that he could not get at his duffel bag; it was buried beneath a mound of other supplies and so wrapped up with ropes it looked like a Chinese puzzle. So he had to settle for whatever the caravaneers dished up. We had finished eating our *bosh-bosh* ration, had slogged a few miles, and were forced to stop in yet another wadi when the loads on the last three camels broke loose. I have been in some miserable places in my time, but that nameless spot was one of the worst. For some reason having to do with desert hydrology, the ground was marshy there. A layer of dried mud, suncracked into chunks resembling fragments of broken pottery, covered the surface of the riverbed. Underneath, it was all spongy slime. Waiting for the drivers to repack the loads, we sunk past our ankles in the muck, raising foul marsh gases and clouds of mosquitoes. Mosquitoes on the desert. It was no easy thing, being a mosquito on a desert, and the arrival of thirty men and twenty camels drove the insects into a feeding frenzy. Singing vampiral arias, they attacked and bit savagely, and no amount of frantic arm-waving could keep them off. Moody reminded me of another menace, the silent menace of the disease-causing snails that were doubtlessly crawling through the mud in which we stood. "Good God, Osman, can't you tell those drivers to get a move on," he said desperately. "This is unbearable." Osman advised him to be patient. A few minutes later, Moody doubled over and started vomiting. The guerrillas paid no attention to him. After all, they had seen whole villages annihilated by disease. His belly emptied, Moody fell to his knees and dry-heaved. I helped him to his feet. Murrah was moved to ask if he was sick. "What does it look like? Of course I'm sick. Eating that stinking slop of yours, who wouldn't get sick?" I pressed my palm against his forehead. He was on fire. Pulling my hand away, he stumbled in the mire on wobbly legs. The mosquitoes keened and dove on us relentlessly. "Damn you, Murrah. Is that all you've got, that stinking mush? Packed my rations so I can't get at them. Stupid buggers—" The sentence ended in another spasm of bilious retching. Offended, Murrah delivered a lecture, telling Moody that at the height of the drought and famine several years ago, the rebels had been forced to eat the rotten carcasses of livestock that had died of thirst. Who did the

Englishman think he was to make these complaints? It
wasn't their duty to cater to his delicate tastes. "Oh, bugger
off, Murrah. Bugger off to hell, you little bastard." I explained to Murrah that Moody was a bit delirious from
fever and hadn't meant what he'd said. "I'm not delirious
and I meant every bloody word of it." I got a couple of
aspirin and an antibiotic from my first-aid kit and forced
them down his throat. He immediately vomited them up.
I gave him another dose, which he managed to keep in
his stomach. "Tell them to unpack that camel. I want my
rations. A can of peaches. Need to keep up my strength.
Peaches. Peaches'll help me keep up my strength." We
bundled him onto one of the animals, where he sat,
slumped over and mumbling about peaches.

The column struggled out of the marsh, striking out
once more across the desert. Osman hollered something
about the delay costing us valuable time and something
else about the danger of being caught in the open in daylight before reaching our next stopping place. He snapped
orders at the caravaneers, who, cursing and grunting,
whacked the camels mercilessly in a futile effort to prod
them along. I was aware, by the increasing resistance of
the land, of climbing a gradual rise. A crepuscular light
began to extinguish the stars. Then the new sun hemor-
rhaged through the sand-haze on the horizon. Ahead, the
camels plodded up a gentle ridge. Farther on, the two
scouts stood on the ridgeline, the sticks of their bodies and
the sticks of their spears outlined against the dawn. A few
guerrillas crouched beside them among clumps of jagged
volcanic rock. One waved his rifle in a signal for the
rest of the column to hurry it up. The oasis, I thought. The
gardens of the Balaka, the oasis, is just the other side of
the ridge. I walked faster, taking the incline with long
strides, passing the camel on whose back the exhausted
Moody dozed, my heart filled with the expectation of seeing green trees and bubbling wells, a hope which turned
to near-despair when I reached the crest and saw a desolation that could have passed for a photograph of the Mar-
tian plains. It was the Sawwa Plateau and it spread before
us for miles, an expanse of red sand relieved only by
patches of black sand and scattered mounds of basalt,

the whole vast sweep of it as flat as a football field. A
green line marked a wadi in the far distance. How far, it
was impossible to tell. Ten miles, twenty, a hundred. Looking at the blistered plateau in the sunrise, I felt as if I
were being given a preview of the end of the world, of the
final holocaust when the sun expands into a red giant and
boils all the seas to steam and burns all living things to
ash. And the rasping wind struck my ears as the dry laughter of that wilderness. "No hope," it hissed in mockery of
my expectations. "No hope, no hope."

The guides loping on ahead, we climbed down the opposite side of the ridge and headed out across the plateau
to Osman's constant litany of *imshi, imshi* and the drivers'
cries of *hut-hut-hut*. We were supposed to have crossed
the Sawwa and been in the shelter of the wadi by sunrise,
Osman said, warning that we would be helpless targets if
government planes caught us on the exposed ground.
"Damned camels," he cursed. "Damn these slow bitches.
Damn them all. Ha! Ha! *Imshi,* you bitches. *Imsheeeee.*"

Within an hour after sunrise, the heat had enough
power to wring a steady stream of sweat from a man. In
another two hours, it would send the mercury to the top
of any ordinary thermometer. By noon, I wondered why
all of us did not ignite from spontaneous combustion. The
fire of the superheated, hardened sand pierced the soles of
my boots, leeching the moisture out of my body from
below while the sun sucked me dry from above. My feet
soon blistered. I started to limp, to feel dizzy, to stumble
over honed shards of volcanic rubble. Slowly, I fell back
until I was alongside the rearguard, then fell behind them,
willy-nilly, like a runner whose wind is spent. And knowing the rebels had no intention of waiting for me, I fought
against the blisters' pain and forced myself to keep pace,
the effort wringing more sweat from me, the sweat drying
instantly to form a salty sticky crust on my skin. My
mouth was full of what tasted like old glue. The wind
picked up, flinging sand into my scorched eyes. *Whap,
whap, whap,* the insulting, demeaning slaps of the wilderness. All along, the mirages teased. There was an insidious
evil in those silent shimmering illusions. I knew what they
were and could explain their causes, but all the scientific

explanations in the books could neither dispel their malev-
olence nor diminish their power to attract. I had to con-
sciously control the impulse to go chasing after them, had
to force back images, roused by the dazzling fantasies, of
the rivers near my home, with their cold clear waters and
lovely northern names, the Silver, the Paint, the Huron,
and the Escanaba.

The column staggered on. The guerrillas and caravaneers took the ordeal in stride, no more affected by the
inclement sun than they had been by the malarial swarms
in the marsh. Only their frequent glances at the sky betrayed their anxiety. Nordstrand strutted at the head of
the caravan, matching the scouts stride for stride, though
with a different rhythm. The tribesmen's relaxed gait,
adopted to conserve energy, suggested humility and a
reconciliation with the desert arising out of a recognition
that it was an indomitable force that demanded submission as the price for survival. The American's rigid,
straight-backed stomp suggested pride, a refusal to submit,
and a belief that he possessed a strength commensurate
with the desert's; a conqueror's walk.

We kept moving, ever toward the wadi that cut through
the middle of the dead plain, its trees sometimes casting
phantom reflections in the mirage, and at other times van-
ishing altogether behind curtains of white-dancing light.
I think we were the only living things out there. I never
saw a single plant, not a lizard, not a fly, nothing but russet
sand broken by blotches of black sand resembling pools
of solidified tar.

We had been on the move some five hours or so, and
the wadi lay two or three miles off when someone up
front gave out a yell and pointed his rifle at a silver dart
trailing white vapor across the sky. We looked up anxious-
ly. It was too high to pose any immediate threat; nevertheless, Osman stepped up the pace. The plane vanished,
but reappeared a short time later. It was several thousand
feet lower, a blunt-nosed MIG describing a rumbling,
predatory circle above us. "Reconnaissance plane," Osman
said. "If he sees us and thinks we're worth it, he'll call for
fighters." He ordered the point to move out on the double.
Then, gesturing at Moody: "Mr. Patrick must come down."

I said that Mr. Patrick had a fever. "I know. I know. He must dismount," Osman answered in his apologetic voice. "If the planes attack, the camels will go wild and throw him. Besides, they have enough weight to carry. He must come down." I relayed this to Moody. Sun- and fever-dazed, he slid limply from the saddle, stumbled forward for perhaps a quarter-mile, then dropped to his hands and knees. The caravan pressed on, itself as indifferent as the desert. Lifting Moody to his feet, I took hold of his waist and draped one of his arms over my neck. I motioned to one of the rebels in the rear to give me a hand. All he did was point at the plane, now making a second pass, and tell me to get moving. "Thanks, you bastard," I snarled in English. I knew he wasn't being cruel in declining to help, but acting out of necessity: Moody was the weak dog in the pack, and if leaving him behind was the price to pay for the pack's survival, he would be left behind. Necessity and Moslem fatalism. For if God willed that Mr. Patrick die in the wilderness, he would die. It was written, and the rebel could do nothing to change what was written. Still I yelled, "You bastards! Goddamned bastards!" I was a little feverish, too, a little off my head, a little touched by the sun.

I walked as quickly as I could, trying to close the widening gap between us and the last man in the file. Above, the plane made another, lower pass, its exhaust smudging the pale sky. Ahead, the caravan pushed forward, increasing the gap until men and animals assumed distorted, wavering shapes in the mirage. Following the faint track they left in the macadam-hard sand, struggling to keep them in sight, I hollered in helpless anger. "Bastards! Help us, God damn you!" The wind blew my voice back into my face. Moody's legs flopped like those of a child taking its first steps. His skin was white and dry with the onset of sunstroke. "Come on, move, you son of a bitch," I said, turning my anger on him. "You goddamned weakling. He's right. A weak sister. *Cunt. Pussy. Move your ass.*" He toddled along, every muscle in him slack as rotten rope. The difference in our height made the going all the more difficult: I had to bend well over to keep his arm from slipping off my neck. Then I saw Nordstrand jogging toward us through the dust raised by the column, his figure magnified by the mirage, so that he looked like a giant. A wave of relief rolled through me when he reached us. "What in the hell's the matter with him?" Fever. Sunstroke. "Knew he wouldn't last, but I thought he'd last longer than this." He shot Moody a glance full of the ambivalent emotions the rescuer feels toward the one being rescued: a pinch of disdain and a large measure of moral superiority. He emptied his canteen over Moody's head, to cool his body temperature, then slung the smaller man over his back in a fireman's carry. He set an incredibly fast pace, stomping his heels as if he meant to wring a cry of pain from the insentient sands. In this way, he caught up with the caravan, paraded past the rear guard, past Osman and Murrah, on up to the point so all could see what he had done, so all could see who was the strong and who the weak. Nordstrand carried Moody the rest of the way to the wadi, never breaking stride.

The plane never came back. Osman thought the pilot had mistaken us for a nomad's caravan. I did not care if he had mistaken us for the retinue of Harun al-Rashid; I was simply thankful not to have been strafed, as I was thankful for the fragmentary shade afforded by the scraggly brush bordering the wadi, for the murky water in its well, and, when it came, for the blessed sunset.

We rested there until midnight. The camels munched happily on the spikelike thorns and we were lulled to sleep by their disgusting digestive rumblings. Then the cry of "Yalla!" awakened us and we were walking again across the grey, desiccated plain. Moody had begun to recover, but was not yet well enough to walk. He rode, slumped at the shoulders and hanging on to the saddle horn with both hands. Murrah, to relieve the boredom, grew loquacious. He chattered away on his favorite topic, politics, and his cant about the people, the masses, the armed struggle, the social struggle, and liberated zones sounded so ludicrous out there I wondered why the desert did not quake with laughter.

"Liberated zones?" I asked, hearing the desperation in my own voice. "Liberated from what? What people? What masses? What're you talking about? There's nothing here,

Murrah. You hear me? Nothing, nothing and more nothing. Nothing minus zero."

"*This* is a liberated zone, Mr. Charlie. There are people here. Look." He pointed to the faint sparking of a far-off campfire. "We are always working among the nomads, teaching them the basics of self-determination. Each clan has its cadre member—"

"Shut up." I wanted to strangle him. I had to endure thirst, heat, and all those soul-shrinking stars, but I was not required to endure that runtish ideologue's chirping.

"This isn't an empty desert, Mr. Charlie."

I almost wept. "Then what the hell is it?"

"You would like to talk about something else?"

"I don't want to talk at all. Too tired."

Murrah grew silent for a while, then, apropos of nothing, asked what I thought of Charlie Chaplin.

"Who?" My voice cracked a little. "What?"

"Charlie Chaplin, the actor."

"*Charlie Chaplin?*"

"Yes, the actor."

"I know. I know. Charlie Chaplin the actor. He's dead, Murrah. He's dead and grave-robbers stole his corpse from a Swiss cemetery."

"He's my favorite actor. What do you think of him—his films, I mean."

"I've only seen *The Great Dictator*. Where, out here, where in the hell did you see—"

"Not here. At film festivals in Moscow. I saw almost all of Chaplin's films. And you've seen only *The Great Dictator*?" Murrah sounded genuinely dismayed. "Not even *Modern Times*?"

"I've seen my own version of modern times."

"*Modern Times,* I think, was the best—"

"I don't want to talk, Murrah. Understand? Not about politics, not about liberated zones, not about Charlie Chaplin."

Murrah said nothing further, and I was thankful for his silence.

We marched on. Each mile we covered looked no different than the mile behind or the one ahead, giving the disconsoling impression we were on a treadmill. Too exhausted to notice any change in the country, I was surprised when we ended up crawling among some hills. I hadn't seen them come up. Real hills. Well, almost—they were actually big humps of craggy lava which aspired to be hills and which rose on either side of a wadi whose bed had the texture and color of flour. The column stopped while the men offered the *salât-issubh,* the prayer before sunrise. Murrah joined them but went through the ritual bowing by rote, pretending to a piousness that came naturally to the others. I collapsed under an enormous margosa, dizzy from hunger, thirst, and fatigue.

By daybreak we were moving down a dusty road through a forest of date palm. A dull, measured thudding echoed in the morning air—a pump. A pump could only mean water. The artesian well. The date palm gave way to corn, pepper, and tomato fields bordered by banana groves. The trees welcomed us with a bowing of broad quill-shaped leaves, beneath which the clumps of banana hung like green candelabra. Peasants stooped and squatted in the fields, whose colors, after the dun reaches of the desert, had the same effect on the eyes as bright light after hours in a dim room. The caravan halted on a hill above the well. It made a wondrous sight: a stream of cold clear water flowing from a pipe, the pump beating rhythmically, and the water pouring into the Wadi Balaka, an ocher ribbon fringed with tall, leaning palm. Black-gowned and black-veiled girls herded a string of donkeys on whose backs waterskins made a luscious, sloshing sound. Looking at them with my inflamed eyes, it required an effort of will not to race down and tear off one of the goatskins and drain it till it was as dry as my throat. Osman sent Yassin down to the well with our canteens. He cautioned us to stay put. Adi Abbas was only twenty kilometers away; the Ethiopians had retaken it in the counteroffensive, and army patrols sometimes ventured into the oasis on rebel-hunts. Guerrillas from the other factions might also be around, and, he added with a fine understanding of the need to maintain our cover, it wouldn't do if they saw us wandering about freely. I didn't care about our cover at that point. All I cared about was water, the cold water springing miraculously from the pipe. Flapping their ugly lips and batting their long eyelashes, the camels folded their spindly legs and knelt as the drivers tied feed bags to their bridles.

Murrah took advantage of the respite to give us another lecture. This one dealt with the horrors of Italian colonialism. The plantation we had passed through, he said, had been the property of one Franco Berlotti until the war drove him back to Italy. He had planted the banana groves, installed the pump, and built the irrigation pipes that ran like steel arteries through the rows of crops. "A real Fascist," Murrah said. "He came here in the thirties, after Mussolini's assassins took over Bejaya." I asked what fascistic acts Bertolli had committed, besides arriving in the wake of Mussolini's troops. Murrah appeared surprised by the question. Berlotti's crimes were self-evident: he was an exploiter, a man who developed the land in the interests of profit, not of the people. He exported his crops to Europe. But, I pointed out, he had developed the land; if he hadn't come, it would have remained a wasteland. Better it had remained a wasteland, Murrah replied. And now that the exploiter was gone, what was to happen to the crops? Would they be distributed among the nomads instead of exported? "Distributed to the nomads?" Murrah laughed. "I suppose we could do that, but why give the nomads a few days of luxury only to have them go back to eating the same idiots' porridge they've eaten all their lives?"

"Absolutely politically correct. No sense in raising their expectations."

I had the impression Murrah had decided never to open himself up to us again: he was hunkering down behind the safe, familiar walls of his ideology, behind the battlements of catchphrases, slogans, and ready-made axioms.

Yassin returned at last with our canteens. I emptied mine in two swallows. The drivers began to unload the camels, which grunted their relief. Osman told us to sling our packs and follow him. Then he, Yassin, Hamad, and Murrah led us down a footpath through alternating patches of sunlight and shade. Yassin insisted on carrying Mr. Jeremy's pack: the humiliated identifying with his humiliator. Along the way, we passed the exploiter Berlotti's house. Murrah could not resist pointing out to us the unjust splendor in which the Italian had lived. I agreed, having decided that the only way to keep Murrah from lecturing me was to pretend I shared his views. "Terrible," I said. The house was a dump, a one-story, adobe-walled building surrounded by tumbledown chicken coops and pigeon roosts. I shook my head in dismay when Murrah pointed at the one luxury, a small swimming pool. Terrible, the son of a bitch had a swimming pool. A greenish scum now coated the surface of the water, pigeon shit speckled the stone deck where the exploiter had once sunned himself. And with my decadent westerner's mind, all I could think of was how pleasant it would be to clean off the algae and take a swim.

We climbed a low hill behind the house up to a thatch shed which was open at both ends. High date palm awninged its sloping roof. Inside, bunches of yellowing bananas hung from circular racks, and a full waterskin, sweating, hung from one of the palm-log rafters. The earthen floor was cool underfoot. The spot was a regular Eden, so I had no objections when Osman told us we would have to confine ourselves there until the caravan left the following night. That said, he went out to join the other three, who were building a fire to brew their morning tea.

Moody collapsed against one of the straw walls. His skin was still dangerously dry, so I filled the tin cup hanging beside the waterskin and handed it to him.

"Thanks, Charlie." He drank greedily. "Should like some peaches to go with this."

I suggested a banana.

"Don't appear ripe enough to me. Besides, you can't be too sure about fruits in this part of the world. Not properly disinfected. Good way to give yourself dysentery." He looked at me imploringly with his grey English schoolboy's eyes. "Feel done in. Mind going back down and getting a tin of peaches from my bag?"

"We're not supposed to leave here. Might run into some bad guys from the other factions."

"Oh, that's nonsense. Ask Osman or one of the others to go along. I'd appreciate it, Charlie. Of course, I shall share the peaches."

Osman went with me. When he saw what had happened, he vowed to find and punish the fools who had done such a bad job of packing Mr. Patrick's belongings. I took a good look at the duffel bag and said that wouldn't be necessary; it hadn't been the drivers' fault. Wrapping what was left in my shirt, I hiked back to the shed. The walk gave me time to dream up an explanation I hoped Moody would find plausible. I had decided to avoid telling him the truth, or what I believed to be the truth, not out of a misguided loyalty to Nordstrand but out of a desire to prevent another confrontation, which the Englishman would be bound to lose.

"Make the most of it," I said, tossing him the peaches.

"Thanks, Charlie," he answered languidly. "Awfully good of you to do this."

Aw-flay.

"We can divide it up and put it in our packs." Opening the shirt, I emptied the contents. "That's it. Four more cans of peaches, two of corned-beef hash, one smoked her-ring—"

"Kippers," Nordstrand interjected. "In England, smoked herring are called kippers."

"—one kippers, two packets of malaria pills, two of halizone, and one enteroviaform."

Moody, a dripping peach-half in his mouth, looked at the pile blankly for a few moments before he realized what I was saying. Then he jumped to his feet.

"What happened?"

"The bag broke open. Looks to me like it chafed against the corner of an ammo crate. Anyhow, it was empty except for this."

"Broke open!"

"Broke open. The way they had it packed—"

"But all those tins spilling out would have made a racket. Why didn't someone say something?"

"Might have fallen out in the soft sand of a wadi. Maybe when everybody was asleep. I don't know."

"Those bastards. Those incompetent woolly-headed bas-tards." His hand trembled when he lit a cigarette. "I told them to be careful. Oh, those bastards."

I told him to calm down, he had a fever and a touch of sunstroke.

"I know I do. Why do you suppose I do? Eating that slop of theirs, that's why. Can't keep my strength up." He began pacing up and down the shed. "Those incompetents. Niggers, that's what they are. Bloody niggers and nothing more. I told them to see that it was lashed up properly. 'Oh yes,' they said. 'All very good, Mr. Patrick.' Those incompetent bastards. How am I going to keep up my strength without those rations?"

The racial epithets, like his fretful pacing, revealed the depth of his anxiety; and I saw then that he had a genuine phobia, an unrealistic terror of malnutrition combined with hypochondria. It was an unusual malady, probably rooted in his background: the provincial Englishman with his regular habits, his eggs and sausages at breakfast, high tea precisely at five, and firm conviction that a man's psychological disposition is ultimately determined by the condition of his intestines. I suppose he looked and sounded ridiculous, but, being prey to irrational fears myself, he did not strike me as at all comic.

"And the medical gear," he went on. "What about that? If one of us comes down with something out here—"

"Calm down, will you? We can make do with what's here and what's in our first-aid kits."

"You are joking, Charlie. That won't last."

"And neither will you."

"Shut up, you son of a bitch." Moody reached as if he meant to pick up the peaches and throw them at Nordstrand, but knowledge of the consequences inhibited him. "Fucking son of a bitch. I will not tolerate any more of your cheap insults."

"Be easy, Moody, will you?"

"No, I won't 'be easy,' Charlie. I'll . . ." He looked outside, at the clearing where Osman and the others sat sipping their tea. "I'll take this up with them. I'm not going to let this sit. Going to have a talk with them about this."

He walked out, veering from side to side from the effects of fever and heat.

I heard him begin to lay into Osman and Murrah:

". . . incompetents . . . told them to . . . hold you responsible . . . we'll have a look . . ." After several minutes of
animated conversation, the three men filed down the path
into the junglelike greenery below the hill.

Nordstrand reached over, plucked a peach-half from
the can, and dropped it into his mouth.

"Have some, Charlie. You heard Moody. He said he'd
share."

"No, thanks."

"Fascinating, isn't it?"

"What is?"

"The way men reveal themselves when they're under
stress. Saw that in Vietnam all the time. Did you hear our
welfare-state liberal? 'Woolly-headed bastards.' 'Niggers.'
Fascinating."

"That's not all that's fascinating."

"And what else is fascinating, Charlie Gage?"

"The duffel bag was new, double-strength canvas. It
should have taken a lot longer than a few days to rip a
hole that size in it. It was also a very neat rip. Had a good
look at it. Somebody cut it open."

"Theft. Somebody broke into the General's pantry."

"No, I don't think anybody stole anything."

"Sabotage, then. Are you implying that someone sabotaged Moody's gear?"

"I wouldn't dignify it by calling it sabotage. More in the
nature of a malicious prank."

"Could it be that you are in reality Sherlock Holmes,
the famous detective? If so, tell me what the culprit's
motives were."

"Moody's got a phobia. He's a hypochondriac. . . ."

"True. True. Proceed, Dr. Holmes."

"Let's say someone had it in for him. Let's say someone
wanted to break his spirit. A good way to do it would be
to prey on his phobia. Emptying out that duffel bag, it's the
same thing as forcing a man who's afraid of heights to
stand on the edge of a cliff, or locking someone with claustrophobia in a closet."

"That is fascinating. Prey on his phobia. Tell me, Dr.
Holmes, is this hypothesis or do you have proof?"

"Hypothesis. Someone cut it open, emptied it out, but

left just enough in there to make it look like it had broken open by accident."

"And is it your intention to present this hypothesis to the victim of the crime?"

"Knock off the bullshit."

"You haven't a shred of evidence, you know, Dr. Holmes."

"Wouldn't do much good if I had. Just make a bad situation worse. There's enough tension between you two as it is."

"You're a smart man, Charlie Gage."

A gust of wind, weighted with the smell of the oasis's foliage, shot through the shed. The odor of vegetation, mingling with those of thatch and ripening fruit, reminded me of Vietnam. Thirsty, I filled the cup from the goatskin bag, which hung from the rafter like a bloated headless corpse, and drank again and again until my gut drew drum-taut against my belt.

More than an hour later, Moody, Osman, and Murrah emerged from the shadows of the date-palm forest and headed up the path to the clearing where Yassin and Hamad, sated with heavily sugared tea, idled in a pillar of greenish-gold light. The Englishman's distress appeared to have had a therapeutic effect on his heatstroke. The color had been restored to his face: it was flamingo pink from sunburn and, judging from his violent gestures, from anger as well. Murrah's shrill voice reached us first.

". . . no right to make accusations, Mr. Patrick . . . not these men . . . our best . . ."

"I have every right, Kasu."

"Mr. Patrick, we searched the entire caravan," Osman said plaintively. "What more . . . discipline, by God . . . have little else, but they have discipline."

The three entered the shed.

"I'm afraid I shall have to ask the both of you to open your packs and submit to a search," Moody announced. "There has been a theft."

Amused by the formal-sounding phrase, Nordstrand stuffed another peach into his mouth and flashed an insolent grin, his teeth plastered with yellow-orange pulp.

"You got a warrant, Moody?"

"Shove it along, you circus strongman. My duffel bag did not break open. It was broken into. Someone stole my rations and medical gear. Our rations and medical gear, I should say."

"Since it's ours, we couldn't have stolen it."

"I'm aware you two could not have been the thieves. These two, however, insist that we search your stuff. Their men did it, of course, and it's the principle of the thing that bothers me. If some of this lot feel bold enough to steal from us now, there's no telling what they'll do next."

"Slit our throats. Cut your balls off. Stake us out on an anthill."

"We can do without your adolescent wisecracks. Now kindly open your pack."

"Since you put it that way, I will. Kindly."

After Nordstrand and I had emptied our packs, Moody turned to the two Bejayans with a look of vindication.

"I hope that satisfied you. You can see for yourselves. Not a damn thing. It was some of your men and I want to know what you intend to do about it."

Murrah, a frown wrinkling his face into a dried black olive, did not answer.

"All right, I'll tell you what I demand you do. You put this matter to right either by recovering what was stolen or by sending someone into Adi Abbas to replace it. I'll give you a list."

"A list?"

"Yes. A list. A list of the items to be replaced."

"Do you mean, Mr. Patrick, we are to send men into Adi Abbas with this list and they are to buy things for you?"

"Yes. If you cannot recover what was stolen, that is."

"There is an Ethiopian brigade in Adi Abbas."

"Not suggesting you attack the place, merely infiltrate a couple of men in there."

"To go shopping for you."

"To replace what your men stole."

"Incredible."

"You won't do it, is that what you're saying?"

"Of course I won't do it."

"And what do you say, Osman? The men are under your direct command."

"Moody," I said, "isn't this getting out of hand?"

"Stay out of this, Charlie. It's between me and them. Osman?"

The old partisan hooked his thumbs into his cartridge belt and shifted his weight from side to side, a movement that came close to an Uncle Tom shuffle. But his eyes were full of resentment at Moody's accusation and demand.

"I can't believe any of my men would steal. They're disciplined fighters."

"I don't dispute that. But see here, Osman, I was in one of the best-disciplined armies in the world and—"

"And so was I," Osman countered, an old memory restoring some of the stiffness to his back. "The same army as you, for four years. Before you were born. I fought with General Wingate's desert group, against the Italians, against the Germans."

"That's quite interesting. You shall have to tell us about it sometime. But it's a bit off the point now."

"I know all about the discipline of the British army, Mr. Patrick."

"Then you also know that the men were always stealing from each other in barracks. It happens in all armies. It's no disgrace. Look, Osman, it's only fair. Since some of your men stole my gear, some of them should replace it. How much of a risk is it, going into the city?"

"A year ago, it would have been no risk at all. Adi Abbas was ours then. But now it's a chance."

"How great a chance?"

"I don't know."

"Yassin and Hamad seem resourceful. Don't you think they could get through?"

"Yes, they could get through, and I would send them for a serious reason. This isn't serious. We have food, Mr. Patrick. We have some medicines. By God, we are not a band of *shifti*. We can take care of you—"

"I prefer taking care of myself, thank you very much." Moody now sounded very much the British officer. "And you're in a sorry state if you don't believe that your men stealing from me is a serious matter."

"Of course that's serious. That isn't what I meant. . . ." Osman trailed off. The Englishman's voice must have stirred another memory, and the memory roused the half-forgotten habit, instilled in him by British army discipline, of saying "Yes, sir" to young lieutenants and captains with accents like Moody's. I suspect his sense of honor also affected him: if his men had committed theft, it was his duty to make it up in some way. Under these forces, Osman began to waver.

"I'll ask Yassin and Hamad if they think they can make it. Will that satisfy you? I'll ask them, but I won't order them."

Murrah said: "No, you won't."

"Eh? Kasu?"

Murrah spoke to him sharply in dialect. The two fell to quarreling, apparently over who had authority in the matter, Murrah's voice a series of vicious, shrewlike squeaks.

With his finely calibrated sense of timing, Nordstrand broke into the argument at the right moment.

"Kasu, Osman, why are you two arguing?" he said, sounding the soul of reason. "There's no argument. You're both trying to tell Mr. Patrick that filling his belly isn't worth the risk of anyone's life, isn't that right?"

"This is between me and them, Nordstrand."

"The hell it is. You're always talking about the mission. All right, suppose Yassin and Hamad went in there, got captured, and talked. The whole goddamned mission would be compromised, wouldn't it? Over what? A can of beans."

"Yes, they could be captured," Murrah piped in, expropriating the idea. "You must consider what would happen if they were captured."

"That is not the issue. Osman just said they could get through. The only issue is whether this matter is important enough to take the risk, and I say it is."

"No, it's not. It's ridiculously unimportant."

"I should think, Nordstrand, that this is a time for us to stick together."

"Why? Because we're white, and they're black?"

"Oh, that is marvelous, coming from you, the man who calls them tar babies."

"And that's marvelous, coming from a man who calls them woolly-headed—"

"Nordstrand! Keep your mouth shut, damn you. I didn't mean that and you know it."

"You don't mean a lot of things."

"We are not here to make debating points. The point is—"

"The point is, no one is going to risk his neck and no one is going to risk compromising this mission just to make you comfortable." Nordstrand stood, rising with the relaxed movements of a superb athlete, and scorched Moody with his fulminating eyes. "You given any thought to how you sound, whining and griping? You actually think you've got a right to ask these men to risk their necks so you can keep that soft belly of yours full." Onstage again, Nordstrand's voice crackled with feigned outrage. He spoke in English, but very slowly and distinctly, apparently to make sure Osman and Murrah understood every word. "These men have been fighting for years on scraps and mush—years, General, and you can't take it for five days. Do you think it was fair, keeping those rations for yourself, while everybody else got to eat stale bread? You see them taking malaria pills? If one of them stole from you, it wouldn't be any wonder, would it? The poor bastard probably hasn't had a square meal in months." He took a breath and cast a glance at the two Bejayans, who appeared to find his performance convincing. "You know you've made yourself look like a weakling in front of them? You know that, don't you? Listen, if you don't like what they're feeding you, why don't you radio Colfax and have him parachute in a food package, direct from Fortnum and Mason. You're worried about getting sick, have him call the National Health Service and they'll send you your personal physician, one of those free-of-charge welfare-state quacks. You think somebody robbed you, call the police. Go on, get the bobby on the corner. That's your style, Moody. That's where you belong, back in London, with the grocers down the street and a doctor just a phone call away and a bobby on the corner."

"Are you quite finished?"

"No, not quite. What Osman and Murrah were trying to tell you was that people like you don't carry any weight with them anymore. They aren't going to fetch and carry for you. Osman, Kasu, isn't that right?"

"Isn't what right?" Murrah asked in return.

"You're not going to listen to Mr. Patrick. If Mr. Patrick tells you to send your men into the city, you're going to tell Mr. Patrick to fuck off."

"I don't understand."

"You-are-not-going-to-pay-any-attention-to-Mr.-Patrick. Mr. Patrick's demands are unreasonable. I agree with you. What he's asking you to do is not reasonable. Isn't that right?"

Their silence answered the question.

"There it is, General."

"I think you've said quite enough."

"Not yet. Where do you get the balls to tell me we ought to stick together when I carried your ass over the desert? Three, four miles, I carried you because you didn't have it in you to walk on your own two feet."

"I don't owe you anything."

"You just remember, it it hadn't been for me, you'd still be out there, so thirsty you'd be drinking your own piss by now. That's what you owe me."

"I don't owe you anything."

"All right. But you owe them something." Nordstrand gestured at Osman and Murrah. "You owe them an apology."

"Don't be absurd." Then, knowing he'd lost and realizing what Nordstrand was up to, Moody attempted as graceful a retreat as possible. "See here, Osman. I've changed my mind for the moment. You needn't ask Yassin and Hamad to try and get through. It won't be necessary. I'll find some other solution. I consider this business ended. Just see to it there isn't any more stealing."

Osman, willing to let it go at that, started to leave. Nordstrand, not content to leave Moody even the cosmetics, laid a hand on one of Osman's thick shoulders.

"Mr. Patrick owes you and Kasu an apology for accusing your men of stealing. I know they didn't steal anything. Mr. Charlie saw it, and he says it was an accident."

"Yes, yes. I agree. An accident. My men are not thieves, by God."

"Then Mr. Patrick owes you an apology."

"I most certainly do not."

"Moody."

"There is every reason to believe someone broke into my gear. I don't owe them a thing."

"I don't understand any of this," Osman said.

"All you need to understand is that Mr. Patrick owes you an apology because he had no right to accuse your men of stealing. He also owes you an apology because he called you and your men woolly-headed bastards and niggers."

I am not sure if they caught the full meaning of the first phrase, but the second was familiar and clear enough to them, and it was like a wedge, widening the breach Moody had opened between them and himself with his hothead charges. Flushing beneath his sunburn, the Englishman flew at the two men.

"That's not true! It's an absolute lie! Him, he's the one, Nordstrand, Mr. Jeremy." Moody spun, waving his arm wildly, smacking a banana bunch off its rack. "He's the one. Do you know what he calls you? Tar babies. Yes, tar babies. That's what he thinks of you."

"Please. Mr. Patrick . . . what . . ."

"What? What indeed. Ah, what's a tar baby? I'll tell you. It's from a fable, an American fable. For a black man. Nordstrand, you bastard, you had no cause to say that in front of them—"

"Mr. Patrick, please, you must calm yourself. You must keep calm in this heat."

"I am telling you what he thinks of you. Tar babies. It's from an American fable. Uncle Remus. Do you know Uncle Remus?"

"Who?"

Moody spun around again to face Osman. "The fable, you bloody idiot." Listening to him stammer and watching him flying nearly out of control, an inner laughter rippled through me as I thought of what had brought him to this state: the loss of a sackful of canned goods. Pork and beans and corned-beef hash, peaches and pears—there was something macabrely amusing in how such trifles, under the right circumstances, could unhinge a man's reason. And that forced you to question the quality of the metal of which the hinges were made. It stood up well enough in the benign climates, but it always crumbled rapidly in the corrosive atmosphere of the intemperate zones.

"Fable?" Osman asked. "I don't understand this talk of fables."

"Uncle Remus, damn you. There's a tar baby in it. A tar baby, it means the same thing as nigger. He called you that. Tar baby. Don't you understand?"

"No, I . . ."

Moody did not let him finish. Whirling again, he pointed at Nordstrand.

"God damn you. God damn your soul."

"Mr. Patrick, you must calm yourself."

"Mr. Patrick has a fever," Nordstrand said.

The Englishman made some guttural noises, picked up the can, flung it at Nordstrand, and missed. Peach juice and peach-halves slid down the thatch wall. Moody then did the worst thing he could have done: he hit Nordstrand in the mouth. The punch had no effect beyond drawing a trickle of blood. And Nordstrand did the worst thing he could have done to Moody: nothing. He just stood there smiling. Humiliated, the Englishman ran out of the shed and went crashing through the underbrush outside.

Osman looked at him, then at Nordstrand in total astonishment.

"Mr. Patrick, he has gone mad?"

"No. Just a fever and too much sun." The American extended his hand. "I guess I'll have to apologize for him. Do you accept?"

"I don't understand, Mr. Jeremy."

In dialect, Murrah explained the situation to him. It dispelled some of his confusion, but his wide, fissured face still wore an astonished look when Nordstrand pressed his hand.

"So, this is all finished now?"

Murrah told him, yes, it was finished. Then, turning his eyes up at the American:

"Mr. Jeremy, did he really say that? 'Niggers'? Is that
how he thinks of us?"

"He didn't mean it," I said. "He has a fever."

"I asked Mr. Jeremy."

"He has a fever," replied Mr. Jeremy, wiping his
mouth with the back of his hand.

"Yes. Perhaps you all do."

———————

We started the following night on the second leg, an eighty-
mile trek to the Malaka Massif, the wind-worn mountain
range that twists through the center of Bejaya like a deformed spinal cord. In moonlight splintered by the spike-
leaved palm, the caravan moved with the scrape of hooves,
the sloshing of the refilled waterskins, the creak of pack
ropes, and the dull jiggling of the camels' nose rings.
Though my swollen, blistered feet protested the renewal
of their torture, though my eyes, revolted by the prospect of staring once more at the desert, wanted to lunge
from their sockets and cling to the cool green trees, I was
relieved to be leaving the oasis. After that scene over the
stolen canned goods, the atmosphere in the shed became
unbearable. For his part, Nordstrand was not content with
his little victory. He evidenced an absolute hatred for
everything about the Englishman, his tics, his gestures, and
would look at him in the way a convict looks at a detested
cellmate with whom he had been locked up for years.
Moody said nothing at all. His manic outburst had given
way to a prolonged depression that made me anxious. He
would sit staring into space for long spells, or count and
recount the remaining supplies of rations and medicines. It
was as if he thought he could miraculously increase them
with those gloomy inventories. No such miracle occurred,
and, worry tracing fine lines across his pink forehead, his
hands would nervously move the tins, the packets of halizone, the plastic bottles of antibiotics and enteroviaform
into various formations: a losing chess-player shifting his
remaining pawns against the onslaught of an opponent
that held all the major pieces—the desert with its bishops

of fever and dysentery, its rooks of hunger and heat, its queen of thirst.

All during the following four-day march to the mountains, Nordstrand never ceased taking potshots at him. The insults were the same, but they seemed to pluck harder at Moody's nerves the deeper we plunged into the embrowned emptiness. He appeared to sense the purpose behind them. Like harassing sniper-fire, they were not serious in themselves, but in what they portended; they were meant to draw a slow, steady trickle of blood, to weaken him in preparation for a deadlier assault. His spirits would revive briefly, and he would give back as good as he got. The two of them clawed at each other with their tongues, but the Englishman's counterattacks had little effect. Nordstrand did not appear to have any vulnerable points, which frustrated the Englishman all the more. He did not know how to cope with a man who could not be reasoned with, insulted, or threatened, who would not submit to anything but a brute force greater than his own. Gradually, Moody stopped striking back. He took the verbal punishment from his adversary not with forbearance but with a kind of acceptance, as if it were his due to be degraded. He withdrew into himself. At the halts, he sat apart from us, sunk in a wounded silence. He spoke to no one, no one spoke to him—Murrah to demonstrate his offence at Moody's racist remarks, Osman because he must have thought the Englishman was a little off his head. As for the others, they had not understood the words Nordstrand and Moody had hurled at each other, but I think they recognized that the two men were exchanging what the Arabs call *hija*—demeaning invective—and that Moody had lost.

We traveled as we had on the first leg, at night and in the early mornings. By day, an unrelentingly clear sky and heat that sucked all the moisture out of us. Sunsets that came like a gift from God. Walking by night, or resting beside a campfire listening to the babble of strange tribal tongues, the tanging of metal pestles grinding bitter Arab coffee. Sleeping in the wadis, those dried corpses of rivers, until the sun induced insomnia. Sometimes we spotted a smuggler's caravan crawling over a distant rocky ridge.

Sometimes we passed a nomad settlement where herds of goats—black and dark brown specks against the desert's beige—scrounged in the sparse vegetation, and the herdsmen stood with their sticks, and mound-shaped huts made of woven twigs humped under the acacia, and emaciated cattle, penned in brushwood corrals, waited for death, either from thirst, starvation, or the slaughterer's knife. There was nothing else, only sand, sun, stars, and wind, the yapping of jackals, the bones of cattle or camels that scavengers' teeth had picked to a pristine white, and a feeling inside myself, against which I struggled constantly, that I could not go any farther.

Nordstrand, on the other hand, walked as if he could go on forever. He somehow drew a vitality from that lifeless land; it was as if he had found a spiritual home in its limitless reaches. Yassin, Hamad, Osman, even Murrah became quite friendly with him, although the latter's chumminess struck me as artificial, a pose he had adopted out of some secret motive. Nordstrand delighted in their attentions. Knowing the Beni-Hamid admired strength, he staged demonstrations to impress them further with his power. At one halt, he held a tug-of-war, pitting himself against six of them, and won easily. He held frequent classes on the arts of Hwrang-Do, teaching Yassin and the other young guerrillas how to kick groins, gouge eyes, and crack ribs.

He made a real hero of himself on our third day out from the oasis, when we were passing a wide shallow ravine where runty trees and tough grasses grew amid the rock. A herd of gazelle were grazing in the ravine. The promise of fresh meat excited everyone. One of the rebels stalked to within a hundred yards of the herd, firing a sloopy snap-shot when some of the males picked up his scent and nervously raised their heads. The gazelle bounded out of the ravine and took off with a series of tense, quick springs, breaking for a low hill a good four hundred yards away. Nordstrand snatched Osman's Enfield, fired once, the bullet kicking dust, then fired again, and a larger cloud of dust rose as a large male went down hard. The rebels cheering, Nordstrand ran off and picked up the animal. He came back with it slung over his shirt. A victorious grin crinkled his sunburned face. The rebel soldiers gathered around him, slapping him on the back and exclaiming, "Look, through the chest, and it was running! Three hundred meters at least. *Mashallah!* What God has willed. Through the chest and three hundred meters. Ya! What a shot, Mr. Jer-ah-mee!" And Mr. Jer-ah-mee, Natty Bumppo in Africa, basked in their praise, and I did not like the savage pleasure with which he watched Yassin and Hamad butcher the carcas with swift, expert strokes of their long knives. Nordstrand's feat of marksmanship was the sole topic of conversation for the rest of the day. The guerrillas and caravaneers talked about it among themselves; they breathlessly related it to the chief of a nomad encampment where we stopped for water. "With one shot through the chest, by God, and it was running!" The chief, an old man with a grey goatee, nodded, proclaimed the foreigner to be the greatest of hunters, and ordered a goat to be slaughtered as a sign of respect.

The caravan halted early that night to allow the rebels time to hold a celebration to honor Mr. Jeremy's achievement and to mark an event: we had entered the traditional tribal homeland of the Beni-Hamid, although it was a mystery to me how anyone could distinguish that part of the desert from any other. A fire was built, and the gazelle roasted over it on a spit. When we had finished eating, the men formed a wide circle around the blaze and sang, while the two scouts did some age-old warrior's dance in the center of the ring. The others kept time by drumming on cooking pots or by clapping rocks together. The dancers circled each other, swinging their swords in mock combat. They were, Murrah informed us in a detached professional tone, reenacting a battle in which the Beni-Hamid had defeated the Christian king of Aksum, a city-state in ancient Ethiopia. "The battle took place more than twelve hundred years ago, but, as you can see, it has not been forgotten. Here, nothing is ever forgotten. We don't have books, gentlemen, we don't have monuments, but we have very long memories." In this way, Murrah let us know he disapproved of reactionary customs like the one we were watching. It did possess a captivating barbarism: the scarred faces of the men burnt-

umber in the embers' glow; the stripped, charred bones of
the gazelle; the smell of its roasted fat; the banging of the
pots; the click-clacking of the rocks; the agile, ritualized
movements of the dancers; and the menacing whisper of
their sword blades. Osman invited Nordstrand to join in,
telling him that the dance was a test. Nordstrand stood and
accepted a sword. He did a fair imitation of the dance,
swinging the three-foot blade as if it were a carving knife.
The rebels expressed their approval with shouts of "Bravo!"
—the Italian word had crept into their vocabulary—and by
calling out his name in rhythm with their drumming, "Jer-
ah-mee, Jer-ah-mee, Jer-ah-mee."

We raised the mountains the following day. Grey-blue
against the pale blue of the sky, they rose out of a plain
so flat it looked as if it had been laid with a carpenter's
level and so hard the hooves of the heaviest camel made no
impression on it. Out in front of us, a vast mirage gleamed
like a lake of molten steel. We crossed the plain in daylight.
There was no fear of an air strike, Osman said. Enemy
aircraft never flew over the plain. I guessed that the Ethiopian air force had decided not to waste bombs on what
the sun had already devastated. The caravan reached the
slag-colored foothills at nightfall and pushed off at dawn
on the final leg, a three-day climb to Jima's camp.

The trip through those mountains was a journey back
to the age of man's beginnings. Winds and flash floods had
eroded the slopes down to the basement rock, down to the
primeval rock over which slouching creatures with heavy
occipital lobes but an erect posture had walked three million years ago.

I could almost feel the presence of those progenitors as
we wound through the massif, almost expected one to poke
his heavy-browed head above an outcropping of pre-Cam-
brian rock.

If the dread of open spaces afflicted my spirit on the
desert, claustrophobia attacked me in those tyrannous
heights. Sheer sandstone cliffs, streaked with greenish-
black seams of granite, loomed over to us to end in peaks
as sharply pointed as cathedral spires. Generally, the caravan stuck to the wadis, the steep mountain trails being too
treacherous for camels. And the narrow wadis, spreading

through the hills like constricted bronchia, conformed to
no discernible pattern If you made one false turn, you
would wind up lost in a chaos of buttes, mounds, and
stony towers carved into fantastic shapes as if by some
deranged sculptor who had re-created the hideous forms
seen in his nightmares. Volcanoes still rumbled in the
Malaka, and we spent the first afternoon picking our way
through a lava field. The razor-sharp igneous rock shredded our boots and the rebels' rubber sandals. It slashed our
flesh. It would sometimes crumble underfoot, tripping us
playfully. A good sense of balance was a must: to fall on
that stuff would have been like falling on a field of broken
glass. As it was, all of us were so cut up that we would
have left a distinct trail of blood if our blood, like our
sweat, had not soaked immediately into the parched,
porous basalt.

On the second day, we struggled up a ravine which a
flash flood had recently turned into a torrent during one of
the downpours that sometimes fall in the highlands. A
dark line on the limestone walls twenty feet above us
marked the depth of the flood, and tall date palm, torn
roots and all, from an oasis upstream were scattered
around like matchsticks. Now that immense volume of
water had vanished without leaving so much as a trickle.
The heat in the ravine expanded your conception of what
heat was. The entrapped air had the aggressiveness of a
living thing.

I kept hobbling along, inspired by Nordstrand. His
boots had also been shredded, his feet clawed by the volcanic rock, and he loved it. He was lost in a state in which
pain is relished because it produces the ecstasy of over-
coming it. He was one of those men destined to thrive on
resistance: the more the land fought him, the deeper his
resolve to fight it back. A measure of the blind ferocity
that had created those awful mountains burned inside him,
drove him on. All the way up, he kept pace with the
guides, who climbed steadily on their lank-muscled legs.

Our torment for that day ended in a place called Kerem.
Not that the name makes any difference; it might just as
well have been called the End of the World. Kerem was a
way station for the caravans, which came in loaded with

salt mined from the Malaka Sink, the dried-up sea lying between the massif and the coastal deserts. The town, if it could be called such, huddled on a flat-topped hill in a broad valley formed by the confluence of two wadis: a row of huts built of lava blocks, a well from which women with tattooed faces and gold rings in their noses were drawing water, the inevitable flock of scrawny goats guarded by spear-carrying nomads whose austere sack-cloth hung loosely over bodies pared to abstractions of the human form, a salt caravan trekking down the wadi, its bed strewn with gravel and chunks of grey rock resembling the rubble of a pulverized city, and all of it surrounded by limestone slopes colored the pale pink of an old scar.

We camped beside Kerem's principal building, a one-story, tin-roofed shack that had been an Ethiopian police post before Jima's rebels seized it. Machine-gun bullets had nibbled bits out of its stone walls. A grenade or small rocket had blown a hole in the roof. It was now manned by a platoon of NIIF partisans as unfriendly as the mountains. Their leader, a black-bearded man who must have practiced scowling in the mirror every morning, greeted Osman icily. The man, Ibrahim Abdel by name, belonged to a Beni-Hamid clan with whom Osman's had an ancestral feud, a debt of blood passed on from generation to generation like a family heirloom. The war had brought it to a temporary truce. And so, despite their belonging to the same tribe and the same faction, the two men regarded each other as if they came from opposite ends of the earth. The post being under the bearded man's command, Osman was required to observe the strictest desert protocol. I think it took them twenty minutes to get through the ritual greetings. It was only then, after incessant invocations of Allah's name had broken down their mutual hostility, that Osman felt it proper to inform the other man that we were going to camp there for the night. Ibrahim Abdel gave a perfunctory nod, as if he were granting us permission. All that out of the way, we were at last allowed to rest.

With Murrah, the three of us sat on straw mats under the corrugated roof of the police station's porch. Pigeons babbled pleasantly. I felt every mile of the two hundred we had traveled from the border, every bruise, blister, and cut. In front of us, Yassin and Hamad blew on the coals of a fire upon which they had set a blackened teakettle and a pot full of the mush that would be our supper. The station faced Kerem's only street, a crooked, rutted pathway, empty except for a few goats nibbling stupidly on garbage, and the village butcher leading a donkey bedecked with the rattling rib cages of slaughtered sheep.

The Arab believes that when Allah created all things and sent them to their places, he assigned each a companion. According to this belief, poverty was sent into the desert accompanied by misery. Poverty and misery were all I saw in that town, the sort of poverty and misery no revolution could ever eradicate. "No hope," whispered the wind blowing down from the sterile heights. "No hope."

"And Jima would change none of this," said Murrah, his thoughts apparently running in the same vein. He waved his hand as if to sweep the village out of existence. "This isn't even the Middle Ages, and Jima would change none of it. Look at that house over there. It's a bridal house." He pointed to a shack some fifty yards down the street. Strips of brightly colored cloth festooned its entrance, making it look pathetically festive against the general drabness. "If you want to see what I mean, I could take you in there and show you."

"I don't think any of us cares to move at the moment," Moody said, the first words he had spoken in days.

"Aren't you interested in the way some of us woolly-headed niggers live, Mr. Patrick?"

"Go to hell."

"C'mon, Charlie Gage. Kasu wants to take us to a wedding."

It was stifling, stinking, and dark inside the hut. Flies hummed in the heat, the only sound. Bolts of cloth similar to those outside hung from the walls, along with various talismen, lengths of camel's hair, carved wooden figures, and leather amulets much like the one Abdul had given Moody. An oblong-shaped form about three feet high occupied the center of the room: the bride, sitting utterly still beneath a goat-hair blanket that covered every inch of her and made her look like a veiled statue. She was so still I wondered if she had suffocated. An old woman sat next to the girl. Flies lighted on her shriveled, tattooed face, but she made no effort to brush them away. Murrah said something to her in dialect. She nodded vaguely without looking at him. Trachoma had blinded her and turned her eyes from black to pearl.

"This girl is probably about fifteen," said Murrah in his professorial voice. "She's to be married in three days. Her husband has never seen her. She must sit this way for the next three days and nights. When it's time, her husband will enter the house and unveil her, but they won't be allowed to fuck for three months."

He uttered the English obscenity self-consciously, rather like a polite lady trying to prove she had overcome her inhibitions.

"Three months," Nordstrand said. "Nothing like spartan self-discipline."

"Three months, and it isn't done for discipline, Mr. Jeremy. It is done because it has always been done that way. When the three months have passed, the husband enters again, bringing the girl a certain gift to demonstrate his manhood. Then he takes her behind the curtain you see there. There's a bed of skin and hides behind it, and the bride is supposed to hold the gift and sing a song in praise of her husband. Then she gets on her hands and knees, and he lifts her gown and he fucks her like that. Like an animal. Our women are mounted like beasts."

Was I missing the point? "I've heard of more bizarre mating rites. The Beni-Hamid don't strike me as all that terrible."

"Perhaps you'd think differently if you saw the gift."

"What is it?" asked Nordstrand.

"I will tell you only that it is what a Beni-Hamid must take from his enemy to become a warrior and a man."

With that enigmatic statement, Murrah walked out. I followed, ducking under the low entranceway, but Nordstrand lingered for a few moments. He stood staring at the girl, at the blue and scarlet strips of cloth, at the weird carved figures and the tribal designs that, like the shrouded bride, like the village, seemed out of another time.

"Mr. Jeremy, you shouldn't stay in there alone," Murrah called back.

Turning sideways to fit through the narrow door, Nordstrand came out. It did not require extraordinary powers of intuition to know that the musky smell inside the house and the mystery of the veiled girl had excited his imagination.

I let Murrah get a few steps ahead of us and, as he prattled on about the necessity to eradicate negative traditions, I whispered to Nordstrand, "Don't even think it."

"Six months out here is a long time. In Vietnam I once had four in one day."

"This isn't Vietnam. You touch a Moslem girl and you'll never touch a second, let alone a third or fourth."

"I did more than touch a Moslem girl in Cairo."

"This isn't Cairo, either."

"I'll bet you got straight A's in geography, Charlie Gage."

"The Beni-Amer have a similar custom," Murrah was saying, "only they wait a year. Bejaya has over one hundred and fifty thousand square kilometers and less than three million people. The Front needs people. The revolution needs them. Almost all the world has too many people, and we don't have enough. Of course. How can we have enough people if married couples must wait months, even a year? Idiocy. Hopeless."

We sat again in the welcome shade of the porch, where Yassin and Hamad had set out cups of heavily sugared tea. Leaning against a palm-log post, languidly sipping, Moody asked, "How was the wedding?"

"The groom was dashing and the bride looked radiant."

"Your tea's getting cold." Moody stood and said it was time to send a situation report. He walked into the station, where the radio had been set up.

"Hopeless," Murrah went on obsessively. His voice sounded like a bat's squeal compared to the soothing coo of the pigeons. "Look at what you saw today between Osman and Ibrahim Abdel. They hate each other. Why? Because their fathers hated each other, and their fathers before them. And if Jima has his way, these feuds will go on forever, and these idiot marriage customs. Jima says,

'No man can escape his destiny, and no nation can escape its past.' That's what he believes. A nation's future is written in its past, and to try to change things is to oppose God's will. Who knows? Maybe he's right. Maybe nothing can be done here without . . ." He paused to drink from his enameled cup, ". . . certain methods."

"What methods?"

"Methods that would erase what is written." Another pause, another sip. "The curse in this part of Africa is nomadism. It breeds tribal thinking and factionalism. It makes men cling to the ways of the past. It pulls us apart when what we need is to be brought together. More than one-third of our people are nomads. That is the root of our problem. So these methods would be those that eradicate nomadism."

"Enforced settlement."

"That's been tried before. The Italians tried it. The British. The emperor. They built houses for the nomads and the nomads put their sheep and cattle in the houses and went on living in tents."

"All right, how would you do it?"

Murrah picked up his cup by the brim, to avoid scalding his fingers, and swirled the tea around.

"The nomads are our kulaks. We should solve their problem as the Soviets solved the problem of the kulaks." In that instant, and only for an instant, all the conflicts within him, between his political creed and the faith of his fathers, between his hope and his growing sense of hopelessness, between the future he saw in his mind and the wretched present he saw with his eyes, transfigured his face into a mask of rage. The appearance and disappearance of that furious expression was like the sudden rise and fall of a curtain: you fancied it had given you a peek at the kind of man Murrah would become if he had power; and the image was made sharper by the words that followed, words wrung from his throat by the torment of his frustrations, words that came almost inaudibly from between his clenched teeth, like a confession made under duress: *"Annihilate them."*

"And Jima?" I asked quietly. There was something extraordinarily private between us at that moment of reve-

lation. I wasn't even sure Nordstrand had quite heard the
two whispered words that had revealed so much.

Murrah did not say anything. He did not have to. His
eyes, radiant with hatred, told me what he intended to do
about Jima if given half the chance.

"And you think we can help you," I said in response
to the unspoken answer. "That's why you've been taking
our side."

"Taking your side? Why should I take your side?" Aware
he had already disclosed too much, Murrah was keeping
the curtain down, but not quite to the floor.

"That was my question."

"If it had been up to me, you would never have come
here."

Yassin walked up, carrying bowls of *gargosh* or *bosh-
bosh*, or God knows what. He laid them in front of us,
serving Mr. Jeremy first. I forced down a couple of mouth-
fuls, idly watching some goats grazing by a stack of grey
acacia logs. As Yassin walked into the station with Moody's
bowl, Murrah remarked:

"And that's why I would have never allowed you to
come. Look at Yassin. You're corrupting us already."

"Corrupting you?"

"Look at Yassin. Look at what you've done to him. I
should say, look at what you've done, Mr. Jeremy. Yassin
admires you. Hamad also. Osman also. And why? Because
you're strong and you shoot well. That's all. They admire
strength and skill with a rifle. Simple warriors' virtues, but
that's all these men are, simple fighters."

"And how has that corrupted them?" asked Nordstrand.

"Because for centuries we listened to foreigners. Always
it was some *ferengei* we listened to. Turks. Italians. En-
lishmen. Ethiopians . . ."

"Russians, Cubans."

"Yes, yes. Them too. It's time we learned to stop listening to strangers. Now you come and they listen to you.
Sometimes I think they would listen to you before they
listen to me. And you've been here only two weeks. In
another two weeks, or five or six, or eight perhaps . . .
well, who knows?"

Despite my inexperience in cryptology, I knew an encoded message when I heard one. I wanted to finish the sentence for him: in another five or six or eight weeks perhaps they would listen to Mr. Jeremy before they would listen to Jima himself. Instead, I took a less direct approach.

"You haven't discouraged them. That business at the border, you took our side."

"Would you have liked it if I hadn't?" He swirled two fingers around in the bowl and popped a doughy, pepper-streaked gob into his mouth. "Think of how hard this journey would have been if you had to make it tied up and blindfolded, as Jima ordered. It was my word that finally convinced them to go against Jima's orders."

"You'll get some argument from me on that."

Murrah looked at Nordstrand intently, his upper lip rising to the top of his jutting teeth.

"Then to avoid an argument, I'll say we worked together to convince them. We can work together, Mr. Jeremy. And also Mr. Patrick, and Mr. Charlie also."

Slowly and cautiously, he was raising the curtain again.

"I thought we were corrupters."

"You are. When something becomes corrupted, it dies, but things die so that other things can be born. So, sometimes corruption is a necessity."

"And if the men eventually become corrupted enough by us, they'll listen only to us, and to you because they'll associate you with us. Then we can all work together to get rid of Jima."

"It is you, not I, Mr. Charlie, who is speaking of disposing of Jima."

"We'll be at his base camp tomorrow, so you thought you'd sound us out now, just to see how far we're willing to go to show our gratitude for your taking our side."

"I am only trying to find out which side you're on, the side of progress or reaction."

"Kasu," I said, "that is a gross oversimplification."

"This is a simple place, without the shadings." He gestured vaguely at the creased and crevassed cliff above the village, its face starkly divided between light and shadow. "And there are some simple things you must understand about Jima."

"You don't have to go into that again. We can guess. He's a reactionary et cetera, et cetera, et cetera."

"No. A religious fanatic, yes, but not a reactionary. A reactionary wants to turn the clock back. But in Bejaya, you cannot turn the clock back any further than it is. Its hands are set on midnight, and Jima is fighting to keep them there. He's fighting because he's an old *shifta* who's always fought, because he enjoys killing Ethiopians, because he has feuds to settle—"

"You know, Murrah," Nordstrand said, "I think you're trying to convert us."

"I'm trying to make you see certain realities about our struggle, since you've chosen to involve yourselves in it."

Nordstrand scraped his bowl clean, drained his tea, and, belching, lounged against one of the crooked posts.

"Who said I'm involved in your struggle?"

"You're here. That means you're involved."

"Tell me something, Mr. Kasu. You said Jima's fighting because he enjoys killing Ethiopians. What's wrong with that?"

"I told you many days ago. We haven't fought a revolution for all these years for nothing. To change the color of a flag."

"I meant, what's wrong with killing for personal reasons?"

"You know what I think of that. These feuds. Killing for revenge—"

"I meant killing when there is no reason except that you want to."

"Only madmen do that."

"Negative, Mr. Kasu. A man can be perfectly sane and kill just for the sake of it."

"If he did that, he wouldn't be sane."

"Listen, haven't you ever wondered what it would be like to kill a man? What's the difference if you kill for revenge, or to change the color of a flag, or for an idea, or just because you want to? He's just as dead. Why is it sane to kill for a political idea and insane to do it for a personal idea?"

"If the idea is correct, it justifies the killing. Why should a sane man kill just to kill?"

"Because each of us wants to be God."

"It's not normal to think that way."

"Each of us wants to be God, but we can't be God by creating life, so we have to take it."

"You are being serious, Mr. Jeremy?"

"I'm always serious, Mr. Kasu."

"This has nothing to do with what we were talking about."

"It does. Listen, I'm here for personal reasons. I don't much care about your struggle one way or the other, which means I don't intend to get mixed up in any of your little intrigues. If you want somebody to help you get rid of Jima, you're wasting your time with me."

"These personal reasons, Mr. Jeremy. Are you here to kill someone and be a god?"

Nordstrand stretched, his movements, like those of a large animal, suggesting enormous power in repose.

"Let's just say I'm not getting mixed up in any of your cheap plots."

"It's you, not I, who are speaking of plots."

"You missed your calling, Mr. Kasu. You should have been a lawyer."

Without making a reply, Murrah stood and walked off. When he was out of earshot, I said, "You didn't answer his question."

"You're a master of the obvious, Charlie Gage."

"I've got the same question. Are you here to play God by killing someone?"

"Hell, I was just baiting him." And Nordstrand gave me a smile which, coy and mocking at the same time, left me unsure as to his sincerity. Perhaps he *had* just been baiting the Bejayan; and yet, there had been an honesty in his voice, an earnestness that aroused an unpleasant expectancy. I wanted to pursue the point, but some inner censor checked me and I changed the subject slightly.

"Do you think that was a good idea, baiting him?"

"Just trying to convince him that we're not going to get mixed up in his bush-league intrigues."

"That wasn't too smart, either. You were too direct with him, telling him he couldn't count on us."

"You want to get mixed up in his bush-league intrigues, Charlie Gage?"

"No. I think it would have been better to have left things a little ambiguous. String him along. Keep him on our side."

"I never did like ambiguities."

"He's obviously got it in his head to do something about Jima, with us or without us. You're forcing him to act on his own. Could be trouble."

"It won't be any trouble I can't handle. You heard him. They listen to me. To *me*, I don't need any Kasu Murrah on my side."

Nordstrand pointed to where the khaki-clad guerrillas and white-robed caravaneers were squatting beneath leaning pillars of campfire smoke. "To me, to me," he repeated, extending both burly, sun-browned arms toward them in a symbolic embrace. "I'm going to make them all mine, Charlie Gage."

"Are you?" I could think of nothing else to say in response to that fantastic, conceited declaration.

"Don't you believe I can do it? They're half mine already."

There was a hum from inside the station as Moody sent the message through the transceiver. The tip of the long, bi-pole antenna showed through the hole in the roof.

"What are you going to do with them? Once, they're yours, that is."

"Whatever I decide."

"That include playing God?"

"You on that tack again? Told you, I was just baiting him."

"I don't completely believe that."

"Know something, Charlie Gage? It'd do you a lot of good to find something you completely believe in."

———————

At the hour when the mountains turned rust red in the waning sun and the *muezzin* began chanting the notes to the *salât il 'asr'*, Moody emerged from the station, rubbing his eyes.

"*Les Miserables*," he said, sounding more or less his old self. "Good novel to use for a book code, because that's how I feel after deciphering Colfax's last. Good news and bad news. Good news first."

Kneeling on one knee, he rolled flat a map of eastern Bejaya, all of it colored varying shades of brown except at the very edge, where it met the coast of the Red Sea.

"The *Challenger*'s been repaired and she's now on a course for the Bab el Mandeb Strait, with the arms aboard. Colfax estimates she'll pass through the strait four to five days from now. So, we won't be going to the old man of the mountain completely empty-handed. That's the good news. The bad news is this: seems that with the delay and all, the Cobra felt it would take too much time to off-load the shipment in Port Sudan, fly it to Nassala, and then have it hauled overland to Jima's base. Instead, the freighter's going to off-load it onto some Yemenite dhows at an island about twenty miles offshore. The island doesn't show on this map. Now then, the dhows will bring the guns ashore here." He pointed to a semicircle of tight contour lines marking a headland called Ras al-Sultan, the Sultan's Head. "That's eighty, maybe ninety miles due east of Jima's base and about half that distance north of a town called Edana. Colfax says we shall have to caravan the stuff in from there. That's more bad news. It's going to be a very rough eighty miles. Sixty of it will be over the Malaka Sink. Salt flats. Temperatures of a hundred and twenty this time of year. Worse yet, Edana's got a sizable Ethiopian garrison. They might have patrols ranging that far north, and if we don't bump into them, there's a chance we'll have a run-in with the FLN. They control most of the countryside east of the Sink. It'll be an awfully tough go, moving that stuff undetected."

Aw-flay.

"We'd have an awfully tough go if we had to move it from Nassala. Six of one, half-dozen of the other."

"Not quite, Charlie. According to Colfax's schedule, the dhows are to come ashore a week from tomorrow, give or take a day. It'll take a caravan three days to make the trip. If you figure in the inevitable delays, the caravan will have to leave day after tomorrow the latest. Meaning there won't be much rest for at least one of us. At least one of us will have to go along to make sure there aren't any balls-ups."

Nordstrand picked up a stick, with which he began tapping the toe of his torn boot.

"You given any thought to who that one's going to be, General?"

"I'll thank you to stop referring to me as 'General.' "

"Will you?"

"Will I what?"

"Thank me. If I call you Moody, Moody, will you say thank you?"

"Really."

Relly.

"Really what, Moody?"

"Really this is hardly the time for these schoolyard games of yours."

"You given any thought to who's going, Moody?"

"No . . ."

"I just called you Moody. Say thank you."

"I'll ignore your stupidity for now. To answer your question, no, I haven't given it any thought."

"You should."

"Not necessary to give it any thought. You're the logical choice, aren't you? You seem to have a zest for roughing it. Well, you'll get your fill of roughing it on this outing. And you say you get things done. Very well. This trip will require someone who gets things done."

"You're getting to be a smart man. Keep working at it and one day you might be as smart as Charlie Gage."

"Speaking of Charlie, he'll remain behind and man the transceiver."

Nordstrand shifted the stick to the other toe. *Tap, tap, tap.*

"And where does that leave you?"

"I'm going with you."

"I thought only one of us was going. Do you think I need the company?"

"I think I ought to. I'm in charge. It's my responsibility."

"You won't go caving in on me again, will you? You

won't have your peaches and pears and your tummy pills.
I'm not going to go carrying you again."

"Don't worry about that. You won't have to perform
any more strong-man acts. And don't make a row about
my going. You don't like the idea, do you?"

Tap, tap, tap. First one toe, then the other. *Tap, tap,
tap.*

"No row. The fact is, I like the idea. The Apollonian
and the Dionysian alone, with no one to referee."

"The what and the what?"

"Haven't you read Nietzsche?"

"No, but I'm pleased you have. Pleased to hear you can
read."

"You should read him."

"Afraid he's not to my taste."

"Try not to be afraid so much, Moody."

———

A sentry, poised on an outcropping far above us, raised
his rifle and hollered a challenge. Echoing and re-echoing,
his call merged into a single sound, a piercing, half-human
cry such as the slouching thing who had lived his clockless
days and uncalendared years in those same mountains
might have uttered in warning or rage. As its last echoes
died away, Osman yelled a response. The sentry answered
with two shots—the signal to come ahead. The caravan
rocked along for another two or three miles, down a broad
wadi blindingly white from the salt blown in from the
Malaka Sink. Like mock snow, salt lay drifted in the draws
and crevasses; it lay in patches on the treeless slopes, cruel
in its evocation of cool alpine meadows.

Turning onto a narrow, stony track, we began the long
climb to Jima's stronghold. The jaded camels were barely
able to negotiate the trail: their wide-spreading, double-
toed hooves, which allowed them to move with ease across
the desert, clopped uncertainly over the loose stones.
Sheer cliffs rose on both sides of the track, gigantic tablets
upon which nature had written the stratigraphic record of
all the ages of the earth. The caravan went on up at a

funereal pace, and there was always a sentry above us,
waving his rifle. Stumbling, the camels kicked rocks into
the chasm that separated the trail from the cliff on the
left. It was no more than ten feet wide, but so deep you
never heard the rocks strike bottom. Fear of falling into
the abyss kept us pressed to the wall on our right. Its
rocky knobs and lava spurs bruised and cut us; the wind
literally rubbed salt into the wounds; the camels gagged
us with their constant farting, and the sun pummeled us.
A couple of hours of this made me savage. You cannot
have your head baked, your feet blistered, and your nostrils clogged with the stench of camels' farts without getting a little nasty. Because it was the closest target, I vented
my rage on the camel in front of me. Every time it farted,
I bashed its haunches with a hiking stick. When it whipped
its head back, spitting and trying to bite me, I cracked its
snout until it bawled with pain. Then I went back to work
on the haunches, whacking and smashing until tufts of hair
started to fall off. "Ya! Mr. Charlie. Good. Good," roared
Osman the camel-hater. "That's the way to treat these
galled bitches. Treat them as you would a wife." He
laughed heartily, quoting an old nomad's proverb. "Beat
your wife every morning—if you don't know the reason
why, she will." The caravan plodded over a high, narrow
pass through which the wind howled, and the wind's channeled force pelted us with sand and salt. That stinging
blast was nature's fillip, a slap in the face administered as
both a reprimand and a reminder of who was boss. Re-
pentant, I stopped beating the animal and, like the other
men, walked on with my head bowed against the wind.
In that fashion, we marched across an open space which
would have been called a highland meadow if the sun had
allowed trees and grasses to grow there. Two of the camels
died. They died the way exhausted camels do, without
preamble, without any fuss or warning. One moment they
were plodding along, apparently healthy: the next moment,
their legs folded beneath them, and they rolled onto their
sides and died. Osman exploded in a fury. Now there
would be another delay as the drivers loaded the cargo
onto the other animals. Worse, one of the camels had
crushed an ammunitions crate in its fall, spilling hundreds

of the small, precious .303 Enfield cartridges. These would have to be gathered up and the crate repaired. "Galled bitches! Useless galled bitches! God damn you!" Osman clubbed the dead beasts on the head. "Bitches! I wish I had killed you myself." The rest of us were inclined to thank the camels. The hot climb had blown all of us, even the all-enduring scouts and the indefatigable Nordstrand. While the drivers went to work, we found what shade we could and rested. Moody, who had an eye for the comfortable spot, discovered an overhang large enough to shelter the two of us. We collapsed under it and drank from our canteens without taking the usual precautions of drinking slowly: I nearly emptied mine, a big, two-quart canteen, in a couple of long drafts. Moody removed a bottle of salt tablets from his front pocket, carefully split one of the pink pills, and handed me half.

"Best take this, Charlie. Keep your strength up. Too bad, but I had enough to last the lot of us in my duffel bag."

I put the tablet in my mouth, attempting to wash it down with a disciplined sip; but the water tasted so good I could not resist draining what was left in the canteen. My mouth dried in the time it took me to screw the cap back on.

Stretched out, Moody was looking at a sheet of yellowed ruled paper he had pulled from the large side-pocket of his bush jacket.

"Remarkable," he said. He wetted his cracked lips with his tongue.

"It isn't remarkable. It's incredible." Waves of light rippled up from the rocky meadow so that I seemed to be looking at the camels and the caravaneers through a distorting lens. "It must be a hundred and thirty degrees."

"Oh, yes. The heat. It is incredible. Didn't mean that. Meant this." He tapped the yellowed paper, which was about the size of a page from a small atlas. "Have a look at this, Charlie. It's really quite remarkable."

Rubbing my eyes, which felt as if someone had gone over them with sandpaper, I looked. Written at the top of the page in block letters were the words: RECORD OF MISDEMEANORS, MALAKA DISTRICT, KEREM SUBDISTRICT,

JAN. 1948–DEC. 1949. Vertical and horizontal lines divided the page. The ruling had been done by hand with painstaking care: the lines were as straight as those in an accounts book and the headings of the columns meticulously printed: DATE. NAME. TRIBE. OFFENSE. DISPOSITION. OFFICER COMMANDING. The signature "J. A. Chancellor" appeared a dozen or so times in a handwriting so precise that each signature looked like a rubber-stamp duplicate of the first. The entries had been written in the same careful hand. "June 8, 1949," read one. "Ali abu Noor. Beni-Hamid. Unauthorized tree-cutting. Fined. J. A. Chancellor."

"Unauthorized tree-cutting," I said. "What the hell is this?"

"Page from a docket. Tore it out of a docket I found in the station house back at Kerem. Been lying in the desk thirty years. It goes back to when Bejaya was under British mandate. That post used to be a kind of courthouse, with the British administrator acting as a policeman, judge, and jury for minor offenses. Quite a remarkable find, wouldn't you say, Charlie?"

"Fining a man for unauthorized tree-cutting sure is remarkable. There aren't a dozen trees inside of ten miles of that place."

"That's just it. Probably there used to be considerably more. Most of them've been cut down since the mandate ended in 'fifty-two. Cutting them was an offense because every last tree was needed to prevent soil erosion and further desertification. I rummaged through the docket. Almost every offense was for cutting down trees or overgrazing herds. Really quite remarkable."

Relly.

"Okay. I give up. What's so remarkable about some colonial fining a tribesman for cutting down a tree?"

"Look at that man's handwriting and tell me if you feel anything."

"Are you going mystical on me?"

"No. Look at his handwriting."

I looked at it and felt nothing except a mild wonder. Why, I asked the Englishman, did this official of the British Empire take such pains to record such a monotonous succession of petty offenses? They did not seem worth recording at all, let alone with such tidiness and attention to detail.

"That's it exactly." Moody sat up suddenly, nearly cracking his head on the overhang. "Why indeed? Why bother? After all, the fate of the empire didn't rest on preventing a lot of nomads from cutting down a few trees, did it? Why indeed? Because it was his duty, that's why. His duty, Charlie, and he did it as best he could."

I said nothing, figuring Moody was again suffering from too much sun. Out in the meadow, the drivers were distributing the loads of the dead camels among the others. Several guerrillas, bowing and stooping, were picking up the scattered cartridges. "Every last one, brothers," Osman barked. "We need every last one." I thought, Good, it'll take them all afternoon to pick up every last one and I'd just as soon stay here, under my rock.

"Difficult to express what it meant to me, finding that docket." Moody was lying down again and fanning himself with his hat. "Saw how foolish I'd been, losing my head back there at Balaka. Afraid I behaved rather badly, accusing those chaps of stealing, taking a poke at Nordstrand."

"You don't have to apologize." I was tempted to tell him how the supplies came to be lost, but then thought, No, no, it wouldn't do anyone any good.

"I'll apologize anyway. Finding that docket, you see, got me to thinking. That man, Chancellor, was a hero. A bloody hero. They ought to have given him the Victoria Cross, because he was more of a hero than all the Kitcheners and Gordons put together. Or heroic in a different way. He was heroic by virtue of his unheroic position: commander of a police subdistrict in a remote district of a mandated territory of no importance to anyone. Judging from the dates on that docket, they did yearlong stretches out at these stations. Doesn't sound like a long time, but they came out to these godforsaken posts alone. Alone, Charlie. Put in charge of a detachment of native police and told to enforce the law, and they did it. Try to imagine what it was like. A whole year out here surrounded by men with swords and spears, no one to talk to, no diversions of any kind, no women, nothing around you but the desert

and these god-awful hills and this god-awful heat, and
your job is to tell the men with the swords and spears that
they can't cut down trees and to fine them if they do.
They must have resented him for that. Can't say I blame
them, either. They must have needed the trees for firewood
and whatnot, and then this white man comes along and
starts fining them left, right, and center for doing something they'd always done. I should think he felt their resentment, too. Don't doubt he went to sleep with his revolver under his pillow now and then. So you'd have to
add fear to the heat, the isolation, the terrible loneliness,
and the boredom. Think of the boredom, Charlie. Week
after week, your little troop of native cops comes in with
some raggedy tribesmen who have done nothing but cut
down a few trees. No tribal wars to settle, no border conflicts to fight in, nothing dramatic or colorful like that, and
so no chance of distinguishing yourself, nothing to look
forward to except a bit of home leave. And at the end of
it all, what? An inadequate pension and maybe a few
stories to tell your grandchildren. Wonder is how chaps
like this Chancellor kept their sanity. He did keep it,
though. That and more. Look at the way those entries are
written. Neat as a pin. Everything filled in and as it should
be—"

"What the hell is this, Pat? Remember the British Empire Week?"

"No, nothing like that. Still, you have to admire men
like Chancellor. Did what was expected of them when
everything around them told them to do the opposite. To
say the hell with it, give up and give in, submit, let yourself go. What does that tell you?"

"I don't know. You seem to have got an awful lot out
of that piece of paper. World's greatest handwriting
analyst."

"It tells me this, Charlie. That Chancellor fellow must
have been a man much like my father, a man who was
moved by fidelity and love."

"Fidelity to what and love of what?"

"Fidelity to standards and love of this place."

I would have laughed if I had had the energy. "*Love*

of this place. I don't think the people who live here—Osman, Murrah, all of them—love this hellhole."

"And I think you're quite wrong. My father was a police commissioner in the Sudan before it got independence. I was raised there till I was ten. That's where I learned Arabic and this dialect. Heard my father speak it —but that's neither here nor there. Point is, my father loved the Sudan. He loved Africa. I do, too. My father passed that love on to me. That's why I'm here: because I love this part of the world and I care about what happens here."

"This love of yours," I asked, "does it include woolly-headed bastards and incompetent niggers?"

"I'm not going to be allowed to forget that, am I? Damn it, you know I was a little off my head then. Fever. Sunstroke."

"Look, I'll let you forget it, if you spare me the love-and-fidelity bullshit."

"You don't believe men can act out of those motives?"

Using the butts of their knife handles as hammers, the guerrillas began repairing the smashed ammo crate. Osman was looking around, puzzled.

"Mr. Charlie," he called loudly, "Mr. Patrick, where are you?"

I poked my head from under the overhang. "Up here."

"Ya! It is almost done."

Shit, I thought, moving again.

"But we are going to rest the camels for a time, until it is not so hot."

"*Al-hamduillah*—Allah be praised," I answered.

Osman laughed. "So now we will make some *tea.* You would like some tea?"

I said we would and drew my head back under the rocky shelf.

"Charlie?"

"What?"

"Don't you believe men can act out of selfless motives?"

"I stopped believing that six months after I stopped believing in the tooth fairy."

"That's very American of you. Nobody does anything

unless there's something in it for him. Everything is done
for personal reasons. You seem to accept that, but you
can't accept that I'm here because I care about this
place."

"All right, let's say you do care. You're full of love
and fidelity, like this Chancellor. So what? What's that got
to do with us? We're not here to fine these people for cutting down trees, are we? We're here to make an army out
of them."

"What's this to do with us? Well . . . of course we're
here to train them . . . that's precisely . . . hard to phrase
this precisely . . . but that will require fidelity, you see,
and, yes, caring, and Nordstrand doesn't have that. He has
his virtues, but those aren't among them. He lacks what
this Chancellor fellow had. No fidelity in him, and no love.
None at all."

"I don't follow."

"You told me what he said the other day. That balderdash about how it is quite all right to kill a man for the
sake of killing because each of us wants to be a god.
Coming from him, that's not balderdash. What I mean is,
I think he was sincere. That's one thing I've learned about
our big friend. He's sincere."

"I still don't follow."

"I think that man is capable of killing someone just for
the hell of it. The fact is, I think you and I are the only
reasons he hasn't shot someone so far. We check him.
That's why I'm going with him to pick up the arms. To act
as a check. Make sure he doesn't do something awful."

"He said all that talk about killing people was just a
way of baiting Murrah."

"You think it was?"

"Could be. I'm not sure."

"Charlie, you don't see that man for what he is."

"Maybe not. Whether I do or not doesn't change the
fact that he's done all right by us so far. You ought to
know about that better than I do."

"I had fever, Charlie. Sunstroke."

"Yeah, I know that. He still carried you, didn't he?
Maybe he didn't do it out of love and fidelity, but he did it.

I know that much, just as I know you're not here because you care about this hellhole."

"Why are you bringing that up again?"

"Because your virtuousness is starting to get on my nerves. Because I know nobody in his right mind takes on a risk like this mission and comes out to a place like this unless he's desperate."

"Really."

"Yes, *relly*."

"And are you desperate, Charlie?"

"Yes."

"About what?"

One of the rebels walked up with two cups of tea. As usual, it was thick with sugar and scalding hot, but it cut the dryness in my throat.

"Well, Charlie? What is it you're so desperate about?"

"It's too complicated to explain. And even if it wasn't, it's too goddamned hot to talk anymore."

"Couldn't be anything so conventional as a woman, could it?"

"My woman troubles ended a long time ago, when I got divorced."

"Didn't know you were divorced. Messy business, that."

"You too?"

"Me? No. Should have said I suppose that's a messy business. No, I was never married. Never engaged, in fact. Had a girl who fancied me when I was in the army. Wrote to each other after I went to Oman. Think she broached the subject in a letter or two, but after . . . well, couldn't really. Doesn't matter. Nothing came of it."

"What about you?"

"What about me?"

"What made you desperate enough to take this on?"

"Why do you insist that I'm desperate? Isn't it presumptuous of you to ascribe your own motives to somebody else?"

Moody lit a cigarette, grimaced at the taste of the hot smoke, and immediately put it out. He started fidgeting with the amulet to occupy his hands.

"Think I'll take advantage of this break and have a bit of kip."

"What happened in Oman, Moody?"

"Nothing happened in Oman. Think I'll have some kip."

Setting down his metal cup, he pulled his hat over his eyes and fell asleep, or pretended to. I tried to get some rest myself, but the crushing heat made me feel that I would suffocate if I lost consciousness. After several minutes of shifting about, Moody sat up and lit another cigarette.

"Bloody hell."

"Couldn't get comfortable myself. Too goddamned hot."

"It's not the heat. It's you, you bastard."

"I'll go find another rock to crawl under if I bother you so much."

"You bloody perceptive bastard."

"That's a backhanded compliment if I ever heard one."

"Everything happened in Oman."

His was the old story of the man who had failed himself. Moody's father, whom he described as a man of old-fashioned, jut-jawed British rectitude, an attribute that had stood him in good stead as a colonial police commissioner, had returned to England after the Sudan became independent. He retired to Essex, where his family had some property and where, helped along by a modest inheritance and his pension, he set himself up as a country gentleman. The family lived a life as regular as the green and gold fields surrounding their comfortable old house. Like most police officers, the elder Moody had a dim view of human nature; years of dealing with murderers and thieves had convinced him that a rigid code of social behavior, the Church, and the Law, especially the Law, were required to prevent men from succumbing to what he called "our base impulses." He raised his two sons and three daughters accordingly, an effort in which his wife was less a wife and lover and more a second-in-command. ("My mother," Moody said, "makes Margaret Thatcher look like a loose woman.") There was grace before every meal, communion on Sundays, and firm reprimands for childhood sins. Visitors always complimented the Moodys on the behavior of their children, headmasters commented on their exemplary deportment at school.

"And we were well behaved. That was our hallmark, children of a police commissioner." Moody smiled in the rueful way of a man recalling a practical joke that had been played on him. "It was easy to be well behaved in that environment," he said. His idea of nature was the benevolent little woods that grew near the house, all cut down to size and fenced in, with nothing more dangerous in it than a fox. As for cities, the family sometimes visited London, but the children were kept confined to the safe neighborhoods. The tough back streets of the East End seemed more distant and mysterious to Moody than the Africa he had known as a child.

"Don't misunderstand me, Charlie. I'm not complaining about my upbringing. In fact, I had a very happy boyhood, but it was all a dream. Naturally, all those compliments about my exemplary behavior affected me. I got rather an idealized image of myself. We all get that, I suppose. I thought I'd always do the right thing. It never occurred to me I was capable of doing the opposite. A dreamworld, Charlie. A dream."

At thirteen, he was packed off to the inevitable boarding school. His father had hoped to send him to Eton or Harrow but, lacking the pedigree and social connections, had to settle for Felstead in Essex. "Another dreamworld," Moody called it. About all it accomplished was to smooth out the rough spots in his Anglo-Irish accent. After graduating, he went on to the London School of Economics (his father disapproved, regarding that slightly left-of-center institution as an outpost of the Kremlin), where he read Arabic and specialized in African studies. Remembrances of his early childhood in the Sudan and the memorabilia his father kept around the house—spears and shields and tribal masks—had stirred in Moody a romantic ambition to return to Africa with the foreign service. He wound up as a desk officer in Whitehall, where the only contact he had with the once-dark, now-twilit continent was through the cables he read from embassies in Khartoum, Lagos, and Dar es Salaam. Moody withstood the monotony for two years, then quit to take a commission in the army. Like the foreign service, the army promised to combine adventure with respectability.

"No need to go into that," Moody said, puffing on another cigarette. "Long on respectability, short on adventure. Posted me in Germany with the British Army of the Rhine, doing my bit for NATO. I was a signals officer. Communications intelligence, actually. I supposed they figured anyone who could master languages like Arabic and To-Bedawyi would find cryptography a lark. Got bored stiff with it and—now I know this'll make me sound a stuffed-shirt—and I found I didn't care much for the men. Found them crude, in fact. Thick-necked bullies, some of them, rather like our big friend Nordstrand. Not as clever. Hadn't read Nietzsche, but the sort who like thumping skulls. Bellies full of beer. Used to put out campfires by pissing on them. Never mind. Word came down asking for volunteers to be seconded to the sultan's army in Oman. Dhofar rebellion was on then, and I signed up without a second thought. The Sultan of Oman—hell, the sound of that got my blood going. I was going to fight for the Sultan of Oman. You know how it is when you're twenty-five. Ready to go anywhere and do anything for no sensible reason."

He told the rest of his story rapidly and in disjointed phrases, chain-smoking cigarettes, his face troubled by the expressions of a man who was not merely recalling a painful experience, but reliving it.

Moody had been in Oman a little under a year, fighting a brutal little war against Marxist terrorists in Dhofar Province, when his unit, a reconnaissance company, was ordered to verify reports of a massacre in a village near the South Yemeni border.

"Don't know why they sent us. Been in the bush too long already. Short of rations, short of water, short of gas for the recce vehicles. Couldn't take the scout cars into those hills anyway. Left them with half the company and hiked up on foot with the other half. Took us nearly three days to get up there. Hills all cut up with wadis, like these here, except they've got more rainfall there and so more trees. Parts of it like a jungle. Heat terrible. Bad as this. Kind of heat that makes you want to scream. Think I had a touch of sunstroke then, too. Too much time in temperate climates, you know. And I was hungry, Charlie. Told you we were short of rations. Top that off, the radio wouldn't transmit properly in those hills. Couldn't get base to understand we needed a helicopter resupply. First time in my life I'd known real hunger, not some pleasant tummy-rumbling before dinner. Know what that does to you after a while? Makes you nasty. Made me as nasty as those scorpions that snuggled up to us out there at night. Rebels made it pleasant, too. Sniped at us quite a lot. Didn't hit anyone, but it worked on our nerves.

"Think I was half off my head when we got to the village. There was me and twenty-odd Arabs and half a dozen Paki mercenaries and my second-in-command, a perfect child of a subaltern, Chamberlain. Old military family. Sandhurst, et cetera. Went out to Oman because it was the only place besides Belfast where a British officer could get himself shot at. Where was I? Oh yes, the village. Shambles. Smelled the place long before we got to it. Must have been three dozen corpses lying about—men, women, children. The kids got to me worst of all. Something especially awful about seeing a child shot to pieces. I do mean pieces. It was a friendly village, you see. Friendly to the sultan, that is, so the terrs had to teach them a lesson. Didn't just shoot them. Shot their bellies open. Know what the human stomach looks like? Greenish brown, like a big mass of spoiled spinach. I'd been out there nine or ten months, but that was the first time I'd seen death on a large scale. And the first time I'd smelled it. Mosque had been blown to rubble. A few people still alive, amazingly. Two or three old men, a couple of women who must have been ten years older than God. Know what the terrs had done to them? Flogged them. Flogged them with thorn branches and laid their backs open. Know why? Because they'd been in the mosque when the rebels attacked. Praying. Practicing Islam was against revolutionary principles, and if keeping principles pure requires shooting up some kids and whipping the hides off some old people, well, it has to be done. That's why they'd blown up the mosque as well. Oh, it was something to see, Charlie. It was something to see, and I wish to God I'd never seen it."

He stopped to take a breath, lit another cigarette, then continued:

"Wish I'd never seen it because something blew in me. It was the kids. All shot up and covered with flies. Blew. Not a figure of speech. I felt it blow. I heard it. Made a sound inside my head like a light bulb when it burns out, a sort of pop. Pop, pop. Yes, a pop. Going on a bit, aren't I? Very well, I shall stick to the facts. That's what they told me at the inquiry. Stick to the facts. Military mind, you know. Subjectivity is not allowed by the king's regulations. All right, here are the facts: We buried the dead and pulled out of there with the old people in tow, and headed back down toward the scout cars. As jolly a business going down as it was going up. Ran out of rations and the damned radio simply wouldn't put out enough signal. Base kept reading us strength two, I think. Maybe three. No matter. We had to eat the dates off the date palm. Nothing wrong with dates. Plenty of vegetable protein. But they dry your mouth up. Like chewing on cotton after a while. And we were short of water as well. Halfway down, we surprised three young Dhofaris who were preparing a little surprise for us. Planting a mine in the track. Three hard cases. Probably been trained in South Yemen by those East German advisers they've got there. Very thorough, the Germans. These three wouldn't answer a question. Wouldn't even give their names. I asked them if they'd had anything to do with that butchery in the village. One of my Arabs cracked one of them in the face. Fellow still wouldn't talk. Another crack, and he spit at me. Not at the Arab, but at me, and I think it was at that same instant that I had a sort of mental snapshot of the scene up at the village. So I shot him. Then I shot the other two. One moment I was looking at them, the next moment I felt the spit strike my face, and the third moment my revolver's bucking in my hand. No proof they'd had a thing to do with the massacre, but I wasn't thinking about that. I just lost control. Killed all three. Killed the three of them. Murdered prisoners of war. That's what rosy-cheeked Chamberlain was shouting. 'Sir! Sir! Stop it! You're murdering them, sir!' And I turned round and pointed my pistol at him and said, 'You're bloody right I've murdered them, Chamberlain, and if you say one word about this, I'll murder you.'"

"You said that?"

"Surprise you? Can't surprise you half as much as it did me. It still surprises me. Oh, I've worked out a rationalization of sorts. You can guess part of it. Hunger, thirst, sun had worn me down. But there was something more. The massacre was my first experience of human evil, and I didn't know how to deal with it. I suppose I had thought the whole world was like Essex. Nothing in my background had prepared me for what I saw. That horror offended my—what? Very well, I'll say it. My good old sense of British decency. It offended my sense of decency, and I wanted to punish someone for it. Anyone. Mind you, it wasn't just the terrs and what they'd done that set me off. I was angry at the dreamworld I'd been raised in. Why hadn't my father prepared me for the way things are? Do you know what I was prepared for? I was prepared to live in Essex, that's all. You can guess what happened next. After we got back to base, Chamberlain reported the prisoner business to our colonel, the senior British officer present. Inquiry, of course, at HQ in Salalah. Recommendation for court-martial. Would've had one, too, if the army hadn't been afraid of a scandal. Some Labour MPs weren't too happy with the role we were playing in Oman, and an English officer being brought up on charges of murdering three prisoners would have made jolly headlines. They solved their problem neatly. Quietly cashiered me. They got some army doctor to say I'd been temporarily insane and then gave me a medical discharge. Oh, they were gentlemen about it. Kept the results of the inquiry out of my records and toned down the doctor's report so I'd have no problems in civilian life. But, in a sense, I was a certified lunatic. Sometimes I wish I could believe that. I wish that were true, but it wasn't my mind I lost in those godforsaken hills. . . ."

"Aren't you being a little hard on yourself? Christ, that kind of thing went on all the time in Vietnam. It happens in every war. It's inevitable."

"That's like telling a man who's been in an auto accident that collisions are inevitable. The point isn't that it happened, but that it happened to me. I thought I'd always do the right thing. I didn't. I was tested and found wanting. That's what the colonel told me after he gave me the news about the arrangement they'd made with the doctor. I recall his words precisely: Never forget them. 'Lieutenant Moody, by the usual standards you ought to be court-martialed, but you have been tried already, young man. You have been tried and found wanting.' Good God, hearing that was as bad as hearing sentence pronounced. The very words my father would've used if he'd been in the colonel's place. I wasn't very proud at that point. I all but got down on my hands and knees and begged the old man for a second chance. Again, I remember precisely what he said. 'Young man, I might consider that if yours was an act of cowardice under fire. But yours was an act of brutality, admittedly an act committed under very unusual circumstances, but an act of brutality nonetheless. And don't you see that to redeem yourself properly you would have to duplicate those circumstances? The chances of that happening are one in a million, and we've no guarantee, you've no guarantee, that you wouldn't do the same thing all over again.'

"He was right, of course, and it has been hell for me ever since. Hell. God, it makes me sick to hear the way the word *guilt* is bandied about these days by people who've never been tested, who will all die with their morals in one piece, full of good opinions of themselves. Fools who think guilt is something you can just pick off a shelf and put back when it's convenient. Quite another matter when you can't put it away. When you wake up with it in the middle of the night. Hell, when you go to the loo with it. Rambling again, aren't I? Drifted after my so-called discharge. Naturally. Couldn't go home and face dear old Dad under those circumstances. Could hardly face myself. Tramped about the Middle East and North Africa. Finally picked up a decent job teaching English to some Sudanese kids in Omdurman. Two years, no, closer to three. Then, as if somebody had decided I shouldn't get off so easily, who should show up as military attaché to our embassy in Khartoum? My old colonel, of course. Saw him at a party the embassy threw for British residents of the area. Queen's birthday was the occasion. I didn't just see him. I was introduced to him by a friend of mine in the consulate. Perfect innocence. He took my arm and led me up to the

old man, and God. I was terrified. The colonel was embarrassed, and I cleared out the next day. Packed a bag and
took the next plane to Cairo. Figured I could lose myself
in a city that size, and I did. Managed to find a teaching
post at the American University. That's where I bumped
into Colfax. The Cobra was studying Arabic. It's enough
to say I was a bit short of money and he made me a generous offer after he'd found out I'd done a spell in Oman. No
sense going into any more detail. Not *germane* to the case,
as my father would say. Father. I must say I miss him
sometimes. Can't help but think that he'd point out the
course I should follow. Odd, a man thirty-three years old
missing his father. I feel as if he's dead."

In the shadow of the overhang, Moody's face looked
aged. The schoolboy freshness had gone out of it, and it
looked old, as old as failure.

"Well, I've confessed, haven't I? You got it out of me,
you persistent bastard. I guess I am desperate. You see,
after I got tied up with Colfax and he told me about this
mission, I had to sign up for it. It would be the only chance
I was likely to get."

"To duplicate the circumstances."

"To duplicate the circumstances." He took out the page
from the old docket, opened it, folded it, opened it again,
the record of a man who had not failed, who had remained
faithful. "I wish to be tried again and to do the right thing
this time."

"You might not, you know. Be tried, I mean."

"I know. But I'll have more of a chance out here than I
would playing schoolteacher in Cairo."

"What if you are and don't do the right thing?"

"I think I've talked enough, Charlie. I've told you more
than I've told any man since it happened. Fact is, except
for the men involved, you're the only one who knows about
this. Never mentioned it to Colfax. Just do me one service.
Keep this from Nordstrand. That son of a bitch would
find some way to take advantage."

"That's one thing I'm still good at, keeping secrets."

The sun was a little less furious in the late afternoon, when
the caravan resumed its slow crawl up the mountains. We
reached another plateau two hours later, after passing
through a defile just wide enough to accommodate the line
of men and animals. The wind mourned and shrieked between the constricting rocks, the place called Bab el Howa,
the Gate of the Wind. Half a mile away, the plateau sloped
up toward a cave-pocked cliff which flung its shadow over
the lava block huts huddled beneath it. As we grew closer
to the camp, I could make out a green flag snapping from
a makeshift pole, machine guns poking their black barrels
from behind parapets of flat rock, knots of armed men
moving around with the lazy aimless saunter all soldiers
adopt in garrison, and a herd of camels, snouts buried in
feed bags because there was no graze for them on that sun-
demolished slope. Heat waves shimmied off the hoods and
roofs of three Land-Rovers and two big trucks parked in
an acacia grove beside the huts. I thought I was seeing
things, and asked Osman how the rebels had managed to
haul those up the mountain. Laughing, he explained that
the opposite side of the plateau was not as steep as the side
we had just climbed. An old caravan trail ran down it,
joining a wadi that spilled into the Malaka Sink. "As good
as a road, that wadi. If we had come up from that side, Mr.
Charlie, we should have made this climb in an hour's
time." It was easy to see why Jima had chosen the place for
his stronghold: it was a natural fortress, unassailable from
the west by any army mad enough to enter those killing
hills and lucky enough to avoid getting lost in the labyrinth
of gorges and ravines. Anyone attacking from the east
would have to cross the formidable Sink. The caves provided shelter in case of an air strike, which was not very
likely: flying a low-level bomb run through the crowded
peaks and cliffs would have required a pilot with the re-
actions of a stunt man and the nervous system of a stone.
And limestone pits collected the sparse rainfall of the wet
season to serve as natural cisterns. It was likewise easy to
see why the Beni-Hamid had acquired their reputation for
ferocity. Eastward lay the part of the massif that had been
underwater in primordial times. A broad wadi wound between the mountains, which the waves and tides of vanished

seas had carved into fantastic arches, chimneys, and baroque pillars, into flinty pyramids and buttes as flat as rooftops. Whole hillsides had sheared away in tremendous landslides, creating cliffs whose faces, cracked in more or less regular lines, resembled the façades of buildings made of huge blocks, and beneath them lay mounds of rubble powdered with saline sand. In the distance, the salt flats of the Sink, the skeleton of a long-dead arm of the Red Sea, stretched away toward the blue coastal hills. The total effect was that of a city whose gigantic structures had been shattered in some unrecorded holocaust, its ruins now laved by a white and waveless sea, covered by a silence as profound as the silence of death, and inhabited by desert hawks, soaring from their rocky nests to ride the thermals on wide dark wings. I had never seen a landscape of such unremitting cruelty. There was nothing in it to arrest the eye, no beauty to quicken the heart, no promise to enliven the spirit. Its one virtue was its sincerity: it promised nothing, nothing is what it gave—not so much as a single blade of grass. Living there had hardened the Beni-Hamid, forcing them to survive either by mining salt from the Sink or by the more interesting pursuit of raiding and robbing those who did. It had made them contemptuous of all those toward whom nature had shown more generosity, and it gave them the notion that Allah had put them there to purify their souls through suffering, because he had chosen them to spread his faith—which they had done with uncompromising zeal.

The two hundred guerrillas in camp welcomed us ceremoniously. They fired their rifles in the air, a traditional greeting, formed ranks behind their green banner in the casual, sloppy fashion with which irregulars perform drill. The flag had crossed swords and some sort of calligraphic inscription emblazoned on it in white. The men presented arms with weapons that looked as if they had come from a mail-order catalogue: Enfields, Mausers, a few Kalashnikovs, an M-14 here, a Belgian FN there, and despite Jima's distrust of Jews, a couple of Israeli Uzis. Several guerrillas had only their tribal swords raised in salute. Their uniforms were equally haphazard, men wearing everything from herdsmen's sackcloth to khaki drill to bell-

bottom jeans. A few recent recruits had only their tribal
dress—white robes thrown togalike over their knobby
shoulders, skirts belted around their waists.

I don't suppose Nordstrand, Moody, and I were any more
impressive in appearance. Our shirts were filthy and card-
board-stiff with dried sweat, our boots and trousers in
tatters, our bearded faces scorched and peeling. We
marched past them as jauntily as our bodies, battered by
almost two weeks of hard traveling, would allow. On some
signal or other, the guerrillas suddenly broke ranks,
swarmed around us, and began singing a slow, haunting
melody in their whispery mountaineers' voices. Startled by
this display, unsure of how to respond, we stood smiling
stupidly at the crowd of black, marked faces, each as
strange as the lyrics to the song.

"Don't worry," Osman assured us. "It's a song of welcome. They're honoring you as guests. Come. This way."

He and Murrah led us along a path toward the caves,
whose dark mouths gaped in the cliff above. The rebels
shambled alongside, still singing, and the air shimmered
with the golden dust raised by their feet. Ending their song
as abruptly as they began it, they took up a chant: *"Jihad,
jihad, hitta al-nasr, inshallah!*—Holy war, holy war, until
victory, if God wills!" They repeated it over and over,
stomping their feet in cadence with the words, raising and
lowering their rifles in time with their feet. Like a football
cheer, the chant was shouted louder with each repetition.
It echoed off the cliff and rolled over the empty mountains,
which echoed it back until it and its repercussions became
one sound, a rushing roar. The guerrillas' eyes grew wild-
er, the repetitive rhythms intoxicating them. There was
something a little frightening in their mindless shouting, a
suggestion of emotions tenuously balanced. They scrambled
with us up the shale-covered slope lying at the foot of the
cliff, all two hundred of them, repeating the chant until I
heard it ringing inside my head and, willy-nilly, almost began yelling it myself. *JIHAD, JIHAD, HITTA AL-NASR,
INSHALLAH!* At last, having shouted themselves hoarse,
they fell silent and finished things off by firing another ragged volley in the air.

"That was quite a demonstration," Moody said, slightly out of breath.

"Yes," Murrah answered in an undertone, so Osman would not hear. "Of sectarian fanaticism."

"Sorry I mentioned it."

Osman and Murrah ushered us into our billet, a short cave with an entrance passageway whose floor angled sharply down into a high, twilit cavern. The angle was such that we could see only the top half of the entrance from the cavern. Sunlight slanted faintly through the mouth, refracting off the back wall, which, composed of a mosaic of rocks glazed by the fires of ancient eruptions, caught our reflections like a broken mirror. It was blessedly cool inside. A row of woven reed beds stood along one wall, the only furniture besides a log table with a kerosene lamp on it, a few straw floor mats, and a tripod supporting a waterskin. I drank from it, but the water did not slake my thirst. The saline air had parched me to a degree that the word *thirst* had no meaning. Falling on one of the bunks, my head whirling from exhaustion, I looked up at the rough vaulted ceiling and thought of the house my father had built, the new ranch house filled with all the conveniences and gadgets modern man uses to insulate himself from the forces of nature. Now I was in a cave in Africa, in man's original home, in the place where the slouching ancestor slept fitfully through fireless nights shattered by the roars and screams of beasts that are now so much fossil.

Yassin, Hamad, and two other men came in lugging our packs and the radio. Yassin, who had become Nordstrand's personal manservant for all practical purposes, asked if Mr. Jer-ah-mee would like some tea. Mr. Jeremy replied that he would.

"Mr. Charlie and I would like some as well," Moody said testily as Yassin turned to go. The Englishman had collapsed on the bunk next to mine. Nordstrand made it a point to remain standing in the presence of the Bejayans. Mr. Jeremy, who never tired, never rested, never slept in the cloth sacks like the other two *ferengei,* but on the naked sands, like the *jebha.* Yassin said, yes, of course he would bring tea for all.

When he and the others were gone, Osman and Murrah let us in on a little fiction they'd concocted to make it easier to explain to Jima why they'd disobeyed his orders. They would tell him that Colfax's message about the arms shipment had arrived the night we crossed the border, not yesterday. That would serve as a plausible excuse for their insubordination, and they would appreciate it if we corroborated their story should Jima ask. We said we would. The two men appeared greatly relieved. Then, in the curt, correct manner of a palace protocol officer, Murrah told us the great man would see us in an hour.

He and Osman left, their fractured reflections rising on the glazed walls as they climbed the ramplike passageway. Then only Nordstrand's reflection remained, a cubist image of himself. He was standing by the table, removing a fresh set of clothes from his pack. Seeing the bulge his diaries made in the canvas bag, I thought of Moody's remark, "You don't see that man for what he is." I was willing to admit I did not, which was not to admit that Moody's vision was any clearer. Each man presents to another a mystery as insoluble as the one he presents to himself.

With his hands resting on his knees and his thin legs folded under him so as not to show the soles of his feet, Jima sat on the floor at one end of the long hut looking like an undernourished buddha. His flag was pegged to the wall behind him, and now we could read the inscription, and the white calligraphy spread across the green field was not meant to challenge or to warn, but to state what Jima regarded as a fact: "Blood shall water the tree of faith." He appeared tall for a Bejayan, five-nine or -ten. A plain uniform covered his slender frame: khaki shorts, knee socks strapped to his legs with old British puttees, a khaki shirt set off by the web lanyard of his automatic. His knotty, grey-speckled hair was cropped close. His black mustache and trim beard, so thin it looked like a chin strap, gave a patriarchal look to his face, a face cratered from a childhood bout wth smallpox. He had a certain presence as he sat there, idollike in his stillness, his nose shaped like a falcon's beak, his dark eyes alert and predatory. When we were a few feet from him, Osman whispered to us to sit and make sure we did not show the bottoms of our feet, which was an insult. This we did, after which Murrah introduced us. Jima neither moved nor spoke. For a very long, very uncomfortable minute, he silently measured us with his deep-set eyes. The intensity in them gave him an almost tangible aura of command. His bodyguards added to that aura. There were about twenty-five altogether, sitting in two ranks along one wall, distinguished from the rank and file by their green armbands and new Kalashnikovs. They also glared at us, all with a deadly serious expression so uniform I wondered if they had staring drills every morning. A table covered with military maps held down by rock paperweights and a Sony transistor radio stood in a corner, the sole furniture. With nothing else to look at, we were forced to meet all those cold glances. I had the impression that Jima and his praetorians were subjecting us to some sort of test, a psychological wrestling match to see who could outstare whom. At last the great man spoke, in the feathery voice of one used to living in a place where a shout could carry for miles: "Peace be unto you." An uncompromising traditionalist, Jima insisted on following the rules of desert etiquette to the letter; and so we exchanged the usual greetings for the next ten minutes, the recitation of stock phrases broken by intervals of silence that made me squirm. A retainer appeared, carrying a copper coffee pot in one hand and a stack of handleless demitasses in the other. He filled the top cup, handed it to Moody, filled the next and handed it to Nordstrand, and so forth, passing out the cups as deftly as a professional dealer does cards. While we sipped the bitter stuff, sweated in the heat, and swatted flies, Jima delivered a lecture of his favorite political theory: the Communist-Zionist conspiracy to crush Islam. It took him a very long time. Kerosene lamps were burning inside the hut before he finished. There is no need to go into detail: it was one of the worst pieces of tortured logic I had ever heard. At first I thought he was leading up to an announcement that Osman and Murrah's explanation notwithstanding, he considered us Zionist spies after all and would hold us prisoner until he had the weapons in his hands. Instead, the diatribe turned out to be a preamble to a speech about his self-appointed mission. This, too, had its bizarre twists of thought. The defeat the rebels suffered in the counteroffensive, he explained, had been the chastisement of an angry God. The leaders of the revolution had offended Allah by allying themselves with the Russians and following the principles of Marxism, which was worse than idolatry. He, Muhammad ibn Idris al-Jima, had been chosen by God to purify the Bejayans' faith and to lead them in a holy war to establish an Islamic state. Victory in this conflict was foreordained, was, in fact, foretold in the holy Koran: *"O ye true believers,"* he quoted, *"if ye assist God by fighting for his religion, he will assist you against your enemies; and will set your feet fast: but as for the infidels, let them perish: and their works shall God render vain."* God had commanded him, he went on, sounding less like a guerrilla general than a Moslem Billy Graham, to remove his army to this secluded camp. God had told him that all those martyred in the cause would gain the paradise promised in the Koran, the garden where rivers flowed. God had instructed him to make the long journey to Khartoum, to meet with the American, Mr. Jack, and to accept the aid of the *ferengei*. At first, he doubted God's word. Yes! He doubted it. He asked. How could God send unbelievers to aid those of the true faith? Then the divine will guided him to read from the Fifth Sura of The Book: *"Thou shalt surely find the most violent of all men in enmity against the true believers to be the Jews and the idolators; and thou shalt surely find among them to be the most inclinable to entertain friendship for the true believers, who say, 'We are Christians.'*

"And you are Christians." A gap-toothed smile broke on Jima's gaunt, pockmarked face. He rose, and with a slight movement of his skeletal hand, gestured to us to stand. We did, stiff-legged. Moody shot a quick glance at his watch. "This is like some bloody papal audience," he muttered under his breath. Moving slowly and deliberately, the sheikh gave each of us an embrace, a gesture which appeared to thaw the collective iciness of his bodyguard.

"These are Christians," he declared, turning to face

them. "As it is written, they are of the faith most inclined to friendship with us. They will be treated as allies and guests. I was wrong, O brothers, to suspect them as spies of the Zionists. . . ."

A sudden coughing fit, so violent I thought it would shake that frail man apart, cut short the confession of his fallibility. The fit lasted a full two minutes, and his air of authority dissolved as the cough racked and shook him. He became nothing more than a sick old man, his chest heaving with the deep, wet, resonant hacking of tuberculosis. Murrah put an arm around his quaking shoulders and led him back to his seat.

"Please calm yourself, O Jima. We have business to talk over. The arms."

The solicitousness in Murrah's tone was belied by the calculating look on his face. You could almost see his brain measuring the severity of the cough, computing the time it would take for the disease to become terminal, deliberating whether he should act or simply wait for sickness to rid him of the old man.

"Yes, Kasu. Business. The arms." The sheikh resumed his buddha-like pose and, the cough subsiding, recovered his aura of command. "Business. Business." The wasted hands gestured, and we again took our seats. "The arms. Gentlemen, what are we to do?"

"What are we to do about what, Jima?" Moody asked.

The question was followed by another long interval of silent staring. The old man then informed Moody that, as the eldest male of the house of Jima, he was heir to the titles bestowed upon his clan by the Ottomans, "Emir of the Malaka, Sultan to the Beni-Hamid," which obliged everyone to address him as "your highness." However, in keeping with the egalitarian principles of Islamic socialism, he had absolved his followers from acknowledging his royal lineage. But he did expect to be shown some respect by being addressed with the formal prefix O.

Baffled, the Englishman said he didn't understand what Jima was driving at.

"You just called him 'Jima,' " Murrah explained in English. "He wants you to address him as 'O Jima.' "

"Oh, yes. I see. Very well, What are we to do about what—O Jima?"

"The change in plans was unfortunate," replied the emir and sultan. "Osman told me the weapons will be delivered near Edana in a few days' time and that a caravan must leave here tomorrow to make the rendezvous. What are we to do? God's will be done."

"I'm afraid I don't understand."

"He means," Murrah said, again in English, "that it will take several days to assemble the number of camels needed to transport the weapons, at least a hundred. Which means we cannot make the rendezvous. So now"—Murrah's voice crackled with disdain—"he is going to rely on God's will to solve the problem."

"Speak in Arabic, Kasu."

"I was explaining the problem to them, O Jima."

"Explain it to them in Arabic. They understand Arabic."

Murrah, nodding deferentially, did as he was told.

"So, you see the difficulties Mr. Jack has caused with his change in plans," Jima said. "Now we must await God's will in this matter."

Moody groped for a diplomatic reply to this display of Moslem fatalism.

"We can't wait, everything's set . . . you see, another change in plans . . . well, we must put our heads together. In the West, we have a saying, 'God helps those who help themselves.' For example, we could take the camels which brought us here—"

"This proverb, what does it mean?"

"It means there are times when men must act on their own."

"No man acts on his own, Mr. Patrick. All is ordered according to God's will."

"Yes, of course . . ."

"As for the camels which brought you here, there aren't enough of them. They also need to be watered, fed, and rested for three days after the journey they've made. By God, I know camels, and those would never survive crossing the dry lake until they've been watered, rested, and fed three days."

"Bloody hell. The dead hand of Islam."

Nordstrand said he had a suggestion.

"I'm handling this."

"You sure are, General. In your usual fucked-up way."

"Speak in Arabic! What is your suggestion, you . . ."

"Mr. Jeremy, O Jima."

"Mr. Jeremy. What is your suggestion?"

Nordstrand said that a few men could take one of the Land-Rovers and meet the dhows at the headland while the camels were being assembled. A Land-Rover could make the coast in a day. The men would then off-load the weapons and wait for the caravan to arrive. Jima objected: it was dangerous to cross the Malaka Sink in a motor vehicle; even in the dry season, there were marshes and swamps. Then take two vehicles, one following in the track of the other: if the first got stuck, the second could pull it free, or, that failing, make the trip to the headland on its own. Yes, yes, Jima responded, but there was another obstacle: all the coast was controlled by Omer Hassab's FLN. If one of their patrols came across the men unloading the weapons, they would attack and seize the arms for themselves; a Land-Rover, even two Land-Rovers, could not carry enough men to provide an adequate defense. One vehicle could be a truck, answered Nordstrand. A truck could carry at least a squad of twelve men, twelve of the bodyguard, whose Kalashnikovs would provide plenty of firepower.

"The FLN also have the Kalash, Mr. Jeremy. Twelve men is hardly enough. And I won't let both trucks go. We have only two. I won't risk losing both. No, twelve will not do."

"At the Battle of Bedr, the Prophet commanded three hundred men and the Meccans had a thousand."

Jima's eyes widened at hearing a foreigner and unbeliever mention Bedr, the battle in which the Moslems won their first victory against the pagan Arabs.

"Nevertheless," Nordstrand went on confidently, "the forces of the Prophet routed the Meccans. That is written, O Jima. It is also written, *Ye have already had a miracle shown you in two armies, which attacked each other: one army fought for God's true religion, but the others were infidels."*

The black eyes widened further and the cratered face beamed in the lantern light like a black moon.

"By God! Listen to this, O brothers! A Christian who knows of Bedr. He knows the numbers of the armies. He knows the words of The Book. You have read from the holy Koran, Mr. Jeremy?"

Mr. Jeremy replied that he had, and to prove he had, said the passage he had just quoted concluded this way:

". . . but the others were infidels: they saw the faithful twice as many as themselves in their eyesight, for God strengtheneth with his help whom he pleaseth."

Jima exclaimed yes, yes, that was how it concluded. This was remarkable, to meet a Christian who knew The Book. And yes, yes, he understood Mr. Jeremy's idea. Omer Hassab's men were infidels—no, worse, they were Communists who said they were Moslems. That made them hypocrites as well. Yes, he saw. The twelve Beni-Hamid would appear twice as many as whatever number might attack them. This was wisdom. Yes, that would be the plan. You, Osman, pick the twelve men, and you, Osman, you and Kasu will accompany Mr. Jeremy in the Land-Rover. You will leave day after tomorrow.

Jima's excitement provoked another spasm of hacking. Moody winced and turned his face aside.

"That will be the plan," Jima rasped, wiping the pinkish spittle from his lips. He then did something which convinced me his mind was as damaged as his lungs. Rising, he walked up to Nordstrand and began to stroke the American's long pale hair, saying he had already heard a great deal about Mr. Jeremy from the fighters. He had heard Mr. Jeremy could fight armed men with only his bare hands, that he had carried a sick comrade on his shoulders, had spoken with great eloquence, and eloquence, as we knew, was a measure of manhood. These were signs not to be ignored. And now this sign: he knew The Book, which was a sign that he had wisdom as well as exceptional strength. Again his fingers languorously stroked Nordstrand's hair. Mr. Jeremy knew of the Battle of Bedr. And it was written that five thousand angels aided the Prophet —peace be upon him—when he defeated the idolators, and the angels wore white and yellow sashes around their heads,

and the sashes hung down over their shoulders. Jima's
feathery voice grew more agitated, his gestures spastic.
Here was another sign, O brothers. The foreigner's gold
hair hung past his shoulders, like the sashes of the angels
at Bedr, and as they aided the army of the Prophet—peace
be upon him—so would this stranger aid the army of
Muhammad Jima. The men in the bodyguard nodded,
yes, yes, it was surely a sign.

Moody and I sat there, astonished at the old man's outburst. Then Moody attempted to bring the matters down
to a less celestial level by asking a few down-to-earth
questions: Did the Land-Rover and the truck have enough
fuel? Were the radiators topped off, the tires in good
condition? Annoyed, Jima waved a hand brusquely. He was
Muhammad ibn Idris al-Jima, Sultan to the Beni-Hamid,
Commander of the National Islamic Independence Front;
he did not trouble himself with such petty problems. If
Mr. Patrick wished to know if the vehicles had enough
fuel, he should ask the men in charge of them. Very well,
Moody responded, speaking quickly to retain some control
of the conversation. Now he had a suggestion to make.

The old man hawked up a gob of bloody phlegm.
"What?"

Moody replied that Nordstrand ought not to travel
with the lightly armed convoy. If it was attacked, there
would be too great a risk of his being captured by the
Ethiopians or the FLN. In either case, the operation would
be compromised and it would be discovered that we were
not the NIIF's prisoners, but its advisers; and no matter
what comparisons Jima made between Mr. Jeremy and
the angels who aided the Prophet, others would say he,
Jima, was being aided by foreign devils—that is, by mercenaries. Therefore, Nordstrand should travel with the
caravan. He would have the safety of numbers, and a
caravan would be less likely to attract attention than a
convoy.

"No."

"Why?"

"Why, O Jima. You will accord me respect, Mr. Patrick."

"Why, O Jima?"

"First, because I order it. Second, because there will be no risk. The convoy will be under God's protection."

Moody's lips gathered to utter an incredulous "What?" but he checked himself and merely shook his head, mumbling, "Daft, the old boy's absolutely daft."

"Speak so I can hear you, and speak in Arabic!"

"I said, very well. He'll go with the convoy. But I insist on going with him—O Jima."

"Now I must ask why. If you think it's a risk for one to go, won't the risk be double if two go?"

"I'm head of this mission. It's only right that I go and share the risk."

Jima waved a hand indifferently.

"As you wish. All three of you can go if you wish. There will be no risk."

"One of us should stay here in case something happens."

"But nothing will happen."

"If it suits you, two of us will go and one stay here."

"As you wish. It's settled. Mr. Jeremy's solved the difficulty. Now we will have some *tea.*"

———

"Did you hear him, Moody? 'Mr. Jeremy's solved the difficulty.' "

Studying the map he had spread on the table, Moody did not say anything. Nordstrand, his shadow rippling grotesquely on the cave wall, walked over to stand behind the Englishman.

"I guess I pulled us through another one, General."

"I thought we agreed you'd stop referring to me as 'General.' "

"Couldn't help it, you look so generallike, studying your map." Nordstrand laid a hand across the back of Moody's neck in what started as a friendly gesture. "I said it looks like I pulled us through another one."

"Yes, yes. It looks that way. Jolly for you. Now get your hands off me."

"It's just a question of knowing which string to pull. With old Bloody Lungs back there it's the religion string.

You ought to learn about those strings if you're going to run anything, General."

Trying to stop another confrontation, I said: "If it's the 'religion string' with Jima, what's all this about us being his allies because we're Christians? I thought he hated Christians."

"Oh, he does, Charlie. Bejayan Christians. He feels it's unnatural for a Bejayan to be anything but Moslem. And Moslems are a bit ambivalent about Christianity. On the one hand, the Koran tells them that we're more friendly to them than the Jews, but on the other hand, we're a mob of unbelievers who fought them for centuries in the Crusades."

"Now it's Professor Moody, Doctor of Middle Eastern studies. Which is it, Moody? Professor or General?"

"We agreed—"

"We didn't agree that I wouldn't call you 'General.' We agreed that you would thank me if I didn't, Moody."

"Infantile."

"Moody. Moody. That's twice. Thank me."

"Incredibly infantile." Without turning to look at the American, Moody reached behind to pull off the hand. Nordstrand's thumb probed for the most sensitive pressure point, found it just below and behind Moody's right ear, and pressed hard. The Englishman sucked in a breath, his hand falling off Nordstrand's wrist.

"Moodeee."

"Insane . . . infan—sadistic bastard . . ." Moody's head twitched and his lips parted from involuntary reflex when the big, hooked thumb dug in deeper, creating a quarter-sized white spot on his sunburned neck.

"Mooodeee."

"Thank you," the Englishman said from between pain-clenched teeth.

"Twice."

"Thank you, thank you."

"That's better." Nordstrand relaxed his grip, and his eyes shone lacquer-bright in the glow of the lamp. "Just reminding you that there'll be only the two of us, and no policemen. No bobbies on the corner, Moody."

Naturalists working in the shining mountain majesties of the North American West have observed a peculiar trait in the mature male grizzly. These giant bears, whose enormous power is so evident that, one would think, they should feel no necessity to demonstrate it, occasionally lumber from their solitary lairs to terrorize packs of cubs, sows, and younger males. They will taunt and tease, snarl, roar, cuff, and claw until the smaller, weaker animals are thoroughly cowed and posture in submission. These attacks are not motivated by any territorial or sexual rivalries. There appears to be no reason for them other than dominance for the sake of dominance.

FOUR

MR. JEREMY

Two days later, I sat by the cave's mouth and watched the truck and the Land-Rover crawling along the wadi hundreds of feet below: two brown dots trailing pale dust. They looked ridiculously small, with the mountains above them and the dry lake before them, vast and white beneath a sun whose hot but passionless kiss drained from it all life and all chance for life. With luck, Moody and Nordstrand would reach the coast by nightfall. With luck, they would make the rendezvous with the dhows. With luck, they would off-load the weapons without being discovered by the FLN or an Ethiopian patrol. With luck, they would keep the cache hidden until the caravan arrived, and the caravan, with luck, would make the return trip loaded down with tons of rifles, machine guns, ammunition, and antitank rockets. There was entirely too much luck involved, I thought, wishing I had the crazy old sheikh's faith in God's protection. Because if luck failed, I would be left on my own in the wilderness. I would be a lost man, and I was not entirely confident I would be able to find my way back. Sitting and watching the convoy's dust trail, I had the uncomfortable feeling that comes when you have no idea of what will happen next. An unpredictable future can be exciting when you are very young and filled with the confidence of ignorance. Life, however, is like war: the more you experience it, the more terrifying it becomes.

In a meditative mood, I stared at the grotesque sculptures of the mountains and tried to come up with some plausible reason why Nordstrand had all but invited me to examine the secret record of his life. But my mind refused to work. There was something disturbing, something thought-destroying about that landscape, with its appearance of a ruined city. It had a sense of enormous age, and gave you a feeling that man did not belong there. And yet he was there. He had always been there, leaving his footprints on the volcanic soil ever since he had learned to walk erect.

The transceiver stood beside me, its long antenna extended. Before he left, Moody had taught me how to use it and explained the laborious business of encoding and decoding. I had just finished sending off a message to the Cobra, informing him that Atropos One and Two had left for the rendezvous at Ras al-Sultan. The copy of *Les Miserables* lay on the ground next to the radio, opened to the page to be used for that day's code, the page which began the chapter entitled "The Elephant's Mansion." I looked again at the old, weird mountains, then at the novel, and Hugo's descriptions of Paris in the early spring turned my thoughts away from Nordstrand and toward Allison. I recalled the weekend we had spent one March in Paris. We stayed at the Montalebert, a small hotel near the Pont Royale. I remembered the room, the view of the rooftops, the chilly weather, grey buildings under grey skies, the waiter who brought us croissants and café au lait in the mornings, and how Allison, for all her public propriety, could be so improper in the privacy of a bedroom. The reverie awakened a feeling that my life had been somehow derailed from its natural track. How could I, a man who had once made love to his wife in a city synonymous with civilization, have ended up in a cave on the African desert? I thought about Allison and the tidy, sensible world she created wherever we went. I had criticized her for it, told her she was living in a dream, shutting out reality, which I equated with the nightmares I recorded for the *L.A. Post* in dispatches of six hundred words or less. I suppose I had been hard on her. Her nerves were not the strongest; she shut out the violent realities of the age because she knew she was not emotionally equipped to deal with them. I also suppose I needed the orderly existence she manufactured with her books and antiques, her copies of *The New Yorker* neatly displayed on spotless coffee tables. Living such a bizarre life, I needed her conventionalism more than I had realized. And yet, I had always felt like an alien in her world. Psychologically, or physically, or both, I had lived most of my life on edges. I had been born on one: Marquette, Michigan, huddled against the cold Canadian gales on the shores of Lake Superior, the edge of the land, the northern border of America. I was a man of the margins, a ragged-edger; so, my ending up in a cave in Africa was not a derailment after all, but another journey to another boundary. Living on edges, however, requires a keen sense of balance, without which you go spinning off into the void; and it was that lost equilibrium I wished to recover.

These jumbled reflections were interrupted by shouts of "Jima! Jima! Jima!" On the stony meadow below, the sheikh was walking to his prayer tent, a black goat-hair affair pitched in the shade of an acacia. Flanked by his bodyguard, he did not acknowledge the shouts of his followers, but walked with the dignity and stately indifference of a celebrity through a crowd of adoring fans. This, I had already learned, was a daily ritual in camp. Jima's mountain base was not only his fortress but also his temple, and he was not only a guerrilla leader but a kind of warrior priest as well. Isolated from all outside influences—that is, from all influences except him—his followers were indoctrinated in the tenets of Islamic socialism and were required to chant his name each time he left his hut to pray. He worshiped Allah, they worshiped him, and his bodyguard made sure everyone joined in.

Not that there were any reluctant worshipers. The Beni-Hamid appeared genuinely in awe of the old man. After their defeat in the counteroffensive, the insurgents needed a man on horseback. They did not want councils and committees, but a flesh-and-blood man who would explain the disaster they had suffered, who would rekindle their ardor with a ringing call to arms, who would point the way. Muhammad Jima was the right man at the right time: the rebels' need for a heroic figure coincided with Jima's need

to be one. He had explained the defeat—it was God's
chastisement. He had issued the call to arms—the rebellion was to be *jihad,* holy war. He had pointed the way—
the rebels were to follow him. This had earned him a
following among the rank and file. It had also earned him
the enmity of the RCC, which charged him with the political transgression of forming a personality cult, ostracized
him, and declared the NIIF to be an outlaw faction. This
did not trouble Jima: the old bandit had been a renegade
all of his life. Now I watched his frail figure stop at the
entrance to the tent, turn to face his followers, and raise
a withered arm. His mouth opened, but I could not hear
his voice at that distance. The response from the crowd
was audible, however: *"Allahu akhbar,"* they shouted, then
took up their frenzied war-chant, waving their rifles, spears,
and swords: *"JIHAD, JIHAD, HITTA AL-NASR, IN-
SHALLAH!"*

The cry, repeated over and over mindlessly, and the
intolerable heat finally drove me back into the cool, dim,
silent cave. The sunlight obliqued off the mirrorlike sheen
of the back wall, where I caught my hazy, distorted reflection. Sitting on my bunk, I knew how I would occupy
myself until Moody and Nordstrand returned. I would
read Nordstrand's diaries. I had planned to all along, and
had pulled them out of his pack the moment after the
convoy started to roll out of camp. What I did not know
then, and what had driven me outside to think and reflect,
was why Nordstrand had again left the lock open, why
he wanted me to read them. I know now. He must have
had a presentiment that something would happen on that
trek to the coast, that he would be given the opportunity
to commit the crime he believed would liberate him; and
out of his overwhelming egotism, he wanted someone to
know the whole of it. Moody was to witness the act itself,
but I had been chosen as the audience for the actions of
his mind, the one who would learn his motives and, presumably, applaud him.

The diaries were stacked on the table. I opened the first
volume, lit the lantern, and began to read. I read for the
next five days and nights (the eight volumes contained
over a thousand pages), read until I thought I would go

blind, squinting at his almost indecipherable scrawl in the lantern light. I read with such absorption that I lost track of time, marking its passage only by the clamor that rose outside whenever Jima went to pray. The caravan left on the third day, but I was only vaguely aware of its departure. Yassin, after I told him I was not to be bothered, left my meals at the mouth of the cave, as if I were some sort of hermit monk. As often as not, I left the bowls of mush untouched. There must have been talk around camp about my sanity because Jima twice summoned me to ask why I was not eating, why I was spending all my time in the dark cave, speaking to no one. I explained my reclusiveness as due to a sensitivity to the sun.

He seemed to accept this excuse, but insisted I keep him company while he listened to the Arabic-language broadcasts of the BBC and the Voice of America on his Sony transistor. When the VOA came on the air, to the strains of "Yankee Doodle," or the BBC announced, "This is London," to the chimes of Big Ben, it was like hearing a transmission from another solar system. In effect, I became the old man's media adviser.

It was during one of these sessions that I heard, at the tail end of one BBC broadcast, that no further word had been received about the fate of three westerners captured by a faction of Bejayan guerrillas, which had demanded half a million dollars for their release. Half a million? We had not been told any ransom money was involved. Oh, yes, replied Jima. Upon our "release," a representative of Mr. Jack would hand over half a million dollars, with which Jima would purchase more arms and equipment. And how was Mr. Jack going to come up with half a million? In so many words, Jima answered that he didn't know and could not care less. While we were on the subject, he asked, why had the United States sent him, the only man in the Horn of Africa with the guts to stand up to the Communists, only three advisers while the Russians and Cubans were sending thousands to the Ethiopians? I gave some sort of muddled answer, all the while resenting profoundly the interruption of my reading of the verbal self-portrait Nordstrand had painted in his tiny backhand.

That was another anomaly, how such a giant of a man

could write in such a small script. I finished reading—decoding, I should say—the last entry on the night of the fifth day. His diaries had brought a light of sorts. It was not a sudden flash, but a gradual illumination, an unfolding. I could discern only vague shapes at first; then, bit by bit, the features of his personality, of his interior landscape, grew distinct. I saw him clearly by the time I closed the last volume, so clearly I almost expected him to materialize in front of me. Did I see him for what he was? I thought I did—we can never be absolutely certain of our vision when we peer into another man's heart. I saw that he was a man unmoved by idealism, by greed, by ambition, or by any of the usual motives. His mainspring was an abiding need to be himself by fulfilling a criminal fantasy that, born of hatred and a fear of what he hated, had seized him in his boyhood, obsessed him, and overmastered him. The picture would not have been so disturbing if it had not been so familiar. I realized that it was a picture of myself, not as I was, but as I could have been. Many of Nordstrand's lusts, his rages and hatreds, were not unknown to me. The demons who dwelled in him dwelled in me, as they do in all men: the attraction to violence, the need to be free from all restrictions, the impulse to follow one's desires wherever they may lead and without regard for others. There was, though, one essential difference: his devils lived much closer to the surface, or, to put it another way, his surface lay much closer to them. The mantle laid over our base rock from birth, which is never as thick as we like to believe, but is yet thick enough to make it so difficult for our demons to emerge that their power is weakened by the time they do—the warm, rich humus which is called civilization never quite stuck to Nordstrand. His moral topsoil was only a fragile crust, and his inherent devils had only to give a prod or two to break free. We are fond of thinking there is an explanation for everything, but I cannot account for that defect; it was just a fact of Nordstrand's existence, a character deformity that, for all I know, he carried from birth.

His birth itself had been all wrong. Jeremy Nordstrand entered existence upside down, that is, right side up, emerging feetfirst with the umbilical cord wrapped around his neck, so that his mother's womb almost became a gallows and his birth a hanging. Having been nearly strangled by the organ which had nourished him, his face was deep blue, and in place of the traditional slap, the doctor had to pummel the infant into taking its first breath.

Apparently, Nordstrand was fascinated by his unusual genesis: he referred to it frequently in the diaries. In one entry, with a phrase characteristic of his violent, morbid romanticism, he described himself as a man "who saw death the same instant I saw life." Otherwise, with a couple of exceptions, he recorded very little about his life before he began keeping his journal. He was ashamed of his childhood because he had been thin and sickly up until twelve or thirteen, the kind of kid other kids love to pick on, the perennial victim of schoolyard bullies. He wrote that his mother had described him as a "fragile boy." Reading those words, it was difficult for me to imagine the man I knew had ever possessed the quality of fragility. In fact, it was difficult to imagine he had ever been a child: you pictured him springing fullblown into life, all six-feet-one and 240 pounds of him.

Despite his frail physique as a child, he harbored a ferocious spirit and a capacity for vengeance so deep it must have been inbred, the result of an aberrant gene. He despised himself for his inability to fight back, for his weakness and cowardice. He wanted his mother to stop nursing his wounds and tell him to go out and stand up for himself; he wanted his father, a placid man who was the town attorney for Walton, Minnesota, to teach him how to fight. But his parents were rather genteel people and he came to see their gentility as one cause of his impotence, and so began to despise them. And he hated every boy who had ever insulted or struck him. He kept a list of their names. Hating them as much as he hated himself, he indulged in fantasies—partly aroused by body-building ads in comic books and by the wrestling matches he liked to watch on television—of turning into a muscular he-man who would exact a terrible retribution. In the end, he did not need to take a body-building course. Nature took care of him. One of those genetic miracles occurred when he reached puberty: in the space of a year, Nordstrand grew six inches, gained fifty pounds, and in his freshman year in high school, won a slot as first-string linebacker for the junior varsity.

The one childhood incident he dwelled on occurred when he was nine. It must have made a vivid and lasting impression because the diary described it in great detail. It centered on a Swede named Knudsen, a heavily built man who kept a sailboat on a small lake outside Walton. One summer afternoon, while Nordstrand was playing on shore, a group of older boys swam out to the boat and capsized it as a prank. They were long gone when Knudsen pulled up in his car to find the center board of his sloop pointing skyward. Nordstrand ran up to tell him what happened, but the tall, powerful figure, his pale face flushed with anger, said, "You little bastard, you and your friends did that," spun the boy around, and kicked him ten feet. Nordstrand landed on his chest, the wind knocked out of him. The big man then picked him up with one hand and slapped him twice in the face with the other, hard enough to leave an impression of his thick fingers on the nine-year-old's face. "You do that again and I'll beat your brains out, you little bastard." The boy ran home. The kick and the slaps were not all that had hurt, but also the injustice, the humiliation, and his utter powerlessness. The angry man had handled him as if he were nothing more than a rag doll. For a long time afterward, he was visited by a recurrent nightmare. A red-faced giant was chasing him. He was trying to escape, but felt a feebleness in his legs and a sickening paralysis in his arms as his pursuer, lunging, grabbed him by the throat. With a half-strangled cry, he would wake up, not sure which was the more terrifying, the man chasing him or the feeling of his own helplessness.

"I want Dad to beat him up," he told his mother after she had soothed his physical pain. "I want Dad to beat Mr. Knudsen's brains out." Christine Nordstrand replied that his father would do no such thing. Civilized people did not behave that way. Besides, his father was the town attorney, a man of the law with a position and a reputation to maintain. No, civilized people did not settle matters with their fists. She had telephoned Knudsen, who had realized his mistake and had promised to come over after dinner and apologize. That night, Thomas Nordstrand sat with his wife and son on the leather sofa in his study, beside a bookshelf lined with buckram-covered copies of the Laws and Statutes of the State of Minnesota. A contrite Knudsen occupied the chair opposite them, explaining that his sloop had been upended before by those punks and that he had simply lost his head when he saw young Jeremy. He extended his hand in apology, and to Nordstrand's everlasting disgust, his father accepted it. His father was a coward, he decided, intimidated by Knudsen's size. Looking at Thomas Nordstrand, the boy felt only hatred and made a promise to himself, took a vow, swore a secret oath: *I'll never be like him.*

Knudsen then turned to the boy and held out his hand, the big hand whose slap the boy still felt in his memory.

"Guess I should shake with you, too, young fella," the tall man said. "You're the one got kicked in the pants. I should of known you weren't the kind of kid to go doing a thing like that."

The kid who would not do a thing like that did not move.

"Jeremy," his mother said. "There's nothing to be afraid of. Mr. Knudsen is apologizing. Shake hands with him."

"No."

"Now Jeremy. Shake hands. C'mon, like a little man. Mr. Knudsen's apologizing to you."

"He should be killed."

"Jeremy! George—the boy's upset. He didn't mean that."

"Did so mean it. He should be killed."

"That's an awful thing to say, Jeremy. Just awful. Go up to your room. Up. Up. Now. March!"

The boy went to his room. There he heard with loathing his mother apologizing for his behavior and his father politely saying good-bye to George Knudsen, and he repeated his oath. *I'll never be like him.*

━━━━━

Jeremy Bennett Nordstrand was as all-American in his bloodlines as he was in his inclination toward violence, a

one-man melting pot, Norwegian and German on his father's side, English and Swedish, with a trace of Chippewa
Indian, on his mother's. His parents, as he described them,
were not unlike my own. They were middle-class followers
of the Middle West's middle way, moderate in their appetites and ambitions, people who sought to score modest
successes rather than to win great victories, who suffered
minor disappointments rather than crushing defeats, and
who occupied the political center, adhering to the balanced
liberalism personified by their fellow Minnesotan Hubert
Humphrey. The odd thing, the thing to make you question
the theory that criminals are the products of social conditioning, was how such a normal couple produced the son
they did. Paradoxically, their very ordinariness was responsible for Jeremy Nordstrand's being what he was. It
was the quality he most despised in them and, early on, he
decided to make his life a contradiction of theirs.

This is not to say that Thomas and Christine Nordstrand's normality was of the ideal *Saturday Evening Post*
variety. Thomas was a somewhat vacillating man, a docile
figure with none of the flair and confidence that had
catapulted many in his graduating class out of small-town
law practices into the ranks of trial lawyers and corporate
attorneys, into judgeships, and, in one case, the state senate.
At the beginning of his career, he had an impulse to enter
politics. But this was in the late 1940s, when service in
World War Two was a sine qua non for anyone seeking
office. Thomas Nordstrand had been kept out of the army
because of a heart condition resulting from a childhood
bout with scarlet fever. The condition also made him wary
of getting into situations that might upset or overexcite
him, and contributed to his retiring nature, his overeager-
ness to compromise, his tendency to avoid struggle.

His only attempt to escape the confines of Walton occurred when his son was three. He passed the Illinois bar
and moved his family to Chicago, where he joined a
LaSalle Street firm. The city intimidated him, and the
family was back in Walton within a year. Disappointed in
himself at first, Thomas Nordstrand later came to terms
with his failure to stick it out in Chicago. The man of the
law said it was fortunate he had discovered his limitations

and his place in life early in his career. His son, as sons are
prone to do, judged him more harshly: his father had
failed to make a go of it in the city out of the same
cowardice that had stopped him from fighting George
Knudsen and made him avoid the army. (Nordstrand had
convinced himself that his father had used the heart condition as an excuse for staying out of the war. It pained
and embarrassed him to go to his friends' houses and see
photographs of their fathers in bemedaled uniforms.)

The portrait of Christine Nordstrand was one of a tall,
rawboned woman, energetic, deeply religious, severe in
appearance and dress, overly concerned with propriety in
speech and behavior, obsessed with cleanliness and order.
It was her religiosity which Nordstrand resented most
deeply. A convert to Catholicism, she went to mass almost
daily, insisted on grace before every meal, compelled her
son to attend catechism classes on Sundays, and then, as
if that were not enough, required him to listen when she
read aloud from the Bible after church. Nordstrand could
bear these sessions only when she gave in to his demands
to read from the Old Testament. The New left him cold,
but something in him responded to the tribal harshness in
the books of Joshua and Exodus. He never tired of hearing
of the annihilation of Jericho, or of Gideon's surprise night
attack, or of David's conquest over Goliath. Though only
a boy, he had already developed an active and violent
imagination, and he pictured himself as a warrior of the
Children of Israel, lopping off Canaanite heads with a
bloodstained sword.

His mother suffered a spell of manic-depression when
she started to go through her change. It was a mild case,
as if the midwestern plains would not permit even madness
to become extreme. Nordstrand was then sixteen. He remembered the night when she suddenly began a long, incoherent monologue about God and the devil, arranged
lighted candles on her bedroom dresser as on an altar, and
then fell into a fit of uncontrolled weeping, the guttering
candles deepening the hollows in her long, gaunt, prairie
woman's face. His father summoned a doctor, who sedated
the hysterical Christine and had her taken to a psychiatric
hospital in Fargo, fifty miles away, across the North Da-

kota line. She remained there only two weeks, was given a
course of drug therapy, and returned home as level as ever.
But, as her husband's heart ailment had made him fearful
of overexertion, her brief descent into insanity had made
her frightened of anything smacking of abnormality. She
became determined to restore her life to its former equilibrium. She would be a normal, healthy woman living a
normal life in a normal household in a normal town. Her
need for normality grew so intense that it became a devi-
ation in itself. She would not allow her "episode" to be
discussed in the house. She joined every ladies' social and
charitable organization in town, each membership card a
certificate of her conventionality. Phobic about dirt and
disorder, she kept the house spotless, required her son and
his football friends to take off their shoes before entering,
and, when troubled by her occasional spells of insomnia,
got out of bed long before dawn to dust, sweep, and vacuum. Sometimes, in an effort to make herself tired enough
to sleep, she rearranged furniture she had rearranged several times only days before; and Nordstrand would walk
down the stairs in the morning feeling he was in a strange
new house. He began referring to her as "the crazy lady."
    The coward and the crazy lady—he despised them both.
He could not bring himself to express his hatred openly,
and it festered in him like an untreated wound, leaking its
emotional pus into every cell of his system. In time, it
extended to the entire town, to everyone in it and everything around it. I had never been to Walton, but I knew
those dull midwestern towns well enough to picture it:
houses, stores, drive-ins, grain silos, a lumber mill and
canning plant surrounded by an immensity of sky and
prairie. The conservatism of middle westerners is not, as
many easterners believe, a political philosophy, but rather
an emotional reaction to their monotonous flatlands, rolling on forever. Though they are often compared to the
sea, the Great Plains do not, like the sea, quicken the spirit
with a promise of new possibilities; they crush it with a
sense of being cut off from possibilities by overwhelming
distances. Deserts can inspire dread, mountains awe, but
the prairies, with their lonely, limitless horizons, inspire
nothing so much as a gnawing unease, a sense of inescap-

able boredom, and a profound caution. The people who live on them cling to their farm and ranch houses, to their cramped little towns, as if in fear of the encompassing emptiness. They are not conservative but intimidated. It has often been my feeling that the Midwest was settled by people who gave up on the idea of manifest destiny, people who were bound for California's gold or Oregon's green, but despaired, rocking in their wagons day after day over mile after dreary mile of buffalo grass, wearied of chasing a horizon that always eluded them, and decided to turn back only to realize they had plunged so far into the vastness that going back was as repulsive as going on. So they stayed put. Oh, they had courage and strength of character—it took those qualities to conquer the prairie, to fight blizzards, drought, locust, Indians, and unbearable loneliness—but they lacked the invincible curiosity to push on and see what lay beyond the horizon. The square and rectangular fields of their farms, the town streets all running at right angles to each other, the roads as straight as a surveyor's traverse, reflect the midwesterners' precision, their dogged persistence and lack of imagination. Without hills, mountains, or meandering valleys to conform to, they had the freedom to create whatever they chose and ended up creating their own conformity by building everything in straight lines. They laid over the brooding enigma of the referenceless plain the dull rationalism of mathematics; they sought to tame its threatening emptiness with Euclidean geometry. Their lives consequently became regular, balanced, and predictable, their emotions as flat as the plains. Television, radio, and superhighways have made them less physically isolated, but life in prairie towns today is not essentially different from what it was half a century ago. There is a feeling of stasis, of inertia and stagnation. They are places where very little happens because no one wants anything to happen.

By the time he reached sixteen, Nordstrand was aware of a fundamental conflict between his turbulent nature and the quiet, measured rhythms of life in Walton. He had an overabundance of wild energy, for which there was no outlet in the town. Football and wrestling siphoned off only some of it. He relished the hard body-contact of both sports; the sweat, the bruises and mat burns delighted him in a way that was almost masochistic. He was elected captain of the football team, not because he was popular (reading between the lines, I had the impression he was regarded as a bully even by the toughest of his teammates), but because he was the logical choice. He had will as well as strength, an ability to compel others to do what he wanted, and a ferocious exuberance. As often as not, his roughness ran to extremes. In one game, he barreled through the line, hit the opposing quarterback with a blind-side tackle, then deliberately twisted the boy's leg, popping his knee and putting him out for the season. Because Nordstrand's side was losing, his coach gave him an approving slap on the back. "Attaway, Jerry," he said. "That's the way to hit 'em." Praise like that encouraged him: it gave him the notion that his ferocity could be a source of rewards.

Though Nordstrand would feel purged after a game or wrestling match, his inner turmoil always came bubbling up again, and he and a few other small-town skull-bashers would prowl high school hangouts looking for action. A source of rewards on the football field, his violence was a cause of trouble off: he began to acquire a reputation as a delinquent after his third arrest for streetfighting. His father's position kept him out of jail.

But his brush with the police reminded him of the restrictions of his life. A few days after one arrest, he stalked the streets alone, filled with an inexplicable rage. The lack of privacy and anonymity in the small town (its population was around 25,000, and it was like an island on that ocean of wheat and grazing land) cramped his field of action. Everyone knew what everyone else was doing. That is the ultimate source of the virtue of small-town people, the presence of public opinion and gossip. Nordstrand felt the pressure, and it made him want to tear the town apart. Every tree offended him. The Victorian houses, with their porches and turrets and air of complacency, made his stomach turn. He despised the people in them, sitting immobilized in the lifeless grey light of television screens.

Nordstrand found temporary release on weekends and school vacations. In the autumn, he hunted the woods and prairies near the White Earth Indian reservation and became a first-rate shot. In the winters, he set traps for small game and, in general, tried to live like his mother's Chippewa forebears. Those were the best times for him. Often, he packed a haversack and sleeping bag and spent two or three days in the open, eating what he shot or caught in his traps. He enjoyed it immensely. He enjoyed stalking and killing, gutting and skinning the game, the sight of fresh blood in the snow, the way a dressed carcass steamed in the cold air. He loved being alone in the wilderness, or what now passes for wilderness. The wild creature within him felt at home there. Camped beside some northern river whose current had once born Chippewa canoes, he felt free, and came to equate freedom with savagery. And he loved the wilderness for the contrast it made with the tranquil predictability of Walton. Out there, he experienced the extremes of the midwestern climate. Arctic winds boomed down from Canada in the winter, carrying the untamed cold of the primeval forests far to the north, a cold that froze the rivers hard as steel and made the snow look blue. Snow buried the wheat fields, covered highways and railroads until the fertile farmland appeared as hostile and dead as a polar ice cap, and that white desolation moved him. He thrilled to the sight of the aurora, bursting silently at night to curtain the stars with its sheetlike flashes. In the summer, the land baked beneath a sultry sun, the long hot spells broken by majestic thunderstorms and, now and then, by tornado funnels dipping darkly down to smash and destroy with capricious fury. He loved the storms most of all, the rain and thunder, the purple-black clouds, the high, tree-bending, branch-cracking winds. He loved these extremes and the extreme emotions they evoked. They satisfied, for a while, his need for contrasts, for the dramatic, for the heights and depths.

In his seventeenth year, the year he began his diary, Nordstrand made a discovery about one of his ancestors and about himself as well. Rummaging in the attic for a hunting coat he had mislaid, he found a padlocked trunk covered by a tarp and hidden beneath a pile of boxes. The lock intrigued him—what secret could the trunk contain that made a lock necessary? Taking a hammer and cold

chisel from the toolshed, he broke the hasp, opened the
trunk, and found stacks of letters and yellowed newspaper
clippings a century old, one or two equally ancient photographs, and a journal whose pages almost crumbled in his
hands and whose cover bore the initials "I.B." He forgot
about hunting and spent the rest of the day reading in
trancelike fascination. When pieced together, the memorabilia comprised a biography of a great-great-grandfather on his mother's side, Isaac Bennett. His story was
the family secret, which Christine Nordstrand had so carefully concealed, for he was the antithesis of her ideal of
propriety and respectability.

Indian fighter, trader, trapper, deserter to the Confederacy, buffalo hunter, outlaw, and murderer, Isaac
Bennett was a wild man of the old northwest frontier. A
letter from one of his cousins described him as a man
subject to terrible rages; he had fled westward after killing
someone in a brawl in his native Ohio. Only twenty years
old at the time, he lost himself in the inaccessible forests
of northern Minnesota, where he became a trapper and
eventually married a half-Chippewa, half-white woman.
Trade in furs took him southward to Walton, then a raw
frontier town of only two hundred people. He established
a trading post there, and might have grown into a fat,
respectable merchant had it not been for the outbreak of
the Civil War and an uprising of the Santee Sioux under
Chief Little Crow.

Bennett had raised a company of local militia—the
First Minnesota Volunteer Cavalry, they called themselves
—and was awaiting assignment to the Union Army when
Little Crow's uprising began. One band raided Walton,
burned Bennett's trading post, murdered his wife—the
Chippewa and the Santee were traditional enemies—and
would have killed his three sons had not a few of his
militiamen arrived to drive off the Indians in time. The
First Minnesota was pressed into service to put down the
uprising. Half mad with grief and rage, Bennett fought
like a man possessed in the battle that ended in Little
Crow's defeat. Three hundred surviving braves were tried
and sentenced to be hanged, but President Lincoln com-
muted the executions of all but thirty-eight. The act of

clemency infuriated Bennett, and he wrote an appeal to General Pope, the departmental commander, for permission to pursue an independent band of twenty-odd marauders who had escaped capture and fled westward. Nordstrand found a letter, signed by Pope, commissioning "I. Bennett, brevet major of the 1st Minnesota Cavalry," to take fifty volunteers and track down the Indians with the object of "bringing them to justice." He was, however, given only two weeks to accomplish the mission, and was forbidden to cross into the sacred Indian lands in the Dakota territories. Pope concluded the letter with a warning to Bennett to keep his "understandable" thirst for revenge in check and a reminder of the instructions he, Pope, had received from Lincoln before the battle with Little Crow: "Take care that the Indians neither escape nor be subject to unlawful violence." Isaac Bennett, however, had his own ideas. "I intend to hang every last one of those butchering devils," he wrote in his private account of the expedition.

With forty-odd half-trained citizen soldiers, a few trappers who had traded with the Santee, and two of his dead wife's Chippewa brothers, he rode out of Walton on October 2, 1862. Instead of two weeks, he took two months, trailing the Sioux band over the Red River into the Dakotas, on up the Sheyenne, then westward across the high plains toward the Missouri: two hundred miles on foot and horseback through country that had hardly been mapped. A big, powerful man, Bennett managed to keep his motley column of farmers and town clerks together, sometimes with his fists, sometimes with a gun, mostly through the force of an implacable will. When, exhausted and hungry, six men asked leave to return home, Bennett told them: "There'll be no goin' back till we have caught them bastards. Even if we got to go all the way to Montana to find 'em. You are under my command, God damn you, so there ain't gonna be no turnin' back till I say so." Four of the six listened to him. Two replied that he had disobeyed Pope's orders; therefore, they were free of any obligation to him. In the record of the court-martial in which Bennett was tried in absentia, one of the survivors testified to what happened next. "Privates Barnes and

Swanson then got on their horses to ride away. Major Bennett, he looked at them and he shot them. He shot them
in the back when they was on their horses and they was
dead when they hit the ground."

The entry in Bennett's journal read: "*Oct. 18.* Barnes
and Swanson executed this day for desertion."

On and on the column pushed, fording streams with
Indian names, riding through expanses of buffalo grass as
high as their stirrups. "*Oct. 21.* Whipped my two brothers-
in-law today because they was talking about cutting out on
me. They are woods Indians and scared of all this open
country. . . . *Nov. 1.* Not cold-trailing anymore. Picked
up Santees' tracks. They are traveling with their women
and kids and are making for a village of Teton Soo some-
ways west of us. . . . *Nov. 6.* Weather turning cold. Five
men deserted last night. If they ever make it back to Minn.,
I will see them hanged. . . . *Nov. 7.* Good news. Captured
an old Teton today. He told us the Santees are only two
days' ride ahead and are slowing down on account of the
women and kids with them."

The column finally surrounded the Indians in a dry wash
somewhere east of the Missouri River. Bennett, hoping to
avoid a prolonged fight, staged a ruse by ordering a squad
of his men to ride around the cornered Santee with brush
piles tied to their horses. The dust raised made it appear
as if the camp were encircled by a full squadron instead
of a company. The Santee, worn out after their long flight,
accepted Bennett's offer of surrender after he promised to
escort them safely back to Minnesota. The Indians were
put in chains the expedition had brought along. For the
next eighteen days, they shuffled behind the horsemen at
the agonizing pace of ten miles a day. The weather turned
bitter and several Santee died en route. This procession
reached the Red River of the North on November 28.
Isaac Bennett, brevet major of volunteer militia, kept his
promise to the Indians: he crossed the frozen Red and
escorted his prisoners back into Minnesota. Then he kept
his promise to himself. In a cottonwood grove, he hanged
the fifteen surviving braves and eight squaws. His men,
who were typical of the Indian-hating militia of that day,
massacred the children, nine of them. "Little savages grow

up to be big ones," Bennett wrote in his journal. He then lowered the corpses, took their scalps as proof he had accomplished his mission, and strung the bodies back up as a lesson to all. "*Nov. 29.* It was a fit retribution for the thing they done. The trouble with Indians is they got no persistence. They fite and then they quit. They do not understand the man who fites and don't quit. This should teach them what they are up against." No doubt it did. A few of Bennett's men, made savage themselves by their ordeal, performed certain surgical operations on the corpses. According to the euphemistic language of the court-martial record, they rode back into Walton with scalps dangling from their rifle barrels and "had attached to their hats the private parts of the Indians, both male and female."

The citizenry of Walton, like most people in frontier towns, were not tenderhearted when it came to Indians, but they had their Victorian sensibilities. They wanted the Santee dead, but they wanted to be spared the details. They also wanted to give a hero's welcome to their local militia, but it was difficult for the boys to cheer and the ladies to kiss the bearded, wind-burned, red-eyed devils who had slaughtered children, who had scalps flying from their rifle barrels, and private parts, both male and female, ornamenting their hats. The townspeople resented Bennett for rubbing their noses in such bloody realities; and when they heard of the summary executions of Barnes and Swanson, they prevailed upon the sheriff to arrest Brevet Major Bennett for murder. The army, however, claimed jurisdiction: General Pope telegraphed the sheriff to keep Bennett in custody until an army escort arrived to take him to departmental headquarters for court-martial. The delay turned to his advantage. Several men from his company, out of some strange loyalty, broke him out of jail. After his escape, he added treason to his crimes by fleeing southward to join the Confederacy. He fought with Bloody Bill Anderson's guerrilla cavalry, whose most famous alumnus was Jesse James. Nothing concrete was heard of Isaac Bennett afterward. According to a letter sent back with Bennett's journal and other personal effects, Bennett was among the outlaws killed when the James and Younger gangs were wiped out in the Northfield, Minnesota, bank robbery in 1876. There was no additional evidence to confirm this romantic, intriguing story. No one knew for sure how he had died. Bennett had vanished so completely it was as if he had never existed.

When he finished reading, Nordstrand felt an immediate spiritual kinship with his ancestor. He was captivated by the man who had led the kind of dangerous, violent life he wanted for himself. He persuaded himself that the legends were true: his great-great-grandfather rode with Jesse James and died in a frontier shoot-out. (Nordstrand was also American in his fascination with the myth of the western outlaw, the myth which makes romantic heroes of men who, if they were around today, would be strapped into electric chairs and forgotten the moment the current was switched off.) For a long time, he stared at a photograph taken of Bennett before he set out after the Santee. It showed him in an army coat, buckskin trousers tucked into high leather boots, and a Union cavalry cap. A revolver was strapped to his waist, a Sharps buffalo rifle cradled in his arms. It was his ancestor's resolution that Nordstrand admired most, the resolution it took to lead his men for two months across a hostile wilderness, to defy orders, to carry out his act of retribution, to break jail and desert to the Confederacy. The last was the most resolute act of all. Treason. In his time, Isaac Bennett would have been forgiven the murder of the Indians. He might have been forgiven the execution of the two soldiers. But treason was unpardonable. Nordstrand saw it as a gesture of contempt. He pictured Bennett riding southward, turning his back on his old life, cutting himself off from it and from all chance of ever returning to it. He knew what Bennett would have done to George Knudsen if Bennett had been his father—he would have beaten that bastard to within an inch of his life or blown his brains out. No sweet reason. No requests for an apology. Bennett had been a man. He rode with Jesse James and died in the Northfield raid. Nordstrand would be like that—tough, pitiless, resolute, a self-contained man owing no allegiances to anyone but himself. In fact, Nordstrand fancied himself a throwback. He became convinced that his unruly nature, the restlessness which made him feel so out of joint with his hometown, were traits inherited from his ancestor and signs that he was destined to live as he did. But the modern world, which the youth equated with the world around Walton, offered no chance for the savage freedom he desired. It was all so tame now. Tame and dull and slack.

Wandering the woods and prairies on his weekend excursions, he dreamed of Bennett's time. The open spaces gave Nordstrand's anarchic imagination the liberty to create whatever visions it chose; and it always chose a vision of annihilation. It wiped out the roads, tore down the telephone poles, toppled the electrical pylons, and erased from the face of the land the rectilinear fields, whose appearance of domestic order and benevolent prosperity revolted him; it burned away the wheat and corn until nothing was left but a virgin plain across whose primitive vastness he saw himself riding, as Isaac Bennett had done.

In imitation of his hero, he began his own diary, starting with the lines "Have begun this diary because have read I.B.'s and I know now what I must do." Actually, he did not have a very clear idea of what he had to do, only a vague notion of the necessity to go someplace where he would have the freedom to act out his fantasy and fulfill his ambition. He had no idea where. At the same time, he was aware of a force binding him to his hometown. He made several plans to run away, but something always stopped him. It was, he decided, a weakness and timidity passed on to him by his father. If a part of him was like Isaac Bennett, another part was like Thomas Nordstrand; and these segments of his divided self warred with each other. He believed the former was the greater part, his true self, but the latter exerted enough pull to inhibit him from acting. Nordstrand feared and despised this side of his character; he feared it would keep him in Walton, turning him into a replica of his father and preventing him from becoming what he wanted to be, a replica of Isaac Bennett.

His hatred of Walton growing until, in his mind, all society and civilization became synonymous with the town, he began to do eccentric little things to show his contempt for it and its way of life. Returning from his forays in the woods, he would swagger around in blood-spattered trousers, a skinning knife hanging from his belt. He fancied it made him appear a wild, dangerous character and shocked the townspeople's Rotarian sensibilities. He drank, whored, and brawled with a few other self-styled tough guys. Parking-lot fistfights. Acts of petty delinquency. Sordid thrustings in backseats with women who expected nothing more. Nordstrand felt especially good coming home one night, bruised and cut from a brawl in a neighboring town, reeking of a slut's cheap perfume, stale beer, and marijuana smoke. He recorded his pleasure on seeing his mother's perplexed and anguished face when she turned on the lights and saw him stumbling up the stairs. Blood from his cut lip dripped onto her pristine carpet, and he saw each drop as a symbol of the scorn he felt for her and her well-ordered world. "Where have you been?" she asked. "Away from you," he snarled. She turned silently away to walk back into the bedroom where his father lay, still sleeping. The sight of the man rapidly turned his drunken elation into loathing, and he felt an almost irresistible urge to drag him out from between the sheets and beat him senseless. He was arrested twice that year, once for assault and battery and once for vandalism—he and a few other delinquents had smashed up some shopping-center windows to alleviate their boredom. With the second arrest, he ended up spending a few nights in the local jail, while his father pulled strings to get the charges dropped. He felt strangely happy in jail. He felt alive. For in the same way that he equated savagery with freedom, he equated criminality with excitement, violence with vitality.

His father's efforts successful, Nordstrand was let go; but his police record got him suspended from the football squad and caused him to lose an athletic scholarship to the University of Minnesota.

His parents decided that he needed discipline and sent him to a stern Jesuit men's college in a northern Minnesota town half as big as Walton and twice as dull. Nordstrand's feelings toward it and its monastic atmosphere went beyond hatred. The sight of its red-brick buildings, sitting complacently in the shade of well-trimmed trees, suffocated him. The requirements to attend mass on Sundays and holy days made him choke with remembrances of his mother's religiosity. He had had so much religion shoved down his throat he was ready to vomit it up. Exasperated by the scholastic lectures on Aquinas, he began reading those thinkers whom the Church had condemned, mostly because the Church had condemned them. Marx, Hegel, Sartre, Nietzsche. Most intelligent young people go through their Marxist, or existentialist, or Nietzchean periods; most get over it, as they get over adolescent skin diseases. Nordstrand was one of the exceptions. He took Nietzsche to heart and, as so many others have done, misinterpreted him. He embraced the German philosopher's denunciations of Christianity and heard in Nietzsche's hatred of weakness an echo of his hatred of the weakness in his father. In Neitzschean doctrine he found a philosophical justification for his ambition to become a strong man above the common run, and in the German's division of world forces into the Dionysian and Apollonian, a neat explanation of the divisions in his own personality.

Nordstrand's diary from his first year at college was a record not of what he did, but of what he thought. Almost every entry was filled with his half-baked, sophomoric reflections on the philosopher of heroes. He had a need to act, he wrote, and to act violently; and this need was driving him toward some dramatic destiny. Destiny, destiny, destiny. The word appeared on every page. He seemed to love it for its own sake. It had a ring to it. He never recorded what his destiny might be, only that its fulfillment would require freedom. He realized that this restlessness was more than physical. He needed more than an escape from the geographical boundaries of places like Walton and Saint Ignatius College for Men; he needed to be liberated from their moral borders as well as from his own inhibitions. He was seeking not simply a place where he could act out his fantasies, but a condition, a realm beyond good and evil. I had a hard time following his logic, but apparently, his thinking went like this: savagery was freedom; society was confinement; therefore, he had to cut the cords of civilization which Walton, his family, and the Jesuits had bound around his spirit; therefore, the strong part of his nature had to overcome the weak, restraining part. "The Dionysian in me must destroy the

Apollonian," he scrawled in one entry. "Otherwise, no matter where I go, I'll always be drawn back." It was just another way of saying that, in imitation of his ancestor, he intended to burn all his bridges with a single, unforgivable act.

The manner in which this self-conquest was to be effected came to him in his sophomore year. It was so obvious he wondered why he had not thought of it before. It was in the newspapers every morning and on television every night: Vietnam. His great-great-grandfather had been a soldier; he would be one. He would go to war in the jungles of Vietnam. War in the jungle—the phrase appealed to him. Though his mind was made up, he did not simply quit school and join the army. That was not Nordstrand's style. He wanted to make a clean, irrevocable break by getting himself expelled. He pondered several courses of action, the bizarre bent of his mind leading him to choose a gesture that would both express his contempt for the Jesuits and leave them no choice but to expel him. He would commit an act of sacrilege. Sacrilege—that word also appealed to him. It was a good, strong word, like treason. After mass one Sunday, he joined his classmates in the dining hall for breakfast. Nordstrand, sitting at the head of the table, parodied the prayers for communion. "For this is my yolk," he said, bowing his head over the eggs in his plate, "and this is my white." He made the sign of the cross, stood, and saying, "In the name of the father, the son, and the holy toast," pulled from behind his lower lip the host he had taken at communion but had not swallowed. He raised the wafer, mimicking the priestly gesture, then dipped it into the egg yolk and swallowed it. The blasphemy had the desired effect: he was expelled the following day.

More than a year later, having passed through basic training, parachute training, ranger training, and officer candidate school, Second Lieutenant Nordstrand became a resident of Firebase X-Ray in the Mekong Delta. It was a Special Forces camp *cum* artillery position, a mean little

patch of mud, bunkers, and ramshackle barracks with
sheet-metal roofs. The other soldiers hated the place, but
Nordstrand found a charm in the surrounding landscape,
with its green paddies sliced by sluggish canals, its heat-
rotted jungles brooding over their primeval secrets. It was
the charm of danger and of being in a place that promised
to fulfill his visions of a violent life. Things did not quite
work out that way. By the time he got to Vietnam, the big
battles were over; fighting had settled into a routine of five-
minute skirmishes. He saw enough action, however, to get
the taste of it and to find that he liked the taste. He saw
enough to win a reputation as a man of raw animal courage, two Bronze Stars for bravery, and a Purple Heart for
the shrapnel wound that had made the indelible mark on
his arm.

As a veteran of that war, I am inclined to use it as an
excuse for my failings and for the failings of all those who
fought there. I have an instinctive sympathy for them, even
the worst of them. Certainly Nordstrand's mind, his soul,
his conscience—whatever you want to call the faculty
which makes us human—was flawed when he went to
Vietnam, but the war aggravated those flaws. It bent and
twisted the warps in his nature until they were beyond
straightening. He had mostly fantasized about violence as
a civilian; he lived it as a soldier. He learned that he had
an exceptional gift for command, but as in all things with
Nordstrand, he pushed it to an extreme. If his diaries were
to be believed, the soldiers in his detachment, a mixed bag
of American Green Berets and Vietnamese, worshiped
him, the latter because he had taken the trouble to learn
their language. He joked with them in Annamese dialect,
quoted from their poets, advised them with native prov-
erbs, and sent them off to be killed or maimed on missions the sole purpose of which was to win more medals
for Jeremy Nordstrand. There were no expressions of
grief, remorse, or pity in his journal. The deaths of his men
did not trouble him at all. He wrote that he felt contempt
for the dead, having come to the remarkable conclusion
that the only men who are killed in war are those who do
not deserve to survive in the first place. He failed to learn
the one lesson the war had to teach: the value of comrade-

ship. He did learn the exercise of power, real power, the power to send men to their deaths. He loved it. He loved it so much that he was known to give incorrect orders for the sheer perverse delight of forcing his men to obey them. He delighted in being unreasonable. Once, while riding convoy, he flew into a rage at an American truck driver who refused to take a wrong turn, as Nordstrand had told him to do. Holding the quaking soldier by the collar (he described the incident with loving detail), he bellowed into the man's face: "You *will* do what I tell you to do, you inferior shit. Got that? I give an order, you follow it, and I don't give a good goddamn if you think it's right or wrong."

There was nothing out there to check him. Firebase X-Ray stood atop a hill at the edge of the U-Minh, a forest near the Cambodian border. Though only a lieutenant, Nordstrand had wound up in command by default. Of its three previous commanders, one had succumbed to malaria, another had been shot, and the third committed suicide. Fever-proof, madness-proof, and apparently bullet-proof as well, only Nordstrand lasted. He outlasted them all.

It is an axiom of western thought that nature has granted us intelligence so we can pursue self-knowledge. The more we are aware of ourselves, the closer we are to perfection. I wonder, though, if limits ought not to be imposed on the pursuit. Perhaps there are things we are not meant to know about ourselves, secrets that, once uncovered, transform us forever, and not necessarily for the better. Nordstrand underwent his sea change one afternoon in the U-Minh, which in Vietnamese means "the Forest of Darkness." Nordstrand's detachment had been assigned to a regular battalion that was sweeping the maze of swamp and rain forest for the hundredth time. It was the only large operation in Vietnam in which he ever took part. A patrol he was leading captured a dozen villagers suspected of giving the Viet Cong sanctuary. A torrential monsoon was blowing. Unable to take the prisoners along and unable to evacuate them because the storm had grounded the battalion's helicopters, Nordstrand radioed the colonel in charge for instructions. The colonel told him to do what he thought best. Without reflecting, realizing immediately the moment had come to commit the unforgivable act that would exile him from the society he scorned, Nordstrand decided it would be best to torture and kill the villagers. He would torture the prisoners by driving bamboo slivers under their fingernails and then, when he had whatever information was to be got from them, execute the lot with his M-16 and leave their bodies as an object lesson to other villagers who collaborated with the guerrillas. There was nothing to stop him. The thought thrilled him. There was nothing, nor anyone, to stop him in the empty jungles. But there was. Nordstrand's Vietnamese irregulars were lining up the prisoners and making them kneel when the colonel came up on the radio: there had been a change in plans. G-2 wanted to question the suspects after all and wanted to badly enough to risk sending up a helicopter in the storm. Nordstrand was to escort them to a landing zone nearby.

The villagers' lives had been spared, but the damage had been done to Lieutenant Nordstrand's soul. He knew he would have tortured and killed them had it not been for that radio call. Only the artificial barrier of military discipline had stopped him. He would have done it. He knew it as surely as he knew the ending to a book he had already read or a movie he had seen. There in the Forest of Darkness he had been given an instant of enlightenment into the darkness within himself, and it was an illumination as strange, as terrible, as magical as a sunburst at midnight. He would have killed them in cold blood. He was capable of it, and, he later wrote, he should have gone through with it, as his ancestor would have done. In ink smeared by raindrops, the entry for the day concluded: "Killing without justification is the closest a man can come to being a god. Once you know you are capable of it, you can never be the same again. I must do what I know I can do. I won't be able to leave here until I have that experience."

But the Army never gave Nordstrand the opportunity. Word of his behavior in the bush reached Headquarters. On one of his fitness reports, he was criticized for "callous disregard for the safety of his men" and "an overaggressiveness"—an Army euphemism for bloodthirstiness. He was pulled back to a desk job in Saigon. Mustered out, he returned to Walton, where he sank into a profound depression, recording that he had failed to escape his old life and felt he never would.

I don't know what he did for the next year. The next entry was dated "Oct. 15, 1973, Tel Aviv, Israel." Nordstrand had taken his savings and, along with several other restless veterans, flown to Israel after the outbreak of the Yom Kippur War. The adventurers volunteered their services to the Israeli army, which replied that it did not need them, thank you. Styling themselves as mercenaries for the benefit of the girls in bikinis, the frustrated soldiers of fortune spent the remainder of the conflict hanging around swimming pools in beach-front hotels. Nordstrand listened with envy to the stories the war correspondents brought back from the front and raged at the circumstances that seemed to be denying him the chance to fulfill his destiny. He raged so much that he got into a fight, was arrested and packed off to jail, where he was visited by an officer from the American consulate. The misadventure might have ended there if the consular officer had been one in fact as well as in name. Something Nordstrand said must have intrigued him. He bailed the American out, interviewed him, checked into his military record, and offered him work. Certain people, the consul said, were looking for a self-reliant young man to supply them with information about the political activities of Palestinian students at the American University in Beirut.

That is how Nordstrand came to be known as November-16 (rated "A-2 reliable") on a computerized roster in the HUMINT (for "human intelligence") section of the Directorate of Operations. His assignment was to pose as a student, befriend the Palestinians by pretending to be an ardent western New Leftist, and, once a week, report on what he learned to his control. He did three years in Beirut, fascinated by the city's atmosphere of intrigue. It was a violent place even before the Lebanese Civil War, an arena for spies and hired gunmen from a dozen different Middle Eastern countries. As for the war, Nordstrand loved it. The roving bands of Moslem and Christian militiamen, the random sniping, the arbitrary shellings, created an environment of total unpredictability that temporarily appeased his appetite for chaos. November-16 proved an adroit and cold-nerved agent, a natural dissembler. He played his role well, became fluent in Arabic, and convinced the Palestinians, about as suspicious, paranoid, and conspiratorial a bunch as could be found anywhere, that he was sympathetic to their cause. In a way he was, though he was more attracted to their terrorist philosophy than to their cause. They were prepared to trample on every law and convention in pursuit of their aim. Nothing counted but the act: a hijacking, an assassination, a kidnapping, a bomb set off in a crowded market. Through action, each *fedayeen* overcame his inertia and created a new self. The romantic worship of violence, violence almost for its own sake—that was their creed, and Nordstrand was drawn irresistibly to them.

At the same time, he informed on them. Nordstrand gave no hints in his diaries of feeling any qualms about his duplicity. Lacking any sort of internal guidance system, he was able simultaneously to befriend and betray the same people. At first, his performance impressed his control. Later, the man had second thoughts, and decided Nordstrand was doing his job too well. This change of heart took place sometime after the war closed down the university. November-16 had vanished for two weeks, then resurfaced with one of the most thorough firsthand reports on the fighting anyone had seen. How had he gotten it? Simple, he replied. He had so won the confidence of the Palestinians that they invited him to join them on the Moslem barricades. He had accepted. Of course, to prove his loyalty, he had been required to shoot now and then at the Christians. His control reprimanded him for taking such a risk without authorization. Nordstrand scoffed at the man's bureaucratic timidity. No one else would have had the guts to do what he had done. Nordstrand was reading spy novels at the time and had applied to become a full-service agent, fancying he could fulfill destiny as a clandestine commando. Parachute drops into remote places on missions of sabotage, night landings on African beaches. His imagination was filled with visions of lurid destruction, exploding oil tanks, collapsing bridges. His application was rejected, largely on the basis of an unfavorable report by his control. Evidently a perceptive man, he had concluded that November-16 (rated "A-2 reliable") had managed to convince the Palestinians he was a rabid fanatic because in fact he was one.

Somehow a copy of the report got into Colfax's hands at the time Operation Atropos was giving its first kicks in the womb of his mind. And somehow the guardian of western civilization found Nordstrand, whose Beirut contract had expired long before, and sent him a plane ticket to Cairo. After several interviews, Colfax showed him the report, saying he ought to regard its unfavorable comments as praise. Resolute men were always regarded with suspicion by the bureaucrats. Then the guardian of western civilization gave him an outline of the project, said he was an ideal candidate for it, and made a speech similar to the one he had made to me. Extremists were needed in an age of extremism, the opportunity in Africa had to be seized now, and so forth. Nordstrand did not thing much of these ideas because ideas bored him, but he was drawn by the chance for action, drawn by the very word *Africa*. Africa: its rivers have been named, its borders marked on maps, its blank spaces filled in, and yet white men still conceive of it as the vast empty place where they will be free to do whatever they imagine. Africa: the name captivated Nordstrand in the way a girl's name captivates her lover; he filled one entire page of his diary with the word. *Africa, Africa, Africa, Africa*. It called him, pulled him, told him it would grant him the fiery climax he sought. He had found the place and the condition. He knew it, as he knew he had found in Thomas Colfax a man who would not try to inhibit him. The mind and the will had met.

———

Moody returned alone. More than a week had passed since he and Nordstrand had left camp. He was riding in the Land-Rover. Its windshield had been blown out. The door on the driver's side looked as if someone had punched holes in it with a giant ice pick. Besides Moody, there were only the river and two guards, sitting on the roof. A crowd of guerrillas pressed around the vehicle, flinging excited questions at the guards, whose answers provoked a burst of yells and a volley of shots fired into the air. Because everyone was speaking in dialect, I couldn't tell if the rebels were firing to celebrate a triumph or mourn a disaster. It had the look of a disaster, but as I shouldered my way through toward Moody, I gathered it was a triumph. Several men slapped me on the back, wild grins on their faces. The Englishman stood on the running board, brushing off the salt and white sand that bleached his clothes and sunburned skin. He had an AK slung over his shoulder.

"Hullo, Charlie," he said with an affected insouciance. "Now I know how Lot's wife felt."

"What happened? Where's the truck? Nordstrand?"

"Dear old Mrs. Lot. Poor girl couldn't resist one last look. I rather think that the destruction of Sodom was a damn sight more pleasant than what I saw. Distant carnage, you know. Vicarious bloodshed. Distant carnage much more pleasant than a close-up."

I picked a shard of glass from the windshield frame. "What went wrong?"

"Why nothing, Charlie." Unslinging the Kalash with a shrug of his shoulder, Moody stepped down and started toward Jima's hut, a train of yelling, cheering rebels behind him. "Can't you tell by the racket? I'm a bearer of good news. Everything went splendidly. Oh, a MIG strafed us. Nothing serious. Lost the truck and three men and some of the ammunition got blown up. Nordstrand shot the plane down. He's really quite the hero now."

"Where is he?"

"Mr. Jeremy is with the caravan. Him and the rest of Jima's praetorian guard. I'd say they're about three days behind us, maybe two if they push it." Moody smiled strangely. Set against his salt-paled face, the red skin ringing his eyes looked like a mask. "They're crossing at night in case the Ethiopians send up any more planes. All things considered, the whole operation went splendidly."

"You don't act like it," I shouted above the hollering and the popping of the rifles.

"We've got the weapons, we lost only three men and the

truck, and, and—this is the important part, Charlie—the tree of faith got a watering. Mr. Jeremy did that as well. Watered the tree of the faith. He makes a splendid gardner, I must say. Splendid."

"You catch another dose of sunstroke?"

"Absolutely not. Look, these are hardly the conditions to carry on a conversation. I must report the jolly news to Jima. He'll be so bloody excited he'll probably cough up enough TB germs to start an epidemic. Do me a favor?"

"Sure."

"Dash off a message to the Cobra. Tell him we made the rendezvous, that the shipment got off-loaded, and that we lost about ten percent of the small-arms ammunition in the strafing. Tell him everything went splendidly."

"All right."

"Do me another favor. Get one of this lot to brew up some tea. I'd rather have a bottle of whiskey, but I don't suppose the old boy has any of that around. Tea will do. See you back in our cozy cave. I'll fill you in then, although I'd prefer not to. I'd like to forget it ever happened, but I don't think I ever shall."

Evah shell.

An hour later, Moody came in carrying a leather bucket he had filled in one of the limestone cisterns.

"I'm going to have a proper wash," he announced. "I'd be a tempting dish, wouldn't I? I've been cooked and seasoned." He gave a strained laugh. "Yes. Parboiled and salted and all set for the pot. What did that pilot—Raymont, wasn't it? Yes. Raymont. What did he tell us? We'll meet people who like to eat people."

"He also told us to watch out for what happens up here." I tapped my temple with a forefinger.

"Do I sound bonkers? I've every right to be, but I'm not."

"You sound a little on edge."

"On the edge of what?" asked Moody, stripping. His body was starkly white except for the shrimp-pink of his lower arms, face, and neck.

"Hysteria."

"Did you get the tea?"

I pointed at the kettle on the table. He filled his canteen cup and drank.

"What was it you were going to tell me?"

"Message get off to Colfax all right?"

"Yes."

"Any response from the Cobra?"

"He sent his congratulations."

"Did he? Marvelous thing, that transceiver. Just press the transmitter button and it sends off a signal to the relay booster at Albara, which shoots it up to a satellite, which sends it back to Cairo, a thousand miles away, all of it at burst so no one can pick it up. A thousand miles. Hard to believe there is such a place as Cairo."

"How about Jima?"

"Oh, delighted at the news. Coughed up a storm. Can't wait to get his hands on his new toys. He's already dreaming about the day he takes the capital."

"What were you going to tell me?"

"In a moment, Charlie. Must have a proper wash first. Collect my thoughts. Tell me, how did you occupy yourself this past week or so?"

"I read."

"Read what?"

"*Les Miserables.* I also listened to the VOA and the BBC on Jima's Sony. He listens to them every day. You'll be pleased to know he prefers the BBC."

"Does he? If we ever get out of here we shall have to tell that to the BBC. The BBC would be delighted to know it has fans even here on the ragged edge. Perhaps they could start a new service. Radio Ragged Edge for all our listeners in the armpits of the world."

After his bath, Moody dipped his clothes in the bucket, wrung them out, then laid them at the cave's mouth to dry in the sun. With a towel wrapped around his waist and rubber shower clogs flip-flopping on his feet, he came back in and poured another cup of the now-tepid tea. Sitting on his bunk, the ankle of each leg resting on the other, he looked like a pink and white yoga in meditation. He drank the tea and smoked a cigarette without speaking. Then he said abruptly:

"We are going to have to figure out some way to get Nordstrand out of here."

"What? Was he hit?"

"Hit? What makes you think he was hit?"

"What the hell are you talking about? You said you were strafed and that we've got to get him out."

"Oh, he wasn't a casualty. Nothing wrong with him physically."

"Naturally this is all making perfect sense."

"I've considered several alternatives. Obviously we won't be able to persuade him to leave. He's determined to see this show through, and no one could persuade that man to do anything he hasn't a mind to. We'd have to use force, but how, Charlie? How? He could take the both of us at once. That's the trouble when you're dealing with a man like him. You aren't left with much choice except to shoot him. Too bad we don't have one of those tranquilizer guns they use on wild animals. We could just pop him with a sedative and stuff him in a cage and off he goes. There's our other problem: even if we did subdue him in some way, we'd have to have him escorted back to the Sudan, but I doubt if we could find one man in this whole lot who would want to see Mr. Jeremy go. They'll really love him when they hear about him shooting that plane down and how he polished off that mob from the FLN. Quite someting. First a gazelle, then a MIG, then men. It's possible we could work something out with Murrah. Murrah really hates him now, but he's got something over our friend Kasu, that bloody little idiot. Nordstrand beat him into it, you know. Threatened to spill the beans to Jima, who wouldn't hesitate to put Kasu to the wall. And of course, we can't rely on Jima. I told him the whole story, including the business about the heads. Wasn't bothered a bit. Fact is, he quite approved. Said they were just Kunama tribesmen, pagans, *kafirs*, the worst of the infidels next to Communists, and since they were with the FLN, he thinks they're Communists as well. Everybody to the left of him is a damned Red. Approved the heads business, too. Quoted to me from the Koran: *When ye encounter the unbelievers, strike off their heads.*"

"You're right. Too bad we don't have a tranquilizer gun. We could use it on you. Might make you coherent."

"You'd be a bit incoherent if you'd seen it." He lit another cigarette. The bright minerals in the cave wall reflected the match light.

"He murdered five men out there."

When I did not respond, Moody asked if it didn't bother me to hear that.

"I won't know if it bothers me until I've heard the details."

"I feel sorry for a man so confused that he doesn't know if murder bothers him or not."

"Listen, Moody. Don't start getting so self-righteous. You've killed men yourself." I expected him to fly off the bunk at me, but he remained fixed in his yogalike pose, as if any movement would shatter him.

"It wasn't like that, Charlie. Not like that at all. I exploded. Didn't know what I was doing until I'd done it. Nordstrand knew. It was as cold-blooded and premeditated as you can get."

"Start over."

"You mean begin from the beginning."

"That's the usual way."

"Very well. The beginning." Bending stiffly and slowly, he crushed the butt of his cigarette on the ground. "Begin from the beginning. Obviously we made it to Ras al-Sultan all right, although it took us a day longer than we'd thought. Vehicles kept bogging down in the salt marshes. We were all a bit edgy when we got to the rendezvous. Well, I was. Worried the dhows had already come in, found us not there, and shoved off. One of our lot kept telling me, '*Allah karim,* Mr. Patrick. God is generous.' As if Allah would make the guns fall out of heaven. Damned Moslem fatalism. We put a couple of lookouts on the headland and hid the vehicles in a big stand of palm near the beach. Rather picturesque actually. Picture-postcard Africa. We waited. Waited all that night and all the next day and the next night. By that time, Osman was sure we were going to be seen by someone, so he ordered everyone to dig in and form a perimeter around the Land-Rover

and truck. Osman's really not a bad chap at heart. He and
I shared the same hole. He talked quite a lot about his
days with Wingate. Most impressed with what he saw in
the war. Of course, he was no more than a boy then, and
all he'd known of war had been tribal skirmishes. With
Wingate, he saw armies of hundreds of thousands, tanks
and big guns left, right, and center. Got it into his head
that the white race was invincible. Not better, you understand, but invincible. Anyhow, he said something that
touched me. He said that here he was, a man in his middle
fifties, right back where he'd been nearly forty years ago,
in a foxhole in the desert."

"Touching and not to the point."

"Oh, but it is. You see, I think Osman admires Nordstrand because Mr. Jeremy fits his conception of the invincible white man. Osman's got a colonial's mentality.
You should have seen him when Nordstrand downed the
MIG. The strafing happened on the third day. The dhows
came in at first light. Just enough light to see. They were
tacking back and forth, waiting for the signal. We popped
a couple of white phosphorus grenades, and they came in,
four of them. Took us all day to off-load. The dhows had
only skeleton crews because of the cargo, and there were
only sixteen of us altogether. Hot work. Worried all the
time a plane would spot us. I'll say this for Nordstrand—
he did the work of five men. Seemed to enjoy the exertion. Never saw so much energy in one man. We hauled
everything from the beach and stacked it up in the stand
of trees, figuring the palms were thick enough for camouflage. The last of it was still on the beach when the MIG
spotted us. Spotted the dhows actually. They'd just shoved
off and were a quarter of a mile out, and the pilot was
smart enough to figure they weren't fishing. He went to
work on them. Lucky for us, not so lucky for them. Two
of them sank, the others caught fire. We ought to have left
that stuff on the beach until he got tired of shooting up
the boats, but Osman got nervous and sent three chaps out
to pick up the crates. Pilot banked towards us, and of
course everyone panicked and opened up on him, Osman
yelling for them to stop shooting because they'd draw fire.

"Which is what happened. The pilot came in low, so

damned low I thought I could see him. Raked the beach
with his cannons, and you would have thought it was the
queen's jubilee when he hit the ammo crates. We didn't
find enough of the three chaps who'd been down there to
fill a mailbag. The pilot banked away and made another
pass. Fired into the trees. Fired blind, I think. Anyway,
he didn't hit any of the weapons, thank God. Shot the
windshield out of the Land-Rover was all. Up he went for
a third pass. I've got to hand it to our Mr. Jeremy. He
does think quickly and he acts without thinking too much.
I don't mind telling you I was scared stiff, Charlie. Never
been strafed before and hope I never am again. Noise of a
jet is simply awful. Could hardly move. Nordstrand figured
the only way to save the shipment from being shot up was
to draw the MIG's fire. He hopped in the truck and backed
it out of the trees and onto the beach. Pilot went for it.
Opened up on the truck with his cannons, and Nordstrand,
cool as you please, was firing back at him with that
twelve-seven they had mounted on the cab. He hit the
damned plane. Hit it in one of its fuel tanks. Had to be
blind luck. Yes, luck. Nordstrand's got that, too. Bloody
plane had shot out the truck's tires, shot the engine to bits,
made splinters out of the sideboards, but it didn't hit Nordstrand and it never hit the gas tank. If either of us had
been on that truck, we would have been blown to tatters.
The MIG burned up in midair and what was left of it
went into the Red Sea. Quite spectacular. It was some show,
Charlie.

"You can imagine the guerrillas' reaction. They yipped
and yapped and cheered and slapped Mr. Jeremy on the
back, embraced him, kissed him on the cheek. If he'd told
them to, they would have kissed his ass. Hell, I would
have at that moment. All I'd been able to think of was that
MIG's twenty-three millimeters hitting all that ordnance
and us splattered over half of Ethiopia. The only one who
didn't join in all the merry-making was Murrah. He just
stood off to one side, looking for all the world as if he were
disappointed we didn't get potted. I asked him what was
eating at him, and he mumbled some nonsense about how
it wasn't good for the movement for the rebels to go making a hero out of a white man. And I said that that par-

ticular white man had saved the weapons and our necks. Well, Murrah looked at the guerrillas all giving Mr. Jeremy three cheers and then at me, and he looked as nasty as that first day at Nassala. 'Better that than this,' he said. Hissed, actually. 'Better that than this.' And I suppose he was right in the end."

Moody shifted his pose. Unfolding his legs, he leaned over and took a bottle of Lomotil from his pack.

"Got cramps, Charlie. Think I've picked up a bug. Too bad we don't have enough antibiotics. This Lomotil stuff just tranquilizes the intestines. Has opium in it, you know."

He washed one of the white tablets down with the tea and picked up the thread of his story.

"The five of them showed up next morning in a Land-Rover. The excitement was over by then. We were just lounging around, waiting for the caravan and hoping we wouldn't get strafed again. All of a sudden Osman dashed up and told us a patrol from the FLN was there and that he had to tie us up to make us look like prisoners. Trouble is, he didn't have any rope. Fancy that. All that hardware and he needed a damned rope. So we just pulled our shirts down across our backs and tried to look as abject as possible. I felt fairly silly, actually. Ever wonder why the Cobra couldn't have found some black agents for this job? Would've made things so much easier. So there we were, playing prisoner, with Osman standing over us, pretending to be guarding us while these five FLN wankers pull up in their Land-Rover. Turned out they were from the FLN base camp ten miles off. They'd heard the strafing and saw the smoke from the evening before and thought they'd have a look at what happened. Of course, they were very interested in what they saw: tons of weapons guarded by some Beni-Hamid a long way from where they were supposed to be. Don't doubt they would have wiped us out and made off with the shipment if we hadn't outnumbered them. Instead, they decided to have a little talk. I'm not entirely sure of the sequence of events, Charlie. While the patrol leader was palavering with Murrah, one of the FLN mob decided to amuse himself with Nordstrand and me. Ugly squat little bastard with an insolent grin on his face, and I suppose you could argue he got what he deserved. 'You Amer-ee-ka?' he said to Nordstrand. 'Fuck Amer-ee-ka.' Think that was the extent of his English. He started to act cute. He took out his knife and mimicked slicing Nordstrand's throat. 'Maybe, huh? Fuck Amer-ee-ka.' Nordstrand couldn't do a thing, of course. Had to play hostage. And I think that's what started Mr. Jeremy off. I mean to say that he was as helpless as if he really were a prisoner and I believe that was his first experience of being helpless, and he didn't like it one bit—"

"No, it wasn't."

"You don't think he minded it?"

"It wasn't the first time he'd felt helpless."

"How the hell do you know that?"

"Nothing. Go ahead."

"What do you mean by 'nothing,' Charlie?"

"Go ahead."

"Very well. Mr. Jeremy didn't like it one bit. You could see it building up in him, in those damned weird green eyes of his. Osman could see it as well and he told that ugly wanker to bugger off. He did, but not before he cut the chin strap of Nordstrand's hat with his knife. Thought for sure Nordstrand was going to break loose and give him a bashing right then. But he just sat there looking. You know how some men can look at a woman and mentally undress her? Nordstrand looked at that man in a way that mentally disassembled him. You could see him tearing that ugly character apart.

"After the ugly one left, Osman spat and said, 'Kunama.' Nordstrand asked him what that meant. Osman went into this long explanation all about how the Kunama were a pagan tribe which the Beni-Hamid had fought and hated for as long as anyone could remember. The whole patrol were Kunama. Osman said we could tell because they had flat noses, not fine ones like the Beni-Hamid, and much darker skin and not a drop of Arab blood in them and they ate dog meat. To top things off, they were pagans. Idol worshipers. Their women had no honor and went about unveiled, and did we know that Kunama husbands gave their wives to visitors? And that Kunama men could change their names whenever they chose? Osman really went on about that name-changing business. You know how these Moslems are about genealogy. And, by God, Osman said, the only thing that prevented him from shooting those insolent Kunama dog-eaters on the spot was the fact that we were united by a common opposition to the Ethiopians. I wish Osman hadn't said that—I mean that business about wanting to shoot them.

"The row started ten, fifteen minutes later. We couldn't tell what was going on. Everybody seemed to be yelling at everybody else. We heard Murrah screeching above them all, then rifle bolts clicking, and then our mob started to square off with the FLN lot. Osman went over to cool things down. Instead, he ended up in the middle of the quarrel. He and Murrah went at it. Really went at it. They talked so fast I could hardly understand a word. From what I could gather, those two were arguing about who was in charge. Next thing I knew, Osman brings his rifle butt up and clouts Murrah in the ribs, knocking him flat. That pretty well established who was in charge. About the same time, our chaps overpowered the five Kunama, took their weapons, and made them kneel down. Osman ordered them tied up, which our fellows did, using the Kunama's shirts for rope. Then Osman came back to us, all lathered up, untied our shirts and told us we were quite free to walk about, do whatever we wished, no need to playact anymore. 'You can thank Kasu for that,' he said. Near as I was able to figure out, the FLN patrol leader, who was chatting with Murrah, asked him what sort of weapons were in the crates, and Murrah, for some stupid reason, told him. Told him everything. Anti-aircraft missiles, anti-tank missiles, the lot. Then the FLN officer, or whatever his rank was, gave Murrah a lecture. Told him this was the FLN area of operations, Jima's men had no damned business being there, and so forth. Cheeky bastard, considering he had only four men with him and we had over a dozen. He then demanded that Murrah turn over some of the weapons to him, as a sort of toll or tax for intruding on the FLN's territory. Amazingly, Murrah started to give in to him, which upset the others a good deal. They hadn't, by God, crossed the Malaka Sink and got themselves strafed to turn over anything to those flat-nosed bastards. Not a bloody cartridge. I guess the FLN bloke saw that he didn't hold any aces and tried scaring our lot. Said there were two hundred men at his base camp, and if his patrol didn't return safely on time, his chums would come looking for him. If the Beni-Hamid thought they could take on two hundred men, that was jolly well fine by him. Our mob stood firm, however, so the patrol leader started to back off. He said, very well, they could do without the arms for now, but they'd take the two prisoners instead. He said he'd heard we were being held for half a million dollars, and half a million would buy them all the missiles they wanted, thank you very much. Hell if I know where he'd heard that."

"Simple. The radio."

"What radio?"

"Your plain old everyday transistor radio. Hell, even the bedouin have got transistors these days. Our kidnapping's been on the news. Heard it myself. Half a million bucks is right. Colfax promised Jima half a million when the mission's over."

"You're joking."

"I lost my sense of humor a long time ago."

"Oh, that's quite marvelous. And if that's an empty promise, I mean, if Colfax doesn't come up with the money . . ."

"There it is. We'll either be staked out on the proverbial anthill or Jima will keep us out here until we're eligible for social security."

"I suppose we shall just have to trust that he's got the money."

"I suppose."

"Where was I?"

"The FLN wanted you two instead of the guns."

"Oh, yes. That's when Murrah did something I really don't understand. He said, no, they couldn't have us because we weren't hostages. We were Jima's advisers."

"Jesus Christ."

"Compromised us. Blew our cover, as the professionals say."

"As they say."

"Did a damned sight more than that. Discredited Jima

and the whole NIIF in one stroke. I gather the FLN fellow was incredulous at first. Muhammad Jima, the famous fighter, the old bandit, the great independent chieftain who said he relied on no one but Allah, had hired white mercenaries? Not exactly mercenaries, Murrah corrected him. Advisers. The FLN leader said it amounted to the same thing, and oh, wouldn't it please Omer Hassab when he heard that the famous warrior Muhammad Jima had to hire mercenaries, and Americans to boot. That's when Osman stepped in and gave Murrah the smack in the ribs. Ought to have banged him in the head if you ask me. The little idiot. The only thing I can figure is that he did that because he must still feel some loyalty to the FLN. Either that or he just panicked and didn't think."

"He was thinking all right, the bastard. He saw his chance and took it."

"What chance?"

"He meant to compromise the mission and discredit Jima."

"Oh? And how do you know that, Charlie? And please don't tell me 'it's nothing.' "

I told him about Murrah sounding out Nordstrand and me back at Kerem. "My theory is that when Nordstrand shut him up, he didn't leave Murrah any choice but to act on his own."

Moody mulled it over for a few minutes. "Well, events proved you right. Nordstrand ought not to have been so unequivocal with him. Murrah jumped at the first opportunity that came along. Cunning little bastard, but not cunning enough. I wonder if he had his next move planned or he did what he did on impulse."

"Knowing that secretive son of a bitch, we can wonder about that until they build ski resorts up here."

"Irrelevant anyway. Moot point. Nordstrand saw to that. Osman was in quite a sweat. He really didn't know what the devil to do with those five prisoners. Obviously he couldn't just let them go, but he was also worried that their boss wasn't bluffing about the two hundred men in the base camp. He figured maybe he could use the five as hostages to bargain our way out of a jam in case their chums came looking for them. So we waited some more.

Waited for that damned caravan. All that day and that night, and no sign of it. No FLN patrols either. Next morning, Osman told us he'd worked out another plan: if the caravan reached us soon, he'd load it up and send it on its way with the prisoners and half his men as guards. He'd stay behind with the other half to divert the attention of any FLN search parties out looking for their chums. He'd start a fire fight or something, anything to keep them occupied while the caravan made off. Nordstrand said, 'That won't be necessary, Osman.' That was all. 'That won't be necessary, Osman,' and he said it in his odd voice. Can't describe it exactly. Somehow calm and not calm at the same time, and the look I'd seen the day before was still in his eyes. It had got into his eyes and stayed there.

"Hot that morning, Charlie. I mean, hotter than usual. Not a gasp of wind. The Red Sea looked like the world's biggest oil slick, and the beach sand was so bright you couldn't look at it. Like looking into the sun itself. Osman and two other men had climbed up the headland to keep a lookout for the caravan. Don't know how anyone could move in that heat, let alone climb a five-hundred-foot hill. No wind and no sound at all except those blasted flies buzzing and buzzing, and the sound of Nordstrand cleaning his rifle. He'd taken the thing apart, detail-stripped it, and had all the parts laid out on his shirt. He was cleaning every last screw in this odd way. Now, I know this is going to sound bizarre, Charlie. You'll think I'm bonkers, but do you know how he was cleaning the rifle?"

"I'll bite."

Moody gave me an embarrassed smile.

"Religiously. It was religious."

"Religious."

"I told you it would sound bizarre."

"It certainly does."

"Well, it's a fact. He was cleaning the AK with total concentration. Completely self-contained. He fondled every damned rod and spring as if it were sacred. He reminded me of a priest getting ready for mass. Do I sound bonkers?"

"Close to it."

"Damn it, Charlie. I know what I saw. You could tell he was getting ready to do something. He was so absorbed in it that when one of our chaps came by to offer him tea, he didn't say a word, didn't look up, didn't acknowledge the fellow's existence. Then he put the rifle back together, took out a magazine, emptied all the cartridges, and cleaned them, all thirty of them. Polished them with the tail of his shirt and reloaded them one by one. Click, click, snick, snick, that's all you heard, the cartridges being shoved back into the magazine, and still another click when he cocked the bolt and put a round in the chamber. The bloke with the tea just squatted there, like a faithful batman, waiting for Mr. Jeremy to finish all this. But when he did, he still didn't say a word. Just leaned back against the tree he was sitting under and stared toward our five prisoners. They were lying under another tree, twenty, maybe twenty-five yards away. The tea *wallah* was looking a bit perplexed by this time and again asked him if he wanted some tea. Nordstrand told him, very softly, 'Get out of here,' and there was no mistaking he meant for him to get out of there. The tea *wallah* trotted off. Then Nordstrand did the oddest thing of all: he started doing deep-breathing exercises. Sort of pumping himself up, like a weightlifter just before he presses a barbell. Pumping himself up and giving off this . . . oh, this air of pent-up energy—"

Exasperated, I said, "Moody, what the hell is the point of all this?"

"The point is that what he did wasn't like what I did. He'd had a whole day and a night to think it over. He got ready for it. Hell, he made a ritual out of it. That's what it was, a ritual. A blood rite if I've ever seen one. All right. I'll come to it. He stood up then, his eyes still on those five Kunama. Four of them were dozing in the heat; the fifth, the one who'd toyed with Nordstrand the day before, was awake sitting against the tree, arms tied behind him. Nordstrand started toward them with the rifle, and I knew what was going to happen. No doubt in my mind. I was scared, Charlie. Almost as scared as when we were strafed. Anyhow, I started after him and I said something like, 'Nordstrand, don't.' He turned around and said, *'I knew you'd*

try, Moody,' and I answered, 'Goddamned right' or something like that, and I leveled my rifle at him. Next thing
I knew, he'd kicked it out of my hand. Odd the things you
remember. I remember it was his right hand because I saw
that scar on his arm, that blue tattoo or whatever it is,
when he hit me. Didn't see the punch, though. Caught me
right here"—Moody pointed to his solar plexus—"and I
went down to my knees feeling as if someone had cinched
a rubber tube around by lungs. No pain that I recall. Just
all my wind gone and a numbness in my arms and legs.
Couldn't move a muscle. I was watching him, knowing
what he was going to do, and I couldn't move. Like a
nightmare really.

"He went up to the one who'd cut his chin strap and
spat in the man's face, and said, "Fuck Amer-eeka' and
started to bring the rifle up—and hesitated. I'm not imagining it. I saw it. I can still see it. He had swung the barrel
halfway up and stopped. Something stayed him, if only for
a second or two. Less than that. Half a second, but something did stay him, and he struggled against it. I'm not
imagining that either. No hallucination, Charlie. I saw him
struggle against whatever was restraining him, and of everything I saw that day, that was the worst. The expression on
Nordstrand's face was awful. Awful. He was . . . well,
transfigured, and then he said something, made a noise,
uttered a word. I think it was a word. It sounded like 'no,'
only it came out very strained, almost like a moan—
'noooooo,' like that. I swear, Charlie, whatever it was that
made him hesitate spoke to him, pleaded with him, and he
struggled against it and denied it with that 'noooo.' All
this happened in an instant, you understand, but you know
how it is in moments like that. Time seems to slow down,
something happens to your perceptions, and you see and
hear things with this horrible clarity, and I saw that expression on his face, almost a tormented look, and I heard
that drawn out 'no,' and then I saw him swing the barrel
all the way up and shove it in that poor sod's mouth.
Fellow's head blew up. Like a hand grenade exploding inside a rotten melon. I think I'd got to my feet by then. I
don't remember. The only thing I recall clearly, and I
damned well wish I didn't, was the man's head disappearing

and feeling something strike my chest, almost where Nordstrand had hit me. Thought for a second a round had rico-
cheted and that I was scuppered. Silly. It was a piece of
the man's skull—I was that close, you see—and for some
reason, that terrified me more than the idea of being shot.
At the same time, Nordstrand spun around and finished
the other four. Didn't take him long. Kalash has a rather
high rate of fire. Three of the four didn't even have time to
move. The last one had got to his knees, and he was trying
to get away like that, walking on his knees with his hands
tied behind his back. Nordstrand emptied what was left
in the magazine into him. The round picked him up and
flipped him over, as if he'd been thrown by some invisible
judo artist. He screamed, either when he was hit or just
before. Must have been just before. Can't say for sure. But
I heard him scream, and then all you could hear was Nordstrand's Kalashnikov sounding like all the murdering machine guns on earth."

Moody paused to light another cigarette. He needed
both hands to steady the match.

"I came to my senses, finally, when it was too late.
Couldn't have done anything to stop him anyway. Ha! I'd
had the feeling he was capable of something like that, almost a premonition, and I'd gone along to make sure he
didn't get out of line. What bloody conceit. I would have
had an easier time keeping a cyclone in line. Strange thing
was, no one else did anything either. The entire horror
probably took thirty seconds from the time Nordstrand
smacked me to the time he pumped the last round into the
last man. And in the end, the others—except for Murrah,
that is—wanted that lot dead. Nordstrand did it for them.
And he wasn't satisfied just to kill them. Had to push it one
step beyond. He was in a regular frenzy, you know. He
beheaded them, Charlie. I mean, he beheaded three of the
four who still had heads. A couple of the rebels had
brought their swords along. Nordstrand ordered one of
them to hand his over, which the fellow did, and damned
quickly, too. I made the mistake of trying to stop him
again, but you might say I wasn't very vigorous about it.
Still, I had to do something. Told him I'd kill him if he
went ahead with it. He just grinned and said, 'Go ahead,'

because he sensed it wasn't in me to kill him. Perhaps I should have, but it wasn't in me. Then Nordstrand lopped the heads off the bodies. One. Two. Three. As automatically as a butcher in a slaughterhouse, but with pleasure. He enjoyed it immensely. The Beni-Hamid didn't mind, either. They were Kunama tribesmen after all. Pagans. Infidels. Idolators. Strike off the unbelievers' heads. He saved the last for Murrah. He dragged Murrah by the shirt over to the corpses and told him to behead the last one. Murrah wouldn't do it, so Nordstrand started to beat him. Rapped him in the chest the way he did me. Nowhere near as hard, but over and over until Murrah was choking and blubbering like a child. Finally, he picked up the sword, but he still couldn't quite bring himself to do it. So then Nordstrand told him that if he didn't, he would be denounced. Jima would learn that he had compromised the mission and had offered to barter away some of the NIIF's weapons to the FLN. In other words, Jima would be told that Murrah was a traitor. The threat worked. Murrah knew he'd be for the firing squad. He was so done in and weak from the beating that he made a mess of the job. Hacked the man's head off, blubbering all the time. When it was over, Mr. Jeremy told the others—no, he made them swear an oath that they'd keep Murrah's betrayal to themselves, but the implication was there: anytime he wants to, Nordstrand can denounce him, and Murrah's a dead man. You see what he was doing, of course. Making Murrah share in the crime and demonstrating his power. Got the others to share in the guilt as well. The bond of blood-guilt, that's what it was, Charlie.

"The horror wasn't quite over. Nordstrand picked up the heads and planted them at the edge of the tree line, then ordered the rebels to take target practice on them. Even if they'd wanted to, they wouldn't have protested. Mr. Jeremy had the power on him, that special power of a man who has just killed. Made quite a sight there on that picturesque beach, the palm trees and the white sand and four heads with bullets pecking all around them, through them, into them. Quite a sight. And you wondered why I wasn't coherent. Damned lucky I'm not stark raving mad."

"What in the hell were you doing all that time?"

"What in the hell do you think? Nothing. I did nothing. Goddamnit, you can go through all your life using a phrase like *petrified with fear,* you can hear others use it, and read it, and never have the slightest idea of what it means until you really are petrified with fear. The thing that frightened me, I mean frightened me the most, was that moment of hesitation. If he hadn't hesitated, I might have understood, if that's the right word. What I mean is that the—atrocity would have been comprehensible if it had been done on impulse or out of pure madness. But Nordstrand knew what he was doing. *He knew what he was doing.* That hesitation—that was his conscience, wouldn't you say? It held him for an instant and he conquered it. Do you see what I'm driving at? A man who can overcome his conscience so deliberately and then go on to do the violence he did . . . a man capable of that . . . do you see what I mean? Damn it, no, you don't. I'm just not making it clear. . . ."

Moody fell suddenly silent. He sat, dappled by the refracted sunlight angling through the cave's mouth, sat so motionless as to be nearly catatonic. He had made himself clear. I did see what he meant. Nordstrand had revealed to him new depths of human darkness, and the revelation had done more than shock him emotionally: it had inflicted upon him a metaphysical trauma that had changed forever his concept of man's capacity for evil. In a toneless, abstracted voice, he went on:

"Osman and the two others came down, blown out. Sweating. They'd heard the shooting. Osman just looked at the mess and said, 'My God.' Not much else to say, I guess. And when he found out what happened, he said it again, 'My God.' And he looked at Mr. Jeremy in this peculiar way. It wasn't exactly fear, and it wasn't admiration, and it wasn't disgust either. It was a kind of awe, rather as if Mr. Jeremy wasn't exactly human, but a phenomenon. As for me, I told you. I didn't do anything. The thing I didn't understand then, still don't, is why he didn't kill me if he was so bent on mayhem. Given the way he hates me, you would have thought I'd be number six—"

"He wanted a witness."

"A witness? He had witnesses."

"He wanted a witness from the outside world, especially a witness like you."

"Charlie, that makes no sense whatsoever. Not that anything else has made much sense the past few days."

As best I could, I tried to explain to Moody that he represented everything Nordstrand despised, that his eyes were the eyes of the civilized world, compelled to watch the outrage by which Nordstrand demonstrated his scorn for its standards and won for himself a terrible liberation. And all the while I was explaining, I kept hearing inside my head that moaning "no" as he resisted and overcame the restraining force that prevents us all from becoming murderers, and hearing that sound, thought to myself, Jesus, he did it, he did it at last, cut himself off entirely, reached escape velocity and boosted himself past the tug of society's moral gravity, out into the void.

Moody said, "You seem to know an awful lot for someone who wasn't even there."

"I didn't have to be there."

"Charlie, right now I feel like smashing that teakettle against the wall. I feel like smashing something and screaming until I'm hoarse."

"Why don't you? Screaming and smashing things are fashionable therapy these days in the States."

"We are not in the States, are we? In conditions like this, one must keep one's head. In any case, the question is, what are we going to do about Nordstrand?"

"A while ago you outlined the options. They come to zero. So I guess we do nothing."

"We can't do nothing."

The Englishman popped off his bunk and gestured frantically.

"Sweet Jesus Christ, Charlie. The man belongs in jail. He's absolutely beyond anyone's control. He is capable of anything. I'd feel safer in a cage with a tiger. Not ashamed to admit that. Given the way he feels about me, I'm quite concerned that I shall be sitting here one fine day and Mr. Jeremy, on some sort of whim, will blow my head off. You said it yourself. He despises me, or I represent everything he despises."

"And that's why he'll never blow your head off. You're

his witness. Listen, if he could, he'd send you back to Sudan to hold a press conference so the whole damned world would know what he's done."

"What rot that is, Charlie. What utter rot. You're the one who's gone bonkers."

"It's not rot, and I'm not bonkers."

There were no terms in my private contract with Nordstrand precluding me from revealing the contents of his diaries. I showed them to Moody and summarized what I had learned from them. It took a few hours. The lantern was burning by the time I finished. Low on fuel, it sputtered inside its smoky mantle and made our shadows jump and twitch like two-dimensional marionettes. Moody listened with the fascination one feels for the grotesque. When I was done, he lay silently on his bunk, smoking and watching the smoke twist and swirl in the nervous flickering of the lamp.

"What you've just told me," he said at last, "is that Nordstrand had it in mind to commit a horror like the one he just did for half his life."

"It comes down to that."

"It was rather like that incident you mentioned when he was at university. He got himself expelled. Now, in a manner of speaking, he's expelled himself from the human race."

"In a manner of speaking."

"All the more reason why we must get him out of here somehow. It's a matter of conscience, wouldn't you say?"

"I'm not so sure about that."

"You're never sure about anything."

"Nordstrand said that about me."

"He's right about a few things."

"Listen, you said it. You'll never be able to persuade him to leave, you can't force him into it, and even if you could, he's got the rebels and Jima behind him, and they don't want him to leave. The way I see it, that leaves you with one option."

"I'm eager to hear it."

"You'll have to kill him."

"Stop joking."

"Said it before, I'll say it again. I lost my sense of humor a long time ago. You'll have to wait till he's asleep, put three bullets in his head, and then hope he doesn't get up."

"Compound murder with murder? I've no intention of killing him."

"And neither do I."

"And you also don't want him to leave, isn't that right, Charlie?"

I said nothing.

"You don't want him out of here, either, do you Charlie? Don't say, 'I don't know.' Talk straight, damn you."

"No, I don't want him out of here."

"Why?"

"Because I want to win."

"Win what?"

"This one. I don't want this mission to fail."

"Again, why?"

"Put it this way. I've got the feeling that if this mission turns out successfully, I'll be different. I mean, I'll be the same."

"You'll be different but you'll be the same. A typical Gageism."

"I meant that I feel I'll be the kind of man I used to be. That's all I'm going to say about it. No more questions on that score. All you'll get is name, rank, and serial number."

"In so many words, you're telling me that we can't 'win' this one without Nordstrand."

"There it is."

Moody stood and paced the width of the cave, shaking his head, the shadow cast by his head flowing over the niches, knobs, and spurs in the rocky wall whose embedded minerals were set aglow by the lantern. Shadow and reflection. Who was to say whether either of us saw anything for what it was?

"Do you condone what he did, Charlie? Is that what you're saying? That this mission is so damned important to you that you condone what he did?"

Moody's voice sounded brittle.

"I don't condone it and I don't condemn it."

"God damn you. *God damn you.*" Now his voice was
like breaking glass. "You don't condone it and you don't
condemn it. How very like you. The master fence-straddler.
What do you do? *What do you do, Charlie?*"

"I accept it."

A little quiver passed through Moody, and he grabbed
the teakettle and flung it against the wall with enough
velocity to send a shower of chipped rock flying.

"You *accept* the massacre and mutilation of five prisoners! You *accept* that! That's all you have to say, you accept it? You disgust me, Gage."

Immediately, he composed himself and struggled to
regain control of his tremulous voice.

"I ought to have bashed you with that kettle. You're
worse than he is in a way. At least he does something. All
you can do is sit back and say 'I don't know' and 'it's
nothing' and that you accept."

The Englishman picked up the kettle, examined the dent
he had put in it, and slammed it back on the table.

"I am going to wait, Charlie. You don't have to worry
about my killing your hero. I'm going to wait for that
murdering bastard to overreach himself. People like him
always do. Then I'll see him out of here, and by God, you
think he wants me to broadcast to the world what he's
done? Well, I will. I will, and I'll see him locked up. Goddamnit, there must be somebody who has jurisdiction in a
case like this. Yes, that's right, I'm going to find the policeman on the corner, and I'll see that he pays."

"The way you paid after what happened in Oman."

"Shut up, you son of a bitch. Shut up."

Nordstrand returned with the caravan two days later. He
acted as though nothing extraordinary had happened, but
the expression Moody had seen in his eyes was still there.
It had got into them and it never left them, becoming as
permanent a feature as the mark on his arm. I had seen
it only once before, in the faces of a patrol emerging from

jungles where they had done something they refused to mention even among themselves, and you had only to look at the unhealthy intensity, the terrible exuberance in their eyes to know it was best not to pry into their secret. Neither Moody nor I ever spoke of the atrocity again. We did not have to. It was there always, an invisible presence except when you glanced at Jeremy Nordstrand's bestial green eyes and saw an image of five headless corpses.

Moody bided his time, waiting for his antagonist to stumble; but Nordstrand proved remarkably surefooted. He was an extremist, but he had an instinctive knowledge of how far he could go. He never made a mistake, and, with time, won even greater loyalty, almost a kind of love, from the rebels. This was after we distributed the weapons and began training the guerrillas. It was a difficult but noble task, lifting the Beni-Hamid out of the darkness of the Bronze Age into the light of the modern, training hands used to gripping sword hilts how to manipulate wire-guided missiles, teaching tribal warriors accustomed to dis-organized charges how to advance by fire and maneuver, instructing products of a preindustrial culture in the art of disassembling and reassembling such complex mechanisms as the 12.7-millimeter anti-aircraft gun. We were agents of progress. We suffered frustrations, of course. Much of the instruction had to be done in sign language because none of us knew the Arabic for such technical terms as *guidance assembly, trajectory, drum magazine feed,* and *joystick* (the lever with which a Sagger antitank missile is guided onto target). Jima hindered us for a while by insisting that his soldiers observe the five daily prayers ordered by Mu-hammad. As three of these occurred between sunrise and sunset, we had to break off training each time the *muezzin* issued the cry "God is great . . . come and pray. . . . There is no God but God, and Muhammad is His Messenger." No argument could persuade the old man to change his mind until Nordstrand found an appropriate passage in the Koran: *When ye march to war in the earth it shall be no crime in you to shorten your prayers.* Nordstrand suggested that these words could also apply to preparing for war. Jima, a deep cough resonating in his frail chest, pondered for several minutes, then consulted his *mullah,* a grey-bearded ancient who advised him on such matters. Yes, the sheikh said finally, they could. Oh, Mr. Jeremy was wise for an unbeliever. Yes, the prayers would be dispensed with. He, Muhammad Jima, the slave of Allah, and so on, declared it.

When, after about three months, we had made an army out of them, Nordstrand got the idea to lead them on a campaign of small-scale raids and ambushes. Then, with a perfectly straight face, he compared his planned campaign to that of Belisarius, the Roman general who had restored the morale of the broken legions by avoiding set-piece battles with the barbarians and engaging them only in hit-and-run actions in which victory for the Romans was assured. Displaying the Germanic side of his personality, he plotted each operation with the precision of a mathematician plotting points on an asymptotic curve. He stayed up nights studying maps and planning for every possible contingency, spent days rehearsing the rebels until each man knew exactly what was expected of him and as little as possible was left to chance. The problem of Nordstrand's visibility was solved by the *mullah,* who was also a kind of witch doctor; he brewed up a black dye similar to kohl. Nordstrand smeared it on his face and hands, shaved off his long hair, and covered his skull with the stuff. From a distance, he looked as if he were wearing an executioner's hood. Before Nordstrand went off on his first outing, Moody, attempting to maintain the appearance of authority, warned him about Colfax's instructions, saying it would be too dangerous: if he were captured, it would be the end of the mission. Nordstrand, throwing back his huge, soot-colored head, laughed, and said: "It won't be dangerous at all, General. It's going to be fun."

The Beni-Hamid had learned their lessons well and passed their final examinations with honors. With the new Belisarius to lead them, they annihilated, in the span of about a month, two Ethiopian supply convoys and a company-sized armored column, captured a small arsenal of weapons and several scout cars, and brought down a couple of MIGs with Strella missiles. The accumulation of these minor victories bolstered the faction's confidence, gained the NIIF a reputation as something more than a mob of bandits, brought in a steady flow of recruits, and elevated Jeremy Nordstrand's status from hero to demigod.

The price of his deification was twenty-six dead ("martyrs," in Murrah's lexicon) and roughly twice that number wounded. The former were the luckier: the wounded fell under the haphazard care of the NIIF's only doctor, a man whose medical training consisted of two years' experience as a male nurse in an Italian-run clinic in the capital. We had missiles, rockets, and AK-47s, but the camp's hospital—it was in one of the caves—was short of almost everything. Tribal robes cut up into battle dressings. Herdsmen's staffs for crutches. *Kat,* a mild narcotic, for pain-killer. Hard and stoic, the Beni-Hamid never cried out. Sometimes we saw them lying on their straw beds, or hopping about like crippled birds on their makeshift crutches, in their shining eyes the removed stare that is the universal expression of men wounded in war; but they never cried out, because it was unmanly and because they believed God made man suffer pain to purify his soul; to cry out, therefore, was to protest against God's will. The smell was the worst part of it, the unique stench of gangrene, of death in life. The doctor used a slaughter knife and woodcutter's saw to amputate diseased limbs, staunching the bleeding with mud packs. In this way, most of his patients attained revolutionary martyrdom.

The young men who survived attained tribal manhood, which was not, among the Beni-Hamid, a matter of reaching a certain age. An inflexible law required a youth to kill one man in battle before he could be initiated as a warrior. Nordstrand's campaign gave them plenty of chances to fulfill their quota. A mass initiation ceremony was held one night not long before we attacked the Ethiopian garrison at Umm-Tajer. The rite, Murrah explained, had origins dating back to the time when the Beni-Hamid were a pagan tribe. Since then, it had become mixed with the practices of bizarre Moslem cults. It was ultrasecret, so that two sentries were posted at the cave to make sure we did not see what no outsider had ever been allowed to witness. The ritual went on all night. And if we could not see it, we could hear it: the thud of drums, lilting shep-

herd's flutes, and howling bedouin fiddles. It was a strange
music, with more of Afrrica than Arabia in it, a sound as
old as those age-worn but ageless mountains. It seemed to
mesmerize Nordstrand. He was drawn to it, and not by
curiosity. I think his exclusion rankled him because he
regarded himself as one of them. Being barred from the
rite struck him as an insult.

Nordstrand had begun to exhibit symptoms of a familiar
spiritual malady, the power disease. He had won the tribesmen's loyalty; for all practical purposes, he was running
the operation and had become Jima's chief adviser and
chief of staff. The lust for authority quickening in him,
he had an audience with Jima at which he demanded that
the rebels recognize his status and triumphs. What did he
have in mind? the sheikh asked. The NIIF was not a regular army that awarded medals and decorations. "I want,"
Nordstrand answered, "the men to call my name as they
call yours." It was an audacious demand, but Jima had
come to regard the American as indispensable to his plans
and acceded to it. When Nordstrand came marching back
from his next sally—another ambush of a government
supply convoy—he received the equivalent of a ticker-tape
parade. Goats were slaughtered in his honor and the still-
warm carcasses laid in his path. The guerrillas who had
remained in camp formed two long lines between which
Nordstrand strutted at the head of his raiding party, his
black camouflage streaked with sweat, his skin burned almost to the Beni-Hamid's coffee brown, his oversized
shaved head swaying in rhythm to the intoxicating sound
of his chanted name: "*Jer-ah-mee, Jer-ah-mee, Jer-ah-
mee.*" The guerrillas had staged this welcome on Jima's
orders, but the emotion in their voices sounded genuine.
They adored him, and their shouts made Moody and me
conscious of our apartness. The Beni-Hamid had all but
adopted Nordstrand, while we two remained outsiders. For
his part, Nordstrand appeared consumed by his glorifica-
tion. He was certainly too swept away to notice Murrah,
standing alone some distance away, his face a black arrow-
head of hatred.

At the opposite end of the spectrum was Osman, the
most ardent of Mr. Jeremy's admirers. By God, he told

Moody and me one idle afternoon, he had been a soldier all his life, and he knew a great fighter when he saw one, and Mr. Jeremy was among the best he had seen since he'd fought with Wingate. This praise came during a conversation in which Osman had been reminiscing about the world war and the coffee farm he had acquired when it was over. The government had granted him the land as a reward for his services against the Italians. He gave up nomadism for the life of a farmer in the northern highlands. It actually rained there once in a while, yes, rained, by God, and the water was good and things could grow. He had seen the farm only a few times in the past ten years. His wife had died years ago, and he had never remarried. The coffee was now cultivated by his eldest son, who had been badly wounded in the rebellion but had recovered, praise be to God. Osman spoke almost nostalgically about the house of sun-dried brick, the rolling hills green with coffee plants, the river running between the hills, and his neighbor's lean cattle watering in the river in the heat of the dry season. Over the passage of time, his visits there grew shorter and the intervals between them longer. He had not been back for two years now. He laughed.

"Do you know why? Because the place bores me. There are times when I think I don't want to go back ever. I get tired of all this fighting and marching sometimes, but I wasn't happy on that farm after the war against the Italians. I thought to myself, What is a Beni-Hamid warrior doing, growing coffee? By God, when this rebellion started, I was happy. It made me happy to carry a rifle again. And there are times, may God forgive me, when I hope we don't win. I hope we don't lose, either. Sometimes I think they are the same, victory and defeat. If we won or lost, the war would be over, and I don't want it to be over. Ya! Mr. Patrick, what do you think of that?"

"Not much," Moody said dryly.

"Mr. Jeremy, he understands. He's a great fighter because he loves fighting. He understands there is an enjoyment in fighting, there is a freedom. The Beni-Hamid have always been free men who fought. We have a saying, you know. 'We are warriors, we are the heirs of glory.' But when the fighting stops, what happens? Men like that Kasu take power. They organize things, and where am I? I am back on my coffee farm, a slave to the seasons and to men like Kasu. Mr. Jeremy, he understands that."

"Yes, he certainly does," replied Moody. "And I don't think you have to worry about your future, Osman. I'm sure your God and Jima and Mr. Jeremy will spare you from the horrors of peace."

Moody: the loss of the rations and medicines eventually had the effect Nordstrand desired. The Englishman had begun to suffer from almost daily attacks of imaginary diseases. Frequently I found him with a thermometer in his mouth. "Feel a bit feverish today," he would say. The reading was invariably normal, which did not reassure him; rather it led him to suspect the instrument was faulty. He caught a mild cough once, and came close to panic, thinking it was the onset of tuberculosis. One morning he declared that he felt unusually weak—protein deficiency, he thought. On another, I found him in the latrine studying his stool with all the absorption of a lab technician. "It's clay-colored, Charlie. Look at it." I answered that there were some things I simply would not do. "Damn it, look. It's clay-colored. That's a symptom of hepatitis."

He became so obsessed with the state of his health that he seemed to forget his promise to find a way to get rid of Nordstrand. He even seemed to forget his personal mission to seek out the circumstances that would enable him to commit an act of mercy in atonement for the act of brutality he had committed years before. He seemed to forget everything except the fear of coming down with some fatal disease and dying unmourned in the wilderness.

Nordstrand wore him down further with his unrelenting insults and mockery; and the fact of what he had done charged each jibe and taunt with a lethal electricity. Every word he spoke to the Englishman, even the most innocuous, conveyed contempt and an implied threat of murderous intent. And despite what I had told him of his role as witness, this undertone of viciousness convinced Moody he was locked up in that cave with a giant, two-legged Doberman, an unpredictable beast who might tear the

life out of him without provocation. That, at least, is my
assumption of what was going on in Moody's mind. We
never spoke of it. But it is an assumption based on his peculiar behavior. He took to sleeping with a loaded Kalashnikov propped next to his bunk, and when that failed to
make him feel safe, he added a nine-millimeter pistol.
Nor did he actually sleep. He just lay on the bunk, refusing
to close his eyes while Nordstrand was awake. That meant
he hardly slept at all because the American, with his manic
energies, stayed awake half the night reading his Nietzsche,
or practicing his Hwrang-Do, or studying a map and plotting some new ambush. All this combined with the climate,
the isolation, and the bleak, hopeless landscape to strip the
insulation on Moody's psychological wiring; it was dangerously near short-circuiting when, getting word of the
PLF's disastrous attack at Umm-Tajer, Jima decided to
seize the town himself.

The word had come from one of our patrols, which had
got it from a smuggler's caravan, which, passing near
Umm-Tajer on its way to the coast, took some of the PLF
wounded to a rebel hospital. Needing a dramatic victory
to restore prestige after its defeats in the counteroffensive,
the Revolutionary Command Council had ordered Adam
Bairu's faction to take the outpost. It stood on the western
slopes of the Malaka Massif, blocking both a main guerrilla supply route to Sudan and access to a nearby oasis,
which, in a land where drought was not a calamity but a
perpetual condition varying only in degree, gave the place
a strategic importance. Apparently, the RCC thought the
garrison would fall easily; it was supposed to be defended
only by a rifle company of the government's half-trained
"peasant militia." Bairu assaulted with five hundred men
and lost half in the first day's fighting. The insurgents' intelligence had been inaccurate. Instead of encountering a
company of conscripts, the PLF ran into the disciplined
fire of a half-battalion of Ethiopian commandos supported
by a platoon of tanks whose canister shot had scythed the
attacking guerrillas. Bairu avoided total disaster by breaking off the assault and dispersing his men into the hills
overlooking the outpost. From there, they put the Ethi-

opians under siege and harassed them with sporadic sniper
and mortar fire.

The news of the Christians' setback made Jima ecstatic.
The situation was almost the reverse of the one in which
Bairu had shamed him long before. What symmetry! The
hand of God was in it. This he told us after calling a war
council to announce his decision to snatch the prize out of
that bastard Bairu's hands. He would capture Umm-Tajer.
The honor of the victory would go to him. And the victory
would put the oasis and the supply line under NIIF control, which would leave the council with two choices: they
would either deal with him or risk another interfactional
war by trying to take the place from him by force. But
they were sensible men; they would deal with him. Yes,
by God, with Umm-Tajer in his hands, the council would
be compelled to listen seriously to his demands. And his
demands would be the integration of the NIIF into the
main rebel army and the seating of Muhammad Jima on
the six-man directorate that ran the council. God willing,
he would do it all in one stroke: take his revenge on
Bairu, give the rebellion the victory it so desperately
needed, and gain power for himself. Once on the directorate, he would eliminate his rivals one by one until only he
remained. From there, hacking and spitting up bloody
phlegm, Jima soared off into more fantasy. Not only did
he intend to take Umm-Tajer; not only did he intend to
hold it. He intended to declare it the provisional capital
of the future Islamic Republic of Bejaya, God willing. He
would see that the news of this feat reached the outside
world; and one day soon, God willing, he would hear on
the Voice of America and the BBC—*his name*. He would
hear that Muhammad Jima had seized the provisional
capital of the Islamic Republic of Bejaya.

Listening to him was at once fascinating and appalling.
The provisional capital of a state that existed only in the
fevered imagination of a diseased old man who wanted to
hear his name spoken on the radio. Murrah and Moody
attempted to bring him back to reality. Murrah suggested
that, assuming we took the place, it was politically premature to declare it a provisional capital. Moreover, he

cautioned, despite the infusion of recruits, the NIIF still mustered under a thousand fighting men: 926 to be exact. Jima raised his eyebrows to show he was impressed with Murrah's exactitude. Not all of the 926 men could take part in the attack, the younger man continued; some, half perhaps, would have to remain behind to guard the base camp. If Bairu had been unable to capture Umm-Tajer with 500 men, what assurance was there of the NIIF seizing it with roughly the same number? Jima dismissed Murrah's arithmetic with a wave of his bony hand. Numbers meant nothing. Had not the Prophet—peace be upon him—been outnumbered at the Battle of Bedr, and had he not put the army of the Meccans to flight? Why? Because God had been with him, as he is with us, Kasu. And just as the Battle of Bedr had been the rock upon which all the Prophet's future successes had been built, the coming battle of Umm-Tajer would be, if God willed it, the foundation of Muhammad Jima's Islamic republic. The sheikh then revealed the degree of his confidence. He intended to risk everything on this one roll of the dice: every available fighting man would take part in the attack. The base camp at Bab el Howa was to be evacuated save for a few men left behind to look after the wounded and sick. Moody interjected at that point. A thousand men could probably take the garrison, he said, but at such cost that the survivors could not hope to hold it against a determined counterattack. Moreover, holding a fixed position against a conventional army violated the principles of irregular warfare; we would be playing the Ethiopians' game. Again, Jima waved his hand disdainfully. He would listen to no more talk of numbers. It was not just a question of numbers, Moody countered. The Ethiopians had tanks, planes, and artillery. They could blow the NIIF out of Umm-Tajer. What was wrong with Mr. Patrick? Had he lost his reason? Why had the faction been supplied with antitank and anti-aircraft rockets? To shoot down enemy planes and blow up enemy tanks. And, the sheikh added, he had recently learned something on the radio. He took hold of the Sony's carrying handle and held it in the air as if to say, "This is a radio." He had learned on the BBC that new fighting had broken out on the Ogaden

desert between the Ethiopians and the Somalis. Most of
the government's air force and armor had been committed;
therefore, we had nothing to fear. The Englishman re-
treated in the face of this fact and tried to hold another
line of defense. He begged the old man not to make any
public announcements declaring Umm-Tajer a provisional
capital. Murrah was right. That would be premature. It
could, in fact, provoke the Ethiopians into launching a
counterattack, whatever their problems with the Somalis.
Jima listened, as thin and rigid as a shotgun barrel, and
about as reasonable. Yes, it would be provocation. He
wanted to provoke the Ethiopians. Let them send their
planes, he would shoot them down. Let them send tanks,
he would destroy them. It would be a further demonstration of the NIIF's power.

Moody, sagging under the weight of the sheikh's fanatical confidence, made one last attempt to dissuade him. The
secrecy of our identities had been preserved by the near-
total isolation of the base camp, he said; evacuating it
would force us to accompany the rebel army to Umm-Tajer
and greatly increase the risk of compromising the mission.

Jima said, "It doesn't matter."

The remark restored some of the Englishman's spark.

"What do you mean, it doesn't matter?" he said in the
brittle voice that usually preceded one of his outbursts.
"That man killed—he butchered—five men to keep this
mission secret." Moody pointed a trembling finger at Nordstrand. "Butchered them, and now you say it doesn't
matter?"

"That was then. Now is now. If it should be discovered
that you've been my advisers and not my hostages, it
won't matter. All that will matter is that I, Muhammad
Jima, hold Umm-Tajer, that I have the weapons to deal
with the Ethiopians' tanks and planes, and that I control
all the supplies which will pass through Umm-Tajer from
Sudan."

"Not all, just some."

"Not some, but most."

"We were ordered not to take part in any actions. For us
to go with you would be to violate our orders. We
couldn't do it without authorization from Cairo."

"Without authorization," Nordstrand cut in loudly. "Who's the authority out here? Why don't you come out with it, weak sister? You haven't got the nerve to go through with this."

"You know, I could have shot you back then at Ras al-Sultan, Nordstrand. I could have and should have."

"But you didn't have the nerve, General Dross. Just like you don't have the nerve to go through with this."

"That's enough! I'll not be insulted any longer."

"It wasn't an insult, it was a statement of fact."

"Speak in Arabic, the both of you!" Jima commanded. "Mr. Patrick, you say you cannot take part in the battle without authorization? Then I say you send a message to Mr. Jack in Cairo with that wonderful device of yours and ask for authorization. I know Mr. Jack and I know he'll give you your authorization. Go now and do that, you and Mr. Charlie. Mr. Jeremy will stay here and help me plan this attack. Ya! Mr. Jeremy, the Italians have a word for *knife*. They call it in their language 'the white arm.' That is you. You are my knife, my sword, my instrument, my white arm."

Moody and I left the old man with his white arm and sent the message to Cairo. The response proved Jima knew Colfax's mind:

Proatropos one Excobra:
Agree prophet's assessment seizing objective key to his gaining seat on directorate. Have examined position on map and think it can be held. Advise Jima to disperse his forces enough to minimize casualties in event of air raid. But not so much as to weaken position's defenses in event major ground counterattack. Re risks mission compromise. If prophet insists you go along, do so. Take all possible precautions to avoid exposure unless situation demands otherwise. If attack successful and results in prophet's instatement on directorate, you are to consider Atropos completed and arrange for exfiltration to Nassala as soon thereafter as possible. Good work so far.

* * *

"And what is all that supposed to mean?" Moody asked rhetorically, wadding up the decoded message and tossing it against the cave wall. "He's sitting on his sweet bottom up in Cairo and looking at a map and he thinks the place can be held. I've seen it on a map as well and I don't think it can be held. That town is sitting on top a small hill in the middle of a valley about four miles square at most, a bloody shooting gallery for aircraft. We're to advise the old man to disperse his men enough to minimize casualties in case of an air raid, but not so much that we've got holes in the line big enough to march a battalion through line-abreast. We're to take precautions to avoid compromise unless the situation demands otherwise. Do you know what all that means, Charlie? Nothing. It is a splendid example of contemporary American double-talk."

"I'd forget about it. I'd just think about getting out of here and collecting what you've got coming. Jima's taking that place is our ticket out of here and the signature on our paycheck."

"Yes, it's like the Housman poem, isn't it?"

"What Housman poem?"

"The 'Epitaph on an Army of Mercenaries.' Do you know it?"

I didn't.

"It goes like this:

These, in the day when heaven was falling,
The hour when earth's foundations fled,
Followed their mercenary calling,
And took their wages and are dead.

"I can't say I care for the 'dead' part. I should very much like to survive this show, although I didn't come here just to survive, did I? And there are times when I wonder if survival is worth the price."

"Look, none of that doomed-young-man crap, all right? I knew too many guys in Vietnam who started talking that way and all of them went home feetfirst."

"Is it worth the price, Charlie? Survival's quite fashionable these days. People say, 'I'm a survivor,' as if that is an achievement. No one questions if surviving is worth what you've got to do to survive."

"It's a lot better than what you have to do not to survive."

"I meant what I said back there." His voice once more took on that fragile sound, the sound of glass cracking. "About Nordstrand."

"Christ, don't tell me you're still thinking of having him shipped out of here. You've got less chance of that than ever. You heard the old man—his 'white arm,' his instrument."

"Oh, yes. That rubbish. But that is not what I meant when I said I meant what I said."

"I'm not tracking."

"About being insulted. I'll not be insulted any longer."

An odd smile broke on his long-jawed face, not so much a smile of confidence as one of acceptance. Then the smile became a little laugh whose tinny sound made me uneasy.

"Charlie."

"What?"

"Do you know what week of the month it is?"

"No."

"Do you know what month it is?"

I thought for several moments, then I laughed. Living in that seasonless, clockless land, I had lost all sense of time.

"It could be January," I said.

"And what if it's not?"

"I suppose it doesn't make any difference."

"It's February. February sixteenth to be exact. One advantage to operating that radio is that I've had to keep track of the days. It's four months and twenty-three days since we crossed the border."

"It still doesn't make any difference."

Moody laughed in that strange way again. No, not strange. I had heard it before and tried to recall where and when and from whom I'd heard it. The memory would not come; it hung on the edge of my conscious mind.

"Doesn't make any difference. That's right, Charlie. Things don't make much difference now, so we are going to have peaches for dinner tonight."

"Right. That follows."

"It's our last tin. I've been saving it, but it doesn't really make any difference if we eat it now or later, does it? So we shall have peaches. You, Nordstrand, and I."

———

We were sitting around the table, its surface papered by the map Nordstrand had used to illustrate the latest product of his tactical genius, the lantern holding the map down at the center, the lantern's light tiger-striping the camouflage on Nordstrand's face, whose eyes glittered with amusement as they stared over the lip of the peach can at Moody, wagging a plastic spoon like a mother scolding a child for bad table manners.

Nordstrand took the can from his lips and passed it to me.

"Let's hear that again, Moody."

I drank some of the peach juice, then handed the can to Moody. He did not take it. Glaring at the American, he sat rigidly with his elbows propped on the table, only his hand moving as it wagged the spoon. I put the tin down in front of him.

"You took two, Nordstrand."

"Two what?"

"Two sips of peach juice, what else? I said that we were to have one sip apiece until it was finished, and you just took two."

"Either you've recovered your nerve or lost it completely."

Moody dipped the spoon into the juice, put it in his mouth, then wagged it again. Nordstrand blinked when a few drops flew over the table into his face.

"I just saw you. I'm not having any hallucinations. That is our last tin, and you took two sips."

"You didn't see anything, Dross."

"And you can stop calling me that."

"Sure I can."

"I'm not allowing you to have this tin until you own up." The spoon wagged emphatically. "You're a selfish bastard, Nordstrand. You haven't the vaguest idea of what it's like to share."

"Stop waving that thing in my face."

"Does it bother you, tough guy?"

"Yes, it does."

Nordstrand could say "hello" in a way that translated into "I'm going to tear your heart out." So you ignored what he said and tuned your ears to the modulations in his voice if you wanted to know when he was joking and when he was being sincere, when the casual sarcasm in him gave way to bone-deep malice, when the puerile bully became the killer. And hearing the flat, dead, ugly way he spoke those three words, "Yes, it does," I told Moody to get hold of himself.

"Do you think I don't have a grip on myself?" he answered, ending the sentence with a burst of unstable giggling. "Do you think I'm afraid of him? I'm not afraid of him." With an idiotic grin on his face, Moody leaned over the table and tapped Nordstrand on the nose with the flat of the spoon. "There. You see, I'm not in the least afraid of him. I'm not afraid of you, you whatever-you-are. Murderer. Yes, that's all it comes down to. A common murderer. Wouldn't you say that's all you are in the last analysis, Nordstrand? A common murderer?"

"I'd murder anyone who stood in my way."

"Undoubtedly. You've already murdered five men who weren't in your way."

"I'd shove a knife into the chest of Jesus Christ himself if he stood in my way."

"Undoubtedly. Undoubtedly you would. But would he die for you if you stabbed him. There's a question. Would Jesus Christ die if Jeremy Nordstrand stabbed him?"

Nordstrand tilted his head to one side coyly. Shorn of hair, it looked even larger, so large as to be almost a deformity.

"I've got another question, General, a better one. Do you know the riddle about the five-hundred-pound gorilla?"

"Of course. What does a five-hundred-pound gorilla do? Anything he wants. The authority of brute force."

"There it is."

"For example, if a five-hundred-pound gorilla wanted to take an extra sip of peach juice, he would. If he wanted to take it all for himself, he would, because no one is going to contest a five-hundred-pound gorilla."

"There it is again."

"There it isn't, there it isn't." Moody's giggle became hysterical and flipped the switch of my memory. Bates. Specialist Fourth Class Bates had laughed that way just before he charged the Viet Cong machine gun that had pinned us down, winning himself a Distinguished Service Cross and a spot on the KIA list for that week. The citation for his medal described his act in the usual Homeric terms, but only we in the squad knew that Bates had not charged the guns to "save the lives of his fellow soldiers." Specialist Fourth Class Bates had committed suicide. He had killed himself because he had been in combat eight months and had seen so many hit beside him without once suffering a scratch himself that he finally became convinced the war was saving him for something special. Then every near-miss struck him not as a sign of his luck but as a taunting reminder of the awful death he was certain awaited him. He could no longer bear the tension of waiting for a horrible inevitability. He could no longer withstand the feeling of being a helpless plaything and decided to have at least some say in the manner of his death, and the crazed laugh he gave just before flipping himself over the wall was a laugh of joy and relief.

"There it isn't," Moody repeated with that same manic cackle. And I knew just how far he had gone over the line when, still laughing, he reached under his bush jacket, drew the nine-millimeter, thumbed the hammer to full cock, and aimed it at the ample target of Nordstrand's head. "You see, Nordstrand, a five-hundred-pound gorilla cannot be contested because he hasn't the intelligence to know what one of these can do." He sat with the spoon in one hand and the gun in the other. "What can one of these do, Jeremy?"

"You've really lost your nerve."

"What can one of these do? If you can't answer that, I'll have to assume you're as stupid as the five-hundred-pound gorilla and be forced to shoot you."

"You haven't got the nerve to shoot anyone."

"Don't be so confident, Mr. Jeremy."

"Stop waving that thing in my face."

Another chuckle bubbled from Moody's lips. "Which thing? Which thing bothers you most, Mr. Jer-ah-mee?"

"Both things."

"You have a choice. One or the other. I think it shall be the spoon. I shall stop waving the spoon in your face." The Englishman let the spoon drop into the can, then held the nine-millimeter in both hands, elbows braced on the table so that his forearms formed a triangle with the pistol at the apex. "That leaves only this. You didn't answer me. What can one of these do to a man, Nordstrand?"

"One of those can put a hole in a man big enough to shove a sewer pipe through it."

"To borrow one of your phrases, there it is."

"To borrow one of yours, there it isn't. That'll blow a hole in you only if the man holding it has the nerve to pull the trigger."

"And of course you don't think I've the nerve."

"You've lost it already, what little of it you had to lose."

Moody stopped smiling and assumed the air of a hurt child.

"Take that back."

"Take what back?"

"That business about losing my nerve."

"I can't take back a fact, General. Your nerves are gone. You've started to see things. You think you saw me take two sips of peach juice."

"I did see you. Oh, I saw you all right. Yes, I did. I saw you, Nordstrand. It is our last tin of peaches and you took an extra sip for yourself. I saw it, you selfish bastard."

"You didn't see anything."

"Take it back."

"You know what I'm going to take back, General? I'm going to take the can of peaches, right out from under that little toy in your hands."

Nordstrand reached across the table. He had misread the Englishman. Moody probably had lost his nerve; he probably had no intention of pulling the trigger; but Nordstrand's mental radar had failed to register that the signals

emanating from Moody were those of a man beyond the
point where nerve or the lack of it had any relevance,
where conscious intention was meaningless. He was in the
condition he had been in Oman years before, under the
rule of blind impulse. And he had not been put there by
a couple of ounces of peach juice It was the conviction
that Nordstrand would kill him eventually, and the inability to bear any longer the pressure of waiting for the
American's final offer: it was the loss of self-respect caused
by all the petty insults that had accumulated into one big
insult. Inside the cave, the pistol crashed like a shell. The
report deafened me, the muzzle flash blinded me, and I
tipped over backward in the chair. Executing a neat back-
flip, I rolled to my feet and expected to see Nordstrand's
brains pasted to the wall behind him. What I did see was
worse in its own way. Nordstrand had not moved. He remained in his chair, staring at the pistol which Moody
waved back and forth, staring with his eyes tinged a feline
yellow by the lantern and with the utter, unnatural calm
of a man more than a little in love with death. Behind
him, and about six inches above his head was the hole the
bullet had bitten out of the wall.

Smiling victoriously, Moody said, "Now do you believe
I've the nerve to press the trigger, Jeremy?"

"Sure."

"If you want to find out if I've got the nerve to put the
next one between your eyes, all you have to do is not do
exactly what I tell you."

"And what's that, exactly?"

"I am going to civilize you, Nordstrand. I am going to
teach you who's the boss here, and I am going to begin
by teaching you to share."

The yellow-green eyes flicked to the Kalashnikov lying
on a bunk, saw it was too far to reach in time, and shifted
back to the muzzle of the nine-millimeter.

"All right, start teaching, General."

"You will stop calling me that, and all your other
moronic nicknames. From now on you'll call me Moody.
Go on, say it. Say, 'All right, start teaching, Moody.' "

Nordstrand did not say anything.

"Have you lost the power of speech, Jeremy?"

Nordstrand said nothing. He stared at the muzzle of the pistol.

"Jeremy, say, 'Start teaching, Moody.' Say it. '*Moody. Moody.*' "

Leaning back in the chair, crossing his hands on his lap, Nordstrand remained silent. Moody stood and, arms extended, pointed the nine-millimeter down to where the American's hands were crossed.

"Say it, damn you, or the next thing you'll say will be in soprano."

Tremors rippled through the Englishman. I saw his finger taking up slack on the trigger and felt enormous relief when Nordstrand said:

"Moody."

"Very good! Oh, that was very good, Nordstrand. You're learning. Let's see if you've learned your first lesson well enough. Say it again. Say '*Moody.*' "

"Moody."

"That's very good. You're a better student than I would have thought, so now I am going to teach you to share. You are going to take this spoon and you are going to feed Charlie and me until all the peach juice is gone. We are going to finish it, the two of us, and you are going to help us, and you are not going to get a drop more. Shall we begin? Charlie, sit down."

"Pat," I said, "Pat . . ."

Arms as stiff and straight as semaphores, he pivoted on his feet to point the automatic at me.

"*I said to sit down.*"

I sat down.

"Go on now, Nordstrand. Take the spoon and feed Charlie."

"Sure, Moody."

Nordstrand plucked the spoon out of the can and held it up over the lamp.

"That's it. That's a good boy, tough guy. Now take a swallow, Charlie."

"Pat, look, his hand isn't even shaking. For Christ's sake, what's the matter with you?"

"Take it, Charlie, or I'll put a round into the tough guy's skull."

I leaned forward, and Nordstrand, his hand steady, put the spoon in my mouth. The juice was warm and sticky-sweet and did not cut the coppery taste of fear in my throat.

The Englishman said, "Again," and Nordstrand gave me another spoonful, then another, and the weird calm emanating from him sharpened that flavor of copper pennies.

"Very good! Oh, very, very good. You are learning to share. Amazing, isn't it, Nordstrand, how much a man like you can learn when a pistol is pointed at him? It concentrates the mind, doesn't it?" Moody let out a hysterical giggle that seemed on the edge of breaking into a sob. "And now you are going to feed the rest to me."

Without saying anything, Nordstrand tipped the can and refilled the spoon. In midair, it was as steady as if it were resting on the table.

"Here you are, Moody. Come and get your peach juice."

"Before I do, I want an answer to a question. A long time ago in Khartoum you were going to tell me what it is about me that offends you so bloody much. Now I want to hear what it is."

"No, you don't."

"Nordstrand, if you don't do precisely——"

"You're not going to shoot, Moody. If you shoot, you won't get your answer, will you? I'm ready to feed you. Come and get it. Come get your peach juice, Moody."

Nordstrand held the spoon a few inches above the lantern's mantle, and Moody was too intoxicated with the confidence that comes from holding a loaded gun to notice the white plastic blackening in the heat.

"All right, Nordstrand, we'll save the question for later. One thing. I've got the hammer on full cock and no slack in the trigger. All you have to do is twitch and you're dead."

"Oh, I don't think you'll shoot, Moody. You'd have too much explaining to do."

Moody cackled again. Smiling faintly, Nordstrand kept

the spoon suspended above the mantle, and now the
plastic had begun to bubble.

"It's night, so it can't be the sun making you laugh
like that, Moody. Must be the moon. You've got moon-
stroke."

"No, no. Not the moon or the sun." The Englishman
chuckled so that he could hardly speak. "It's what you
just said. I'd have too much explaining to do. To whom,
Jeremy, to whom? The police? You said it yourself months
ago. There aren't any policemen out here."

"That's right. No policemen." Nordstrand extended the
spoon, which now resembled a kind of flattened, toasted
marshmallow. "Come and get your peach juice, Moody.
I can't hold this thing here forever."

"Remember now, not even a twitch."

Moody drew the pistol to his abdomen, so Nordstrand
could not grab it, and leaned over the table, the tip of his
tongue sticking out. He must have caught the smell of the
melting plastic, because he jerked his head back at the
last moment, but not before Nordstrand jammed the scalding juice and the scorched spoon into his mouth. He cried
out and dropped the pistol, tearing with both hands at the
spoon fused to his lower lip, and the concentrated potential energy in Nordstrand exploded, his legs and arms a
kinetic blur of synchronized jabs and kicks, the table over-
turning, the lantern tumbling to burst like a miniature
napalm bomb, setting a new straw mat afire as Moody flew
backward and fell against a jagged wall.

Straddling the prone Moody, Nordstrand shoved the
spoon down his throat.

"Come get your peach juice, weak sister. Come and get
it."

The Englishman made a gagging noise and his legs
moved with the reflective spasms of a man being strangled.

"Had enough peach juice or do you want me to feed
you some more?"

Moody gurgled something.

"I understand that to mean you want some more,"
Nordstrand said, twisting the spoon. I yelled, "Stop it!"
and grabbed the Kalashnikov by the barrel, swinging the
rifle butt against his lateral muscles. They were as thick

and hard as construction pine, so the blow had little deterrent effect. It just made him angrier. Springing off Moody's chest, he let me have it with a flurry of punches in the midsection that numbed my arms and made the filaments of my nerves feel as hot as short-circuited wires. I dropped the rifle, genuflected on both knees, then fell sideways, my lungs sucking for air.

Nordstrand pounced on Moody again, wrapped the thong of the amulet around the Englishman's neck, and started to garrote him with it.

"You still want to hear what it is about you that offends me, Dross? You still want to hear?"

Moody clutched at the leather cord.

"Answer me."

"Let go," Moody gasped.

"Your existence, that's what offends me. You got that?"

The Englishman clawed to relieve the pressure around his windpipe.

"I said your existence, General Dross. The very fact that you are offends me. Now have you got it?"

Moody nodded weakly, the implication quite clear that Nordstrand only had to tighten his grip to wipe out the existence that offended him. The fire had quickly consumed the mat. Nothing remained but the lingering odors of kerosene and burned straw, a few charred strands, and a rectangle of faint embers in whose light Nordstrand's black-dyed, rage-contorted face looked as if it had been disfigured by the flames.

Moody finally managed to get the tips of fingers between his throat and the thong, and forced out a few words:

"What do you want?"

"Who's the boss, Moody?"

"What do you want?"

"Who's the boss?"

"What do you want from me, Nordstrand?"

Nordstrand, one knee jammed into the Englishman's back, twisted the cord.

"Who's the boss?"

The movement of Moody's head might have been a gesture or simply a reflex to the tightening of the cord.

"Let's hear it, General. Who's the boss?"

I had got back to my feet by then and had taken hold of the rifle barrel, meaning to take another swing at Nordstrand, when I caught the strangely serene expression on Moody's face. It was the serenity of surrender. He must have known all along he had hardly a chance of winning a confrontation with the American; but he had not wanted to win as much as he wanted an end to the constant insults and humiliations. He wanted all of it to end, and he ended it by giving the answer Nordstrand wanted:

"You are."

———

It was a gift from God, Jima said quietly, passing the field glasses to Nordstrand. *Allahu akhbar.* He uttered the sacred phrase rapturously. God *was* great. He *did* reward those who were patient and endured. How he had endured! How patient he had been, praying for two years for an opportunity such as this. Smiling, his gap-teeth dirty yellow, Jima described how he would exact his vengeance: after we captured Umm-Tajer, if God willed, he would invite Bairu to come down from his position in the hills to share in the victory. Then he would take that Christian son of a Christian whore by the neck and pay him back tenfold. He would piss in his mouth, he would make him lick the dirt off a donkey's hooves, he would chop off the arrogant hand which had refused to shake his.

"I will take my price," the sheikh cackled when he had finished cataloging the humiliations he would inflict on his rival. "In the twenty-second *sura,* the *sura* of the pilgrimage, it is written that God will assist whoever takes a vengeance equal to the injury which had been done to him."

"What's you're planning hardly sounds equal," I said, crouching in the shade of a wedge-shaped boulder.

"O Jima."

"It hardly sounds equal, O Jima. All he did was refuse to shake your hand."

"That's true. That's all he did. I will be just, Mr. Charlie. I will be just, but I shall also take my price."

He was shaken by a cough so loud I thought it could be heard by the Ethiopians, huddled in their garrison a thousand feet below. On the slope behind us, feasts for scorpions and flies, bellies already threatening to pop the buttons on their blood-mottled shirts, sprawled the bodies of the PLF guerrillas Jima's scouts had killed the night before. The corpses had drawn the inevitable vultures. Black against the blue sky, they rode the thermals above us, wheeling, gliding, waiting for the living to leave so they could dive down and get their share of the dead. There had been five guerrillas on the hilltop where we now lay, glassing Umm-Tajer. The four dead had died without a sound; the scouts had been quick and efficient with their knives. The fifth had been taken alive. Bound and gagged, he sat a short distance from us. His knees were drawn into his chest. Like all prisoners of war, he appeared relieved to find himself still alive but uncertain as to how long he would remain that way. At his feet lay the Japanese walkie-talkie he and the others had used to communicate with Bairu's headquarters in the hills on the far side of the valley. Whenever a call came through, Yassin, who was guarding him, loosened his gag, held the radio to his lips and a knife to his throat, and told him what to say. The knife was extraneous. The swift, silent deaths of his comrades had made the man very cooperative. He had told us the locations of Adam Bairu's command post, that the PLF forces besieging Umm-Tajer numbered under three hundred, that these were scattered in small bands like his among the surrounding ridges, and that the Ethiopian soldiers were concentrated within the garrison perimeter at the south end of the town, leaving the north end lightly guarded.

Nordstrand studied the garrison's defenses through the powerful artillery-spotter's glasses. Occasionally, he put the binoculars down to fill in the sketch he was drawing of the Ethiopian positions. The new Belisarius was planning this attack with more than his usual thoroughness and enthusiasm. The effort absorbed him totally. It consumed him. All the destructive energies in his insubordinate soul were concentrated on annihilating a couple of hundred soldiers and a handful of tanks.

We moved as little as possible on the hilltop, and our stillness emboldened the vultures. They rode the updrafts on their wide dark wings; but seeing no movement below, they descended with each gliding circle until we could make out their white underbellies and the lappets dangling like obscene earrings from their bare, pink heads.

Finishing his sketch, Nordstrand handed the field glasses to me.

"Have a look, Charlie Gage. We couldn't ask for a better setup. It looks like one of those field problems they used to give us in OCS."

Umm-Tajer perched atop a hill which, oblong and bare, fissured and grey, resembled a petrified brain. The hill rose well above the trees of the oasis and lay in the center of the narrow valley below, between two ridges that embraced it like a scorpion's pincers. We were on the eastern ridge, the main forces of Bairu's PLF on the western. The Ethiopians' only route of retreat was the caravan trail that passed between the tips of the pincers about two miles south of the outpost, then ran down the foothills toward the open desert and the Sudanese border 120 miles away. My heart drumming against the baking rock, I swept the binoculars over the town's small, blue-domed mosque and the warrens of straw- and tin-roofed shacks to where the Ethiopians' green, yellow, and red flag hung above the barracks—long, buff-colored buildings ringed by handbags and a perimeter of foxholes. The men inside the foxholes looked like toy soldiers. Near the headquarters building, identifiable by its high radio antenna, one of the Russian T-54s squatted hull-down behind a rocky knoll. It had been painted desert beige and its long gun was aimed at the pass between the pincerlike ridges, and it did not look like a toy. Even at that distance, it looked lethal. Dark brown objects specked the slope just beneath the last line of perimeter wire. Distorted by the heat shimmer, they had first appeared through the lenses as clumps of brush. A second glance revealed them to be the corpses of the PLF guerrillas who had tried to storm the outpost nearly two weeks before. The bodies lay alone, or in huddled bunches. A line of them clogged one of the shallow ravines fissuring the hillside. Half a dozen hung from the outer wire like bits of flotsam left ashore by an outgoing tide. They lay in the hot sun unburied and unwept. Even the vultures ignored them: the choice parts had been eaten long ago.

"If it's a field problem," I said to Nordstrand, "I can see a few people who didn't solve it."

"Went at it like amateurs, Charlie Gage. All this bullshit about how they've been fighting seventeen years. They haven't got seventeen years' experience, just one year's experience repeated seventeen times. They should have attacked from the north, the way we're going to do, and assaulted through the town and hit the Ethiopians from behind. The houses would have made natural tank obstacles. Instead, that dross staged a frontal attack against the strongest part of the line—"

His analysis of Adam Bairu's flawed tactics was cut short by a sound like that of firecrackers exploding inside a sewer pipe. The PLF's mortars were firing from the ridgeline opposite. I began to count to twenty by thousands: at eighteen, a cluster of grey puffs appeared around the tank. The 82s' dull, flat explosions reached us a few seconds later.

"Amateurs," Nordstrand sneered. "Might as well throw rocks at that T-54 as try to knock it out with mortars."

"Think they might be aiming for the headquarters building."

"They're still amateurs."

Through the smoke, I saw the tank's turret revolve, the gun elevating and moving from side to side like the snout of some prehistoric dragon picking up a scent. It stopped and fired, flame and smoke jetting from its muzzle. The shell burst on the western ridge an instant later; then we heard the almost simultaneous reports of the gun and the shell, both reverberating through the valley until they fused into a single roar, diminishing with each echo.

The noise excited Jima. He snatched the field glasses from me, focused them on his future provisional capital, then on the ridgeline, where another tank shell threw up a geyser of black smoke.

"Ya! Bairu!" he spat, his wasted lungs convulsing from the effort. "Ya! You dog-eating son of a Christian whore!

Your mother's vulva, you bastard! I pray to God they don't kill you. I want you to live so I can piss in your mouth."

With some effort, we persuaded him to stop his exalted cursing. Our reconnaissance done, we left Yassin and a few others to take care of the prisoner and keep an eye on the outpost, then filed down the steep trail on the reverse slope toward the wadi where Jima's army waited. Seeing our movements, the vultures flew upward a short distance and resumed their vigil. Halfway down, we caught sight of the army, stretched out along the wadi for more than a mile. Looking at the men, some crouched beside small, smokeless fires over which their morning tea bubbled, some cleaning their rifles, some filling waterskins in a well, at the string of tethered mules with ammunition crates lashed to their backs, at the trucks and Land-Rovers, dust-filmed and battered after the hard, five-day ride from the old base camp, at the baggage camels kneeling in the white shale of the riverbed, at the grove of leaning date palm, their green heightened by the backdrop of barren mountains, at the mountains whose every draw, crease, and ravine showed in stark relief in sunlight so bright that all the sky seemed a sun—looking and hearing the muted, ragged firing from beyond the ridge, I felt my throat tighten and something move within my chest.

Jima called another council when we reached the encampment. Osman and Murrah were there, along with a dozen headmen who served as the NIIF's equivalent of company officers. Moody also attended, docile now, and happy in a way. Nordstrand had left him alone since his submission, had stopped harassing and mocking him. His lips bore scabs where they had been burned by the overheated spoon. We all gathered around Jima and Nordstrand, who, with an AK slung across his back, a Russian automatic attached to his belt, and the field glasses hanging from the thick, truncated pyramid that was his neck, was very much in his element. Squatting Arab-fashion, he took his sketch from his pocket and, using it as a blueprint, built a model of the outpost out of rocks and sand. He said the reconnaissance revealed no need for major amendments to his original plan.

It was simple enough. The NIIF would be divided into four companies of roughly two hundred men each: two attack companies, a reserve company, and an ambush company. Leaving the reserve in the wadi to guard the supply train, the rest of the column would move out at dusk and scale the ridgeline. Jima, his bodyguard, and the mortar crews would establish a position there while the attack companies deployed under cover of darkness. The mortars would open with a barrage at midnight. Advancing behind the shellfire, the first attack company would stage a frontal assault to divert the Ethiopians' attention while the second advanced through the town from the north and struck the garrison from behind. Unless they had orders to fight to the death, the Ethiopians would likely try to save their tanks and armored personnel carriers by withdrawing through the pass. The ambush, armed with Saggers and RPGs, would be waiting there to finish them off. He, Nordstrand, would go with the second attack company, I with the ambush, and Moody remain with the reserve.

To this, Moody voiced an unexpected objection: our instructions to avoid direct participation in combat were still valid; therefore wouldn't it be best if all three of us stayed with the reserve?

With a slight grin, Nordstrand softly touched the scabs on Moody's lips with the stick he had been using as a pointer.

"I thought everything was settled between you and me, General."

"It is."

"Then why are you making an issue?"

Moody reached for his talisman, fondled it briefly, then let his hand fall limply into his lap. Closing his eyes for a moment, he leaned his head back as if overcome by an immense fatigue that went beyond mere physical exhaustion.

"Moody?"

"Just thought I'd say that for the record."

"There isn't any record."

The *mullah*, a goateed man of indeterminate age, worked on our camouflage for the rest of the morning. The dye had to be applied in layers, to allow it to soak into the pores and avoid streaking. Feeling as if we were getting ready for a minstrel show, I looked at myself in the tin-plate mirror and said:

"This isn't going to fool anyone within half a mile."

"It'll be night, Charlie Gage, and there's only a quarter moon. Someone would have to be real close up to see what we are. Real close and then"—Nordstrand mimed twisting a knife into a man's ribs. "Let's have a look."

I handed him the mirror. He turned his head this way and that, admiring the *mullah*'s cosmetic work. His hair had been shaved to stubble again, and his head resembled a giant fire-blackened skull.

"This will do," he said. "This will do."

"How many bald-headed, six-foot, two-hundred-and-forty-pound Bejayans have you seen?"

"Night, Charlie Gage. Night and a quarter moon." Nordstrand laughed. "They'll mistake me for a Nubian."

Opening his pack, he pulled out what looked like a bed-sheet. It was actually two white, ceremonial Beni-Hamid robes sewn together to fit him. Standing, he slipped it over his shoulders and extended his arms so the wide sleeves hung down like those of a monk's cassock. Nordstrand twirled once and, dipping one arm to the corner of the sleeve, brushed the ground, straightened himself, then dipped the other arm.

"What do I look like?" he asked in Arabic.

A squad of rebels lounging nearby laughed and clapped.

"Ya! Mr. Jer-ah-mee!"

"Mr. Jer-ah-mee!" echoed Nordstrand. Another twirl, another dip of his arms, the white sleeves billowing elegantly.

"What do I look like?"

"Like one of us. Ya! Mr. Jer-ah-mee, you look like one of us, only bigger."

He danced up to them.

"Yes, I look like one of you. And after tonight, I will be one of you."

"Yes, yes," one of the rebels, an older man, answered.

"After tonight, God willing. One of us, Mr. Jer-ah-mee."

Then, to their applause, Mr. Jeremy whirled and twirled back to me and stood over me, white-gowned, dark-headed.

"What was all that about?"

"Just a little performance for the troops, something to amuse the cannon fodder before they get their heads shot off."

"I meant that business about your being one of them."

"Jima's promised to initiate me into the tribe if the attack goes successfully." He said this offhandedly, as if tribal initiations were something he did once a week. "I'm going to be one of them, Charlie Gage."

"You can't be. You're one of us."

"I'm as good as one of them already. And after tonight, it'll be official."

The idea appeared to have gripped Nordstrand's imagination as tightly as the notion of a provisional capital had seized Jima's. He, a white man from the biggest industrial nation on earth, would be made a member of a nomadic African tribe. He would become one of them. It was necessary to be one of them to complete his plans. I asked, what plans?

He looked at me as if the answer were self-evident.

"You know what they are, Charlie Gage. You've read them."

"I haven't seen these plans of yours in writing."

"Yes, you have."

The green irises, their light intensified by the contrast with his artificially darkened face, flicked to the corners of his eyes and gazed down at his pack. Unable to tell if he was probing, if he really knew or merely suspected, I decided to play it safe.

"I don't know what you're getting at."

"Are you afraid, Charlie Gage?"

"No," I lied.

"You don't have to be. I know you've read them, and I don't mind." He sat beside me cross-legged. For several minutes, it was as though no one else were in that wadi. We were as good as alone, bound by a shared secret, isolated by it. "The fact is, I wanted you to read them. I knew you would understand because you and me, Charlie

Gage, you and me, we've got more in common than you think."

"And less than you think," I said, more to assert myself than to state a fact. For I was all too aware of the things that made for a kinship between us.

Nordstrand made no reply. Uncrossing his legs, he stretched out on his side with a movement at once indolent and powerful, crooked his arm, and rested his head in his palm. Then, staring past me at the dust-chalked rocks on the wadi's bank, he spoke of his grand design in the levelest of voices and with a cold, arresting clarity.

"When we take Umm-Tajer, it won't be the end of the mission, it will be the beninning. The beginning of my mission. I'm free now, free of all the stinking petty standards the dross invent so they can feel safe. I freed myself when I blew the life out of those germs back there on that beach, and I've been wondering ever since, what am I going to do with this freedom? I know now. Expand it. Stretch it to its limits, beyond its limits. I've been a catalyst to this rebellion. I've changed it forever by the things I've done, and I'm bound, *bound* to see the change through until it's complete. I've made an army out of these people, and now I'm going to make them and Jima the node of the rebellion." He paused momentarily to savor the last phrase. "The node of the rebellion, Charlie Gage, and when that's done, I'm going to make a nation of them. I'm going to beat them, hammer them, mold them into a nation, and in exchange for that, I'm going to see that Jima makes me a very special citizen of his republic. You know, in the past men like me built countries so they could plunder them or ruin them or both. Riches and power, that's what they wanted. But there were a few men back then, men like me, men like Gordon, who didn't want riches or power. They wanted freedom. So I'm not going to tear a fortune out of this place. There isn't one to be had here anyway. What is here is worth more than all the oil and all the gold on earth—emptiness, room, space, the space to be free to do what all men want to do but haven't the guts or the nerve to do. *Whatever they choose.* That's an old dream. It's in Genesis. I remember it from when the crazy lady forced me to listen to her Bible readings. *Hereafter they*

will not be restrained from doing whatever they determine.
There it is. To be free to do whatever I choose. Whatever I
imagine, I'll do. By God, I'm going to create a new realm
of existence for myself out here. I've already begun. I've
taken the first step, and the next step is to commit myself
totally to this place and to these people. My people. I'm
going to become one with them, and they'll be one with
me. Do you see?"

I said nothing because I could think of nothing to say in
response to this extraordinary monologue, which would
not have been so disturbing had it been the raving of a
madman. My feelings at that moment were the same as
those I had had when I listened to him spouting his ideas
in Khartoum: a kind of emotional arrest created by equal
measures of attraction and repulsion. I recognized that his
vision of a life without restraints was the very vision that
has inspired the great butchers of this century; but he also
aroused the fascination we often feel toward rogues and
renegades and even cold-blooded killers, toward all those
who do things we publicly condemn but privately admire
because they are our surrogates, acting out criminal fantasies we dare not act out ourselves.

"Well, Charlie Gage? Do you see?"

"No," I lied.

"I'll make it simple for you. I'm not going back. I'm
staying here."

"You can't . . ."

"I never meant to go back. This is the place I've been
looking for for half my life. Why do you suppose I
brought all those diaries along? Because I never intended to
go back, because those diaries are a part of me, and I
didn't want to leave even a part of me behind."

"You don't belong here, Nordstrand."

"Not at this moment, but after I've become one of
them, I'll belong."

"If I didn't know you better, I'd say you ought to be
locked up for the rest of your life."

"But you know me. You've read the diaries. You've got
a streak of the pure metal in you, and you know I've got
to stay. It's destiny. It's simple as that. It's the fulfillment

of destiny. I've got to stay here just as you've got to go back." He paused again, and sat upright. His eyes were frightening in their intensity. "And now you listen to this. When you get back, you tell Colfax what I've done and why. You tell the whole goddamned world if you can. My life out here is going to be an art. It's going to be an artistic act, and I want all the dross out there to know about it. I want them to know there's at least one man on this fucking planet with the guts and the nerve to do anything he decides."

I remained silent. His future life was to be one long gesture of contempt for the world, and I was to broadcast it to the world. I was to be the poet who would sing the deeds of the Nietzschean hero, the instrument that would make final his self-created alienation.

"Do you see what I want you to do?"

"Yes, goddamnit. I see."

"And I expect you'll do it."

I nodded, the gesture more a reflex than a signal of assent.

"You're a smart man, Charlie Gage."

With that, he rose and walked off with his martial stride toward the column of men and animals, strung out like beads along the length of the wadi. As I watched him, the thought of shooting him occurred to me. There was no other way to stop him, and a man with his ideas and his capacity for translating them into action was too dangerous to be allowed to run around loose. And I would have emptied my pistol into that broad back of his, even at the risk of having his loyal followers shoot me in revenge. If I really had had a streak of "pure metal" in me, if I had had the strength to overcome my gravitation toward Nordstrand, I would have killed him as I would a wild animal that's broken out of its cage.

The commander of the ambush company was Ibrahim Abdel, the scowling, bad-tempered young man we had met at Kerem months—it seemed decades—before. My pres-

ence offended him a great deal: he regarded it as an insult
to his professional competence. Why was I there? he asked
in a whisper as we huddled behind a natural stone parapet
above the pass. Were he and his men considered so un-
trustworthy that a foreigner had to show them how to lay
an ambush? Then he snarled something to the effect that,
as a Christian, I belonged with Bairu's Copts or with the
Ethiopians for that matter.

With that out of his system, Ibrahim Abdel fell into a
sullen silence. I was relieved. An ambush is not the best
place to conduct an argument, even in whispers. There
were about 170 of us altogether, deployed in a semicircle
on the gently sloping finger on the east side of the pass.
The pass, its sand a leprous white in the light of the quarter moon, was about six hundred yards wide and roughly
half that distance long, giving us clear fields of fire. On the
other hand, the Ethiopians' tanks and armored personnel
carriers would have plenty of room to maneuver. I would
have positioned half the company on the west side, to
catch a withdrawing column in a crossfire, but the high
ground there rose straight up for a good hundred feet.
The cliff's shadow fell on the pass like the shadow of a
building on a snow-covered square. Two miles northward,
Umm-Tajer showed as a grey hump rising out of the pale
sand and flintstone of the valley floor. I could not see the
town or the garrison, only the outline of the hill and the
silhouette of the mosque's dome and minaret.

To soothe Ibrahim Abdel's injured pride, I whispered
that he had done a creditable job of laying the ambush.
And he had. The two dozen missile crews had been deployed at the midpoint of the semicircle, the point farthest
from the pass. This gave them enough distance to "gather"
the Saggers onto the correct trajectory and range in on
their targets. The guerrillas with the bazooka-like RPGs
held the ground downslope, and riflemen and machine
gunners protected the ambush's flanks against a possible
infantry counterattack. All in all, it was a well-laid trap,
a fine application of the ancient art of bushwhacking. The
strange thing was to see the rebels lying or crouching behind the twentieth-century gadgetry with tribal swords
slung across their backs; it was as though they did not

completely trust the destructive products of industrial civilization. Or perhaps they did not find the impersonality of modern warfare to their taste, and were hoping for the bloody intimacy of a hand-to-hand fight. Certainly Ibrahim Abdel's guerrillas did not care for this ambush business. On the march to the pass, lugging the valise-like missile cases that made them resemble a procession of tourists or refugees, they had grumbled about their subordinate mission. They wanted to be in on the seizure of the town, even though they knew that half the attackers were likely to be killed or maimed in the attempt. The idea of death did not trouble them half as much as it would western soldiers, for they believed that to die in battle was to purchase an admission ticket to immortality.

At the ambush site, they displayed a good deal of restlessness. They were the grandsons of mounted warriors who had galloped down from highland strongholds to plunder and raid, and they retained their ancestors' cavalry spirit. They had that hothearted eagerness for the quick rush and the charge that is often mistaken for reckless courage but which is actually an inability to sit still. Their natural impatience made them unsuited to so strenuous an exercise in patience as an ambush. They fidgeted constantly and shifted the positions of their bodies, knocking bits of rock and shale down the hillside. To my ears, their sensitivity heightened by anxiety, these tiny cascades sounded like avalanches. I told Ibrahim Abdel that if he did not settle the men down, we would be detected by the Ethiopians, or, more likely, by the PLF, who must have some men posted near the pass. Bristling, he said he didn't need me to advise him on how to handle his men.

"All right, then I'll quiet them." I rose to one knee. Taking hold of my arm, Ibrahim Abdel pulled me down.

"You will stay here."

He stood, and in a crouch, moved along the firing line, cautioning his men to stop moving about like undisciplined children.

"Are they quiet enough for you now?" he asked when he came back. "Is their behavior to your satisfaction, Mr. Charlie?"

I said nothing. The friction between us seemed ridic-

ulously petty under the circumstances. My watch read
eleven thirty. Half an hour to go. Leaning against a rock,
I watched a scorpion burrowing past my feet. I noticed
every detail, every grain of moon-refracting sand shifted
by the scorpion's movements, the tips of its legs, its stinger
curving out of the sand, and every detail seemed important.
Then, feeling an overwhelming fatigue, I closed my eyes
and nodded off. I saw a yellowed, lateen-rigged sail filled
with wind, a blue and heaving sea, an Arab pilot with one
weathered hand on the helm and the other pointing past
the dhow's fo'c'sle toward a tree-fringed shore in the
distance, the coast of India.

The bombardment opened. There was no transition between sleep and wakefulness, between dream and reality.
One instant I was looking at the Indian coast, the next at
the mortar tubes flickering on the ridgeline. The shells
burst on the Ethiopian barracks with a stroboscopic flashing and a sound like the chug of a laboring steam locomo-
tive. The Ethiopian commandos were not amateurs and
didn't take long to respond. Only a few minutes passed
before their tanks opened a counterbattery, the cannon
making a sharp crack that could be heard above the duller
explosions of Jima's mortars. Then a huge pillar of flame
erupted from the outpost. It rose for two hundred feet, like
the jet of an enormous gas lamp, lighting up half the valley,
the barracks, the mosque, and the squat huts of the town. I
guessed one of our shells had made a lucky hit on the fuel
dump. The first company started its attack. If I had had
field glasses, I probably could have seen them in the brilliant glare of the burning diesel oil. To the naked eye, only
the muzzle flashes were visible: a red-orange twinkling on
the hillside below the garrison's perimeter. As the Ethiopians returned fire, red and green tracers streaked between
them and the line of attacking rebels, and illumination
flares, hanging in the air like paper lanterns, made it all
look quite festive. We knew the main attack had begun
when grenades and shells started bursting in the streets behind the outpost. One after another, the brush and thatch
roofs of the houses blazed, the line of flames suggesting a
torchlight parade. Watching the fires springing up, I pictured Nordstrand dashing between them and wondered if

he was at last sating his lust for destruction and if he had finally found the intensity he had always sought from life.

Ibrahim Abdel's men watched the battle with fascination. And it was fascinating, a spectacle, a sound-and-light show, fuel drums burning like enormous votive candles to a fugue of thumping shells and the stuttering choruses sung by rifles and machine guns.

The volume gradually diminished until there was total silence, broken suddenly by an eruption of tank fire. Then silence again. Several minutes passed. Or perhaps it was several seconds. Or an hour. Time was warped out of all shape. Ibrahim Abdel wiped his hands on his shorts and asked no one in particular, "What's happening?" Something exploded at the base of the hill and was engulfed in rolling white-orange flames. It might have been a tank struck by an RPG. The blast was followed by heavy machine-gun fire that sounded like a piece of cardboard flapping against the spokes of a bicycle wheel, only amplified a hundred times. Then I caught another sound and, my heart doing a clumsy tap dance against my breastbone, I cried in English, "It's worked! Their tanks are pulling out! Pulling out! It's worked!" Ibrahim Abdel looked at me as if I had gone mental on him. I repeated myself in Arabic, and he responded with praises to Allah. Now all could hear the rising-falling whine of diesel engines and the weird screeching of tank treads. Someone on the captured outpost had the presence of mind to remember us and sent up several illumination rounds with a mortar. We saw them then, unreal-looking in the unreal light of the flares: five T-54s and three or four armored personnel carriers, rolling fast, throwing up rooster-tails of dust shimmering in the wavering flares, the tanks with their turrets facing rearward and firing on the garrison to cover their withdrawal, and those fifty-ton monsters bearing down on us at full throttle, looking as if they could squash us like so many insects. Sweat oiled my palms, my mouth was dry, but the symptoms of this natural fear were not unpleasant. Having suffered so long from a free-floating dread, I found it a positive joy to be afraid of something.

The flares swung to the ground, sputtered for a few moments, and went out. Several more whooshed skyward. The

Ethiopians were not stupid. They must have figured the pass would be ambushed, and swung their guns around and started shelling us. Firing blind and low on ammunition, their barrage was desultory and inaccurate, the rounds crashing randomly a good hundred yards downhill. Still, the crazed whoop the high-velocity shells made before exploding unnerved some of the men, and my gut felt the way it does in a dropping elevator as several guerrillas let off a volley of RPGs before the tanks were in the killing zone. Spotting the backblasts, the tankers started strafing us with high explosive, then canister. The canister was the worst. The shot smacked against the rocks like hail driven by a cyclonic wind. It was all chaos, noise, and smoke, men screaming, things hissing and cracking. Ibrahim Abdel panicked. Convinced the Ethiopians were going to try to roll up our right flank, he stood, ran off to the left, and began pulling men to set up a new line perpendicular to the old. I yelled to him that the slope on the right was too steep and rocky for a tank assault, that he had to keep his men in place, the Ethiopians had no choice but to run the pass. He gave me a shove and hollered back, "I know what I'm doing, you bastard." He knew what he was doing. In the next instant, he and half the men with him, struck by a blast of canister, fell as if they'd been swiped by an invisible giant hand. Now crawling, now running, I somehow managed to get the stunned survivors back in place. I was in something of a panic myself. I was afraid—of Nordstrand. Of Nordstrand! I was afraid he would blame me if the ambush failed.

The Ethiopians were running the pass, and doing it coolheadedly, too. They had maneuvered into echelon—a staggered line extending from one side of the pass to the other, with the vulnerable APCs farthest from the ambush. The formation presented as small a target as possible and allowed each tank to put direct fire on us without being masked by the others. Two of our missile crews launched their Saggers. They were easy weapons to operate. The projectile paid out fine electrical wires attached to the joystick; tracking the missile by its bright taillight, the operator guided it onto target much as he might fly a model airplane. But it required a good deal of nerve when under fire, and one of the crews lacked the nerve. They sent the missile over the column. It burst harmlessly against the cliff. The second slammed into the T-54 nearest us with a clang like that of a sledgehammer striking a boiler plate, then an earsplitting blast that blew the tank's turret off. It burned beautifully, and its ammunition exploded, sending up gorgeous fiery streamers. That was when the Ethiopians made their mistake. They were only a few minutes from clearing the pass, but instead of continuing on, the remaining tanks wheeled suddenly and came at us, the beetle-shaped APCs following, spraying us with machine-gun fire. The Beni-Hamid had regained their composure and held fast. A dozen missiles flew down the slope, taillights bobbing over the contours of the land. Instantly all four tanks and one of the carriers were transformed into pyres. We caught the stench of broiling flesh mixed in with the smell of burning diesel fuel. It must have been the terror of suffering a similar incineration that made the infantrymen and the drivers in the other APCs try to break out on foot. They ran out of the flaming vehicles, shooting wildly as they ran, and their movements in the light of the flames were like those of figures in a film run at the wrong speed, jerky and somehow comical.

The rebels fired into them until, moved by some common impulse, they rose and charged, some screaming, *"Allah ma'ana*—God is with us." Maybe he was, but I think it was the devil who charged with those wild men. They had slung or simply dropped their rifles and went running full tilt with their tribal swords drawn. In a moment, they had gone from twentieth-century warfare back to the Bronze Age. They. We. *We.* For I was running with them, carried by the same bloodthirsty tide that was carrying them. It was magnificent in its own way. After the roars and rattles of tanks, and all the dueling between machines, there was something wonderfully tribal in the sight of men charging with swords, in the sound of their voices, calling the name of their god. The Ethiopians—there could not have been fifteen left—started to throw their weapons down and their hands up. They might as well have tried surrendering to a

tidal wave. The Beni-Hamid swept down on them, and
then it wasn't even the Bronze Age any longer; it was the
epoch before governments existed to declare wars, before
the word *war* or any other word had been spoken; it was
the time when our naked progenitors went at each other
with clubs and rocks. The Ethiopians died amid half-human grunts, amid the crash of sword blades against rifle
stocks and the barely audible gag of throats slashed by
knives. I was in among them, not myself any longer. Or,
worse, perhaps I was myself, totally myself, a man released
from all doubts, anxieties, and inhibitions. In the phantas-
mal mingling of moonlight and firelight, I saw an Ethiopian
soldier running away. He was stumbling through the soft
sand and gravel. I went after him. I ran effortlessly, ran with
what felt like the exhilarating speed and grace of a lion
running down a gazelle. The soldier's short stride was no
match for my long legs. Lunging, I tackled him and locked
my arms around his neck. His neck felt very small. I
wrenched his head back as hard as I could. He made a gurgling noise. I snapped his head again, gritting my teeth
until I thought my jawbone would break. There was the
sound of a twig breaking underfoot. The soldier's body
convulsed beneath me, his legs gave a few rapid kicks,
and then he lay still. I stood over him, my lungs burning
and my arms so knotted I had trouble straightening them.
When I did, I reached down and rolled the body over.
The Ethiopian's mouth was half-open, his eyes wide, white,
and forever blind. I had never killed a man before. In combat, you could never be sure if the distant figures falling
out there in the rice paddies had been hit by your bullets
or someone else's. There wasn't any doubt about who had
killed this one. You are what you do. Looking down into
his blank eyes, I waited to feel shame or remorse or some
of the other emotions you are supposed to feel; but it was
too early for emotion. All I felt were the stiffness in my
arms and a tremendous thirst. I unsnapped my canteen.
It was nearly empty, so I had to tilt my head far back to
drink. The Southern Cross was shining in its usual place.

In the morning, we saw the reserve company and the baggage animals moving down the ridgeline toward the outpost. A short time later, the NIIF's green and white banner was raised over Umm-Tajer. Muhammad Jima had won his provisional capital, though much of it was a ruin. The rebels around me whooped and fired their rifles in the air when the flag went up. Its raising also drew some sporadic sniping from the PLF guerrillas in the hills off to the west. The sniping wasn't serious, merely a gesture of protest over being robbed of the prize they regarded as theirs.

Smoke from the rubble of the Ethiopian barracks and from the still-burning tanks rose in narrow funnels which merged and spread to form a haze that hung over the valley like a translucent canopy. Through it we could see the first vultures arriving from their distant roosts. A few glided down and, talons thrust forward, wings set to brake, landed at the head of the pass. As ugly and clumsy on the ground as they were beautiful and graceful in flight, they waited at the fringes of the battlefield, hopping and jostling each other to establish dominance. Their clucking resembled laughter. It occurred to me that a hyena's cry also sounded like laughter, and that corpses' lips were often drawn into a grin, and I wondered if the dead and the creatures which fed on the dead saw a joke the rest of us missed.

Our dead—I thought of them as ours, although I knew they belonged to no one—were buried in a mass grave dug with the shovels we found on the two undamaged personnel carriers. The company had suffered seventeen killed; Ibrahim Abdel's body was among them, punctured in a dozen places by canister shot. We left the Ethiopians to the vultures, except for the crews who had been sealed inside the tanks and the infantrymen who had been immolated in the other APC. Their bodies had been reduced to charred, child-sized figures fused to each other and to the scorched wreckage, so that burned man and burned metal were all one blackened lump. I did bury the soldier I had killed by piling rocks over his corpse. My conscience had begun to throb, like a wound after the first, nerve-numbing shock has worn off, and I thought I could quiet it by giving the Ethiopian a burial.

The cheerful work done, we loaded our seriously

wounded and the captured enemy weapons onto the APCs.
A couple of men figured out how to operate the vehicles,
cranked up the engines, and started down the caravan
road toward Umm-Tajer. The slightly wounded rode atop
the carriers or on the fenders while the rest tramped behind. The novelty of riding raised the injured men's spirits;
bloodied and bandaged, their hands pounding a rhythm
on the armor plate, they sang a slow Arabic war chant.

> Oh yes! The sun is shining
> Where the date palm shades the sands.
> Oh yes! The sun his shining
> Where the women carry water from the wells.
> Oh yes! The sun is shining
> Where the men ride their camels to the wars.
> And they'll fight and kill with honor
> If God wills.
> And they'll fight and die with honor
> If God wills.

The column moved past the hulk of the first tank we had
destroyed. Its turret lay beside it, and one of the crewmen
lay beside the turret. He was burned to cinders from the
waist down, but freakishly his head and shoulders had
escaped the flames, and his hair, ruffled by the wind, looked
disturbingly lifelike. Still the rebels sang:

> And they'll fight and kill with honor
> If God wills.
> And they'll fight and die with honor
> If God wills.

Listening to them, I began singing "The Minstrel Boy"
to myself. I had heard it sung by my grandfather, a displaced Irishman who had wound up among the Swedes and
Finns of upper Michigan:

> The Minstrel Boy to the wars has gone
> In the ranks of death you'll find him.

* * *

But I could remember none of the lyrics beyond "in the ranks of death you'll find him." The phrase repeated itself over and over in my mind, which was not the mind I had possessed the night before. That was why I could not recall the rest of the words to the song. I was no longer thinking with the same mind, seeing with the same eyes, hearing with the same ears. I had killed a man with my bare hands. Nothing could ever be the same again. I could never be the same again. A man plumbs his soul in war, entering depths where there is not enough light to make standard judgments: and I was unable to judge my act or to assign a value to the transformation I had undergone. I wasn't the better for what I had done, but I could not say I was the worse, either. All I could say with conviction was that I felt totally and irrevocably changed.

The rest of the day and the two days following were spent tidying up. The dead had to be buried, the wounded treated. The civilians who had not evacuated Umm-Tajer and who had survived the fighting were put to work cleaning up the debris and making Jima's provisional capital look a little less provisional. Using barbed wire cannibalized from the outpost's perimeter fence, the Beni-Hamid built their first prison. This to contain the twenty-odd Ethiopians captured in the assault. Murrah was made their warden and given the job of reeducating them. No doubt the two machine guns guarding the prison compound helped his students concentrate. Barbed wire and machine guns: the Beni-Hamid had definitely entered the twentieth century.

In the meantime, a truce was arranged with the PLF, who continued to hold their positions on the western ridge. Adam Bairu accepted Jima's invitation to come down for talks aimed at patching up their factional and personal squabble. Because he knew the Christian from his days with the PLF, Murrah acted as mediator. Nordstrand, Moody, and I were not allowed to see his arrival. Jima decided that compromising the mission mattered after all. To avoid our being discovered, he confined us to quarters—an abandoned hut as dismal and dark as the cave we had lived in in the mountains. Guards were posted at the door to make it appear we were captives in case Bairu heard any strange stories from the villagers about the three white men who had been seen walking about, two with their faces painted black.

We waited in our make-believe cell all that afternoon. We were never displayed to Bairu, so I figured he hadn't heard anything out of the ordinary. In the evening, Jima summoned us to his new headquarters, a stucco building near the mosque. It had been the living quarters of the Ethiopian garrison commander, a major whose papers, letters, and photographs still littered the floor. Two of Jima's bodyguards presented arms sloppily as we ducked through the doorway, over which a green flag hung from a pole and flung its oath at all who saw it: "Blood shall water the tree of faith." The old man was sitting behind the officer's desk, its surface cleared except for a copy of the Koran. Osman and two bodyguards flanked him. The latter also presented arms, then drew up three chairs.

"Please, sit down, gentlemen," Jima said. "I've good news, but first we will have some tea."

A retainer brought us the tea. It was peculiar to see the desert chieftain, the ex-bandit, the dusty guerrilla, ensconced behind a desk instead of sitting beside a campfire. His manner was also peculiar. Only three days before he had been screaming obscene curses into the wind; now his demeanor was grave—was, I would say, presidential. This, combined with the guards' formal salutes, the flag hanging over the doorway, and the chairs arranged in front of the desk, gave the impression Jima wished to create. I detected in him the first symptoms of that political and psychological malady the French call *folie des grandeurs*.

His folly was not without some basis in reality. When we finished tea, he told us that his talks with Bairu—his inaugural venture into diplomacy—had been a great success. No, he had not humiliated the man; the NIIF's quick victory, in contrast with the PLF's prolonged failure, had been humiliation enough. Besides, he was now above petty jealousies. What Jima had done was to give the Christian a lecture on the facts of life, mixed with a few fictions. He reminded Bairu that he had seen the firepower of the NIIF, that he, Jima, had captured Umm-Tajer with only part of his army, that thousands more of his followers were assembling in the Malaka Highlands. The NIIF now controlled one of the main supply routes to Sudan. Weapons destined for the other factions would end up in his hands. He controlled the wells at the oasis; if he chose, he could deny them to PLF and FLN patrols passing through the area—let them fight with their tongues out, by God. However, he wished to avoid such measures. He preferred co-operation, not factional strife. This was a time for unity, not division. If the Command Council wanted his cooperation, they could get it by seating him on the directorate. At that point, Jima related, Bairu protested that it was not in his power to decide who could be seated on the directorate. That was a matter for the council; moreover, the directorate's six seats were already filled.

"I told him then, 'Then take your men and go away from this place, go to the council and discuss my offer. As for the seats being filled, empty one of them or create a seventh.' Those were his choices."

The combination of reason, bluff, and threats worked. Bairu agreed to withdraw his men the next morning and present Jima's ultimatum to the council. He would propose that the council hold a "unity conference," to which Jima would be invited for a "democratic dialogue" to discuss integrating the NIIF into the rest of the rebel army. Jima rejected the offer. He, the victor of Umm-Tajer, the man who had given the insurgency its first triumph in a year, would not make a pilgrimage to council headquarters like some lowly bedouin seeking a favor from his sheikh. No, he would not, by God. He and the council should meet halfway, literally as well as figuratively: the "democratic dialogue" should be held at the town of Karu, a desert crossroads roughly an equal distance from headquarters and Umm-Tajer in a neutral zone where none of the factions claimed exclusive control. Bairu argued against the demand. The area around Karu was not as secure as it had been before the government counteroffensive; traveling there would expose the council members, and Jima as well, to the risk of an air raid or an ambush.

"I told him I was no merchant to bargain in a bazaar. If the council wouldn't meet me in Karu, then they could meet me here, in my provisional capital. They could come to me like bedouin. And if that didn't suit them, they could not count on my cooperation. They could count on me as an enemy. They could fight me as well as the Ethiopians. 'How would you like that, Bairu?' I said. 'Another civil war among us?' "

Without any cards to play, the Christian capitulated. He would propose the conference be held at Karu, and promised to relay the council's decision to Jima within a fortnight.

The old man paused, glancing at each of us, the black disks of his pupils bright around the edges, like two tiny eclipsed suns.

"He listened to me because I've won, God be praised. He listened to me because now he must listen to me. O, it is as it is written, gentlemen. *He who is armed keeps his house: his well is defiled who does not hold his enemies from it with his sword; he who is weak, him shall men injure, he who is strong, him shall men honor.*"

With that, he dismissed us, and we returned to the hut. Something Jima had said put Nordstrand in a strangely quiet mood. Pensive and preoccupied, he sat on his bunk without moving. Then, struck by one of his mysterious inspirations, he pulled the maps from his haversack, spread them on the dirt floor, and spent a good hour squinting at them in the lantern light. Folding them suddenly, he bolted out the door without a word. I watched him striding up the dusty street in the dark toward Jima's quarters. He didn't return until past midnight.

Waking up, I asked, "What the hell was all that about?"

"Nothing." He stuffed the maps back in his pack. The expression on his face was at once triumphant and secretive.

"What do you mean, nothing? You were with him for three hours."

"With who?"

"Jima."

"I went for a long walk. I didn't see Jima."

"Look, we're nearly at the end of this. You don't have to play games with me."

"I went for a walk."

Nordstrand moved toward the bunk in which I sat upright. He moved toward me, a mass of muscle exuding an implacable will.

"Right, Charlie Gage? I went for a walk. I didn't see Jima."

"Right," I answered bitterly. "You went for a walk."

"You're a smart man, Charlie Gage."

━━━━━━━

I ceased to be a smart man at the victory celebration, which was held the following night, an event that ended with Nordstrand's initiation. The ceremony took place in the rubble of the garrison and began innocently enough with a feast. The headquarters barracks, its roof blown off, two of its walls pulverized and the other two punctured by bullet holes, its floor littered with burned papers, smashed filing cabinets, pieces of a long-range radio, and broken furniture, served as the feast hall. Goats were being roasted whole on what had been the Ethiopians' parade ground. The animals had been expropriated from the villagers, who were of course eager to express their gratitude to the men who had liberated them. Jima had shed his khaki uniform, and his air of presidential pomposity, and had put on a set of snowy tribal robes. Again the desert chieftain, he sat on one of the straw mats that had been spread on the floor, his face caramel-colored in the glow of the kerosene lamps placed here and there to give light. Camel saddles had been laid down and covered with folded goatskins, upon which fifty-odd men sat or reclined, their Kalashnikovs making a startling contrast against their robes. When we took our seats, Jima beckoned some retainers, who floated in with copper coffee pots in one hand and stacks of cups in the other. The lackey assigned to serve us filled the top cup and passed it to Nordstrand, the second to me, the third to Moody. We could hear the fires crackling outside, dogs barking in the village, and jackals howling dismally in the hills. The savor of roasting goat mingled with another, less pleasant smell that lingered in the air despite all our burial work. It seemed to have soaked into the broken walls around us, that death-stink.

We drank the customary three cups, after which the retainers left. They returned shortly with huge steaming cooking pots suspended from carrying poles. These were set down in a cleared space in the center of the circle of mats and saddles, great black iron pots filled with mounds of rice yellowed by melted fat and mixed with chunks of fried intestine, liver, heart, and lung. The smell brought murmurings from the meat-starved crowd; but this being an occasion of some solemnity, everyone had to put on his best desert manners and wait for Jima's signal to eat. At last he gave it. Intoning, *"Bismillah ar-rahman ar-rahim* —In the name of God, the all-compassionate, the all-merciful," he dipped the fingers of his right hand into a pot, and we attacked the food ravenously, scooping out gobs of meat, guts, and rice.

When the pots had been licked clean, a ruffle of tribal drums announced the main course. Another procession of retainers filed in, carrying the goats on high triangular wooden stands that looked like police barricades. The gutted, roasted animals were draped over the center pole, hoofless legs hanging down, cooked heads, with the eyes fried white and pink mouths gaping, propped up with small pegs driven through the lower jaws. Layers of brown meat and muscle covered the shoulders and flanks. We attacked the carcasses like a pack of starving dogs, ripping and tearing slabs of flesh with our hands, breaking off ribs and legs to gnaw on the bones, wiping our grease-coated lips with our arms, then plunging in for more until there was little left except the fire-browned skulls and tatters of sinew dangling from broken rib cages. Sated, everyone collapsed on the mats and languidly cleansed their hands and mouths in the washing bowls the retainers brought around. A round of tea was served, followed by a special treat: *kat*. The retainer brought in bundles of the narcotic plant. For the next hour, the only sound was the rustling of branches as we tore off the leaves, wadded them into lumps resembling uncured tobacco, and chewed and sucked, sucked and chewed. Its initial effect no more potent than a shot of whiskey, it gradually induced a languorous euphoria. Lying back against a saddle, feeling for the first time in months a release from all pain, physical and otherwise, I watched Osman and the other tribesmen filing out of the ruin, their mouths bulging with *kat,* their robes lovely and white. They built a great bonfire on the parade ground and grouped themselves around it; white wraiths in the twitching orange light of the flames. Only Jima, a few of his bodyguards, Nordstrand, Moody, and I remained inside the shell of the building.

Jima, looking at us with the dark suns of his eyes, said it was now time to honor Mr. Jeremy. His voice came from a long way away. Mr. Jeremy had been the strongest among us and was, therefore, most deserving of honor, Jima went on in the tone of a proud father. He planned and led the attack while you, Mr. Patrick, had advised against it. You, Mr. Patrick, thought the Ethiopians would bomb us, but we've been here four days now and no planes have come. Mr. Jeremy was right, and your advice was wrong, Mr. Patrick.

Moody appeared baffled and asked, in what way was Mr. Jeremy to be honored?

"He is to be made a member of the house of the Beni-Hamid."

"He means I'm going to become one of them."

"Yes, I understand that, Jeremy."

"Speak in Arabic!"

"I said that's very interesting."

"O Jima."

"O Jima."

Narcotized, Moody had spoken with an exaggerated slowness. Though *kat* is a mild drug, we had taken nothing stronger than tea in six months, and the *kat* coursed through us like a powerful tranquilizer. Outside, the fire rose and fell in bright sheets.

"Mr. Jeremy's not of our blood or of our faith, but we believe a man can be our brother by the covenant of the deed. And Mr. Jeremy is our brother by covenant. He fulfilled the requirements for becoming a warrior on the night we fought for this place. Osman witnessed it and took the proof. It won't be an insult to you, Mr. Patrick, or to you, Mr. Charlie, if I say that you haven't done what is required, and so cannot be members of our house?"

In my memory, there was the crack of a twig broken underfoot and the soldier's body quivering as the life went out of him, and an inner voice cried, I have! I have! I am also one of you!

"No insult," Moody replied. "I'm sure the ceremony will be interesting from an ethnological point of view."

"I'll not ask you again to speak in Arabic, Mr. Patrick."

"I said I'm sure it will be interesting."

"O Jima."

"O Jima."

"But you and Mr. Charlie will be allowed to attend, which is itself an honor for foreigners."

He smiled faintly. Chewed *kat* formed a greenish goo around his lips.

The sheikh rose from his cross-legged seat, and as he walked lightly outside toward the fire, a solitary drum took up a slow, solemn beat and the tribesmen began chanting, "Jima, Jima, Jima, Jeee-mah!" Then: "Jer-ah-mee, Jer-ah-mee, Jer-ah-mee." Hearing his name, Nord-strand adopted a pose of great dignity, as if he were walk-ing down the aisle at Westminster, about to be knighted. Outside the circles of pale-robed tribesmen sat a dozen or so musicians with flutes, hourglass drums, and single-string fiddles. They joined in the chant as we approached. "Jima, Jer-ah-mee, Jima, Jer-ah-mee." The mood was one of religious fervor. One of the bodyguards pointed to a spot just outside the rings of seated men and rather sternly told Moody and me to sit down. This we did. The Englishman whispered:

"Don't like this already, Charlie. Maybe it is an honor, but I feel as if I just walked into the wrong church."

Jima and the bodyguard ushered Nordstrand to the place of honor, a big reed mat laid in a gap in the inner circle and covered with more bundles of *kat*. Everyone chewed and sucked on the stuff. Osman was sitting on the mat with a blanket folded on his lap. It was an odd-looking cloth, not dull but glossy, more like a well-rubbed hide

than a blanket. With Nordstrand beside him, Jima sat
down, folding his wire-thin legs beneath him.

The fiddles began screeching and the flutes blowing
the shrill notes of a classical Arabic melody, untempered,
plaintive, and monotonous, unpleasant to the western ear.
Then the hourglass drums joined in and one of the tribesmen sang the refrain to a chant which the others echoed
back in the high, faint voices of men who live where the
flap of a hawk's wing can be heard for a mile. I couldn't
understand a word—they were singing in a dialect—but I
heard in the chant and drumbeat a sound antiphonal to
the squealing flutes and fiddles, a more primitive sound,
a cry that came out of the heart of old Africa. Singing, the
men in the inner ring rose and began to dance slowly
around the fire, slowly, moving only their legs, holding
themselves stiffly from the waist up, the expressions in
their eyes trancelike, as if the music had bewitched them.
The *mullah,* wearing a black gown over a white wide-
sleeved robe, suddenly appeared in the center of the ring.
I had no idea where he'd come from; he just appeared, as
though he had sprung out of flames. He was a wisp of an
old man, with a pointy face accentuated by a grey, spade-
shaped goatee; he held a book in one hand and a string
of beads clacking in the other. The *mullah* danced alone,
his movements lithe and fluid. He pranced lightly on his
toes, made quick, graceful whirls, and capered with a
fawnlike gaiety that contrasted with the measured, funereal
circling of the younger men, their bare feet stomping
against the bare earth. The outer circle, singing the repetitive chant, green drool trickling from their mouths, started
to clap in time with the hide drums, to clap and sway.
Their clapping, the thud of the drums, the voices, the
stamping of naked feet, the swaying bodies, and the white
swirl of the *mullah*'s billowing sleeves created a strange
enchantment. The meaning of the ritual was a mystery to
me, the lyrics of the song incomprehensible, and yet there
was something familiar in the cadence of drum and chant,
chant and drum. It seemed to awaken a memory in me,
a memory not my own but one passed on to me, of savage
hymns sung long ago. The rhythms matched the most elemental rhythms within me, my heartbeat and the throb of

my pulse, and I felt a stirring, difficult to suppress, in a
deep and hidden part of myself resonant with the earliest
ages of man.

After it had gone on for a quarter of an hour or so, the
music began to have a narcotic effect far stronger than the
kat. It deadened the mind and unstrung the will. Nordstrand appeared to have been hypnotized by it. His head
swayed and his half-closed eyes wore the enraptured look
of the dancers. Lumps of *kat* swelled his cheeks. Appre-
hension passed through me when I looked at him, though
I couldn't tell if the drug and the music had actually cast
a spell over him or if he was merely pretending they had,
if his beguiled air was theater or reality or something in
between.

The tempo increased. A series of high, quick notes ran
from the flutes, the fiddles cried more insistently, and the
drummers' hands became a blur. Pairing off, the dancers
drew their swords and twirled and stomped around each
other, swinging the blades in ritualized mock combat. It
was a kind of barbaric ballet: men leaping and lunging,
scarred faces sweat-glistening in the firelight, swords glinting silver. Then half the dancers flung themselves in the
dust and lay still. With torsos rocking back and forth,
their partners stood over them while the outer ring of men
went on chanting and clapping. Without breaking step,
the *mullah* undid the clasp of his black gown, let it slip
to his feet, and held out his arms, displaying the white of
the robe underneath. At this gesture, the prostrate dancers
leapt to their feet, formed the ring anew, and again began
dancing around the priest. They let out a sound imitating
the ululation of women lamenting the dead, a shrill, vi-
brating howl that reminded me of nothing so much as a
cage full of deranged birds.

"Well I'll be damned," Moody said under his breath.

"What is it?" I kept my voice low even though no one
would have heard me if I'd shouted.

"Dervishism. What the priest just did, that's a dervish
symbol of resurrection and the conquest of death."

Now all in white, the *mullah* gamboled around the ring,
genuflecting in front of each tribesman, his knee not quite

touching the earth. His movements became more feminine.
A lascivious smile broke on his pointed face, his hooded
eyes wore a look half-dreamy and half-lustful. As he began
the third turn around, he moved toward one of the dancers.
The hand holding the beads reached for the man's face;
his long, bony fingers extended, withdrew, and extended
again to caress the tribal markings on the warrior's cheeks,
which he then kissed with a lingering lover's kiss. Sleeves
whirling, he spun on to the next man, and again the slender fingers traced the V-shaped grooves of the markings.
To the next and the next and the next he gave the same
caress and the same lingering, unnatural kiss, his headdress
sweeping behind him and the dancers' frantic steps raising
a pall of dust that glowed like volcanic ash in the firelight.

Osman, holding the blanket under one arm, stood and
led Nordstrand to the *mullah*. The action reminded me of
the way a sponsor guides a confirmand to the bishop.
Nordstrand appeared to be in a stupor, his eyes transfixed
by the priest's twirling figure. The flutes and fiddles had
grown quiet, the wild ululating stopped. There were only
the drums, to which the tribesmen danced ever faster, until
they all merged into a spinning blur of black and white.
The drumming slowed suddenly, and with a discipline and
grace any choreographer would have admired, the dancers
adjusted their steps to the new rhythm, broke the circle,
formed the lines, and stomped and clapped and flung their
heads violently from side to side. Osman and Nordstrand
stood at one end of the corridor of gyrating bodies; the
mullah, executing a series of arabesques, reeled between
the lines up to Nordstrand. Osman said something to the
American, who then leaned his head forward. The priest
stretched out his hands; his fingers, five charred sticks,
stroked Nordstrand's face; then with a flick of those fingers,
he stilled the drumming and halted the dance. The abrupt
silence was as disturbing as the noise had been. For several moments, the hypnotic drums continued to throb inside my head. By degrees, I became aware of the hissing
wind, in whose gusts the fire rose and fell, of the dogs
baying in the town, and the jackals laughing in the distance.
Osman and the *mullah* were engaged in an unintelligible

conversation to which the exhausted dancers, chests heaving, listened attentively. I asked Moody if he could make out what the two men were saying.

"Parts of it," he answered in a strained whisper. "The priest's asked Osman why this stranger should be brought into their house. Osman said he's their brother by covenant. Didn't understand a word after that—wait . . . all right . . . now Osman's said Nordstrand's done what the law requires . . . killed a man in . . . can't quite make it out . . . something to the effect that he's killed a man in personal combat. . . . He, Osman—that is—saw it . . . killed him with . . ."

At that point, Osman drew a long, curved knife from beneath the folds of his robes and held it up in his free hand. The priest muttered something which Moody described as "absolute mumbo jumbo."

"Is this still a dervish ceremony?" My lips were pressed against Moody's ear, my head turned to one side. The Englishman said, "Good Christ!" and I snapped my head around to see the priest swiftly and skillfully slash Nordstrand's cheeks with the knife. Blood streaming down his face, the American shut his eyes against the pain. The *mullah* was practiced in the operation and took a very short time to finish it. A kind of celebratory song lilted from the tribesmen's throats as the knife flicked and flashed. The priest wiped Nordstrand's face with a cloth. When his hand withdrew, I saw that the glistening wounds were the chevron-shaped tribal markings of the Beni-Hamid. And the sight of Nordstrand's skin branded with their mark was at once grotesque, awful, and ludicrous. I didn't know whether to laugh or scream at his revolting attempt to deny what he was and the world he came from by becoming something he was not and committing himself to a world in which he had no place.

After the priest had completed his cosmetic surgery, Osman made a long speech. It was, according to Moody's halting translation, an account of how Mr. Jer-ah-mee had killed the Ethiopian, the deed by which he had made himself their brother, though he was not of their blood, not of their faith, and so forth. The law demanded that proof be taken. He, Osman, had taken it. Mumbling a kind of incantation, something to the effect that a Beni-Hamid warrior gains his manhood by robbing an enemy of his, Osman unfolded the object in his arms and hung it, by a thong attached for that purpose, around Nordstrand's neck. It draped over his front like a brown leather apron. My eyes traced the oval-shaped outline of the hide—yes, it was a hide—from the incision made across the chest, down past the abdomen to where the skin of the penis drooped like an empty balloon. I breathed in sharply, as much from the surprise as from the horror of what I saw—I had taken it for a blanket or an animal hide. One thinks odd thoughts at such moments, and my first thoughts ran to technique. I wondered how Osman had done it, where and when he had learned the art of skinning a man. Osman, the aging soldier who had fought with Wingate, the tired warrior who had spoken bemusedly of his high-land coffee farm, had done *that*.

In a kind of trance myself, I watched the priest embrace Nordstrand; pressing himself against the—well, the hide, he planted on the American's mutilated flesh the same voluptuous kiss he had given the others. The *mullah*'s frail body shuddered as if in consummation. The drums commenced beating again, the tribesmen resumed the dance, their limbs twitching like marionettes'. His arms flung out wide, smiling, his face blood-smeared and streaked with the black camouflage paint, Nordstrand executed a slow turn to display the proof of his manhood to his chanting, clapping, writhing brothers. Natty Bumppo in Africa. The man who lived apart in the wilds. And I saw in Nord-strand's movement another kind of turning, a turning of his back on all civilization and on all society except for the savage brotherhood that had embraced him. He had meant what he said; there would be no going back.

The rite lost all semblance of order. The pattern to the music dissolved into a delirious noise, the dancing became a chaotic whirling of white robes and jerking limbs. Some of the Beni-Hamid began to shout their war cry. Others took it up, and it rose and swelled above the urgent boom of the drums: *"Jihad, jihad, hitta al-nasr, inshallah!"* Nord-strand stood in the midst of them, a head taller than the tallest. His green-rimmed mouth opened, distorting the red-streaming scars beneath his eyes; it opened wide and voraciously, it yawned, black as the entrance to a cave, the mouth of a man of insatiable appetites. Then he too bellowed the chant.

With a grunt of disgust, Moody got up and walked away quickly. I followed him. Leaving was a matter of conscience. To have watched that profane ritual any longer would have been to take part in it. I felt tainted as it was, for having seen as much as I had, for having felt that moment of captivation when the music reached down into me, down through the stratum of civilization to pluck a deep and primal chord.

It was a night full of stars, and we were grateful for the cool blessing of the wind from the mountains. Moody and I walked without talking, but both of us sensed we had come to a turning. Heading toward our hut in the village, we passed the wrecked barracks. A knot of the retainers who had served us at the feast squatted around the embers of a cooking fire; lips shellacked with grease and fat, they gnawed on their portion, the skulls of the sheep. I glanced back at the figures rioting around the soaring blaze, then craned my neck to look at the cold, fixed fire of the Southern Cross. An image of Nordstrand draped in a human skin rose unsummoned in my mind, hovered in midair between me and the constellation, and sent a fresh wave of revulsion through me. It had been one thing to hear Nordstrand talking about what he meant to do, but quite another to see him do it, to see him turn his back on everything and lose himself so completely. He had said the taking of Umm-Tajer would not be the end of the mission, but the beginning. And it was just the beginning. There would be more horrors and greater bloodshed because his lust for violence was like an addiction, requiring ever larger doses to satiate it. Murdering five men had not satisfied him. The battle had not satisfied him, and this latest outrage would not satisfy him. No catharsis would ever purge the murderous poisons within him. His appetite was limitless. I had feared him, had respected his strength, had admired the power of his convictions; but now all I felt toward him was an immeasurable disgust. He had come to Africa seeking a forbidden liberty, the freedom of the man in isolation, and the price of that freedom was an enslavement to his miscreant impulses. And so I had a moment of enlightenment. I had had to kill to gain it, to cast myself into the darkness to see, but at least I saw him for what he was: neither madman nor monster, but the embodiment of all that was wrong with me, all that is wrong with our crippled natures.

FIVE

RIFT VALLEY FEVER

We passed the prison compound, behind whose barbed-wire coils the Ethiopian prisoners slept huddled up against the chill desert night. A few sat awake, watching the fire flickering where their barracks had been, listening to the wild drumming. At sling arms, the rebel guards sauntered outside the wire with that air of boredom and arrogance common to prison guards everywhere. One of the Ethiopians muttered something. The sentry nearest lit a cigarette and passed it to him. A second guard, in a jocular mood, taunted another of the captured soldiers.

"Ya! Ismail," the sentry called to his friend. "This one said he wanted his letters returned. 'And do you have the eyes of a leopard that you can see in the dark?' I asked him. He said he wished to read them in the morning. They were letters from his wife. I told him, 'Very well, you may read them in the morning, but your wife's letters bear a strange scent, my friend. We've used them for toilet paper.'"

This elicited a burst of harsh laughter from the other sentry. A familiar, high-pitched voice ordered them to be still and to leave the prisoners alone.

"If things ever go badly for us, you could be in their place and they in yours."

"No danger of that, Kasu," a guard retorted. "The Ethiopians don't take prisoners."

Murrah made no reply. Then, spotting Moody and me,

he called in English and in a tone edged with mockery:
"Good evening, gentlemen."

We said nothing. Murrah, who had been standing by
the compound's makeshift wooden gate, strutted toward
us.

"I thought you would still be at the celebration. You
were privileged, you know. It's very rare that foreigners
are allowed to witness it."

His squealing voice was as grating as ever.

"Ya! Mr. Charlie, do you remember when I showed
you the bridal house in Kerem some months ago? I told
you that a Beni-Hamid warrior must present a certain gift
to his bride as proof of his manhood, but I wouldn't tell
you what the gift was. Now I think you have seen the
gift. Your Mr. Jeremy has it." His face eased into a sneer.
"I'm eager to hear your impression of this custom."

I did not say anything.

"Come, tell me. Speak plainly."

"It's awful."

"Awful. Yes, awful." The jeering smile faded from his
lips. "Idiocy, that's what it is. Idiocy and savagery. Isn't
that what your impression of us is now? That we're savages? 'Woolly-headed niggers,' eh? Monkeys in a zoo.
Drums and blood rites. Jima would change none of that,
and maybe you'd be right to think of us as woolly-headed
niggers, monkeys in a zoo."

"We haven't said any such thing, Kasu."

"Now you see what you three have done to us. Now
you see it. Look at it."

"We've seen quite enough, thank you. And we haven't
done a bloody thing."

"You're destroying us, especially that madman over
there." He gestured at the distant fire. "All those men,
and, yes, Jima too, they may say they owe the victory here
to their Allah, but in their hearts they believe they owe it
to him. To *him*. Is that independence, to believe they owe
something to a man like that? That murderer of yours?"

"He isn't ours," I said. "Not anymore."

"What did you expect us to do anyway?" Moody's voice
sounded tired. "At any rate, you'll be rid of us soon

enough. If the council meets Jima's terms, we'll be ordered
out of here. You know that."

"What's that?"

"We'll be ordered out of here if Jima's put on the
directorate—"

"What did Mr. Charlie say?"

"I said he isn't ours anymore."

Murrah measured us with his eyes. It was obvious he
sensed the change in us but, in his usual cautious, indirect
way, he wasn't about to do anything abrupt.

"Not yours," he said. Cupping his hands against the
wind, he struck a match and lit a cigarette. "Not yours
anymore."

"How about a cigarette, Kasu. I'm fresh out and could
use one."

Murrah handed Moody a cigarette.

"And you say you'll be ordered out if—*when*—Jima is
put on the directorate. What will you do if Mr. Jeremy
doesn't follow those orders?"

"He's the boss," Moody replied.

"I'm serious."

"So am I."

"And you would allow him to stay here? He means to
stay here, doesn't he? Isn't that what you meant when you
said he isn't yours anymore, Mr. Charlie? He's ours now."

"Something like that."

"And you'd let him stay also? You'd just leave, accept-
ing no responsibility for what happened afterwards?"

"Since I haven't got much idea of what you're getting
at, and even less of an idea of what's going to happen, no,
I don't accept responsibility."

"You heard Jima before we left for this place. Once he's
on the directorate, he'll get rid of the others one by one
until only he is left. Muhammad Jima, the great dictator.
He wasn't boasting. That wasn't Arab rhetoric. It was a
vow, Mr. Charlie."

"Isn't this all a bit hypothetical?"

"I don't understand."

"Jima isn't on the directorate yet. He may never be."

"True. But I must think about what will happen if he is.

He's done a lot with only a few hundred men and the weapons you've given him. I must think about what he'll be able to do with many more men, and more weapons, and—oh, yes, the half-million dollars you people are going to hand over to him."

"Really, Kasu. It is all quite hypothetical. Even if he does get on, how much harm can he do? The Beni-Hamid are a minority tribe after all—"

Murrah's voice went up the scale. "And Idi Amin's tribe was a minority tribe! And he seized power with the help of foreigners. Oh, yes, the British and the Israelis. His chief adviser was an Englishman. Yes! One of your polite Englishman, Mr. Patrick, helped Idi Amin build the prisons where men's heads were smashed in with hammers. Oh, yes, he was from a minority Moslem tribe, and what did he do? He made his minority tribe a majority by murdering the others, thousands of them. And your Mr. Jeremy, what will he be? He'll be to Jima what that Englishman was to Idi Amin."

"I think you're getting carried away with yourself. Just what is it you're trying to say?"

Calming himself, Murrah gave a little vulpine grin and jerked his thumb at the prison enclosure.

"What have they got to do with anything?"

"Those poor devils. They're terrified, being held like this. Only one thing terrifies them more: being sent back to Ethiopia. The government's issued a decree that any soldier who is captured is to be considered a traitor and executed if he returns. An intelligent policy. It makes for a problem. A problem for me and for them. We can't hold them forever."

"Meaning what? You're going to save the government the trouble by shooting them yourself?"

"Absolutely not." Murrah's tone was aggrieved. "No, I've been trying to convince them they should join the EDRP."

"Oh, just what we jolly well need, a new set of initials. What is the EDRP?"

It was, Murrah explained, the Ethiopian People's Democratic Union, a guerrilla group fighting in Ethiopia proper.

Their base was in the province immediately south of Bejaya.

"We've cooperated with them and sent them prisoners before. My plan was to release these men and have them escorted to the province border. It isn't far from here, three days' march at most. There we could turn them over to the EDRP and not have the responsibility for them. Jima agreed with the plan. We were going to move them in a few days' time." Murrah paused, stopped in midsentence, and glanced at one of his sentries. "No, not here," he said. "Not even in English. We'll walk."

He snapped an order at the guard, then started down the crooked, darkened street. A row of roofless, fire-blackened huts stood on one side, empty except for the ravenous dogs scavenging in the rubble. A sentry stepped out of a shadowed doorway and challenged us. A few of the surviving civilians, fearing an Ethiopian air raid, had filtered out of the town. Jima regarded this as an insult and as tantamount to desertion; and not wishing to preside over a provisional capital with no population, he had posted guards with orders to shoot any villager trying to run off. Murrah identified us and the guard waved and greeted us with a "*masalkhair*—God grant you a happy evening."

"*Masal el full*—An evening of fragrance," Murrah replied with a hint of irony. The only fragrance, besides the smell of charred wood, was the odor filtering through the dirt of the shallow graves hurriedly dug wherever the dead had been found.

We walked to the northern edge of the village—Umm-Tajer was only half a mile from one end to the other. Below, the hillside Nordstrand's guerrillas had scaled before launching their sneak attack dropped steeply to the valley floor, a monochromatic expanse of gravel dotted with black acacia. The oasis was an ink smear a short way off. The mountains rose in the distance, as treeless as the moon that shone on them.

Moody flopped down on the lip of the hill.

"Well, Kasu, you were saying?"

"What are Mr. Jeremy and Jima planning to do with the prisoners?"

"How the devil should we know?"

"Perhaps Mr. Jeremy still is yours a little?"

"We don't know," I said. "As far as we know, nothing."

"I told you the plan was to escort the prisoners to the border and turn them over to the EDRP. Last night, I went to talk over the arrangements with Jima, but Jima's guards told me I had to wait. He was having a meeting with your Mr. Jeremy. Jeremy can talk to him as long as he pleases, but I have to wait. They talked for a very long time, and when Mr. Jeremy left, I saw he was carrying some maps. Then I went in to discuss this matter of the prisoners. Jima became very excited. I was not to release them, he told me. I told him we didn't have enough food to care for them for much longer. Jima said that was not a problem. They would not be with us much longer. But I was not to release them. He had found a use for them. He would tell me nothing more, except this: I was to continue to promise the Ethiopians they would be released to the EDRP. 'And will they?' I asked Jima. 'Oh, yes, yes, yes,' he said, but I didn't believe him. So they are planning to do something with the prisoners, and I thought you gentlemen might know."

"We don't know."

"He *is* still yours a little."

"I told you we don't know. Look, I was awake when Nordstrand got back from the meeting. I asked him what he'd been up to. He said he hadn't met with anyone. He said he'd gone for a walk."

"And you believed him?"

"Of course not."

Murrah dropped into a squat and, picking up a stick, idly drew designs in the sand. Turning away from his doodling, he looked me up and down, gauging my sincerity.

"That's what he told me," I said.

"So, it's being kept secret even from you. It must be a very interesting plan if it's being kept from you."

"You know it's possible that they didn't talk about the prisoners at all."

"Yes, possible, but I think they did. Perhaps you gentlemen could find out what they discussed."

"And?"

"And tell me."

Having grown accustomed to Murrah's circumspect manner, I had no idea how to respond to this direct statement.

Moody said, "I rather think it's time for a bit of kip."

"Kip?"

"Sleep, although I'm not sure I'll be able to sleep after what I've seen tonight," Moody answered, but did not stand to leave.

A gust of high wind fanned across the valley, rattling the acacia branches and blowing with a dry sibilance through the leaves of the palm in the oasis. From the opposite direction came the laughing of some unseen sentries sharing a joke and, farther off, the muted drumming—a reminder of what we had seen and of how close we were to the world of the tom-tom.

"After what you've seen," Murrah said stridently, "do you have any idea of what it will be like here if Jima takes power?"

"Hypothetical again. Jima is a long way from that."

"What does it mean, that word."

"It means 'conditional, depending on something,' " Moody answered. "In this case, it means 'something that might happen.' "

"Might happen. So can you imagine Jima content with just being a member of the directorate?"

I said, no, I couldn't imagine it. Whatever he was Muhammad Jima was not a complaisant committeeman.

"You're wise, Mr. Charlie."

"I'm a smart man all right."

"Jima would not be content simply to be a voice. He wishes to be a voice of the revolution. He's a natural Leninist."

Moody laughed at this preposterous statement.

"Oh, I should love to see the old boy's reaction to that. Muhammad Jima, the fanatic anti-Communist, a natural Leninist. That is more than farfetched, Kasu."

Murrah, still scratching designs in the arid earth, piped in reply, "Jima is a bandit at heart. He's a renegade, and

in the end, what is Leninism but the politics of the renegade?"

"And that sounds odd coming from a Marxist."

"You forget, I'm not the Marxist I once was. And even
when I was, I don't think I was a Leninist. Leninism is the
outlaw's ideology. Where was Lenin when the revolution
began and what was he? An outlaw and a fugitive living
in Switzerland. But he understood one principle: the man
who wins is not always the man with the most numbers or
the greatest firepower. It is the man who applies decisive
force at the decisive point at the decisive time. How do you
suppose he won? You don't believe those silly portraits by
the Soviet artists, do you? Those silly portraits that show
so many thousands of Bolsheviks attacking the Winter
Palace? There weren't twenty thousand Bolsheviks in all
Russia at the time. No, Lenin simply stormed through the
palace with a handful of henchmen and brought Keren-
ski's stupid little parliament to an end at gunpoint. Yes,
Mr. Patrick. They just pointed pistol at the heads of those
bourgeois parliamentarians and told them the session was
over, the game was up. Lenin's men were gangsters and
their revolution was armed robbery. They stole an entire
country, the biggest country on earth. Jima's never read
Lenin of course, but he understands the principle by instinct. He's an outlaw. He has the gangster's mind, like
your Mr. Jeremy. And if Jima gets on the directorate, believe me, he'll steal Bejaya."

"Kasu, all this political salon chatter is quite interesting,
but what's it leading to? After all, the whole purpose of
this operation—"

"I know the purpose of your operation. Put Jima on the
directorate so you'll have someone who'll help you keep
that base of yours at Albara. My God, the stupidity of you
people is incredible. British and Israeli agents made an
operation to put Idi Amin in power so they could have
someone who would play their game. Were you pleased
with the result? The British got a man who made fools of
them, the Zionists got a black Hitler, and the Africans—
your woolly-headed niggers, Mr. Patrick—got massacred."

"Do stop reminding me of that remark and do stop
lecturing me and come to the point."

"I have no point to come to. Not yet."

"Then what the devil is all this chatter? I'd like a bit of kip."

"I've been thinking about some things these past days. Alone. When I saw you tonight, I thought perhaps . . . I don't know how to say it."

"*You* at a loss for words?"

"You thought we might be interested in hearing your thoughts," I said.

"I thought that now you could be trusted."

"We can and we're interested."

"But you never answered me if you could find what Jima discussed with Mr. Jeremy and tell me."

"We'll do it." Whatever Jima and Nordstrand were planning, Murrah clearly meant to stop them. And I was obliged to help him. It was an obligation not to Murrah but to myself, and it required me to do something. No matter how extreme, mere repulsion at Nordstrand's self-excommunication was not enough to divorce myself from him. I had, by my own act of killing, followed him into moral exile. Only by acting now could I hope to break the covenant that bound us and save myself from becoming as irrevocably lost as he.

"So, you'll do it then," Murrah said, speaking quietly for a change. "Good. Now Mr. Patrick can have his 'kip.' "

"We're still interested in your thoughts."

"Oh, they're nothing. They were thoughts on certain objective realities."

"Objective realities. That's a Leninist phrase if I ever heard one."

"Yes, it is. What is the objective reality of Jima's charm? Why does he command such loyalty? That's what I was thinking about. What's his secret? He came along in a time of defeats and he gave us victories, with Mr. Jeremy's help, of course. He gave us this victory here, so now the fighters think he is invincible and they would follow him to fight the devil because my people will do anything for a man who is strong, who is successful. The Beni-Hamid are a very loyal people to the strong man. They have one fault, though. They're not a constant people. They have no mercy for the weak and no tolerance for failure. Let their strong man falter just once, let him make one mistake, and they'll pounce on him like jackals and eat him. So I thought, what would the fighters think of their Jima if his victory here became a defeat? What would they do if he made a mistake? They would be finished with him." Murrah dropped his stick and made a cleansing motion with his hands. "Finished. *Khalas*. And he's already making his mistake. He wants to hold this place, but he hasn't the strength to hold it. Nine hundred of us took this place from the Ethiopians in a night, and now there are only seven hundred of us left. Which means the Ethiopians could take it from us as easily as we took it from them, especially if they come with their planes."

"We've been through that. Precisely what I told him, but I can't say I performed well as a military oracle. We haven't seen a single plane."

"Because now the Ethiopians are busy with the Somalis in the Ogaden. These problems they have with the Somalis happen every year, like the rains. They start and then they're over. So I was thinking. What will the Ethiopians do when their troubles in the Ogaden are over? I have made the correct analysis of objective realities, and I know they will make a big counterattack when they hear Jima has declared this place a provisional capital. They could not allow him such a propaganda victory."

"This is plowed ground as well, Kasu. Of course the Ethiopians will regard it as a provocation. But I should think it'll be some time before they hear that this miserable little dung heap is a capital. Their intelligence isn't all that good."

"Jima is helping their intelligence. As you know, he wishes to hear his name on the radio." Murrah let out a squealy little laugh. "Muhammad Jima, the great dictator, wishes to become famous on the BBC and the Voice of America. And so on the very morning he raised his flag, he asked me to make propaganda for him. I was to write an announcement of what had been done here and that Umm-Tajer was now the provisional capital, give it to some couriers and see they brought it to our underground in Sudan, who will pass it on to the Sudanese press."

"That bloody fool."

I laughed to myself. If Jima was a natural Leninist, he was also a natural public relations man: he had no sooner won his victory than he sent out a press release announcing it.

"Yes, yes. That bloody fool. I wrote very good propaganda, gentlemen. I'm good at that. I made the announcement very provocative."

"Awfully clever, Kasu. You mean you made sure it was written in such a way as to goad the Ethiopians into counterattacking?"

"To what?"

"Goad them. Provoke them."

"It is you, not I who is saying that, Mr. Patrick. I only made good propaganda. I'm a political officer. That's what I'm supposed to do."

"Good Christ, what are you trying to do? Bring the temple down on all our heads? You're as great a bloody fool as he is."

"I only made good propaganda."

"At any rate, we—I mean, he's got enough to handle whatever the Ethiopians throw at him. How many SAM-7s has he got, Charlie?"

"Twenty launchers, five rounds to each launcher. Even if four out of every five rounds missed, that's enough to shoot down better than half the combat aircraft they've got."

"Yes, I've thought of that, too. It would make him even more a hero. Muhammad Jima, destroyer of the Ethiopian air force." Rising from his squat, Murrah took a pebble and tossed it with the awkward, bent-armed motion of one unpracticed in throwing. "But suppose the missiles failed to fire? Or, so there would be no suspicion of sabotage, suppose some of the missiles fired properly and others not? You're an expert on these weapons, Mr. Charlie. Can they be made to not fire properly?"

I did not react immediately to this incredible suggestion. Murrah had made it without changing the inflection in his voice, so that it sounded like nothing more than casual conjecture.

"Can that sort of thing be done, Mr. Charlie?"

"Yes," I answered, more than a little shaken by the

audacity of the idea. "The best way is to neutralize the heat-seeking device in the nose cone. You disconnect the circuits between the infrared head and the synchro motor. That would make the missiles veer off course."

"I don't understand that."

"It's a technical problem."

"I really do think this chat's gone far enough. I think it's time we all got a bit of kip."

"I'll find out what Nordstrand's planning with Jima, but count me out of anything else, Kasu. If there's an air raid, I want to see those MIGs shot down. I don't want any bombs falling on my head."

"When a small tumor is cut out sometimes other parts of the body must suffer."

"I'm not a part of this body."

"But you are. You have been these past six months. You can't escape that, Mr. Charlie."

"Count me out. I'm not going to go sabotaging any missiles for you."

"It is you, not I, who is speaking of sabotaging missiles."

"That's the word you used two minutes ago. Sabotage."

"It was hypothetical."

———

Sharing the small, hot, dim, stifling room with Nordstrand was appalling. It was appalling to listen to him, to feel his presence, and, most appalling of all, to look at his disfigured face. The scars had begun to scab over and looked all the more gruesome, but Nordstrand wore them, the marks of his self-imposed exile, as proudly as a soldier wears his wounds. The sight of them always disinterred the memory of the priest's quick knife, the hideous syncopation of drums, flutes, and tribal chants, and of Nordstrand with the smooth brown length of human flesh draped from his neck, submitting to the priest's kiss and caress. I would remember it as one remembers a terrifying hallucination, and remembering, would look at him and feel as though I were caged with some strange and rabid animal. As Moody had done weeks before, I took to sleeping with my pistol on, afraid Nordstrand would pounce on the Englishman or me without warning or motive. Did I say sleep? I hardly slept at all. Lying on my musty straw mattress, I suffered through intervals of troubled unconsciousness broken by spells of the most acute consciousness, that hyperawareness which usually precedes a collapse into madness.

Nordstrand took to wearing a tribal costume all the time, the white robe reaching no farther than his knees. He exchanged his boots for sandals, adorned himself with a bone necklace, kept his head shaved, and had the *mullah* redo his camouflage whenever it began to fade. "I'm a giant Nubian," he would say, examining his paint-blackened face in the tin mirror. "A gi-*ant Nu*-bee-an." I thought he looked like a man who had not only stared into the fire but had shoved his head into it.

One afternoon, some five or six days after his True Brothers had made him a member of the club, he flew into a rage—at the sun. The sun was too bright, goddamnit; the sunlight hurt his eyes. He cursed the sun as if he meant to snuff it out with his bare hands. And he would have if he had had the power. Instead, he demanded to be supplied with a pair of sunglasses. He made the demand to Osman, the truest of his True Brothers, who replied that he doubted sunglasses could be found in a place like Umm-Tajer. "God damn you, you *will* find me a pair, understand? This sun you've got here bothers my eyes," Mr. Jeremy stormed, as if the brightness of the sunlight were Osman's fault. And Osman came up with a pair. They had belonged to one of the guerrillas, who must have got them from a smuggler, because they were a very fancy pair of one-way, wraparound aviator's glasses. When Nordstrand put them on, their opaque silver lenses combined with the camouflage, the pink scars, and his shaved skull to make him look like something you might see in a very bad dream. He wore them all day, and then at night when he was in the hut and the lamp was lit. The lamp, he complained, also bothered his eyes, and one night he commanded Moody to turn it down. When the Englishman said it was turned down as far as it would go, Nordstrand roared, "Then we'll just put it out for good," picked it up, threw it against a wall, and almost burned us out.

That demented act pushed conditions beyond the appalling into the intolerable. And yet, they had to be tolerated. To avoid arousing his suspicions, I had to pretend nothing had changed when, in fact, everything had changed; and the feigning strained my nerves until I thought they would burn up like wires carrying a voltage beyond their capacity. In the most cautious, circumspect ways, I tried to pry out of him some hint of what he and Jima were cooking up together, and I would hear the falseness in my voice, I would hear my voice echoing back at me. One afternoon when Nordstrand was off somewhere, I dug out his diaries and searched them for clues. They yielded nothing but more gibberish about the fulfillment of his destiny and the transformation of the NIIF into the "node of the rebellion." One half-legible fragment said he had now won the complete trust of the Beni-Hamid, without which "it" could not be done. This entry ended with a quote from Nietzsche: "Everything I touch becomes light, everything I let go of, coal; I am certainly fire." Then I took the maps he had studied so carefully before running off to his secret conference with Jima. I stared at them, trying to force them to surrender their secret. He had circled Karu, which, like Umm-Tajer, was a town surrounded by mountains and accessible only by a couple of well-defined caravan tracks. Nordstrand had drawn a line parallel to one of the trails, which led through a wadi. The line ended at a narrow pass, which he had marked with another circle. The marks were as enigmatic as the words in the diary, and giving up on my detective work, I placed everything back in his haversack.

Walking outside to rest my eyes, I caught something in my peripheral vision that tripped an alarm in my peripheral consciousness. Something was different, different and wrong. Crouched beneath the prehistoric mountains, the town looked the same—houses and shells of houses, roofless houses and houses with tin roofs still intact, heat waves rippling off the tin. The sky. The sky was wrong. It had a cloud in it, the first cloud I had seen in that sky in nearly six months, a high, thin, moving white cloud that was not a meteorological phenomenon. It was an omen: the vapor trail of a reconnaissance plane.

Another vapor trail scribbled another silent warning the

next morning. More warnings came later through the guerrillas' intelligence network: a salt caravan trekking westward from the Malaka Sink reported seeing "many" Ethiopian planes taking off and landing at the airbase at Edana; a band of nomads moving their herds to meet the coming rainy season said they had passed near a government outpost in the province south of Bejaya and saw "many" soldiers arriving in strange aircraft that had no wings. All these portents Jima airily ignored. He was preoccupied with his Sony shortwave, waiting to hear his name pronounced by the outside world. It was, at last, first at the very end of a broadcast from Radio Cairo; then the BBC's Africa Service picked it up: unconfirmed reports reaching Khartoum that Bejayan rebels seized a strategic town in heavy fighting recently . . . rebels are believed to belong to the National Islamic Independence Front . . . led by Sheikh Muhammad Jima, who broke ranks with the guerrilla leadership more than a year ago. . . .

Muhammad Jima! Now the world knew his name.

Muhammad Jima, media star, received another present shortly afterward. It came in the form of two haggard couriers who arrived in a Land-Rover with the equivalent of an engraved invitation. The Command Council had agreed to convene a "unity conference" at Karu, where, in a "democratic dialogue," it hoped to "reconcile the contradictions" between the NIIF and the other factions. The meeting was set for two weeks from now. Three of the six members of the directorate would attend, including Bairu and Hassab. Jima coughed with joy and immediately went to offer prayers to Allah, from whom all things came. And while he prayed, two more planes swept overhead for a closer look at us; flying at near stall-speed they were out of the SAM-7s' range, but low enough for me to make them out through Nordstrand's field glasses: MIG-19s fitted out as photo reconnaissance aircraft. My imagination went to work, and I could almost hear the high-speed cameras clicking, and pictured Russian and Cuban advisers studying photographs at their headquarters in Addis Ababa.

"We have got to convince that man to start doing something," Moody said. "You and I, Charlie. I don't want Mr. Jeremy around."

We managed to get a private audience with the sheikh
after his prayers were done. A guard ushered Moody and
me inside the "presidential palace." (Jima's *folie des grandeurs* had grown more virulent, and that is what he now
called his two-story stucco shack.) Some changes in interior
decoration had been made. The place had been cleaned
up. The downstairs room had been converted into a waiting
room that doubled as a barracks for the bodyguard. A
dozen of them lounged about, cleaning their rifles and
endlessly sipping cups of tea. A rude table stood where the
desk had been—the latter had been moved upstairs to
Jima's private quarters. Osman, sweat beading his forehead, hulked behind the table. In addition to being chief
of the bodyguard, he now served as a kind of mayor. He
had to handle many annoying and commonplace problems.
Villagers complaining that the rebels were stealing their
livestock, trampling their meager gardens, making shameful advances to their daughters. Nomads flocking in from
the surrounding countryside petitioning Jima to settle petty
disputes over water and grazing rights. These goddamned
civilians. On top of all that, he had to make sure no more
of the townspeople sneaked off. Goddamned civilians
didn't have any nerve, any confidence in the NIIF's ability
to protect them. Looking at him, stocky and grandfatherly
in appearance, listening to him grumble like any bureaucrat about administrative trivia, I had to remind myself
that he was the same man who had flayed a man's corpse.

Curtly, I told him we hadn't come to listen to his problems.

"Of course, of course. This way."

He led us up a short flight of stairs that threatened to
crumble beneath our weight. In the upper room, the lou-
vered shutters of the paneless window had been closed
against the harsh sunlight. Wrapped in ribbons of light
and shadow, Jima sat behind his desk. It was bare except
for the usual copy of the Koran and his Sony, its antenna
extended. The old man was back in uniform—khaki shirt,
puttees, leather Sam Browne belt—and as with Osman, I
had to remind myself that I had seen this same man pre-
siding over a primitive blood rite. I saw him then as a
figure jammed in a kind of cultural and temporal doorway,

with one shoulder touching the world of the automatic rifle and the transistor radio and the other the world of the spear and the tribal drum.

We suffered through the infuriatingly slow litany of civilities, the usual calls for tea. When all that was out of the way, Jima folded his emaciated hands and asked what was so urgent.

Moody came to the point: all signs pointed to a major ground and air counterattack. Jima had only seven hundred men in fighting condition, more than a hundred wounded to care for, nearly a hundred civilians to watch over, and all of them concentrated in this punch bowl of a valley. One sustained air raid and he would lose half his men, perhaps everything. And if, as reports indicated, the Ethiopians were planning to launch an assualt with helicopter-borne infantry, the game would be up. The wisest course of action would be to evacuate. . . .

Jima waved his hand. He could not have looked more stunned or angry if we had suggested that he convert to Judaism.

"This isn't advice you're giving me. By God, it's treason. Telling me to abandon what we won at such cost. My victory here has been on the radio, gentlemen, the *whole world* knows of it, and you are advising me to run away?"

"No," Moody replied, "we're asking you, O Jima, to withdraw. Pull out, draw the Ethiopians in, then hit them."

"In other words, having taken this town from those *kafirs,* I am to give it back to them so I can fight them for it again. You gentlemen must be mad. *Ya Allah!* If Osman here, or any of my people, came to me with such advice, I'd have them shot. Ye-es! Executed on the spot. Where is Mr. Jeremy? Mr. Jeremy is my adviser. Where is he? Is this *his* advice as well?"

We fumbled and fudged our way through that one.

"You know, Mr. Jeremy is right about you. You lack nerve. A man should be afraid only when there is danger. You two are frightened of dangers that might be because you have no faith. It is the absence of faith that causes your absence of nerve. *Allah karim,"* he said, meaning that God, in his generosity, would take care of everything. *"Allah karim, Allah karim."*

The fatalistic phrase seemed to strike the Englishman physically.

"Very well—O Jima. Do you think you could give God some assistance by ordering your men to start digging in? They haven't done a thing since we took this place. Nothing. Not so much as a trench."

"Eh?"

"Trenches! Fortifications! Order them to start digging. And order at least half of them to occupy the high ground. You've got all of them bottled up down here just to make sure none of the civilians run off. A few bombs would wipe out the lot."

"O Jima. Why must I keep reminding you to say that, Mr. Patrick?"

"O Jima."

"And will it quiet your heart if I give those orders?"

We nodded.

"Then I'll give them. Now get out of my sight, the both of you."

As we stood to go, the furious expression on Jima's face composed itself into an arid smile.

"Perhaps it will also quiet your hearts to know that in two weeks' time, I'll have many more than seven hundred men, more than enough to hold this town. I'll have enough to take Albara itself if I choose."

And where was he to get this vast army? We would find out when it was time, he answered cryptically. And what if the Ethiopians attacked before then?

"*Allah karim.* Don't worry."

Walking outside, I thought of his remark—he would have enough men to seize the capital—remembered the lines on Nordstrand's maps, and felt an unpleasant fullness in my head. A wipeout. They had to be planning a wipeout at Karu. There would be no dialogue, democratic or otherwise.

———————

Like the nomadic warriors of the past, the Huns, the Visigoths, and the Arab horsemen they claimed as ancestors, the Beni-Hamid tended to extremes. Periods of furious activity gave way to near-total inertia. The battle for Umm-Tajer having sated temporarily their need for fighting, they had fallen into the comfortable indolence of occupation troops. The romantic view of the desert nomad holds that he is something like a cowboy, a man who willingly accepts the hardships of his existence because he knows they are the price he pays for freedom. In fact, the nomad despises the hardships; he doesn't like drinking muddy water, eating mush and unleavened bread, sleeping on rocky ground; and he doesn't love the desert. It is to him a thing of unremitting cruelty, a superior enemy to which he must submit. Far from scorning comforts, he dreams of them (whence comes the Koranic dream of paradise, a garden filled with sweet water and women), and he takes full advantage of them if they are offered to him. Umm-Tajer was a squalid place to me, but to men who had lived most of their lives in the open or in tents, it was as close to Edenic as anything they were likely to find in this world. They found it a novelty to sleep with roofs over their heads and with walls to shield them from the cold night winds; the straw beds in the huts were as down to backs accustomed to lying on gravel where scorpions crawled; they delighted in lolling around the oasis, where there was shade from the sun and clear water in the wells and dates for the picking; a few of the young girls who had remained in the village had proved willing; when the men had a hungering for fresh meat, all they had to do was shove a Kalashnikov in the face of some defenseless shepherd and expropriate a few goats in the name of the revolution; and then, bellies full, how pleasant to recline beside campfires reciting love ballads and oral poetry handed down from past generations, the epic sagas of ancient battles. As Osman had told us, the Beni-Hamid liked to describe themselves as "warriors and the heirs of glory."

And it proved very difficult to force men who saw themselves as heirs of glory to dig foxholes and trenches. That was common labor, demeaning and beneath their warrior dignity. Besides, defensive warfare was as alien to them as snow. It was only with the greatest effort that Moody and I got them to scrape out a few shallow shelter trenches and fighting holes. Even then, some of them impressed villagers as labor gangs and forced them to wield the shovels. None of them wanted to go up on the ridges, where there would be no dates for the picking, no fresh meat, and no willing young girls. Finally, Osman, who understood what was coming, ordered a few guerrilla "officers" at gunpoint to take their men up. Up they went, reluctantly, sullenly, leading mules laden with waterskins in which the well's sweet water would soon putrify. Watching the unhappy column trudging up the mountainside, I saw that the hard, sharp instrument we had fashioned was already growing rusty and dull, and looking at the pitiful defensive works, which would not protect any of them from anything more lethal than a mortar shell, I saw a first-class catastrophe in the making. Nordstrand, with the loyalty he commanded from them, would have been a help to us; but he spent most of his time huddling in more conferences with Jima. Apparently their mysterious little plans needed some refinement.

In this way, three days passed. By the third day, Moody was frantic and spooked. He took a tour of the perimeter, said he could punch a hole through it with a platoon of Sandhurst cadets, and announced that he'd come to a decision: he was going to radio Colfax for authorization to exfiltrate immediately.

"We've earned our pay, Charlie. We don't have to muck it here any longer, waiting to hear what they decide in this democratic dialogue they're going to hold."

Nordstrand was off conferring with Jima for the third time in as many days. Moody quickly assembled the transceiver, coded the message, and tapped it out. "Ethiopian counter attack imminent . . . position here untenable . . . request (beg, plead) permission to begin exfiltration immediately." A red light on the black facia winked, indicating the message had gone through, but no reply came. "Must have been garbled at the other end," the Englishman said, and retransmitted. We waited twenty minutes or so, usually the time it took to decode the incoming traffic and send a reply. Again, there was none. Moody disassembled the radio, tinkered with various circuits and switches, could find nothing wrong, and sent out a third repeat. We waited another twenty minutes, thirty, forty-five. Nothing.

"Must be atmospherics. Or perhaps the hills around here are blocking the signal somehow." Moody's effort to control the rising panic in his voice was not very successful. "Look, I'm going to have this thing hauled up to some higher ground and try transmitting from there."

Moody rounded up a few men. They were lashing the transceiver to a mule when Nordstrand returned. Dressed in his gone-native outfit, face carboned, his carnivore's eyes hidden behind the silvered lenses, he came down the rutted street with his usual head-down charge. I guessed he was lost in thought, because he tripped over a palm log anyone but a blind man could have seen. Recovering his balance instantly, he spotted Moody and veered off in that direction. It was then that I noticed the scars had become inflamed, swelling his cheeks into two red oblong lumps. He was sweating heavily.

"What the hell have you got there, Moody?"

"What the hell does it look like? The radio."

"And just where you heading with the radio?"

"Bugger off, you bastard."

"Where're you heading with that goddamned radio?"

"I said bugger off, Nordstrand."

"General, I thought things were settled between you and me."

"It's time they got unsettled again."

"You little yellow limey sphincter. *I'll* unsettle things."

Nordstrand reached under the folds of his robe, drew an automatic and fired three or four rounds at the transceiver. The men who had been loading it onto the mule flung themselves out of the way, the mule screamed and, gut-shot, trotted down the street trailing a length of bluish-grey intestine before it realized it was dead and rolled over onto its side, the radio beneath it.

With Nordstrand laughing maniacally behind us, Moody and I ran up to the animal, Moody hollering back at the American, "You insane bastard. I'll kill you, god damn you, so help me, I'll kill you, you insane bastard."

The rebels, more than a little perplexed by the assassination of the mule, helped me roll the carcass over onto its other side.

"Cut off, Charlie. Jesus. Jesus, he's cut us off."

"All right! Shut up."

"We are entirely cut off out here."

The radio's metal case had been crushed by the mule's weight. I prised it open with a knife, and yes, we were cut off. The transceiver facia was a mass of smashed dials and bent switches, and the transistor circuits showing through a hole in the facia were in their own way as sickening a sight as the gut hanging out of the mule's torn belly.

"*We are cut off, Charlie.*"

"*Shut up,* god damn you."

I looked behind. Nordstrand had gone back into the hut. A small crowd of civilians had gathered in the street to see what the commotion was. The heat shimmer gave their figures a look of insubstantiality.

"I'm going to kill that maniac. So help me, I'll kill him. He shot the radio to pieces."

"He didn't shoot it."

"Look at it, you fool! Isn't anyone sane around here? Look at it. Goddamned hole right through it."

"There's no bullet hole in the case, Moody."

"What are you now, Charlie? A detective?"

"There's no bullet hole in the case. He missed it, Pat. He fired at it from ten feet away and missed it."

"What do I give a damn about his marksmanship? Result's the same, isn't it? Radio's a pile of junk and we are cut off. So help me I've a good mind to go in there right now and blow that madman's head off."

The rebels said they were going to find another animal to haul the carcass away. A cloud of flies hummed around the gooey mass oozing from the holes the nine-millimeters had plowed through the mule's side.

"You blow his head off and Jima'll have you against a wall five minutes later."

"I'll tell you one thing. I'm moving my gear out of there. If I'm around that psychotic another five minutes I'll kill him."

"All right. All right. Go camp somewhere else then. Just keep your head. Nordstrand's going blind."

I dreamt that night. Dark-limbed figures swathed in white danced in the dream. The priest's face appeared, bloated to several times its normal size and distorted by its ravisher's smile. He raised a long knife to cut someone's face— my face. The knife glinted in a huge flame that rose, fell, rose again, and peaked in the wind. Then I felt the blade dig into my flesh, a scalding rush of pain, and someone moaned in the background. *I am certainly fire, I am fire, I am fire.*

"I'm on fire. I'm on fire."

Semiconscious, not yet able to distinguish nightmare from reality, I heard the voice coming from what seemed a mile away. "On fire. Fire."

I sat upright, instinctively closing my fingers around the butt-grip of my automatic. Faint moonlight slanting through the glassless window showed Nordstrand rolling from side to side on his cot.

"Burning up," he said in a tight voice, as if he was speaking through clenched teeth. "I'm on fire."

"Nordstrand," I whispered. "You awake?"

"No sleep for hours. Burning up."

I got a flashlight from my pack. The beam pierced the cavelike darkness and fell on Nordstrand's face, drenched in sweat. Pus leaked from the scabrous scars.

"Turn that goddamned light off. Hurts my eyes." His lips worked slowly, painfully.

I flicked off the flashlight and lit a new kerosene lamp, hoping he would not fly into a rage and smash it.

"Told you, turn that goddamned light off."

"I did. I've got the lamp on."

"Turn it down. Hurts my eyes."

"It's down as low as I can get it."

"I'm on fire."

I laid the back of my hand across his forehead. He certainly was on fire. Nordstrand pulled my hand away and, shielding his eyes, swung himself into a sitting position. The movement appeared to require all his strength.

"Gage, you don't do something about that light and I'll break your arms."

"In a minute. Lie back. You've got one hell of a fever."

"I haven't got any fever . . . just hot is all—" He broke

off and slumped backward, striking his head against the wall. "Not sick . . . can't be . . . I've got to be there . . . never do it right without me."

Taking the lantern, I went out and walked to the neighboring shack where Moody had moved himself. I woke him and told him Nordstrand was in bad shape, on the edge of delirium.

"Good," the Englishman replied sleepily. "Hope it's terminal."

"Get your medical kit."

"I hope he dies from whatever it is."

"C'mon. You're our resident hypochondriac. Maybe you know what it is."

"Who cares what it is as long as he dies from it."

"Get your goddamned kit and let's go."

Nordstrand had lapsed into a half-conscious state. While I held the lamp, Moody shoved a thermometer into his mouth. He had to pry his jaw open to do it. Then he pressed the fiery, puscous sores, and Nordstrand shuddered and gave out a moan, the first time I had seen him show pain.

"Light . . . out . . . out of my eyes . . . hurts my eyes," he mumbled with his tongue against the roof of his mouth.

Moody removed the thermometer. Squinting, he held it up to the light and sucked in a breath.

"This couldn't have come on him all of a sudden. Must have had a fever for some time now."

"What is it?"

"A hundred and five."

"What would give him a temperature like that?"

"Any number of things. Severe case of typhoid or hepatitis could do it, but he hasn't got any other symptoms of those. He does have tetanus for sure. Fever. Stiffness in his facial muscles and joints. I'd say it was the knife that did it. Osman used it to . . . well, you know what Osman did with it. It was probably crawling with filth. Absolutely tetanus, but I don't understand the blindness, the sensitivity to light."

"No," Nordstrand groaned. "No-ooo."

"He must have something else as well."

"No tetanus . . . won't stop me that way, weak sister."

Conscious again, Nordstrand heaved himself to his feet and stood, wobbling, his bear's eyes slitted against the lantern light. "Won't stop me with that . . . one stroke and it'll be over . . . one clean stroke . . . thought things settled . . . you goddamned shit-licker . . ." He swiped at Moody's head, but, nearly blind, missed by several inches and pawed the air, the force of his swing toppling him over.

"Can't see with that light . . . can't . . . Gage, you bastard . . . trying to stop me too?" He got to his hands and knees, then to one knee, like a boxer taking the mandatory eight. "You trying to stop me with this tetanus crap? Who told you? Jima? Knew Moody would try, but not you. No convictions, trouble with both of you." He stood again, rocking from side to side. His mouth formed a rigid, crooked, crazy grin. "Oh, that you would become cocky . . . oh, if you would still have convictions . . . Nietzsche."

"Take it easy. Lie back. You've got tetanus and a temperature of a hundred and five."

"No tetanus. Bastard."

Nordstrand lurched toward me. I shoved him back. He staggered a moment or two, tottery as a drunk, then collapsed onto the bed and into unconsciousness.

"Here. Give him these." Moody handed me two tetracycline tablets. "They are the very last we've got. If that gear hadn't been lost, we'd have enough to take care of him. I'll fetch the medic."

The medic, or doctor, as he liked to style himself, came in carrying a canvas kit bag and wearing a makeshift surgical apron imprinted with floral patterns of dried bloodstains. He was irritated by this interruption. He had, he told us in a peevish tone, just finished an emergency amputation of a man dying of gangrene. He had 120 casualties to look after, and only two men to assist him, both incompetents, and his only medicines were those captured from the Ethiopians. He did not appreciate being called away to treat someone with a mere fever, even if that someone was Mr. Jeremy.

"Mr. Jeremy has considerably more than a mere fever," said Moody. "And if anything happens, Jima will hold you responsible."

The warning cut short the medic's complaint. He examined Nordstrand, gave him a shot of penicillin, and wrapped him in a heavy goat-hair blanket to sweat the poisons out of him. Then he gave his diagnosis:

"Mr. Jeremy is very sick."

"That's quite brilliant. Sick with what?"

The medic confirmed blood poisoning. Nordstrand's peculiar blindness was actually photophobia (the man appeared pleased by the way he tossed off the professional-sounding word), an intolerance to light. It's cause was probably Rift Valley Fever. "It's a common disease," the medic went on in his musical English. "In most cases, the impairment of vision is mild and temporary. But Mr. Jeremy appears to have an extreme case."

"Meaning what?"

"The impairment could become permanent. He could even go blind if he's not treated properly. And the tetanus, that could kill him. I don't have any more tetanus vaccine. I can give him a little antibiotic each day, only a half-dosage. I haven't enough. That could make him well enough to travel in a few days. Then you must take him to Sudan. They have proper doctors there."

"It's two hundred kilometers to Sudan. He couldn't possibly make the trip on camelback."

"Perhaps Jima will give you one of the captured Land-Rovers. You could make it in two days, a day if you're lucky."

"Jima is rather fond of his Land-Rovers. Part of his armored corps, you know."

The medic shrugged fatalistically.

"Whatever God wills."

Nordstrand's temperature climbed to a hundred and six the next day, where it held briefly before rising another degree. An extreme case. Sweat poured from him in mercury streams, and his skin was so hot to touch I wondered why he did not burst into flame. *I am certainly fire.* It would be a fitting end, I thought. His physical fever consuming his body as the other infections had consumed his spirit until nothing remained of Nordstrand but cinder and ash.

His delirium increased in proportion to his temperature. His fever-cracked lips moving slowly, he raved incoherently, uttered a few lucid phrases, raved some more. An ambush . . . had to be there . . . no margin for error . . . victory in a single stroke. Then, sinking into a condition where hallucination merges with reality, he thought I was Jima and began arguing with me in a mixture of Arabic and English. What laws, Jima? The laws of hospitality? What laws? No laws except the ones you make. I'll see that it doesn't fail . . . in one stroke . . . why did you tell Gage and Moody . . . damned Arabs can't keep their mouths shut . . . my throat's on fire. Water. Moody doesn't like the water . . . weak sister . . . you will be the node of the rebellion . . . in the Koran, Jima, *What hinders me from killing thee? Nothing.* Nothing hinders you from killing them . . . a perfect ambush, Jima. Destined to do it . . . a man must follow his nature, you understand that? His nature is his fate . . . also in the Koran, isn't it . . . the Chapter of the Night Journey . . . fate . . . a man's . . . *every man's fate is bound around his neck like a collar which he cannot get off* . . . only twenty-five men . . . the best . . . it will be shaped like the English letter *L*, here . . . yes . . . the Chapter of the Night Journey. Night, dark. Eyes all right in the dark now, but I'm burning up . . . thirsty . . . Yassin! *Jib myim* . . . bring me water."

The medic came again and pumped another half-dose of penicillin into him, lanced the blackish-red poisons from his facial sores, dressed them, and applied gauze patches to his eyes.

"That should ease the photophobia," he said. "Try to keep his temperature down. Another degree or two and he'll be dead. Don't touch the dressings. Rift Valley Fever is very contagious. It's communicated through contact with the diseased tissue."

Once again pleased with his professional terminology, the medic slung his kit over his shoulder and left. Moody, paling at the word *contagious*, walked behind him, saying he would try to persuade Jima to give us a Land-Rover and guides for an evacuation.

Nordstrand kept raving about his thirst. I took the goat-skin from its peg on the wall, shoved the spigot in his mouth, and squirted a jet of water down his parched throat. He vomited it up immediately, so I held a damp cloth to his lips, recoiling when my arm brushed against the dressings, sticky and stained a purplish yellow.

Nordstrand regained consciousness a quarter of an hour later. I should say he passed from total delirium into a state of partial lucidity. Propping himself on his elbows, his movements like those of a man heavily sedated, he plucked the patches from his eyes, which gleamed with an unhealthy iridescence.

"Jesus, Jesus!" He shut his eyes against the stabs of light lancing through the window. "I can't see!"

I replaced the gauze, then hung a blanket over the window so that the sunlight became a faint translucence, like the glow from a distant fire.

"Is that better?"

"Better."

"You've got an interesting condition, Nordstrand. You can only see when you're blindfolded."

"That you, Charlie Gage?"

I said it was.

"Ache. Ache all over. Hardly talk."

"You were just talking plenty."

"Had this dream. Dreamt someone said I'm going to be evacked to Sudan. Can't go. Not finished yet. It can't go through without me."

"No margin for error, right?"

"Right. None."

"You weren't dreaming. That was the medic. He said you've got to be evacuated to Sudan as soon as you're well enough to travel. You've got tetanus, an acute case of Rift Valley Fever, and a temperature that would kill most people."

At this, he bolted upright, the blanket falling away to reveal his sweat-drenched shirt.

"Can't go . . . I've got to see it through . . . this fever, it won't stop me . . ."

"Listen. It causes temporary blindness. If you don't take

it easy, it'll be permanent, and you won't see anything through, ever."

"I've got to be there. I've got to see it happen. Get this, Charlie Gage. I'm counting on you not to let them evacuate me. You understand? I've got to see this one thing through. It would be a fulfillment." His arm, the arm that bore the ineradicable mark of his old wound, reached out and he gripped my wrist. "*A fulfillment.*"

"I'll give it to you straight. You might not make it." I paused to measure the blow. "You might die if your fever gets any worse."

His only reaction was to turn his blinded, scarred, and swollen face toward me and repeat hoarsely: "A fulfillment."

"Did you hear me?"

"I heard you."

"You've got a temperature of one hundred and seven. It's usually all over at a hundred and nine or ten." I paused again, to let that sink in. Nordstrand's head fell back against the cot and he lay with his white-patched eyes facing the ceiling. He lay like that for a long time. A momentary spasm, like a heatstroke convulsion, racked him. Then he raised his arm again, and again took hold of my wrist, and I looked at the scar the shrapnel had left, ugly and indelible, like the mark of Cain.

"It's got to go through, with me or without me."

Yes, yes, it had to go through, with him or without.

"Do you know what the secret of the Roman legions was, Charlie? Before they turned into dross? Do you know how they won?"

No, I didn't know.

"By the terror of their name, Charlie Gage. That's what we're going to do. Inflict them with terror."

Right, that's what we would do.

"The secret to winning wars like this one is terror, Charlie Gage. *Inflict terror.*"

I nodded, though he could not see me. That was the ticket, all right. A little terror went a long way.

"You're the only one besides me who can make sure they do it right. I want you to handle it if I'm not on my feet. You and me, Charlie Gage, we've . . ."

"We've got more in common than I thought."

"That's right. Get my maps out of my pack. Follow what I say. Listen closely, Charlie. There won't be any margin for error."

He gave me the details—not all of them because he occasionally plunged into delusionary gibberish: but I heard enough to gain a new appreciation of the lengths to which Nordstrand would go to fulfill his peculiar desires, of the fecundity of his morbid imagination, and of his genius. Yes, genius, for the plan did reflect a kind of appalling brilliance.

While he spoke, his hand never relaxed its grip on my wrist. My forearm was tingling with numbness when he finished. The effort had completely exhausted him, and he spoke in a whisper.

"That's it, Charlie Gage. You'll handle it if I can't."

I said, yes, I would, and I almost meant it. My first reaction to his scheme was one of unholy excitement. It could work! I exclaimed to myself, the thought not my own. The words seemed to charge from his brain, advance through our linked arms, and invade and occupy my mind. It could work! I had an image of him then, whirling in the abyss with his arms outstretched and beckoning me to follow; and I saw myself, tottering on the brink, feeling the temptation some people experience on high bridges or the roofs of skyscrapers, the irrational temptation to jump. It was remarkable. He was remarkable. Prostrate and half-deranged with fever, his will continued to exert some inexplicable power over mine. I resisted him, took a step back from the brink as it were, and tried to pry his fingers loose from my wrist. He tightened them, dug them into my flesh.

"Where are you going?"

"Nowhere. You need some rest."

He relaxed his hold slightly.

"Terror, Charlie Gage. *Inflict terror.*"

And I tore loose from him and ran outside.

I ran on up the dusty, dung-spattered, heat-tormented street toward the prisoners' compound, ran quickly to avoid thinking and the paralysis that comes from thinking.

Murrah, his child-sized bush hat pushed low over his eyes, was standing by the gate and smoking idly.

I slowed to a walk, so I wouldn't draw any attention, and approached him with a casual air.

"Mr. Charlie . . ."

"Let's talk about the great dictator."

Murrah's agile mind picked up the code.

"In the film, the great dictator was a comic figure."

"This one isn't so funny anymore." I had been breathing sand for six months, and the short run had made my lungs raw. Breathing hard, I gave him the highlights. He showed no emotion, said nothing and did nothing except to pull out another cigarette and light it off the stub of the first.

"The prisoners and the ambush are going to move out from here three days before the conference. That'll give them time to get into position, and that gives us"—I stressed the pronoun—"four days to do something."

"So, it's to be a type of coup, Mr. Charlie."

"Coup, assassination, you can call it whatever you like. It's murder, mass murder, and we've got four days to do something about it."

Murrah cocked his head toward the sky, where a vapor trail dissolved into an imitation of a high stratus cloud.

"The Ethiopians, they'll attack before then, I think. In a day or two, perhaps even in hours."

"Let's hope so," I said, not believing I had said it. "If he's busy with them, he won't have time to stage any coup."

"And what if he wins the battle? What will he do then? Then he will have the time and the power to do whatever he wishes."

It was not a statement but an appeal.

"So you see, it's not just a question of stopping him this one time, but of stopping him for good, Mr. Charlie."

"Are we speaking hypothetically again?"

"No."

"All right, I'll do it."

"How?"

"You are going to pass the word that I want to inspect the missiles. We're expecting an air raid, and I'm worried that the missiles have taken a good deal of knocking about and I want to make sure they'll fire properly. Understood?"

"Pass the word?"

"Tell the men, the fighters, your future martyrs. Tell them that the missile crews are to come to me as soon as possible for an inspection."

"Mr. Charlie, if I do that, and then it's discovered what you've done—"

I wrapped one hand around the back of Murrah's neck and pressed my thumb into the hollow behind his ear.

"Don't play with me, Kasu. You're not getting any free lunches. You're in this, and you'll do exactly as I say."

"Too risky," he said, wincing against the pressure on his nerve.

"How would you like it if Jima found out about what you did back at Ras el-Sultan? How you betrayed him to your old chums from the FLN?"

Murrah gave me a nod of acquiescence.

"You can start by finding me a screwdriver and a pair of pliers."

Murrah laughed sardonically at this request. There were no such tools in Umm-Tajer because there were no machines.

"There used to be machines—tanks and APCs. Some of the Ethiopians' tools must be lying around."

"I'll try, Mr. Charlie."

"You'll do it."

Walking back down the street toward the hut, I felt myself crossing the psychological no-man's-land that lies between a decision to do something desperate and the actual doing of it. A tightness, like the onset of a heart attack, clutched my chest, my head swam, and the mosque with its limestone minaret, the shacks hedging both sides of the street, even the earth I was walking on, seemed as insubstantial as the mirage rippling up from the valley below, seemed on the verge of a sudden dissolution that would leave me alone and adrift in referenceless space.

Three of Jima's bodyguards were standing by the door of the hut. Their demeanor was not casual, like that of the other guerrillas sauntering about. They exuded vigilance. Paranoia stabbed me. *They know, I thought. They know.*

They've found out already. I waved to them, convinced my every move betrayed me. They returned the gesture, but I imagined them following me with suspicious eyes as I opened the door and the voice inside my head cried again, *They know, they know.*

Jima, the medic, and Moody were inside, the medic bending over Nordstrand, who was sleeping fitfully.

"You will give whatever is needed to make him well again," Jima snapped, "or by God I'll have your head."

The phrase was not a figure of speech. Compliantly, the medic removed an antibiotic Syrette from his kit and pumped a full dosage into Nordstrand's arm. Then he placed three more Syrettes in Moody's hand, instructing him to administer one shot each day, and left without another word.

"God willing, Mr. Jeremy will be well again," Jima said, speaking to no one in particular. He gently stroked Nordstrand's damp forehead, a gesture of tenderness that disgusted me. "You will be well again, Mr. Jeremy."

"What the hell is all this?"

"Have a guess," Moody answered with false cheerfulness. "The old boy won't allow Nordstrand to be evacuated. Told him what the medic said. He fetched the poor fellow and ordered him to get Mr. Jeremy back on his feet, shortages or no. Did you see our three friends outside? Jima's got it into his head that we might try to spirit Nordstrand out of here on our own. Those three are there to make sure we stay put. We're confined to base, so to speak. Can't leave the city limits."

"*Wha-at?*"

"We're as good as marooned, Charlie."

"Speak in Arabic, the both of you."

A marooned man is prone to recklessness. Deciding to take another blind leap, I turned to Jima and told him Moody and I would have to leave in four days.

I could sense him turning on his aura of command, amplifying the power of a will unaccustomed to opposition.

Nordstrand, I went on, had told me about the ambush and instructed me to lead it in case he hadn't recovered in time.

Jima only gave me a sidelong, skeptical glance.

"What ambush, Mr. Charlie?"

"You know what ambush."

"I don't believe he told you anything."

"Then how did I find out about it? Only you and he knew about it. Did you tell me?"

"Don't be impertinent. You are to lead the ambush if he isn't well? *You*. You're not capable of it."

"Apparently Nordstrand thinks I am. I'll need Moody to help me."

"I don't believe you."

"Then wake him and ask him."

Jima started toward Nordstrand's cot, then hesitated.

"Wake him and ask him. Now."

"He told you. Who have you told?"

"No one."

"And you won't tell anyone, either."

"Absolutely."

"God willing, Mr. Jeremy will be well."

"*Inshallah*."

Jima opened the door to leave, then stopped and closed it.

"I'm curious. Now that you know of it, what do you think of it?"

"It could work."

"It must work."

"It will be very risky. It will require precise timing and absolute secrecy."

"That's why I want Mr. Jeremy to lead it."

"If there are any survivors . . ."

"There won't be any survivors."

"But if there are . . ."

"If Mr. Jeremy leads it, there won't be any survivors."

"I'm sure of that. But in case there are . . . tell me if I understand this correctly. By agreeing to your request to hold this conference—"

"My *demand*, Mr. Charlie."

"By agreeing to your demand for this conference, the men who take part in it will be your guests. To turn on them this way would . . ." I paused, searching for the right Arabic phrase . . . "it would violate the code of hospitality. That code is very important, isn't it? Almost sacred?"

Jima's nod was nearly imperceptible in the dim light.

"Then why are you planning to break it?"

"That is an impertinent question."

"Did you ask me what I thought about this plan because you have some doubts about it?"

"That is a very impertinent question."

"I'm curious too."

He thumped his fist against his sunken chest, and answered fiercely:

"You want to know why? Because of this. This thing that's eating me." He struck his chest again, as if he meant to beat the tuberculosis out of his lungs. "And because I have no sons who could do my work for me. I have been cursed with daughters. For twenty years I've dreamed of seeing an Islamic Republic in Bejaya. For twenty years I've fought for it, fought everybody, by God. For twenty years I've waited. I no longer have the time to wait. I no longer have the time to fight both my enemies and the Ethiopians, but I will see an Islamic Republic in Bejaya. I will see that day. Do you hear me? If this plan works, God willing, it will hasten that day. It will take care of my enemies in one stroke. One stroke, by God, and leave me free to take care of the Ethiopians. Those bastards want a 'unity conference,' do they? Well, they'll get one. All the factions will be united under Muhammad Jima, and with that many men and these weapons, I'll defeat the Ethiopians in a year, if God wills."

"One stroke. That's what Mr. Jeremy said to me. One stroke."

"Yes! One stroke. Bairu, Hassab, and the third man. *Khalas.*"

"That still leaves the three who won't be at the conference."

"They won't learn anything. There will be no survivors!"

Out of the corner of my eye, I saw a perplexed Moody staring at us. He opened his mouth to say something. I gestured to him to keep silent.

"So now you know why, Mr. Charlie, but I don't think you understand, because you're young and have your health, God be praised. You don't know what it's like not to have time." Jima cracked open the door, admitting a rectangle of light in which his pocked sun-dried face, its creases almost indistinguishable from the tribal markings, took on a muddy brown color. "You don't know what it's like to be a sick old man."

The words "sick old man," with their implied appeal to pity, made me vaguely nauseous.

"If you and Mr. Patrick lead the ambush and it fails, you won't live. You know that, don't you?"

"The arrangement is, the three of us alive for half a million dollars."

Jima shrugged indifferently.

"I can always say you were killed by the Ethiopians."

After he left, Moody demanded to know the meaning behind all this cryptic talk about an ambush. Nordstrand stirred just then and muttered something incomprehensible, the words falling off to a succession of labored breaths.

"Outside," I said.

The afternoon sun was piercing after the twilight inside. We sat in the shade of a house on the opposite side of the street, which was no wider than an alley. Our watchdogs smiled amicably but, with subtle changes in posture and slight movements of their rifles, warned us not to stray far. An old man, the skin of his feet dust-grey and cracked, shuffled by, leading a donkey with brush piles on its back.

With a twig, I drew a crude map in the dirt, trying to look as if I were merely doodling.

"The council's headquarters are somewhere out here." I pointed to my representation of the mountains east of Karu. "The supposition is that Bairu, Hassab, and the others will come to this conference in style, that is, by Land-Rover. The only decent route between their headquarters and Karu is this wadi." I pointed to the squiggly line I had drawn. "It leads through this pass here. That's where the ambush will be sprung."

"One stroke. How tidy. Who does the ambushing?"

"Twenty-five men from Jima's bodyguard. They're most loyal to him and most likely to keep their mouths shut—at least for a while, for long enough. They'll be dressed in

Ethiopian uniforms that were stripped off the corpses after we took this place. That's the pleasant part."

Standing off to one side, a group of four or five small children watched us intently, fear and curiosity commingled in their eyes.

"The ambush party is going to have the prisoners in tow. The plan is to tell them that they're being taken to the provincial border to be handed over to the EDRP. They'll be tied up and blindfolded, so they won't know where they are or what the hell is going on. The whole bunch are to move out of here at night, so no one else knows what's going on either. Okay. The ambush sets in. Hassab's and Bairu's convoy comes rattling through the pass, fat, dumb, and happy. *Ratta-tat-tat, boom-boom,* so much for the democratic dialogue. They're annihilated. No survivors. Jima's won the ball game."

"You seem to have got ahead of yourself."

"The bodyguard will be camouflaged as Ethiopians, remember? The idea is to make it look as if government soldiers have sprung the ambush. If he's nothing else, Nordstrand's thorough. He's figured the convoy will be traveling under armed escort, and that the escort will shoot back after the ambush is sprung. If any of the Beni-Hamid are killed, their bodies will be left at the ambush site to make the hoax look authentic. The tribal markings would identify them, but I suppose he's figured some way to take care of that. Blow their faces off, I suppose. That's also where the prisoners come in. A handful of them are going to be with the ambush, and they'll be massacred and their corpses will be scattered around in case none of Jima's men are killed. The rest will be with Jima at Karu, and they'll be executed after Jima gets word the ambush has been sprung. He'll message council headquarters, telling them that Bairu, Hassab, and the others have been killed in an ambush. He promises to find the Ethiopian bastards who did it. He waits a day or two, then sends another message: his men have tracked down the Ethiopians and killed them. Jima invites the other members for a look. The corpses at Karu are put on display. They'll be stage props. See the dead Ethiopians. Then a tour of the ambush site.

More dead Ethiopians. Jima is now the man of the hour. The NIIF has avenged the killers of the revolution's leaders. Jima then fills two of the vacant seats with men of his own choosing. Being the man of the hour, he fills the third with himself and elects himself chairman of the directorate. He's it. The number one. The node of the rebellion."

"The what?"

"Nordstrand's phrase."

"Nordstrand thought up this entire monstrosity?"

"Oh, he dreamed up the concept, and I guess Jima added the details. Kind of a joint project."

Moody rested his head against the wall. With his eyes closed, his skin parched and peeling from exposure, he looked as if he had aged a decade in the past six months. The children continued to stare at us, all of them perfectly still except when they swatted at the flies which lighted on their umber faces. The boldest, a boy of seven or eight, took a few steps toward us, then hesitated, uncertain if he should come any closer.

"It's an awfully complicated plan, Charlie. Something could go wrong with it."

"It's not that complicated, and I'm going on the assumption that it'll work."

"I wonder what would happen if we walked in there right now and put Mr. Jeremy out of his misery."

"I told you a long time ago, the only way to get rid of him would be to kill him. Too late for that now. We've got three of Jima's goons on the door."

His fear overcome by fascination, the boy approached me. Tentatively he poked my forearm, then looked at his fingertip to see if my white color had come off. Amused, one of the guards told him that if he rubbed hard enough the *ferengei*'s paleness would peel off like paint.

"Go on," I said. "Rub hard."

"You speak Arabic."

"Yes."

"You speak Arabic, but you're the color of a white camel."

The guards roared with laughter.

"Your friend speaks Arabic too?"

"Of course," called another of the guards. "Also having the color of a camel, he too speaks Arabic."

"Yes, I speak Arabic," Moody said. "And I want you to go away."

The boy stood fast, staring at Moody's tanned face, grey eyes, and light hair.

"It's said in the village that you and your friends are prisoners of the *jebha*. Is that true?"

"What're you, a bloody spy?"

"*Shu?*"

"Yes, we're prisoners."

Timidly at first, then with vigor, the boy rubbed my arm with his knuckles until a red spot appeared.

"There. You see. My whiteness has gone away and I've turned red."

Captivated, he watched the redness fade. In a playful mood, he rubbed again, his brows knit with concentration.

"What have you got in mind, Charlie?"

"Murrah reckons the Ethiopians are going to counterattack in a day or two at most. I'm going to give them every chance to win. Then there won't be any Jima to spring any ambushes. No NIIF either."

"Right, Charlie. And maybe no us. You're talking about those SAM-7s, aren't you?"

"I am. Disassemble the IR warhead, disconnect the circuits to the servo motor, and you've got an unguided missile."

"Charlie. You do realize what you're saying, don't you? We'd be sabotaging our own mission, for God's sake." Moody's voice was low but intense. "A sustained air raid would blow this wretched little valley into dust."

"It's dust already."

"The red won't stay!" the boy cried in frustration. "The red won't stay."

"Ya, boy!" one of the guards laughed. "Whoever heard of a red camel?"

The boy tried again, rubbing until my skin felt raw as sandpaper.

"The bombs'll fall on them as well. These kids."

"Goddamnit, I know that. You were always bitching about my indecisiveness. Your problem is that you want to commit the perfect act, the act with no unpleasant consequences. You want to act, but you don't want your morals to suffer. It's a question of balancing one thing against the other. If Jima's willing to go these lengths to get power, you can imagine what he'll do to hold on to it. Don't imagine. I can predict it. Jima won't be able to keep the assassinations secret. At least one of the men who was in on the ambush will start talking. It's inevitable, and Jima knows it. What he doesn't know is which one. The best way to make sure none of them talks is to kill all of them. Then he'll have to kill whoever kills them, and so on, and we'll be ultimately responsible. Murrah's right on that score. We'll be responsible if we don't do something to stop him."

"Murrah. And what do you think will happen here if his sort take over? They won't install any Swiss democracy. That's also predictable."

"At least those other devils are trying to change things. At least they want to bring this place out of the Bronze Age. At least they're not holding ceremonies like the one we saw. It's a case of choosing your devil, Moody."

"The red won't stay!" the boy cried again. A guard motioned with a rifle and told him to run along and leave the foreigners alone.

"You heard him. Run along now."

"Do you have a gift?"

"Gift?"

"*Bakshish.*"

"Bloody hell. No. I mean, *la, la*—no, no. Wait. Here take this."

Moody took a box of cigarettes from his shirt pocket and handed him the foil wrapper. Scratching his robe, which appeared to be made of old sandbags stitched together, the boy held the wrapper and gazed in wonder at its silvery glint.

"What is this?"

"In English, it's called tinfoil."

"What is English?"

"It's a language. In the language of English, that is called tinfoil. Ti-in-foy-al."

"Tinfoal."

"Let's not talk politics, Charlie. The one thing I really don't understand is why you committed us to leading that ambush if Nordstrand can't. And he won't. The condition he's in, he won't be in any sort of shape to lead any ambushes in only four days."

"That's an insurance policy in case the Ethiopians don't attack. It's also our ticket out of here. If it comes to that, we'll lead the column out of here. Then, one fine night along the way, we'll steal one of the Land-Rovers and take off for Sudan. I figure the ambush party will forget about shooting anybody up and take off after us. We'll be just like the heroes in the westerns, drawing the bad guys off. As for Mr. Jeremy, sorry about that. He stays here with his blood brothers."

"We'll steal a Land-Rover and just buzz off into the desert. Heroes in the westerns. Of course. Do be serious, Charlie."

I answered Moody by pulling the antibiotic Syrettes from his pocket, breaking them, and spilling the fluid on the ground.

"Now Nordstrand doesn't have a prayer in hell of recovering on time."

"Tinfoal, is that right?"

"Yes, that's right," Moody answered irritably.

"Tinfoal." The boy held the wrapper out flat, turning it this way and that. "Why, it's like a mirror! A mirror made of paper."

"Yes. I've given you a paper mirror. Now you go. Understand? Go. Go."

The boy smiled brightly. Flies clung to the corners of his mouth, nibbling on the crumbs of food left from his last meal.

"Charlie, really. If there is an air raid and kids like this one are blown to tatters, do you really think you could live with that on your conscience?"

"I don't know. I'm just getting reacquainted with my conscience."

"You've given me a paper mirror. You are my friend, even if you're a prisoner of the *jebha*."

Turning suddenly, he ran toward the other children and exclaimed, "The foreigner has given me a tinfoal. A tinfoal is a paper mirror." Then they all went down the street, jabbering excitedly about the camel-colored man who had given them a paper mirror.

———

Jeremy Nordstrand was a miracle of human genetics. Nature had designed him for survival, like a shark. Unable to bear the thought of the ambush taking place without him, he issued a general call-up of his body's natural defenses. They too obeyed unquestioningly his implacable will, closed ranks, and fought to repel the alien disease that had invaded him. Within thirty-six hours, his temperature dipped five degrees, the stiffness in his joints began to relax, his vision grew clearer, and the inflammation on his face cooled. He was able to walk about, though unsteadily; he could look into the light, though he still had to wear sunglasses. He had literally commanded himself to recover, and I was afraid he would on time, and had no idea of what I would do if he did.

While he rested inside, Moody and I sat in the cool morning air, eating our usual breakfast of boiled mush, wafer-thin loaves of bread, and sweetened tea. Smoke from cooking-fires rose in thin plumes, then were blown away by the wind that clouded the air with reddish dust and carried a warning of the crushing heat to come. A couple of dogs quarreled nearby, pigeons babbled under the eaves of the hut, and a camel knelt in front of another shack down the street, chewing on a thornbush clump.

I ate slowly and read *Les Miserables,* which now had no cryptographic value. Jean Valjean's journey through the Paris sewer system, I hoped, would take my mind off the terrors of the underworld I had entered. In terms of the technical problems, sabotaging the Strella missiles had been easier than I had thought. The projectiles were about the size of a bazooka rocket, so it was simply a matter of breaking the circuits to the synchro motor, which is connected to the heat-seeking sensors in the warhead and adjusts the tail fins to guide the missile in flight, rather like a radio-controlled model plane. Disconnecting the wires would make the projectiles fly off course; they would ap-

pear to have been improperly aimed rather than sabotaged.
I had managed to get to more than half the weapons. The
rest were with the crews up on the ridgeline, and I planned
to work on them next.

It was a simple mechanical task, but another matter
psychologically. I was not insensitive to the possible consequences of what I had done. Doubt and guilt gnawed
at me, and I could not look at the ragged children, the
women and old people without my imagination conjuring
visions of them blown apart by bombs. And I was plagued
by the thought that things had not changed as much as I
cared to believe. *A man's fate is like a collar which he
cannot get off.* And it seemed my fate was to be an accomplice. I had been Colfax's accomplice, then Nordstrand's,
and now I was abetting whatever scheme Kasu Murrah
had in mind. That was not what I wanted for myself.
The young men in my graduating class had ambitions to
be foreign-service officers, corporation executives, poets,
scholars, chemists, bankers, but all I had ever wanted to
be was a hero. As a boy I'd had visions of myself playing
Jim Hawkins to Robert Newton's Long John Silver, the
two of us side by side on a pitching quarterdeck as we
went a-yo-ho-hoing out of Porto Bello to battle Spanish
galleons in secret Caribbean coves. I had wanted to test
my strength and try my luck on my own. And when I
joined the paratroopers, I dreamed of splendid battles in
which men died Hollywood deaths, of marching in victory
parades through storms of confetti while lovely girls broke
from the crowds to press their breasts against my chest,
bright with valor's badges.

The camel sensed them first. Out of the corner of my
eye, I saw it prick its ears and lift its gourd-shaped head;
then it heaved itself to its feet, bawling and scuffing the
earth nervously before stumbling off on its hobbled legs.
The two dogs stopped nipping at each other and sent up
a frantic barking, and a he-goat clopped by us at full trot,
bleating.

The camel's owner came out of his house and ran after
the beast, cursing, his curses suddenly obliterated by a
deafening howl. They came out of the sun, too fast to see
until they were past, streaking over the minaret, orange

flames from their rockets flashing under their backsweeping wings, their twenty-three-millimeter cannon winking
and stuttering, the rockets bursting on the NIIF positions
on the ridgeline. The four MIG-21s climbed steeply in a
smudge of exhaust, banked, and dove to strafe the ridge
again. Nordstrand's guards stared at the planes as if they
were apparitions. Then, recovering from their surprise,
two of them boosted the third onto the roof of the hut,
where he crouched, pointed his Kalashnikov skyward, and
emptied a magazine, the spent cartridges clattering against
the tin roof. Within seconds, every guerrilla in Umm-Tajer
was firing panicky, profligate bursts—the fighters were out
of effective small-arms range—so that the stammering of
machine guns and automatic rifles blended into a single
sound. It was like the cracking of a great falling tree, only
prolonged over several minutes. *Thumpthump, thumpthump.* A salvo of Strellas went up. And the missiles were
like stars, red shooting stars, shooting upward instead of
down. Most of them missed, but one locked onto its target.
The pilot saw it and tried to evade it, first by pushing the
MIG into a near-vertical climb, then looping her over into
a near-vertical dive. The fireball followed the parabola, as
if attached to the plane by an invisible cord. Rapidly, remorselessly, it closed the distance. A reverberating *boom.*
Flaming, the fighter dropped straight down and burst like
a sun in the foothills beyond the pass. The rebel soldier
on the rooftop, looking at the flames and smoke roiling up
from the wreckage, yelled something, a cheer, a curse—I
couldn't tell which. The other two shoved Moody and me
inside, where Nordstrand was bellowing like a blinded bull,
"Where's my rifle. *Where's my rifle!*"

Moody dove under a cot and lay with his hands folded
over the back of his head. He pressed himself against the
earth, muttering, "Goddamnit, goddamnit." It was more
a prayer than a curse. "Goddamnit, goddamnit." The cartridge casings kept clanging against the rooftop.

"*Where's my rifle!*"

The old Nordstrand had been resurrected. In a fury,
his sunglasses lying crushed where he had fallen on them,
he pawed at the air, picked up his cot, flung it across the
room, and, not finding his AK under there, tipped my cot

over just as the hut shuddered and the waterskin suspended from the beam swung like a misshapen pendulum. Slivers of daylight suddenly pierced the room from above. Things smacked into the walls. There was a scraping noise overhead, then a soft thud as the guerrilla's body slid down the roof and fell to the street. The door flew open. The other two rebels dragged him in. His dead eyes stared toward the slender shafts of sunlight falling through the holes the bomb shrapnel had torn in the roof.

"It's all right," one of the guerrillas declared, turning to me with a lunatic's grin. "It's all right. I shot one of them down. I shot one of the planes down, by God!"

He did not have a magazine in his rifle, but everything was all right.

"Goddamnit, goddamnit."

"WHERE'S MY RIFLE!"

"It isn't here." Smelling like sewer gas, smoke from the bomb rolled down the street. Another crash and the hut swayed to one side, then to the other before it settled. "Get down, Nordstrand! Get down!"

He picked up the dead man's rifle, tore the cartridge belt from his waist, and bulled out the doorway. I saw him through the haze, running in a crouch, propelled by his natural ferocity to seek some violent culmination to his life. And I hoped he would do the world a favor by finding it.

The first bombardment lasted half an hour, or maybe an hour, or maybe two, or maybe ten years. The MIGs concentrated on the ridgeline, so most of the town was still intact. At some point, their ordnance spent, they flew off. Panic among the civilians was almost immediate. I went out into the street and saw them, running and stumbling, some with cardboard suitcases atop their heads, some lugging sacks, some tugging terrified donkeys and camels loaded down with bedding, leather buckets, waterskins, and pots and pans, some piling their belongings into creaking wooden carts. Despite their alarm, the quick, efficient way they had packed up told you they had done this before. They were veteran refugees. Their flight was not a stampede. Fifty or sixty of them streamed past the hut, black-robed women carrying squalling children, an old man

hippety-hopping on his walking stick, a half-dozen children
with stunned, uncomprehending eyes riding in a lurching,
mule-drawn cart. I looked for the face of the boy with
the paper mirror, but couldn't find it. The small column
raised a cloud of beige dust that mingled with sooty smoke
rolling down from the ridge to form a dark brown haze
overhead. A scout car filled with guerrillas sped up and
blocked the civilians' path. Standing rather grandly behind
the machine gun mounted on the cab, a rebel soldier
shouted at the villagers to return to their homes. One of
the planes had been shot down, the others driven off.
There was nothing more to fear. The civilians knew better
and streamed around the car like water around a rock.
The guerrilla fired a burst into the air. The people kept
moving. He swung the machine gun around and aimed it
at them, and I screamed "NO!" and muttered a silent
prayer of thanks when he raised the muzzle and fired another perfunctory volley over their heads. They trudged
on downhill into the valley, joining another, smaller file,
and then the whole procession of people and livestock and
carts plodded toward the pass, beyond which the pall from
the downed plane bent far over in the wind.

The second wave came—I guess it was ten or fifteen
minutes later. Eight planes this time, flying in two echelons.
I suspected the pilots spoke Spanish. Anyway, they were
fliers with some experience in taking evasive action from
anti-aircraft missiles. As the Strellas streaked up after
them, the pilots put their planes into sharp, violent, rivet-
popping turns, turning the "cold" side of their planes toward the uprushing scarlet fireballs. Not that the maneuvers
were necessary. This volley of SAM-7s came from the
perimeter around the town; they were the missiles I had
worked on and they sailed off harmlessly into space to
explode somewhere off in the mountains. One by one,
the planes peeled off, climbed, and then came down toward the village in screaming dives. For a moment, the
picture was hypnotizing: the MIGs nosing down out of
the smoke-hazed sky, tracer rounds forming a tangled
mesh of flashing light through which black bombs tumbled,
a plane hit by machine-gun fire trailing flames from its
wings and going down in a long, somehow lovely slide be-

fore it splattered against the slope of the ridge. The guerrillas in the scout car cheered its crash. Then the whole
world seemed to vibrate. The houses, the mosque, and the
ridges beyond shimmied and blurred before my eyes; it was
as though I were looking at them through the foggy window of a car racing over a bumpy road. An instant of silence. Then, as the delayed-fuse, five-hundred-pounders
went off, a curtain of smoke and pulverized earth rising
where the mosque had been, eruptions of such violence
you thought you were witnessing a reenactment of the
volcanic upheavals that had first formed that land. Fragments of the mosque's dome and walls, chunks of the
minaret, clods of dirt, tin roofs, lengths of wood, went
whirling through the air. A sound of things being rended,
split, torn, shattered. A cloud of debris flew down the
street toward me, came at me like a rolling wave. A hot
wind flattened my shirt and pulled my skin taut as I went
down. When I looked up, amazed to find myself still alive,
the scout car was over on its side, the rebels' crumpled
bodies lying around it or beneath it. Another of our guards
had been killed—the force of the blast had driven a stick
through his chest. But the same caprice that had killed
him had left the other man untouched. He smiled at me
again. I saw his lips move, but couldn't hear a word he
said. I could hear nothing except an angry buzz in my
inner ear. The mosque and the houses for some distance
around it—that is, one-fourth of the town—were gone.
The mosque had been transformed into a pile of white
stone, except for a half-wall still standing, the minaret
chopped in half, and the shacks reduced to mounds of dust,
petty anthills sprinkled with bits of junk, bits of bodies,
bits of bits.

Looking behind, I saw the roof of the hut bent back
like the top of a tin can.

Moody.

"Moody, *Moody,* MOODY." My voice seemed to be
coming from ten miles way.

The grinning rebel soldier was still grinning at me, his
lips still working. I heard him faintly through the buzzing.

"Everything's all right. I shot down another. Did you
see it?"

He still did not have a magazine in his rifle.

"Moody!"

"Here."

He was still lying under the cot, alive and curled up in the fetal position. Back to the womb. Back to the womb before your doom. Womb doom. *Doom-doom-doom-doom.* That was the sound the heavy 12.7-millimeter machine guns were making. *Doom-doom-doom-doom.*

"Let's go, Moody. Out of here."

Another eruption. A piece of shrapnel sailed through the opening in the roof and buried itself in the wall. It was as big as a railroad spike.

"Here," Moody yelled madly. "All here. Present and accounted for, all of me. So far."

Somehow I dragged him out of there. Somehow we made it to the cover of a ravine on the hillside below the village. Umm-Tajer was being pounded back into its component dust. Bombs and rockets only had to fall near the Beni-Hamid's perimeter to blast them out of their shallow, ineffectual trenches. Not a hundred yards above me, I saw one man spring out of his foxhole like a jack-in-the-box. He broke apart in midair.

In time, Moody recovered from his funk, and I got most of my hearing back. A knot of rebel soldiers with dust-covered faces and the eyes of walking dead came staggering down the ravine. Some had thrown away their weapons. Two were supporting a wounded companion. Falling behind the others, they set the injured man down and collapsed beside us.

"*Jima—mayit,*" one said to me. "Jima's dead."

"Nordstrand. What about Nordstrand?" Moody asked in English.

"What?"

"Mr. Jer-ah-mee."

"Don't know. Jima's dead. It's finished."

But there were still men on the perimeter and on the ridge who did not believe it was finished, fierce men who faced the howling gale of high explosive and howled right back. Their machine guns kept clattering at the three MIGs swooping down on the ridgeline. Remorseless mechanical hawks. It must have been pretty awful on the high ground: the volcanic rock probably doubled the shrapnel effect of the bombs. The second wave left. The third arrived. Four planes. The rumble of the bombs rolled and echoed off the hills, the noise like that of a massive sheet of tinplate shaking in a wind. They worked us over in shifts. Industrial-age warfare visited upon the Bronze Age.

Bit by bit, the NIIF began to break up. In the distance, ant-sized figures, black against the grey rocks, were scrambling down from the ridge. Others, individually or in small bands, were running out of the hell that had once been a town. Bit by bit, it was breaking up, like a ship wave-pounded against a reef.

We flattened ourselves as a MIG screeched overhead and loosed a salvo of rockets, blowing up rubble. Moody, tentatively raising his head, gazed at the brownish-black plumes rising just above us.

"Charlie."

"No. Leave that murdering bastard in there. He's probably dead anyway."

"Even if he's dead."

"No."

"You—we brought this on."

"If anyone's got a reason for leaving him in there, you do."

"That's why I can't leave him."

Cahnt liv him.

"You do see, don't you?"

Dunchyew.

"I've got to do it."

"Your *beau geste,* Moody. Your fine deed of mercy. You *asshole.* Go on, go do it."

He stood, and bent low, ran up the ravine.

I could do nothing but follow him.

Except for the saw-toothed half-wall of the mosque, the broken stalk of the minaret, and a few intact houses, Umm-T   had been wiped from existence. The Ethiopians had meant to do more than retake the town; they had meant to make an example of it. It looked like a miniaturized version of Hiroshima. Fires burned here and there. A dead camel lay beside the timbers of a splintered porch, its greenish-brown guts a feast for the indestructible flies. Running, lying flat when one of the MIGs made another pass, running again, Moody and I made for the old garrison perimeter. Whatever opposition the Beni-Hamid were offering was being offered from there, from the Ethiopians' deep trench lines and dugouts. Smoke and dust turned noon into dusk. A squad of beaten ash-coated rebels ran past us in the opposite direction and looked at us as if we were mad. *Jima—mayiṭ. Mayit. Mayit.* I guessed he was. His once and future presidential palace was a crater ringed by a corona of flaming debris. We cringed behind the smoldering hulk of one of the captured APCs as the MIGs swooped down for yet another pass, engines singing their earsplitting arias, cannons chewing up the earth. I tend to get religious in moments of crisis, and I started to say a Hail Mary. I could remember only the last line of the prayer. *Now and at the hour of our death. Amen.* The guerrilla who had been manning the APC's machine gun hung upside down from the hatch. His face was only a couple of feet above mine. The coagulated blood on it looked like tallow. His hair, just like the hair of the Ethiopian tank crewman I had seen several centuries before, was ruffled by the wind. And the contrast between his dead face and the lifelike movement of his hair made me want to scream. *Now and at the hour of our death. Amen.* The planes whined away. Crouching, we waited for them to strafe us again. Instead, they climbed and winged over the hills to the north. Homeward bound. Back to the officers' club for a beer. The bombardment of the ridgeline continued for a while longer, a steady, sonorous rumbling. Then all the planes ended their runs and flew off, pursued by machine-gun tracers. *I caused this*, I thought. *I caused this.* Moody took off again, running toward the garrison perimeter, still two hundred yards away. A long two hundred yards. I followed him through the beige and black smog, past the torso of a child who had not got out in time. *Now and at the hour of our death. Amen.* Past a leg lying all by itself in the middle of the street, past the shredded perimeter wire, past the barracks building, which had been converted into the rebels' hospital and which was now a charnel house of dead and twice-wounded men, past the prison compound, the worst sight of all. It had taken a direct hit, perhaps two, and the men I had sought to save from massacre were all dead or dying. *I caused this. Now and at the hour of our death. Amen.*

"Moody, we're not going to find him in this mess." My voice sounded on the edge of cracking. The ragged edge between now and the hour of our death, between madness and what passes for sanity. The man of the margins.

"I'll find him, damn it. You can go back if you want to."

I laughed hysterically.

"*Back?* Back where?"

"I'll find him."

It seemed like a hallucination at first: a Land-Rover came rattling out of the fog. It had more holes in it than a cheese grater, but it was running somehow, and a file of fifty-odd men shambled behind it. Their gait and their dazed eyes, staring out from soot-covered faces, made them look like survivors of a mine disaster. Again, we heard the words, *Jima—mayit.* They hung in the air like an echo, and pronounced a summation.

Kasu Murrah was riding in the passenger seat. He hadn't a mark on him. I figured he had managed to find himself a nice, deep, safe hole to hide in. Showing no emotion when he saw us, he ordered the driver to stop and said matter-of-factly:

"Mr. Charlie. You did it."

I laughed hysterically. Yes, yes, I had done it, all right. I had caused this. I swept my arm over the ruins and the dead. There were no sounds except the crackling of the flames, the shouts of some survivors up ahead, and the popping of small-arms ammunition cooking off in fires.

Murrah gestured at the ragged column behind him. They were all the men he could find. The others were dead or dying, or had run off. Murrah said he and his survivors were evacuating Umm-Tajer immediately and would retreat to Karu. Moody and I were to join them. It was our only chance of escape before the Ethiopian infantry attacked.

"We've got to find Nordstrand first," Moody said levelly.

Murrah revealed a ribbon of pink gum above his jutting teeth.

"He must be dead. There's no one left but us. No one."

"I am not leaving without Nordstrand."

"All dead."

"Who's doing that shouting up there, then?"

"I'm not risking lives for that murderer of yours."

It was a different Moody than the one I had known for six months who sprang onto the running board, threw an armlock around Murrah's neck, and jammed a pistol against his temple.

"Over there," he shouted at the driver. "*Yallah imshi!*"

The Land-Rover bumped forward. The startled driver popped the clutch and stalled the engine. Murrah groped for his AK, which was propped against the front seat. I ran over to the driver's side, shoved him out of the way, and grabbing the AK with one hand, restarted the engine with the other. In first gear, we jounced through the murk and over the cratered crest of a knoll and saw Nordstrand occupying a trench with Osman and a dozen remnants of Jima's bodyguard. Sweating heavily from fever and exertion, he was deploying them, a mere squad, when we got there. His moment of apotheosis. He was Gordon of Khartoum, Custer at the Little Big Horn, ready to go out in a blaze of self-destructive madness.

Slamming on the brakes, I laid the rifle down and leaped out of the Land-Rover. Nordstrand, half of him showing above the trench parapet, turned and peered through the smoke with his weakened eyes.

"It's me. Gage." I spoke as calmly as I could and approached him as you might a wild animal.

"I see you, Charlie Gage. How many men have you got with you?"

"Fifty, maybe sixty."

"All right! Divide 'em up into five-man teams. Put three teams to cover the south end of the perimeter—"

"Let's go. It's finished. We're clearing out of here."

Nordstrand vaulted out of the trench.

"*I said*, divide 'em into five-man teams and put three teams to cover the south end of the perimeter. . . ."

From far off, I heard a faint, familiar sound, but its meaning did not register immediately.

"And I said we're pulling out. We're falling back on Karu. It's finished. You're going with us."

"I do not retreat." He waved his rifle at the men in the trench. The outlaw and his gang. "And they don't retreat, either. We're going to hold here. You want to cut and run, then cut and run, you and the rest of the dross. The pure stuff stays with me."

I took a few steps toward him. I considered going back for the rifle but rejected the idea, feeling I owed it to Moody to make every effort to get Nordstrand out of there alive. The noise was louder now. *Bop-bop-bop-bop.* I kept walking toward him.

"This isn't the time for speeches," I said. *"Let's go.* You're going back."

"You're a smart man, Charlie Gage, and you're right. No time for lengthy speeches."

Nordstrand came at me then—in a rush. He came with his bear's head swaying from side to side and his bear's eyes fixed not on me but on something beyond me. He meant to kill me, of course. He wanted to stay in the wilderness. I wanted to bring him out. I was in his way, and he had never permitted anything to stand in his way. I stood as fixed as a tree, moving only inwardly with a racing heart, a sick, fluttering gut, and a drunken wooziness in my head—the symptoms of my nameless terror. And in that instant, the instant before Nordstrand struck at me, gratitude rushed through me. I felt grateful—to Nordstrand. At last my dread had assumed a concrete form. It was six-feet-one and 240 pounds. It had acquired a name: Jeremy Nordstrand. It possessed an object: the evil he embodied, the evil of unrestrained brute force, of the capricious violence that lies sleeping in the prison of our hearts, waiting to be roused and released.

All this took place in a moment. Then he was on me, swinging, meaning to finish me with that favorite punch of his, the one that drives your nose into your skull, but his movements lacked their usual lethal certitude. His fading eyes betrayed him. The punch slammed into my shoulder, numbing my right arm down to my wrist, and that sensation filled me with a wild joy. He had missed. His eyes had gone bad and he had missed. With the strength that surprised even me, I let go with my good arm, caught him flush on the jaw, and fractured my hand. Feeling had returned to my right, so I hit him with that, four right crosses to the temple. It took that many to put him down and one more to keep him there, and if he hadn't been half-blind and debilitated by fever, you could not have knocked him off his feet with a tire iron. Nordstrand sat up, a rivulet of blood running out of the corner of his mouth. He sat propped on his elbows, his eyes cloudy and dazed, his expression incredulous. Before he could recover, I rushed him and kicked him, first in the ribs, then square in the chest. The air hissed from his lungs.

I expected one of his True Brothers to cut me down. None did. I suppose they were a little stunned by the sight of a defeated Nordstrand. Or perhaps they were distracted by the peculiar noise the wind was carrying from somewhere beyond the mountain's rim. *Bop-bop-bop-bop.*

I was in a fury, but clearheaded enough to remember what Murrah had said about the Beni-Hamid, and something Moody had done a few days before, and a certain sound Nordstrand had made when the Englishman touched the infected sores on his face. I wanted that sound from him, needed it if I was to prevent Osman and the others from killing me. Straddling Nordstrand, I whipped the back of my hand across the inflammation, once, twice, three times. Still it didn't come, and I wondered, Doesn't he have any nerves at all? Once more and again, putting all my weight and strength behind the slaps, until it finally burst from him: a cry of human pain. Only then did I back off.

Nordstrand staggered to his feet, clutched at his face, and groaned. The men in the trench looked at him, disbelieving. His mastery over them had rested on his invincible strength. Now their brother by covenant, the man who had set himself up as a demigod, had shown himself to be a man of common clay and weakness. He had exhibited the one failing the Ben-Hamid could not abide. Their exacting, primitive code demanded that pain be endured but never expressed. All those wounded men—never once had any of them cried out, for to cry out under any circumstances was contemptible.

"That's it, Nordstrand. It's finished. Now let's go."

He stood staring at me, raised one arm, then let it drop flaccidly, a gesture suggesting submission. But I knew his mind better than I knew my own. When his cavernous mouth opened, I knew the order he was going to give before he gave it.

"*Kill him!*"

No one did anything.

"KILL HIM!" The voice boomed as it always had. A couple of tribesmen, responding to it reflexively, started to raise their rifles. But they did not fire. They had heard his contemptible cry, and the command he had just given was a further admission of weakness. He had been injured by me; the code required that he exact his own retribution, not order others to do it for him.

"YOU BASTARDS, KILL HIM!" The voice quavered with frustrated rage, and recognition at last flickering in the green eyes, Nordstrand drew his pistol and got off one ill-aimed shot before I dived into a bomb crater a few yards away.

Bop-bop-bop-bop. The noise was much louder, and its familiarity dried up my mouth. Three or four rebel soldiers leaped into the crater beside me, loosing long bursts at the Russian troop-carrying helicopters spiraling down for a landing. Small arms crackled from the ridge, where a few iron men still held out. At the same time, I heard Osman shouting, "Mr. Jer-ah-mee!" His voice was suddenly cut short by an explosion of rifle fire. Scrambling out of the crater, I saw that Nordstrand's display of vulnerability had proved too great a temptation for Murrah. He had been unable to restrain himself from striking back at the man who had held the power of life or death over him. Flinging open the Land-Rover door, knocking Moody off the running board, he had emptied half a magazine at Nordstrand before Moody was able to wrestle the weapon out of his hands. And Osman, in a last gesture of his outmoded, absurd fidelity, had leaped from the trench and thrown himself in the line of fire. The old man's body lay atop the American, who was sprawled on his back.

The helicopters had begun to touch down in the valley, a mile or so north of us, their rotors creating small sandstorms through which the Ethiopian infantry came running. Some fanned out and started to assault the ridge, from which the NIIF holdouts fired raggedly. Their resistance allowed us to organize something resembling an orderly withdrawal.

Feeling an immense exhaustion, I pulled Osman's corpse off Nordstrand. He was still alive. He had taken one bullet through the leg, another had creased his forehead, and ricocheting fragments had punctured his face. Quickly, pressured by the firing and the roaring of the choppers, Moody tore Nordstrand's robes into strips, bound two around his smashed calf as a tourniquet, and the third around his forehead, which the tiny wounds speckled like a pox.

"Hurry it up, goddamnit."

"I am, goddamnit."

Mortars started crumpling at the far end of the village, or what used to be a village.

"This isn't going to work, for Christ's sake. He'll bleed to death before we get help."

"The attempt's got to be made, Charlie."

Crump. Crumpcrumpcrump. A walking barrage. The last of the choppers was landing. The firing from the ridge swelled in volume. Tracers sought the aircraft. One, hit in its tail rotor, began to buck and dip, then to spin on its own axis, spewing bodies like some death-dealing merry-go-round.

"Hurry it up, for God's sake."

Murrah's column of stragglers took off, breaking for the safety of the pass before the enemy infantry blocked it. Murrah remained with us.

Finally, the tourniquets tied off, Moody and I lifted the heavy body and laid it in the back of the Land-Rover. Then I saw why Murrah had stayed. He had not been in so much of a hurry that he hadn't had time to load it up with SAM-7 launchers and projectiles. Perhaps he meant to have me repair them. The weapons would be his ticket of readmission to either the FLN or PLF. They would give him considerable cachet when he marched into Karu to inform Bairu and Hassab that Jima and the NIIF were finished.

Who could say, maybe they would give him a command as a reward. Remembering Murrah's proposed solution to the problem of nomadism, I tossed the weapons out as Moody got behind the wheel and started after the retreating column, Murrah protesting what I had done, the mortars crashing behind us.

Rocking, bouncing, we headed down the caravan track. The Land-Rover's transmission must have been damaged in the bombing: the shift was jammed in low gear, and Moody couldn't get more than ten miles an hour out of the straining engines. I rode in back with Nordstrand. He was still in shock. Blood leaked from the dressing on his forehead into his eyes. "Can't see," he moaned. I told him it was his fever, Rift Valley Fever. He had had it a long time.

Catching up with Murrah's bedraggled army, we took on a few badly wounded men, then drove on ahead, the rebels in the file turning their heads against the dust thrown up by the wheels. Moody was careful not to get too far ahead—broken and dispirited as they were, those fifty men were the only protection we had. Behind us, the ridgeline and the hilltop where Umm-Tajer had stood were wreathed in smoke, reminding me of pictures I had seen of active volcanoes. There was still a good deal of firing. I could see the Ethiopians, dark little moving dots, fighting their way up to the ridge. Battalion strength at least. We passed the hulks of the tanks destroyed in the ambush, drove through the pass, then wound on down through the foothills, reaching the open desert just before dusk. The immensity of sand, its red relieved only by scattered clumps of scrub acacia, looked endless under the dying sun. We stopped to rest and to give the stragglers time to catch up.

Murrah, livid at me for disposing of his arsenal, told us we would not be accompanying the column to Karu. Moody replied we had to.

"Why? For him? That murderer of yours?"

"All right, yes. For him."

"Impossible. How could I explain it? And I don't think there are any doctors in Karu. No, you're not going there."

"Just where are we going?"

"Sudan. You, Mr. Charlie, and that murderer of yours. You want to save him? Very well, save him. Take him to Sudan, to Nassala. There are doctors in Sudan who'll save your murderer."

"Now see here, Kasu—"

"Don't speak to me like that."

"We can't possibly make it on our own with a wounded man. You know that."

"I know that, yes, I know. I'll be generous. In exchange for Mr. Charlie's services, shall we say? You can have the Land-Rover and I'll give you two men who know the way."

Turning on his heel, he walked down the file of exhausted men slumped by the trailside and asked for volunteers. He got more than he expected, for the Beni-Hamid had never experienced the terror of a sustained air raid. They knew what lay ahead: they would be shoved into the ranks of the FLN or the PLF to fight again and, after the disaster they had just survived, few of them had the desire for any more battles. The prospect of crossing 120 miles of desert was preferable: the Sudan and safety lay at the end of the journey. Guiding us out would be a respectable form of desertion. So much for the idea that dying with a sword in your hand was a ticket to paradise. In the end, Murrah chose Nordstrand's old batman, Yassin, and another boy called Rashid.

"They know the way," he said. "You can make it in two days, *inshallah*, as Jima would have said. You will leave now. It's better to travel at night." He paused, then handed Moody a waterskin attached to a length of rope. "And you may have this also."

"It's empty."

"*Allah karim,*" said Yassin. "And I know the wells on the way."

"Yes, yes," Murrah added with a certain vicious satisfaction. "God is generous."

"He shall have to be."

"You should leave now. If that murderer is around me any longer, I'll kill him."

"You tried that already."

"Ye-es. But maybe it's better this way. Now Mr. Jeremy

will die slowly and in a lot of pain. I'll enjoy thinking about him, dying slowly and in a lot of pain." We saw Murrah's buck-toothed grin for the last time. "Slowly and in great pain—God willing."

Without saying another word, Murrah moved off and ordered the men to their feet. They rose slowly, reluctantly, then trudged away, some with their rifles slung, some with their weapons braced across their backs, some without any weapons at all. Murrah marched at the head, with the tight, mechanical movements of a windup toy. The little tin soldier. Soon, they were only a dark line on the red desolation, and I felt the emptiness and hostility of the desert as never before. I felt like a castaway who had been shoved in a launch, given a chart, a compass, and a few days' rations, and told to row for land.

Moody clambered into the back of the Land-Rover, saying he wanted to improve the makeshift battle dressings. Sitting beside Nordstrand, he looked like an ambulance attendant. Unconscious, Nordstrand was silent. I got behind the wheel, my fractured hand throbbing. Yassin and Rashid slid into the front seat beside me. Having spent all their short lives on foot or camelback, riding in a motor vehicle struck them as an exciting novelty. Like the idea of escaping the war for a while, it restored their spirits. They were only twenty, after all, with youth's resiliency in catastrophe.

When I switched on the ignition, the fuel gauge read only a quarter full. I pointed this out to Yassin, who said, "Don't worry."

"*Allah karim*, right?"

"*Aiwa! Allah karim.*"

"I don't suppose he's so generous that he'll make a gas station appear out of nowhere."

"*Yallah!* Mr. Charlie. *Yallah, yallah.*"

"Go? Where?"

"Follow this caravan trail. Ahead, there is a turning, another trail that leads to Nassala. I know it. I've traveled it . . . oh, many times."

We bounced along for five miles or so, and there appeared to be a turning every few hundred yards—trails, gullies, wadis. We were losing light quickly, but Yassin sat as confidently as a city kid riding through a familiar neighborhood full of well-marked street signs.

Finally, he said, "There. There, Mr. Charlie. The turning, where I said it would be. It goes to Nassala." He pointed to a shallow ditch pounded into the sand by the passage of caravans. Or maybe it was a wadi. Or a game track followed by herds of migrating gazelle. Anyway, I couldn't see what distinguished it from all the others we had passed.

"Don't worry, Mr. Charlie. This is the right trail. I've traveled it plenty of times, believe me. Don't worry. You will be the *sheikh al-kara*—the leader of the caravan—and I your guide, unto death or the Sudan!"

Unto death or the Sudan. It was one of the grand-sounding Arabic phrases, full of poetic bravado, but no more than a phrase. I don't believe Yassin had the slightest inkling that it was to be death for him, Rashid, Moody, and Nordstrand. He could not have known, as he exclaimed happily, "unto death or the Sudan," that the five of us were ordained to play out a bloody little epilogue. It was, as the Arabs had it, written. All would die but me. I was destined, by the caprice that governs the universe, to survive and bear witness and to perform my own final act of loyalty to Jeremy Nordstrand.

———

I had a crippling headache when I woke up and opened my eyes to the light pressing through the screens as through a thick white gauze. Multicolored spots sparkled in the air, changing their patterns constantly; it was as though I were looking through the lens of an endlessly revolving kaleidoscope. Can't see, I thought. He kept saying he couldn't see, almost up to the end. Then he saw. *I see! I see!* he said. He said he saw. The words repeated themselves over and over inside my head, like the lyrics of a nursery rhyme or an advertising jingle. *I see! I see! He said he saw.*

I was lying on a bed, the first bed I had felt beneath me in—how long was it? Anyhow, a bed, an old-fashioned one, its foot and headrest made of iron tubing. The tubing was painted white, and the sheets were white, white, clean, and cool. Cool. That heat. If that heat had been eternal, it would have been hell, or one of the more punishing regions of purgatory. *I see! I see! He said he saw.* I blinked my eyes several times, but could not make the kaleidoscopic twinkling vanish. Through the shimmering, ever-shifting patterns, I made out a paddle fan turning overhead, the bleached planks of a well-scrubbed floor meeting colorless walls, screened windows, and two straight-backed chairs. Bandages swathed my feet. I wondered why bandages covered my feet, then recalled, in the fragmentary way you recall a dream, the stretch of black volcanic hills rising abruptly from the rust-red desert. The remains of those ancient volcanoes stood alone, vestiges of some other time. Yassin. Yassin led us through them after he had lost his way in the storm—assuming, that is, he had known where he was going in the first place. The razor-edge lava shredded our boots, and we walked on it until our feet looked as if they had been gnawed by dogs. My left hand was also bandaged, the hand I had fractured against Nordstrand's jaw. Had I hurt it that badly? No. Some other injury. I had hit someone else. I had hit—who? Facts, I needed facts. I needed to cling to a few facts. I am Charles Robert Gage, I thought, a journalist, a man who deals in facts. I also wished I could see more clearly. *I see! I see! He said he saw.* Raising my left hand to rub my eyes, I felt a resistance and heard something rattling above and behind me. An intravenous tube was inserted in the back of my hand; it did not have enough slack, so the metal rod holding the I.V. bottle nearly toppled when I moved my arm. The clear liquid in the bottle was almost gone. Looking at the container with the plastic tubing running from its cap to my hand brought a memory of the field hospital. That was when I had been known as Gage, C.R. Sgt. 2945041, A/1/503, meaning I was Sergeant Charles R. Gage of A Company, First Battalion, 503rd Airborne Infantry. One good thing about the army—you always knew who you were and where you belonged. I could have used that kind of certainty as I lay in the bed, not knowing where I was, or how I had got there, or what had happened to me.

The door opened. A dark man wearing a white uniform walked through the curtain of dancing lights, detached the empty bottle, and replaced it with a fresh one, testing the metal valve to make sure the fluid flowed freely. Pulling up one of the chairs, he attached a blood-pressure gauge to my arm and was squeezing the bulb when he noticed that my eyes were open.

"Mr. Gage! You are awake?" he asked in singsong African English.

I nodded.

"Very good, Mr. Gage. I will tell the doctor as soon as I am finished."

He took my blood pressure and pulse, which he said were also very good, then shook out a thermometer.

"Where am I?" Actually, it came out sounding like "Wammi" because my lips moved as though coated by some not quite hardened glue and my tongue felt like a big, stiff dry sponge.

"Excuse me?"

"Where . . . am . . . I?"

"Nassala. You are in a government clinic in Nassala."

"Nassala? Sudan?"

"Of course. Nassala is in Sudan."

The male nurse put the thermometer in my mouth and waited the required three minutes. My lips stuck to the glass as he removed it. My temperature, he said, was not so very good, but down from yesterday, only forty degrees.

"Was tha in Fahrenha?" Despite years of living abroad, I had never got used to the Celsius scale.

"Excuse me, I cannot understand you." The musical voice lifted pleasantly.

"What . . . is . . . forty . . . degrees . . . in . . . Fahrenheit?"

"Oh, I do not know. I will tell the doctor you are conscious. You have been in a coma for"—he checked his watch—"nearly thirty-six hours."

"Whave Iga? Whzeeze?"

"Excuse me?"

"Duh-zee-eeze."

"I will get the doctor."

He left, returning shortly with another dark man in a white uniform. That was all I could see through the colorful flashing—dark faces, white uniforms.

The doctor looked at the clipboard upon which the nurse had recorded my blood pressure, pulse rate, and temperature; then he lifted my eyelids, flashing a little penlight in my pupils. That done, he turned to the nurse and said in Arabic:

"His blood pressure is near normal now. Little danger of a stroke."

"Duh-zee-eeze. Whzeeze Iga got?"

The doctor turned his head toward me and asked how I felt. I said I felt as if someone were pounding tenpenny nails through my skull. I couldn't see clearly, and every muscle and joint in me was sore. He hardly understood a word. He asked if I felt well enough to talk. I said I did except for the fact that I could hardly talk. What disease did I have? Was it Rift Valley Fever?

"No. No disease at all, Mr. Gage," the doctor said. "You have sunstroke, malnutrition, some slight infection from the injuries in your foot, and dehydration, very bad dehydration. Your temperature was forty-two degrees when they brought you in here. You were quite off your head. You struck the man from your consulate. Do you remember any of that?"

"A little."

"You struck him; then—coma. We were all day cooling you down yesterday and last night, too. We may have to continue today if your temperature doesn't go down to thirty-nine." Pausing, he glanced at the I.V. bottle. "That's a saline solution, Mr. Gage. To replace all the salt you lost."

The doctor paused.

"I'll tell the major and the man from your consulate that you're awake. They want to talk to you. Do you think you can?"

I nodded again.

He and the male nurse left. To take my mind off the pain in my skull and joints, I tried to convert forty degrees Celsius to Fahrenheit. Was the formula centigrade multiplied by five-ninths or nine-fifths? Nine-fifths. Multiply centigrade by nine-fifths and add thirty-two. All right. Nine times forty equals . . . equals . . . equals three hundred sixty. And three hundred sixty divided by five equals —what? Five goes into thirty-six seven times, carry one. Yes, I see. *I see! I see! He said he saw.* What did he see? Moody, who I thought had gone mad, was convinced Nordstrand had seen the faces of the men he had butchered, the faces of his victims coming to haunt him and terrorize him (*inflict terror*) and to make the last hours of his life hours of exquisite mental anguish. *I see! I see!* Carry one. Makes five into ten. Two. What was the first number of the quotient? Facts. I needed facts, beginning with the most elemental and unequivocal—that is, mathematical facts. The first number was thirty-six divided by five. Seven. Seventy-two. Seventy-two plus thirty-two equals one hundred and four. My temperature is one hundred four. Feeling excited by my ability to do simple arithmetic in my head, I converted forty-two degrees Celsius. Because the quotient ended in a fraction, the calculation took me some time. One hundred and seven point six. Sweet baby Jesus. I had had a temperature of one-oh-seven-point-six. It was a fact, but not one I cared to contemplate. Another degree would have caused permanent brain damage, two degrees more, death.

The door opened. Two men entered the room, one white, one black. Salt and pepper. The white man wore civilian dress, the black an olive-drab uniform set off smartly by a polished Sam Browne belt. I could see nothing more. The sparkling, varicolored spots blurred the details of their features. The former, speaking with a peculiar accent, made some perfunctory inquiries as to how I was feeling. He then introduced himself as Henry Carr, consular officer from the American embassy in Khartoum, and explained blithely that he was there to give me advice and whatever protection the government of the United States could offer an American citizen under criminal investigation by the government of Sudan.

"Criminal investigation?" A thrill of fear went through me; then I remembered that I had struck him. Assault and battery, I guessed.

Henry Carr rested a calming hand on my shoulder.

"Take it easy, Mr. Gage. We promised the doctor we wouldn't excite you. This is just a formality, believe me. It won't take more than a few minutes. The major here has to fill out a report. That's all. Just paperwork. So my first piece of advice to you is to answer his questions as best you can."

"Can't talk very well."

"Can you write?"

I held up my bandaged hand. The fingers were free, but as stiff as an arthritic's.

With a certain false joviality, Henry Carr said, "Maybe you can't write with that hand, but you sure can hit with it. You pack quite a wallop. That was quite a wallop you gave me."

He pointed to his right eye. A purple half-moon shone beneath it. *A wallop?* I thought. *You pack quite a wallop?* The outmoded slang was as odd as his accent. Looking at the bruises, the memory came to me, though vaguely. I had been ranting something about completing the mission and being owed fifteen thousand dollars. And Carr, not realizing the state I was in, said, "Afraid your boss overreached himself this time. We don't owe you a thing." Then I hit him, after which everything went black.

"Sorry hit you," I said. "That what this all about?"

"I wonder if we ought not to put this off till tomorrow," Carr said to the major. "The swelling of his tongue should go down by then and he'll be able to speak more clearly."

"We've been waiting nearly two days now." The major spoke with the same musical tone as the nurse, only his voice was an official-sounding basso.

"All right. I think you can get through this somehow."

Carr sat on one of the chairs and lit a cigarette. He had a short, muscular physique, jet-black hair, spoke with that strange accent, and yet something about him reminded me of Colfax. The way he moved and his manner, cautious but sure, casual but watchful. "Afraid your boss overreached himself this time. We don't owe you a thing." *We?*

"Who are you?"

"Who am I? It's no damn business of yours, Mr. Gage, but I am Major Atallah. I'm in command of the border police here. That means I will ask the questions."

"Not you. Him." I pointed at Carr. "Who are you?"

"Do you see, major? The man isn't even in his right senses yet. If you keep questioning him, I might have to make a protest."

"This is not a matter of some tourist with an expired visa, Mr. Carr."

"I know that. That's why I think we should put this off until he's in better shape."

"I want this matter cleared up today."

"Who are you?"

"I've already told you, Mr. Gage. Henry Carr, from the consular section of the American embassy. I'm here to give you whatever help I can."

"Naconslit. Yurna fom conslit."

Rising, Carr walked to the bedside and produced a laminated I.D. card. It had what appeared to be his photograph on it, but for all I could see, it might have been his driver's license.

"This, does it satisfy you, Mr. Gage?"

"Can't see clearly. Eyes bad."

"Right. Doctor said the sunlight did some damage. Nothing permanent."

"Yurna fom conslit. Wha all this?"

Carr again turned to the Sudanese police officer.

"Major, if you've got to question him now, could you give me a few minutes with him alone? He's been through a lot. He's confused, I think, and I think your uniform makes him a little nervous."

"It shouldn't if he hasn't done anything."

"I'm sure he hasn't. He's a well-known and respected journalist in the States. I think I can clear up a few things for him if you give me a minute or two with him. Hey! I'd appreciate it, major."

"I certainly wouldn't want the well-known and respected journalist to write that he was mistreated by the Sudanese authorities."

"I didn't mean to imply that."

"You did, all the same."

"Well, I'm sorry."

"A few minutes. No more."

"Thank you, major. We appreciate your cooperation."

Major Atallah sneered at that remark and walked out. The instant the door closed, Henry Carr peeled off the patronizing, consular officer's manner like a coat that fit him too tightly. Resting one hand on the bedstead and the other on my shoulder, he stood over me and looked down at my face.

"A few minutes isn't much time, so I've got to come to the point. You are in deep shit, my friend. Not just in trouble with the Sudanese, but with us. Got that? *Us*. Do you hear me or did the sun bake your eardrums, too?"

I said I heard him. Hungarian, I decided. The accent was Hungarian. A refugee who fled the 'fifty-six uprising. He must have learned the tough-guy English by reading detective novels.

"As far as you're concerned, Gage, I'm Henry Carr from the U.S. consulate in Khartoum. You ask any more stupid-ass questions like the one you just did or make any more stupid-ass remarks, and I'll turn you over to the major. If he wants to, he can hang you, or put you in the cooler until you're very old and very grey."

In the cooler? The current slang is "slammer," Henry Carr.

"You're under suspicion of murder and a crime that's not even on the books."

At the word *murder,* I forgot all about Carr's habits of speech.

"When the border police found you, you had those two things with you, wrapped up in a bloodstained shirt, and a pistol that had been fired, and a knife. I'll abbreviate. They know you and those other two were kidnapped. It's been on the news—"

"Not kidnapped."

"As far as everyone but you and me are concerned, you three were kidnapped by Bejayan guerrillas. Just like I'm from the consulate. I'll tell you what I think the major thinks. He thinks you three escaped somehow, got lost on the desert, and ran out of water and food. Then you killed your pals and cut them up for lunch. Cannibalism, in other words."

A cry rose in my throat, but my swollen tongue choked it off.

"That's crazy. Moody suicide. Took those 'cause couldn't carry both bodies with me. Had to bring something to bury."

"Don't cop any pleas with me. I don't know what went on out there. I'll find out when the major's through. Just get this straight. The major doesn't give a rat's ass if you killed a thousand people and made a banquet out of all of them, so long as you did it on Ethiopian soil. Tell him what you want, but you make sure he's convinced you didn't do a thing on the Sudanese side of the border. How are you receiving me, Gage? Loud and clear?"

I nodded.

"Another thing, When you talk to the major, Nordstrand is Fredricks and Moody is Anson."

"Forgot about that. Cryptonyms."

"Start remembering. And remember this: I'm all that stands between you and the major. I can take care of him even if he wants to throw the book at you. But if we want to, if we feel we have to, we can do things to you that'll make you want a rope around your neck. That means no more stupid-ass questions. Still loud and clear?"

When the major returned, I told him a story that contained enough truth in it to sound plausible. He jotted in his notebook, sometimes with the bored demeanor of a bureaucrat going through the motions, at other times with the sharp-eyed skepticism of a cop listening to a patently false alibi. He questioned various points of my account, then cross-questioned my answers, trying to trip me up. All this took a good three hours. When he was finished, he slapped his notebook in his hand and contemplated me with a pained look.

"We come now to the difficult part. A band of Beni-Amer found you, Mr. Gage. You were lying beside one of their wells. Evidently you had been trying to fill a waterskin, but didn't have the strength to pull it up and collapsed. By the way, it's lucky for you you did collapse.

Out here a man caught stealing water seldom lives to drink it."

"What's the difficult part?"

"The difficult part." He blew out his cheeks. "The Beni-Amer found you near a village on our side of the frontier. They alerted one of our border patrols. The patrol found you with two"—he blew out his cheeks again—"with two hearts. Two human hearts, wrapped in a shirt you had tied to your back. Also a seven-shot pistol with five rounds in the magazine and powder grains in the barrel. Also a knife."

I opened my mouth to speak. He silenced me with an upraised hand.

"Why did you cut out your companions' hearts, Mr. Gage?"

I told him the truth. I did not want to leave their bodies unburied in the wilderness, but could not carry their corpses out. So I decided to take from them their most essential part: the heart. It had seemed the fitting thing to do under the circumstances; but now, looking at the revulsion in the major's eyes, I realized I had been living in another dimension then.

"Why their hearts?" he asked incredulously. "If you had to do such a thing, why didn't you take a hand, for fingerprint identification? No one can identify a heart. My God."

I said I had not been thinking about identification. My only thought had been not to leave their hearts in an alien land.

"When a man is struggling to survive, he sometimes does things he would never think of doing otherwise." Major Atallah appeared genuinely vexed by his own suggestion. I thought I'd help him out by stating it directly.

"I didn't eat them."

"I didn't mean . . . I've never run into a case like this. Never. It's unique." Quickly his troubled air changed into one of abrupt officiousness. "Forget that for now. The village you were found in is more than ten kilometers inside the Sudan. Is that where you killed your friends?"

"I told you. Beni-Hamid. Rebels. Beni-Hamid killed them."

"I'm sorry. I forgot. The Beni-Hamid. We know them. A nasty lot."

Yes, nasty.

"The border patrol searched the area around the village. They found no bodies. No graves. And the—the body parts with you were badly decomposed. To me that says their deaths occurred some time before. Some time and some distance."

I nodded. Major Atallah obviously wanted the unique case off his hands; he was feeding me hints, rather like a teacher who wants a student to pass a quiz because it would be too much trouble to flunk him.

"So, it appears that whatever happened, it happened on the Ethiopian side."

Yes, I said. Definitely. Absolutely. Everything happened in Ethiopia.

He slipped his notebook into the side pocket of his green tunic.

"It's a strange country, Ethiopia."

I gestured in assent. Henry Carr rose from the chair.

"Would you say that's enough for today, major? Mr. Gage should not be under too much stress."

"You take very good care of your respected journalists, don't you, Mr. Carr?"

"We try to look out for the welfare of all American citizens. That's the consulate's job."

"I'm finished for now. Mr. Gage should remain here for a while. For the sake of his health."

"For the sake of his health, Mr. Gage won't be going anywhere, major."

———

By the next morning my headache had subsided to a dull throbbing, the swelling in my tongue had gone down, and my temperature hovered only two degrees above normal. My vision remained blurred, however. I was paid another visit by the doctor, who told me I would have to remain under observation for a few more days "to make sure there is no brain damage or circulatory problems." As for my eyes, I was suffering from an affliction similar to snow blindness, "an excess of light" as the doctor phrased it. *I see! I see! He said he saw.* There was no need to worry: my eyesight would clear up shortly.

Later, Henry Carr came in carrying a large attaché case and wearing a smartly tailored powder-blue safari suit. Without so much as a "good morning," he pulled up a chair next to the bed, took a cassette recorder out of the case, and set it on the nightstand.

"Shall we begin?"

"Begin what?"

"Your speech has improved. You don't sound like a four-year-old anymore, compañero."

Compañero?

"Where do you want me to begin?"

"I want you to begin by telling me what really happened out there. You can start with what happened to Moody and Nordstrand. Then we'll back up and start from day one."

"Why not just start with day one?"

"I've got my reasons. Don't be a pain in the ass, Gage. What happened to Moody and Nordstrand?"

I was in neither the condition nor the position to argue. My only problem was my memory, which was as blurred and fragmented as my vision.

"Just tell me what you remember." Carr pushed the "record" button.

All right, Mr. Carr. What I remember. Just don't interrupt me. I might lose the thread. I remember Yassin shouting, "*Allah karim,*" after we'd squeezed the last drop of gasoline out of the Land-Rover. He had found a stray camel and was leading it toward us by its nose ring, and shouting, "*Allah karim,*" which means "God is generous," Mr. Carr. We built a travois out of some heavy acacia branches, laid Nordstrand on it, and hitched it to the camel. That was on the first day after the Ethiopians retook Umm-Tajer. Moody had already begun to show some peculiar signs. He was acting strangely, flaky, spooky—do you understand what I'm saying, Mr. Carr? Saving Nordstrand was becoming an obsession with him because he believed it would be a way of saving himself. When the Land-Rover ran out of fuel, his only concern was Nordstrand. How

would we get Nordstrand out on foot? You have to understand that Nordstrand had been wounded, and was sick,
but to go into that, I'd have to start from day one, and you
don't want to start from day one. Then Yassin spotted the
camel, grazing on a ridge a good mile away. "You must
get that animal," Moody told him. "We're lost without it."
Yassin got it. Oh, yes . . . I said that already. He got it
and said it had been a gift from God. Moody would listen
to none of that. He said to him: "I don't want to hear any
nonsense. We'll have to get through this on our wits and
luck, and it was luck, that's all, luck that that camel
turned up." Yassin didn't care for that, you know; the
Beni-Hamid are very religious, fanatical in fact.

Well, it was all walking after that. Slow, slow walking,
the travois bumping over the rocks, and toppling Nordstrand over a couple of times. He was in terrible pain by
then, and kept moaning, "I can't see. I can't see." I think
the shock of his wounds and the dirt and no medicine
brought on a relapse of Rift Valley Fever, Mr. Carr, but
I wasn't sure, and I'm still not sure, and I didn't really
care, walking in all that sun, wind, and sand. Sun. Wind.
Sand. Two days. Four days. Six. Can't recall how many
days we walked. However many days it was, each day was
alike, a repetitive hell. Red sand and gravel, black sand
and basalt, and blinded by red-hot waves shimmering in
the air and teased by mirages, beaten by the sun. The wind
rubbed our eyes raw and cracked our lips. Moody's lips
looked like a hot dog split by the heat of a campfire. The
sand we slept on sucked what little moisture was left in us.
Know what that sand was like? Each grain was a miniature
leech, sucking water from us instead of blood. Yassin
found wells. Sometimes the wells had water in them. Sometimes they didn't. And when they did, it was a brown
sludge that looked and smelled like shit, Mr. Carr; we
drank shit, that's what. The water in one well was so bad
Moody and I vomited it up. The Englishman asked Yassin
why, if we were on the correct route, so many of the wells
were dry. Yassin made the mistake of answering, "Don't
worry, Mr. Patrick, God is generous and will provide us
water." Thought Moody was going to strangle him right
there. "We're lost, aren't we? We are lost," he said. "Ad-

mit it, god damn your soul. You don't know where we are." Then Nordstrand started moaning again. "I can't see. I can't see." His eyelids were encrusted with dried blood and they opened and closed very slowly, and his leg-wound was a big festering lump that drew flies like a dung heap. Moody lifted Nordstrand's head and tipped the spigot of the waterskin in his mouth, and I remember—you asked me to tell what I remember—thinking, Die, you bastard. Die, die, die. But he didn't die. He wouldn't. He was a genetic miracle. He was a remarkable man in his way.

More walking. Sand. Wind. Sun. Sun. Wind. Sand. Walking without shelter and without rest through storms of light, storms of it; that light out there came at you like a storm. Eating nothing but the lizards Yassin and Rashid found under the rocks—looked like gecko lizards, some of them, and some like scaled-down gila monsters, and that's what we ate, lizards, we ate lizards and drank shit, and our bellies started to cave in. Yassin and Rashid were thinking about death. I knew they were thinking about death because they got even more religious, so religious every other word was *Allah*—well, no, not every other word, it just seemed that way. What a sun! It seemed to stay directly overhead all day, all day it was like high noon, and when it really was high noon, I thought the sun was about six feet above the ground because it made our clothes smell like they'd been under a steam press for too long. Sunset always struck me as a miracle.

One night we were staggering down a wadi and we found an abandoned nomads' settlement. The tribesmen had moved into the high pastures, where—I couldn't believe it—it was raining. I mean, I couldn't believe it was raining anywhere on earth, but it was raining in the mountains, Yassin said; it was the time of the little rains and that's when I realized it must be April and I'd been in the desert seven months. The nomads had taken everything with them, but the well had water, more shit-water, Mr. Carr, and Yassin found a small sack of ground maize tucked away in one of the brushwood huts. The discovery unbalanced him. He really got religion then. He shook the sack in front of Moody's face and he started yelling, "There, God is generous, you unbelieving bastard. You

can't say God is not generous. Don't tell me He is not
generous because He is. *Mashallah!* What God has willed!
Mashallah! Mr. Patrick. See what God has willed. God
led me to this sack of grain, not luck, and not your wits,
but God. *Mashallah!*" Moody was sitting by the fire. The
fire flared brightly because the temperature dropped sharply at night and made the wind blow harder. And did God
have the generosity to lead you to a pot in which to cook
the grain? he asked Yassin, who said he would find something. He didn't find anything. He dug a hole with a knife
and lined it with rocks. "I'll pour the grain in this and
build a fire around it." Then Moody said: "Has your
generous God shown you the way to Sudan? How far is it
to the Sudan?" Yassin replied, "Not far." The Englishman
jumped up like a scorpion had bit him. He looked a hundred years old in the firelight; the skin was flaking off his
face like paint off a weathered house. "Not far! How far
is not far? A day, two days, a week? Why don't you admit
you're lost? The trail we've been following isn't the right
one. It can't be. In all this time, we have seen exactly one
stray camel, but not a single caravan, not a village with a
soul in it, not one decent well. If this were the right trail,
we'd be in the Sudan by now." Yassin said nothing, kept
lining the hole with rocks. The quiet Rashid spoke instead.
We are not lost, this was the correct trail, he had been
keeping direction by the sun and stars, we had not reached
the Sudan because we had covered only ten, at most fifteen
kilometers a day. Rashid pointed at Nordstrand. "Because
of him. But for him, we would now be in Nassala, eating
goat's meat and drinking tea. This is the time for Mr.
Jeremy to die." Moody shouted: "Don't give me any of
your fatalism. Do you hear me? I won't have it. We are
not leaving Nordstrand." Rashid just shrugged and said:
"Then it is time for all of us to die." That's what he said,
but I saw something light up in his eyes, the idea of desert-
ing the three of us, or perhaps killing us, I don't know, but
he wasn't as ready to die as he pretended to be. Later on,
while he and Yassin slept, I warned Moody that if he
didn't stop pushing them so hard they would take off and
leave us. "Let them," Moody said. "It won't make any
difference. They're as lost as we are." I stayed awake all

night, listening to the jackals and never taking my eyes off those two Beni-Hamid, all night until dawn. Dawn. If sunset was a miracle, dawn was a curse, a red curse. We had to travel in daylight you see, because Yassin and Rashid didn't know the route so well that they could follow it in darkness.

What I remember. I remember amputating Nordstrand's leg. It might have been the next night. I remember it was at night, the night before the storm. Nordstrand got up from the travois and stood on his good leg, balancing himself by holding on to an acacia branch. He was a genetic miracle, oh, yes, I already told you that, but he was. Anyone else would have been killed by that ordeal, but he got up, stood and spoke, and I couldn't believe it. He wasn't even a man. He was the survival principle made flesh and blood, the incarnation of the wild forces of nature itself, so help me; he was as indestructible as a shark. He stood and spoke! You should have seen him with his lips swollen to the size of sausages, and his skin blistered, and his face slashed by the marks, the marks a kind of purple color in the light of the campfire—I'd explain those marks, but I'd have to start from day one, and you don't want me to start from day one, so I'll just say they were Beni-Hamid tribal marks—and they had a purple color and his blind green eyes stared out from above the markings while he stood on his good leg, the wounded leg bloated to nearly twice its size below the knee, the skin blackish green and giving off a stench that made your eyes water if you got close enough; you should have seen him, Mr. Carr. *"Where are we going?"* His voice sounded like the wind in the dry acacia. I told him, and all he said was, "I can't see, I can't see." Moody tried to get him to lie down again. Nordstrand's lips formed a snarl or grin, I couldn't tell which, and he spoke again: "Not bringing me out, not yet, weak sister . . . the terror of their name . . . inflict terror . . . Osman! Machine guns on the short leg on the L fire down the axis of the convoy . . . wait till the whole convoy is in the pass . . . five minute burst, then reload, and a second burst at ground level to finish the wounded . . . aim for their boots, and there'll be no survivors . . . one stroke . . . Have to complete the mission, you understand that,

dross?" He raved like that, and I could explain his ravings
if you'd let me start from day one. He tried to take a step,
and went down. The gangrenous leg crumpled beneath
him. It smelled very bad, so I took it off.

I took it off with Yassin's knife while the other three
held him down. Hacking through the bone was the hardest
part. I thought it would kill him, hoped it would, but it
didn't. He screamed. Up until then he'd borne his pain because he was a remarkable man in his way. But the amputation tore from him a scream that drove through my ears
like a spike. Yassin stanched the hemorrhaging with mud
dredged up from the well we had camped beside, mud that
would harden in the sun, Yassin said; and it did, hardened
until it was like a plaster cast. Nordstrand raved all that
night and all the next day. Have you ever been wounded,
Mr. Carr? If you have, you'll know there is nothing more
isolating than deep bone pain. The whole world ceases to
exist and there is only you and your agony. But Nordstrand
was a little different. He got company in his loneliness. He
said he saw faces, faces coming at him, horrible faces, and
he swatted his arms like a man under attack from a swarm
of bees and cried: "Get away, get away, get away," his
arms all the time batting the air as if he could somehow
wipe out whatever visions had come to haunt him in his
isolation. Moody never left his side. He sprinkled water on
his lips and asked, over and over, what faces he saw. They
were just faces, and he swatted at them and hollered, "GET
AWAY FROM ME."

I think it was a little while after sunrise that Nordstrand's body started to tremble, and his breathing grew
shallow. I was certain he was dying. And Moody was certain also. Moody, I should explain, was very spooky by
that time, flaky, strange—do you understand what I'm saying, Mr. Carr? The sun had got to him. An excess of light.
Oh, he spoke clearly, he spoke with the clarity you sometimes hear in psychiatric wards. His theory was that the
old Nordstrand was dying, and that the new one, con-
ceived in agony, the first true, prolonged agony Nordstrand
had ever known, was being born. And in that interval between death and birth, Nordstrand's rapid, shallow gasps
began to form words, the dying man's last words, so to

speak, and the baby's first: "I see! I see!" He said he saw, Mr. Carr. What? I'm not sure. Maybe nothing, maybe he was just raving, but his eyes widened as if they actually had seen something, something damned awful, I imagine, because there was terror in those blind eyes, and that cry, "I see! I see!" was not one of joyous enlightenment, no, it was long and drawn out and came from deep down, more shrill and terrible than the scream he'd let out when I amputated his leg; a howl of despair, that's what it was— you would have said that's what it was if you had heard it. I'll tell you, compared to the way he cried "I see! I see!" the most dismal wail of the most moon-maddened jackal sounded like a lullaby.

Moody smiled when he heard it. It scared the hell out of me, but the Englishman smiled. The sun, you know. Moody said the cry was a cry of guilt. His theory was that Nordstrand's intense pain had put him in contact with the current of human suffering that flows through the world. His agony forced upon him an awareness of all human agony, especially the agony he had inflicted, and that, Moody claimed, was what he saw, the agony of his victims, and he felt guilty, and there was in his guilt an implied repentance, or so Moody said, and guilt and repentance were Nordstrand's passport back into the community of men. I'm not saying I agreed with Moody. No, I thought he was crazy. The sun, you know. An excess of light. He was having visions in the desert. Still, he made me wonder what Nordstrand saw, what it was that made him cry so horribly. So Moody became more determined than ever to save Nordstrand because, he said, Nordstrand now more than ever was worth saving. It was our obligation to bring him out. And that marvelous, insane obsession, combined with the storm, finally drove poor old Moody right off the edge. Are you following me, Mr. Carr?

Henry Carr pushed the "stop" button and said: "I'm not following any of this, Gage."

"That's because you wouldn't let me start from day one."

"I want to know what happened to Moody and Nordstrand, not all this bullshit about seeing things."

"What Nordstrand saw was one of the things that happened to Nordstrand. It might have been the most important thing that ever happened to him because I worked out my own theory about what he saw. He saw his soul."

"You're the one who's had too much sun. His soul? What the hell are you, Gage, a priest?"

"I didn't mean it in that sense. The word is just a figure of speech. Maybe it'd make more sense if I said that Nordstrand saw himself. He saw himself for what he was."

"No, that doesn't make any sense, either."

"Goddamnit, he saw himself for what he was. That's what terrified him."

"Think we'd better go on and get this over with. Then we'll try it from day one."

"Moody was probably right, though. Whether he saw the people he killed or himself for what he was, it was a kind of salvation."

"Gage. I know you've had a rough time, but will you knock off this born-again, glory-hallelujah crap? I want facts, my friend. Facts."

And I said I wanted facts too, but not for the same reason. You, Mr. Carr, want facts because you think they'll explain something. Well, I've dealt with facts for years, newspaper facts, and I know facts don't explain anything, just as I know there is a truth beyond mere facts, a truth we are sometimes, rarely, sometimes only once in a lifetime, allowed to glimpse. So why do I want facts? Because I can't live without them. In that sense, facts are no different than their presumed opposite, illusions. Facts and illusions, Mr. Carr, are necessary for our psychological survival. They are the saving pieces of driftwood we cling to in an ocean of futility, ambiguity, and darkness, but they don't explain a damn thing.

Carr punched the "record" button. "Let's go on, Gage, and a little less emphasis on metaphysics."

"Where was I?"

Carr waved a hand in exasperation. "How do I know? Something about a storm."

It began as a brown smudge on the horizon, and by noon it filled a quarter of the western sky. The wind picked up. Dust started falling on us, a sort of dry rain. Wind, a lot of wind, but in spite of the wind, the air felt

the way it does in Indochina, webbed so thick it was difficult to breathe. Ahead, huge billows of sand were swirling
toward the sky. Sand and wind, that factual enough for
you? Yassin, who was in the lead. picked up the pace,
making for a ridgeline two or three miles off, only two or
three miles. Rashid, bringing up the rear, whacked the
tiring camel into a half-trot, and the travois bounced over
the rocky ground, and the jarring cracked Nordstrand's
mud-plaster cast. Moody wanted to halt there; we'd get lost
if we were caught in the storm. Yassin said we'd be buried
if we didn't get into the lee of the ridge. So we went on,
and the ridge vanished under the whirling brown cloud—
it came like that, a whirling cloud, like a heavy squall at
sea it was suddenly on us and it roared down on us, like
a squall, like a wave, a wave of sand driven by gale-force
winds, so that each grain smacked our faces like buckshot.
You want facts? The fact was, we were marching through
a sulfur-colored darkness, and sometimes an opening would
appear in that yellow cloud and give us a glimpse of the
ridge. Then we couldn't see. Nordstrand could see, but
we couldn't, marching head-down against that wind. Finally, it became impossible to look up for even an instant
without feeling as if the sand was going to tear your eyes
out and shred the skin off your face. We stopped and
turned our backs to it, unhitched the travois, and knelt
the camel beside it, and the wind rose and howled and
flung sand against the animal until it was half-buried. I
don't know how long we stayed there. You couldn't tell
night from day. Not too long, I suppose. There are sandstorms that go on for days, even weeks, and that one was
to a bad storm what a cloudburst is to a hurricane, but it
was bad enough. It was daylight when the wind let up. It
was light, but we couldn't see the ridge. The ridge had dis-
appeared. For a few moments, I thought the storm had
just blown it out of existence, but if it had, it had blown
in a new feature, a range of these low, black volcanic hills.
Yassin and Rashid looked at the hills, and they were both
very confused. No, the wind hadn't obliterated the ridge
and replaced it with those lava rocks. Somehow, in the
time we had trudged through the storm, we became lost,
just as Moody had feared. He was too worn out to say

anything, but Yassin saw the anger in him, and said, oh so soothingly, that we were not too far from the trail. He knew those black hills, by God, they were just south of the ridge, and there was a well on the other side. "How do you know we're south of the ridge?" Moody asked him. I remember the question because I remember how Moody looked when he asked it, remember his eyes shoved back in their sockets and his face as lank as a skull, and I remember his voice had this spooky tone to it, an unbalanced sound. "How do I know?" Yassin asked back. "Why, because they are, Mr. Patrick. They're south of the ridge. We only have to go north some little distance, then west, and in one day, Sudan." We set off again, over those cheerful hills. The sun hammered against the black rocks, and the rocks flung the heat back, so we were scorched from below and above. The doubled heat evaporated the little water we had left in the goatskin. Yassin had lied about the well, of course. There wasn't any well anywhere. He'd lied to preserve his status as a guide and to avoid losing face, which the Arabs call "blackening the face," and he'd gambled that luck or God's generosity would make a well appear out of nowhere. Nordstrand was hardly breathing by then. He should have stopped breathing long before, and maybe you could say it would have been good if he had stopped breathing the day he was born, strangling on the umbilical cord. Moody kept asking, "Where's the well, where is it, damn your soul?" And Yassin kept answering, "Be patient, Mr. Patrick, it's not far." You wanted to know what happened to Moody, I'll tell you, Mr. Carr. This is what happened:

Moody stopped walking and said:

"Mr. Jeremy is dying."

"I know, I know," Yassin said. "We must keep going. North some little distance, then west to the well, and in one day, Sudan, *inshallah*."

"Mr. Jeremy is dying because you got us lost. You insisted on traveling through the storm and got us lost."

Rashid stood beside Yassin and told Moody to be patient, we would surely find a well.

"Ah! Not *the* well, but *a* well. And how are we to find this magical well? Through God's generosity?"

That's when Yassin snapped. He snapped all at once. He was starved and thirsty, like all of us. Like all of us, he was suffering from the sun, from an excess of light, Mr. Carr.

"Yes!" he said loudly. "Because God is generous and will lead us to a well, as he led us to the grain, as he led us to this camel. I am sick of you blaspheming God. What do you know, you filthy *kafir*? *Ferengei,* what do any of you know? I am a believer, and a Beni-Hamid, and I'll praise God and his generosity with my last breath." He commenced to hop about as if the rocks had become hot coals. "Praise be to God! Praise be to God! God is generous! God is generous! Praise be to God!"

"If you had relied on common sense instead of God, we wouldn't be lost."

Under different circumstances, I would have found all this amusing, Mr. Carr. There we were, twenty-four hours at best from dying of thirst, and those two were arguing theology. Then Rashid told Moody everything had been his fault.

"My fault?"

"Yes. If you had not insisted on taking Mr. Jeremy, we would have been in the Sudan by now. Yes, long ago. We would now be in Nassala eating bread and olives, drinking tea and sweet water. The fault is yours because you refused to believe it is Mr. Jeremy's time to die."

"You can't just leave a man to die."

"If his death is written, you must leave him."

"It isn't written. Nothing is written, you ignorant bastards."

"Ignorant bastards!" Yassin shouted—well, no, it wasn't a shout, his throat being too dry to shout. "Ignorant bastards, is that what we are? *Quss ummakh.*"

Moody said, "Don't insult me," because Mr. Carr, *quss ummakh* means "your mother's vulva," and is one of the stronger insults you can make in Arabic.

"*Quss ummakh.*" Yassin was giggling and danced a kind of jig on the hot stones. "Your mother's vulva. Praise be to God! Praise be to God! Your mother's vulva."

"Don't insult me, you stupid bastard."

"*Quss ummakh.*" And Yassin cocked his head and spat

in Moody's face, and that is when life played its little joke on the Englishman. He was exhausted, he was frustrated and in desperate circumstances and someone had just spat in his face. Life gave him what he'd been seeking all along. It duplicated the circumstances—you would understand what I mean by that if you'd allowed me to start from day one—but it duplicated them at a moment when he was least prepared for them, which caused him to duplicate his behavior. The instant after the spit struck his face, he pulled out his pistol and pumped five or six rounds into those two. The range was point-blank, so he didn't miss, and the big nine-millimeters spun both men around before they fell.

It didn't take long for Moody to catch on. A couple of seconds. He saw the jest. He was laughing, in fact, in a funny way, laughing and crying at the same time, laughing and crying and saying, "Oh my God, no, no, no, no," and looking at his pistol as if it had gone off by itself, just the way he did in Oman a long time ago. I knew what he was going to do, so I walked toward him very slowly and told him that I was the only witness and that, as far as I was concerned, I hadn't seen anything.

But he kept saying, "No, no, no, dear Jesus, no."

I moved a little closer, holding my hand out. "Listen, Pat," I said, "please listen. There won't be any court-martial this time, no disgrace."

"Got rounds left, Charlie. Please don't make me have to shoot you." He was backing away from me.

"You don't have to. Please don't, Pat. No one saw any-thing but me, and I'm not talking."

"I've seen it. That's all that matters, isn't it?"

He was still laughing in that funny, flaky way when he raised the pistol to his temple. I tried to bring him down with a flying tackle, but I hardly had the strength to walk, let alone to make a ten-foot lunge. I was in midair when the pistol went off.

What else do I remember? I don't remember clearly what I did after he shot himself. I have a foggy recollection of trying to revive Yassin and Rashid—the sun, you know —because I couldn't bear the thought of their dying with-out someone knowing they had died, of their bodies lying out there for ten or twenty or a hundred years until their bones were found by someone who couldn't know those bones once belonged to two human beings named Yassin and Rashid. And I recall cradling Moody's smashed skull. I might have cried, although I doubt it. There wasn't enough water left in me for that, nor enough of whatever else is required for tears. Moody. The General. His flaw wasn't the streak of irrational violence in him; it was his inability to accept that part of himself. He wanted so much to be like that man whose dockets we'd found away up there in the mountains—I'll tell you about that when we start from day one—wanted to be the Englishman of the movies and legend, cool and level and decent while chaos swirled around him. Moody, the General, was the best of us, Mr. Carr. None of us was any good, but Moody was the best, the best of the worst, which is more than I can say for myself and infinitely more than I can say for the remarkable Nordstrand. Moody had failed again the standard he tried to live by, but at least he tried, tried to touch what is good in our natures. Oh, his reach exceeded his grasp, but that wasn't important. The important thing was, he tried, he stretched out his arm and tried to reach out beyond the muck and slime and darkness. He made the attempt.

And that, Mr. Carr, is what happened to Patrick Moody.

And this, Mr. Carr, is what happened to Jeremy Bennett Nordstrand: I killed him.

He was still alive. Of course he was alive. The genetic miracle refused to die. He was lying on the travois, breathing shallowly, and, you know, I was convinced he was going to make it through, he was going to survive somehow; he was savage nature's very own child. But he owed a debt, a very heavy debt. He had paid a part of it, but no amount of pain he could ever suffer would be enough to settle the balance. And there was no one but me to square his account. He had said it himself so many times— there were no policemen out there. No judges, lawyers, or courts, either. He owed a debt, but I owed him a debt: he had shown me my dread, Mr. Carr, he became the material manifestation of the thing that threatened to destroy me, and he gave me the chance to fight and subdue it.

Really, I didn't know what to do at first. I thought for a long time, long enough for the vultures to come calling. Those crooked-necked bastards came gliding down and formed one of their chuckling circles, and I was sitting so still one of them hopped up to me and almost gave me a little peck, and got the surprise of his life when I whirled around and smacked him in his disgusting pink head, and yelled, "Not yet, you filthy sonsabitches. Not yet!" It was then that I had one of those moments I told you about, a glimpse of a truth beyond the facts. If Moody had been right about Nordstrand, then I would do him a favor by killing him. If he had been graced with guilt and repentance, then it was best for him to die in that condition. In other words, I could make him pay his debt and pay my debt with the same act. I looked down at that enormous, unconscious hulk and didn't think anymore. I took out my pistol and shot him. Twice. Twice in the head.

Also without thinking, I got Yassin's knife and cut out Nordstrand's and Moody's hearts, and the strange thing was, they looked the same. I expected Nordstrand's to look different, to be marked, like his face, like his arm, but it looked the same as Moody's. You already know why I cut out their hearts. That was my final act of loyalty, to take the most essential part and see that it wasn't buried on alien soil, to see that there was something left to bury and mourn. Oh, I had thought of slinging their bodies on the camel's back, but I didn't have the strength—Nordstrand weighed two-forty, Mr. Carr—and anyway, I doubted the camel could carry them both because the animal was on its last legs—it died the next day as a matter of fact. Another fact for you: the camel died. It died the way they do, just folded up its legs and quit.

So there I was. Up the creek without a paddle, in the desert without a camel, but I wasn't ready to quit. You see, I got it into my head that I was destined to survive and bear witness. That's one of the things that kept me going all across the desert. That, and the strips of meat I fileted off the camel, and the water I got by puncturing its belly. A camel doesn't store water in its hump, Mr. Carr, it stores it in a part of its belly, and I sliced its gut with the knife, and held the waterskin underneath, and managed to draw a pint or two. It smelled awful, naturally, but it kept me going—it and the raw meat, and the conviction I had to survive to bear witness. And, oh yes, most important of all, the belief that someone had to bring out their hearts for burial.

I almost forgot illusions. Illusions got me through. I told you that illusions, like facts, are necessary for psychological survival. Sometimes you have to choose illusions. You see, if I toted up the facts of my predicament, I would have gone crazy or killed myself or both. Crossing that desert was a little like getting through life, Mr. Carr, I had to dream up little fantasies so I wouldn't see the reality of my situation too clearly. To put it another way, I drove myself a little crazy to prevent myself from going completely crazy. I pretended that the mirages I saw really were water, pretended they were the waters of the Arabian Sea, and that I was not lost and alone in a wilderness, but sailing an Arab dhow to India, and the tree lines in the distance my imagination transformed into the coast of India. The tree lines bordered the wadis—that's how I traveled, from wadi to wadi, always westward, pretending I was at sea until I actually believed I was at sea. I lost touch with reality. After all, if reality means you're alone and lost, with nothing to eat but raw rotting meat and nothing to drink but the water from a camel's belly, and the odds are that you'll die of thirst, which is a very bad death, by the way, then it's a good idea to lose touch, isn't it? But that isn't factual in the sense you mean facts. Facts. The one part of my mind kept direction by the sun and stars. I traveled only at night and in the early mornings, keeping the sun behind me in the mornings and noting the position of the Southern Cross at night, and keeping it there. Sun. Stars. Facts.

And those facts and my half-craziness paid off, didn't they? I reckon I'd been on the move three days, maybe four, when I saw the palm trees around the village. I had no feeling by then. I couldn't feel the weight of the waterskin, or the rope digging into my shoulders, or the weight of the hearts tugging on my back, or anything at all. You know the rest. I found the village well, but the major was wrong when he said I collapsed. I went to sleep. The rope was too short! I lowered the waterskin down into the well, and the rope was too short by ten feet, and that was the only time I really felt frightened. To have come that far and to die of thirst because of ten lousy feet of rope, so I just laid down and went to sleep, figuring dying of thirst in my sleep wouldn't be painful. Then the villagers found me, and that's it, Mr. Carr. Now you know the facts of what happened. Moody killed himself and I killed Nordstrand out there in Ethiopia among those terrible hot black rocks. Everything happened in Ethiopia."

Henry Carr punched the "stop" button again, ejected the cassette, marked it, and put it in the attaché case. Then he propped his elbow on the nightstand, placed his hand under his chin, two fingers alongside his cheek, and stared at me for a long time.

"In other words, my friend," he said finally, "you killed without authorization an agent of the United States government."

"I killed a man who deserved to be killed."

"You killed without authorization an agent of your government."

"I killed a man who would have been called a mass murderer if he'd done what he'd done in some place where they've got lawyers and cops."

"Gage, you're being a pain in the ass again. I said I wanted facts, and when I cut away all the bullshit and metaphysics and poetry from your story, one fact stands out: you terminated a U.S. agent named Jeremy Nordstrand without authorization."

"All right. Fine. Have it your way. I terminated him. I suppose that's what you meant yesterday when you said I'm in deep trouble with you people. I committed an unauthorized termination."

Henry Carr smiled brightly. With his dark hair, olive complexion, and toothpaste-advertisement smile he reminded me of Ali Mahmoud. (Ali Mahmoud—I saw him as a figure standing at the distant entrance to the nightmare, the gatekeeper, so to speak, and now here was another smiling face at the exit. If I had come to an exit.)

"That isn't what I meant," Carr said. "A little white lie.

Let's say you could be in deep trouble. Just trying to scare you into talking facts. And one fact is, we're just as glad those two are out of the way. It makes things easier." He inserted another cassette. "All right. Day one, and no metaphysics, and no tales about desert survival this time. Just facts. What was done, when it was done, who did it. I want to hear the facts about this fiasco from day one."

"Talk to Colfax about that."

"We already did, but he was a little removed from the scene of the action. You were there. You wanted to be a witness? Okay, let's hear the testimony, Mr. Witness."

"You get nothing from me but name, rank, and serial number until I hear a few things from you."

"Like what?"

"Like what you mean by saying I could be in trouble. Like why you don't owe me anything. Like why 'my boss' overreached himself. Let's try those for openers."

"Most of that's classified."

"So is most of what I've got."

"No sweat. I've got clearance."

"So do I."

"No, you don't. Compañero, with the clearance you've got, you wouldn't be allowed to read the wrapper on the shit paper in the men's room."

"I was cleared for Atropos—compañero."

Carr wiped a square forefinger over his sweating forehead.

"I can tell you this much. You weren't cleared for Atropos, because Atropos wasn't cleared. Colfax ran off the reservation."

"This is no time for metaphors."

"Atropos was a renegade operation. It wasn't cleared by anybody. It wasn't even seen by anybody except Colfax's Chinaman. Except for those two and you three, nobody knew Atropos existed until about a month ago."

If I had any capital left in my emotional portfolio, I would have reacted to that disclosure. I am not sure how, but I would have reacted. As it was, the news just stunned me briefly, like a mild electric shock.

"Let's hear some explanation."

"Classified."

"Fine. Know what you'll get from me? The hole in the doughnut."

"Listen, Gage . . ."

"No cheap threats. One advantage to going through what I've just been through is that nothing scares you anymore. Fact is, I'll do the threatening. How'd you like to see this whole sweet story in *The New York Times*? Or if that doesn't bother you, how about if I just get out of this bed and give you another wallop? Maybe five or six wallops. I pack quite a wallop, remember? I'll turn your face into raspberry jam."

"Take it easy, Gage." Carr scrutinized me for several minutes. Then:

"All right. This much and no more. Your boss was very ambitious. His career was at a dead end because he'd done so much time in Vietnam. He'd thought that's where the action was. Every one of our people who was over there either got a pink slip or was shoved off into a corner because we'd lost, and they were associated with that loss. They were all tarred with the same brush. Want to know what Colfax was doing in Cairo? Economic intelligence. He was counting Egyptian cotton balls. So he dreamed up Atropos and talked it over with his Chinaman topside—"

"What the hell is a Chinaman?"

"A patron, a sponsor. Those two decided that Atropos would be their little secret. They were afraid that if they submitted it to the directorate of operations for approval, it would either get axed or end up in front of one of those congressional committees, then get leaked to the press. The deal was, if Atropos worked, the Chinaman would see to it that Colfax's career got out of the doldrums. Help him along, put in a good word for him to the right people. The Chinaman let Colfax work out the details. The only time he stuck his two cents in was when Colfax pushed this Nordstrand guy to run the operation in the field. The Chinaman had copies of Nordstrand's military record in Vietnam. He also had a report that had been written on Nordstrand when he was working for us in Beirut. None of that made a favorable impression. I guess this Nordstrand came out looking unstable—unmanageable. A real wild man. We're used to that type in this business, but the Chinaman figured there was enough risk in a mission like Atropos without having a cowboy in charge. He told Colfax to get himself another man to head up the operation. Otherwise, he would pull out his support. So Colfax didn't put up any argument. Like I said, he was very ambitious. Crazy ambitious. He actually thought he was going to be director someday. He thought he was destined for it. He thought he was going to be the guy who'd control all the networks and have little chitchats with the President in the oval office. He'd pulled off a stunt in Cuba in the old days. Went ashore with some anti-Castro rebels, which he wasn't supposed to do, and blew up a sugar refinery. Get chewed out for it by one department, but you know how bureaucracies are: another department gave him a commendation. That gave him the idea that success justifies everything. He used to say that to us: success justifies everything. So, the only thing I can figure is that he got the idea he could get away with this if it was successful. He got so crazy in the head he thought he could get away with it, and he damned near did. End of explanation."

"I don't believe that. I don't believe he and this Chinaman you're talking about could run an operation without anybody knowing."

"Hey! Whatever else was wrong with him, your boss was a talented guy. If anybody could pull off a hoax like this, he could."

"A hoax. That's what you call it? A hoax?"

"That's what it was, compañero."

"What's this 'compañero' business? You and Colfax blow up that refinery together?"

"Not likely. I was probably guarding the refinery. My original name was Carbonell. I used to work for Mr. Castro, then I said a few uncomplimentary things about El Presidente and had to light out on a fishing boat to Florida. Long story, also classified. Now I'm here, keeping tabs on what my old compañeros are up to in Ethiopia."

"Right. That makes sense. Where's Colfax now?"

"Dead. Administratively dead. He's in research, reading magazines. Finished, in other words. Washed up."

"And just how did you uncover his hoax?"

"You want me to tie up all the loose ends, Gage?"

"Just some."

"Sorry. Can't do it. Classified. Compromise too many people."

"I'd like to know where he came up with a quarter-million to pay for the guns. And where was he going to come up with a half-million in ransom money, it he was running this show on his lonesome?"

"His source for the half-million's classified. He embezzled the quarter-million from Inter-Arab. He was smart enough to figure his creative accounting wouldn't stand up under an audit, so he worked out a sweetheart deal with this Greek, some Greek with a name I can't pronounce. You know who I mean, Gage, the Greek who shipped the guns for him."

"Boxavenides."

"Helluva name, isn't it? The Greek scuttled his own ship and collected the insurance, two and a half million dollars, and gave ten percent to Colfax. Colfax put it back in the company's account. The trouble was, this Boxwhatits then scuttled Colfax."

"Scuttled him how?"

"Blew his cover. In the press. See, four crewmen drowned when that ship went down, so the inquiry got a paragraph or two in the papers. They held it in Athens. Some kind of admiralty court. I guess this Greek had paid off the court, because they cleared him so he could collect. He kept his bargain with Colfax, but then he turned around and made a statement that he was running guns into Ethiopia for the U.S. of A., and mentioned Tom's name. Don't know why he did that, but he did."

"Revenge. It was his way of getting even. Colfax wasn't smart enough to figure some people won't be yours forever."

"Maybe you can explain that later. Anyway we had to pull Tom out of Cairo. . . ."

"The radio. That's why we couldn't get through on the radio."

"Right. He wasn't there to say hello. We pulled him out and, naturally, asked him, What the hell is going on here?

He stonewalled us but we got persuasive, and that, Gage, is how we found out about his little hoax. It might interest you to know that after he gave us the code, we messaged you people to get out of there. We didn't get any response. How come? I've sung my song. Start singing yours."

"Nordstrand wrecked the radio. I'll tell you about that."

"I know you will. No more questions now, Gage. I've told you more than you'll ever need to know."

He punched "record" and I gave him the facts he wanted. It was dark by the time I finished. Henry Carr, formerly Carbonell, did not appear to be affected by the recitation of facts. He simply shoved the tape recorder into his black case and snapped the locks shut crisply.

"This Nordstrand," he said as he opened the door to leave, "he was some piece of business."

Yeah, some piece of business.

"How do you figure a guy like that, Gage?"

"You wouldn't want to hear it. Not factual. Metaphysics."

"The recorder's off."

"He lacked restraint and he couldn't love."

"See you in a day or two, Gage."

Two days later, after I'd breakfasted on olives and eggs, the first food I'd been able to keep down since landing in the clinic, Henry Carr returned with his attaché case and a fresh safari suit. This one was dark green and made him look like a forest ranger. Sitting down, he opened the case and pulled out a copy of the *International Herald Tribune* which he laid on my lap.

"You're mildly famous, Gage. Page one. Only a few paragraphs below the fold, but page one."

I flipped the newspaper over. In the far right-hand corner, I caught the headline: U.S. NEWSMAN ESCAPES GUERRILLA CAPTORS. My eyesight had improved only slightly but I was able to read the story, essentially the same story I told the major.

"You bastard," I said. "Who put this out?"

"You read the story. A high U.S. official."

"You want me to do something. What is it?"

"Flesh out the story. Put a little human interest in it.

You know, desert survival, desperate escape, high adventure. In other words, I want you to be interviewed. They're waiting outside."

"Who is?"

"The three wire services, the BBC, the VOA, and your alma mater, the *L.A. Post,* of course. Would have liked to have got the *Times* down here, but short notice, and Sudan's a little off the beaten track."

"I don't get it. Let's just let it die."

"You said something the other day that bothered me. Something about seeing the whole sweet story in *The New York Times.* You can guess why we don't want the whole sweet story in the *Times* or anywhere. We don't want you to give in to your journalistic impulses, in other words. If you do, our first option would be to put out an unsourced piece including all that pleasant business about your killing Nordstrand and cutting out their hearts, with a little background on your psychiatric record. That's the most pleasant thing we could do to you. You can imagine what the others are, and now I'm not making any cheap threats. I promise you, Gage, we'll do things to you that'll make you wish I'd turned you over to the major for a hanging. Here. I talked to Washington. They thought we owed you something after all."

He dipped into a pocket of the case and withdrew an airline ticket to New York via London. Inside this ticket was a check for fifteen thousand dollars.

"Hush money."

"Not hush money. We want you to talk, to sing a song. And the song you'll sing is that the three of you were kidnapped and held for six months. Then you made a break, but the other two were killed in the attempt. You managed to survive."

I kept the ticket and tore the check into quarters and neatly laid the pieces on Henry Carr's lap.

"That really is stupid, you know. I wasn't kidding about what we can do."

"Don't worry. I'll say what you want me to say. I just don't want to make money for doing it."

"Why the hell not?"

"It makes a difference."

"Right. Fifteen thousand dollars' difference. Have it your way. I'm going to get them now, Gage."

"Go ahead."

Carr leaned forward aggressively, his face still slightly indistinct through the lights that continued to sparkle in front of my eyes. Behind him, the white morning light shone through the web of window screening. I would do as he asked not out of fear of what might happen to me if I refused to, but out of a determination to conceal what Nordstrand had done. He would have wanted me to tell the world he despised about the crimes by which he had manifested his contempt but I had performed my last gesture of loyalty to him. I closed my eyes for an instant, and my imagination arranged the shifting lights into a familiar pattern: it was a radiant portrait of a dhow sailing across a blue and unambiguous sea. The image burst when Henry Carr said:

"I'll be listening to your song, and I don't want to hear you hit any false notes."

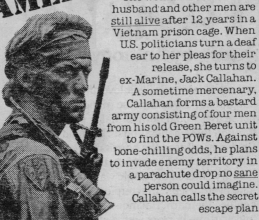